A
SHADE
OF
DIFFERENCE
BY
ALLEN DRURY

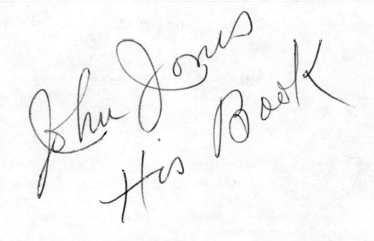

John Jones
His Book

Also by Allen Drury

ADVISE AND CONSENT

A SHADE OF DIFFERENCE

A SHADE
OF DIFFERENCE

A Novel By ALLEN DRURY

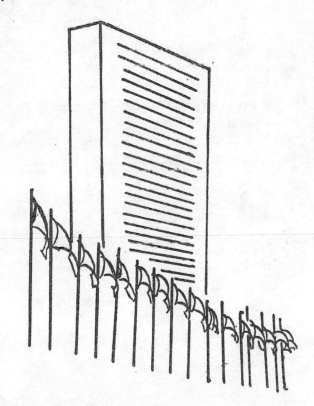

Doubleday & Company, Inc., Garden City, New York, 1962

Drawings and jacket design by Anne Drury Killiany
Jacket painting by Alice Smith

Dedicated to the men and women
of the Secretariat and to those
delegations that genuinely work
for peace in Turtle Bay.

Events surrounding the nomination of Robert A. Leffingwell to be Secretary of State, the death of Senator Brigham Anderson, the Soviet and American moon expeditions, and other previous matters mentioned in this novel will be found related in full in the novel ADVISE AND CONSENT by the same author.

Grateful acknowledgment for assistance kindly and generously given is made to:

Dr. V. John Murgolo, concerning medical matters. Earl Mazo, concerning his home town of Charleston. Matthew Gordon and other good friends of the Press Section and the Secretariat of the United Nations.

Excerpt from speech of Senator Harold Fry to the General Assembly, "Hal Fry's Book":

"Oh, Mr. President! How does mankind stand, in this awful hour? Where does it find, in all its pomp and pride and power, the answer to its own fateful divisions? Where on this globe, where in this universe, is there any help for us? Who will come to our aid, who have failed so badly in our trusteeship of the bounteous and lovely earth? Who will save us, if we do not save ourselves?

"I say to you, my friends, no one will. No one will. We are wedded to one another, it may be to our death, it may be to our living. We cannot escape one another, however hard we try. Though we fly to the moon and far beyond, we shall take with us what is in our hearts, and if it be not pure, we shall slaughter one another where'er we meet, as surely on some outward star as here on earth.

"*This* is the human condition—that we cannot flee from one another. For good, for ill, we await ourselves behind every door, down every street, at the end of every passageway. We try to remain apart: we fail. We try to hide: we are exposed. Behind every issue here, behind the myriad quarrels that make up the angry world, we await, always and forever, our own discovery. And nothing makes us better than we are.

"Mr. President, I beg of you, here in this body of which men have hoped so much and for which they have already done so much, let us love one another!

"*Let us love one another!*

"It is all we have left."

CONTENTS

MAJOR CHARACTERS OF THE NOVEL

At the United Nations:

His Royal Highness Terence Wolowo Ajkaje ("Ahdge-kah-gee") the M'Bulu of Mbuele; "Terrible Terry"

Senator Harold Fry of West Virginia, acting head of the U. S. Delegation

Senator Lafe Smith of Iowa, member of the U. S. Delegation

Felix Labaiya-Sofra ("Lah-buy-uh-Soaf-ra"), Ambassador of Panama

Lord Claude Maudulayne, the British Ambassador

Raoul Barre, the French Ambassador

Krishna Khaleel, Ambassador of India

Vasily Tashikov, Ambassador of the U.S.S.R.

The Secretary-General

Other Ambassadors and delegates

Members of the Secretariat

The Press

In Washington:

Harley M. Hudson of Michigan, President of the United States

Lucille, his wife

Orrin Knox, Secretary of State

Beth, his wife

Senator Robert D. Munson of Michigan, Majority Leader of the U. S. Senate

Dolly, his wife

Representative Cullee Hamilton of California

Sue-Dan, his wife

Maudie, their maid

The Speaker of the House

Senator Seabright B. Cooley, President Pro Tempore of the U. S. Senate

Representative J. B. "Jawbone" Swarthman of South Carolina, Chairman of the House Foreign Affairs Committee

In Washington (continued):
Senator Thomas August of Minnesota, Chairman of the Senate Foreign
   Relations Committee
Señora Patsy Jason Labaiya, wife of the Ambassador of Panama
Governor Edward Jason of California, her brother
Robert A. Leffingwell, Director of the President's Commission on Admin-
   istrative Reform
Mr. Justice Thomas Buckmaster Davis of the U. S. Supreme Court
Other Senators and Representatives
The Press

In Geneva:
The Chairman of the Council of Ministers of the U.S.S.R.
Other officials of the U.S.S.R.

One

TERRIBLE TERRY'S BOOK

In the great pearl-gray slab of a room that is the North Delegates' Lounge of the United Nations in New York the late-September sun slanted down through the massive east windows and fell across the green carpets, the crowded chairs and sofas, the little knots of delegates standing or sitting or milling about in the midmorning hours before the General Assembly's seven committees began. Riding over their noisy hubbub came the heavy voices of the young ladies at the telephone desk, relaying via the public-address system their bored yet insistent summonses to the myriad sons of man:

"Mr. Sadu-Nalim of the delegation of Iran, please call the Delegates' Lounge! . . . Senator Fry of the United States, please! . . . Ambassador Labaiya-Sofra of the delegation of Panama, please call the Delegates' Lounge! . . . His Royal Highness the M'Bulu of Mbuele, please . . . Secretary Knox of the United States . . ."

Surveying the immense and noisy chamber from his vantage point near the door, Senator Harold Fry of West Virginia, one of the two Senate members and acting head of the United States delegation, wondered with some impatience where Orrin Knox was now. The Secretary of State had been in town two days and Hal Fry had hardly seen him for ten minutes at a time, so busy had the Secretary been with conferences, diplomatic receptions, U.S. delegation business, and what Senator Fry termed with some disparagement "giving beads to the natives." Not that he was above giving a few himself, he thought wryly as he waved with vigorous cordiality to a passing Nigerian and bestowed a glowing smile upon the delegate from Gabon; but at least he could take it or leave it. Secretary Knox seemed to be going about it with a determination that bordered on the grim; Orrin acted at moments as though the fate of the world depended upon it. Which, of course, Senator Fry conceded abruptly with a loud "Hello!" to the delegate of Nepal, it quite possibly did.

A momentary look of concentration and unease touched his face at the thought, an expression of sudden melancholy that went almost as soon as it appeared. The Ambassador of India materialized at his elbow and seized upon it with unfailing accuracy.

"My dear Hal," Krishna Khaleel said with his air of half-jocular concern, "first you are being so jolly with everybody and then suddenly you look so sad. What is the matter with the Great Republic of the West this morning? Or is it only the distinguished delegate who feels something unsettling in his tummy, perhaps?"

"My tummy's all right, K.K.," Senator Fry said. "In fact, I was at the Guinean reception last night and ate like a horse. I'm just wondering where Orrin is."

"Ah, yes," said Krishna Khaleel with a little agreeing hiss. "Orrin is so *busy* since he arrived here. Does he think the United States depends on him alone?"

"He has been known to feel that way," Senator Fry said with a little smile that the Indian Ambassador answered at once.

"Even now, he feels that way? With Harley in the White House and—"

"Even now," Hal Fry agreed. "And perhaps with some reason. After all, it isn't as though Harley were the greatest President who ever—"

"No, indeed," the Indian Ambassador said quickly. "But we like him, Hal. We all like him. The world thinks highly of your President. He lacks the dramatics of his predecessor, but there is something very—solid about him. And of course Geneva was dramatic enough."

"Oh, yes," Senator Fry said, thinking of that fantastic event which had astounded the earth and flabbergasted the universe. "Geneva was dramatic enough, all right . . . Isn't that Terrible Terry over there?"

"Where?" Krishna Khaleel demanded, peering toward the bar. "I assume if it is he will be accompanied by the British Ambassador. The United Kingdom can't seem to leave him alone these days."

"I should hope not," Hal Fry said dryly. "I hear Terry's going to make quite a speech in the plenary session of the General Assembly Friday morning."

"He can be counted upon," the Indian Ambassador said with equal dryness.

"Why do you people give him such a play, anyway?" the Senator from West Virginia inquired. "Just to embarrass the rest of us?"

"All the Asian-African states think he has a very good case, you know, Hal. He is one of the last gasps of colonialism. Or his situation is, anyway."

" 'All the Asian-African states,' " Senator Fry mimicked. "As if you all agreed on anything for more than five minutes at a time."

"On some things," the Indian Ambassador said. "On some things. We do agree on Terence Wolowo Ajkaje the M'Bulu of Mbuele."

"Terence Woe-loe-woe Ahdge-kah-gee the Mmmbooloo of Mmmbweelee," the Senator from West Virginia said, rolling it out with considerable sarcasm. "Quite a title for a Harvard graduate."

"And the London School of Economics," Krishna Khaleel said with a smile. "And Oxford . . . Now," he said abruptly, "what is the S.-G. doing, talking to Felix Labaiya?"

Far down the room, under the great wooden slab above the bar that bears the carved map of the world, the Senator from West Virginia saw the tall figure of the Secretary-General bending down to the dark, clever face and short, animated body of the Ambassador of Panama.

"I don't know," he said. "Shall we go ask?"

"I'm tempted," the Indian Ambassador said, as two sheiks from Mauretania went billowing whitely by. "I wonder if it's the draft resolution Guinea put in yesterday in the Fifth Committee? Guinea, you know, wants to send a UN observer force to Gorotoland to see what the real situation is."

"Guinea always wants to meddle in everything," Senator Fry said. Krishna Khaleel smiled broadly.

"So do we," he said. "And Ghana. And Mali. And Nigeria. And Indonesia. And Ceylon. And—"

"And the Soviet Union," Hal Fry said. "And, lately, Panama. What's the matter with Felix Labaiya, anyway?"

"The Ambassador of Belgium, please," said the young lady at the phone desk. "*L'Ambassadeur de Belgique, s'il vous plaît.*"

"He is leaning more and more in that direction," Krishna Khaleel said in the thoughtful tone of UN delegates who know very well which direction they mean. "But why don't you ask his wife? After all, he's married to an American. North American, I should say."

Hal Fry shrugged. "No one gets anything out of Patsy Labaiya. She's as much of a closemouthed crackpot as all the rest of her family."

"I hear," the Indian Ambassador said, "that her brother has plans to run for a very important office next year and that Bob Leffingwell may resign from the Administration to help him."

"Governors of California have run for it before," Senator Fry said, "but don't believe all the gossip you hear. Here come Her Majesty's distinguished Ambassador and Terry, so we'll get a chance to explore all your most delicious suspicions in that sector."

"Hal, old boy," Lord Claude Maudulayne said, peering at him in an amiable way, "of course you know His Royal Highness the M'Bulu of Mbuele."

"I haven't had the pleasure," Senator Fry said, shaking hands cordially. "Shall we go sit by the window? There seem to be some seats empty over there, if we move fast."

"Right," the British Ambassador said, grasping his tall companion by the arm and steering him toward the glass wall just in time to forestall three rosy Swedes and a small brown man from Madagascar who were heading for the only available chairs. "I can't stay too long, though. Have to go to the First Committee and help Orrin hold off the Soviets on the Panamanian resolution."

"Typical British understatement!" the Indian Ambassador cried with a laugh. "Of course the Panamanian resolution is directed at the U.K., not the U.S. Orrin will be helping *you.*"

"K.K.," Lord Maudulayne said, "you always see through me. Always. But of course," he added more seriously, "the resolution is slightly directed at the United States, too, you know. I think you can take the reference to 'unfair treatment of minority peoples' as being—er—pointed. I'm quite sure it is intended that way."

"I'm quite sure it is," Senator Fry said. "What do you make of all this, Your Highness?"

"I think you should call me Terry," the M'Bulu said in the guttural voice of his people and the clipped accent of his educators; and he conferred a dazzling smile upon Hal Fry, who returned it vigorously. "I think everyone should be friends," he added with a gesture that was soon to become familiar to them—holding his hands out palms upward with a graceful, charming little shrug. "That is why I am here with His Lordship—even though the United Kingdom and I are engaged in a rather—delicate—discussion at the moment."

"I expect him to give us jolly old what-for in plenary Friday morning," Lord Maudulayne said with a chuckle, and the M'Bulu of Mbuele chuckled right back.

"I expect I will. Gorotoland is quite important to me. It has been in my family since roughly the time William of Normandy acquired your island. Or so," he said with a wry little smile that removed some of the sting, "tradition says. It isn't written down anywhere. They tell it on the drums."

"We haven't any desire to take it away from your family, you know," Lord Maudulayne said mildly. "In fact, you can have your freedom. The Whittle-Hornsby Report promises that, and far be it from Her Majesty's Govern—"

"Now," Terrible Terry said with utter finality.

"If you were only ready," the British Ambassador said.

"Now," the M'Bulu said, and with a bland, faraway look he concentrated his gaze upon a heavily-laden barge struggling slowly up the East River in the hazy autumn sun and for the moment said no more. When he spoke again it was in a tone of restrained but quite ferocious indignation.

"The only place in the whole of Black Africa which is still unable to break free. Dahomey is free. Chad is free. Gabon is free. And what are Dahomey and Chad and Gabon? Nothing but bare places in the sun!"

"Angola and Mozambique—" Lord Maudulayne ventured to mention the Portuguese colonies, but the M'Bulu brushed them aside with an angry wave.

"Their time will come," he promised with great certainty, "and not far off. But our time is now."

"Two hundred high-school graduates in two million people," Lord Maudulayne said in a bleak tone. "One hundred and two college-educated men and women. Thirty-three doctors. Twenty engineers. Forty-one trained administrators."

"Not a very good record for you, is it?" Terrible Terry asked pleasantly, and the Indian Ambassador gave an appreciative little chuckle. His British colleague sighed.

"We could have integrated you so well with the Rhodesias, if only you had been willing. We had all the plans ready, but you wouldn't accept."

"No!" the M'Bulu said with all the fierce vigor of his twenty-nine years, and for just a second Senator Fry had a vivid and uncomfortable vision of human sacrifice around a ritual fire in the thorn-tree country. "No!"

"Secretary Knox of the United States," the young lady at the microphone said earnestly. "Secretary Knox of the United States, please call the Delegates' Lounge!"

"Yes, Secretary Knox," Hal Fry said in a humorous way that broke the tension, "please do, because I want to see you before I go to Fifth Committee. I want to know what to say to Guinea when they bring up that resolution."

"And the U.S.S.R.," the M'Bulu said in a tone that dismissed other matters and came back to good nature. "Mr. Tashikov tells me they plan something very vigorous. We had an interesting talk yesterday on many things."

"And he promised you complete Soviet support on immediate independence," Senator Fry said.

"Of course."

"Of course," Lord Maudulayne agreed. "Beware."

"Yes," said Krishna Khaleel quite unexpectedly, "do beware, Your Highness. Accept support where you can find it, when you need it—but without strings. They have no claim on you now. Don't give them any. These people. They are not playing simple little games in this world or in this UN. They do not come to this house to offer generosities they do not expect to exact tribute for. They are in this house for what they can get. Do not be fooled by them."

"K.K.," Senator Fry said, "how consistent can you be? Every time it comes to an issue here you line up with them as dutifully as though—"

"I resent that, Hal!" the Indian Ambassador said with real anger. "I resent that. India does what she does because she believes it to be best. It has nothing to do with the Soviet Union. It does not even always coincide with the Soviet Union. Often it is different from them. We take our own positions. We are not fools about them, Hal! I resent that!"

"Well, it's sometimes very hard to see," Senator Fry remarked. "And very confusing for the rest of us. Anyway, here's Orrin at last, and I guess maybe we should talk of other things."

"Your Secretary looks more friendly than I had expected," the M'Bulu observed, "and not so formidable for one who engineered Geneva."

"He has a tart tongue and a tart reputation," Hal Fry said, "but the latter is somewhat exaggerated. And I think the President had quite a lot to do with Geneva. Where are you off to, Claude?"

"First Committee for me, old boy," Lord Maudulayne said. "I'll wait and go in with Orrin. Possibly His Highness would like to go with us. If you see Raoul Barre before I do, tell him I shall meet him for lunch at 1:15 in the Delegates' Dining Room. Why don't you join us? Possibly the M'Bulu will do the same."

"I see," Terrible Terry said with amusement, "that I am not to be let out of sight."

"Oh, now!" Lord Maudulayne said, and his youthful companion gave again his hands-out, palms-upward gesture.

"I have a wicked sense of humor," he confessed merrily. "That is where I got the nickname Terrible Terry. My sense of humor used to distress everyone in England so."

"Still does, old boy," the British Ambassador said, and they all joined in his rueful laughter as the American Secretary of State, working his way slowly through the outstretched hands and dutifully smiling faces of a dozen different nationalities, approached them at last.

"I'm sorry to be late, Hal," he said without preliminaries, "but I got tied up talking to LeGage Shelby at U.S. headquarters across the street. And you know how it is across the street. I should have come straight here, as you recommended."

"You'll learn if you stay awhile," Senator Fry said. "Do you know Terrible —His Royal Highness the M'Bulu of Mbuele?"

"My pleasure," Orrin Knox said. "I've been looking forward to meeting you for some time, Your Highness."

"Call him Terry," Hal Fry said. "Everybody does. Orrin, do you have any instructions for me for Fifth Committee?"

"No different than you've had right along," the Secretary said, "but come over here. Excuse us, gentlemen."

Staring out the great window at the gleaming river, outwardly placid, actually swift-racing in the autumn light, he asked abruptly: "How are you feeling?"

"I'm all right," Hal Fry said with some surprise. "I'm feeling fine. Why?"

"You looked quite odd for a minute last night at the Guinean reception," Orrin said. "A very strange expression. I didn't know whether you were going to faint or what."

"Was it that obvious?" Senator Fry asked in some annoyance. "I don't think anybody saw it but me. What was it?"

"Just my eyes," Hal Fry said. "A little reddish tinge for a minute. It went right away. Just overtired, I think. It startled me, though, which is why I showed it, I guess."

"Well, take it easy," Orrin Knox said. "That's orders."

"You're very thoughtful. I will, as much as one can around this place."

"I don't want the acting chief delegate dropping by the wayside now that the permanent Ambassador is incapacitated too."

"How's he doing?"

"So-so. I was by Harkness Pavilion this morning. Still oxygen tent."

"Hearts are occupational in the public business, I guess," Senator Fry said with a sigh. "How's yours?"

"I'm too ornery to die," Orrin Knox said, turning back to the others. "Everybody knows that. Well, gentlemen, I expect the committees are beginning, and we should probably all run along. Take care of the interests of the United States in Fifth Committee, K.K. I know we can count on you."

"M. Raoul Barre, s'il vous plait," the young lady said politely to the enormous room, now emptying slowly as the delegates headed for committees. "M. l'Ambassadeur de France, s'il vous plait."

"Always joking, Orrin," the Indian Ambassador said. "It is a side that has developed in you since your new responsibilities."

"Since Geneva, I'd say," Lord Maudulayne remarked. "Nothing like tasting the joys of defiance, eh, old chap?"

"Defiance, nothing," Secretary Knox said. "We had no choice."

"Does it ever seem like a dream?" the M'Bulu asked, and for a long moment the Secretary appraised him with a steady glance. Then he tossed off, "A bad one," tersely, and started to turn away.

"But I wanted to talk to you for a moment," Terrible Terry said, holding out a restraining hand.

"Very well," Orrin Knox said, dropping onto a sofa. "I'll talk. See you later, Hal. Claude, do you want to stay—or is that forbidden, Your Highness?"

"Why," the M'Bulu said with a charming smile, "nothing would please me more." He too sat on the sofa and arranged his brilliant robes. "Mr. Secretary, I want to visit your country and be entertained at the White House. I think it would enhance my cause."

"Well!" Orrin Knox said. "There's nothing bashful about that. I should think it would, indeed."

"And diminish ours," Lord Maudulayne said, too surprised and annoyed to be polite about it.

"Possibly," Terrible Terry agreed placidly. "But I think it would be nice."

"Is this a formal request?" the Secretary inquired in a thoughtful tone that showed he was giving it serious consideration.

"It is," the M'Bulu said with equal gravity.

"Oh, I say," Claude Maudulayne said. "Now, really—"

"You could always give a reception for me at the Embassy," Terry said blandly, "prior to the White House dinner."

"Oh, dinner?" Orrin Knox said. "Is that all you want? Isn't there anything more we can do for you?"

"I think that will be sufficient," the M'Bulu said with a jolly laugh.

"What an extraordinary thing," the Secretary said. "If I were still in the Senate, I'd tell you that it was nonsense and forget it. Now I'm at State, I have to be more diplomatic. Do you mind if I consult with the President? He might have different ideas, you know. It's just possible he won't want to rearrange everything for a—a rather minor African prince."

"Now," Terry said with a sudden anger in his enormous eyes, "you go too far, Mr. Secretary. Really too far."

"That was just as though I were still in the Senate," Orrin Knox said nonchalantly, waving to the Secretary-General, who had paused across the room to talk to two members of the Soviet delegation. "I don't mean it, really. But really, now—"

"You entertain distinguished foreign visitors all the time," the M'Bulu pointed out in a reasonable tone. "Surely I'm no different."

"Well, except as you're still fighting your case in the UN and it would put us in a position of opposing our allies—"

"A position of post-Geneva," the M'Bulu said softly. "Perhaps it is more necessary now than it might once have been."

"You're a very clever young man," Orrin Knox said without guile. "I wonder what you really want on these shores?"

"I want only the freedom which is due my country," Terrible Terry said. "I don't think that's so extraordinary."

"I wonder . . . I wonder. Where do you want to go in the United States?"

"I heard so much about South Carolina when I was at Harvard, but I never got a chance to go down there. I should like to go there now."

"I am not at all sure you would be welcome in South Carolina," the Secretary remarked. Terrible Terry smiled.

"I am prepared to chance it."

"I am afraid we could not permit it," Orrin Knox said. The gorgeous figure exploded in a happy, sarcastic laugh.

"How can you prevent it? I'm no Communist diplomat you can keep chained to New York or Washington."

"Possibly the British can restrain you."

"They wouldn't dare!" the M'Bulu said scornfully, and Lord Maudulayne sighed.

"Right you are," he said. "We wouldn't dare. Nor, my old friend from the Senate, would you."

"So, you see?" Terrible Terry demanded in happy triumph. "It is all so simple, and we might as well all co-operate."

"When would you like to go?" Orrin Knox asked.

"The invitation is for tomorrow noon," the M'Bulu said, and at his listeners' looks of surprise he laughed again—in innocent merriment, as the Secretary remarked in the privacy of his own mind, in inno-cent merri-ment.

"And what invitation is this?" he asked.

"The Jason Foundation is giving a luncheon for me in Charleston," Terry said proudly. "Señora Labaiya's brother, the Governor of California, will introduce me."

"Patsy Jason Labaiya's family fortune is behind that," the Secretary informed Lord Maudulayne. "It does much good and causes some trouble, like all foundations. So Ted Jason will be there too? I thought the California legislature was in special session. Why don't you go out there instead? Maybe you could address them."

"I have several invitations to be on television here that I have to keep," the M'Bulu said proudly. "It all helps."

"I'm sure it does. Well, I'll talk to the President. How about letting him designate a member of Congress to go with you as his representative?"

"And my guard?" Terry suggested with a smile. "Who—Senator Cooley? I'm sure that would guarantee me safe-conduct in South Carolina!"

"He might just surprise you and do it," the Secretary said. "There are a few tricks left in old Seab yet. No, I was thinking of Cullee Hamilton, as a matter of fact. He's one of our young Representatives, from California. A very fine one. And a Negro."

"I know him," the M'Bulu said, and for just a second a contemplative and not too pleasant expression came into his eyes. "He visited my capital of Molobangwe last year for the House Foreign Affairs Committee."

"Did you like him?" the Secretary asked. Terrible Terry's expression changed to something indefinable. He shrugged.

"He has a pretty wife." He stood up briskly, his robes showering down about him in glittering cascade. "Very well, I'll take old Cullee, then, if that's what you want. And you will talk to the President. Maybe Thursday night, if he's free. Then I can have the day Thursday for seeing people in Washington."

"It takes time to arrange a White House dinner," Orrin Knox said.

"He can do it," Terry said complacently, and the Secretary thought: Go down through layer after layer after layer and you still find something tenaciously and terribly childlike underneath.

The M'Bulu smiled happily. "That way, I can still be back here in plenty of time for my speech Friday morning."

"Full of praise for the United States, no doubt," Orrin Knox suggested. The M'Bulu gave his charming palms-out gesture.

"I am sure of it! Your Excellency—" he shook hands with the British Ambassador. "Mr. Secretary—" he repeated with Orrin Knox. "I just want to say good morning to the S.-G. before I drop in on the First Committee. I shall see you there, no doubt, discussing my important little country."

"See you there, Your Highness," Orrin Knox agreed, and caught himself even as the M'Bulu did—"Terry."

"Good cheer," the glamorous visitor said. "Good cheer, both!"

"Mr. Fibay-Toku of Upper Volta, please," said the young lady at the microphone. "Mr. Fibay-Toku of Upper Volta, please call the Delegates' Lounge."

A moment later the Secretary and the Ambassador could see the M'Bulu on the other side of the enormous room, now almost deserted as the hour neared eleven and the UN's committees prepared to convene. He had hailed the Secretary-General with an easy familiarity, and they were standing near the entrance where the races of mankind passed in and out: both tall, both stately, both handsome, both alert, the one clad in the glittering robes of his homeland, the other in a dark-blue business suit, subtly different, yet subtly alike.

"What an extraordinary young man," Orrin Knox remarked.

"Trouble," Claude Maudulayne remarked. "Trouble for us both."

"Why don't you give him his little seat in the UN and his God-given right to make boring speeches to the General Assembly and get headlines in the New York *Times?* That's all they want, most of these petty little politicians who come out of the bush. It's the great bauble of the century."

"We have given a definite promise, at a definite time, under definite conditions," the British Ambassador said doggedly. "It is only a year away, and even then they will be so poorly prepared it may mean chaos. Her Majesty's Government will simply not turn loose an undiscipline mob if we can help it, until there is some chance of orderly transition."

"Here comes Terry, ready or no," the Secretary said in a mocking tone.

"For you, too," Lord Maudulayne said. Then he added with a rare show of bitterness, "After all, it *is* post-Geneva. And we all know what that means."

"Yes," Orrin Knox conceded, "we all do."

"Miss Mahdrahani of India, please," the young lady said. "Miss Mahdra-hani of the delegation of India, please call the Delegates' Lounge."

2

Now it was autumn, the time of blowing leaves and warm, regretful weather; and yet it did not take any great feat of imagination or effort of will for the Secretary of State to return himself instantly to the terrible tensions of the bright spring days six months ago when he and his colleagues from the Senate had taken off for Geneva from Washington's National Airport. As he matched the loping stride of Lord Maudulayne along the low, swoop-ing corridors past the constantly recurring glassy vistas of the United Nations building to Conference Room 4 and the inevitable wrangle that awaited them there in First Committee, he could remember very well each detail of that strange, unlikely episode. It had brought a new emphasis to the world, produced a major and not yet clearly understood shift in the East-West confrontation, given to the United States at once new stature and a new need for friends. Partly it had been the President's doing, partly his. Neither they nor anyone else was quite sure, even now, exactly what had been wrought in those two fantastic, terror-haunted days when it seemed that it would take but a breath—a whisper—and catastrophe beyond imagin-ing would be visited at once upon the human race.

Well: it hadn't been, and for that, Orrin Knox thought grimly, the good Lord Himself was probably responsible, since His children were so unclear about how it happened. The good Lord and the instincts of nearly two centuries of freedom, which had stood them in good stead when the final chips, or what seemed to be the final chips, were down.

There had been little conversation in the plane, he recalled, as it had hissed out across the empty wastes of the Atlantic. The President, much heartened by the enormous crowd that had come out to see them off with such loving fervor at the airport, had soon dropped off to sleep—"One time when it can really be called the sleep of the just," the Senate Majority Leader, Bob Munson of Michigan, had remarked to Orrin with an affectionate glance at the dozing Chief Executive—and the rest had occupied themselves with magazines, or brief, murmured conversations, or their own occasional naps. Senator Tom August of Minnesota, chairman of the Senate Foreign Relations Committee, had looked about nervously for a while, staring with deep intensity at the water until Senator Warren Strickland, the Senate Minority Leader, had finally asked, "Well, Tom, and what are the wild waves saying?" At this inquiry, which seemed to disrupt some obscure train of thought that probably only he could follow, the senior Senator from Minnesota had peered up in his startled, owl-like way, mumbled something unintelligible, and finally buried his nose in an old copy of *Life*. (ROBERT A. LEFFINGWELL, the caption on the cover portrait said; WILL THE

SENATE SAY YES? The recent nominee for Secretary of State, photographed at a moment before he knew that the Senate would say NO, looked out upon the world with a confident and self-satisfied air.) Shortly before the chief petty officers came in to start arranging things for lunch, Bob Munson had come over and sat down beside Orrin Knox, and for a time their conversation, first cautiously and then with increasing candor and trust, had ranged over events that neither of them in the rush of recent days had found time to discuss with one another: the long, bitter Senate battle over the Leffingwell nomination; the devious yet ultimately goodhearted machinations of Senator Seab Cooley of South Carolina; the contest between Orrin, then senior Senator from Illinois, and the late President; the President's death; the sudden yet curiously reassuring ascension of Vice President Harley M. Hudson of Michigan to the Presidential chair; and the dark tragedy, which had cost them so much in pain and sorrow and yet curiously given them much, too, in renewed strength and dedication, of Brigham Anderson of Utah, beginning to recede already into an endurable memory, the dark things forgotten and the kindly, decent, generous, and straightforward personality beginning to come into its own as they wanted to remember it and as he would have wanted them to remember it.

Recalling that conversation, and recalling Brig, the Secretary of State was aware for a second that the bright autumn day beyond the glass which at almost every turning commingled the United Nations with all outdoors had become shadowed over. With an effort he shook off the profound depression that sometimes came over him when he thought of that shocking suicide, so necessary in some ways yet so unnecessary in others, and told himself that he must not think of things that would weaken or distract him now that he was about to enter First Committee and try to walk the delicate tightrope between loyalty to the British ally beside him and the savage onslaught he knew was coming from the Soviet Ambassador as he heaped ridicule and scorn upon the plan for gradual emancipation of Terrible Terry's Gorotoland. The M'Bulu—that clever, willful, deviously determined young man. What game was he playing, and where did it fit on the chessboard of Soviet-American relations? There was a place for it, he was quite sure, but whether it would be on his side of the board or Vasily Tashikov's, he did not know. But he was sure the M'Bulu knew, and he contemplated for a rueful moment the perils that can sometimes arise from an education at Oxford, the London School of Economics, and Harvard University, fused into one shrewd brain and fired with a fierce ambition.

After their luncheon on the plane, he remembered as he paused in the long, red-carpeted corridor to greet the delegate from Cameroun, two ladies from Nicaragua, and the Ceylonese who was executive director of the Economic and Social Council, a certain practical animation had come upon the Geneva-bound party. With the meal they had put past things away and begun to think seriously about what lay ahead. Harley—even now, six months after his accession, Orrin still referred to the President by his given name in his thoughts and sometimes, embarrassingly, in face-to-face conversation—had moved, with the same surprising sure-footedness that had characterized all his actions in the first hectic week of his Administration, to put the problem in the perspective he deemed best for the country.

"Orrin will probably tell me I'm all wet," he had begun with a little smile at the Secretary, "but I think the best thing for us to do is keep calm and follow my lead." He looked at the glistening waters far below, beginning to turn silvery in the flat rays of the afternoon sun as the day declined and night raced toward them out of Europe. "I do have one, you know," he added in a tone that chided them with a little humorous mildness for thinking he might not. "Even though I think maybe I'll just keep it to myself for a while."

"But, Mr. President—" Orrin had begun with some impatience.

"Even though we too have now landed an expedition successfully on the moon," the President continued calmly, "in the eyes of the world we go to Geneva, to some degree, under Soviet threat. They demanded that we go, and the Presi—my predecessor—had already accepted before our own expedition landed. So when I followed through on his acceptance, it appeared that we were yielding to threat and were afraid to stay away. You understand, of course," he added quietly, so that if they did not understand it, there would be no doubt, "that we were not. I was not. I thought it best to go letting them think that. I think it is still best to let them think that."

"I don't quite see—" Bob Munson began in a puzzled tone.

"Surprise has its advantages," the President said. "One lesson I learned from *him*," he commented with a sudden chuckle, and for a moment they could see the predecessor he referred to, so strong, so dominant, so determined, so devoted to the country, and so full of tricks. "Would he ever be surprised to see me now!"

"He's not the only one," Tom August blurted out, and then corrected himself hastily. "That is, Mr. President—I mean—" But the President led their laughter, and after a moment the Senator from Minnesota stopped blushing and joined in, timidly at first, but with a growing assurance.

"We don't sound at all like a group of men on their way to surrender their country," Senator Strickland observed with satisfaction, and the President smiled.

"No more are we; though, as I say, I think it's just as well they continue to think there's at least an outside chance. They're awfully cocky after that broadcast from the moon and that big stout ultimatum to get to Geneva. And here we are, of course, getting to Geneva. So let them dream. I have an idea or two about it."

"My only worry, Mr. President," Bob Munson said, "is whether we should have let them think, even for a minute, that we were giving in. I rather wondered, in fact, why you didn't tell them to go to hell the minute you took over."

"I believe in giving his head to an opponent who's riding for a fall," the President said. "It makes the tumble that much more emphatic. Don't worry, Bob. We'll work it out."

"I certainly hope so," Orrin Knox said; and after a moment, explosively, "by God, we'd better!"

And thinking now of the reactions all around the world to that lonely flight across to Geneva, scene of so many blasted hopes and dead ideals, he was aware that he had not been the only one so desperately concerned. Not since Munich had the world waited in quite such fearful expectancy for an international event, and on the short-wave radio as they rode along they could hear the tongues of the nations raised in varying degrees of near-hysteria to chronicle their journey. When they touched down briefly at Shannon, a silent throng had crowded to the gates and along the edges of the field, never stirring, never speaking, as they stepped out to take the air and look about them. Then as they lifted off a great cheer had arisen, touching them deeply. Back in their seats they found that newspapers had been put aboard, and the crisis was made even more emphatic and insistent for them. "WORLD ON BRINK OF DISASTER," the London *Daily Mail* exclaimed. "WILL U.S. CAPITULATE?" the *News-Chronicle* wanted to know. "GRAVE CONCERN," the London *Times* admitted; "P.M. TO ADDRESS HOUSE." "WAR?" demanded the *Express*. And from their own country, flown up from Paris in the day's overseas editions, the New York *Times* carried an eight-column, three-line banner which began "WORLD AWAITS FATEFUL CONFERENCE," while the New York *Herald Tribune* warned that "HUMANITY MAY FACE EXTINCTION IF PARLEY FAILS."

But here was humanity six months later still alive and kicking, and as he and the British Ambassador emerged from the elevator on the lower level and started over the tan and orange Ecuadorian carpets toward the group of delegates, guards, and press standing about the entrance to Conference Room 4, the Secretary of State thought with an ironic conviction that it would probably be a while yet before that condition changed. Whether Geneva had made it less likely or more so that ultimate catastrophe would overtake the world, no one could say with certainty at the moment; but that it had been absolutely imperative for the United States that the conference conclude as it did, there was not now, nor had there been then, the slightest doubt.

Of this, as they became airborne again and turned south for the Continent, they were instinctively aware, although they did not know at the moment just how the President intended to achieve it. He remained bafflingly exclusive about his thoughts, so much so that there were moments when his Senate colleagues came close to dressing him down as though he were still the kindly, rather bumbling, rather timorous, and uncertain Vice President they had known for the past seven years. Senator Munson, indeed, had at one moment started to exclaim, "For God's sake, Harley!" but had thought better of it and ended in a muffled expletive which did not, however, conceal his definite opinions on the subject. This amused the President.

"Now, Bob," he said, "and all of you: take it easy. I'm worried about this—" his eyes darkened and a sudden look of disturbing sadness touched his face for a moment—"but suppose I were to show any outward signs of it, or even let myself really feel it inside? Why, you'd be scared to death. I remember how it is, it's only been a week since I was on the other side of it. There comes a moment sooner or later in any real crisis when the most important thing in the world is to help the man in the White House stay on an even keel, because if he starts to crack, then everything starts to crack. You don't *want* me to show concern, really; the most absolutely necessary thing in the world for the United States right now is that I *not* show concern. So don't push me into showing it, because if you force me to show it I may begin to feel it, and then nobody could tell what might happen." He looked at them one by one, an expression of absolute trust and candor that they found very touching. "Now, isn't that right?"

"Yes, Harley," Bob Munson said after a moment, "that's right . . . O.K., I won't press. But I do think we should have a little more co-ordinated planning for what we're going to do. Don't you, Orrin?" An amused glint came into his eyes. "After all, you're always so busy about things, and you are Secretary of State. I'm surprised you're not raising hell on the subject."

"Well," Orrin said with an answering smile, "I do assume that at some point along the way the President is going to take the Secretary of State into his confidence—and all of us, in fact. But you know Harley. He has a fearful ego underneath it all."

"Oh, sure," the President said. "Oh, sure, sure. I really think you boys ought to give Orrin a medal. He's really showing great restraint for a man who thinks he ought to be where I am. And may well be, one of these days."

At this reference to his long-standing ambitions for the White House, which had been more customary from the late Chief Executive than Orrin expected them to be from his successor, the Secretary of State gave a rather rueful smile and shook his head.

"No, I've learned my lesson. I tried—and tried—and it didn't work out—and then suddenly you appointed me and said you wouldn't run to succeed yourself next year—and now it does seem a possibility again—but I've stopped worrying about it. You can only take so much of this he's down, he's up, he's down, he's up business, you know. If it happens, it happens. If it doesn't, well, I can always go back to law, I suppose."

"You've turned Knox into a philosopher," Senator Munson said. "None of us thought it could be done."

"If I know Orrin," the President said, "this reformation will last until the next time he gets up a head of steam about something. Then watch out!"

"Right now," the Secretary said, "I'm generating a head of steam about the Russians. You may have to hold me down in Geneva, Harl—Mr. President. I suppose it would be quite possible to say something there that would blow up the world."

"Oh, dear," Tom August said. "I hope not."

"It would," the President said quietly. "And of course you're just joking now, Orrin. You wouldn't say anything irresponsible."

"No. But it is hard to avoid a little irritation now and then."

"There's the understatement of the week," Warren Strickland remarked.

"We're on the moon, too," the President pointed out. "Our cards are just as good as theirs, when all is said and done, even though they've succeeded in stampeding a lot of the rest of the world into thinking they're miraculously ten thousand miles ahead."

"The crowd at Shannon didn't seem to think so," Senator Strickland said, and the President nodded.

"An enormous goodwill goes with us. Apparently they feel we mean well."

"Oh, yes," Orrin Knox said, "they always feel we mean well. They can kick us around six and nine-tenths days of the week, but now and again, on the remaining one-tenth of the seventh day, they will sometimes reluctantly admit that we mean well."

The President shrugged.

"Well. That in itself is something . . ." He looked below, where the darkness held England, and suddenly leaned forward. "Now, what's that?"

"It looks to me," Bob Munson said as they all peered out, "like bonfires. You don't suppose," he said half humorously, "they're for us, do you?"

"I'll have the radioman check," the President said, reached for the intercom, and gave the order. In a moment the copilot appeared in the doorway.

"It is for us, sir! We just checked the Air Ministry and the government has suggested that all along the route the people light fires for us. The Ministry says they're doing it in France, too. We're going to be lighted all the way in."

"Well, what do you know," the President said softly. "So we come to Geneva on a path of light . . . Tell the pilot to turn on the landing lights and keep sweeping them down to the ground and up again at one-minute intervals from now on. That way they'll know that we know and that we appreciate it."

And so they had proceeded, the little beacons flaring out of the darkness far below, the lights of the plane gravely responding as it sped on south over England, the Channel, and France: an exchange of messages, profoundly moving, which emphasized the fearful loneliness of their journey yet gave them much heartening for it.

It would be a long time if ever, he realized as he and Claude Maudulayne entered First Committee and began to move toward their neighboring seats at the left of the inner horseshoe of blue-leather chairs, before any of them would forget the highway of light they had traveled down in the closing moments of their flight. At last the President had broken the silence. "I am always impressed with the enormous kindness of ordinary people. If I have that to support me, I can take my chances with the rest."

The feeling had been heightened when they landed at Cointrin Airport and, transferring to limousines provided by UN headquarters in Geneva, rode into the city along Route de Meyrin and Rue de la Servette. The citizenry was out in force. American flags showed everywhere, people stood eight and ten deep along the way, and the cheers that began for them at the airport swelled steadily as they drove along. Here, too, was the emphasis on light, springing from some atavistic instinct in the human race, going back so far into ancient night that the mind could not follow even if the mind dared. Torches and flares danced everywhere, and as they turned into Rue de Lausanne and proceeded slowly past the League of Nations building along Lake Geneva to the villa hastily procured for them by the UN, a solid wall of flame kept them company on the left and threw the giant shadows of their progress out across the night-dark water.

At the villa they were informed that the Russians would be expecting them at 10 A.M. the next morning at the Palais des Nations. The President sent word back that they would be there at 3 P.M., and after a little desultory small talk and a nightcap with several very nervous officials of UN/Geneva, they bade one another good night and went off to bed.

Off to bed and, in his own case, Orrin remembered, right off to sleep. He had been interested to find next morning that the others had done the same. Bob Munson explained it simply enough: "I don't know whether it was the bonfires, or what, but suddenly last night I got the conviction that this is going to work out all right. If so many nice people think so highly of us, how can we fail?"

They had all agreed; but of course, the Secretary thought as he watched the delegate of Ghana coming into First Committee with Vasily Tashikov, the gorgeous M'Bulu, and a pallid little man from Hungary, the world did not run on such simple lines. It took more than the good wishes of nice people to carry on the affairs of humanity: it took guts and character and tenacity, and now and again a flair for the dramatic, which the President, again to their surprised relief, presently proved that he had.

Ranging back now over their two meetings with the Soviets in Geneva, while First Committee filled up and gradually began to get under way, in true UN fashion, half an hour late, Orrin Knox could see that Harley's strategy from the first had been exactly right for the situation that confronted him. His offhand dismissal of the Russian demand that the Americans appear at 10 A.M. had of course given him the world's headlines immediately, and he had never once let them slip away from him thereafter. He had held a press conference at 11 and another at 2 P.M. At each, with calm good nature, he had proceeded to reduce the Soviet position to one, essentially, of bad manners, and rather ridiculous bad manners at that. He had been confident but not boastful about the progress of the American moon landing, respectful but not overawed by the Russians' parallel endeavor. The whole confrontation here in Geneva, he had implied, was rather unnecessary and not a little stupid. Simply by his manner, tone, and general deportment, he had managed to convey to the world a picture of a man not in the slightest hurried, harried, intimidated, or upset.

It was no wonder that when they arrived in the gorgeous spring afternoon at the Palais des Nations amid the screaming sirens and sputtering exhausts of their motorcycle escort, the Soviets should have been awaiting them with obvious impatience and a steadily mounting anger. But when the Chairman of the Council of Ministers came down the steps to meet the car, advancing slowly in his dour, slab-sided, and characteristically suspicious way, the President shook hands with an almost absent-minded cordiality and then commented on the weather.

"What a beautiful spring day, Mr. Chairman!" he exclaimed. "I am so glad you offered me the opportunity to see Geneva for the first time, and in such a lovely season of the year. I am quite glad now that I decided to come."

At this Tashikov, with whom Orrin supposed he would have to deal very shortly as the delegate from Yugoslavia, rapped the gavel for First Committee to come to order, had leaned forward and muttered something harshly in the Chairman's ear. The Chairman had nodded in the grimly thoughtful fashion familiar from a million photographs and television glimpses and snapped out, "Da, it is beautiful!" and turning on his heel had trudged doggedly up the steps. The President waved to the cameras with a broad smile and wink that amused all but the Soviet photographers, shrugged elaborately, beckoned to his companions, and started, in a deliberately leisurely fashion, to follow.

His host, if that was the proper designation, had disappeared down the hallway when the American party entered the building. With another shrug and a humorous look about, the President continued past the long line of guards standing at attention and the massed flags of the two nations intermingled with exact mathematical equality by the UN/Geneva protocol office, until he came to the heavily-guarded bronze doors of the Assembly Hall and there found some three hundred reporters clamoring without success to get in. He then precipitated the crisis of the day.

"I don't know where the Chairman has gone to," he said to Tashikov, who was waiting at the door, "but you can tell him that my predecessor accepted this invitation on the sole understanding that this meeting would be open to the press, radio, and television of the world. I agreed to honor his acceptance on the same understanding. Is the meeting to be open?"

"Mr. President," the Soviet Ambassador began coldly, "my government felt it would save you embarrassment in the eyes of the world if—"

"Is it!" the President snapped, and Tashikov snapped back, "It is not!"

"Very well," the President said without a moment's hesitation. "Come along, gentlemen."

And he had swung about and led them, startled but having the sense to conceal it, back to the entrance, back to the steps, back to the waiting limousines, and so, with a roar and a flourish and the inevitable scream of sirens, back along the dazzling blue lake in the gleaming bright sun and the warm whipping wind to the villa.

There he collapsed into an enormous overstuffed chair with a little grunt of satisfaction and a happy smile.

"Now," he said with what was for him a surprising use of profanity, "let's see what the bastards make of that."

"My God, Mr. President," Bob Munson had said, and not entirely joking either, "hadn't you better check and see if Washington is still there?"

"Washington is still there," the President had responded in the same vigorous vein. "Washington will be there a damned sight longer than these sons of bitches. Have a drink, everybody. I'm perfectly happy, but you all look as though you might need it."

"Yes," Orrin Knox agreed, "I think we do."

Now, as he put on his earphone for the simultaneous translation in First Committee and switched the dial over the six channels to English on Channel 2, he could remember with satisfaction Tashikov's appearance when he came to the villa at 6 P.M. The Soviet Ambassador had been white-faced and quivering, both at the situation and at the Secretary's insistence on meeting him in front of the press in the villa's ballroom. Under the anger Orrin could sense an uneasy and growing uncertainty. It had not been alleviated, he knew, when he informed the Ambassador tersely that the President had given orders that he was not to be disturbed for the rest of the night.

"I thought he was entertaining the Chairman at a state dinner at 9 P.M.," Tashikov had said angrily. "And the Chairman will entertain him tomorrow night. That was the agreement."

"Agreements can be broken," the Secretary had taken some satisfaction in pointing out, "as you have already proved this day. Anyway, I think it's just as well to get away from this standard nonsense about how much everybody loves everybody at these international conferences. You didn't ask us here to be friendly. You thought you would bring us here to destroy us. Well: you haven't; nor will you. Now, state your business, and if it's worthwhile, I'll tell the President. That's my function."

"We cannot possibly agree to open the conference to the press!" the Ambassador said.

"We can't possibly agree to attend unless it is open," the Secretary replied. "Tell the Chairman. Good night."

And taking a leaf from the President's book, he turned on his heel and went back to the private quarters where the White House communications center had set up an enormous bank of transmitters and receivers, over which he could hear the frantic commentators of his own country telling the world how horribly dangerous the American delegation's behavior was and how irresponsibly it jeopardized the world's hopes for peace.

Watching Tashikov now as he launched into another of his high-pitched tirades against the United States, translated word for word and smug inflection for smug inflection by the UN translator, Orrin Knox recalled with a grim amusement the Ambassador's three subsequent visits to the villa that night: at 8 P.M., at 11, and, finally, at 1 A.M. Each time their conversation had been roughly the same, and each time it seemed to be briefer; and yet the Secretary of State had the growing conviction that all he had to do was stand firm and presently he would win out. At the last he had gestured to all the cameras, the reporters, and the television gear before which they were standing. "Do you know what you're doing, Mr. Ambassador? You're making yourself utterly and completely absurd."

"Very well," Tashikov had said with a black anger that sounded, at last, completely genuine, "if that is your attitude, your blood be on your own heads, Americans!"

But at 3 A.M., after they had all gone to bed, a courier had come and awakened the Secretary: the Russians would meet them at the Palais des Nations at 3 P.M., and the conference would be open.

"Imperialist colonializers . . . oppressing the just aspirations of the peoples for freedom . . . destroyers of human rights . . . enemies of justice . . ." The idealistic phrases of the liberty-loving friends of Hungary, Poland, Rumania, Bulgaria, Czechoslovakia, Albania, East Germany, and the Baltic states came to him in violent precision over the earphone as he watched the Soviet Ambassador pounding and gesticulating across the curved horseshoe of seats in First Committee. He had heard it all so many times before—so infinitely many times. But never, he was sure, with quite the ominous and portentous contempt with which it had been hurled at the President and his companions by the Chairman of the Council of Ministers as he delivered his three-hour denunciation in Geneva.

After one or two futile attempts to interrupt, the President had sat back with an expression both amused and bored while the torrent of invective flooded in upon them through the same UN earphones and apparatus of translation. In fact, it could have been the same translator: there was the same precise rendering of emphasis and inflection, a mimicry so perfect as to border, unconsciously or perhaps not, on parody. The gist of the first two and a half hours of it differed little from what had been coming out of Moscow ever since the Soviets began their calculated campaign of world imperialism at the end of the Second World War. "I don't think they like us," Bob Munson had confided at one point, leaning across to Orrin behind the President's chair. "I'm saddened," the Secretary had replied with a cheerful amusement that caused an uneasy little ripple through the ranks of the Soviet delegation.

In the final half hour, however, the Chairman, looking about with his angry scowl and customary hostile expression, had gotten down to business. It was not a pleasant prospect that he laid out before the world; although it was, as Warren Strickland remarked later, no different from the prospect presented so often in the past by his late predecessor before that worthy's abrupt and unexpected demise. It just sounded uglier, reduced to bald essentials and stripped of the grins, the proverbs, and the bouncy banging-about.

"Gospodin!" he had begun, giving to that word, as versatile as the French alors!, a fateful and somber inflection: "Gentlemen, attend me well. You have come here at the direction of the Government of the U.S.S.R., after great and overpowering gains by the U.S.S.R., to hear what the U.S.S.R. requires of your country in the interests of world peace. It is this:

"You will at once abandon the imperialist military alliance known as the North Atlantic Treaty Organization, and will assist with all possible speed in the liquidation of the NATO armed forces. This to be accomplished not later than one month from today.

"You will abandon all military and naval bases of whatever nature on the continents of Europe, Asia, Africa, South and North America, exclusive of the United States, retaining only those bases not more than ten miles from the shores of the continental United States. This to be accomplished not later than one month from today.

"You will terminate at once all missile and space exploration projects of the United States, transferring immediately to the U.S.S.R. control of all such projects and their personnel.

"You will terminate at once the experimental programs of the United States in the field of nuclear, thermonuclear, chemical, germ, and other super-weapons, transferring immediately to the U.S.S.R. control of all such projects and their personnel.

"You will reduce the Army of the United States to one hundred thousand officers and men, effective two months from today.

"You will reduce the Navy of the United States to ten battleships, five destroyers, and thirty supporting vessels, with suitable complements. You will discharge all other naval personnel and transfer to the United Nations Security Council title and control of all other vessels presently in the United States Navy.

"You will immediately destroy, under supervision of the United Nations Security Council, all nuclear-powered submarines in the United States Navy and immediately discharge their personnel.

"You will immediately disband and destroy, under supervision of the United Nations Security Council, the Air Force of the United States and most particularly the Strategic Air Command.

"You will abrogate at once all treaties of alliance, mutual assistance or defense, between the government of the United States and other governments.

"You will take immediate steps to make certain that persons friendly to the U.S.S.R. are brought into the Cabinet of the President and other high offices of your government, and you will take steps also immediately to assure a friendly attitude toward the government of the U.S.S.R. on the part of the press, radio, television, and motion picture industries of the United States.

"You will prepare to receive in Washington not later than one week from today commissioners of the U.S.S.R., who will advise you on carrying out this agreement.

"You will appoint immediately two representatives to sit with the representatives of the U.S.S.R., the Afro-Asian States, the People's Republics of Europe, the People's Republics of the Caribbean and Latin America, and a representative of the Secretary-General of the United Nations, to supervise the carrying-out of all the terms of this agreement."

He paused and looked up and down the long table, and only the whirring of the television cameras and the sounds of pencils racing over paper in the press areas along the walls broke the silence. His gaze came back to that of the President, who looked at him with impassive curiosity from directly across the table. He gave a sudden cough and an impatient, angry shake of his head.

"Now, gentlemen," he said, "these terms may at first glance seem harsh and difficult for you to accept. Be assured it is not the intention of the U.S.S.R. to be harsh but only to do what is obviously necessary to guarantee the peace of the world. Our sole interest lies in removing the causes of friction and of war. We have tried for many years without success to persuade the United States to abandon policies which could lead only to war. The United States has persisted in these policies even though it has been obvious to the world that they could have only one conclusion, a conclusion which would be disastrous for all mankind.

"Now the time has come to change these false and wrongheaded policies. Soviet science has placed in our hands the means to do so. We would be betraying our responsibility to the human race if we did not exercise this new power to make the United States abandon its mad drive toward war and adopt policies desired by all the peace-loving peoples of the earth. That is our sole interest, gentlemen. We are here in the cause of peace. Do not, I beg of you, stand in the way of the world's yearning for peace."

He paused, and this time it was the President who coughed, a perfunctory and rather disinterested little sound which he emphasized by smiling politely and saying, "Excuse me," in a friendly voice. The Chairman frowned but went on.

"You are asking yourselves, as the watching world may no doubt be asking, why should you yield to these Soviet cries for peace? Why should the great United States abandon its drive toward war and rejoin the community of the world's peace-loving peoples? Are there not profits to be gained by continuing to pursue a policy of war? Is there not power to be gained by continuing to pursue a policy of war? Gentlemen, do not believe it! No, gentlemen, that day is vanished forever. To continue on such a course is to follow an empty dream, to get holes in your shoes chasing a swamp fog.

"Why, gentlemen, do you think"—and here a heavy sarcasm came into his voice—"do you think there are only radio transmitters in the Soviet expedition to the moon? Do you think that is all we sent up there? Do you think it is just a contest in radio broadcasts that exists between our two countries? No, gentlemen, we—(the translator hesitated and then produced)—tucked in— we tucked in a little something else along with the bread and cheese to keep us healthy when we reached the moon. We did not want to rob you of this contest in radio broadcasts, but we wanted to be sure that we had some other argument available when we asked you to come here and accept guarantees for peace.

"That argument is up there too, gentlemen. It needs only a signal from us and it will suddenly be down here on earth again, falling on Washington and New York and Chicago and St. Louis and Denver and San Francisco and all your other fine cities. That is our argument, gentlemen, and you must not stand in the way of it. And, gentlemen! We cannot necessarily be sure that these are the only cities it will hit if you force us to use it. It may also hit

London and Paris and Rome and many other capitals in the former imperialist alliance ring of the United States. We should not like this to happen, but if you force us to use our argument, gentlemen, we might not be able to control it entirely. This would be a heavy responsibility for the United States to assume, gentlemen. The results would be very sad for the world." He glanced at the watching cameras. "The world is right there now, gentlemen. What do you have to say to it, yes or no?"

And with a gesture that did indeed bring suddenly into the room the watching presence of humanity around the globe—Americans in their pleasant homes, Russians in their dark cities and mud-daubed huts, English in their clubs, Malays in Singapore, a white-robed Nigerian in Lagos, some Indians in New Delhi, little excited groups in the sunny alleys of Rome, a sheepherder in New Zealand, businessmen in Rio, tribal chieftains huddled around a squeaky receiver in Jebel-el-Druz, vividly dressed Malagasys in Tananarive, a frightened group of tourists in Tahiti, and many and many a million more on that bright spring day—he folded his arms abruptly and sat back with an intent and listening scowl. A silence again fell on the room, broken as before only by the busy whirring of cameras and a little stir here and there among the press, as history quieted down and prepared to attend the President of the United States.

"Mr. Chairman," he began slowly, leaning forward to rest his elbows on the arms of his chair and look with a candid appraisal at his opponent, "I would like to think that I am in the presence of a sane man instead of a maniac, for if I am in the presence of a maniac, then this world, so beautiful in the spring, does not have much longer to live."

He paused, and there was an audible intake of breath around the room and, no doubt, around the earth. But he appeared not to notice and after a moment resumed in a curiously detached voice, as though he were addressing, not the Russians, but the world, as indeed he was.

"I came here with my delegation, composed of old friends of mine from the Senate of the United States, thinking we would find serious and sober proposals for easing the tensions that afflict our poor common humanity." He stopped and his glance went slowly up and down the Russian side. "Instead," he said, and a new vigor came into his voice, "we are confronted with utter frivolity. Yes, gentlemen, with utter and complete frivolity. With the most irresponsible playing with the destinies of mankind. With something so monstrous it would under other conditions be considered a joke, though an evil and despicable one."

"*Gospodin—*" the Chairman began angrily, but the President went on.

"Evil and despicable!" he said, with all the intensity of one coming from a small town in Michigan confronted suddenly with something dirty and unexpected in the middle of the living-room rug. "Evil and despicable! *How dare you*, Mr. Chairman?"

"*Gospodin—*" the Chairman said softly, but again the President brushed him aside.

"We have heard here every dream of every Soviet leader since the end of

World War II, boiled down to essence and presented with a straight face. Get out of this! Get out of that! Scrap your defenses! Abandon your friends! Give the world to Communism! Forget your responsibilities to humankind and surrender to us! All the dearest fantasies of the Kremlin have been rolled up in one and presented to us here complete with threats. *Gospodin,*" he said, giving the word an angry and sarcastic emphasis, "*you* attend *me* well, and I will give you the answer of the United States.

"We will never accept your ridiculous proposals. We will never abandon our duty to the world. We will never betray our friends. We will never shirk our destiny or our responsibility." And he concluded slowly, with a softness to match the Chairman's own, "Never. Never. Never . . .

"And so what will you do now? Blow up the United States? Destroy the globe? Use upon humanity all those rockets which, as your predecessor was so fond of telling us before you disposed of him, you 'produce like sausage?' Gentlemen, there are two sausage factories in this world. There are two bomb factories in this world. There are nuclear submarines with nuclear weapons beneath the seas of this world. There is everything in this world to destroy not only us but you as well. *Gospodin,* do you really think we will not use it? And do you think you will gain anything thereby?

"Mr. Chairman," he said, and at last he spoke directly to the man who scowled upon him from across the table, "do you not see what you have done by this threat of terror, not only this threat but all the others you have flung upon the world over the years? You have made terror ridiculous. We have so much terror at our fingertips, you and I, that there is no more terror. It no longer makes sense. It is absurd.

"Blow us up, then! And we will blow you up, then! And let us together blow up the world, then! And that will be the end of humanity, then! And what will that accomplish, can you tell me?

"You are childish and unworthy to be trusted with your great responsibilities. And I and my delegation," he concluded quietly, "have nothing more to say or do here. If you wish to meet us in the United Nations to conduct negotiations with a decent respect for our mutual needs and the needs of humanity, we shall be there as always. Right now," he said in four words that were so simple they dignified the moment better than oratory could, "we are going home."

And he rose slowly, and with a friendly nod to his countrymen, who also rose as in a daze and followed him, he walked with his sturdy, plodding gait down the long table past the cameras, past the guards, down the steps, into the limousine, and once again in screaming procession beside the blue lake in the warm wind along the Rue de Lausanne to the villa in the bright spring sun.

And the world did not collapse or the skies fall, Secretary Knox thought as he watched Tashikov come to the end of his indignant peroration and prepare to make way for a few words from Ghana prior to First Committee's vote on the Panamanian resolution to have the General Assembly take up immediate independence for Terrible Terry's Gorotoland. Yet for a little while it had seemed that they might and the globe had awaited with fearful trepidation what would happen next.

"My God, Harley!" Bob Munson had said when they were alone in the villa. "My God!"

"What else could I do?" the President asked simply. "Really, what else could I do?"

And that was it, of course: there was nothing else. But as they rode back to Cointrin Airport that evening they were not, despite the outward appearance of calm they managed to muster, at all sure what lay in wait for them or for the world. No further word of any kind had come from the Russians, and anything from kidnaping to an immediate nuclear holocaust could have greeted them. This time the crowds were small. No one cheered. There were little gestures and waves now and again, and it was not difficult to tell that they were again being wished well. But a terrible terror lay on the world. No one at all felt like demonstrations now.

Presently the plane was airborne and the lovely city faded in the night. Fog and clouds came on soon after they lifted off, and Europe, the Channel, and England were hidden from them. It was just as well, for they did not really think that any bonfires were burning for them now. What they were going home to they did not know, either: whether there would be cities or a country left, although the President had received no word of anything unusual from Washington, and so it seemed likely things were all right, at least for the moment.

Somewhere out from Ireland they broke above the clouds into a clear moonlit night. It was then that Tom August, peering up at earth's companion floating serenely above, said suddenly, "Great God, what's that?"

For a moment, somewhere far out between moon and earth, a tiny red rose blossomed in the endless depths of night—blossomed and grew infinitely brighter for a lovely, horrible minute filled with death and beauty and insane fear, and then began slowly to fade and fade, until at last it disappeared altogether. It was not repeated, and no one had ever been able to discover since whether it had been a shot that failed or simply a Soviet gesture for whatever propaganda value might accrue. It caused great headlines next day, but nobody knew. It was not repeated.

And now here they were in First Committee, Soviet pressure unrelenting but the direct ultimatum, at least for the time being, laid aside. The world had gulped, shifted, adjusted, changed: nobody could say quite how much, or quite in what direction, whether toward or away from the men of Moscow, toward or away from those of Washington. The event, however, had brought an even greater tension to affairs, given many lesser powers a bargaining position they had never known before. The middle nations, the so-called neutrals, the youthful governments of Africa and the uncommitted states, had become even more important now. The contest had reverted to diplomacy and the battle had become even more vicious, using every means at hand. Including, Orrin Knox thought uneasily as he watched Senator Lafe Smith of Iowa come in across the room with a wave and a cheerful grin, the

M'Bulu of Mbuele, that glittering young man who now moved gracefully to the podium and prepared, with a respectful yet confident air, to address the chair.

Terrible Terry no doubt had some surprises up his sleeve for the West: all that education hadn't been wasted on this particular product of the bush. Nor was it entirely clear why he should suddenly wish to visit South Carolina.

"Trouble for both of us," the British Ambassador had said. It might well prove true, though perhaps it could be kept within bounds if Washington would co-operate. If the President would make a gesture, if Cullee Hamilton would perform a possibly distasteful task, if Seab Cooley would not be too obstreperous and unmanageable, if— Ten thousand ifs: such was the unrelenting nature of his new life as Secretary of State.

He thought wistfully of the Senate, some two hundred miles to the south, and now at three minutes to noon preparing to convene, as the M'Bulu said politely, "Mr. Chairman," and began.

3

A month later, after Terrible Terry has cut his swath through the United Nations, the United States, and the affairs of mankind; after Felix Labaiya and his wife and her family have advanced their various ambitions in their various ways; and after Cullee Hamilton and Harold Fry have, each in his own fashion, come to terms with the imperatives of personal need and the obligations of national integrity, the Majority Leader of the United States Senate will look back and wonder why he ever went along with Orrin's idea in the first place.

He will be able to understand it as an intellectual proposition, but he still will not be entirely convinced of its wisdom: a tribute, he will suspect, to that universal state of confusion in which men everywhere, confronted by the necessity for making great decisions on great events, proceed along paths they cannot anticipate toward conclusions they cannot foresee. He will wonder then if the Secretary of State, impressed with the need for charting a careful diplomatic course in the wake of Geneva, may not have gone too far in his willingness to adapt himself to both the supposed attitudes of certain foreign states and the known prejudices of certain domestic critics, some of the latter more noted for their ability to raise hell than for their capacity to understand issues.

Contemplating the results of it all, Senator Robert Munson of Michigan will be inclined to think that the first reactions in Washington were the right ones; although, being aware with what imperfect knowledge and imperfect understanding the human race moves toward its mysterious and shrouded destiny, he will conclude honestly that, after all, the decisions taken may have been the right ones, or, at any rate, no worse than any others that might have been adopted.

Right now, however, as he takes his position at the first desk, center aisle, of the Senate and prepares to bow his head to another of the Senate Chaplain's maundering prayers, the senior Senator from Michigan is not concerned with such philosophic musings as this. Right now the M'Bulu of Mbuele and all the events and people about to be involved with him are among the least important items in the world of Bob Munson. He is aware that the United Nations is engaged in one more controversy about one more would-be African state, and he has followed its general outlines in the press. But he is much more concerned at the moment with the practical problems involved in bringing to conclusion the Senate's debate on the foreign aid bill, and in pushing his balky and cantankerous colleagues toward an adjournment that is already, in late September, several weeks overdue.

It has not been his idea, Senator Munson reflects with some impatience as the clock reaches noon, the President Pro Tempore bangs his gavel, and the Rev. Carney Birch, Chaplain of the Senate, snuffles into another of his admonitory open letters to the Senate and the Lord, to let the Congressional session run on so long. Certainly he and the Speaker of the House would have liked to wind it up a month ago; only the President has seemed to want it prolonged. Since his return from Geneva and the growing public praise and acclaim which have mounted steadily as the world has begun to realize that it will not be blown up because of his actions, Harley has been displaying what Senator Arly Richardson of Arkansas has referred to with his customary sarcasm as "a great urge to play President."

Leaving aside the fact that Harley of course is the President and definitely not playing at it, Arly's casual cloakroom crack nonetheless does express a certain wry attitude on the part of the President's former colleagues on Capitol Hill. The Executive whom *Time* magazine now hails respectfully as "the man the Soviets couldn't scare," and whom the editorial cartoonist of the Washington *Post* now pictures with a certain homespun strength that was hardly noticeable in his drawings when Harley first took office, is obviously enjoying his job. Not only that, he is using it to attempt to push through certain reforms which, like most other reforms of the human, haphazard, peculiar, and peculiarly successful American system, are long overdue. Possibly spurred on by Robert A. Leffingwell, who is receiving great press commendation as director of the President's Commission on Administrative Reform, the President has already proposed a sweeping overhaul of the Defense Department and its allied missile and space programs, a streamlining of the Foreign Service and the overseas information activities of the government, and even, God save the mark, a new farm program. This last has already caused some revision in the Congressional estimates of what he will do next year when his party holds its national nominating convention. "I really believed he meant it when he said he wouldn't run again," Senator Stanley Danta of Connecticut has just been quoted by *Newsweek*, "but when I saw that new farm bill I knew he'd changed his mind."

Whether he has or not (and, queried at his press conference a week ago, the President would only chuckle and say, "My, my, you boys must be hard up for news if you can't think of a better question than that"), and whether his burst of executive activity since returning from Geneva has been his idea or Bob Leffingwell's, the fact remains that he has given Bob Munson a busy summer. The Majority Leader has been held to his duties as rigorously as he ever was during the tenure of the President's predecessor. He has not complained about this, for, after all, it is his job, and it has also given his wife Dolly a chance to hold at least four extra garden parties at "Vagaries," that great white house in Rock Creek Park, that she wouldn't have held if they had returned to Michigan earlier in the summer. But the instinct of twenty-three years in the Senate, the last twelve of them as Majority Leader, tells him that the time has come to get the Congress out of Washington and give its members a chance to rest up from one another.

There comes a point, as Bob Munson is well aware, when Senators and Representatives have been together long enough and it is much better for the country if they can just go away, return home or travel or whatever, and forget the problems of legislating for a while. In a system resting so subtly but inescapably upon the delicate balances of human likes and dislikes, familiarity does not necessarily breed contempt but it does breed an eventual irascibility which, toward session's end, makes the functionings of American democracy rather more subject to personal pitfalls that they should ideally be.

A fast windup to the aid debate—about two more days, Bob Munson estimates—an opportunity for a few last-minute speeches and dramatics by those Senators and Representatives who always have to have the last word for the sake of the political record and whatever headlines it may bring them, and then—home.

So thinks Robert M. Munson as Senator Tom August of Minnesota rises in the Senate to make his concluding speech on the aid bill and at the United Nations the M'Bulu of Mbuele begins to set in train the series of events that will add another ten days to the session and bring to the UN and to both houses of Congress one of the most violent and embittered controversies of recent years.

Unaware of these thoughts of adjournment passing through the mind of the Majority Leader, but fully in accord with their general import, the President Pro Tempore of the Senate is also anxious to get away. Seabright B. Cooley of South Carolina is just turned seventy-six—his colleagues spent all day yesterday trying to outdo one another in paying him tribute, except for Fred Van Ackerman of Wyoming, who deliberately stayed away with the sour comment to the press that he "wasn't interested in soft-soaping senility"—and he fully apprehends that he had best get on home to South Carolina and do some visiting around the state if he wishes to retain his gradually slipping hold upon it. The basic sources of his political power are as ancient as himself, and many of them, indeed, are gone. A great name and a great reputation, great battles in the cause of Carolina and the South, have carried him through election after election; but he is conscious now that new generations, new interests, new industries, and new money in the state are threatening his position as never before.

"Seab won't leave the Senate until they carry him out on a stretcher," Senator John DeWilton of Vermont remarked the other day. The old man knows with a lively awareness that he can be carried out just as effectively on a ballot box. New leaders walk the streets of Barnwell and new voices exchange the softly accented passwords of power in the moss-hung gardens of Charleston. Seab Cooley still commands great respect in his native state, but his instinct is not playing him false: there are whispers everywhere, an urge for someone new, a feeling, sometimes vague but increasingly articulate, that South Carolina should have a younger and more vigorous spokesman in the Senate.

"Younger and more vigorous, my God!" his junior colleague, H. Harper Graham, comments to his fellow Senator. "Could anybody be more vigorous than Seab?" But Harper Graham knows the talk, too, and Seab Cooley has good reason to believe that among those who would not be at all averse to seeing him defeated is Harper Graham himself, melancholy, dark-visaged, filled with ambition and temper almost as great as his own, burning like a dark flame in the Senate. He would not put it past Harper at all to actively seek his political downfall, Seab concludes, and the thought brings an ominous scowl to his face for a moment as he sees his colleague entering at the back of the big brown chamber. Then the look passes almost as it comes and is replaced by the sleepy, self-satisfied expression his fellow Senators know all too well. "What's that old scallywag cooking up now?" Powell Hanson of North Dakota murmurs to Blair Sykes of Texas as they enter the Senate together, and they speculate for an idle and amused moment that he is probably dreaming up some way to get Harper Graham: so well-known to the Senate is the nature of the bond that unites the senior and junior Senators from South Carolina.

Actually, as is so often the case with Seab, the somnolent look conceals a mind at work on much more far-ranging matters than merely how to remove the threat of a bothersome colleague. "Getting Harper" is part of it, but his entire political problem is what engages him now, and the self-satisfied expression is really due to one of those flashes of intuition—or inspiration—"or hashish, or whatever it is," as Senator John Winthrop of Massachusetts once put it—which occasionally show the senior Senator from South Carolina how to work his way out of difficult situations.

It is not even, in this case, anything particularly specific, nor is it associated with the man on whom his eye happens to fall just now; it is just that Seab is reminded that on one issue, at least, neither Harper Graham nor any other successful politician in South Carolina can afford to take a position different from his. The man he sees is Cullee Hamilton, the young colored Congressman from California, but the thought Cullee immediately inspires in the mind of Seab Cooley is not one that directly concerns him; it is simply a generalized reaction, prompted by his presence, going back into the bitter past of a troubled region, stirred by emotions as new as tomorrow's headlines, as old as the tears of time. It is not an especially original thought, but in a political sense it works; and contrary to much violently expressed northern opinion, which conveniently forgets such areas as Chicago, Detroit, and Harlem, it does not work simply because politicians both white and black make use of it for their own selfish purposes. It works because the overwhelming majority of his fellow southerners, like Seab himself, are absolutely convinced of it by birth, by tradition, and by belief. This poses many deeply tragic problems, but the Senator and his fellow citizens can no more change on that particular subject than they could fly, unassisted, to the stars.

By the same token, neither can Cullee Hamilton, as he stands at the center door of the Senate chamber looking about for California's junior Senator, the dashing and slightly overdapper Raymond Robert Smith. There is a bill involving a proposed water viaduct in the San Fernando Valley which is on the Senate calendar awaiting action, and Cullee, aware that this is important to a number of constituents in his sprawling district just north of Los Angeles, wants Ray Smith's help in persuading Bob Munson to pass it through the Senate by unanimous consent in what everybody believes to be these closing hours of the Congressional session.

Cullee already has the Speaker's promise to pass it through the House tomorrow—the Speaker has always been fond of him, personally as well as politically, and Cullee has been well-favored by that powerful gentleman ever since the start of his first term five years ago—but the Senate Majority Leader is another matter. He has rather more on his mind than the Speaker does at the moment, the Senate being customarily more cluttered up with last-minute odds and ends than the House each year when adjournment approaches, and it will take a little extra assistance to get Cullee's bill approved. Not that he anticipates any great difficulty, but it is a matter of timing and that takes care. In this Ray Smith, for all that he is something of a laughing-stock to his colleagues in their cloakroom conversations, can be of real assistance, particularly since those San Fernando Valley constituents are vitally important to him, too. Ray is up for re-election next year, and he is as sharply conscious of his constituency as Seab Cooley is of his. The fact that he too is in rather shaky condition may provide the extra spur to successful action on Cullee Hamilton's bill. An extra spur to Cullee, too, Cullee thinks wryly, if only he were as ambitious as Sue-Dan and as full of git-up-and-go as she constantly tells him he ought to be.

The thought of his wife, though it appears to be a circuitous and indirect way to approach it, and though they would both be surprised at the parallel and for the moment unable to see it, brings him to the very point that is just passing through the clever old mind of the President Pro Tempore of the Senate as their eyes meet for a brief moment across the crowded chamber. He and Seab Cooley do not really know one another, having had only one brief and uncomfortable talk on carefully innocuous matters when Cullee testified at a Senate Judiciary Committee hearing three years ago, but there is a certain instinctive understanding between them; "perhaps," as Cullee told himself dryly at the time, "because we're both Southerners." Possibly for this reason it occurs to each of them in this fleeting instant now that the other may be thinking of the subject of race. Both are right, though there is a shade of difference in their thoughts. Seab is thinking of it in terms of his problem in South Carolina, Cullee, much more basically, in terms of his wife.

"Why don't you run against fancy-nancy Smith for the Senate next year?" she keeps asking in her taunting way. "Because you're afraid a nigger can't make it, even in California?" And when he winces at the expression she laughs and says it again three times. "I know you don't like that word, my poor little Cullee," she tells him in mock-soothing tones. "That's a bad word us enlightened people don't use. But it's true, isn't it, nigger, nigger, nigger?"

It is all he can do at such moments, Cullee admits to himself, to keep from slapping her straight across the face; except that it is, as the M'Bulu of Mbuele has already indicated to the Secretary of State, a beautiful face, and it happens to belong to a girl with whom the young Congressman from California is in love in a way so fundamental he can't help himself. So his only response is a tired sigh and the comment, "Why do you say things like that, Sue-Dan? You know it only bothers me, and what does it gain for you? Do you like to bother me? Haven't you got better games to play than that?" But her response, as so often, is an apparently instant loss of interest. "You sigh an awful lot, lately," she says, and with another little laugh she picks up the cat and a magazine, sinks into a chair, and seemingly becomes lost to the world as she studies the printed page and croons soft endearments to the cat.

Thinking of such scenes, which are becoming increasingly frequent of late, the Congressman sighs again and gives an unconscious, instinctive jerk of his right shoulder, as though someone were trying to hit him and he were ducking the blow. His eyes are troubled behind their gold-rimmed glasses, and across his handsome scholarly face, with its high cheekbones, classic brow, and full lips, an expression of trouble, both innocent and obvious, passes briefly. Ray Smith, approaching him unnoticed from the left, does poke him with a friendly fist and asks, "What's the matter, Cullee? Somebody walking over your grave?" The Congressman shakes his head and looks down at the shorter Senator with a quickly concealing smile.

"I'm worried about water. Are we going to help those folks in the San Fernando Valley? Looks to me like we've got to if we're to be elected next year." Ray Smith grins back and says with a playfulness just a trifle too exaggerated, "Elected to what, Cullee?" And abruptly the Congressman realizes that Ray Smith and his wife agree. He's actually afraid of me, he thinks, and it is impossible to deny a thrill of ego at that. He thinks maybe I could beat him, if I wanted to; or at any rate, he isn't sure he could beat me. And he asks himself again, as he has on many more occasions than he has ever let on to Sue-Dan: why not? Why shouldn't I? California's different; they're more progressive out there. Somebody has to break the ice, and why shouldn't I? Out there, maybe a man could.

Thus his thoughts again parallel Seab Cooley's, and now almost identically.

There is the same commingling of passionate belief, personal ambition, and practical politics; the only added ingredient being that Cullee, a much younger man reared in a much different age, is able to stand back for a second and think to himself with an ironic and troubled amazement how fantastic this America is, which lets one man seek office on one basis in one state and another man seek office on almost the diametrically opposite basis in another state. How broad this umbrella, which covers so many children, he thinks; and underneath the joshing, uncomfortable conversation he is attempting to carry on with Senator Smith a deeper melancholy comes as he adds to himself: and will they ever rest together in harmony and peace, or will they always betray the ultimate reality of brotherhood and love that is the great final promise of the American dream?

But now, he chides himself, you're talking like an editorial writer, and the whole thing is a lot more basic than that. The whole thing at the moment, in fact, is as basic as Sue-Dan Hamilton and what she thinks when she goes to bed with Cullee Hamilton; because while this still happens very often it is beginning to become obvious to one participant, at least, that the other doesn't think too much of it. Certainly not as much as she used to in the first wild months of a union that seemed at the time so inevitable it couldn't be stopped. Now he is beginning to find it possible to think that under certain conditions it *could* be stopped; and the thought terrifies him, for what would life be like without little old Sue-Dan? But even here a basic, ironic honesty still intrudes. You'd get along, boy, his mind tells him; you'd get along. But his body adds instantly, it wouldn't be the same. Oh, no, indeed. It wouldn't be the same.

At once there leaps into his mind—by now Ray Smith is really quite worried that the Congressman does intend to run against him, because he seems so absent-minded and unresponsive to all of Ray's sallies and there surely can be only one explanation for that: Cullee's so busy thinking how to beat him that he isn't able to concentrate on small talk—a picture of hot, dusty Molobangwe, capital of Gorotoland, lying in the blazing sun of distant Africa. He recalls the mud-and-wattle huts, the cattle and chickens in the streets, the guttural, rapid, curiously clicking sound of Terrible Terry's native tongue, and in the rambling, ramshackle European structure, left over from an early ill-fated Christian mission, which now serves as the royal palace, a peculiar conversation with his elusive and half-naked host. The talk appeared to center around politics and the M'Bulu's impatient and uneasy relationship with the British, but underneath it all Cullee had the impression that it concerned Sue-Dan.

They had been in Molobangwe for a week at the request of the House Foreign Affairs Committee, and the visit had proved, so far, quite disappointing. "Why don't you run along over there and see what's up with that boy?" Representative J. B. ("Jawbone") Swarthman of South Carolina, chairman of the committee, had suggested in his lazy drawl. "Mebbe he'll let you in on things he wouldn't tell the rest of us." It was indicative of the working relationships in the Congress that neither Cullee nor Jawbone made any point of this practical reference to his color.

Jawbone's assumption, however, had been false, and this had been very disturbing. In Africa he soon began to feel that he was being received, not as a fellow Negro, but as a prying and probably hostile American. Despite his preliminary reading, he had been a little too goodhearted to expect this, and so his first visit to Africa was proving something of a shock. The conversation with Terry had served to increase this unhappy realization that in a continent of tribes he was regarded as the representative of just another one, and that probably inimical. The whole thing was so foreign to his idealism about his own background, both racial and national, and his exhilaration at the great African surge to independence that was contemporaneous with his college years and start in public life, that he was having considerable difficulty accepting it. Consequently he did not pay too much attention to the M'Bulu's rambling, if charming, discourse. Except that, at the end of it, he had gathered enough to be able to report later to the committee in Washington that there was probably real trouble coming with the British; and to carry away in the back of his mind the feeling that Terence Ajkaje, given half a chance, would love to appropriate his wife.

Whether Sue-Dan fully understood this he never knew directly, except as he was male enough to know when his female was desired by another male. He did realize that she was conscious of it to some extent, and perhaps bothered by it a little. He preferred to think that she had not encouraged it, and indeed there was little opportunity during their long, jolting rides through the back country in Terry's old American jeep that had come down to Gorotoland through the mysterious channels of jungle and desert trade from some unknown long-ago battleground far to the north. His wife had been circumspect and noncommittal in the presence of the M'Bulu, who alternated between showing off his gorgeous robes and appearing stripped to a breechclout with his magnificent torso rippling like molten ebony in the sun. Sue-Dan had professed to be unimpressed by all this, and had even remarked sardonically at one point, "For a man with as many pretty clothes as you've got, Terry, you sure do like to undress." Terry had given her his charming smile and exploded into delighted laughter. After that, save for his final talk alone with the Congressman when they had both sat around half-naked drinking native wine in the steaming hot room that had once resounded to "Rock of Ages" thumped out on a pump organ, the M'Bulu had been ceremoniously and fully clothed.

And now, Cullee thinks uneasily, Terry is at the United Nations and his argument with the British is front-page news, and sooner or later their paths will probably cross again. In fact, he is almost sure they will, for although he has turned down Jawbone's suggestion that he "trot along down to that Jason party for the Emm-booloo in Charleston," he is sure Terry won't miss the chance to come through Washington on his way back to New York and create as many headlines as possible for himself in the process. And he, as the most popular, well-liked, and respected Negro in Congress, will indubitably be expected to be on hand at some point along the line.

He decides, as he stands there by the Senate door responding with a tenth of his mind and attention to the nervous chatter of Senator Smith, that both he and Sue-Dan will stay out of it as much as possible. Patsy Labaiya and her family can whoop it up for old Terry as much as they like, but he, Cullee Hamilton, will do only the minimum that he absolutely has to; and Terry can be a white man's pet nigger if he is willing to lend himself to the Jasons' patronizing ways, but he, Cullee Hamilton, having been down that road and back on several occasions, will be damned if he will do the same. And he is also not disposed, given the present uncertain state of his marital situation, to encourage any stray sparks in igniting any stray dynamite that may be lying around.

He frowns, driving Ray Smith almost frantic, and after an absent-minded expression of thanks for Ray's help on the San Fernando Valley viaduct, meets Seab Cooley's eyes once more, gives a polite nod which is politely returned, goes out the swinging doors of the Senate, and starts back down the long, dim marble corridor, crowded with tourists who think he is probably a clerk, to the House.

At this final exchange of glances, five charming ladies whose presence in the Family Gallery is unnoted by the two participants exchange glances of their own and, with them, amused smiles and a significant nod or two. Beth Knox, wife of the Secretary of State, has come to the Hill to have lunch with Dolly Munson, wife of the Majority Leader. In the corridors on the street level two floors down they have, just a few moments before, run into Kitty Maudulayne, wife of the British Ambassador; Celestine Barre, wife of the French Ambassador; and Patsy Labaiya, wife of the Ambassador of Panama, dressed as always in one of her bright, garish dresses and bright, garish hats. Since no one of any prominence can be seen in Washington with anyone else of any prominence without half a dozen people immediately speculating on the significance of it all, Beth and Dolly have both been instantly struck by this odd conjunction of Britain, France, and Panama. Both have perceived some of its possible implications in view of recent developments at the UN, and it has taken only the slightest and most elusive of feminine communications to produce a unanimous and hearty invitation to join the luncheon party. This has been promptly accepted by Kitty, who loves politics and gossip; by Celestine, who has approved with her gravely silent smile; and by Patsy, who interrupts her own rush of conversation long enough to cry, "My dears, we'd be simply DELIGHTED," and then goes on talking about her own opinion that the recent and surprising marriage of that perennial prowler about town, Senator Lafe Smith of Iowa, may already be on the verge of breaking up. It has been her DISTINCT impression, Patsy informs her companions, two passing newspapermen, a Capitol cop, and a group of tourists from Nebraska, that ALL IS NOT WELL in that household. Why, do THEY know that at Dolly's last garden party at "Vagaries," Lafe and little Irene were seen by Justice Tommy Davis of the

Supreme Court VIOLENTLY arguing behind one of the rhododendrons, and now that Lafe is up there at the United Nations, Patsy's husband, HER husband, Felix, says it's common talk that Lafe is— But here the Senators' private elevator arrives and swallows them up, leaving behind two disappointed newspapermen, one grinning cop, and six puzzled but thoroughly intrigued tourists from Nebraska.

Now in the Family Gallery, where, as Dolly murmurs to Beth, even Patsy Labaiya has to shut up, they have dutifully stood for Carney Birch's prayer and then settled down to watch the Senate for a little while before going back down for their 12:30 luncheon reservation in the Senators' Dining Room. Beth says she can't stay away from the Senate even though Orrin is at State, now—"it's always been home to us, and I guess it will always be"—and now that Dolly has finally landed Bob Munson after long and diligent effort, she is finding that she, too, is drawn constantly to the best show in town. The best, and, with the House, the most important, in the opinion of the Congressional wives. The ambassadorial, knowing that here in these chambers United States foreign policies are implemented and American money is approved for distribution abroad, are inclined to agree.

While Tom August drones on about the aid bill, interrupted occasionally by heckling questions from Paul Hendershot of Indiana and Victor Ennis of California, five busy minds of five busy ladies click away like efficient little machines. Beth Knox, thinking over the telephone call that comes faithfully from Orrin every day that he is away from her, recalls that last night he expressed a genuine worry about the latest developments at the UN. The M'Bulu of Mbuele is vividly present in Beth's mind, for Orrin has told her without embroidery exactly the problems posed by that shrewd young figure: the possibility that the United States, though it will do its best to seek a compromise, may yet have to break with Britain on the issue; the possibility that France, still courting the favor of the young African states she released to independence, may also find herself forced to certain imperatives of national interest; the possibility, not yet supported by real proof but always present, that the Soviets may seek and in Gorotoland possibly find one more African foothold; and the Secretary's additional uneasy feeling that "this boy is a hell-raiser and I don't know where he will jump next."

Added to that, Beth's own feeling of incompleteness when Orrin is away, and she has a good deal to contemplate as Tom August rambles along; added also the fact that just before she left the big comfortable house in Spring Valley for the Hill she received another phone call, this one from Springfield, Illinois. Her son Hal and her daughter-in-law, Senator Stanley Danta's daughter Crystal, had burbled over with the news that the Knoxes would presently be grandparents. This too, understandably, gives her much to think about.

For Dolly Munson, reflecting her husband's concern with getting the Senate session concluded, the problems are also of a domestic, though somewhat less emotional, nature: whether she should have one last quick cocktail party and buffet at "Vagaries" on Saturday night, or whether Congress will have left town by then so that everyone of any importance will be gone—whether she should tell the advance crew of servants to leave for Michigan to open the house in Grosse Pointe next Monday or whether she and Bob should stay over a week and just enjoy Washington and the Valley of Virginia in the beautiful fall weather without having to worry about the Senate, Congress, government, social obligations, or anything else—whether it might not even be best for Bob to take him away altogether, arrange a quick reservation on Cunard to Europe, and do their relaxing in London and Rome. Being married to the Majority Leader has brought with it many subtle responsibilities Dolly never really found out about in her first unhappy marriage. The basic problem of how to take care of a man, which Beth knew instinctively on the day she first met Orrin in college, is only now being fully understood by Dolly.

Kitty Maudulayne, who, like Beth, never doubted from the moment she first saw Claude come riding over the green meadows and stone fences of Crale that this was what life had planned for her, is also concerned to some extent with domestic matters and the possibility of a brief vacation. But being Kitty, loving politics, and very thoroughly aware of the problems implicit in representing a steadily withdrawing power in a world of aggressively advancing forces, she is also vitally concerned with matters at the UN. They come sharply into focus as she watches the handsome young Congressman from California nod briefly to Senator Cooley and leave the chamber. "My dear," Patsy Labaiya whispers loudly behind her hand, "some of them look like BLACK GREEK GODS!" Kitty responds with a brightly absentminded smile and, as she does so, catches the thoughtful eye of Celestine Barre. She knows at once that the wife of the French Ambassador is also reminded of color, and so of Africa, and so of Gorotoland, and of Terry, and of the UN, where events may soon take a turning that could conceivably bring to an end an association possessed of a warmth notably pleasant and notably close in the annals of the Washington diplomatic corps.

This, Kitty thinks with a real regret, will be too bad if it happens; but if it must, she knows there is nothing for it but to smile and say the usual cordially empty things and make the best of it. These necessary estrangements occur in international politics as in domestic—indeed, it has been quite unusual that the Ambassadors of the two major West European powers and their wives should have been good friends at all, so many are the points of friction between their countries—but Kitty is one of the world's nicest people and quite capable of not liking what her husband's profession requires them to do. She knows that he doesn't like it, either, for he told her before going up to New York a couple of days ago that "things may get a little sticky with Raoul and Celestine, but let's keep on with it as long as we can." So they are both hoping that what is known at the United Nations as "The Problem of Gorotoland" may be settled without too intense a strain upon either their personal or national relationships with the Barres. But they are aware that the chances of so pleasant a solution are slim, especially since the Russians, with their grim determination to inflame every friction and destroy every hope for peace, will be busily working on an Anglo-French split along with all their other little projects.

She looks again at Celestine with a smile that holds both worry and affection, and Celestine smiles back in much the same way. Patsy Labaiya, sitting between them, suddenly asks, "Why doesn't that OLD FUDDY-DUDDY sit down?" in a whisper so loud that Tom August actually looks up at the gallery with a startled and annoyed expression. The Problem of Gorotoland is temporarily forgotten as all the ladies again exchange amused smiles.

Actually on this occasion, as on so many others, the wife of the Ambassador of Panama is proceeding, with methods that have often proved effective before, in pursuit of purposes that most people usually do not suspect. All of her present companions are aware that there is a lot more to Patsy Jason Labaiya than appears on the ostensibly rattlebrained surface, but this knowledge is not shared by the general public or even by many people in Washington.

"Patsy Labaiya is a very clever woman," Beth Knox remarked to her husband when they came home from the diplomatic reception where they had met her for the first time, but Orrin only snorted. "She is? She conceals it well." "Beautifully," Beth agreed, and suggested that he file the fact away somewhere in his mind for future use.

But Orrin had apparently dismissed it, even though he made no attempt to hide from his wife the fact that he considered Patsy's brother to be someone worthy of the greatest respect and wariness in the political arena. Nobody had ever called Edward Jason, Governor of California, a stupid man, and Beth could not understand why it was so difficult for Orrin to imagine that some of the family brains might have been conferred upon his sister. Possibly it was because the Governor could conceivably pose some threat to Orrin's ultimate ambitions that Orrin was willing to concede his abilities and not do the same for Patsy; or possibly it was just that men in politics, even more than men in other lines of endeavor, tend to be unwilling to accord full equality of intelligence to women. Nonetheless, of the five ladies sitting so cordially together in the Family Gallery, not one is under any illusions about the wife of Felix Labaiya-Sofra.

As for Patsy herself, she too at this moment is thinking with the deep concentration of which she is capable about the M'Bulu of Mbuele and the place where he fits in with the family plans to win the White House for her brother. The Jasons are no different from the Adameses, the Harrisons, the Roosevelts, the Tafts, the Kennedys. No more numerous than the first, no less ambitious than the last, they too see no reason why one or more of their number should not occupy the fearful seat of power at 1600 Pennsylvania Avenue. Her brother is willing, her cousins are eager to help, her aunts and uncles are prepared to spend as many millions as may be required to win the primaries and add the White House to the other family possessions, and in Patsy's clever mind the whole thing boils down to the question, "What are we waiting for?" That the principal thing they are waiting for is Orrin Knox lends an extra little ironic fillip to this chance meeting with the Secretary's wife; and the game is lent an extra zip by the fact that Patsy assumes that Beth must be as aware of its ironies as she. Beth is, but it says much about the two of them that Beth can sometimes relax and stop thinking about the next election, whereas Patsy Labaiya, like the rest of her family, never does.

Into this situation the visit of the M'Dulu of Mbuele to the United Nations has come as an unexpected bonus, a fortuitous circumstance that must, like everything else, be examined for its value to the cause of Ted Jason and used for whatever it may be worth therein. The luncheon in Charleston tomorrow was originally the half-amused, not quite serious idea of Bob Leffingwell, passed along to her at the last garden party at "Vagaries"; but the idea of bringing it under the aegis of the Jason Foundation and making of the guest list as powerful a cross section of influential opinion-makers as the nation affords, was Patsy's own. California, despite its fantastic growth, has had relatively few racial explosions of late, and the Governor has consequently had few opportunities to associate himself with the politically suitable side of this politically useful question. Felix had called her from the UN a month ago to suggest that the M'Bulu could be very useful to the family plans if handled right, and her brother, apprised of this, had promised to make himself available for whatever she could arrange. The gain among the Negro vote, they hope, may be very substantial.

Therefore the luncheon has its values, both immediate and long-range; and it is lent an extra piquancy and excitement by the inspiration, also hers, of holding it in Seab Cooley's Charleston. Thank God, Patsy Labaiya tells herself with a scornful glance down at the white-haired figure of the President Pro Tempore, slumped in the Vice President's chair on the dais, her brother isn't an insincere racist demagogue like THAT.

As for Bob Leffingwell, it may well be that a direct approach should be made to him about joining the Jason forces. In six months' time, aided by the President's generosity in salvaging his career by appointing him director of the Commission on Administrative Reform, he has managed to recoup a good deal of the ground he lost when the Senate defeated his nomination for Secretary of State. There is a disposition in the country to be fair to a man who has, after all, been defeated and humiliated by a Senate rejection and who has now, in the wake of that defeat, gone to work diligently and faithfully for the President who rescued him from what could have been a disastrous end to his public usefulness. The attitude of most of his fellow citizens has been: if the President is willing to give him another chance, the country should too. In general, the country has.

The only thing that might interfere with Patsy's plans to bring him into her brother's camp, in fact, is the possibility that he might feel so much gratitude and loyalty to Harley Hudson that he would not wish to take a position that could bring him into conflict with Harley's plans for next year. But this would only be true, she suspects, were the President to reverse his announced decision and decide to run again. If he were, as all indications now suggest, to step aside in favor of Orrin Knox, then Bob Leffingwell might feel perfectly free to join those who wish to defeat Orrin. Particularly since everyone knows how he feels about the Secretary of State, even though he has been careful to keep his rare public references suitably decorous.

In some ways, Patsy concludes with some annoyance, it is really that old character in the White House who is her brother's principal obstacle even more than Orrin Knox. Like so many, she never thought much of him as Vice President and she doesn't think much of him now, in spite of all his Geneva triumphs and recent executive energetics.

"My dear," she had told the Speaker not a week ago at Senator Winthrop's cocktail party at the Mayflower, "after all, *what did he do* at Geneva? He just said No. ANYBODY can say NO." The Speaker had looked at her quizzically from his wise old eyes. "All depends on who you say No to, seems to me," he had said. "Sometimes it's not so easy." "Poof!" she said. "I knew they wouldn't do anything." "Oh?" said the Speaker. "Well, maybe you knew that, Patsy, but, to tell you the truth *I* was scared as hell." "Well," she had gone on, "supposing it WAS a real threat? What else could he have done?" The Speaker had given her that same long, quizzical look. "Some men might have run, and thrown us all down the drain doing it. Harley didn't. When guts were needed, Harley had 'em. Maybe you don't value that. I do." "Why, here's Stanley Danta," she had cried, turning away and bestowing a kiss on the Senator from Connecticut. "Stanley, the Speaker's putting me in my place about the President, and do you know? I MAY DESERVE IT!"

But she didn't think she did, and it is with a continuing impatience now that she considers the way most of the press and the country are continuing to fawn upon the President. Possibly he deserves some credit for doing what he had to do with a real show of courage, and she is willing to concede him that; but, really, this adulation is approaching the ridiculous. It is also making it quite difficult to challenge him politically, or to make any really solid plans about next year until he makes clear what he intends to do. Like everyone in Washington, Patsy never takes a denial of Presidential ambition to mean what it says, and neither she nor anyone else can believe that a man sitting in the White House will willingly vacate the premises until the Constitution says he absolutely must. Harley, having acceded to office with only twenty-one months of his predecessor's term remaining, faces no bar whatsoever to two full terms for himself if he so desires and can persuade the voters to approve. Right now his stock is so high that there seems little doubt that the voters, if requested, will do just that.

Whether he will ask them, however, remains his secret; and now, as Patsy Labaiya decides she has been silent long enough and must make some whispered comment to try to persuade the other ladies, unsuccessfully, that she has not really been thinking like a little engine every minute, he is contemplating it quite seriously as he sits a mile away in the study on the second floor of the White House waiting for his lunch. It is a room that holds many memories of many Presidents, but the one he associates it with most often and most poignantly is the midnight conference last spring when his predecessor attempted to dissuade Brigham Anderson from his plans to reveal the truth about Bob Leffingwell. The President has thought many times of that talk, with all its implications and difficulties and terrible national imperatives, which, in the final rendering of judgment, required from his predecessor duplicity and from Brigham Anderson his life.

"Suppose you were sitting here—" his predecessor had said. Well, now he was, and he could see things now that he couldn't see then, even though he would never, he honestly believes, have permitted events to carry him to the point of no return to which they had carried the late President.

To even contemplate for a second running again is, he tells himself, sheer insanity. It is a terrible job, one of the most terrible ever devised by human ingenuity to meet the need of men to have an organized society; why should anyone subject himself willingly to its fierce demands? Yet, he concedes, it exerts a powerful hold, conferring great rewards in return for the human toll it exacts upon those who occupy it.

So far he has conducted it with honor, he believes, and with a courage that cannot help pleasing him as he thinks back on the rather scornful and patronizing attitudes of Washington in his Vice Presidential days. Events have given him the opportunity to achieve the basic ambition of most men, which is to make the world accept them at their own evaluation. He thanks God every day that he possessed the character to do it when the time came. There are still moments, however, when he wonders with awe how it ever came about, in the mysterious movements of human destiny, and his emotion deepens as he recalls the searing moment of revelation he had as he approached the great bronze doors of the Assembly Hall in Geneva that first fateful afternoon.

Now, my boy, he had admonished himself with a deep breath, you've really got to act like the President. Quite suddenly, like a flash of light that almost stopped him where he stood, came the thought: *I don't have to 'act like' the President. I am the President.*

After that, he had proceeded as though under some other guidance than his own. He had preferred to consider it divine, for that had been his family upbringing, and while he knew Harley Hudson had character that few people suspected, he also knew it wasn't quite as good as all that. Accordingly on his return from Geneva he had declared a day of national prayer and thanksgiving and had led it himself by attending a solemn convocation at the Washington Cathedral. He was gratified to note that it had been joined by all denominations and, so far as press estimates could tell, by well over a hundred million of his countrymen. From that moment, too, he noted with an inner irony, had begun the steady change in press estimation and public attitude which had now resulted, six months later, in making him the most popular Chief Executive in recent years.

At first, he would admit, this had been a highly uncertain and chancy proposition. With very few exceptions, the major elements of the American news community had greeted with an alarm approaching hysteria his treatment of the Russians in Geneva. So violent and vitriolic had been the attacks upon him from his own country, he remembers now, that it had seemed for forty-eight hours as though the United States, at least as represented by its major communications media, had turned into one gigantic yawp of bellowing agony at the thought of the possible consequences of maintaining national integrity in the face of the Soviet threat. He would not blame anybody for being afraid, he remembered telling Bob Munson in his only show of real anger at the time. God knew he was afraid himself. But at least he wasn't acting like a sniveling baby about it.

Twenty-four hours later, of course, after the Soviets had made their monstrously preposterous demands, press, radio, and TV had swung completely about, given him the most absolute support, and poured out upon the Russians a scorn at least as vitriolic as that they had so recently flung at him. But he could never forget that first headlong rush to condemn him, without hesitation, without judgment, without waiting to ascertain the facts, *without waiting to see*—the automatic assumption that their own country must per se be wrong and stubborn and pigheaded and without justification, and that the enemy by the same token must have reason and justice on his side.

Of his own inner turmoil and the terrible weakening effect upon him of these attacks by his own countrymen at a moment of absolute decision for the United States, he said nothing publicly then, and it was only after he had been back a few weeks that he made his feelings clear. He had given a stag dinner for some of the nation's top publishers and unburdened himself a little.

"Do you have any idea what it is like to try to face the world and protect the United States with a lot of you boys yapping at my heels all the time?" he had asked with a mildness that had removed some, but not too much, of the sting. "To do your best to defeat the people whose major consistent aim is quite literally to destroy the United States of America and then pick up the papers or listen to radio or television and find yourself called a traitor and a fool and a—'an aging child playing with the fires of world destruction,' as my good friend from the *Post*, here, put it? I'd expect to read that kind of stuff in *Pravda*, but I must confess I was a little surprised to turn around from facing the Soviets and find my back full of American knives."

They had taken it with a rueful laugh and a round of applause, but they hadn't liked it at all. Well, he hadn't liked what they had done, either, and he had gone on to tell them quietly, "There were a couple of moments there when you almost had me convinced that I was wrong and ought to give in. You just stop and think where we would all be tonight if I had, and then ask yourselves how well you have served your country lately."

The next day the inevitable inside reports from "informed sources" had carried his off-the-record comments to the public. "A face-to-face dressing-down of the American press," the AP described it. "Veteran observers have rarely heard the President so angry," the UPI agreed. "H.H. DOES AN H.S.T.," the Washington *Daily News* reported cheerfully; "GIVES US HELL." But he had announced with a friendly smile at the start of his next press conference that he had "decided I'm not going to answer any questions on White House stag dinners," the correspondents had laughed, and the flurry had died down. When he noted a couple of weeks later that it had really died down, and that the press had apparently decided that his popularity was such as to make a real attack upon him unwise, he had known with a feeling of genuine triumph that he had won a major victory.

"They have a right to criticize," he told Orrin next day, "and I don't think one in ten does it with any but the best of motives. But damn it, they've got to realize this isn't a tea party we're in with these people. They've got to do it responsibly."

"They will," the Secretary replied, "as long as you're as popular as you are. My advice is to make the most of it while it lasts."

And so he has, the President thinks as he looks out the window at the Washington Monument surging whitely upward into the soft autumn sky and waits a trifle impatiently for his lunch. Six months is a short time in which to judge a Presidential stewardship, or any other kind for that matter; but starting with Geneva, which he regards now as being in all likelihood one of the supreme turning points in history, he feels that he has served his people well so far. The immediate and more easily tackled aspects of the world situation have yielded to a firm hand and a forceful approach. The problem and the atmosphere summed up in what the press has come to refer to tersely as "P.G."—post-Geneva—is another matter. And on that, the President thinks with a sigh and a sudden unhappy expression that destroys the normal amicability of his pleasantly plain face, the vision is dim and the way is not yet clear.

Whether it ever will be—whether, in truth, it ever has been, for any Administration at any time, in the delicate and uncertain area of relations with other powers—he does not know. Here too he is trying to do his best: to transform the psychological shock and advantage of his actions in Geneva into a lasting and long-range policy that will gradually restore a balanced sanity to world affairs and, indeed, place the United States once again in the lead. This last aim he does not mention, save to his Secretary of State, for he knows that it too would draw down upon him the scorn of elements in the country which are either afraid of Soviet reaction or still in the grip of the strange philosophy of the Forties and Fifties that the United States should be satisfied to seek no more than a timid and uneasy equality with its most deadly enemy. Like all who understand the ultimate implications of the American Revolution, the President is something of a revolutionist himself. He is prepared to advance the cause of genuine freedom wherever and whenever and however he can, now that he has succeeded in putting at least a temporary halt to the headlong Russian campaign of imperialism, subversion, hypocrisy, and hate.

But the ways in which these purposes can be achieved remain, P.G., obscure. For the task the President feels he has a diplomatic team as good as any and probably better than most. The Secretary of State is proving to be considerably more diplomatic in his diplomacy than his past performance as a Senator might have indicated, and at the UN the United States has a delegation, able and hard-working, upon most of whose members the President feels he can rely with implicit confidence and trust.

Thinking for a moment of Harold Fry, acting head of the delegation during the lingering and probably fatal heart illness of the Permanent Ambassador, the President smiles in an affectionate way. The senior Senator from West Virginia, with his easygoing nature, steady humor, and stubborn dedication in the cause of the United States, may not be as subtle in his methods as might sometimes seem advisable. Yet he inspires, at the UN as in the Senate, a warm regard and a deep and abiding trust in his integrity and good faith. Lafe Smith of Iowa, replacing Clarence Wannamaker of Montana, who asked to be relieved to return to his Senate duties, is—well, Lafe Smith, liking everybody, liked by everybody, hard-working and able, with the extra ingredient of an attitude toward sex which, the President suspects, makes him more understandable and endearing to a good many delegations than some more strait-laced Americans who have served at the UN in the past. Possibly Lafe's recent marriage has curtailed his energies and activities, but the President rather doubts it. Unless Lafe has changed mightily, he has probably already strengthened relations with half the young ladies in the Secretariat. Around the world in eighty days, the President thinks with a mild chuckle at his mild joke, and decides he will have to josh Lafe about it when the Senator is next in Washington.

The remainder of the delegation, composed in the usual pattern, consists of the customary State Department advisers and staff and, with an exact attention to the nation's minorities, a Catholic, a Negro, and a Jew. Of these last, the Negro is the only one who arouses some uneasiness in the mind of the President, who has been wary of changing the delegation left him by his predecessor. LeGage Shelby is something of a problem, and the President, at something of a loss how to solve it, frowns as he considers the rather fiercely clever young man who heads Defenders of Equality For You (DEFY) and has been in the vanguard of the increasingly vigorous drive to overturn the hard-dying racial patterns of the South.

It is not that 'Gage Shelby has been openly opposed to United States policy, but he has managed to convey to both his own government and the United Nations as a whole that he is not entirely happy with such attitudes as those concerning Red China, now awaiting admission in two years' time under the compromise finally worked out by Yugoslavia and Ceylon; the patient tolerance toward France and her still-uneasy relations with the Algerians; the continuing insistence of the President on adequate disarmament safeguards in the face of the steady and terrifying growth in the "atomic club," now numbering eleven nations, including Communist China; and the situation in the Caribbean, where the Republic of Panama seems of late to be working with elements not overly friendly to the United States.

'Gage has done a great deal of what he calls, with a sardonic grin, "black missionary work" among the African states; but neither Hal Fry nor the President has been entirely satisfied that all of it was in line with what Washington desired. "It isn't that I'm out of step with you, Mr. President," LeGage had told him recently with a disarming smile; "I'm just an inch or two ahead." Such candor had momentarily stopped the President, as he was sure LeGage had known it would, and he had only said mildly, "Well, you understand of course that it is advisable for all of us to proceed along the same general line if we are to present a united front to the world." "Absolutely," LeGage had said, again with the disarming grin. "You and I couldn't see more eye to eye on anything, Mr. President."

But, the President thinks now, of this he is not so sure; and how to handle LeGage within the context in which he must be handled is among the more annoying, if not major, problems that now concern the occupant of 1600 Pennsylvania Avenue. DEFY, a youthful and turbulent offshoot of the National Association for the Advancement of Colored People, formed out of the impatience of the younger generation with the cautious older, commands the loyalties of many of the nation's Negroes in the college and young-married levels. It was for this reason that the President's predecessor appointed LeGage to the delegation a year ago and, shortly before his death, announced his intention of appointing him again. The President has gone along with it for reasons that are as practical as his predecessor's: the simple fact that LeGage is well on his way to becoming one of the nation's major colored politicians, plus the fact that the increasing prominence of the new African states seems to make him a natural for the UN assignment. Now the President wishes he had chosen someone like Cullee Hamilton, even though under the custom which governs appointment of the United States delegation, the Senate and House alternate in providing two delegates each year, and this is a Senate year.

Somewhere, the President recalls, he has heard that Cullee and LeGage roomed together at Howard University right here in Washington, and it is quite possible that the young Congressman from California may have some useful insights into the chairman of DEFY that would prove helpful to the White House. He makes a mental note to talk to him about it if the opportunity arises and thinks with genuine pleasure of his few brief contacts with Cullee in the past. He has always found him eminently sensible, he thinks approvingly—and then assures himself hastily that he doesn't mean that as patronizingly as it might sound if said aloud. Cullee has not been sensible in the negative sense that Seab Cooley might use the word in describing a Negro; rather, he has seemed sensible to the President in the sense of his understanding of the needs of all parties involved in what the President considers the major domestic problem, human, economic, emotional, and moral, of twentieth-century America.

"I don't think we should move too fast," Cullee had said three years ago when the then Vice President had asked him to drop by his Senate office for a private chat after the Congressman had testified before the Senate Judiciary Committee, "but we should *move*. That's the important thing. We've got to keep moving. History won't let us stop now."

There was, the President was pleased to find, an absence of the customary cant, true but fatuous in its false emphasis, about "the eyes of the world are on you, America." There was just a firm insistence on America being true to what America ought to be, irrespective of what anybody else might think. Just because there were certain things that America, being America, must necessarily do and certain high standards that she must eventually live up to if she were to be ultimately whole.

Compared with LeGage, who is always giving lengthy interviews about "America's solemn obligation in the eyes of humanity," and "America's duty to see that she does not disappoint humanity's hopes," this is a very sensible position on Cullee's part. It is not demogogic—indeed, the Congressman is so calm-spoken and mild in outward bearing that political Washington sometimes wonders how he ever got elected in the first place—and it is not the sort of thing to win big headlines in the papers. But it is, the President suspects, an attitude that, matched by a similar attitude on the part of responsible whites both North and South, will ultimately provide a solution if solution is to be found.

If solution is found!

He snorts, startling the butler bringing in his lunch.

It has to be found.

He sighs at the unending complexity of the problems that beset the President, and instantly a hundred pressing urgencies rush into his mind. Trouble in Asia—trouble in Africa—trouble in the Middle East—trouble in Latin America—disarmament talks—a slight sag in business—unemployment rising—missile program still lagging behind the Russians—new integration crisis possible any moment in South Carolina—the space program—maintaining the moon expedition, readying another—Governor Edward Jason of California and his ambitions—Orrin's ambitions—his own ambitions and/or lack of them—criticism by America's enemies—criticism by America's friends —the United Nations—anti-American riots in Lima, West Germany, Manila, Capetown, Panama City—bills he must sign—people he must see—things he must worry about . . . it never ends. And always, overriding all else, the constant evil pressures from the Communist world, inflaming every problem, increasing every difficulty, negating every hope for peace in a blind, insensate drive toward world destruction so automatic by now that he doubts if the Kremlin could reverse itself and rejoin the decent purposes of a decent humanity even if it wanted to.

He finds it difficult not to feel that this is, as Bob Munson remarked to him the other day with a surprising melancholy, a haunted autumn; indeed, a haunted era. "The weather's too beautiful," the Majority Leader had said; "I don't trust it." Whether there are valid grounds for this premonitory sadness, the President does not know; probably no more than at any time in the past decade or, if the world is so fortunate as to have one, the next decade. But he, too, cannot escape the frequently recurring feeling that things everywhere are moving toward some sort of climax, one that may come a month from now, a year, two years, a day, a minute: who knows? Ever since the last war the Russians have engaged in a relentless and unceasing campaign to push tensions everywhere to their absolute peak; and the human animal does not live forever under such conditions without an explosive release into violence—it is simply beyond human nature.

War may come, the President feels, for no other reason than that the Soviets have deliberately created so many tensions in so many places that there is nothing else that can logically happen except war; and he sighs again as he contemplates the possibilities of such a holocaust and wonders what, if anything, a man even in his position can do to stop it.

Sometimes he considers the struggling masses of the earth and it seems to him that their leaders are no more than chips on a tide, flung this way and that by the necessities of national security and self-interest and the pressures of the inarticulate yet insistent millions below. No sane man aware of the facts wants to destroy the world; but who, nowadays, is sane, and who has all the facts? Even he, on whom so many heavy responsibilities and desperate hopes devolve, often thinks that he possesses no greater light to see by than anyone else in the fitful darkness that rests upon the twentieth century.

Lost in such thoughts he does not realize for a moment that he has stopped with his sandwich halfway to his mouth and is staring blankly out at the Washington Monument, the river, and autumn-tawny Virginia beyond. Then he starts, gives his head a rueful shake, and bites firmly into the ham and lettuce sandwich sent up from the White House kitchen. He had asked for chicken, he recalls with an ironic smile: even here, the President is powerless to set the course. Like the rest of the world, he will take what the kitchen sends him and make the best of it.

He wonders if anyone else undergoes such prolonged and self-scarifying appraisals as he has found himself called upon to undertake since he entered the White House; and concludes that probably many do, though possibly none with quite the direct and agonizing personal involvement of the President.

"The buck stops here," Harry Truman had put it, in a sign he kept on his desk. "I am all alone," Harley's own predecessor had remarked in a tone of absolute desolation, in a secret telephone call Harley had never told anyone about, on the morning after Brigham Anderson's death. In a world of problems that range from men on the moon to the relatively minor yet important matter of a difficult member of the United States delegation at the UN, the President now realizes to the full the import of both these comments, at once curiously pathetic and deeply terrifying, on the office he now occupies.

As for the United Nations, which he has thus returned to in the course of his absent-minded and preoccupied lunching, he wonders how the session is going today and what Orrin will have to report when he calls in later. The Problem of Gorotoland is not a simple one either, filled as it is with implications of an argument with allies, and the President contemplates it with real misgivings. Trouble anywhere is sooner or later trouble for the United States in these times, and in the person of the M'Bulu of Mbuele he can sense all sorts of potentials for trouble. He thinks for a moment of putting in a call to the Secretary-General, just to get another point of view on the situation, but then abandons it for the time being. The S.-G. he considers a friend of his, they had enjoyed a warm and cordial talk when he addressed the opening session of the General Assembly—but the thought occurs to him that perhaps he should hold in reserve against a time of real need any further direct contact. It might be interpreted now as going behind Orrin's back, and that would be most unfortunate. Nonetheless he wonders whether the Secretary-General, agent of an organization with such great potential capabilities but so little real power, is ever moved by such philosophizings as those which come to him who has so much real power as head of a state whose capabilities are felt wherever men live.

If he were to make the phone call, instead of abandoning it for a later day, he would find that the Secretary-General, sitting in his office on the thirty-eighth floor of the Secretariat building, is indeed filled with a comparable concern. He has changed the chaste decor left him by his predecessor— there is more color in the room and a livelier atmosphere in which to conduct negotiations—yet far below in the General Assembly Hall, the Security Council, the noisy lounges, and the bustling corridors, the rulers of earth remain as obdurate and contentious and far apart as ever.

For this, the S.-G. thinks moodily, he is not to blame, yet he cannot avoid feeling, as other idealistic men in his position have felt before him, that he bears a major responsibility. Like them, he has come into office to find his powers ill-defined, his duties circumscribed by the conflicting national interests of more than a hundred nations, and his office the focus for a constant tug of war between the Communist and non-Communist worlds. Indeed, he would not be here were it not for this constant conflict; and the fact that he is here, in and of itself automatically makes him almost impotent.

Remembering his election, outcome of two months of bitter struggle between East and West, the S.-G. sometimes wishes one of the other candidates had received sufficient votes: then at least the issue would be clear. But the East would not accept the West's candidates, the West rejected those of the East. Finally his name had been mentioned, almost as an afterthought, by the British. Within two days sentiment in the lounges, the corridors, and the delegation headquarters scattered through midtown Manhattan had coalesced in his favor and he had been elected. *"Il n'est pas un Pape de Rome,"* Raoul Barre had commented to the prime minister of the Secretary-General's country. *"Il est un Pape d'Avignon."* And in truth, for ineffectualness and inability to do the things the salvation of the world so clearly demanded, he was.

For this state of affairs, he reflects, the Communists are largely responsible, for their constant attacks upon the office of the Secretary-General and their steady hammering at the morale of the Secretariat have inevitably, in time, begun to produce some of the results they desire. The attack begun by the late Chairman of the Council of Ministers during his raucous attendance at the Fifteenth General Assembly has borne its evil fruit and been continued by his successors. Now both the office of the Secretary-General and the Secretariat are closer to real impotence than they have ever been.

Even during the high point reached in the early stages of the crisis in the

Congo, their powers and influence at best had not been very great; now they have declined to a sort of innocuous and ineffective housekeeping that not all the earnest editorials at the time of his election have been able to redress.

"It is with renewed hope," the New York Times had commented then, "that the world hails the election of a new Secretary-General. Now, if ever, the United Nations has a chance to halt the decline of recent years and climb back to the high plateau of goodwill and sound endeavor that men everywhere still hope to find in the world organization."

Well, the hope had not been justified, because men everywhere did not hope to find the goodwill and sound endeavor so dutifully invoked by the Times. A great many of them just hoped to find one more mechanism for their own unchanging plans for world conquest. And their campaign to reduce the United Nations to just such a mechanism has made ominous and steady strides ever since. Endless debates, endless arguments, endless demands for impossible concessions, disorderly sessions of the General Assembly, frivolous demands for special sessions of the Security Council—there is no limit to the vicious ingenuity with which they frustrate the decent hopes of mankind.

Now, he thinks as he goes into his private apartment off the office to see whether his heavy beard needs a quick shave before he goes down to lunch with Terence Ajkaje and the Soviet Ambassador in the Delegates' Dining Room on the fourth floor, all is tenuous and uncertain and the future is dimmer than it has ever seemed, even in the great slab-sided glass monolith that houses the United Nations. "We fly on a wing and a prayer," his American deputy had told a luncheon meeting of the United Nations Correspondents Association a week ago, "if we fly at all."

Yet there is, he tells himself with a sort of angry hopelessness, such great potential for good in the flimsy shield, riddled with national self-interest and competing sovereign claims, which men erected in San Francisco in 1945 in one more desperately hopeful attempt to protect themselves against the dismal winds that howl down the reaches of history. Only yesterday he had stopped by the offices of the Technical Assistance Fund on the twenty-ninth floor and been shown proudly by its director an enormous map of the world with little colored pins scattered over the surface, each representing a UN mission. Sometimes the mission consisted of eight or ten people; sometimes, in the vast expanse of some desert nation or the steaming jungles of another's almost impenetrable heartland, the pin would represent just one man --just one, for so many hundreds of thousands of square miles, so many millions of people. But it was a start—it was a start. Here and there in the darkness the UN was lighting little lights.

"Maybe a hundred years from now it will all add up to something," he had remarked somewhat bitterly to the director, a doughty little Welshman grown gray in the service of the world organization.

"It is the hope in which we live," the director had replied; and had added gravely, "In which we *have* to live."

Technical assistance—the United Nations Children's Fund—the United

Nations Relief and Works Agency for Palestine Refugees—the United Nations Korean Reconstruction Agency—the United Nations High Commission for Refugees—the United Nations Emergency Force—the United Nations Special Fund—the Economic and Social Council—the Trusteeship Council—the Economic Commissions for Europe, Asia, and the Far East, Latin America and Africa—the United Nations Conciliation Commission for Palestine—the United Nations Advisory Commission on the Congo—the United Nations Refugee Assistance for South Africa—the United Nations this, the United Nations that—

It is a proud roll call, even if it does represent a defiance pathetically tiny of the forces that conspire to threaten humankind everywhere. At least, the Secretary-General thinks with an ironic grimness, you can get East-West agreement on stamping out malaria in the jungles, and on inoculating natives against yaws, and on teaching a peasant how to plow a straight furrow, and on building a dam here and there to protect the crops and generate power. Maybe that, in the long run, is a work of the United Nations far more hopeful and far more lasting than all the bitter political wrangles that go on in the Assembly and the Security Council. Here in Turtle Bay on the East River, in the sheer marble-and-green-glass shaft of the Secretariat, he is aware that dedicated people from all the races of man are working in the light of a fragile promise and a desperate hope. They are people as human, as imperfect, as subject to red tape and petty ambition and simple error as people everywhere, yet for the most part he has found them to be earnest and idealistic and devoted to the world organization and the good of humanity. He sometimes wishes that those who freely criticize the UN could know, as he knows, the patient, persistent, day-by-day work of the organization as it attempts, so doggedly and under such great handicaps, to push back the night that threatens to engulf the world. The night is so black and the light is so feeble. But it shines. That is the important thing: it shines.

And so, he thinks with an abrupt bitterness as he pauses for a moment to stare out his apartment's glass wall at the steel and concrete crags of Manhattan that balance his office's East River view over Brooklyn on the other side, one manages to convince oneself that it all adds up to something and really does encourage hope, and that the vicious political conflicts of the UN are really less important than its small, snail-like progressions in the area of social, economic, and human relations. One can almost persuade oneself that a Communist pounding on his desk to stop free debate, or an African sneering at a white man, or a white man bitterly denouncing another white man, can all be wiped out by sweetness and light in the Economic and Social Council or a tentative glow of compassion in the Children's Fund. It would be nice to think so, but he knows the thought is not tenable for long. It is the fearful bitternesses that really matter; it is the terrifying divisions that really control man's fate, not the temporary and tiny co-operations.

And here he knows, as any honest man must know, that the outlook is not promising and the future is not bright. Ever since Geneva the neutral states have been beating a path to his door. The burden of each has been essentially the same: Protect us.

"Protect you!" he had finally blown up at the smugly self-righteous representative of China. "Protect you, when you did everything you could to subvert the Congo, and always try to play your own imperialist game in Africa! Why should I protect you, even if the Charter and the big powers gave me the authority to do it?"

The Ghanaian had been angrily resentful and accused him of being a lackey of the British; but the S.-G.'s barb had sunk home, and it had been fully justified. They all wanted to follow their own cheap, self-serving little ends, and then when the going got rough they wanted a man whose powers they had blandly connived to diminish to come running and help them out. When they get scared, he thinks, they turn tail fast enough; but it is almost too late for them to do so, because bit by bit they have helped to whittle away the always flimsy powers of his office until now it is an almost empty shell.

In the aftermath of the dramatic confrontation between the American President and the Soviet Chairman at Geneva, this fact annoys and frustrates him increasingly as the tensions heighten. He does what he can to ameliorate differences; tries his best to serve as a bridge between East and West; is respected by the United States, treated with contempt by the Soviet Empire and its colonies, beseeched by the Africans and Asians, ignored by the Latin Americans, patronized by the French, criticized by the British, advised by the Indians, given hearty admonitions by the Canadians, and made much of by the American press. This last gives him some little wry amusement at times. He may be a figurehead to some, but he does rate well with the New York *Times*, the *Post*, and the *Herald Tribune*. This is not such insignificant support, either, since most delegates to the UN are sensitive to the writings of the metropolitan press and eager to find themselves mentioned in its pages.

Today they should all be quite happy, for The Problem of Gorotoland is receiving its full share of attention, and discussions concerning it are being followed most attentively by all channels of communication. He is not surprised that this should be so, for he has followed the career of Terence Ajkaje ever since he met him in London ten years ago. It is not unexpected that the M'Bulu should have been able to take a matter so dear to the hearts of the press and raise it with skilled showmanship to a major international issue. It would be surprising, in fact, if he did not do so, adept as he is at parlaying his flair for the dramatic into big news. Combine big news with a moral issue, however clouded by events in Molobangwe and elsewhere, and headlines, radio reports, and television commentaries are bound to follow, in America. It is no wonder that the UN, which in its standard legal parlance is "seized of" issues when it assumes jurisdiction over them, should be seized indeed of Terrible Terry.

The thought of this brings a smile to the Secretary-General's face for a second as he drops world problems to concentrate on his beard. "I don't have five-o'clock shadow," he remembers telling Senator Fry of the United States the other day; "with me, it is more like 9 A.M." "It isn't noticeable," Hal Fry assured him, "but if it bothers you, why don't you give in and let it grow?" The Secretary-General had shaken his head with a smile. "That's only for northerners like the Ethiopians. I wouldn't want to get people confused."

He decides now that he can probably get by without a shave until time to get ready for the Turkish reception at the Waldorf tonight, especially since he doesn't want to run the risk of cutting his chin again. He frowns as he notes the tiny clot of dried blood from the morning's accident, but against the black skin it shows hardly at all, and after a moment he forgets it and turns away. Then he leaves the beautiful apartment with its sensational view of New York, walks past the pleasant office with its sensational view of Brooklyn and the river, quickly paces off the long corridor to the elevator, pushes the bell, and, after a moment, steps in. The Javanese girl who operates the elevator greets him respectfully; he responds, and then stands with hands clasped behind him and head thoughtfully bowed as they glide swiftly downward to the halls and corridors far below where the bickering heirs of Adam conduct their talkative and tendentious business.

4

It was at moments like this, the M'Bulu told himself with a happy satisfaction, when everything seemed to conspire to give his talents and abilities their greatest possible scope, that the world could not possibly avoid admitting that he was as dashing and effective a figure as he knew himself to be. Here he was, child of Gorotoland, heir to a threadbare kingdom, "a minor princeling," as the London *Times* had dared to call him recently, and here was all the world, in solemn assembly arrayed, attentive to his every word. At least, most of them were attentive. The British Ambassador was, you could be sure of that, for all his outward bland imperviousness; and the American Secretary of State, and the Soviet Ambassador, and indeed nearly everyone else around the globe, for today almost every seat in the big pale mahogany-and-blue bowl of First Committee was filled. Only Cameroun and Congo Brazzaville were absent, and he knew what he thought of them, particularly Cameroun. He made a mental reference to Cameroun's ancestors which was not complimentary, rearranged his gorgeous green and gold robes with a spiteful flourish, drew himself to his full six-feet-seven, and turned to the Yugoslav delegate in the Chair with a suitable dignity as all those on the floor and in the press and public galleries who did not speak English adjusted their earphones and prepared to listen attentively.

"Mr. Chairman," he said soberly in his chopped, guttural accent, "I must thank you on behalf of my people in Gorotoland for permitting me to appear here before this august committee of the United Nations on this matter so dear to their hearts. A long period of desperate suffering under a ruthless colonialism"—he was aware of the slightest hint of motion from Lord Maudulayne and found it difficult to refrain from a broad grin—"has made their hearts desperate for freedom, Mr. Chairman. They look to you, the United Nations, to release them from their bondage. Now." A sudden fierce look flared on his face and he banged his massive fist on the rostrum with an explosive force. *"Now!"*

There was a burst of applause from many delegates and some desk-pounding by the Communist bloc. He acknowledged it all with a bow and went gravely on.

"I shall not delay you with a further recounting of the terrible struggles of my people to achieve independence. The distinguished Soviet delegate has already given you that sorry story this morning. It is one that does no credit to the colonial power which has been responsible." He looked squarely at Lord Maudulayne, who returned the look with the slightest of ironic winks that clearly conveyed the comment: Why, you hypocritical little pip-squeak. Terry broke into a sunny smile and marveled at how effectively he could make his tone change altogether.

"But, Mr. Chairman," he cried, "at last there is hope! Hope from the United Nations! Hope from the United States and the Soviet Union! Hope, not least, from the United Kingdom itself, which, remembering at last its traditional regard for the rights and liberties of men, now moves forward boldly to assist in the solution of this problem. Yes, Mr. Chairman, we look to the United Kingdom for the decision humanity and justice dictate! Give us your votes and support and we know the U.K. will join happily in immediate independence for Gorotoland! *Now!"*

Again there was the burst of applause, the pounding by the Communists. In the midst of it the British Ambassador raised his hand for recognition.

"Mr. Chairman," he said from his seat in a flatly impassive tone that instantly silenced the chamber, "exercising briefly the right of reply, I simply wish to reiterate again that Her Majesty's Government have entered into a solemn obligation to establish the independence of Gorotoland in one year's time. There has been, to my knowledge, no change in this position to warrant the assumption just made by His Royal Highness. Nor can there be, until the territory achieves adequate preparation for self-government. Surely His Highness is aware of that."

And he pushed aside his microphone with an air of tired distaste, amid renewed desk-pounding by the Soviets and considerable stirring and muttering throughout the room. At the rostrum the M'Bulu permitted an expression of sadness to disturb his primordially handsome face, but when he replied it was in a tone of patient tolerance.

"Mr. Chairman, the distinguished delegate of the United Kingdom— whom I like to consider," he added, with a wistful smile, "my good personal friend, however these differences of policy may divide us—is, as usual succinct and to the point. Naturally I am aware of the commitments undertaken by Her Majesty's Government. I am also aware that history does not always wait upon formal commitments. I am also aware"—and his voice began to rise again—"that freedom is impatient! Justice is impatient! Gorotoland is impatient! What is the right thing to do is impatient! Her Majesty's Government should remember that, too!

"But, Mr. Chairman," he said, and he permitted his voice to modulate gently, "I am hopeful. I am always hopeful. There are signs of friendship and assistance from many quarters.

"Tomorrow I shall visit a famous city in the southern United States, and there I shall find friends and support. I shall visit Washington, D.C., and there, I understand, the President of the United States, that great man whom we all admire"—there was a thump from Vasily Tashikov, answering laughter from others, and with a sudden grin Terry amended his statement—"whom *some* of us admire, will entertain me at a dinner in the White House. And also, though we have our differences here, I understand that the distinguished delegate of the U.K. and his delightful wife, who is known to many of you, will entertain for me at a reception at Her Majesty's Embassy. So, you see, though we argue here and have our differences in this great house of the nations, we are still all friends. I think we should all," he added with a commanding gesture that started and encouraged the responding applause, "be very pleased by these indications of humanity and friendliness which mean that no real bitterness can linger here."

"That's what you say," Orrin Knox murmured to Lord Maudulayne, who replied with an ironic snort. "I defy you to get up now and say all this isn't so," he whispered back. "You see how simple it is. Seek and ye shall find. Demand and ye shall get. The powers of the West are but as sheep, and a little child is leading them."

"Little child, my hat," said Orrin Knox. "Some child!"

But in this, as the M'Bulu bowed low and prepared to move on to the peroration of his brief address, the Secretary of State might possibly have been mistaken; for behind the broad-planed face and towering body before them at the rostrum there were many complex things, and one of them might well have been a little child. Certainly Terrible Terry was filled with a happiness so tense and excited that it might, in other surroundings, have been expressed with a child's exuberance—a certain kind of child. The kind who might, in a moment of exhilaration, kill a lion with a spear, or catch a running wildebeest on foot, or, perhaps, castrate an enemy tribesman over a slow-burning fire and then roast the results for dinner.

For there was much to the M'Bulu of Mbuele that of course could not be known to great sections of the rest of the world, though it was clearly understood by many of his compatriots from the vast upsurging continent who, like himself, now appeared amid the trappings of Western civilization in the gleaming glass citadel of the UN. Many an echo from the savage depths of mankind was present, though not all white men were sensitive enough to perceive it in the bustling lounges, the long, murmurous corridors, and the contentious conference rooms on the East River. No tribal drums sounded in Turtle Bay, but their faint, insistent beat was never far from many ears; and in few did they beat with quite the commanding note that they sounded for Terence Wolowo Ajkaje.

It would have been important for many men to find out why, had there been time and not ten thousand other things to think about, for an understanding of his background and purposes might have permitted some more reasoned attempt to be forewarned and thus forearmed. But possibly even that would not have been enough. Intelligent anticipation can only go so far, even under the best of circumstances; and the M'Bulu was one of history's sports in an age that encouraged them: extremely smart, extremely clever, deceptive, misleading, erratic, but, as many were now to find out to their sorrow, erratic with a plan.

That the plan was not his own, but that he should have been able to lend himself to it so willingly and improve upon it so brilliantly in his own right, was a tribute to a mind that had traveled a long way since it first became sentient in Gorotoland. Now as he stood in First Committee gathering his thoughts for his final comments before the vote on Panama's resolution to have the General Assembly take up The Problem of Gorotoland, he was thinking with an approving awe of that predestined forward progress which had brought him to the point where he could sway the nations of the world. It had not appeared at first that he would even live to maturity, let alone achieve so high a dignity in the councils of the earth.

He had been born, twenty-nine years before, to the seventh wife of the 136th chief in direct descent from the legendary first M'Bulu, the great warrior Molobangwe. Many were the tales of this great one, and numerous the rival chieftains he was said to have killed to consolidate his power. One by one he had subjugated seven warring tribes, carefully marrying all the widows he created with each new conquest. ("You call George Washington the father of *your* country," Terry was fond of remarking during his year at Harvard. "You should have seen the man I'm descended from.") By the time he died peacefully on his pallet at the reputed age of eighty-one— the last M'Bulu for some years to expire so uneventfully—Molobangwe had carved for himself a sizable kingdom and done more than any other one man to populate it with the dominant Goroto people.

The kingdom, consisting of a small area of mountain highlands, some dusty plains and sparse grasslands, a few elusive streams, and two fair-sized, sedgy lakes, was favored by nature just sufficiently to permit its people a bare subsistence if they worked from sunup to sundown from the day of birth to the day of death. The populace, filled with the innumerable progeny of the late warrior king, was almost fatally diverted from this necessary diligence for the better part of half a century, for it was immediately torn apart by rival claimants to the vacant throne. (When he was at Oxford, Terry liked to refer to this as "our Wars of the Roses," which sometimes made his listeners wince.) Out of the constant raiding, fighting, and general bloodshed there rapidly appeared and violently disappeared the first thirty-one of the 137 M'Bulus. With the thirty-eighth, a great-nephew in the female line of the great Molobangwe (although which female, tribal elders were never entirely clear), there finally arose a youth firm enough and strong enough to once

again impose upon his warring people much the same *pax virilis* as that
imposed by his fertile forebear.

By a brisk policy of beheading his enemies and impregnating their wives,
he managed in ten years, time to pacify Gorotoland and turn its people once
again to the problem of eking out a living in the highlands, where some of
them hunted, and on the plains, where the remainder grazed their cattle.
He must in his way, as his descendant the 137th M'Bulu sometimes thought
with real respect, have been something of a statesman, for he was able to
work out a trading relationship between the hunters and the grazers that permitted them to live together in peace instead of existing forever at each
other's throats, as was so often the case elsewhere in Africa. He also chose
for his seat of government the town of Mbuele in the highlands, thus adding
to his title for all time the name of its first capital. It was only several hundred years later that the capital came down to Molobangwe on the plains
as the result of a marriage between the two leading families in the nation;
a choice that Terrible Terry deplored but which he could not change even
in the mid-twentieth century, so rigid were the iron rules of tribal custom
that still bound the ruler of Gorotoland to this day.

The centuries passed and other M'Bulus succeeded the pacifier of mountain and plain; in Europe and Asia civilization advanced across the hemi-
spheres, great states rose and fell, wars and revolutions and dynastic enterprises swept the earth, men drew maps and navigated the globe, developed
science and theology and medicine, began to think, first in idle dreams and
then with mounting excitement, beyond the planet to the stars. In Gorotoland, as in the rest of Black Africa, life never changed from one century to
the next. Men were born, lived, and died in accordance with ancient
ritual. Tradition, superstition, terror, and ignorance ruled the life of the people. Around succeeding M'Bulus and the elder priests who presently came
to form their council of state there encrusted an inflexible way of doing
things that raised men barely above the beasts they hunted and the beasts
they grazed and kept them there, apparently forever.

So ages passed to the middle of what was known, in distant regions out
of sight and out of mind, as the nineteenth century.

And then suddenly the white man was everywhere in Africa, adventuring
after gold, after diamonds, sometimes, encouraged by willing rulers such as
the present M'Bulu's grandfather, after slaves; pushing up river valleys,
landing along the endless coasts, trading, colonizing, bringing an impatient,
pushing, ambitious, violent, explosive, restless, never-fulfilled and never-
satisfied civilization to all but the most inaccessible parts of the black continent. Some sentimentalists found it fashionable now to bemoan this invasion, alternating between ruthlessness and paternalism, and to deplore the
passing of the noble savagery which had prevailed before. Terrible Terry
was not among them. If it hadn't happened, he wouldn't be here now addressing the First Committee of this wobbly parliament of man; nor would
he be able to command the attention of NBC, ABC, CBS, *Time, Life,*

or the New York *Times*. Savage innocence? They could have it! He would take "Meet the Press" any day.

For Gorotoland, the transition to British rule was sanguine and abrupt. A small exploratory expedition sent out by the Royal Geographic Society came innocently one day to Molobangwe in the sun. Fifteen savage minutes later its members were mercifully beyond sensation as a surprised and indignant reception committee readied them for lunch. The response of the Crown was inevitable and immediate. Two weeks later a full-scale military expedition appeared on the horizon, and by sundown a thousand of the M'Bulu's finest warriors were dead, seven members of his Council of Elders were hanging from nearby thorn trees, and he and twenty-nine of his wives were in abject and ignominious captivity. Life was simpler in those days when there was no First Committee to appeal to, and the whole thing was decided with a dispatch no longer permitted in seeking solutions to the world's more irritating problems. Disraeli turned up one morning at Windsor with good news for the Queen and, graciously if a trifle vaguely, she accepted one more jewel in her diadem and Gorotoland joined that long list of rather inadvertent and absent-minded conquests which turned the map crimson and, for a time now gone forever, gave the sun something to shine upon wherever it went.

There ensued a period of uneasy dominion which inculcated deep in the Goroto people and their ruler those traits of dissembling, deviousness, and deceit which were, though few who watched him at the rostrum now were aware of it, so much a part of the 137th M'Bulu. It went against the grain to give up slavery, ritual sacrifices, and the privilege of devouring one's opponents; and back in the highlands, none of these pleasant customs ever died, despite the earnest efforts of the sweating, sandy-haired, red-faced, mustachioed, exasperated but terribly, terribly self-controlled young men who came out from London to do their best for the Empire and, quite sincerely, for the natives. The natives never really did desire all this well-meant attention, having been much happier in a state of self-ruled slaughter and their own precarious trade balance between hill and plain.

Toward the end something approaching a grudging tolerance for the colonizers finally became general in Gorotoland—they tried so hard, and were so inexplicably just, and it was so easy to pull the wool over their eyes and go right on doing what one had always done—but there was never at any time any real affection or loyalty. Not even when, with the country's population pushing toward two million, thanks to white man's administration, white man's medicine, and white man's peace, the British instituted a modest but definite program of sending a few of the brighter youths away to be educated in the white man's world. This was regarded as one more example of an innate and baffling foolishness on their part, but it did not take long for the ruling family and the Council of Elders to perceive that this was a good thing and they had better allow a certain number to get in on it. This number, a fact known to Terry but unknown to Lord Maudulayne when they had argued the matter earlier that morning, was decided by the natives themselves. Education was restricted to those selected by the then M'Bulu and his immediate advisers and it was, they thought then, in their best interest to extend it to no more than a handful. Later, when independence swept Africa and the M'Bulu's grandson was hurtled on the tide of it into his demand for immediate freedom, the grandson could have wished it had been more broadly based to provide him with a greater corps of potential administrators. But by then, of course, it was too late.

For himself, however, Terence (a tribute to the Resident, who professed to be pleased) Wolowo Ajkaje could not complain, once he had surmounted the apparently insurmountable obstacle of being born to the seventh wife of his late father. Ahead of him in the succession were four half brothers, and for thirteen of his years in the dusty royal compounds of Molobangwe it seemed likely that he would never be anything more than a very secondary brother of whoever succeeded to the throne, providing that worthy allowed him and the other brothers to live at all once he came to power. Indeed, there was considerable danger that some such sudden termination of his career might occur even before his father passed from the picture, so violent were the intrafamily feuds that surrounded the succession. But the genius of his more notable ancestors, having skipped his father and several preceding M'Bulus, seemed to have lodged in Terry, and with a shrewdness beyond his years he dissembled his brains, hid his clever and overactive intelligence, and went about with an air of stumbling stupidity that provoked loud cries of indignation, but nothing worse, from his father's other wives.

To his mother, whom he only wished he could have brought along to see him at the United Nations, and would have had she not been Regent and also badly crippled with arthritis, the M'Bulu felt that he owed most of his native abilities. He had never forgotten a wild night in his sixth year when a thunderstorm had seemed to come up from all of Africa below them to the south. Without a word his mother had taken him firmly by the hand and slipped away from the compound to a great bare baobab tree that stood on a little rise looking toward the mountains. There, with a sort of wild crooning chant whose echoes in memory could still make him shiver, she had implored the assistance of their ancestors and all the tribal gods for one, single, all-consuming purpose: "Make my son M'Bulu! Make my son M'Bulu! Make—my—son—M'Bulu!" At the height of the storm the ancestors and gods had reached down and, in a blinding flash of light, hurled them both insensate to the ground. "Damn-fool woman is lucky the lightning didn't kill them both," the Resident had grumbled hopelessly the next morning when they were still resting from the shock in the little makeshift hospital in Molobangwe; but neither he nor his mother ever doubted that they had been given a pledge of divine assistance for her ambitions, which thereafter became his own.

It took six years for the gods and ancestors to contrive the means to do it in the crowded compounds, but suddenly one day after his mother had passed silently outside a window overlooking a fireplace where a broth was being prepared for his two oldest half brothers, the gods and ancestors began to make good on their pledge. Within two hours his half brothers were rolling in agony in the dust, and a couple of hours after that his father had two less heirs. Inevitably this stirred sharp suspicions in Gorotoland, but the gods and ancestors had been as good as their bond: his mother had not been seen, and her protestations of innocence were so loud and aggrieved that everyone soon believed her and turned instead upon one of the Council of Elders, who presently vanished somewhere in the highlands and was heard from no more, despite the Resident's earnest attempts for six months to find him.

A short time after that, the gods and ancestors intervened again, apparently on this occasion entirely on their own volition. The younger of his two remaining half brothers contracted a genuine case of pneumonia in the midst of the rainy season and was carried off in three days. That left one, a boy of fourteen, one year older than himself, son of his father's fifth wife; and now, it seemed to Terry, it was time for the gods and ancestors to again take an active hand in his destiny.

It took him several months to decide how to help them go about it, but the approach of the annual puberty rites, held in a great cave in the highlands near the ancient capital of Mbuele, gave him the idea. The year before, in preparation for their own participation later, he and his brother had been permitted to watch in wide-eyed excitement from the outer reaches of the cave as the ceremony, in which the older men of the tribe were mingled with the novitiate youths, reached its peak. There came a moment when, elders and young stark naked and inflamed with fermented banana beer, standing in a great circle in the dimly lit cave, the ceremony reached a climax and everyone became so busy that no normal male could concentrate on anything but the sensations of his own body. Terry was normal enough in that, but he was abnormal in his powers of concentration and will. That moment, it seemed to him, would be the ideal moment for the gods and ancestors to insert a knife between the ribs of his half-conscious, half-blind, all-animal brother.

And so, as events went forward, it came about. With great presence of mind he concealed the knife beforehand; pretended to drink but refrained from it; and when the final moment came, did what the gods and ancestors intended him to do and then eased his dying brother gently down upon a nearby rock, unnoticed in the general grunting frenzy all around. Instead of fleeing the cave, he simply moved to another part of it, until he was on the other side of the fiercely quaking circle. And when, some hours later, the first spent novitiate staggered awake and tripped across the cold body of his brother, it was by then much too late for anyone to discover how the gods and ancestors had performed so foul a deed. (Far away in America, *Time* magazine took its first notice of Terrible Terry in an account of the strange series of royal fatalities in Gorotoland, entitled "A Little Fresh Heir." But of course no one in Gorotoland ever saw it, and it was soon forgotten by the rest of the world, for although it was an example of shrewd speculation, the facts to support it could not be proved.)

Thus at thirteen Terence Ajkaje became the heir apparent to Gorotoland, and a fortunate absence of any but female children in the huts of his father's remaining five wives made it unnecessary for him and his mother to seek any more divine assistance. They could now proceed to prepare him, with the rather dazed concurrence of his father, who could not understand why the gods and ancestors had bereft him of so many heirs, for the throne. In the boy and his mother the British found both the material and the appreciation for what they were trying to do in education. There was no doubt, the Resident reported to London, that the heir to Gorotoland was as bright as a whip, or possibly three or four whips. He recommended every encouragement, and that was what the Colonial Office, in its ponderous but eventually efficient fashion, set out to provide.

Recalling now the stages of his education as he stared blandly down upon Lord Maudulayne and the rest in First Committee, the M'Bulu of Mbuele could not escape a small ironic bow in the confines of his mind to those who had opened the doors of the world for him. You did it well, you British, he said in a silent conversation that Claude Maudulayne could not hear but would not have been surprised about if he had; oh, yes, you did it well. More fools you, but—you did it well.

First had come shoes and European clothing, and an awkward period of practicing with them that lasted until time to leave for the trip to Mombasa and the slow steamer up the east coast, through Suez into the Mediterranean, and so past the soft green shores of fertile France to the misty little island that now, in the aftermath of her second great war, was saying good-by with increasing speed to all the lands on so many continents and across so many seas over which she had for so long held dominion. The British were a revelation to Terry, as they are to most who visit them at home; and in some strange way he both resented and admired, could not understand and yet could not ever entirely escape, they had left their mark upon him forever, no matter who the savage that lurked beneath.

In fact, he told himself now with irony that was not quite irony and sarcasm not entirely sarcastic as he readied his concluding words of appeal to the nations sitting silently before him, there would always be in Gorotoland some little piece of blackness that would be forever England; and whether he or the English would ever understand the curious love-hate of it, either in Gorotoland or in so many other places in Asia and Africa where their stuffy, proud, and strangely gallant cavalcade had passed, he very much doubted.

This, however, was a mature thought now, long after that first unforgettable passage up the Solent into Southampton Water; the ride into London on the tootling train through the tidy little fields, green with a greenness even the highlands of Gorotoland could not match; and his first excited introduction to the strange ways and strange world of the white man. The junior clerk from the Colonial Office who shepherded him from dockside to the capital was one who took his duties seriously and was also gifted with the ability to address children as adults without being patronizing about it.

Long before the train pulled into Waterloo Station he had broken through the awed reserve of his royal charge and Terry was asking questions so fast his mentor found it difficult to keep up. (To this day the M'Bulu still received an occasional letter, increasingly wistful and concerned, from his old friend. Recently he had stopped replying.) By the time he was taken off to Eton a week later, he had been given a quick but thorough introduction to the major relics of the English past and in some subtle, understated way been given to feel that he was fortunate indeed to have the opportunity to add its heritage to his own. He was not, at first, prepared to accept this without a struggle, until somewhere early in his public-school career, when he suddenly perceived the basic element in the heritage: a willingness to accord to one's opponent a decency and fairness as great as one's own. Then he began to see how vulnerable this made his hosts, and after that he had the key to his future and that of Gorotoland firmly in his grasp. A boy who had the purposeful determination to murder his brother at the age of thirteen did not need a great deal of assistance from outsiders in getting where he wanted to go; but the English, just by being English, gave him all they could.

Academically, his record was brilliant from the first, and by the time he was ready to enter Oxford the judgment of the Resident had been more than justified. At Magdalen the story continued, and, accompanying it, with a sort of offhand air that greatly impressed his schoolmates, the steady development of that reputation that soon earned him the sobriquet "Terrible Terry." There was not much that Terence Ajkaje, heir of Gorotoland and veteran of puberty rites, did not know about sex, in all the infinite varieties that fascinated the students of Oxford as they fascinate students everywhere. Being big, handsome, and black gave him an added advantage, and in very short order he was welcomed in many circles, some rather peculiar and all quite influential, both at the University and in London. A secret contempt, which did not need much encouragement to get started, began to fill his mind for the self-righteous, tightly controlled whites who preached such lofty morals and, at least in his experience, did such avid and hungry things when you took off your clothes for them.

Inevitably he soon became the darling of the sensational press. "African Prince Cited," the London *Times* would murmur discreetly; "TERRIBLE TERRY BOPS COPS, JUGGED AGAIN," the *Express* would roar. A series of escapades and a growing string of well-publicized dates with titled young ladies made him the pet of the columnists and the darling of the gossips. The final accolade came just before he left England, in a valedictory personality sketch in the *Daily Mail*: "TERRY JOINS 'SET': PRINCESS FINDS HIM AMUSING."

Behind the window dressing, most of it both socially enjoyable and physically refreshing, a mind like a razor busily stowed away all the information it received, both textual and human, at Oxford and during a year's postgraduate study at the London School of Economics. It also, on a few quieter, unpublicized trips upcountry with his old mentor from the Colonial Office, gave him as much insight as a foreigner could ever achieve into the enigma of Britain: a tiny country, filled with a thousand surprises, each a thousand years old, that never quite divulged its innermost realities to anyone who wasn't native. As a tribalist, he eventually concluded with some ironic amusement that he was in the presence of another tribe, and one he would never completely understand: very ancient, going back very far into the past, surrounded by haunted scenes and haunted memories and heroes and heroines and deep-dyed villains who had never really died. "But all these people are still alive!" he had finally exclaimed in amused amazement to his mentor as they studied some ruined haunt of Hotspur in the west; and so it seemed, in this lovely little land where, eating lunch in some ancient inn set in an emerald valley in the hills, one might almost expect to hear in the courtyard a rattle and a clatter and a whicker and a whinny and, looking out, see Great Elizabeth, all silks and jewels and spangled things, descending from her coach; and, being startled but not at all surprised, say politely, "Why, yes, ma'am. But I had thought you were in London."

So England left her mark, for all that he had sampled some of her most superficial as well as most impressive aspects, and for all that he headed home to Gorotoland determined to put to use all his British-conferred knowledge to break his ties with Britain just as rapidly as he could. In Molobangwe he found his father, now in his early seventies, failing badly; but although he and his mother had one more talk concerning the possibilities of again seeking the aid of the gods and ancestors to hasten his accession to the throne, they decided that it would be neither necessary nor wise. Independence was sweeping Africa now, and the world was suddenly acutely conscious of everything that went on there; it would not suit his purposes to have "Fresh Heir" taken out of the files and brought up to date. He decided instead, after securing by blood-oath the acquiescence of the Council of Elders in the unheard-of proposition that his mother should serve as Regent during his father's decline, to go off to the United States and take another postgraduate year, this time at Harvard. Before he left, he married three wives and spent an intensive two weeks alternating among them night and day in the firm determination to leave behind as many heirs as possible. He was pleased to learn a month after he left that all were pregnant.

In the United States he went about as determined to absorb impressions and knowledge as he had been in Britain. He arrived with his reputation fairly well established, and while he had decided that it would be best to play down the "Terrible Terry" side of it, at least in public (in private, he found himself as eagerly pursued in Harvard Yard and along the gaudier reaches of the eastern seaboard as he had ever been in Oxford and London), he put the rest of it to good use.

Great racial ferment was under way in America, too, which was one reason he had wanted to go there, and he promptly found himself in great demand from many groups in both races as a speaker and adviser on African affairs.

"While his own country is still struggling to achieve the full forms of democracy," *The Reporter* announced in an admiring article, "the basic freedoms and liberties of its citizens are being daily strengthened with new guarantees."

This was news to Terry, but he said, "Oh, yes, oh, yes," with complacent quickness and a brisk confirming nod when he was asked about it on "Face the Nation." Self-delusion, he rapidly found, was the principal characteristic of mid-century America, and this made the country willing sucker bait for anyone who could offer a reasonable facsimile of idealism and goodwill. The word was enough, provided it was applied to humanitarian causes, and nobody bothered to check behind the word for either facts or ultimate intentions. It never occurred to him to appreciate the genuine goodwill toward man from which this sometimes terrifying naïveté arose, since in his country, as in so many others, disinterested goodwill toward man was a concept that simply did not exist. He concluded soon that many Americans were fools in this regard, and one night when he had been invited to be one of the principal speakers at a Brotherhood Week banquet in New York he decided to put it to the test.

"It has been wonderful to have this fine roast beef," he began, looking out upon the glittering audience agleam with diamonds and humanitarian impulse. "In my country, you know, we eat *people*. This is quite a change."

They had roared with happy laughter and considered him the most charming spoofer. After that he adopted a sort of sardonic double-talk with his American hosts which they always took with absolute seriousness. The British, he decided, always believed that you were *going* to tell them the truth, and eventually caught up with you if you lied; the Americans always believed that you *were* telling them the truth, and never caught up with you if you lied. He still found this puzzling, at times, but it did not stop him from using the fact with the most calculating ruthlessness to advance his personal and national ambitions.

In contrast to what he found in America, the harsh dynamism of Soviet Russia and the steady hammering advance of Communism upon the citadels of the West had deeply impressed him. He had deliberately refrained from giving himself the experience of studying in Moscow, even though the Soviet Government had secretly invited him on several occasions; his business was with the West and he did not wish to alienate it unduly. Possibly if he had gone there he would have been less impressed and less willing to be gullible about it. But to him, as an African watching the world convulsion go forward after the Second World War, seeing the confused and ineffectual way the West attempted to withstand it, perceiving in it all the opportunities it held for the clever little mice to play while the great cats were at one another's throats, he inevitably came to admire and respect the Soviet approach. It was as cruel, as brutal, as heartless, and as cold blooded as his own. The words were roseate, the principles were noble, the slogans were as ringing as any to be found in the West; but, underneath, the undeviating purpose and aim was as deceitful, as deceptive, as devious and unprincipled and greedy for power as anything to be found in Africa. The Communists talked as volubly as the West of shining goals; but the Communists acted, too, and the talk turned out to be a lie: and the lie worked. No one with a background such as Terry's could fail to be impressed by that.

It was no wonder that since his father's deep senility he had permitted the secret entry of Soviet and Chinese Communist advisers and technicians into Gorotoland, that Communist arms were being secretly assembled in the highlands, and that in the past two years he had come increasingly to rely upon his younger cousin (making sure, of course, that the cousin was always attended by tribesmen absolutely loyal to himself), who had accepted Moscow's invitation and had spent three years in Russia.

At Harvard, where he audited a number of classes and participated in a number of forums and other intellectual exercises concerning emergent Africa, he found himself looked to as an authority both on what should be done there and in the United States as well. There were several incidents involving colored students (one was a star trackman named Cullee Hamilton), and during each he was interviewed, questioned, and quoted. He made his statements suitably fervent and solemn, and was given much attention as a youthful symbol of the wave of independence and dawning justice that was racing across Africa and finding many echoes at the lunch counters and campuses of America.

And this reputation, he thought contemptuously now, he still retained as he launched upon his final comments to the First Committee, despite the fact that Gorotoland had a tribal caste system as terrible as India's, despite the fact that his government still connived at secret slavery, despite the hushed-up massacre of the United Opposition Party two years ago and the ritual sacrifices that still went on in the cave at Mbuele. The British were beginning to catch onto him, but in the United States he still remained the shining knight jousting with the forces of colonialist evil. Occasionally some disturbing question would be raised by someone, some embarrassing disclosure would creep into the pages of the papers; he could always count upon a dozen influential defenders to spring to his side, pooh-pooh it all away, write indignant editorials denouncing the suspicious, or offer the world some other equally impressive example of hardheaded realism on the subject. There were a great many people in academic, literary, and journalistic circles of the United States, he had been happily surprised to learn, who simply *did not want* to admit the seamy side of their chosen idols: too much of their own reputations was involved. Having committed themselves to certain people and causes, they could not abandon the commitment without admitting that they had been fools. And none of them, if it could possibly be avoided by sufficiently loud, sarcastic, indignant, and self-defensive noise, would do that.

So, while he knew Claude Maudulayne and Orrin Knox and Vasily Tashikov and a good deal of the rest of the world assessed him for exactly what he was, he was calmly confident—as he rolled out his concluding sentences about "help us achieve true liberty for Gorotoland—help us join the nations of mankind, upright and unafraid"—that he could count on much friendly support in America. It gave an extra power to his peroration as it resounded now in First Committee just prior to the vote on the resolution offered by Felix Labaiya-Sofra in the name of Panama:

"Oh, Mr. Chairman"—he told himself, with a sudden reversion to the happy excitement that made his heart feel like bursting, how beautifully he was performing, here at the UN—"we cry out in Gorotoland! The world cries with us! Freedom for my poor oppressed people. Freedom—*now!*" And once again he crashed his enormous fist down on the rostrum while the Communist bloc banged and pounded and applause rippled over floor and public galleries. And once more he found Lord Maudulayne raising his hand and, with an ironic little bow, started to step aside. But the British Ambassador halted him with a gesture.

"Mr. Chairman, I would just like to put one question to His Royal Highness before the vote. Is he aware that Soviet and Chinese technicians are in his country illegally and that arms from Communist sources are being smuggled into the highlands to a secret point there?"

An exaggerated expression of surprise came over the M'Bulu's face, followed by a broad smile.

"Well, Mr. Chairman, if Her Majesty's Government really think outworn charges about Communism will delay this vote on freedom for Gorotoland, I think they are mistaken. Why *is* it, Mr. Chairman, that everyone—*everyone* in the West who wishes to stop the forward march of peoples always—*always*—tries to scare the world with Communism? Do they not understand that this is old stuff now? Do they not know that the peoples of the world can no longer be frightened with it? Do they not know the world simply does not believe it any longer? Mr. Chairman," he said gravely, "I again ask your help for my poor enslaved country. I have no more to say, distinguished delegates. It is in your hands."

And with a flourish of his gleaming robes he stalked from the rostrum without another glance at the British Ambassador, who seemed for a second, but only a second, at a loss.

"Very well, Mr. Chairman," he said matter-of-factly, "I wonder if the Ambassador of Panama would read his resolution to us, so that we may all hear it again before we vote, bearing in mind the question I have just put to His Highness, which is based on very well-authenticated information reaching Her Majesty's Government from very reliable sources within Gorotoland."

There was a stir, and into it Patsy Labaiya's husband spoke from the floor.

"It is irregular, Mr. Chairman," he said, a frown on his shrewd dark face and a characteristic sharpness in his tone. "I see no reason why I should read the resolution. Let the distinguished delegate of the U.K. resume his seat and let the *rapporteur* read it, if that is the desire of the committee."

"I will read it," said the Yugoslav delegate in the chair, and proceeded to do so as Lord Maudulayne resumed his seat and the Secretary of State passed him a note that said, "We have intended to vote with you all along at this stage, but watch what the press will make of it." Claude Maudulayne nodded rather grimly and tore up the note.

"Whereas," the Yugoslav delegate said in his thick but recognizable

English, "it is the legitimate desire of all colonial peoples to achieve independence, and,

"Whereas, it is the purpose of the United Nations to encourage and support all such legitimate aspirations of all colonial peoples everywhere, and,

"Whereas, it is the intention of the United Nations, furthermore, that all states should speed the easing of racial tensions, whether springing from the colonialist past or any other cause—"

"Damn it," Claude Maudulayne whispered, "I still don't like that language. And neither should you."

"He wanted 'imperialist past' and it's taken us six days of negotiating to get agreement on 'colonialist,'" Orrin Knox whispered back. "The Asians and Africans wouldn't permit any further change. Be thankful for small favors."

"And, whereas the Territory of Gorotoland is the outstanding area at the moment where these purposes may be achieved most speedily,

"Now, therefore, it is the recommendation of the General Assembly that the United Nations do all in its power to persuade the United Kingdom to grant immediate independence to the Territory of Gorotoland."

"Roll call!" the Soviet Ambassador shouted. "Roll call!"

"If the distinguished Soviet delegate will wait until I put the question," the Yugoslav delegate said with some asperity. "The question is, does the First Committee approve this resolution and recommend its referral to, and adoption by, the General Assembly?"

"Does the First Committee approve immediate independence for Gorotoland!" Vasily Tashikov said loudly.

"That is not the question," the Yugoslav delegate said with a pout. "I have stated the question. A roll call has been requested." He reached into a small box before him and, in the UN custom, drew the name of the first nation to be called, the others to follow in their alphabetical order in English. "We will start with the Malagasy Republic."

"*Oui*," said Malagasy.

"Mali."

"*Oui*."

"Mauritania."

"*Oui*."

"Mexico."

"*Sí*."

"Mongolia."

"Yes."

"Morocco."

"*Oui*."

"Nepal."

"Abstention."

"Netherlands."

"No."

"New Zealand."

"No."

"Nicaragua."

"*Abstención.*"

"Niger."

"*Oui.*"

"Nigeria."

"Yes."

"Seems to be a landslide," NBC/UN whispered to the London *Daily Mail* in the press gallery. "Serves us jolly well right," the *Daily Mail* responded dourly. "Imagine trying to stop genuine independence in this day and age." "Nothing to the reports of Communism, then?" NBC inquired. The *Express* snorted. "You Yanks are hipped on the subject just like Terry said. Why don't you come off it?" "O.K.," NBC said with a shrug. "I just wanted the official word." "You got it from Maudulayne, right enough," the *Daily Mail* said, "but that doesn't mean it's true. Listen to South Africa! What could you expect?"

"No," said South Africa.

"Spain."

"No."

"It appears you have a very handsome victory," the Secretary-General murmured to the M'Bulu. "I cannot complain," said Terrible Terry.

"Turkey," said the *rapporteur*.

"No."

"Uganda."

"Yes."

"Ukrainian S.S.R."

"*Da.*"

"U.S.S.R."

"*Da.*"

"United Arab Republic."

"Yes."

"United Kingdom."

"No," Claude Maudulayne said firmly.

"Here we go," said NBC, leaning forward.

"United States."

"No," said Orrin Knox with equal firmness, and there was a sound of released tension through the room.

"Afghanistan," the *rapporteur* went on, going back to the head of the alphabet after running through the U's, V's, W's, and Y's. "Albania . . . Algeria . . . Argentina . . . Australia . . ."

"The vote on the draft resolution submitted by Panama," the Yugoslav delegate said presently, "is 51 Yes, 23 No, 36 abstentions, others absent. The resolution is adopted and referred to the General Assembly.

"If there is no other business, this meeting of First Committee is adjourned until tomorrow at 10 A.M., when we will consider General Assembly draft resolution 6 stroke 98, proposals for suspension of nuclear testing by the eleven nuclear powers."

At the door, as the delegates crowded out, the M'Bulu of Mbuele, halted by many congratulatory handshakes, awaited with a happy smile the approach of the British Ambassador and the American Secretary of State.

"There," he said comfortably. "It was not so bad, was it, Your Lordship?" Claude Maudulayne shrugged.

"It was an interesting advisory. And that, of course, is all it was."

"But with the weight of world opinion behind it," the M'Bulu said, somewhat less sunnily.

"If it passes the General Assembly, possibly."

"Surely you don't think you can stop it!" Terry said with an anger he made noticeably louder as the press began to approach.

"Who knows?" the British Ambassador said. "We want some answers on those reports I mentioned before H. M.'s Government would be willing to relax their very determined opposition."

"Reports!" Terry demanded. "Who told you about 'reports'?"

"I'm not going to tell you," Lord Maudulayne said with a cheerful smile at the press. "I don't want the poor beggars eaten. There's the matter of the slave trade, too."

"Come now," said the London *Daily Express* in a peremptory tone. "Surely H. M.'s Government aren't going to bring out those old chestnuts!"

"Aren't you interested in whether they might be true?" Claude Maudulayne inquired mildly.

"I know they're not," the *Express* said flatly. "I've been to Gorotoland and seen for myself, haven't I, Your Highness?" He turned to the Secretary of State with an impatient air. "Mr. Secretary, why did the U.S. vote with the U.K.?"

"We feel the program of independence for Gorotoland is well timed and well phased, on the whole," Orrin said, "and in any event, if it is not, we aren't so sure this kind of pressure is the way to help the situation. We haven't decided what to do when it comes before the Assembly."

"Then we may be for it there," the New York *Times* said quickly. Orrin shrugged.

"Wait until it gets there and see."

"Is it because you're afraid of the blacks?" the *Express* inquired. The Secretary's expression hardened, and it was Terry who came to the rescue.

"Enough, enough!" he cried with an infectious gaiety. "Enough of such solemn talk! Ahead of me lies my delightful visit to the southern United States, my dinner at the White House, my reception at Her Majesty's Embassy, the chance to renew old acquaintances and make new friends for Gorotoland. Enough, enough!" And he burst into a roar of delighted laughter that quite startled his listeners.

"Enough, indeed," the Secretary of State agreed dryly. "How about some lunch?"

"Alas, I have contracted to meet the distinguished Ambassador of the Soviet Union and the Secretary-General for lunch," Terrible Terry said. "Possibly next week, if I may be so bold as to request a rain check."

"Fine with me," Orrin said. "Claude? A quick one, because I have a lot of telephoning to do to Washington."

"All caused by me?" the M'Bulu asked coyly. The Secretary smiled at the attentive press.

"You do love to be the center of things, don't you? No, not entirely by you. There are other things that concern the government of the United States."

"Ah," said Terry. "But none more important, surely."

And in this, as the Secretary of State was to reflect in glum retrospect two days later, the M'Bulu was to be proven entirely correct.

5

The crowded elevator arrived at the fourth floor and two Indians, three Sudanese, a Cypriote, two French correspondents, three American correspondents, a graying secretary from the Economic and Social Council, and the junior United States Senator from Iowa stepped off. The others rapidly found their luncheon companions and dispersed from the humming little entryway to the Delegates' Dining Room, but the Senator paused a moment to watch the hubbub of arrivals, greetings, handshakes, and exclamations in half a hundred tongues before wandering to the reservations desk to get his table number.

"Senator Smith of the United States," he said with the intimately boyish grin that always fluttered feminine hearts, and the large Brunhilde behind the desk, true to her sex, gave a pleased titter and obediently skimmed through her reservation book with a swiftly ingratiating pencil.

"Table 47, Senator Smits," she informed him with a dazzling display of teeth, and Lafe Smith reached over and patted her on the cheek.

"I can always count on you, can't I?"

"Oh, yess, Senator Smits!" she assured him with a hearty giggle. "For annnysssing!"

"Ah, ah!" he said. "You'll be giving me ideas."

"Oh, *Senator* Smits!" she exclaimed, turning away with a wink and a blush to the grave Pakistani who was pretending not to hear this intimate exchange. Senator Fry, approaching his colleague from the rear, poked him in the small of the back.

"That was a disgusting exhibition," he observed. Lafe grunted and swung about with an amiable grin.

"Hi, buddy. I just have to keep in practice."

"I thought you were a sedate old married man now," Hal Fry remarked. For a moment his companion lost his cheerful expression.

"Yes," he said. "Who are you waiting for?"

"Nobody in particular. I thought I might run into you. And you?"

"Well, I took a table for two," Lafe said, "and—actually—"

Senator Fry shook his head.

"All right. I'll run along. I won't even ask who she is."

"But I don't know who she is." Lafe grinned. "Yet."

"Oh, come on, now. I don't believe even you are that good. Particularly right here in front of God and the UN."

"As a matter of fact, there's a little nurse in the Medical Service, and—I don't know, you understand, she may be married with ten kids, but when I was in there the other day to get some cold pills she seemed—uh—friendly, as it were."

"I'll bet, 'as it were,'" Hal Fry said. "What does Irene think of this?" Again a shadow filmed his colleague's eyes.

"If she doesn't like it," he said shortly, "it's her own damned fault. If, of course," he added pleasantly, "it's any of your business."

"Sorry," Hal said. "Your love life is so much a part of Washington, you know, that even up here one expects to be kept informed. But forgive me if I'm intruding."

"You are and I do," Senator Smith said, good nature restored. "There's that little lady now." He stared intently at a group of girls getting off the elevator, but none responded.

"There goes that little lady now," Senator Fry remarked after they had passed. Lafe smiled.

"Very significant. Don't have to tell an old campaigner like me what it means to be deliberately ignored. I may even have to have some more cold pills this afternoon."

"You ought to be ashamed of yourself," his colleague told him, not entirely in jest.

"Oh, I may be pure as the driven snow these days, for all you know," the Senator from Iowa said. He frowned. "About as pure as my wife. But that's another story. How was Fifth Committee? Are the administrative and budget vultures still after poor old Uncle Sam?"

"Always. Why don't we wait for a minute and see if Orrin comes up?"

"O.K. I'll ask Miss Fluoristan of 1896 to give us a table for four."

"I'll ask her. You've titillated the poor girl enough for one day."

"Titillated!" Lafe Smith repeated dreamily. "What an obscene, delightful word. Can't you just see me with my naked hands around her naked—and my naked—and her naked—and—"

"All right," Hal Fry said hastily. "Save that for the next time Tashikov makes a speech in the Assembly and I need something to keep me awake. Not here. I'll be back in a second."

"There's that little guy from Gabon," Lafe said with a shift to seriousness. "I want to ask him something, anyway. See you in a minute."

Their errands completed, they met again by the entrance to the blue-and-white dining room just as the Secretary of State and the British Ambas-

sador came out of the elevator and moved to the reservation desk. Hal hailed
them, and in a moment they were on their way in together. By doing a little
quick reshuffling that would a few minutes later badly upset four lady members of the Friends of the United Nations of Pipestone, Minnesota, Miss
Fluoristan had managed to give them the prize table that sits in the north-
east corner of the great glass-walled room looking straight up the East River
to the Queensborough Bridge and beyond. The gentle autumn haze had
lifted a little; the sun was bright and almost hot upon the river, ruffled by
a freshening breeze. Oil barges and sightseeing boats trudged busily up and
down, and over the bridge beyond the apartment buildings of Beekman
Place and Sutton Place they could see a stream of tiny cars constantly coming
and going.

"Well," Orrin said as they settled down and ordered drinks before turning
to the menu, "and how was Trusteeship Committee?"

"You know Fourth Committee," Lafe said. "Flick, flick, flick from our little
friends in Moscow, as always. Guess what we talked about this morning:
just the same thing you did in First Committee—Gorotoland. I must say that
boy has his groundwork well laid."

"He's a shrewd fellow," Hal Fry agreed. "We even had to spend an hour
on it in Fifth Committee, too. Did you vote in First?"

"We did," the Secretary said. "And he won, substantially."

"And we lost," Senator Fry said. "Substantially."

"We did."

"I'm not so sure, with all respects to you, Claude, that this is a wise position for us to take," Hal Fry observed. "I have a good many qualms on this
one."

The British Ambassador looked argumentative, but the Secretary shrugged.

"The press asked. I told them. I said we regarded the commitment made by
Britain on independence as well phased and well timed. And in any event,
I said, we didn't feel that the situation would be helped by this kind of pres-
sure. I said I didn't know what we'd do in the General Assembly."

"Once in a while," Lafe observed, "I'd like to see us be consistent all the
way through, you know? If we're against it, let's be against it. If we're for it,
let's be for it. All the way."

"Well," Orrin said. "We may be."

"We would appreciate that," Claude Maudulayne said. The Secretary
smiled.

"Or, again, we may not be," he said cheerfully, and then sobered at once.
"No. I don't mean to be frivolous about it, but there is much to be said on
Terry's side of it, even admitting Communist infiltration, hidden slave trade,
ritual sacrifices, and all. After all, most of the rest of Africa is free now,
and—"

"Yes," the British Ambassador said, "and look at it! Just look at it! Sinking
back into tribalism in a dozen areas, abandoning all the protections of liberty,
all the safeguards of the human being that some of us tried to give them over
so many hard years—"

"Maybe they never really wanted them," Hal Fry suggested. "Maybe they just wanted to be left alone to slaughter one another down the ages."

"Well," Claude Maudulayne said. "I must be fair, too. Of course there are some who have tried. Julius Nyerere has tried. Nigeria has tried. Some others have tried. But look at those who haven't, starting with Ghana. But you'd never know it," he said bitterly, "to read some of the press."

"There are certain major elements of the press that occupy a curious position relative to the United Nations," the Secretary of State said thoughtfully. "They decide arbitrarily that *it is best* for their readers to believe certain things about certain areas of the globe. It rather confuses things . . . Speaking of our troubles," he said as they finished giving the pretty Japanese waitress their orders, "wouldn't you like to eavesdrop on that conversation down there by the window?"

"I must say Tashikov and Terry look happy," Senator Fry observed. "The Secretary-General doesn't seem so cheerful."

"What a hell of a spot he's on, really," Lafe said. "Those damned bastards chipping away at him every minute of every day; the organization slipping, really, ever since the Congo, nothing in sight to indicate the trend is going to change—Orrin," he concluded abruptly, "why don't we have the S.-G. to lunch someday? I think we ought to make more of a fuss over him. The poor guy needs help."

"We do as much as we can, don't we?" the Secretary asked. "Without making it too obvious. We can't afford to court the charge that he's an American stooge."

"There isn't a charge in the world that we try to avoid," Senator Fry remarked, "that the Communists don't make anyway. So why should we worry what they say? I think we ought to work with him more closely, too."

"I don't think he'll do it," Orrin Knox said. "Oh, he'll lunch with us, I'm sure. But look at him now. He wouldn't be any more relaxed or communicative than he's being with them."

And indeed it did appear to many eyes around the room that the Secretary-General was not entirely at ease in his present company. This was correct, for he was not. He found himself, in fact, wondering with some asperity how it was that his host the Soviet Ambassador could always succeed in placing him at a disadvantage, and concluded that it was by exactly the same means that the Communists used to put everyone at a disadvantage: simply by taking the forms of polite and civilized custom and twisting them around with complete selfishness and ruthless inconsideration to serve their own ends. A luncheon invitation from the head of a delegation was something one in his position did not normally turn down without a valid excuse if he were in New York: so all Tashikov had to do was ask. And then all he had to do was extend the invitation to the heir to Gorotoland, and there were the three of them in the eye of the world, obviously in cahoots and crowing about the vote in First Committee.

Such, at any rate, was the exact impression he knew the Soviet Ambassador wanted to give when he had ordered champagne and started the luncheon with a toast. The toast had been only the standard "To peace!" but when he forced them to clink glasses with a big, obvious gesture and then grinned triumphantly around the dining room, it was obvious to everyone that they were saluting Terry's triumph. Particularly when that exuberant young man had gulped down his drink, refilled his glass, and gulped that down, too, with a sunny smile upon the world. For him, at least, there was no subterfuge; he *was* celebrating his triumph.

"Mr. Secretary-General," he said, "this is a wonderful day for my people. And indeed for all people like us, don't you think?"

The Secretary-General stiffened slightly at this reference to their mutual color and responded with a circumspect courtesy.

"I can understand Your Highness' satisfaction."

"Aren't you satisfied too?" the M'Bulu demanded in some surprise. Their Soviet host chortled.

"The Secretary-General can't afford to be satisfied or dissatisfied, can you, Mr. Secretary-General? It is beyond the scope of the Charter."

The S.-G. smiled, a trifle bleakly. "And on the letter of the Charter, Your Highness," he said, "you will find that the distinguished Soviet delegate is a very fine and meticulous expert. The spirit of the Charter is sometimes something else again."

"We do not understand spirits in my country," Vasily Tashikov said blandly. "We are practical people. We consider spirits the same as ghosts. The ghost of the West," he remarked with a sudden ironic chuckle in which the M'Bulu joined with spontaneous delight.

"I love the UN," he said simply. "Everyone is so witty and amusing here. You are fortunate to be in your position, Mr. Secretary-General. It is a great honor as well as responsibility."

"Yes," the Secretary-General said in a polite tone that warned off further comment along that line. Terrible Terry got the message but plunged right on.

"You can do so much for Africa now. So much more than you could when you were delegate from Nigeria. We all look to you."

"The Secretary-General," Vasily Tashikov said, spearing a large bite of steak, "tries to remember, occasionally, that he comes from Africa. Most of the time he is more anxious to be liked by everyone everywhere. Is that not true, Mr. Secretary-General?"

"I conceive it my duty," the S.-G. said stiffly, "to be as impartial as possible. However difficult the distinguished Soviet delegate and his associates may try to make it for me to be so."

"We try to understand you," the Soviet Ambassador said with a mock wistfulness. "We attempt to exercise every charity in seeing your point of view. It is only when you consistently play the imperialist game of the West that we find ourselves baffled and saddened that one we thought a good friend should so betray the cause of human freedom. It is sad."

"You attempt to destroy my office and the United Nations every day in the world," the Secretary-General said bluntly. "*That* is what is sad. If you people devoted one-tenth of the energy to building up the world that you do to tearing it down, what a wonderful world it would be."

"You see, Your Highness?" Vasily Tashikov said with a show of frustration. "He persists in these historical fallacies."

"I do not know about this," the M'Bulu said in a placating tone. "All I know is that we regard him as a great defender of our liberties in Africa, and we in Gorotoland, particularly, are counting upon him to aid us in our struggle to be free."

"The point is," the Secretary-General said sharply, "that I can't help anybody much. This man and his country have virtually destroyed my office and the UN itself."

"But without the Secretary-General," Terry objected with a sunny disbelief, "where would any of us be?"

"That is exactly it," the S.-G. said grimly. "It is the question you should ask yourselves before it is too late altogether."

"You are turning a delightful luncheon into a debate," the Soviet Ambassador said regretfully. "And everyone is watching. It *is* sad, on such a happy day for our young friend's country."

"Yes, really," the M'Bulu said. "You are much too gloomy, Mr. Secretary-General. We should all be friends! That is what the UN is for, is it not?"

"Who knows?" the S.-G. said, giving him a sharp, appraising glance. "What do you intend to use it for?"

" 'Use it for'?" the M'Bulu echoed. "For the independence of my country. And, after that, for the benefit of mankind. If Gorotoland can contribute to it."

"Mmmhmm," the Secretary-General said. "Anyone who has sufficient goodwill and integrity can contribute to it. Some do not."

"We would like to expel them," the Soviet Ambassador agreed, "but it is so difficult, with the veto."

"Accccchhhh!" the Secretary-General said, an indescribable combination of disgust, distaste, and dislike. "What a mockery you make of it."

A look of amusement and, the S.-G. thought, understanding of some secret nature he could not interpret passed between his companions. Again the M'Bulu gave his hearty laugh and held out his hands in his palms-up gesture.

"Mr. Secretary-General, I think you are much too gloomy. Be of good faith, Mr. Secretary-General! Be of good cheer! It is a great day and all will come right for humanity!"

"Let me tell you something, Your Highness," the Secretary-General said. "I served some considerable time as delegate before being elected to this office, and I will tell you something you should know. And that is that nothing good comes of the kind of game you are playing here."

"What game?" Terry demanded in blank bewilderment.

"I tell you that as one African to another," the Secretary-General added quietly, and for a long moment they stared at one another until the M'Bulu's eyes dropped. But he covered it, again, with an infectious laugh.

"You speak in riddles, Mr. Secretary-General. Riddles, riddles. All I want is for us to be happy and enjoy the happy day for my country. Will you not drink to that? I think our friends the Secretary of State and the distinguished British Ambassador will think you are not comfortable being with me unless we have a little show of happiness."

"The Secretary-General does not dare to appear happy in my presence," Vasily Tashikov said with a laugh. "The world would think he was forgiving me for pointing out the historical facts about his position as agent for the colonialist powers. The world would think he was finally agreeing to the facts. Nobody in the West wants to agree to facts. That causes all our troubles here."

"Very well," the Secretary-General said, lifting his glass. "To the fact of human decency, which survives everything, even you."

"To the human decency of the freedom-loving peoples," the Soviet Ambassador said amicably. "I will stop there."

"To everybody!" the M'Bulu said with a flashing smile. "Let us make it unanimous."

"Now, what was that all about?" Hal Fry inquired. "The S.-G. looked as though he were drinking vinegar."

"Drinking the blood of the West," Claude Maudulayne said, "if Tashikov had anything to do with preparing the tipple. But Terry looked happy."

"Terry always looks happy," Lafe Smith said. "Terry is having a ball. I understand Harley's going to entertain him in Washington, and you folks are going to give him a reception at the Embassy, and the Jasons are going to roll out the red carpet in Charleston, and everything's really going to be great. It's the talk of the Lounge. Does Harley know all about this?"

"No, I doubt if he does, yet," Orrin said. "I've got to call him before his press conference so he'll be prepared for it if they ask him. Actually I think we can get out of it at the White House with just a little buffet or something; maybe Foreign Relations Committee, Foreign Affairs Committee, a few correspondents to give him the publicity he wants, and that ought to do it. And as for you, Claude, it's none of my business, but the smaller that reception the better, it seems to me."

"Oh, yes. We'll keep it down. They'll hardly know he's been in town. We hope."

"Good," Orrin said as he signed the check for the delegates' discount, "we'll hope so, too. Hal, why don't you go take a nap?"

"Do I look that tired?" Senator Fry asked with a smile. "I'm really not."

"Keep an eye on this man for me, Lafe," the Secretary said. "He worries me, suddenly."

"It isn't anything," Hal Fry said with some annoyance.

"What?" Lafe asked in concern. The Senator from West Virginia looked even more annoyed.

"Now here's Orrin making a federal case of it. I'm just having a little blurring of vision, a little reddish thing. Very temporary. Nothing serious. It's only happened twice—"

"In twenty-four hours," the Secretary of State said. "I saw you blink just now."

"—and it's just a little tiredness. Maybe I will lie down, but only for a little while."

"Let me take you to the doctor's office," Lafe suggested. "That would be an even better excuse than cold pills."

"Excuse for what?" Orrin asked. "No, don't tell me. It can only be one of the nurses."

"Raoul was telling me yesterday that the delegate from Senegal describes you as 'le chasseur formidable,'" Lord Maudulayne said. "You're the envy of the entire UN."

"I don't really deserve it, you know," Lafe said. "No, really I don't," he repeated when they all laughed. "But I suppose it gives people something to gossip about in the Lounge . . . Well, let's be off. Fourth Committee's going back at three and I want to run across the street to delegation headquarters and check my Washington mail before the meeting starts."

"I'll come with you," Hal said.

"Rest," Orrin told him.

"Call Harley," Hal replied. "You worry about the cares of the world and I'll worry about me."

"It's no care, really," the Secretary said as they walked out of the dining room to the smiles and nods and little bows of many delegates who stopped their eating to watch them go. "You know that fatherly manner Harley's developed lately. Terry will be charmed to pieces and all will be well."

And as he turned at the door to give a cheerful farewell wave to the glittering M'Bulu, who waved cheerfully back, he actually believed it.

6

"What I can't understand," the St. Louis Post-Dispatch remarked rather sourly as the Washington press corps drifted into the New State Department auditorium, "is why this press conference was called three hours early."

"I suspect the President's going to take off for the Upper Peninsula of Michigan tonight," the Houston Post said. "The word isn't out officially yet, but I understand he wants to spend a few days up there in the back woods."

"Oh, God," the Washington Star said with a groan. "More roughing it around the campfire for America's Finest."

"Just because you don't like to fish," said the Baltimore Sun. "Anyway, let the great man have his fun. He has a tough job. It says here."

"Oh, it is," the Arkansas Gazette agreed. "Nobody said it wasn't."

"I still think Governor Jason could do it better," the Herald Tribune said.

"What's this thing the Jason Foundation's throwing for that African gook?" the Memphis Commercial Appeal inquired. "I understand they're going to serve white man Bordelaise. You boys better stay away from there."

"Only bureau chiefs and columnists got invited," the Philadelphia *Inquirer* said. "You don't suppose they'll be eaten, do you?"

"You're living in a dreamworld," the *Post Dispatch* said. "No such luck. Ooops! Everybody up!"

"Please be seated," the President said, taking his customary stand at the high rostrum with the microphones, his press staff beside him in a row, the White House stenographer at one side transcribing busily. Before him in the auditorium he saw some two hundred members of the press corps in various stages of alertness, in back of them and on the sides the waiting television cameras. What he had begun by referring to as "my weekly ordeal" and had now come to regard as "my weekly picnic" was about to begin. He hadn't much for them this time, but if he knew the press corps they'd develop something before the senior wire-service man put an end to it by crying, "Thank you, Mr. President!" and they risked life and limb racing for the telephones.

"I really haven't much today," he said. "The Ambassador of the Ivory Coast presented his credentials this morning. I had a short talk with the Ambassador of Rumania on a possible food grant there. The head of the World Bank and I had a short talk on the world economic situation, and the Secretary of Labor reported that unemployment has risen slightly—the Labor Department is releasing those figures later this afternoon. I have some new postmaster appointments and some new Generals in the Air Force, which I shall send down to the Senate tomorrow in the hope they'll advise and consent to them. I shall take off tonight for my fishing camp on the Upper Peninsula of Michigan for a five-day visit, and if any of you want to go along for a taste of life in the great outdoors, you'll be welcome. Now I'll answer any questions you have."

Fifteen were on their feet at once. He picked a familiar face and nodded.

"Mr. President," the AP said, "is it true that the government of India has invited you to make a formal visit in the spring?"

"That is under consideration."

"Mr. President," said the Chicago *Daily News,* "since your Administration is deliberately withholding so much news from the public about current missile developments, do you think the country would be justified in becoming alarmed by the situation?"

The President started to look indignant but then thought better of it.

"No, I stopped beating my wife yesterday. You can ask her."

"Well, Mr. President," the *Daily News* said as his colleagues laughed, "that is all very well, but—"

"I don't believe we are withholding information. If we are, write me a letter through the press office with specific examples and I'll see what I can do about it. Next question?"

"Mr. President," UPI said, "are you satisfied with the progress of the nuclear control talks at the UN?"

"They are never satisfactory," the President said with a frank unhappiness. "They are always too slow and they never really come to grips with the problem."

"Is that the Communists' fault or ours, Mr. President?" the Washington *Post* asked quickly.

"I prefer to think it's theirs," the President said. "Do you have some information to the contrary?"

"No, sir," the *Post* said. "I just wondered if you were satisfied that we were doing all we can."

"I am doing all I can."

"Yes, sir," said the *Post*.

"Mr. President," the New York *Times* said, "we have a question from our bureau at the United Nations. They understand up there that you are going to give a formal White House dinner for Terrible Terry—the M'Bulu of Mbuele, that is—that African prince from Gorotoland—"

"I know who he is. Who tells them that?"

"Apparently he did," the *Times* said.

"I haven't heard about it."

"Mr. President," the Los Angeles *Times* said, "you mean that he is inviting himself to dinner without your knowledge?"

"Apparently so," the President said with a chuckle. *Ebony* magazine was on his feet at once, looking indignant.

"Mr. President," he demanded, "do you mean to say, sir, that you are against entertaining visiting African dignitaries?"

"Now, I don't recall saying that," the President replied mildly. "Of course I am not against entertaining the official representatives of other countries. I do it all the time."

"Who makes them official, Mr. President?" *Ebony* demanded in the same tone. The President looked surprised.

"I don't quite understand your question."

"I mean," *Ebony* said, "are they officials because somebody says they are, or because *they are?*"

The correspondents laughed, but the President only smiled patiently.

"I still don't quite see it, but I suppose you mean would I receive Prince Terry if the British Government said they didn't want me to?"

"Do you feel he has to have British permission, or do you feel he is a dignitary in his own right?" *Ebony* persisted, as the other correspondents began to fidget.

"Knock it off, Uncle Tom," the Philadelphia *Bulletin* murmured to the Providence *Journal*, "knock it off."

"It is my understanding that Gorotoland is not an independent nation," the President said. "If I am wrong, you can correct me."

"Then will you receive him, sir?" the New York *Times* asked. The President smiled.

"I receive everyone who wishes to see me."

"The question is, sir," the *Times* persisted, "will you give him a formal White House dinner, as he says you will?"

"Well," the President said, beginning to show a little irritation at last, "I can't do it this weekend because I'm going away to Michigan. I can't stay around and entertain for every little character that comes to town."

"Oh, oh," the *Christian Science Monitor* whispered to CBS. "That does it."

"Mr. President," the *Air Force Journal* said, leaping up a fraction of a second before twelve colleagues, "is it planned to launch another moon expedition before the end of the year?"

"I have no comment on that."

"The families of the men who are there seem to be getting a little concerned, Mr. Presi—" the *Air Force Journal* said.

"The men will be maintained. That's all."

"Yes, sir."

Ten reporters were on their feet. He chose the El Paso *Times*.

"Mr. President, sir," she said, "why are you going fishing right at this time when world problems are so pressing?"

"Come along with me," he said as they all laughed, "and you'll find it will give you a much healthier outlook on all those pressing world problems. Seriously, I haven't had a vacation since Geneva and I think it's time I had one. Any objections?"

"No, Mr. President," she said. "I don't object. Some people do, though."

"Let 'em," he said cheerfully.

"My, my," the Denver *Post* remarked *sotto voce* to the Chicago *Tribune*. "Aren't we getting big and important."

"Just to go back for a minute to Terrible Terry, Mr. President," the Louisville *Courier-Journal* said, "we are to understand, then, that you know of no official dinner for him, you don't expect to stay here to see him, and there wouldn't be a dinner for him even if you did?"

"That's about it," the President said. "Don't get me wrong. I'm not unfriendly to him, but of course he won't be here in a status in which I can entertain him formally."

"Thank *you*, Mr. President!" the AP cried, and they tumbled headlong up the plushly carpeted steps out of the big orange-and-blue auditorium to the waiting telephones as the President watched them go with an amused shake of the head.

"Felix," said the New York *Times*/UN in the Delegates' Lounge, "what do you think of this? The President says he won't stay around to entertain Terry and wouldn't entertain him even if he did stay around. He says he's going fishing and he thinks Terry's a little character. How about that?"

"I don't think," said the Ambassador of Panama, "that our African friends will like it one little bit."

"Does it make your resolution on Gorotoland even more important?" the *Times* suggested.

Felix Labaiya-Sofra gave his characteristic thin-lipped smile and his dark eyes snapped.

"Its wisdom becomes more obvious every day."

"Do you think the President should stay and entertain Terry?" the *Times* persisted.

"I think any President who wished to make friends for the United States would do so," the Panamanian Ambassador said. "The United States," he added coldly, "does not have so many friends she can afford to waste them."

"Can I quote you?"

"Please do," said Felix Labaiya.

"Of course," said the delegate of Guinea to NBC with an air of deepest injury, "the President knows what he wishes to do. But it is a distinct shock to us. We are indignant and horrified."

"If the President had deliberately set out to insult the entire Afro-Asian world," the delegate of the United Arab Republic said sternly to *Paris-Match,* "I do not see how he could have done a better job. I am surprised and disappointed."

"We are disappointed," said the delegate of Ghana. "We are not surprised."

"I should hardly think it would be well received in Africa," the French Ambassador said, "but that is the President's problem."

"It might perhaps have been better to do as His Highness desired," said the Ambassador of the Argentine, "but we would not wish to enter into a matter that is between the United States and the African states."

"It is typical Yankee imperialism!" said the delegate of Cuba.

"I am puzzled by his decision," the Indian Ambassador observed cautiously to CBS, "but I would wish to study it further before saying anything about it."

"A bit thick, under the circumstances, wasn't it?" asked the Canadian delegate cheerfully.

"As Africans," said the delegate of Mali to the *Daily Mail,* who nodded vigorous agreement, "we are personally affronted. I think we can promise you there will be the gravest consequences."

"Oh, no," said the British Ambassador with a bland expression that didn't quite come off, "I wouldn't want to make any comment at all."

"Oh, no!" said the M'Bulu of Mbuele with a sunny smile. "I wouldn't want to make *any* comment *at all!*"

"It's my fault," the Secretary of State said. "I should have tried to reach you earlier, but I just assumed you were having your press conference at the usual time."

"And of course I just assumed that everything was in order up there," the President said with a trace of annoyance in his tone. The Secretary glanced across First Avenue at the green and silver shaft of the Secretariat Building, caught now by the slanting golden rays of the late-afternoon sun, and laughed rather grimly.

"Nothing is ever in order up here. Particularly with everybody in Africa big as life and twice as self-important. I don't think that reference to 'little character' was especially fortunate."

"It wasn't. But I knew how I meant it, and the press knew how I meant it—"

"—but the world didn't," Orrin said. "Or, anyway, a good portion of the world is pretending it didn't to suit its own devious purposes."

"Why are they such chintzy souls all the time?" the President asked in mild wonderment. "They know perfectly well—"

"It's like Alice in Wonderland. They do it 'cause it teases. For no other reason at all, except to embarrass us. That's the great game in the world, you see. We're out front, so we're fair target. That's for the jealous and spiteful ones. For those who really want to tear us down, of course, the game is less frivolous and lighthearted."

"Do you know where the line is that separates the two?" the President inquired dryly. The Secretary snorted.

"It's a little difficult to find, in some areas. I do think it would be wise to modify your plans somewhat. I ran into Raoul Barre just before I came across the street and he said he has already found great consternation and excitement among the former French colonies. Apparently they still come running to him with their troubles up here, and he thinks you would be well advised to think of some graceful excuse and change your plans."

"Oh, for heaven's sake," the President said in a tone of disgust. "How can I? Do you mean I have to be at the beck and call of every little two-bit international scalawag who wants to hold a gun at my head? It's blackmail."

"Sure," Orrin Knox said cheerfully, "that's exactly what it is. And everybody knows it. The most delightfully cynical double life goes on up here all the time about almost everything. Of a political nature, anyway."

"Now, Orrin," the President said. "God knows I don't have much side to me, but I do have some concept of the dignity of my office, and I can't let it appear that Terence Ajkaje is leading it around on a string. It's beneath the office. It's beneath the United States."

"That," said the Secretary of State, "is exactly the point Raoul was making, in an indirect way. He's not so sure it is."

"Have we fallen that low?" the President demanded. "I don't believe it. And neither do you."

"No. But—"

"And, furthermore, I must say all this hardly sounds like *you*. What's become of the fearless fighting Senator from Illinois? I thought I was appointing a Secretary of State with some starch in his soul."

"Now, Harley," the Secretary said sharply, "you know that isn't fair."

"Well," the President conceded, "you're right; it isn't. I apologize. But it does seem to me—"

"God knows I'd like to tell the little worm to go to hell," Orrin said, "but, you see, he isn't a little worm in the eyes of his fellow Africans, the press, and the New York cocktail circuit. Or if he is, they're doing an awfully good job of keeping it quiet. He floats around this place on a wave of favorable publicity that hasn't been matched since Castro spoke to the newspaper editors. He's the world symbol of freedom and liberty at the moment. It doesn't make any difference that he's really the exact opposite. It's the public image that counts, and I must say the public image is crowned with laurel and ten feet high."

"Even so," the President said with a stubborn note that his Cabinet had come to recognize, "I am afraid I can't possibly change my plans for him."

"Raoul suggested that perhaps you could say that last-minute legislation needed your attention, so you had decided to put off the fishing trip until next week—"

"There isn't anything that can't wait to be signed until I get back."

"—and then you could arrange to have possibly just a small buffet at the White House," Orrin went on calmly, "with perhaps the members of Foreign Relations and Foreign Affairs committees and a few of the top correspondents so he can get the publicity he wants—"

"I said I'm not changing my plans. Now, what else is on your mind?"

"I feel as Raoul does," the Secretary said earnestly, "that perhaps under the circumstances it would be best to find a good excuse and do it. The world doesn't deal in realities any more, you know; it deals in public fictions."

"I know. And I am determined that the public fiction about the United States will be that it does not yield to every little passing wind of hysteria that blows. Haven't I made that clear already, at Geneva and elsewhere?"

"You have done beautifully," the Secretary of State said soberly, "and, like you, I think the public fiction will coincide most closely with reality if that is the picture of us you can educate the world to accept. But there is a genuine feeling up here that we must take into account. And in that context—"

"I know what it is," the President said. "It's a feeling of blown-up ego that has the whole world out of balance. Sometimes I think the end result of the United Nations has been to give unimportant little states nobody would ever have heard of a chance to inflate themselves out of all proportion to their actual weight in things. It's ridiculous that we let the tail swing the cat the way we do."

"But you understand why it is," Orrin Knox suggested. The President sighed.

"Yes, I understand why it is. The more real power you have, the less you can afford to exercise it, and the less real power you have, the more you can throw it around. It's a sign of how topsy-turvy our world is."

"So you do think perhaps, then, that you can—" the Secretary began, and was conscious at once of a change of atmosphere at the other end of the line.

"No, indeed," the President said crisply. "This is one of those times I feel it won't do to give in."

"I'd rather do it gracefully now than find we had to later," Orrin observed.

"I can't conceive of any situation in which we'd 'have to later.' Anyway, Ted Jason and his little luncheon in Charleston ought to give him all the headlines he wants."

"LeGage Shelby won't be happy, either," the Secretary told him with an ironic amusement.

"LeGage Shelby is the least of my worries. Are you coming back down tonight?"

"Yes, I think so. I don't feel I can be away from the department more than a couple of days without a lot of things getting out from under me. Not that they don't when I'm there, of course; but I feel better about it when I'm on the spot. At least I can prevent some of it."

"Now, surely," the President said with a mocking irony that exactly mimicked some other voices of the past, "you don't think that some obscure little clerk in some obscure little bureau lost China, do you?"

"Obscure little clerks in obscure little bureaus can do a hell of a lot of damage in a government like this, and it's either naïve or disingenuous to say they can't. However, it's more a matter of good administration that I'm concerned with. So, I'll be back in town late tonight if you want to reach me before you go to Michigan."

"I'm going to Michigan at six. Do you and Beth like trout?"

"Love 'em."

"I'll bring you a dozen. And, of course, you can always reach me through the White House switchboard if you need me."

"Sure thing," Orrin Knox said. "Have a good rest. You deserve it."

"Thanks," said the President. "I will."

And that, the Secretary thought as he returned the direct phone to the White House to its receiver and swung back to the pile of papers that confronted him on his desk, was what could still happen with Harley. For the most part he had settled into the Presidency with a sure skill that had, in the case of Geneva, risen to an instinctive brilliance. But there was still a stubborn streak, certainly not decreased by the adulation that had followed his actions in the Swiss city, and a certain willful blindness about things, on occasion.

Of course Orrin could see his position that the United States must not be "on a string to Terence Ajkaje," but, by the same token, the President's press conference remark and his decision not to entertain the M'Bulu was already an issue and rapidly becoming more so at the UN. The episode was exactly the sort of thing that the neutralist states, encouraged by the Communists, loved to fret about and worry away at until it had grown to a size out of all proportion to its real worth. And in this recurring and oft-repeated process, of course, the lure of a good story and a major controversy always brought the eager co-operation of the news corps. It was already top news in the New York *Post* and the New York *World-Telegram and Sun,* whose late-afternoon editions were on the desk before him. "PRESIDENT SNUBS AFRICANS," said the former. "HASSLE DEVELOPS ON WHITE HOUSE BID TO TERRY," said the latter.

As far as he was concerned, the Secretary thought with some annoyance, he would love to kick the bucket over the moon along with Harley and not worry about it any more. He smiled as he recalled the President's remark about his own newly found diplomacy: he certainly had become a diplomat since leaving the Senate. But in the democratic system each job had its own imperatives, as each had its own prerogatives and privileges, and you inevitably found yourself adapting to the style of new responsibilities when you took them on. It was all very well to rise and denounce something in the Senate—and he thought for a wistful moment of what fun it would be to do it, just once more—but in the delicate area of international relationships it was not so easy or advisable to do so. Of course the Communists could, that was their stock in trade—but the United States could not. It would, ironically enough, shock all those powers that watched the Soviet performances with a secret envy and approval. They would never accept it from America. It would be much too uncomfortable to have two great powers acting like great powers. As long as the United States confined itself to acid rejoinders and refused to take the offensive, everybody could pretend it wasn't so.

He swung again to the window and stared thoughtfully across at the UN buildings against the backdrop of the darkening river and Brooklyn, now becoming dotted with early-evening lights as the day swiftly faded. On a sudden impulse he picked up a phone, had his secretary verify an appointment, clapped on his hat and coat, and hurried over.

"You know, Seab," the Majority Leader murmured as they sat side by side in the Senate and listened with half an ear to the foreign aid debate droning on, "you ought to take yourself a cruise when this is over. Get away from it all. Relax. Rejuvenate. Regain your youth."

His seatmate gave a chuckle and peered at him through half-closed eyes.

"Now, Bob, you know exactly where I'm going to be doing my cruising this fall. You know exactly where, Bob. In the great state of South Carolina, Bob. That's where."

"Things getting a little rough for you, are they?" Bob Munson asked. "I didn't know that could ever happen to you, Seab."

The senior Senator from South Carolina chuckled.

"Oh, yes, sir. Oh—yes—sir. Even to poor old beleaguered Seabright B. Cooley, servant of the people these fifty years, Bob. The little mice are nibblin', Bob. They're nibblin' at me. *But,*" he said with a sudden emphasis, "I still know a thing or two, Bob. I'm not through yet. Or even near it."

"What are you going to do?" the Majority Leader asked with the impersonal curiosity of one political technician to another. "Get involved in the race issue?"

"I'd rather not," Seab Cooley said soberly, "if I can avoid it, Bob. It's bad enough at best, and I don't want to be stirring it around. Unless they push us too hard, Bob. If they push us too hard, Bob, then you'll hear from me. Yes, sir, you'll surely—hear—from—me."

"Mmm-hmm. I expect we will. Well, we'll try to get you out of here to-morrow night, Seab. The Speaker and I wouldn't want Harper Graham and those other boys to have a free hand against you one minute longer than we can help it."

"Where is he?" Senator Cooley said, hunching himself around and peering dourly over the Senate. "Where is that devious fellow, Bob?"

"I don't see your distinguished colleague," the Majority Leader said. "Probably on the phone to South Carolina right this minute lining up votes against you, Seab."

"It won't do him any good, Bob," Senator Cooley said calmly. "It won't do him any good at all."

"Well, I hope not," Senator Munson said truthfully, "but you never know. Mr. President!" he said, jumping to his feet as Paul Hendershot of Indiana concluded a lengthy attack on the bill. Powell Hanson of North Dakota, in the chair, gave him recognition. "Mr. President, I should like to advise Senators that it is the leadership's intention to hold the Senate in session late tonight, possibly until ten o'clock or midnight, in the hope that we can conclude action on the pending measure."

"Mr. President," said Raymond Robert Smith of California, "I think we should have a quorum call so that a majority of the Senate can hear that important announcement by the Majority Leader. I so move a quorum call, Mr. President."

"Now, what is that all about?" Senator Munson muttered in some annoyance to Senator Cooley as he resumed his chair and looked about the Senate at the handful of Senators present. "We don't need a quorum until at least eight o'clock. We won't begin voting on anything until then."

"Maybe he has a delegation in town from California and wants the Senate to look busy for them," the Senator from South Carolina suggested dryly. "Or maybe he wants to read us something for the Congressional Record. The old Record gets mighty important when you come to run for re-election, Bob. Maybe you noticed I've been using it a little myself recently."

"I had, Seab," the Majority Leader said, "but I just thought you had come across something of unusual merit that should be recorded for posterity—and sent out under your frank to the voters, of course. Well, if Ray Smith has something, it probably concerns movies, agriculture, or irrigation. I expect we'll have to listen."

What the junior Senator from California had, however, concerned neither movies, nor agriculture, nor irrigation, and in very short order it became apparent to his colleagues that it might behoove them to listen. He arose with a serious expression as Powell Hanson announced that, fifty-four Senators having answered to their names, a quorum was present. Arly Richardson of Arkansas leaned over to Elizabeth Ames Adams of Kansas. "Oh-oh," he said. "Ray's The-Gravity-of-This-Cannot-Be-Minimized attitude. I wonder what up." "Undue Japanese competition for Southern California industries," Bessie Adams whispered wickedly back. "They've found a new process for mass-producing crackpots."

"Mr. President," the Senator from California said earnestly, "I wish to call the Senate's attention to a surprising and, I think, most disturbing development today in our relations with the great continent of Africa. I am informed, Mr. President, that the President of the United States has withdrawn plans to entertain one of the most distinguished representatives of the African continent, and, indeed, is leaving for Michigan to go fishing for five days and won't even see him while he is in Washington. I refer, of course, to His Royal Highness the M'Bulu of Mbuele, certainly one of the most outstanding and noteworthy members of the great Negro race—"

"I knew he was afraid of Cullee Hamilton running against him," Cecil Hathaway of Delaware whispered to Murfee Andrews of Kentucky, "but I didn't know he was *that* afraid."

"—and one who deserves, if anyone does, the recognition that should by rights be conferred upon him by the President."

"Mr. President," Bob Munson said, "will the Senator yield? Is it not the fact that His Highness' country is still under British rule and he is not yet the head of an independent state? Might this not explain the President's action?"

"I do not know what explains it, Mr. President," said Ray Smith severely, "unless it is shortsightedness of the most flagrant kind. Certainly a representative of the great Negro race—"

"He's practically terrified," Murfee Andrews whispered to Cecil Hathaway.

"—deserves better treatment than this from the President of the United States. How are we to hold up our heads at the United Nations, Mr. President? How are we to convince the African states that we are truly their friend? How are we to convince the world that we mean it when we talk of equal rights, equal justice, and life, liberty, and the pursuit of happiness for all men?"

"Mr. President," said the senior Senator from South Carolina with an ominous gentleness, "will the distinguished Senator from California yield?"

"Mr. President," Senator Smith said hastily, "I do not wish to get into an argument with the disting—"

"Oh, Mr. President," Senator Cooley said. "Now, I do not entertain at all the idea of getting into an argument with the distinguished Senator from California in this matter. But is it not true that in Gorotoland where this Emboohoo of Embewley—"

"M'Bulu of Mbuele," Ray Smith corrected nervously.

"Emboohoo of Embewley," Seab Cooley repeated firmly, "lives, there is reason to believe that slavery still exists? Is it not rumored that human sacrifices and even cannibalism can still be found there? Are there not even signs of Russian and Chinese Communist infiltration?"

"Oh, well, Mr. President," Senator Smith said with a relieved scornfulness, "don't tell me the Senator from South Carolina is going to trot out old charges of Communist infiltration! Now, that is ridiculous, Mr. President."

"Is it?" Seab Cooley asked mildly. "Well, sir, I wouldn't know about that. The Senator from California is much more of an expert on Communism than I am, that's true, Mr. President. He knows *much* more about it than I do."

"What does the Senator mean by that?" Ray Smith demanded with a nervous anger. "I resent that, Mr. President!"

"Now, Mr. President," Senator Cooley said with a sad patience, "I don't know what the Senator from California is talking about. I do think there is reason to believe that this African fellow that the President won't entertain— and, in my opinion, wisely won't entertain—is not all the Senator from California says he is. Representative of the great Negro race! Mr. President, I know representatives of the great Negro race. I know them in my own state, Mr. President, and, yes, I know them in the state of the Senator from California. The distinguished Representative from that state, Mr. Cullee Hamilton, Mr. President. There is a great representative of the great Negro race." He fixed the junior Senator from California with a steady glance and his voice dropped to a siren's whisper. "*Does he deny it*, Mr. President? Does he deny that Representative Hamilton is a great representative of the great Negro race?"

"Why, no," Senator Smith said nervously. "Why, no. Why, of course not. I don't deny that Representative Hamilton is a great representative of his race."

"Worthy even to be a United States Senator, Mr. President," Seab Cooley said softly.

"Why, er—er—why, yes, I suppose so," said Ray Smith helplessly.

"This is murder," Sam Eastwood of Colorado murmured to Alexander Chabot of Louisiana. "Somebody ought to stop it." Alec Chabot smiled and shrugged in his dapper way.

"Now, Mr. President!" Seab Cooley said, raising his voice suddenly, bringing his fist high over his head and crashing it down on his desk in his characteristic gesture, "I think the Senator from California should apologize to his fellow Californian, that great Negro Congressman who is even worthy to be a United States Senator, for mentioning him in the same breath with this—this—adventurer from Africa whom our President has wisely refused to entertain. He should apologize to him, Mr. President! He—should—apologize—to—him!"

"This 'adventurer,' as you call him," Ray Smith said, his tone rising slightly in pitch, "is going to be entertained in your own state tomorrow, Senator! Of course you know that!"

"Oh, yes," Seab Cooley said, "I know that. A pack of adventurers will entertain him, Mr. President. An ambitious family with its eye on the White

House. The ragtag and bobtail of the American press, Mr. President. Oh, yes, they will all be there in my state of South Carolina making a Roman holiday for this adventurer. They will all be there!"

"And among them, Mr. President," Senator Smith said in the same high-pitched, icy way, "the governor of my own state of California, the Honorable Edward Jason. I think the Senator from South Carolina owes *him* an apology, Mr. President, for using such language about him. To say nothing of the distinguished audience that will honor His Highness the M'Bulu."

"They may do honor to *him*, Mr. President," Seab Cooley roared, "but they do dishonor to the white race! And they do dishonor to the great state of South Carolina! When you dishonor the white race, Mr. President, you dishonor South Carolina. When you dishonor South Carolina, you dishonor the white race! Dishonor, Mr. President! Dishonor! That is what this kinky-haired kinkajou brings to America!"

"Mr. President," the Majority Leader said calmly, "if the Senator will yield—if whichever Senator has the floor will yield; I've lost track—I think we have had enough of this discussion of the M'Bulu and might now get back to the foreign aid bill, if we could. I think the Senator from California has made the point to his constituents that he wished to make, and I think the Senator from South Carolina has made the point to his constituents that he wished to make. At any rate, Mr. President, I think we should at least try to get back to the pending business. Is that agreeable to the two Senators?"

"I still think the President is making a shocking mistake that will seriously damage the United States," Ray Smith said doggedly.

"I still think the Senator owes an apology to his great Negro colleague who is worthy to be Senator, to my state of South Carolina, and to the white race, Mr. President," Senator Cooley said. "But," he added sadly, "if he is going to remain obdurate in his contumacy, I can only watch him go with a sorrowing eye, a mourning heart, and a 'Farewell, brother!'"

"That was a great performance," Bob Munson whispered sarcastically as they resumed their seats. "That was worthy of Booth in his best days."

"I said I still know a thing or two, Bob," his seatmate said. He gave a satisfied chuckle. "I still do."

7

"Mr. Shelby of the United States, please," said the young lady at the telephone desk in heavy accents. "Mr. Shelby of the United States, please call the Delegates' Lounge . . . Señora Del Rio of Peru, please call the Delegates' Lounge . . . Signor Vitelli of Italy, please . . ."

"Don't go away, Felix," LeGage Shelby said. "I'll be back in a minute, I want to talk to you about this."

The Panamanian Ambassador nodded.

"Surely," he said. "I shall call Patsy while you're gone if I can find a phone."

"Tell her I'll certainly be in Charleston for the luncheon," 'Gage Shelby said.

"I think she knows," said Felix Labaiya, and watched his companion swing away to the telephone desk in his pantherlike, self-important way. A peculiar expression gleamed for a moment in the eyes of the Ambassador of Panama: the expression reserved by the users for the used. Then he spied an Indian concluding a conversation on one of the instruments at one of the small tables along the wall and, with a quick step, moved toward it just in time to take it from under the nose of a Norwegian with the same idea. The Norwegian gave a sour smile, shrugged, and walked away. Felix dropped into the leather armchair alongside the table, dialed 9 for outside, and then dialed his home. From Dumbarton Avenue in Georgetown his wife answered immediately. The housekeeper, he deduced, was busy with dinner and Patsy was upstairs in the bedroom taking her usual rest before the meal. His voice took on the direct, impersonal note it usually held when he addressed his wife on the telephone. He had once explained to her that he did not believe in using the instrument for romance. Someone might be listening.

"This is Felix," he said. "I am in the Delegates' Lounge, as you can hear"—he put a hand over his right ear to shut out the booming loudspeaker, now calling for Mr. Hirosaki of Japan, please—"and everyone up here is quite excited about the President's comments on Terry. It is ideally timed for us."

"Everyone here is terribly excited, too," she said in a pleased tone of voice. "In fact, everyone is FURIOUS. Wouldn't you know that old fool would put his foot in his mouth? Leave it to him! But, more fun for us. They've already had a big row about it in the Senate."

"Oh? Were you there?"

"I was earlier, but then I had to go and have lunch with Beth Knox and Dolly Munson and Kitty Maudulayne and Celestine Barre—"

"An interesting group," her husband observed with a smile that sent some warmth over the wire. Patsy chuckled.

"Yes, wasn't that a combination? But VERY interesting. Beth isn't worried at all," she added less cheerily.

"She will be," the Panamanian Ambassador promised, again with a smile. His wife laughed.

"Yes. Well, I started the row, anyway, because the minute the news came over the wire—" Felix winced as he always did at the thought of the wire-service teletypes tapping away in the Dumbarton Avenue study; but it was Patsy's money, and who was he to quibble? Just Patsy's husband. "I got right on the phone and called Ray Smith, and do you know—he went right on the floor and made the most magnificent speech about it . . . At least," she said more thoughtfully, "I THINK it was magnificent. The reports aren't too clear yet, because Seab Cooley got into it somehow and you know how he can confuse the issue when he wants to. I don't see why that old mountebank DOESN'T DROP DEAD. I really don't. Anyway, it's now a big issue down here, too. Which is all to the good for the luncheon. Now we'll really get attention."

"I never doubted it," Felix said with an irony he knew she didn't miss. "When the Jasons go to work on something, I've found they rarely fail. Why don't you buy us the Canal and give it to us for a birthday present?"

"Wait until Ted's elected," she said cheerfully. "We may be able to work something out. What's happening up there?"

"Much discussion, much excitement, much annoyance. The Africans are very exercised, the Asians are upset. The Europeans are baffled and the Communists are happy. All in all, one grand mess."

"Will it help your resolution?"

"Certainly. I don't see any possibility of its failing now. Even if it gets blocked in the Assembly, I think it may be possible to get it to the Security Council as a threat to world peace. Particularly with this assist from the President."

"Felix," his wife said, "I may be dense, but exactly how does the problem of Gorotoland affect peace? I mean, I can see that as a moral matter, possibly, as a nice thing to do, an idealistic gesture, it makes sense. But I don't quite see how it rates as a threat to peace if Terry doesn't get his independence until the date the British have promised him. After all, a year isn't so long to wait. Just how does it come under UN procedure in the form you've presented it?"

"UN procedure," Felix Labaiya said dryly, "never was very exact, and it's becoming less so every day. It's already been attacked on just the grounds you say. The British tried to keep it out of First Committee, where it really doesn't belong, with just that argument. But we've all learned things from the Russians. You can get the UN to do whatever you want it to if you just present it with something loudly enough and insist that it act. Maybe ten years ago sentiment for precedent could have been mustered to block the whole thing at the outset. Now you can get the Afro-Asians to go along with anything, provided certain of the big powers are against it. Once upon a time Britain could have got enough votes to have the whole thing thrown out. She doesn't dare try it today. Not even with U.S. help."

"Yes, but what I mean is, *why?* Why is it so vital that Gorotoland be freed at once? Why is it such an issue? Why is everybody suddenly so wild on the subject?"

"Specifically, why am I? Well, to me it's simply a matter of common justice. Nearly all of Africa is free, just as the M'Bulu says, and it's about time the rest of it was, too. And with Soviet help I felt it could be done most directly in the form in which I've presented it."

"Why did the Soviets choose you?" Patsy Labaiya asked. The Ambassador made a small, disgusted "Tchk!" sound and his tone sharpened noticeably.

"No one chose *me*. No one chose anybody. It was my idea all along. I happened to mention the matter to Tashikov one day at lunch and he said they would be glad to help if they could. I've told you all that."

"Yes, I know. But it still puzzles me."

"Puzzling or not, it seems to be working perfectly all right. And of course the whole thing builds up beautifully for the luncheon and Ted. Would he like to come back up here with me and watch the final voting, or does he have to go right back to California?"

"I expect he'll have to go back," Patsy said, "but you can talk it over in Charleston. He does want to come back through here and see the President; I know that."

"Oh? That's intriguing."

"Yes, very. It's a courtesy call, of course, but—"

"One of those where you put your pistols on the table when you sit down," her husband suggested with a smile. She laughed.

"Probably. Well, I'm delighted everything's going so well. Things are all set for the luncheon, too. It's going to be wonderful."

"LeGage Shelby wanted me to be sure and tell you he would be there."

"I'm so surprised," Patsy said ironically. "If there was anyone I thought would stay away, it was 'Gage Shelby. He hates headlines so . . . The one who says he *is* going to stay away, of course, is Cullee Hamilton, and he's the one we really should have."

"Can't your brother do anything with him? If he wants to run for Senator, I should think he'd need Ted's support. Surely that provides some leverage."

"California's a funny state," Patsy said. "Just when you think you've got political leverage on someone, you find the leverage isn't there and you fall flat on your face. The voters are too independent to co-operate. So is Cullee. Ted can offer his support, and it may be of some assistance, but his opposition wouldn't hurt much. Everybody runs on his own out there. I certainly wish he would come, though. He's so respectable. You know what 'Gage is."

"Yes," said Felix Labaiya. "And here he comes now, so I'd better conclude."

"I wish you were here," his wife said in a voice that suddenly changed completely. "Right *here*."

"Yes," he said, thinking dryly, Well, that's dutiful; I must be dutiful too. He put a little fervor in his voice. "We must discuss all that in Charleston."

"Is that a promise?"

"A promise."

"I'll hold you to it," she said. "Tell 'Gage I'm absolutely thrilled to death that he will be with us."

"He will be thrilled that you are thrilled," Felix said. "Good-by, now."

"How is she?" LeGage asked, dropping into the armchair on the other side of the table. "Well, I hope."

"So excited about the luncheon she cannot see straight," Felix said, and they both laughed pleasantly over the fiction, which neither believed, that Patsy was ever so excited about anything that she couldn't see straight.

"Ah, yes," 'Gage said dreamily. "That will be quite an affair, particularly with Justice Davis about to hand down a decision on that appeal for injunction on the school integration case. *Quite* an affair. Is Cullee coming?"

Felix frowned.

"Apparently he is not." 'Gage frowned too.

"What's the matter with that boy?" he asked in an exasperated voice.

"Doesn't he know this is a chance to stand together and really strike a blow for something constructive? I ought to talk to that boy."

"I thought you had," the Panamanian Ambassador said in some surprise. "And if you haven't, why haven't you? And if you haven't, why don't you?"

LeGage gave an embarrassed little laugh.

"Well, you don't exactly understand the relationship between old Cullee and me. We were roommates at Howard, you know; we understand each other pretty well; and—well, he doesn't take much from me without getting mad. I can't push him; he gets stubborn. He's already mad at me about something else down there, a bill that DEFY wanted to have passed, and—I just don't know whether it would do any good for me to talk to him about the luncheon or not. That's why I haven't, because I haven't been sure. I thought it might just make it worse."

Felix Labaiya gave him a skeptical and appraising smile.

"Don't tell me there's someone who has the great LeGage Shelby intimidated. I do not believe it. What does this Cullee have that I don't know about? I shall have to cultivate him when I am in Washington."

"He's worth it," LeGage said. "He's really quite a boy."

"You sound as though you genuinely admire him. This, too, is rare."

'Gage Shelby smiled, somewhat uncomfortably.

"Let's just say he can—do things I can't do." A rarely honest expression crossed his face for a moment, and his companion realized that only a very genuine emotion could produce such a result in one who normally lived behind several brassy and self-protective layers. "He's got guts about some things I haven't," LeGage said simply. "Let's put it that way."

"And by the same token," the Ambassador said firmly, "you can do things he can't do. And you have the guts to do them, too. Such as lead DEFY to new victories and deal so splendidly with our friends of the Afro-Asian bloc here."

"That was one of the Nigerians on the phone just now," 'Gage said with a pleased smile, distracted to more comfortable matters. "They're having a conference in half an hour about your resolution and they want me to be there."

"Have you cleared it with the Secretary?" Felix asked with a certain mocking note that did not escape his companion. LeGage smiled.

"Nope. But he needn't worry. I'm just supposed to explain the fine points to them if they ask me."

"They regard you still as an outsider," the Panamanian Ambassador said. LeGage gave him a scornful look.

"Shucks, man. They don't *really* take me in. I'm not a Negro. I'm an *American*. We Americans, we got it made, you see. They're jealous of *us* . . . Got it made!" he said with a sudden deep bitterness. "Oh, brother. Have we got it made."

"Well," said Felix Labaiya-Sofra with a quiet conviction. "You will have. One of these days."

"Yes!" his companion said with a sudden naked fierceness in his voice, though his face retained its usual sardonic mask. "Yes, man. You just bet we will."

"Have you seen Terry?" Felix asked with a deliberate change of tone. LeGage laughed.

"Terry's in the recording studios being interviewed by the networks. In another hour he'll be the most from coast to coast. That boy never had it so good. He's really riding high."

"Well," Felix said, "I can't be at your Afro-Asian conference, because they would never ask me, but you take them a message from me. You tell them," he said, his eyes narrowing as he looked down the lounge to the bar, where delegates and press now clustered, drinking and gossiping beneath the wooden map of the world, "that I, of course, deeply deplore the unfortunate and insulting attitude of the President of the United States toward His Highness and, indeed, toward all African states generally. You tell them that I intend to push my resolution with unrelenting vigor until it is adopted by the United Nations. You tell them I shall never flag or fail in the cause of freedom and opposition to colonialist domination of which, as a Panamanian, I know something."

"Say, now!" 'Gage Shelby said with a laugh. "That's quite a speech, Felix, boy."

"You tell them," the Panamanian Ambassador repeated in a completely humorless tone.

"I'll tell them . . . Can I fly down to Charleston with you tomorrow?"

"Gladly. And, look. Why don't you call Cullee? We really do need him, and I'm sure this is something sufficiently important to overcome your strange and uncharacteristic reluctance."

"We-ell," LeGage said, looking doubtful. "I'll think about it."

"He really does have you scared, doesn't he?" the Panamanian Ambassador said. LeGage grinned.

"Not exactly scared. You just don't understand about Cullee and me. That boy's got *character*."

"And you haven't?"

"Sometimes when I'm around him," LeGage admitted, not altogether humorously, "I'm not so sure."

They stood for a moment silent in the glass-walled living room on the thirty-eighth floor, looking out over First Avenue to the fantastic spectacle of New York flung upward to the sky, a last shred of sunset dying behind the city's silhouette, the lights coming on in a hundred skyscrapers, an impression of overwhelming life, cruel, challenging, ruthless, beautiful. The Secretary-General shook his head.

"Fabulous city. Fabulous. Words can never do it justice. It has to be lived to be believed. You are lucky to have it in your country."

The Secretary of State smiled.

"Sometimes yes, sometimes no. But you're right; there is nothing like it.

In some ways it is hardly America, but there's no denying it's the twentieth century."

"Would you like a drink?" the Secretary-General asked. "I have some sherry, or something stronger."

"Sherry will be fine," the Secretary said. "I've got to cut down on this UN high life. I don't see how you regulars stand it."

"It took me a while to arrive at a happy compromise," the S.-G. admitted with a smile. "The British left us a drinking tradition in Lagos, but it's nothing like this."

"Of course I suppose it has its purpose, as much as in Washington. A good deal of your business gets done at receptions, cocktail parties, and dinners, I've observed."

"Even more than yours," the Secretary-General said, "because of course in Washington you deal in the substance of power. You can really make things happen. Here we deal only in power's shadow. We can only talk. We can't make much of anything happen."

"Sometimes the talk can be very important," the Secretary said, staring into the amber depths of his glass. "World public opinion can be a powerful thing."

"It can be as powerful as you let it be," the Secretary-General said quietly. "That is something you in the United States sometimes forget. The decision on how powerful always rests with you, because if you desire you can always ignore it. Possibly you would prefer not to remember this, for it is perhaps easier not to accept the obligations remembering would impose upon you."

"Surely you are not suggesting that we ignore world opinion! You don't want *us* to have Hungaries, now, do you? Surely not as an African you don't. Even less as Secretary-General."

The Secretary-General stared across at the vast glowing peaks and canyons of Manhattan, the enormous buildings afire now with a million lights, and his eyes looked as far away as Lagos.

"No, of course not. But sometimes I wonder—I wonder if perhaps your reluctance to be tough doesn't play directly into the hands of the Soviets who would destroy you—destroy me—destroy the UN." He smiled ruefully. "Why did you seek me out?"

"Partly to get acquainted. Partly to assess whatever damage the President may have done in his press conference."

"Ah, yes, the President. A great man, in his unpretentious way. But I know little about the reaction. My African colleagues for the most part no longer talk to me. I am relatively isolated in this position, which is exactly the way the Soviets want it."

"But surely some of your friends talk to you still," the Secretary objected. "Or, if not, your own appraisal is sufficient and well informed, I'm sure."

The Secretary-General shrugged.

"Obviously the President's remark was ill-advised and thoughtless, even though anyone with an ounce of sense and an iota of goodwill can perceive exactly what he meant. You understand, of course, that there are plenty of people in this house who possess a great deal of sense and not one speak of goodwill. His refusal to see the M'Bulu, while also understandable, was perhaps even more unfortunate. There I think possibly he was ill-advised."

"He wasn't advised at all," the Secretary said bluntly. "I failed him, because I didn't know that he had advanced the hour of his press conference. It was an understandable human error."

"The world turns these days on understandable human errors to which understanding is refused," the Secretary-General said. "It is the business of many here not to understand. No amount of explanation could erase now either the general impression left by the remarks or the decision not to see Terry. I am afraid the United States cannot ignore entirely the situation thus created."

"But it's such a stupid tempest in a teapot!" the Secretary exploded. "Such utter silly nonsense. Particularly when you take into account that—that little —adventurer."

The Secretary-General smiled, a sudden gleam of white teeth against black skin, and his eyes filled with a quizzical amusement.

"He is that. He is all of that. He is not a nice young man, the heir to Gorotoland. But marvelously popular in your country. Let us see—it is just past six." And, crossing to an outsize television set, he turned it on and switched rapidly over the channels. On two of them Terrible Terry was already appearing, talking with slow earnestness on one, grinning and waving happily on the other. The Secretary-General snapped off the machine with a sardonic expression and returned to his chair. "It is a wonderful medium for the dissemination of information. I am sure Orrin Knox, or anyone else giving a true picture of the M'Bulu, would receive equal attention."

The Secretary smiled.

"You just don't understand our free society . . . You think, then, that we should now undertake the hopeless task of appeasing the unappeasable. That was the idea with which I came here, but I wanted confirmation."

"Some gestures should be made, I think. They will not appease Terry, and he may not accept them, but at least you will have made them. It is important to give the Afro-Asian states the idea that you are humbling yourselves. They love that."

"I take it you tell me that as an African," the Secretary said dryly. The Secretary-General smiled.

"Sometimes I can understand the point of view. However, I tell you basically as Secretary-General, who wishes to do what he can to remove unnecessary frictions from the path of co-operation here. God knows there are enough necessary ones."

"Yes. Well: the President is on his way to Michigan right now, so that part of it can't be helped. But maybe we can fix up something else for his royal importance."

"The Jasons are apparently going to do what they can to help in Charleston," the Secretary-General observed. The Secretary of State snorted.

"That's a great crew. I mean, something in Washington."

"Good luck," the Secretary-General said. "Will I be seeing you at the Turkish reception this evening?"

"No, I think I'm going back to Washington around eight. I'll probably be back next week for the Assembly debate. I'll see you then."

"Call on me any time. I like to think I can be of some use to someone."

"Oh, come now," the Secretary said. "It isn't that bad."

"Almost," the Secretary-General said. "Almost, my friend."

And that was symptomatic of the UN at this stage of its existence, the Secretary thought as he walked down the long corridor to the elevator, descended thirty-eight floors, and emerged from the Delegates' Entrance to cross the furious homebound rush on First Avenue just before it funneled into F.D.R. Drive up the East River. A pervasive questioning filled the gleaming glass structure of the nations, "this house," as so many of them called it. If only the performance equaled the potential—if only: that bitter, annoying, frustrating phrase. If only—the world's troubles would be over.

Well, he thought as he entered U.S. delegation headquarters and returned to his office, not in his lifetime, probably, and probably not in the lifetime of anyone now living. Attack, struggle, and fall back; attack, struggle, and fall back. Maybe a little less back each time; that was the most one could hope for. He marveled at his own patience and thought again of the President's comment on his changing attitude of late. He smiled. This was not like impatient Orrin Knox. Impatient Orrin Knox was learning, in the crucible of world events. Impatient Orrin Knox might really be a statesman, someday, if he kept at it long enough.

He paused for a moment to stare out his office window, his eyes traveling up the lighted Secretariat Building to the top floor, where he had just been. The private apartment was still illuminated and a tiny figure was still standing in the window staring out at fabulous Manhattan. Moved by some sentimental impulse, the Secretary raised his arm and waved, but there was no response, and indeed it was ridiculous to suppose that out of all that fantastic jumble of buildings the S.-G. should be looking at Orrin's window. But he felt better for the gesture as he turned back to his desk, put through a call to Washington, and prepared to take the next step in his plans for easing the situation.

It was a lonely office the S.-G. had, he thought with a shiver. All the offices that bore men's hopes were lonely—his own, he realized too, not least among them.

I shall see that gorgeous figure stalking down endless corridors in my dreams, Hal Fry thought as he emerged from the restricted delegates' area into the Main Concourse of the UN, and there it was again. His first instinct was to let it go, but this was superseded instantly by duty, and he hurried forward, calling "Terry!" As the M'Bulu swung about with a pleased smile, the Senator became conscious of hurrying feet behind him, and he and the Indian Ambassador arrived together at their objective in the center of the echoing expanse of lobby, emptied now of its usual thronging tourists and occupied only by a small trickle of secretaries, clerks, and delegates going home.

"My two good friends!" the M'Bulu exclaimed. "Always together, a really genuine international friendship."

"It wasn't my intention," Hal Fry said amicably, "but I heard the patter of little feet and there he was."

"Oh, if I am not welcome, Hal—" Krishna Khaleel began, but the Senator from West Virginia waved him silent.

"Nonsense, I haven't any secrets to hide. I just want to know what our young friend here is going to do to us as a result of the President's rather undiplomatic—frankness."

Terrible Terry smiled and made his hands-out, palms-up gesture with a graceful shrug.

"I am not doing anything to anyone. I am the one who is having things done to me. I am simply awaiting with interest to see—what next!"

"Mmm," Hal Fry said. "Well, we hope there won't be any 'what next,' at least of that kind. And, of course, he didn't mean any personal disrespect to you. You know that."

Again the M'Bulu shrugged and smiled.

"Who can say what is in the mind of another?"

The Senator from West Virginia snorted.

"Half the world, apparently, or so I hear around the corridors. The things they read into the President's mind are quite something."

"I regret he gave them the opportunity," Terry said, and this time he did not smile. Hal Fry looked at him for a second, debating several tactics, and then chose, characteristically, the most direct.

"Who gave who the opportunity? I don't recall that you were invited. As I remember it, you demanded to be asked. A self-invited guest need not necessarily expect the same cordial reception as one who is invited. Isn't that right?"

"Oh, now, Hal," the Indian Ambassador said, "I do not think we should get into a public argument right here in the lobby of the UN—"

"I'm not getting into an argument," Senator Fry said reasonably, "and, anyway, it's late. There's hardly anybody around. Let him answer if he will. Or am I," he said with a sudden amiable grin, "being entirely too Western and direct?"

The M'Bulu gave a merry laugh and shook his head.

"You are being very American—let us put it that way. And I, perhaps, was being too—civilized when I thought I could depend on the famed hospitality of your country. Apparently it is very selective. It does not extend to those whose skins are black."

"That's a lie, and you know it. From Kwame Nkrumah and Sekou Touré right on up, African leaders have been entertained at the White House."

"Then I do not see why I am unworthy," Terry said harshly. "Am I any different than they are? How, tell me. How?"

"You do not represent an independent state," Senator Fry said patiently. "That is how."

"It seems to us a very precious distinction," Krishna Khaleel said in a superior tone. "I must confess, Hal, it does seem splitting hairs."

"I suppose," the Senator said. "Or, at any rate, you're all going to act as though you thought so if you think you can make a little propaganda from it."

"Who is this 'all' who is going to do this?" the M'Bulu asked in bewilderment. "Who is conducting this sinister conspiracy against the great United States? Is she really so alone in the world? I am sorry for you, America!"

The Senator from West Virginia smiled.

"I know. I know. I am talking of shadows, and here at the UN everyone is calm and well-intentioned and kindly toward one another, nobody uses empty pretexts to attack anyone else, love and harmony fill the air, and we are all friends and companions in the great adventure of world peace. I salute you as you join our ranks, o noble son of Africa. May your days be long and your efforts fruitful. We shall look to you to lead us from the darkness into light."

"Hal, Hal," K.K. protested. "Now you are not being serious again. How is it possible to keep you to the serious point?"

"How fortunate," the M'Bulu said with a quick irony, "that I do keep to it. What would you advise me, then, Senator? What should one who is—in the words of your President—'a little character,' do now? Should I cancel my visit to South Carolina? Should I give up my plans to visit Washington? Should I steal away silently, as suggested in effect by the United States, with no doubt the close concurrence of the United Kingdom, and be seen and heard no more? Do you think that would make the Afro-Asian states feel more kindly toward your country?"

"That is right, Hal," Krishna Khaleel said solemnly. "You must think of the Asian-African states."

"I think if I were you," Hal Fry said as the M'Bulu disposed himself on one of the long, low benches where the tourists gather and looked out across the dark, swift-racing river to the giant neon Pepsi-Cola sign over Brooklyn, "that I would go to South Carolina as planned and go to Washington as planned. I'm sure you haven't the slightest intention of abandoning either idea, and I suspect that in Washington it will be possible for you to see many people important to your cause. I haven't talked to the Secretary since noon, but I think probably you will find that he is arranging opportunities for you to see members of the Congress, perhaps, and others with whom you might wish to confer. Possibly," he said, hoping to goodness it was true, "he is arranging some suitable social event for you. I am quite sure that you will be made welcome in Washington."

Terrible Terry gave him a long, thoughtful look and then smiled.

"By everyone save the one man who counts most. No," he said, all amiability suddenly gone, "I do not think my colleagues from Africa are so mistaken in their reactions. I think their instincts tell them truly when, through me, they are being insulted. I think it will take some substantial amends in Washington to make up to them for this."

"I believe you will have them," Hal Fry said with a calculated indifference. "K.K., are you going back to the Waldorf?"

"No, thank you, Hal," the Indian Ambassador said importantly. "Not yet. I wish to discuss some matters with His Highness, if you will excuse us now."

The Senator from West Virginia shrugged.

"Surely. Will I see you at the Turkish reception?"

"I shall be there!" Terrible Terry said with a sudden happy eagerness. "I would not miss anything of this wonderful UN."

"Keep smiling, K.K.," Hal Fry said. And, recalling another conversation at the height of the Leffingwell controversy some months ago, he added dryly, "It won't matter in a hundred years."

But the Indian Ambassador preferred not to be amused. Instead, he looked offended.

"Possibly not, Hal. But it matters now. Most assuredly."

And so, because of this damnable twentieth-century habit of inflaming everything out of all proportion, it did. The Senator from West Virginia was very conscious of the two of them talking behind him as he put on his coat and hat and walked along the great empty lobby toward the Public Entrance. This was typical of his days since becoming acting head of the delegation: a series of little talks and arguments, an endless attempt to do justice to the United States position and still be fair to others, the grinding burden of truth denied and falsehood enthroned that weighted down the UN. There were moments when this left him deeply depressed. If men knew the truth and yet persisted in denying it with a straight face, how were the nations ever to arrive at a stable world?

And yet one had to keep trying. The favorite cliché here in Turtle Bay was to say quickly, "Why, of course the UN will continue. It's got to. There isn't anything else." Along with the cliché went the most candid cataloguing of all the handicaps that made its success most problematical. Oh, yes, they would say cheerfully, this is wrong and that is wrong, and this won't work and that won't work, the Russians hate the Americans and the Americans distrust the Russians, and the Jews won't accept *that* and you know very well the Arabs won't accept *that*, and the Africans are angry about *that* and the Asians about *that* and the Latin Americans think so-and-so and the Europeans think thus-and-such, and you know nothing can possibly be achieved *there* and nothing can be done *there*—but, It's Got To. There Isn't Anything Else.

He sighed, feeling suddenly extraordinarily tired and sapped of energy with an abruptness that startled him for a moment; perhaps he hadn't rested long enough, though at Orrin's insistence he had gone back to delegation headquarters and slept for half an hour or so. It was true that in the last couple of weeks something had seemed to be a little wrong with his health: nothing he could quite put his finger on, a fleeting moment of complete tiredness, such as he was experiencing now, gone almost as soon as it came; the little odd reddish flickering of vision, a sudden flash of white, that he had noticed a couple of times in the past few days; an odd little rash on one arm. Maybe he was working too hard, but if so he wasn't about to admit it to anyone yet. The General Assembly was really just getting under way, and there was a great deal to be done to serve the American cause: his country, to use another cliché which was also valid, needed him. He had never shirked a public duty yet, and now in mid-fifties he wasn't about to shirk this one, if he could get by with a little more rest and care for the abrupt, puzzling, but really quite slight deterioration in his physical condition. And besides, he told himself wryly, he was one of the cliché-repeaters too. He too had acquired a deep devotion to the strange, troubled, gloomy-hopeful organization. Like everyone else, he too believed that It's Got To. There Isn't Anything Else.

In the open space before the bronze doors given by Canada, he paused for a moment to glance at the incongruous but somehow fitting trio that guarded the gates: to his far right, off near the wall, the statue of naked Zeus, gift of Greece, with his old man's head and his young man's body with its half-erection; the model of the first Sputnik hanging insolently above the entryway; and high on the left the two-hundred-pound, gold-plated pendulum of the Netherlands on its seventy-five-foot stainless-steel wire, swinging slowly and inexorably back and forth as it crossed a metal ring below, endlessly demonstrating the rotation of the earth.

Zeus and Sputnik and the sure, impersonal turning of the globe: a fitting galaxy of Fates to preside over mankind's latest joint endeavor.

"It is a privilege to live this day and tomorrow," Queen Juliana had said in donating the pendulum; the words were inscribed on the steel pillar supporting the ring. Everyone who labored in the organization could certainly agree with that, Hal Fry reflected. Today and tomorrow—and stop there. Take them as they came—and stop there. No one cared, or dared, to look beyond.

He sighed as he emerged onto the plaza and the cool nip of the autumn night air hit him in the face. He must hurry over to the delegation and tell Orrin to get busy on the task of rolling out a substitute red carpet for an angry and vindictive M'Bulu who had no intention of being mollified by anything less than abject amends on the part of the United States. There had not been much attempt to conceal the injured spitefulness beneath the spurious outward amicability. He walked toward the roar of First Avenue and the glittering mass of Manhattan, hoping that the Secretary of State would already be at work doing those things that would have to be done to appease an injured ego which, unappeased, could cause much damage.

And so, of course, Orrin was, being at that moment on the phone to Senator Munson in Washington, getting the Majority Leader's acquiescence to a temporary delay in Senate adjournment and securing from him Dolly's aid in giving a small private dinner party that might, hopefully, give the M'Bulu's hurt feelings the comforting they wanted in Washington.

8

There appeared shortly thereafter on the little screen the visage, alert and intelligently terrierlike, of one of the nation's top commentators. Smoothly and ably, as he did every night at this time except Saturdays and Sundays, he proceeded to put the whole thing in perspective for his faithful audience:

"It is already apparent tonight that the President of the United States has pulled something of an international boo-boo in his cavalier treatment of the young African leader known by the unusual title of the M'Bulu of Mbuele. Terence Wolowo Ajkaje, hereditary crown prince of British-held Gorotoland, perhaps expected a little too much when he confidently predicted here at the United Nations earlier today that he would receive the red-carpet welcome usually reserved for heads of states and major royalty in Washington. But he perhaps had the right to expect at least a modest version of it, and even this much the President seems determined to deny him. The President, in fact, has left the capital for a five-day fishing trip on the eve of the M'Bulu's visit. Behind him he has left a United Nations abuzz with what many delegates, particularly those from Africa and Asia, seem determined to regard as a deliberate insult to the whole African continent.

"The rights and wrongs of this dispute are already buried beneath automatic layers of prejudice, East and West, that make it virtually impossible to get at the basic justice of it. Let it suffice to say that what the United Nations sees most clearly is that a symbol of emergent Africa, a Western-educated leader who might be expected to bring his people into the democratic camp, has been publicly, and it would seem deliberately, snubbed by the President of the West's greatest democracy. This cannot help but have serious consequences here in several areas not directly connected with the immediate event.

"There is, for instance, the resolution introduced by the Ambassador of Panama, Felix Labaiya-Sofra, which would bring strong United Nations recommendation that independence be granted to Gorotoland immediately instead of at the end of the one-year period now promised by Britain. Señor Labaiya and the M'Bulu won the first stage of that battle in the United Nations First, or Political, Committee this afternoon by a vote of 51 to 23. Now the argument moves to the Assembly. The United States voted with Britain in First Committee today, but there were strong indications that this unity of Western viewpoint may not hold in the Assembly. The Soviet Union, of course, voted for the Panamanian resolution and thereby again gave dramatic proof to the African-Asian states that she favors their cause and desires a speedy and complete break with all vestiges of the colonial past. If the United States should vote against Britain in later stages of the debate on Ambassador Labaiya's resolution, it would indicate that this country, too, has decided to step up its attempts to compete more directly in the sweepstakes for Africa's friendship.

"Against this background, the President's snub to the M'Bulu seems doubly puzzling to observers here at the United Nations. For those observers interested in domestic politics, there is an added factor that intrigues them. One thing the M'Bulu will definitely do is attend a private luncheon in his honor to be held tomorrow in Charleston, South Carolina, under the auspices of the Jason Foundation. The Jason Foundation, of course, is one of the family foundations of Edward Jason, Governor of California, who may well seek the Presidential nomination of the President's party next year if the President follows through on his announced intention not to seek re-election. And another director of the Foundation, of course, is the Governor's sister Patsy, who is the wife of Ambassador Labaiya, author of the Gorotoland resolution. Thus are domestic and international politics dramatically linked in this argument at the United Nations, to which the President has now, by his snub to one of the most intelligent, most worthwhile, and most hopeful young figures out of Africa, added the fuel of personal controversy."

And now, Patsy Labaiya told herself with a pleased anticipation as she snapped off a further comment on Japan's latest atomic tests, I shall see if I can't add a little more to that personal controversy. The phone rang twice at a handsome home just off Sixteenth Street near the Woodner and a soft and slightly sulky voice answered, "This is the Hamiltons' residence."

"Is this Sue-Dan—Mrs. Hamilton?" Patsy asked, adding hurriedly, "This is Patsy Labaiya, Sue-Dan. I believe we met at the Pakistan Embassy last month, didn't we?"

"Yes, we did," the voice said, somewhat less sulky and more cordial. "How are you, Mrs. Labaiya?"

"Patsy. Why, I'm fine, thank you, just fine. And how are you and the Congressman these days?"

"Oh, we're fine, too."

"Well, that's good."

"Yes, ma'am."

"Oh, for heaven's sake, don't ma'am me," Patsy said in an annoyed tone. "I hate that. Particularly from someone in your—your position."

"Yes, ma'am," said Sue-Dan evenly. There was a silence and then, impersonally, "How is everything with you and the Ambassador?"

"Oh, we're fine, too, thank you," Patsy said, beginning to feel a little on edge about this and rather sorry she had called in the first place. After all, she didn't have to take this kind of insolence. Jasons usually didn't. But she filled her voice with a cordiality that fooled her listener not at all and pursued her objective.

"I was wondering, Sue-Dan, if you could help me persuade that distinguished husband of yours—distinguished *and* handsome, I might say—"

"Lots of ladies seem to think so," Sue-Dan observed politely. Patsy flushed and, in spite of her best intentions, found it impossible not to retaliate.

"I'm sure you're pleased," she said smoothly. "Well, as I was saying, I wonder if you could help me persuade him that he really should come down to Charleston tomorrow and be one of our head-table guests at the luncheon in honor of Terence Ajkaje—you know, from Gorotoland. The M'Bulu of Mbuele."

"I know Terry."

"Oh? Then why don't you come too? I think it would be very nice to have you there with him."

"I usually leave most of that official business to Cullee. Anyway, I doubt if he would like me to come along to see Terry. He doesn't approve of Terry."

"I'm sorry to hear that," Patsy said, and she genuinely was, for it complicated several plans. "I hope, though, that this wouldn't prevent him from doing honor to a fellow—er—a fellow—"

"Nigger?" Sue-Dan said blandly, and was pleased to hear a gasp at the other end. "I really wouldn't know. I expect Cullee just doesn't like him."

"But, surely," Patsy said, trying not to sound flustered, "in his capacity as a distinguished visitor to this country—"

"I wouldn't know about that, really. Cullee doesn't pay much attention to frills when he likes somebody or doesn't. And I do know he doesn't think too much of Terry. So I couldn't say."

"Well, will you tell him I called?"

"Oh, sure, I'll tell him."

"Will you tell him what I wanted, and that I may call again later, when he's home? I suppose you do expect him home from the Hill soon?"

"Yes, ma'am. He'll be here, and I'll tell him."

"And look, Sue-Dan," Patsy said rather desperately, "why don't you and I have lunch together some day soon? I feel I should know you better. I think we would have a lot to talk about."

"Where?"

"Why—er—why, I don't know. How about the City Tavern?"

"Would they take me?"

"I should think they would if I said so."

"Mmm-hmm. Well, no, thank you, ma'am. Unless you'd like to join me at something like some Hot Shoppe somewhere."

Damn her, anyway, Patsy thought furiously; she knows perfectly well we've got to have Cullee's support in California.

"Look, Sue-Dan," she said pleasantly, "I don't really think either one of us is going to gain anything by playing games with the other, now, are we? It's important to me to know you better. It is not entirely unimportant, I might point out, for you and your husband to know me better, considering his plans and my brother's plans for next year. I would like to take you to lunch. Next Tuesday. At twelve-thirty. I shall pick you up at your house. All right?"

"Why, yes," Sue-Dan said agreeably. "I expect that would be all right."

"Thank you, Sue-Dan."

"Thank you . . . Patsy."

And, with a wicked little laugh that came clearly over the wire, she hung up. Patsy turned away in genuine irritation. They were all alike, all alike. She told herself sternly, however, that she must get over that thought and calm herself down to call Cullee back later, because Cullee wasn't one of those who was "all alike." Cullee was quality and a very important man to the Jason family. But she pitied him his wife. How on earth did he stand it?

In this thought, she would have been interested to know, she was not alone; for now as he ran hastily through the accumulation of letters to be signed that his secretary had put before him, affixing his flowing signature carefully to each, the young Congressman from California was unhappily thinking much the same thing. His mind, temporarily diverted from the subject by his visit to the Senate and his uncomfortable chat with Ray Smith, had returned to it again as soon as he started back down the long corridor to the House.

Nothing he had found in that chamber had done much to divert him again. The House, operating as usual under the five-minute rule, was hearing a long parade of short speeches on a bill to tighten minor provisions of the Taft-Hartley Act. The bill was not going to pass—everybody knew it—and so both proponents and opponents were just going through the motions while they waited for the customarily laggard Senate to wind up its business so that both houses could adjourn for the year and go home. Cullee dutifully presented his five minutes of opposition and then for a while sat toward the back of the room; the House at work on a dull bill, he had found, was the best place in the world in which to concentrate free from distraction. Late in the afternoon the Speaker came by, took the seat beside him, and chatted for a few minutes about life in general and next year in particular.

"You going to run against Ray Smith?" he asked, and Cullee, who felt obligated in many ways to the powerful old man who had befriended him and encouraged his career from the first, answered with complete honesty, "I don't know at the moment, Mr. Speaker, but I'm leaning."

"Toward or away from?" the Speaker asked, and Cullee smiled.

"Depends on which wind happens to be blowing. Mostly toward, I guess."

"You've got powerful support in 'the other body,'" the Speaker said, using the term with which House members are accustomed to refer formally to the Senate. "Bet you'd be surprised to know who it is."

"Victor Ennis?" Cullee asked, thinking possibly California's senior Senator had abandoned his increasingly uneasy neutrality to take the plunge, but prepared to be surprised if it were for him.

"Guess again," the Speaker said with a chuckle. "No, sir, you've got powerful support from the South, my boy. A certain very distinguished southern Senator."

The memory of his polite exchange of nods with the President Pro Tempore of the Senate flashed across Cullee's mind. He began to laugh.

"Don't tell me Seab Cooley—" he said, and the Speaker chuckled again.

"Yes, sir, you should have heard him. They tell me he had poor old Ray Smith backed right against the wall and admitting in public that you were fully equipped to be United States Senator. Practically had him urging the people of California to vote for you, way I heard tell."

"That I should like to have heard. Poor Ray! He does have his troubles, and I guess I'm no help to them."

"Why should you be?" the Speaker asked in some surprise. "This isn't any charity ward. It's politics."

"I know, but—" the Congressman began. The Speaker stopped him with a fatherly squeeze of his knee.

"You run. You owe it to the country and to California. Don't like to get maudlin about these things, but you also owe it to your people. Think it over," he admonished as he rose to go back to the Chair for the vote on the Taft-Hartley amendments. "Think it over, hear?"

And while the few remaining five-minute speeches were delivered, and then through the lopsided roll call, Cullee found that he was thinking it over, for this was a diversion important enough to take him away from the thought of Sue-Dan—though, of course, it inevitably led back to her, for she was gaining support all the time, and he was losing, in their running argument about what he should do. About all he needed now was for LeGage to call and put the pressure on him, and he would really be in a mood to blow up and tell them all to go to hell. He was not at all amused ten minutes later when this turned out to be mental telepathy and a page boy came up to tell him he was wanted on the phone in the cloakroom. "A Mr. Shelby," the boy said, and was quite startled by the Congressman's expression and the tone in which he said, "Oh, for—all *right*, I'll take it!"

"Cullee, boy!" 'Gage's voice came cheerily over the line in one of the private booths. "How's the great statesman in our next-to-most-deliberative body?"

"I'm fine," Cullee said, without giving much. "How's our greatest civil rightser?"

"Always busy," LeGage said, not so cheerily. "Think you've got 'em stopped coming in the doors and they come in the windows. Looks now as though something's going to pop in South Carolina."

"Oh?"

"Yes. Justice Tommy Davis has just handed down an order upholding our appeal in the Charleston case. They're ordered to integrate immediately."

"Well, you'll be down there tomorrow," Cullee said in a mocking tone. "You can wrap all that up in no time."

"I don't know about that," LeGage said thoughtfully. "DEFY'll have some pickets out, but South Carolina's a tough one. They're really mean down there."

"Check with Seab Cooley. He's a friend of mine."

"*What?*"

"Sorry. Confidential Congress business. Look, 'Gage. I've got to get back to the floor in a minute. We've got an important vote coming up—"

"Oh, damn it, you always use that 'got to get back to the floor' routine on me. Why don't you ever be nice to me, Cullee? I'm a friend of yours."

"Yes, boy, I know. We slept together all through college. In the same room, that is."

"Well, damn it, you always hold me off, when we know each other a lot better than anybody else knows us. We need each other, Cullee. We're both fighting for the same thing."

"Different ways."

"All right, Mr. High and Mighty. So you're a Congressman and I'm head of DEFY. Who's bigger?"

"Want to test it out against me in California next year? Maybe you can lick me."

"Oh, damn it, I *don't want* to lick you. I want you where you are, doing the job you're doing. Or even a better one."

"Sure. Now *you* tell me to run for the Senate. That'll really kill it."

"Cullee," LeGage said patiently, and the Congressman could tell he was close to that point of emotionally frayed nerves to which he could so easily drive him, "please lay off me? I didn't call to get in a fight. I called because Felix Labaiya asked me to. He thinks you ought to be down there in Charleston tomorrow at that luncheon for Terry."

"You agree with him?"

"I suppose I'd better say no, so you'll do it."

"Well, I don't care whether you do or not, really. But I'm not going."

"Why not?"

"Because I just don't like to be patronized by the Jasons, for one thing. Ted just sees one thing when he looks at me, and you too, and that's the Colored Vote. Furthermore, Terry doesn't mean any good for this country, and I don't want to be part of whatever he may have in mind, even if you do. Also, I've seen him on his home grounds and he isn't much. Why, hell! All this white sentimentalizing over that little two-bit belly bumper from the bush. He isn't worth *that*."

"He isn't little," LeGage objected mildly. "He's six-foot-seven."

"I'm talking about inside, not outside," the Congressman snapped. "Why, hell! I'll bet he's all over television right this minute. Yes, Your Highness. No, Your Highness. Tell us poor ignorant white folks about all you noble black fighters for freedom in Africa, Your Highness. Crap all over the United States, Your Highness. We love it, Your Highness. It's how we prove we're a great enlightened nation, Your Highness. Acchhkk. They make me sick!"

"What's the matter, boy?" LeGage asked with a sarcasm he knew would infuriate but could never resist when Cullee got in this mood. "He try to run off with your wife?"

"And leave my wife out of it," the Congressman said ominously. "Good-by."

"*Cullee.* Please, Cullee, don't hang up ye—oh, *God* damn it."

And that's the way it always was with 'Gage, Cullee thought bitterly as he went back into the chamber; why in the hell doesn't he leave me alone? They had been on each other's nerves from the day they met, they had never stopped being on each other's nerves one minute since, and they would always have this tension between them if they lived to be a hundred. "I think you and I are too much alike," he had told his clever, driving roommate after one of the earliest of their many furious arguments in the room at Howard; "maybe I'd best move out." But 'Gage, instantly contrite, had begged him not to—"We've got to stick together, boy. Who else is there for us to talk to?"— and some combination of like, dislike, affection, annoyance, love, hate, whatever, had kept them together, bickering through their school years and bickering still. It was true that they did know each other better than anyone else did, and that included 'Gage's placidly limited wife and the hellcat he himself happened to have drawn in the Lord's sardonic lottery. When things got unhappiest for him, he could always think—and it was genuinely comforting, he would admit— Well, I'll bet 'Gage knows how I feel; and he was sure 'Gage did, and that 'Gage often thought the same about him, although they rarely came even as close to touching on it as 'Gage had done just now. It was a curious and apparently unbreakable relationship, whose possible implications they had finally faced one time in senior year in a completely candid discussion that certainly didn't change matters any. "Well, it's obvious neither of us is a woman," Cullee had said, "but I guess we can't live with each other or without each other." "You make me awful mad sometimes," 'Gage had agreed, "but I expect if I was ever really—really—in trouble, I'd come to you." "Me, too," Cullee said, and they had shaken hands very solemnly, at twenty-one. Then divergent paths to the same objectives had brought increasing criticism, increasing nagging, growing uneasiness and sharpness between them, inflamed and embittered the tensions of their youth, made their friendship ever harder to live with, or without. Damn it all, why did he have to be such an annoying bastard?

On the House floor he found only a handful of members remaining for the final speeches of the day, the "special orders" without time limitation after regular House business is done, in which those who desire can present their arguments about this, their exhortations about that, rarely listened to by their colleagues but, once in the Record, available to be sent out under frank to presumably interested constituents. He left the floor; dropped by the Speaker's office for fifteen minutes of what that gentleman referred to as "the usual libation," a little late-afternoon ceremony that he reserved for the more powerful chairmen and his special favorites among the younger members; and then went on to his own office in the Old House Office Building, cleaned up the mail, and dismissed his staff. He called home to say he was coming; got the maid, Maudie, who informed him when he asked for Sue-Dan that "she's resting and can't be disturbed"; and closed the huge mahogany door to his office with a crash so vigorous that a policeman at the guard desk far down the corridor looked up startled from his copy of the *Evening Star*. He waved, the cop waved back, and then he took the elevator to the basement, got his Lincoln Continental out of the garage, and drove off through the heavy traffic of homebound Washington, negotiating automatically and hardly conscious of the crush of cars around him all the way through town and up Sixteenth Street.

Arrived home, he went on into the house, again punctuating his mood with the door from the carport. The sound brought Maudie immediately to the living room. She was a woman of sixty who reminded him a good deal of his mother, and she always treated him as though she were.

"A mighty big noise from a big man," she said, pausing to plump the pillows on the sofa. "Suppose the world's ending, maybe, or something?"

"It may be," he said darkly. "Could just be, old Maudie."

"Not likely tonight," she said. "Not likely tonight. Let me take that hat and coat and get you a drink."

"Thanks," he said, tossing the garments to her. "The usual."

"Martinis made by the devil," she observed disapprovingly, "but if you want one, I expect I have to make it."

"Expect so, Maudie," he said, more cheerfully, "seeing as how you're a devil."

"You get along, now. Don't see you growing any angel wings, Mr. Congressman." Her voice underwent the subtle change it always did when she referred to the lady of the house. "Shall I mix one for *her* too?"

He shrugged.

"I don't know. Is she up? Ask her."

"Oh, she's not up," Maudie said. "You wouldn't think she'd be up and waiting for her husband after his day at the office, would you? That not the girl *you* married."

"O.K., if you know so much about it, old woman, maybe she just likes to wait for me in bed. How about that?"

"You needn't be flaunting it," Maudie said tartly. "Even suppose it's true. Which," she added, "I don't."

"All right," he said, suddenly sterner, "get along out, now, and mix those drinks. I'll take it up to her. Then," he added wickedly, "maybe you can put off dinner an hour, Maudie, and think about it, down here in the kitchen."

"Hmph," she said. "Little boy like to talk about getting the moon, but once he got it, what he got? Just plain old cheese. Not gold and silver at all, just plain old cheese."

"All right, get along, I said!" he repeated sharply. "And hurry it up!"

"I'm gettin'," she said grumpily. "Don't resh me."

So much for that, he thought angrily as he went to the television set and snapped it on. So much for God damn that. Little boy *will* get the moon and see what it's made of. But even as the screen began to light up and there appeared upon it exactly the bland and happy face he expected to see, he knew the answer. Maudie's answer. Just plain old cheese.

"Of course," the M'Bulu was remarking in a film clip taken out on the concrete expanse of the plaza with the Secretariat Building looming most impressively behind him, "I am sure the United States does not wish to be in the position of being discourteous or inconsiderate to Africa. But—" he shrugged and gave his charming gesture and smile. "But—"

"Then you think, Your Highness," the network correspondent asked eagerly, "that the President definitely should have canceled his trip to Michigan to remain in Washington and entertain you?"

"Oh, I would not want to disturb the President's plans," Terrible Terry said politely. "He knows what is best for his own health. And, I assume, for his country. But—" And again the charming shrug and smile.

"Then you *do* think he should have stayed?"

The M'Bulu laughed.

"Now you are attempting to get me to be critical of the President."

"Oh, no," the network correspondent objected, but Terry went on.

"I think the President is a great man. I am sure that if he decided to insult Africa, he had reasons for it. And I am sure they make sense to him. Even if," he added wistfully, "they leave all of us in Africa somewhat puzzled."

"You would say that the United States, then, has definitely lost ground in Africa as a result of the President's snub?"

Again the M'Bulu shrugged and smiled.

"I would not want to pass judgment, but—well, yes, I think the United States definitely will have to regain some lost ground. If, of course, the United States cares what we in Africa think. Sometimes we are not so sure."

Cullee made a disgusted sound and snapped off the set as Maudie returned with the drinks.

"A great man, Maudie. He's going to tell the United States what to do. I think maybe he's also going to lead us poor black folks out of slavery, if he has the time."

"Pfoof," she said. "'T's all I can say. Pfoof! Here's your drinks."

"Thank you," he said, starting up the stairs. As he did so, she laughed suddenly. "Bet she's still listening to him. What do you bet?"

"You know I'd lose, Maudie. Don't hurry dinner."

"You going to be mighty embarrassed when you find you have forty-five minutes to kill," she called, but he didn't deign an answer.

Nor, he thought as he kicked open the bedroom door and went in carrying the tray, was there any particular answer to make. Most of the older women of his race had an instinct for going straight to the jugular, particularly in matters involving life, death, love, and other fundamentals. Maudie had sensed it out, all right, though she had never before voiced it so frankly. By the same token, maybe she had made him face it more honestly than he had up to now. The thought did not give him a pleasant expression as he came into the room, and the shrewd little fox-face that greeted him from among the pillows and lacy things of the bed threw it back to him without an instant's hesitation. Of course the bedroom television set was blaring too, and of course Terry was still on it, though on another channel. He put the drinks on the night table, went over to the machine, and snapped it off with a vicious twist of his fingers. Sue-Dan promptly switched it back on again with the remote-control mechanism beside the bed.

"Leave it off!" he demanded, and after a long look and a moment sufficiently prolonged to tease him she complied with a little chuckle.

"What's the matter? You don't want to hear your old friend Terry?"

"No."

"Big man. Real famous now. Better look him up, Cullee. It might help your career."

"How's that?" he demanded, going to the closet and taking off his coat and tie, tossing his shirt on a chair, putting his glasses carefully on the bureau, coming back to sit on the edge of the bed as he unlaced his shoes. "What's he got to do with my career?"

"Patsy Labaiya called a while ago. She thinks you ought to go to Charleston for that luncheon."

"LeGage Shelby called a while ago," he said in a voice that mimicked her own sarcastic tones. "He thinks I ought to go to Charleston for that luncheon."

She laughed.

"Cullee's other wife. You can say no to Patsy, but sure enough you aren't going to say no to 'Gage. Now, are you?"

"Yes," he said levelly, "I did say no to him."

"And had another fight."

"And had another fight."

"Could be the Jasons could help you when you run for Senator next year," she observed dreamily, nestling down in the pillows with a luxuriant air.

"*If* I run for Senator," he corrected, slipping out of his trousers and draping them over the chair with his shirt.

"Oh," she said, as he sat again on the edge of the bed. "I expect you will."

"The Speaker thinks I should," he admitted, and for the first time since he had entered the room Sue-Dan looked genuinely pleased.

"Good for him. He's got some sense, that old man."

"He's got plenty of sense," Cullee said, starting to strip off his undershirt. He was conscious of an immediate tensing alongside.

"What you got in mind, Cullee?" she asked sharply. He gave a sarcastic laugh.

"I just like to get undressed and run around naked. Isn't that what you been thinking right along? Surely, now, you haven't been thinking anything *else*, little Sue-Dan."

Her eyes looked enormous, though not, he thought bitterly, from any fear or anticipation of him. She played this game all the time.

"I'm tired."

"I'm tired," he mimicked. "So am I tired. But I'm not tired right *here*. See that, Sue-Dan? Terry isn't the only big man. You got a big man too."

"Why can't you ever leave me alone?" she demanded angrily, starting to roll out the other side of the bed; but he reached an arm across and pinned her down with one enormous hand as he reached down with the other, ripped off his shorts, and dropped them on the floor.

"I've got to show you who Cullee's wife really is," he said huskily, stripping back the blankets and clambering over her. "I think maybe you forgot since the last time."

"I haven't forgotten anything," she said through her teeth, struggling fiercely under him.

"Then stop it," he said angrily, his face an inch from hers, his powerfully muscled athlete's body slowly and inexorably crushing down upon her. "Just stop it. God damn it, do you mean I have to rape my own wife?"

Suddenly her struggles ceased as quickly as they had begun, her arms went around him, the world became a place of wild confusion, until at last they cried out together in hoarse, incoherent exclamation and a quietness descended.

"Now get off me," she whispered abruptly with a harshness that broke the mood at once. "Just get off me, big man. You've proved it, whatever it was you wanted to prove. *Get off me.*"

"You just can't help but be good, even when you hate me, can you, Sue-Dan?" he said with an equally harsh sarcasm as he started to comply. "You're just a natural-born lay, Mrs. Congressman Hamilton."

"Better not let anybody else find it out," she said shrewishly, and he swung back one huge hand, caught her wrist, and again pinned her down helpless on the bed, leaning over so close his face was again an inch from hers.

"Better not *you* ever let anybody else find it out," he whispered with a menace that he was pleased to note made her look genuinely terrified. "Or I not promise what I do to you, little Sue-Dan."

And as abruptly as he had pinned her down he released her, stood up, stretched, and went into the bathroom. She remained motionless where she was, not stirring until the phone rang as he came out, toweling vigorously and starting toward his drink. She lifted the receiver and, in a tone as casual as though she had been mending socks, asked who it was. Then with an expression of surprise she said respectfully, "Yes, Mr. Secretary, just a minute. Here he is."

The car radio was on as they swung out of Forty-eighth Street onto Massachusetts Avenue in Spring Valley and started the run across town to the Sheraton-Park on Sixteenth Street, and once again much was being said about the troubles of the M'Bulu. By this time, the Secretary of State noted, the public was being given the general impression that the President had told the Savior He couldn't walk on the water. Apparently the Secretary's companion had the same reaction to the broadcast, for he gave a slow chuckle and shifted a little in his seat.

"Orrin," he said, "what in the world—what—in—the—world—did Harley do to that young man? Must have been something terrible, Orrin. I can't remember things getting so stirred up since you and I did all those awful things to Mr. Robert—A.—Leffingwell. Can you, Orrin?"

"Well, it's all very unfortunate," the Secretary said as he drove briskly down nearly deserted Mass. Avenue. "I missed giving Harley the pitch by half an hour, and consequently the sky has fallen in. Or, at any rate, all our eager friends, allies, and enemies would like to have us think so. It's amazing how unanimous they can get when it's a case of embarrassing the United States."

Senator Cooley chuckled.

"Seems to me like you're getting a mite prickly in your new job, Orrin. Think of what a gray world it would be for them if we weren't around to embarrass."

"It's so damned childish, that's what gets me. Grown men and grown nations—because many of them are grown that do it; it isn't always the babies who might possibly be excused on the ground they don't know any better—yapping at our heels on the slightest pretext they can find. Listen to that: 'British reaction tonight is harshly critical of the President—'"

"Maybe there comes a time in the life of a nation," Seab Cooley said, "when you haven't got much more to do but react. Maybe you get hypersensitive and waspish just because you're sick and sad inside that nobody any more cares enough to react to *you* like that. Could be a lesson for us someday, too, you know, Orrin."

"'Far-called our navies melt away,'" the Secretary quoted with an ironic note. "'On dune and headland sinks the fire . . .' Yes, I suppose so, Seab. But not yet awhile. Not yet awhile, God willing and God grant us strength. We have an awful lot to do before we reach that point, I do believe. And so do they believe, all of them, when you come right down to it. Just suppose there were no United States to bulwark the world? Where would all the yappers be then?"

"Ground up and sold for hamburger at Moscow Meat Factory No. 1," Senator Cooley said with a dry chuckle. "Yes, sir, ground up and sold for hamburger at Moscow Meat Factory No. 1."

"Exactly," the Secretary of State agreed as they swung around Ward Circle past American University and continued the long plunge down Massachusetts Avenue toward the center of town. "That's why I sometimes find it a little hard to be as dutifully polite as I'm suppose to be in this job."

"Kind of hard for Orrin Knox to hold it in, isn't it?" The pugnacious old face looked solemn, but there was a puckish gleam in the eyes. "*Good* for you, Orrin! *Good* for you!"

"So Beth tells me. She tells me I may be a great man someday if I can just stand the discipline of it."

"Very kind woman, Beth," the Senator from South Carolina said. "Very kind of you both to invite me to dinner tonight."

"Oh, I had a motive," Orrin said cheerfully. "Aside from always being glad to see you, of course, which we both are. I want your help in dealing with the M'Bulu, Seab. I'm really taking him rather seriously. I have to, now."

"What do you think would happen, Orrin, if sometime the United States just refused to take some over-inflated episode seriously? If the United States just said, 'Now, you all just run along and stop bothering us. We just never heard about it, so you all just run along.' Would the world really come to an end, Orrin? Or would they respect us the more for being strong enough to do it?"

"Yes, that's all very fine, Seab," the Secretary said as he turned left on Idaho Avenue to Woodley Road and then turned right toward Connecticut Avenue, "but it isn't very practical in the nervous situation the world has got itself into. You've no idea the way they go twittering around that UN aviary up there like a flock of sparrows in a high wind. And if you happen to believe in it then you have to take it into account. You can't just dismiss it cavalierly. We're committed to it, and that automatically means that everybody from the biggest power to the littlest can put his oar into what we do. So—we have the M'Bulu. And the M'Bulu, as you gather, is making the most of it."

"Mmmm. That's why you're going to see young Cullee."

"Yes. I think he can help. You could, too, Seab, if you would."

"How's that?"

"Just by keeping quiet. Just by not inflaming the situation any more than necessary."

"If you mean be kind to Ray Smith—" Seab began with a humorous air. Orrin snorted.

"Ray's a fool. I hope Cullee runs and beats him. No, have your fun with Ray, if you want to. But tomorrow, for instance—do what you can to keep this luncheon from boiling over into something unpleasant in Charleston."

"I haven't been invited. You know that, Orrin. Wouldn't invite the Senators from South Carolina. Might put the curse of respectability on it. The Jasons can't have that."

"Respectability in South Carolina, you must remember, Seab. Other places your presence might not be considered respectable."

"I might just go, you know, Orrin," Senator Cooley said gently. "I just might, now."

"That's exactly what I mean, Seab. That's exactly the sort of thing. Please don't. It's too important to play games with."

"I'm not playing games, Orrin. I'm protecting my state."

"And the political future of Seab Cooley," the Secretary said. His companion chuckled.

"Looks to me like the political future of Orrin Knox is involved too. Ted Jason's going to get a mighty lot of mileage out of this with the colored folks, Orrin."

"Well," the Secretary said bluntly, "that may be. But we've got to hope it will be as orderly as possible and that they'll get out of there without some sort of incident or other. That's where you can be of assistance, Seab. Just help keep the noise down to a minimum, O.K.?"

"Least I can do, if I don't go, is issue a statement, Orrin. You know I've got to do at least that much, now."

"All right, issue your statement. But tell your friends not to start any funny business."

"It isn't always my friends who start the funny business, Orrin. We have elements that aren't so well-mannered about these things. Can't say they're my friends, though. Necessarily."

"They vote for you. They'll listen to you. I'm asking your help, Seab. Please."

"What are you going to do for him when he gets to Washington, Orrin?"

"I said please, Seab."

The senior Senator from South Carolina smiled.

"Now, Orrin, you know perfectly well I'm not going to give you any answer to that. I'm just going to keep you guessing. I'm a vicious, evil old man, Orrin. Everybody knows that. But I'll say this: Within the necessary limits of what I have to do to protect myself politically, Orrin, I won't stir things up for you. I'll help you with your kinky-haired kinkajou."

The Secretary laughed as they turned right off Cathedral Avenue onto Connecticut and headed down toward the rambling, comfortable old Sheraton-Park Hotel, where Seab had his apartment.

"The first thing you can do is stop repeating that phrase. You had your fun with it this afternoon, and that annoyed the Africans enough. Don't use it again. What do you think of Cullee?" he asked abruptly. His companion shrugged.

"For an educated colored man, I think he does very well. He seems to be a well-mannered fellow. I haven't any argument with him."

"Lucky Cullee," Orrin Knox remarked. Seab chuckled as they swung under the portico.

"Lucky Seab, maybe. Don't ever quote me, though, Orrin. I'd deny it, Orrin, so don't ever quote me. Seriously," he said as the Secretary eased the car to a stop, "I think he's a good boy, Orrin. Got more sense in him than they usually have. I wish him well, Orrin. You can tell him I said so, Orrin. Just say: 'Seab Cooley said to say he wishes you well.'" He chuckled. "That'll puzzle him, Orrin. That'll give him something to think about." He held out his hand and shook Orrin's firmly as the doorman leaped to open the door. "Thank you again for the pleasant dinner. Getting to an age where I appreciate small kindnesses, Orrin. Seventy-six." For a second the Secretary thought he was about to be party to a rare moment of pathos with the senior Senator from South Carolina. But he might have known. "And not dead yet," Seab Cooley said with pugnacious satisfaction. "Not dead yet and not about to be, Orrin! Not about to be! Good night, now. And good luck with your kinky-haired kinkajou."

"Thank you, Seab," the Secretary said. "I'm counting on you. Take care of yourself."

But whether he could count on a Seab hard pressed and "running scared," he thought as he swung the car down the curving drive and back to Connecticut for the Klingle Road–Piney Branch connection through Rock Creek Park to Sixteenth Street, he was not at all sure. The drive from Silver Spring had taken nearly twenty minutes, and he wondered if it had accomplished so much after all. Now more news was on the radio, reiterating his problem. He switched swiftly to music and sighed as he heard a time-check. Almost 10 P.M. Quite an hour to come calling on Cullee, but he hadn't landed from

New York until almost eight, and then it had taken some time to get home and have dinner, and he hadn't wanted to rush Seab. Like everyone in Washington, he still had great respect for Seab's abilities to cause trouble, seventy-six or no.

Curious, though, he reflected as he passed the Woodner on Sixteenth and prepared to swing off a block to the street where the Hamiltons lived, that little message to the Congressman. Curious the whole white-black relationship in the South, that compound of love, hate, tolerance, and intolerance, understanding and misunderstanding, laughter and anger, that he as a Northerner could never fully comprehend. Black-white did not mix so well in his native Illinois, particularly in Chicago, where the proud pretensions of the North went down the drain in the ugly frictions that never eased and often flared. And as for Harlem, that black ghetto existing side by side with all the airy, patronizing pretenses of the white New York cultural world—the South, he thought, need not bow its head too low. The city of its chief critics was no sweet-smelling rose on the face of the earth, that was sure, "fabulous" though it might appear to the Secretary-General and anyone else with an ounce of romance in his soul. A great crawling abyss lay just below the surface of the romance, and it would be a long time, if ever, before New York could say truthfully that its own reality was such as to justify the superior, arrogant intolerance so many of its more publicized residents unfailingly displayed toward other people's shortcomings.

He parked his car in the neat neighborhood—what did the houses run here, he wondered, $25,000, $35,000, $40,000? He estimated that the one before him with its broad lawn and neatly kept shrubs and gardens must be well over $30,000. The door was opened as he started up the walk. Cullee greeted him dressed in razor-pressed navy-blue slacks, white tie and shirt, a loose gray cashmere sweater—a combination of neat informality exactly right for the occasion, Orrin thought as he extended his hand.

"Cullee," he said cordially, "you are very kind to see me at this hour, and I appreciate it."

"Not at all, Senator," the Congressman said, using the old title Orrin had borne so long and still liked to hear. "I'm honored that you would come here to me . . . I'll have to apologize for my wife," he said as he led his guest into the warmly furnished living room and gestured to a chair. "She had a headache and went to bed early."

"Just as well I didn't bring Beth, then. I was going to, and she said no woman wanted to entertain another at 10 P.M. while their men talked business. I guess she was right." He smiled and looked approvingly around the room. "I see you're like we are. You like comfortable things. We'll have to have you out soon."

"Thank you," Cullee said. "We'd like to come. Yes, I'm a comfort boy, myself, and I've managed to persuade Sue-Dan to go along with me. Her taste rather runs to the frilly, you know, but I hardly thought that would suit a man my size."

"What was it? Football?"

"Track."

"That's right, of course. The Olympics, and so on—"

The Congressman smiled, a reminiscent look in his eye.

"That was fun. I really enjoyed beating those puffed-up boys from the Communist bloc. I think they thought because I was a Negro I'd betray the United States. They had," he remarked with satisfaction, "another think coming. Cigarette?"

"No, thanks; I don't."

"Me, either, but one has to make the gesture."

They smiled at one another with great amiability, and the Secretary remarked thoughtfully, "You know, it's nice to see you again. We never did get to know each other very well on the Hill, but now that I'm at State maybe we can get together more often. Frankly, I'd like your help with the Africans. They're my biggest headache at the moment."

Cullee laughed.

"Got lots of big ideas, haven't they? Terry, for instance."

"Terry is why I'm here, as a matter of fact," Orrin said. His host nodded.

"I thought so. He's a bad boy."

"You bet he is," the Secretary agreed with feeling. "You were out in Gorotoland last year, weren't you?"

"Yes; Jawbone Swarthman asked me to go out for the Foreign Affairs Committee, so we did. Terry showed us around for about a week." He smiled. "Didn't give us any human flesh to eat or show us any sacrifices, but we got a pretty good picture of the civilized side. It isn't much. Personally, I don't blame Britain."

"We start pretty much in agreement, then. I don't, either."

"But we may not be able to support her in the General Assembly," the Congressman suggested. The Secretary's face clouded.

"I wouldn't want it officially confirmed, but we may not. We just aren't sure yet, so please don't say anything."

"It stops here. What can I do to help with Terry?"

"First of all, I hope you'll go to that luncheon in Charleston tomorrow," Orrin said and then, as a stubborn look came instantly to his host's face, went firmly on, "and when he returns here to Washington, I hope you'll pretty well stay right with him all the time he's here. I want somebody I can trust to keep an eye on him."

Cullee smiled and for a moment his face lost the stubborn look.

"I'm flattered by that, right enough, but I'm afraid I can't do it."

"I wish you would. It would be a great help to me. It would be a great help to the country, I think."

"You don't understand," the Congressman said. "I—I don't like him, for one thing. He's kind of—unclean, inside, I think. We didn't get along too well when Sue-Dan and I were out there—"

"He told me this morning he thought you had a pretty wife," the Secretary said, and his tone brought an answering smile from Cullee.

"He's got half a dozen of his own; why pick on mine? But—aside from not liking him personally—it's difficult to explain to you, Senator, but—I just resent the way you—you people—are fawning all over him here. He isn't worth it."

"By 'you people,' I take it, you mean 'you white people,' is that right?" Cullee nodded. "It isn't my doing," Orrin Knox said shortly. "The only fawning I'm doing is a strictly political necessity—internationally political, that is. Harley got us rather in a mess, I'm afraid, by not being too tactful this afternoon at his press conference. Now it's up to me to bail us out. Everybody at the UN who wants to embarrass the U.S., and that's just about everybody, has seized upon it to make a big rumpus, as you know. You've seen television and heard the news."

"Yes, and I'd like to help if I could, but—I'm not sure I could do much, anyway. Also, I resent playing tail on Ted Jason's kite. He just wants me around because I'm colored. It's all part of his schemes for next year. You know that, Senator."

"Maybe that's the only reason I'm here," Orrin Knox said with a calculated bluntness on which several things were riding; but he thought it best to meet it head on. "Maybe I'm just trying to line you up on *my* side. After all, you know, the colored vote's the colored vote."

His host looked at him without expression for a long moment before smiling and shaking his head.

"No, I don't think so. I don't think so. I have a lot of respect for Orrin Knox, I may say, and I don't think so. Oh, of course you'd like my support, and you need the colored vote, there's no doubt of that. But I really think you're working on the problem you've got right now. I really do."

"One problem at a time," Orrin said with a rueful smile, and Cullee smiled too.

"That's a good motto."

"Well, let *me* ask *you*— Do you think you can run for Senator out there if you antagonize the Governor and don't help him with his plans?"

His host shrugged, but the Secretary could see the gesture covered a more troubled mind than the Congressman wanted to admit.

"Who knows? I don't know that I'll even run, yet. And if I do, I expect I'll get along, with Ted or without him. In California, you know, we're all pretty independent of one another."

The Secretary looked at his watch.

"Well," he said with a deliberate matter-of-factness, "I expect I'd better run. It's getting late. I'm sorry you won't help me, but—" Cullee held up an admonitory hand.

"Sit down, Senator. Wait a minute. Let me think . . . I hate to—well, to be frank with you, it doesn't sound very modest, but I just hate to lend my name and prestige to that overdressed piece of nothing. I do represent something, to my people and—"

"And to mine."

"Yes, maybe to yours, too. At least, I hope so. I try to be a good Congressman and a good representative of my race."

"The best," Orrin Knox said without flattery.

"That's why I hesitate, you see?" Cullee Hamilton said. "It means something, if I do a thing. It's a responsibility."

"It is indeed. A very great one, which you carry supremely well. Of course you know I wouldn't ask your help if that weren't the case."

Cullee laughed, rather helplessly.

"You meet me coming around the barn the other side . . . All right. I'll do it."

"Good," said Orrin Knox, rising briskly and shaking hands. "I'm very pleased and very grateful. I know the President will be too"—he gave a wry smile—"after he realizes that we're gradually getting this thing worked out for him."

Cullee smiled.

"He's a great guy, but I guess this time he just didn't stop to think."

"I'd be out of a job," Orrin Knox said, "if all the people in this world who ought to stop and think stopped and thought. Well, then. You'll be at the luncheon and then squire him around town afterwards."

"O.K.," Cullee said without enthusiasm. "You understand I'm not cutting any rugs for joy about it, but I'll do my best to put a good face on it for you."

"Good man. I really meant it about getting together, too. You come have lunch with me at the Department sometime in the next week or two—I'll have my secretary call and make a date. And Beth and I would like to have you two out. I meant that, too."

"I'd be pleased," Cullee said with a genuinely flattered smile.

"We'll work it out," the Secretary said. He stopped on the doorstep. "Oh, one thing. I almost forgot. I have a message for you from our dinner guest this evening. I'll quote him exactly. He said, 'I wish him well. You can tell him I said so. Just say: "Seab Cooley said to say he wishes you well."' There, I think I've made it about as repetitious as he does."

Again the Congressman looked genuinely pleased.

"That was very kind of him. You know," he added thoughtfully, leaning against the doorjamb, "it's a funny thing, and I expect you northerners wouldn't understand it, but in a curious way I think that old man and I really quite like each other. We'll never agree on my race, and no doubt he's been guilty of a lot of bad things toward it, but—you tell him I said I wish him well, too. He's one of the last of his kind, and, on its own terms, I expect it wasn't such a bad kind, in lots of ways. You tell him what I said."

"Maybe you should tell him yourself," the Secretary suggested. His host dismissed it with a laugh.

"No. To quote my mother, God rest her soul, that wouldn't be fittin'. It just wouldn't be fittin'. I could do it, but he wouldn't know how to take it. So you be our messenger, Mr. Secretary. We both trust you."

Orrin Knox laughed.

"Good. And good night, Cullee. It's a great relief to have your help."

"Any time I can. Give my regards to Mrs. Knox."

And so, the Secretary told himself with some satisfaction as he began the long drive back to Spring Valley, he had done about as much as he could do to appease little Mr. Self-Importance from Gorotoland. He would call Hal or Lafe as soon as he got back to the house—both would be at the Turkish party at the Waldorf, and he could reach one or the other there—and get the word to the M'Bulu that he would have a formal luncheon with the Foreign Relations and Foreign Affairs Committees on Friday and then on Friday night be entertained at "Vagaries" by the Knoxes, the Munsons, and a lot of other highfalutin folk. These honors, together with the reception at the British Embassy, should be enough to calm him down. In fact, considering all the handicaps that had surrounded the matter, the Secretary congratulated himself as he swung up Massachusetts Avenue again that he had done about as good a job as anyone could do on such short notice of handling the problem presented to the United States by the M'Bulu of Mbuele.

What he could not know, of course, was that the M'Bulu, dancing gaily with a lady delegate from Malaya at the Waldorf, wasn't really anywhere near as concerned about this particular problem as he had chosen to sound all day long. Terrible Terry, although no one knew it but himself, had kept an eye on the news and now had another problem altogether in store for the United States.

9

For the better part of two hundred years, "Harmony" had stood on the Battery in Charleston with an air of calm and stately dignity that often belied the activities that went on inside. Behind the great white pillars in the great high-ceilinged rooms, some of war's beginnings had been plotted and many of war's bitter consequences had been felt. Proud men who debated conquering the North over brandy and cigars in the mansion's oak-paneled living room had come home to that same room minus legs or arms or eyes and carrying in their hearts the bitter foreknowledge of the North's cold unforgiveness. The passions and tempers of four proud families had swept in and out of the broad hallways and across the broad lawns, velvet-soft in the years of plenty, scraggly and weed-grown in the years of adversity, velvet again as prosperity slowly returned to a beaten but still unhumbled people. Original Ashtons had given way to Boyds; Boyds eventually yielding, after the war, to Middletons; Middletons, dwindled down at last to two ancient spinsters, giving over, after a later and yet more monstrous war that began in 1939, to Jasons. Yet even with these last, regarded as rich, intruding Yankees, fawned over to their faces and despised behind their backs by their soft-talking, professionally cordial Southern neighbors, "Harmony" had always managed, under all conditions, to maintain its dignity, its air of solid magnificence, its outward aspect of stately and serene gentility.

Until today.

Today, things were happening to "Harmony."

The process had begun around 9 A.M. when three trucks filled with cameras and electronic equipment, each emblazoned with the name of a national network, had roared down the quietly gracious thoroughfare to turn abruptly into "Harmony's" winding drive. Loud-spoken men had leaped to earth, their voices raucous in the golden morning, and for an hour or more there had been great noise and disturbance in the neighborhood. When it finally subsided, long black cables snaked from the trucks up "Harmony's" stately steps and into "Harmony's" stately halls, and at every vantage point in the mansion—in the living room, the parlor, the ballroom, and the banquet hall; on the verandas and here and there at strategic intervals about the lawn, television cameras now stood poised and ready to capture famous people and witness historic events. Operators and technicians lounged about, exchanging loud and irreverent conversations on the affairs of nations and of men as they drank coffee furnished by the crew of servants busily at work in "Harmony's" kitchens, and it was obvious to everyone for blocks around that something of vast import was soon to take place.

Shortly after 11 A.M. this knowledge was strengthened by the arrival of two chartered buses labeled "JASON FOUNDATION—PRESS," just in from Municipal Airport, where their occupants—reporters, correspondents, columnists, editors, and photographers—had been met by Jason-furnished transportation after their Jason-financed flights from New York, Washington, Chicago, Los Angeles, Denver, and other centers of publicity and communication. Again the soft morning air was troubled with the cries of old hands at the game greeting one another, the ribald comments of professionals surveying the sort of spectacle they had all seen so often before, the cynical, half-resentful jesting of men and women who knew they were being used but knew also that their profession made it impossible for them to escape being used. Another coffee line soon formed under the great oaks and the air was filled with gossip and speculation about the luncheon to come, its principal guest, its principal organizers, and the pertinence of it all to political events both foreign and domestic. So quietly that hardly anyone at "Harmony" noticed, shades were drawn on the windows of the two houses overlooking the old mansion and a deliberate hush descended on the Battery. Against it the noise and bustle in that one place, emphasized by the surrounding silence, appeared to take on the volume of a small but crowded midway at a circus. This was undoubtedly the intention of those who had drawn the shades, but the gesture was lost upon the people at "Harmony." None of them paid any attention, and the rising tide of sound kept right on rising.

Promptly at noon the first of what soon became a steady procession of sleek black chauffeured Cadillacs came along the Battery, turned into the winding approach to the mansion, and discharged its passengers under the gleaming portico. From this car there emerged four people, Edward Jason, Governor of California; his sister, Señora Labaiya-Sofra; his brother-in-law, the Ambassador of Panama; and the guest of honor. Cameras whirred, flashbulbs popped, newsmen pressed forward.

"Governor, do you have any comment to make on the President's treatment of His Royal Highness? Governor, would you care to comment on the United States attitude toward Africa? Governor, are you ready to announce your candidacy for President?"

To all of these, particularly the last, which brought general laughter in which he joined, the Governor of California gave his pleasant, statesmanlike smile and a friendly, "No comment, ladies and gentlemen. This is the M'Bulu's day. Talk to him."

"But, Governor," the San Francisco *Chronicle* said, "surely you have *some* comment to make on what has been happening in the last couple of days?"

"I'm going to make a little speech," Edward Jason said, patting his breast pocket. His dark eyes sobered for a second, his deep tan looking beautifully impressive contrasted with his silver eyebrows and silver hair. His fine head came up in the challenging gesture he had adopted from another Governor of California who not so long ago had followed to its successful conclusion the road upon which he himself was now embarked. "Listen to the speech. I think it will make my position clear."

"Your Highness, then. Has Your Highness received any communication from the United States Government since yesterday?"

Terrible Terry, his green and gold robes crowned today by a cap and tassel of brilliant purple that raised his total height to seven feet, gave his shrug and happy smile.

"Oh, I received something last night. Not a formal communication, you understand; but the distinguished delegate of the United States to the United Nations transmitted invitations to me from the Secretary of State. There will be a luncheon, I believe, on Friday. And a party Friday night after the British Embassy reception. A private party."

"Will this satisfy you as a substitute for being entertained by the President, Your Royal Highness?"

Again the shrug and smile.

"Is a little stone a substitute for bread?" he asked, as they all laughed. "I think not. But, like the Governor—I too have a speech. Will you listen?"

"Oh, yes," someone assured him. "We'll listen." "We wouldn't miss it for anything," said someone else.

Amid more laughter, the official party turned and went in.

There followed in quick procession other distinguished guests, faithfully recorded by television and still cameras, evoking appropriate comments from the press as its members busily jotted down names and noted the degree of fame.

Herbert Jason, cousin of the Governor and Señora Labaiya, Nobel Prize-winning scientist and genius in the field of electronics, arrived with two elderly Jason aunts and the director of the Jason Foundation. Four members of the Senate and five from the House, all from northern or western states, followed in succeeding cars. Several editors from the smaller and more agitated journals came next, looking suitably self-important. Various members of the upper echelons of the metropolitan press: editors, editorialists, special writers, columnists; three or four book publishers of the desperately concerned variety—they too passed within the portals.

Following came some of the more famous leaders of a certain highly vocal sector of American intellectual thought, the headline-lovers who sign petitions and get up memorials, the profound thinkers who are to be found one week seeking "FAIR PLAY FOR DICTATOR X," who has just shot ten thousand innocent victims, and the next urging "JUSTICE FOR MOE GINSBERG," now waxing pale in Dannemora after having given atomic secrets to Russia and done his best to destroy his own country.

It was, in fact, a sort of Walpurgis Noon of all the professional phonies and intellectual flotsam of America, washed up on "Harmony's" broad lawns, and given an extra twitter this day because the word was out that next week there would be a full-page "FAIR PLAY FOR GOROTOLAND" ad in the New York *Times* and *everybody* but *everybody* would have his name on it.

Finally, quite late in the flow of arrivals, not appearing until almost a hundred guests had entered "Harmony," came a trio that again brought press and cameras surging forward. In rather surprising conjunction the director of the President's Commission on Administrative Reform, the chairman of DEFY, and the young colored Congressman from California arrived together to be faced with the usual onslaught of questions.

"Mr. Leffingwell, sir, do you have any comment to make on the President's refusal to entertain the M'Bulu? Mr. Shelby, what do you think the United States can do to regain the ground we have lost at the UN? Congressman, do you think His Highness' reception here will please the Negroes of America?"

"I have no comment," Bob Leffingwell said easily. "I work for the President, you know." They laughed appreciatively; he posed for pictures and vanished within. LeGage was a little more elaborate.

"Yes, I think the United States has lost ground," he said slowly, "with the Africans and also with the Asian states. Through this thing with the M'Bulu and also, as always, because of domestic conditions here in this country. Speaking as a member of the United States delegation, I am happy to be here with His Highness. Speaking as chairman of DEFY, I would hope that the United States would continue to press forward vigorously to end segregation wherever and whenever it exists. Including," he said after a significant pause that they leaped upon at once, "this city."

"Does that mean DEFY is going to get into the school situation here, 'Gage?" the Chicago *Defender* asked quickly. LeGage got the solemn self-important look that always made his ex-roommate want to kick him.

"I wouldn't want to say anything at all on that," he said with great emphasis. "Anything at all."

"How about you, Congressman?" the *Defender* said. "How do you think the Negroes of America feel about the M'Bulu's visit here to this city which is about to become the scene of another battle for human rights?"

"Quite a question," Cullee observed. "I'll ask you one. You're a Negro: How do you feel?"

"It's my business to ask the questions, Congressman," the *Defender* said sharply. "It's yours to answer."

"I can't speak for the Negroes of America."

"Some of us would like to think you could, Congressman," *Ebony* magazine told him, while the white press crowded closer, intrigued by this developing intramural argument.

"Well," the Congressman said shortly, "I don't. I don't know how all the Negroes in America feel about it, any more than *you* know how all the Negroes of America feel about it. Speaking as a member of the Congress of the United States—one member—I hope the M'Bulu will have a pleasant and enjoyable visit and go home thinking well of us."

"What do you think about the integration crisis here?" the *Afro-American* asked. Cullee gave him a long look and started to turn away.

"When a crisis develops, then maybe I'll comment on it."

"You doubt it will?" *Ebony* demanded. Cullee's eyes flashed at the tone.

"If you have anything to do with it, yes," he snapped, knowing that he shouldn't give way to anger but unable to refrain from it. There was something so smug about the way certain of his fellows always approached the question. "Come on, 'Gage," he said, taking him by the arm and swinging him around and into the mansion.

"That boy's been associating with whites so long he's practically white himself," he heard the *Defender* murmur behind him.

"Get to be a great man when you get to Congress," *Ebony* agreed. "Apt to forget where you came from."

"Now, what did you want to do that for?" LeGage demanded in a fierce whisper, yanking his arm free and pulling Cullee aside once they got inside the door. "Why do you have to make your own people mad at you? They can do you a lot of damage if you keep on acting uppity. And they will, too."

"Ah, I get so sick of them," Cullee said with an equal fierceness. "Integration, integration, integration, as though that were the answer to everything. We've got a hell of a long way to go and a hell of a lot more to do, boy, and don't tell me we haven't. Maybe we better stop being so worried over what we demand and ask ourselves whether we deserve it when we get it."

"You get awful sick about a lot of things, seems to me," 'Gage told him softly as Felix and Patsy Labaiya began to converge upon them from different corners of the room. His eyes suddenly flashed with anger and a drained, tense expression that Cullee hadn't seen for a long time came over his face.

"You say Terry's a white man's nigger," he whispered. "How about the Congressman who has ten times more whites than Negroes in his district? Maybe he's become a white man's nigger too, because he has to be to get elected. Now you listen to me, white pet. The time's coming and soon when you're going to be for us or against us. You remember that, Cullee. You just remember it."

The Congressman gave him a contemptuous stare as Patsy advanced burbling, with hand outstretched, and Felix came smoothly forward.

"I'll remember it," he said "Don't *you* get too big for your britches, either,

And, 'Gage. Do me a favor and just leave me alone, will you? I think that would be best."

For a second before the Labaiyas were upon them and talk was no longer possible, hurt, protest, anger, and an agonized mixture of dislike and regret passed across LeGage's face. Then without a word he flung away, past the Labaiyas, whom he was apparently too blinded by emotion to see, and on into the crowded living room, where a noisy throng was gathered worshipfully around the M'Bulu, holding court.

"Nobody quarrels with the intensity of old friends," Felix said with a bland smile that apparently dismissed it. "Cullee, we are happy to have you with us."

After five minutes of innocuous chitchat, however, Cullee noticed, the Ambassador glided quietly away and was presently to be seen off in a corner engaged in earnest conversation with the still-agitated chairman of DEFY.

What this meant, the Congressman did not have much time to speculate, for very shortly gongs began to toll through the halls of "Harmony," and presently the guests of the Jason Foundation were crowding in to take their places at the two enormous tables that had been prepared for them. The doors giving onto the central hall had been flung open in both living room and banquet room so that the two had in effect been connected into one huge dining area. At one end in a seat of honor Terrible Terry, flanked by LeGage and Robert A. Leffingwell, took his place amid much loud applause and eager cries of greeting; opposite him at the other end the Governor of California gracefully acknowledged a similar ovation as he took his seat, flanked by his sister and brother-in-law. Television cameras around the walls peered up and down the tables to catch this distinguished guest with a piece of shrimp halfway into an open mouth, that distinguished guest mopping surreptitiously at a spot of spilled soup on the tablecloth before him. Those distinguished members of the press who were guests could be seen here and there down the table, eating busily with the rest; those other newsmen who were actually working stood against the walls among the cameras jotting notes on the appearance and behavior of the notables thus glamorously displayed before them. In hushed voices the network commentators identified the major guests for the audiences that would see them that evening in taped reports on half a dozen national news shows.

There came presently the time of surfeit and speeches, and with a flourish the director of the Jason Foundation presented the Governor of California. Ted Jason rose and everyone agreed he had never looked so handsome and distinguished as he did making a graceful little speech of welcome to introduce the honored guest.

It was a shame, he pointed out, that under the laws of South Carolina Negroes and whites could not associate at a public gathering, and therefore it had been impossible to hire a suitable hall for their distinguished guest this day. By the same token, however, it was fortunate for the Jason Foundation that this was so, for it had given the Foundation and, he might add, himself and his family, a chance to do particular honor to this great fighter for Negro freedom who had come to them from Africa. (Loud applause.)

It was a shame also that the Government of the United States had seen fit to treat in so cavalier a fashion so fine and worthy a visitor to these shores. (Hisses and boos.) But here, too, the President's failure was his, and his family's good fortune, because it permitted them to extend on behalf of the people of the United States—who, he knew, did not agree with their President on this particular matter—a fond and cordial welcome to break bread with many of the greatest leaders of American thought. (Further warm applause.)

It was also especially pleasing this day to have with them the great young Negro Congressman from California and the dynamic, fighting young chairman of DEFY, both of whom had done so much in the unceasing struggle to bring true liberty and justice to this great land of ours. (Renewed applause, shouts and whistles.)

He was pleased to say that as a Californian, and as Governor of California, he was particularly proud of Cullee Hamilton, who fully lived up to the finest traditions of his race and of a state where he, the Governor, would say without undue modesty that great advances had been made under his Administration, and would continue to be made, for the great Negro race. (Wild applause, some standing.)

This gathering today, he hoped, would prove both an apology and a recompense for the slur and slap at the peoples of Africa implicit in the President's mistaken treatment of the M'Bulu. And it was particularly fitting that it should be held here in this city, which was about to become the newest battleground in the struggle of America's own Negro people to achieve full equality under law. (Significant laughter, cheers, and applause.) He hoped this word would be carried back to the residents of the city, even though their newspapers and radio stations had seen fit to boycott the luncheon. (Sarcastic amusement; cries of "Shame! Shame!") And even though their senior Senator, the *Honorable* Seabright B. Cooley, had seen fit to issue a statement in Washington denouncing the gathering as "an insult to South Carolina." If he, Ted Jason, weren't Governor of California and a proud resident of that state, he would be tempted to run for Senator right here next year and see if he couldn't remove what was *really* an insult to South Carolina. Anyway, he fully intended to help whoever should do so. (Great applause and cheers; shouts of "Sink Seab!")

And so, without further ado, he would present the guest of honor they all wanted to hear, that brilliant, dedicated, fearless fighter for the freedom of his people and all peoples, His Royal Highness the M'Bulu of Mbuele. (Wild and prolonged applause, audience standing and shouting.)

There followed one of Terrible Terry's most effective speeches, filled with an impression of intelligence, idealism, and fierce internal anger which, taken together with his towering physical presence and his gorgeous robes, made fair ladies sigh and strong men be thankful they weren't meeting him alone in a dark alley. As he railed at the United States, poured sarcasm on the

United Kingdom, and repeatedly claimed for himself the role of symbol of all Africa, the television cameras had a field day around the tables, recording the Governor of California, dignified and approving; Robert A. Leffingwell, gravely attentive; the Panamanian Ambassador, breaking his customary impassivity with sudden sharp bursts of applause; his wife, eager and ecstatic; the chairman of DEFY, his eyes gleaming and an expression of fervent approval approaching hero worship in them; and the M'Bulu himself, gigantic and magnificent in his scathing denunciation of the enemies of Africa and the Negro race, whom he professed to have found at work in the United Nations and the city of Washington. Only the Congressman from California sat quietly and without noticeable response, on his face a peculiar combination of amusement, skepticism, patient boredom, and something that some perceptive viewers might characterize as contempt. The commentators couldn't make much of his attitude, and after a couple of desultory glimpses the cameras left him and concentrated on the others.

After half an hour of this there came one more slashing attack on the United States, one more magnificent defiance of "those too blind to see the road of history that lies before them," and the speaker was done. Amid frantic applause and another standing ovation, the newspaper reporters fled to the telephones which had been thoughtfully provided in "Harmony's" library upstairs and began to file their stories. "TERRY RAPS U.S., U.K., AND U.N. 'SABOTEURS'" the New York Post reported in the streets of Megalopolis an hour later. "COLORED RULER HITS LOCAL SEGREGATION," said the Charleston News and Courier, which had decided to cover the story, after all.

And once more, as the happy throng broke up into chatting, excited groups for coffee on the lawn prior to being taken away again in Cadillacs and buses to the various transportation terminals, the Panamanian Ambassador drew the chairman of DEFY aside for five minutes' earnest conversation, in which they were presently joined, briefly but apparently for some concrete purpose, by the guest of honor.

A few moments later the Congressman from California was on the phone to the Secretary of State in Washington to report, "So far, so good, aside from words, and I guess we can stand them." The Secretary thanked him, wished him well, and invited him to lunch at the Department next day. He accepted with pleasure but had to call back ten miuntes later and cancel because the M'Bulu had informed him of a new development. The Jasons had invited him to stay over, he said, and use the house—the family had to leave right away, its members explained regretfully in the hearing of the press, but he might stay on and make use of all "Harmony's" facilities if he wished to see the historic old city and its surrounding area. "Does that invitation include me, too?" Cullee had asked Patsy Labaiya, and with only a moment's hesitation she had cried, "But of COURSE it does, Cullee! Do be our guest!" So he had changed his plans, he told Orrin Knox—or had them changed for him, rather.

"Well, old Cullee," Terry said an hour later, stretching out to his full length on one of the outsize double beds in "Harmony's" master bedroom, "imagine seeing you here in Charleston. I feel very flattered you decided to come and hear me."

"I want to do all proper honors to a famous symbol of my race," the Congressman said calmly from where he half sat, half stretched on the other bed. Terry laughed aloud.

"I know how sincerely you mean that. I know very well how sincerely you mean it, old Cullee, my friend from Congress. Where's that pretty little wife of yours?"

"She's in Washington," Cullee said evenly. "Where are yours?"

"Molobangwe," Terry said, and chuckled. "I was afraid I'd shock my strait-laced admirers in the United States if I brought them along." He stretched again, like the jungle cat he was. "I wish I had one of them here right now. I could use her."

"I'm sure," the Congressman said. "Did you think of asking Patsy Labaiya?"

The M'Bulu gave a shout of laughter, sat up, and then dropped back full-length upon the bed.

"I doubt if the notable tolerance of the Jason family would go that far. I'm sure the Governor didn't raise his sister to sleep with a Negro. Tell me about this Charleston, though. We ought to be able to find something interesting here tonight."

"Is that why you decided to stay over?"

"Oh," the M'Bulu said airily, "many reasons, many reasons, Cullee, friend. Tell me: are *you* staying to spy on me for the distinguished Secretary of State?"

"Yes," Cullee said, "I am. Are you going to give me trouble?"

Again Terry gave the shout of laughter.

"Keep close and see."

"I shall. What did you think of the luncheon?"

The M'Bulu gave him a sardonic wink.

"Why, I think it was a great success. I got publicity for my cause. Ted Jason got publicity for his cause. And all those nice, wide-eyed, twittering fools who attended as guests were able to tell each other how enlightened and progressive and full of love for humanity they are. And they also got a chance to hear a big black man tell their country to go to hell, which seems to be what they like best . . . Cullee?" He frowned. "Why do so many Americans like to hear their own country attacked? Gorotoland isn't much, as you know, but you don't catch me or any of my people failing to defend it in the face of strangers. Why are so many Americans the other way?"

The Congressman winced and shook his head.

"I don't know; I can't explain it. I never have known how to explain it. I just don't happen to be one of their kind, you might remember. This country has been good to me and I don't knock it."

"Even when it does what it does to your people?" Terry asked.

"Even when it does what it does to your people?" he said, returning to it as they started out three hours later, after a sumptuous candlelit dinner proffered by servants who tended them in impassive and expressionless silence, for a walk in the soft autumn twilight. The walk was Terry's idea, and at first he had been disposed to make it in full regalia, or at least had teased his companion into thinking he would. It was not until Cullee became really angry in his protests that the M'Bulu had admitted blandly that he had intended to change into a conservative Western business suit right along.

"But I had you worried, didn't I, old Cullee?" he asked mischievously as they left "Harmony" and started along the Battery toward East Bay Street, one of the Jason Foundation Cadillacs following at a discreet distance a block behind. "You thought I was going to start out and create an incident right tonight, didn't you?"

He uttered his charming laugh and gave Cullee's shoulders a fraternal squeeze with one long arm.

"Relax. I wouldn't do a thing like that to you, my friend. Think of the headlines it would make: 'CONGRESSMAN AND TERRY INVOLVED IN RIOT.' I couldn't do that to *you*, Cullee."

"I think I could handle it if you did," the Congressman said, "but it would be simpler if you didn't."

"You wish to refrain from disturbances and protect the country," the M'Bulu said, "even when it does what it does to your people?"

The question hung in the gentle air as they walked along. The Congressman started twice to answer, then stopped. Finally he said with a frown, "You'd never understand, so forget it."

"But I might. A former graduate student at Harvard? Surely I know something about the United States!"

"Only how to make trouble. I think you know that pretty well."

"Come," the M'Bulu said as they reached Tradd Street, taking him by the arm and waving up the Cadillac, which put on a spurt of speed and drew sleekly alongside. "Let us go and see them in their native habitat, your people and mine. I would like to walk there rather than in front of all these fine white houses. I feel more at home. Perhaps it will suggest some thoughts to us. Take us somewhere near the Old Railroad Depot," he told the chauffeur, who, like all "Harmony's" servants, received his order without visible reaction. Cullee had no choice but to clamber in, and the Cadillac rolled off.

"Now," the M'Bulu said, after he had stopped the car and they had alighted and left it, again following discreetly a block behind, "here they are, the happy American Negroes." A group of youngsters was playing ball down a side street, gossiping neighbors were talking over fences or rocking on porches; a drowsy peace rested on the colored sections of the city. Indeed, the M'Bulu and the Congressman furnished the only excitement of the moment: two such tall and stately men did not often walk with such a lordly air together down those humble streets. A little eddy of comment and discussion followed them as they moved slowly along. Terrible Terry was not disposed to let the mood of the moment rest. "What do you think of this?"

"They look happy enough to me," Cullee said. "They *are* happy, as a matter of fact."

"Right now. Oh, yes, surely, right now. As long as they don't try to stir off their porches or play in some other street. But suppose," he said dreamily, "suppose someone were to say to them suddenly"—and he half raised his voice as his companion caught his arm—" 'Come with me, my friends, and we will go have a fish fry on the Battery. Come with me to "Harmony," where they like Negroes, and we will make "Harmony's" neighbors like them too.' " His voice dropped and he shrugged off Cullee's hand. "What then, my friend? Would they be happy then?"

"Keep your voice down," the Congressman said quietly. "I don't want to have to slug you."

Terrible Terry threw back his head and gave a shout of delighted laughter that caused heads up and down the block to turn and a little wave of answering, appreciative laughter to eddy in the wake of his.

"It would be a fair match, Cullee. Six-feet—what, four?—against six-feet-seven, and I guess about equal in weight, give or take a few pounds. Yes, it would be quite a match. But again," he said with a mischievous chuckle, "that incident. 'CONGRESSMAN AND TERRY BRAWL IN STREET.' No, no, we cannot have that, my upright and self-righteous friend . . . So they are all very happy, are they?"

"No. But they can't get happier by your methods in this country."

"And what have they achieved by your methods?" the M'Bulu asked as they strolled along, avoiding a jacks game, detouring around two games of hopscotch, narrowly averting head-on collisions by fast footwork as a flying wedge of boys and girls from eight to twelve came shrieking and laughing down the street. "Well, let us see. One thing, of course, they have," he said elaborately, "is a Congressman from California. And one from Michigan. And one from New York. And one from Chicago. And also, of course, some of them do drive big cars and many of them have television sets, for all of which they will be paying their own usurers 50 per cent interest for a hundred years to come. And their brave leaders like yourself, aided by some of those desperately enlightened whites, have managed to get *Brer Rabbit* removed from some schools, and nowadays when the white folks sing about Basin Street it isn't 'where the dark and the light folks meet' any more; it's where the *people* meet. And when somebody beats his feet on the Mississippi mud, it isn't the *darkies* who do it; it's the *people* who do it. And a well-picked handful here in the South do attend a few schools now that they didn't once upon a time, and there's public transportation they can use now, and some lunch counters where they can eat . . . Oh, yes, there's been great progress, Congressman. But does a single one of *them* respect you or want you around?" he demanded with a sudden fierce challenge that made passers-by hesitate and glance at him with a quick curiosity. "Tell me that. *Tell me that!*"

"Orrin Knox likes me," Cullee said with a deliberate sarcasm, "and Ted Jason likes you. There's two."

"And both for the same reason," Terry said spitefully. "For their own political advantage. At least that old fool of a President of yours is honest. He doesn't think much of me and he won't pretend he does, no matter what the consequences." His eyes darkened and he spat out the words: "I hate this pious, pretending country!"

"I know you do," Cullee Hamilton said in a tired fashion that suddenly made him seem much older than he was, "and I think it is too bad that you have to suffer us and we have to suffer you. I happen to love this country—I was born here; at least with all its faults it's mine; and even if I didn't love it, your saying you hate it would make me do so. Now, I'd suggest we get on back. I'm tired and I'm going to read awhile and then turn in. I'm not leaving you loose in Charleston tonight. So come along, Your Royal Highness. Whistle up your Cadillac and let's us poor oppressed colored folk ride back to the Battery where we belong."

The M'Bulu looked at him appraisingly, and for a moment Cullee wasn't sure but what he would have to make good on his threat and persuade him to come by physical means. But Terry once again threw back his head and laughed, turning to wave up the Cadillac as he did so.

"You're so persuasive, Cullee, friend, and so logical. I just couldn't refuse Sue-Dan's husband anything."

"Fine," Cullee said, exercising great restraint and managing to make a joke of it, which he knew disappointed his companion; "if I can count on that, we'll get along."

"Oh, we'll get along," Terry said as they got in the car and started the short ride back to "Harmony." "No doubt of that . . ."

"Two numbers in New York for you to call," the butler said as they re-entered the stately house.

"No other calls?" Terry asked sharply.

"No," the butler said.

"I'll take them in the library."

Fifteen minutes later he rejoined Cullee, by now comfortable in pajamas and slippers and starting to read, in the bedroom.

"Well," he said with an amused air. "Imagine that. My friends in the United Kingdom have just issued a White Paper on Gorotoland. It seems we conduct human sacrifices, we eat people, we deal in slavery, and, worst of all, we're accepting help from the Communists."

"It's all true, isn't it?" Cullee asked. Terrible Terry didn't answer directly, but gave him instead a cheerful grin.

"You know very well that not one of those fools who attended the luncheon today will believe it. Nor will most of your press and television. That was the New York *Post* asking me if I considered it a pack of lies. I said I did. You see, they make it easy for you. They put the words in your mouth and all you have to do is agree."

"I think you're not much," the Congressman observed, without looking up from his book. The M'Bulu's grin increased.

"But in this country they make it so easy for you to get away with it."

And as he went whistling and humming about the room getting undressed and ready for bed, his companion reflected that, for all those unscrupulous enough to take advantage of the fact, this was unfortunately all too true. There was a sort of perverse and self-defeating innocence about America which made her easy game for the phonies, the self-serving criticizers, the sly and subtle enemies of freedom and decency in the world. The eternal baby-faced innocent, waiting wide-eyed for the pie in the face from the villains in the cheap comedy of international errors put on by the Communists and their stooges—that was his country. With a sudden fierce anguish he thought: I will help you. And instantly deflated himself with the thought: What can you do, one little colored Congressman? One little white man's pet, as LeGage put it? One little nigger, as his wife put it?

"Better call the Secretary and tell him I've been a good boy," Terry suggested cheerfully as he got into bed. "Well!" he added as the phone rang on the nightstand between them. "There he is now."

But it was not the Secretary, and he was not calling Cullee. The call again was for Terry, and when, in great glee, he told Cullee all about it a moment later the Congressman tried in great alarm and anger to persuade him to abandon what was apparently a carefully conceived plan by the M'Bulu and certain of his friends. Terry, however, would have none of it. All he would do was suggest mockingly that Cullee might like to come along.

"We need our great Negro Congressman at a time like this," he kept saying. "Your people need you, Cullee."

The Congressman, terribly disturbed, lay awake long after the M'Bulu had dropped off to sleep and started to snore heavily; for he was torn between what he knew he should do for his country and what he knew he could not do because of his race, and he was aware now that there was not longer anything at all amusing about the visit of Terrible Terry to the United States.

10

In much the same fashion as "Harmony," the Henry Middleton School had also grown old and dignified with the years, and like "Harmony" it too was experiencing strange things on this fine fall morning following the M'Bulu's luncheon. Again the soft autumnal haze lay upon the city, lending an atmosphere of somnolent peace drastically challenged by events now proceeding at the stately institution just below Broad Street.

Here, too, the television crews, the reporters, and the press photographers were gathered, indeed had begun to gather as early as 6 A.M. Here too were the gossiping knots of newsmen, the impromptu coffee lines at nearby stores, the peering eyes of television, the atmosphere of expectancy and excitement. But here there was a difference, for there was in the air around Henry Middleton School an ugly unease, a tense and explosive sense of violence that filled the bland morning air with a definite and inescapable menace.

Partly this came from the city policemen who stood about, sullen and nervous, in the streets, on the steps, and on the grounds of the school. More insistently, perhaps, it came from the steadily growing group of white women who clustered near the approaches to the grounds, talking together in hurried, raucous fashion, broken now and again by squeals of excitement and loud, nervous shrieks of laughter. Studied objectively, with an eye to their sloppy clothing, their half-combed hair, and the ostentatious vulgarity of their out-cries, it could be seen that these ladies were not the cream of Charleston society. It did not matter; nor was it necessary that gentler ladies should do the task that was being done by these cordial dames. Those who were there were white, and that was quite sufficient to make the point they wished to make to the little gathering of Negroes that stood about, silent, sullen, and equally nervous, at a corner some one hundred yards down the street.

To this little group, which carried one rather shamefaced DEFY banner and could not have numbered more than ten or twelve, the ladies of the schoolyard gave frequent and noisy greeting.

"Go on home, you God-damned niggers!" they would scream, making sure the television cameras were turned upon them. "We don't want no niggers messing with our kids!" Banners, too, waved gallantly in the breeze: "THIS IS A WHITE SCHOOL: NO NIGERS NEED APPLY" and "KEEP YOUR BLACK BASTIDS IN YOUR OWN BACK YARD."

Now as the hour neared eight-thirty the excitement increased and the tension mounted. CBS and ABC had by this time interviewed some ten of these Christian souls and were about to extend equal privilege to the Negroes, already tapped by NBC. These operations, too, had provoked a certain attention from the chorus of Graces clustered near the steps. "Why don't you northern nigger-lovers go home?" one disheveled charmer yelled, while a companion, for no pertinent reason that the cameramen could see, but which they dutifully photographed, made obscene motions with her belly. "Why don't you take these burrheads back to New York with you? We don't want 'em!"

For these kindly suggestions there did not seem, at the moment, any rational rejoinder that the newsmen and television crews could make, even though a few were provoked to mutter angry comments to one another. One such comment was overheard by a policeman, and the cameraman responsible was promptly arrested for disturbing the peace. This made for a diversionary scuffle as other cameramen sought to take pictures of the police throwing a cordon around their colleague. The outcry of the ladies grew even louder, more excited, and more obscene.

Ten minutes went by in these pursuits, and it was almost time for the school bell to ring. A sudden hush descended upon the raucous crowd as they looked down the street toward the little group of Negroes. The police hurriedly formed parallel lines along the walk that led to the entrance to the school. The Negroes seemed to gather more tightly together. A silence, infinitely tense, infinitely menacing, fell upon the street. The world of reason, the world in which decent people tried to understand and help one another, the universe where kindly folk tried to make sense of humanity's eternal contradictions, the places where Christians tried to live like Christians, even the many areas where whites and blacks existed tolerantly together, were suddenly far away. Abruptly there was no more world, no more anything but a silent street, filled with anger, blindness, hurt, and hate. Slowly the school bell began to toll and, as if commanded by some great director, there came from everyone, white and black alike, a sudden expulsion of pent-up breath.

At the doorway there appeared the figure of the school superintendent, his voice quavering and cracking with strain as he raised it against the clamor of the bell and shouted, "This school has no choice but to obey the law and we intend to do it!" So great was the tension that no one shouted back. Nor did anyone need to. The silence was more ominous than any spoken word.

For perhaps five minutes, while the bell completed its call and ceased, the silence held, the tension stretching and twisting and turning like a living thing, whipping hearts to a furious pace, straining eyes, catching breath short, making muscles ache with the frozen postures of bodies that did not know in exactly what fashion they would be called upon to perform, but knowing that in a split second's time the demand would probably come.

Perhaps five minutes—and then, quite suddenly from a side street, unexpected and stunning in its abrupt appearance, there turned into Melton Avenue and drove to the school entrance, with a slow but inexorable pace that forced the silent women to fall back before it, a long black Cadillac.

From it, while the crowd watched with the same tense silence, now heightened by bafflement and curiosity, there descended two persons. One was a little colored girl of six, wide-eyed and frightened and hanging desperately to the enormous hand that gently held her own. The other was a figure seven feet tall, dressed in gorgeous robes of gold and green, wearing a purple-tasseled cap and walking with a calm and lordly disdain straight for the center of the group of women who blocked the entrance to the school.

So astounded were the ladies that for perhaps another two minutes, while the new arrivals bore down upon them, there seemed to be no reaction at all. Only the press photographers, dancing frantically in front of the advancing figures as they sought effective angles from which to snap them, only the short, excited expletives of the television cameramen trying to picture everyone at once, only the sharply-drawn breaths of newsmen scribbling frantically on their note pads, broke the silence. Not until the stately progression of the two disparate figures, the little girl terrified to the point of tears, her stately companion looking straight ahead with a composed fierceness that struck genuine terror into his viewers, reached the gates and started in, did the tension break. Then it was the belly-manipulator who suddenly screamed in a high, frantic voice, "Don't let the black bastards in," and ran forward, hesitant but determined, to try to block the way.

At once the silence dissolved into a wild outcry of shouts and screams and catcalls as a handful of her sisters surged forward behind her. Seven strong, they stood shouting before the M'Bulu, and for just a moment, while the little girl started to cry and hid behind his robes, he surveyed them with a withering distaste. Then he bent down and with one gentle, scooping movement lifted the little girl to his arms. And then he resumed his progress, step by step with a blind fury on his face that, even more than his physical presence, made them fall back before him. The last to give way was the belly-shaker herself, still screaming obscenities, but now with a high, terrified note of mounting frenzy and fear in her voice. Contemptuously the M'Bulu trod on her foot and she gave a sudden yelp of pain and hobbled away to the side. The police surged forward, but they too hesitated before the giant figure, awesome in its controlled fury. The pause was long enough for the M'Bulu and his tiny terrified burden to pass within the gates and begin to mount, step by step while the photographers scrambled frantically to record each foot of progress, up the stairs to the waiting superintendent.

At the top, the M'Bulu paused beside the superintendent, who looked terrified himself, and, turning with the little girl in his arms, looked back upon the once-more silent crowd. It made a magnificent picture (the AP photographer who took it would subsequently win first prize in the annual White House News Photographers' Contest), and he held it for a long moment. Then he turned, gave the little girl a gentle kiss, gently put her down, gently disengaged her hand from his and transferred it to the shaking hand of the superintendent, and, turning once more, resumed his stately progress back down the steps toward the waiting limousine.

As he passed out the gates the fury of the ladies broke again through their fear, and although this time they kept a careful distance, they did offer him tokens of their esteem. From all sides eggs, rotten tomatoes, bricks, sticks, and rocks, thrown in wild excitement and without very good aim, began to rain upon him. Only one of the more solid objects struck home, a small stone that landed solidly on his right temple. He stopped as blood spurted suddenly down his face and raised a hand to it with an expression of surprise, faithfully recorded by the jostling photographers. Then he moved slowly on while the barrage resumed. By the time he reached the car, his gorgeous robes were stained and draggled from head to foot with broken eggs and splattered tomatoes; and these too he displayed for the photographers as he turned once more and looked at the screaming crowd with an utter contempt before slowly entering the car.

Then he was driven away, while behind him the last shreds of the soft peace of morning vanished altogether as the gentle ladies of the schoolyard, bitter with a wild frustrated fury, yelled and spat and caterwauled.

So acted His Royal Highness Terence Wolowo Ajkaje the M'Bulu of Mbuele, heir to Gorotoland, son of Africa, between 8:35 and 8:49 of a fine fall morning in the city of Charleston, South Carolina. The consequences were immediate and, as he and his friends had known they would be, worldwide.

By 9:30 A.M. extras were on the streets of New York, radio and television commentators were busily relaying the news, and across the nation and the world in a mounting babel of voices in a thousand tongues and dialects the word was being carried to the farthest corners of the globe.

By 10 A.M. business at the United Nations had virtually come to a standstill as delegates gathered in buzzing groups in the corridors, in the lounges, in conference rooms, in every available corner and cranny of the vast glass building, to exchange excited comments. The British Ambassador was observed to be, for once, openly concerned. The Soviet Ambassador and the Ambassador of Panama were observed to smile, not blatantly, but with a solid satisfaction. Senator Fry of the American delegation was seen to look tired and worried, Senator Smith to lose his customary affability. LeGage Shelby was not to be seen, though many from Asia and Africa wished to seek him out.

By 10:37 Edward Jason, Governor of California, had issued a statement in Washington, where he was visiting his sister, expressing on behalf of himself and his family "the greatest sorrow, dismay, and condemnation for this lawless episode in our adopted state of South Carolina."

By 10:38 the switchboard of the New York *Times* was besieged by excited callers wishing to add their names to next week's "FAIR PLAY FOR GORO-TOLAND" advertisement.

By 10:46 A.M. (4:46 Greenwich) a question was being asked by the Opposition in Parliament, and two minutes later the Prime Minister was launched upon one of his gracefully obfuscatory replies which managed to chide the M'Bulu, uphold the M'Bulu, chide the United States, uphold the United States, comfort the white race and encourage the black, and all in the most charming, amicable, pragmatic, and fatherly language.

By 11 A.M. the State Department had gathered itself together sufficiently to issue a statement on behalf of the Secretary expressing deepest regret, and hard on its heels at 11:15 the White House issued one from the President conveying his personal apologies to the M'Bulu and announcing that he was canceling his vacation stay in Michigan in order to return to the capital at once and both confer with, and entertain, the nation's distinguished visitor. ("I think we've got things in fairly good shape," Orrin Knox had begun when the call came through from the Upper Peninsula. "Dolly's going to give a dinner party for him—" "Dolly, hell!" the President snapped back with a rare profanity. "I'm going to come back and entertain the little bastard myself. He's got his White House party.") In his statement the President also expressed the hope, in language fair but firm, that South Carolina would see fit speedily to comply with the rulings of the courts.

By 11:45 the President had been hanged in effigy at Henry Middleton School.

By 12 noon Eastern Time, or 2 A.M. Japanese Time, the first of what the Secretary of State was later to label in his own mind as "Anti-American Riots, M'Bulu Series" was under way in Tokyo, where several hundred well-paid youths were serpentining angrily in front of the American Embassy and threatening to knock down its gates.

By 12:30 P.M. similar demonstrations were under way in Moscow, Jakarta, Cairo, Stanleyville, Mombasa, Lagos, and Accra.

By 1:15 they had also begun in Casablanca, Rome, Paris, London, Caracas, Havana, Port-au-Prince, Rio, and Panama City.

By 1:22, having disposed of routine business, both houses of the Congress of the United States were engaged in angry debate, with the senior Senator from South Carolina making a furious denunciation of the M'Bulu in the upper chamber and his colleague, Representative J. B. Swarthman of South Carolina, chairman of the House Foreign Affairs Committee, doing likewise in the House. Both were being constantly heckled by Senators from North and West, in the one case, and Congressmen from Chicago, Detroit, and New York, in the other.

By 1:35 three famous television programs had announced that the M'Bulu had accepted their invitations to appear, and in New York both the Overseas Press Club and the United Nations Correspondents Association were able to announce the same.

By 2:36 *Life* magazine disclosed that it had signed an exclusive contract with the M'Bulu for a first-person account of his experiences in South Carolina.

At 3 P.M. the British Embassy in Washington announced that the M'Bulu would arrive shortly at National Airport and would be entertained at a reception tomorrow night prior to the White House dinner.

At 3:31 P.M. the plane carrying the M'Bulu touched down at National Airport, and to the waiting reporters he gave only a graceful greeting and the news that instead of spending the night at the Embassy, as the Ambassador had invited him to do, he would instead stay with his old and dear friend the Congressman from California, here at his side. To the insistent demands of the reporters the old and dear friend refused comment. He did manage to keep a calm outward aspect and a pleasant if firm attitude, but as they finally gave up and started to turn away he seemed to let down and for a moment looked terribly unhappy, as though he were being harried and haunted by many things. Fortunately none of the press perceived this. Only Terry perceived it, with an ironic smile. "Cheer up, old Cullee," he said. "Everything's going our way."

In newspapers all over the world the news of the M'Bulu's courageous gesture and its worldwide repercussions rated banner headlines. The news about the British White Paper on Gorotoland merited only passing mention in many papers and none at all in some. It was freely predicted everywhere that the Panamanian resolution on immediate freedom for Gorotoland would now be passed at once by the United Nations.

11

And so it always was, the M'Bulu told himself, at each stage of his forward progress when he acted truly and forcefully as his instincts and his destiny told him he should: his brothers died, the way to the throne opened for him, the citadels of white society fell, the U.K. retreated before the claims of Gorotoland, the UN rallied to his cause, and the proud Americans were humbled in their own front yard. The gods had answered on that wild night in the storm when his mother had cried out, and they were with him still. Who else could have been so noble? Who else could have been so brave?

"No one," he said fiercely aloud. "No one." Beside him in the British Embassy limousine bringing them from the house off Sixteenth Street to the reception in the stately Embassy on Massachusetts Avenue his hostess stirred and turned to look at him in some surprise.

"No one what, Terry?" Sue-Dan said.

"No one can do what I can," the M'Bulu replied, with so crystalline a certainty that her initial impulse to be sarcastic died halfway. "They all go down before me, don't they, Cullee, friend?"

The Congressman, staring out the window, deep in his own thoughts, at first did not reply. Then he gave his guest a sidelong glance in which tiredness, distaste, disapproval, and a lingering trace of reluctant envy fought with one another.

"You're a great man, all right, Terry," he said finally. "There's no doubt about it now. You're the greatest thing that ever hit these United States."

The M'Bulu gave his merry laugh and his graceful palms-out shrug.

"Anyone could have done what I did. Anyone who loved his own people. And was brave enough."

"Cullee's smart," his wife said with a sudden sharp sarcasm. "He thinks that's better than being brave."

"I invited him to go with me," Terry said with a wistful regret. "I gave him every chance. He preferred to be—objective."

"I don't know what I married," Sue-Dan said viciously, and was pleased to see her husband's hands knot furiously in his lap. "I swear I don't."

"You're not the only one who wonders that," he said, and deliberately turned his back to stare again out the window. He felt her fingers claw into his arm with ferocious strength.

"Don't you turn your back on me, Cullee Hamilton!" she said shrilly, and up front the British chauffeur, completely expressionless, pressed a button. A glass wall slid neatly up into place to close him off from their discussion. "Don't you treat me like dirt. You're the dirt! Where were you when your own people needed you? You let Terry do it! You let a foreigner do it! Someone had to come from Africa and do the job you should have done! And you call yourself a Negro!"

"I thought you called it nigger, Sue-Dan," he said evenly. "Now, I'm not going to argue with you—"

"How can you?" she demanded, still in the same shrill way. "How can you, when I've got a jellyfish for a husband? Terry's the only man in this car!"

"Well, now," the M'Bulu said soothingly, "I'm sure I didn't mean to start a family argument—"

"You stay out of this!" she snapped, so sharply that he gave a startled laugh and sank back against the seat.

"You can have her, Cullee! She's too much for me. I've got half a dozen at home, but this little girl's got more spirit than all of them together. Mercy!" he said with a delicate precision incongruous with his bulk. "Has this little girl got spirit!"

"It's a good thing I have," Sue-Dan said scornfully, "because Cullee hasn't. Won't help his own people. Won't run for Senator. Won't anything."

"I swear to God," the Congressman said, "someday I'm going to—"

"Going to, nothing! You couldn't. It might upset the white folks, and then you wouldn't be elected any more. You'd have to go back to being a ditch-digger or whatever job the white folks'd let you have. Or maybe," she added with a shrewish instinct for hurtfulness, " 'Gage would let you sweep up his office."

"That LeGage," the M'Bulu said dreamily. "There's a great leader of his people who knows how to lead. I like LeGage."

"I suppose he put you up to this," Cullee said.

"We discussed it," Terry admitted, "but it really was my idea. DEFY is going to help, now I've done it, but I thought of it. After all, it was so obvious. It ties in so well with so many things. I'm just surprised no one ever thought of it before. Kwame could have done it. Sekou had the chance. It would have been a natural for poor Patrice. But no one thought of it but me. No one!" An expression of fierce pride came to his face. "No one but Terry!"

"It was a great and noble action," the Congressman said, spitting out the words with a genuine distaste. The M'Bulu shrugged and, in one of his abrupt transitions, gave his sunny smile.

"So your press is telling the world. And so the world believes. Who am I to deny it?"

"At least it showed the white man," Sue-Dan said with a satisfaction that sounded quite ferocious. "At least, my poor Cullee, it showed the white man."

"That isn't all, either," Terrible Terry said happily. "Let me tell you," he said as the limousine neared the Embassy and they saw ahead a crush of traffic, cops, and arriving vehicles, "what else is going to happen."

And as they approached the stately iron-scrolled gates and the police, alerted by the standards of Gorotoland and the United Kingdom flapping together from the fenders, moved to clear the way for their arrival, he proceeded to do so with an arrogant pleasure that seemed to delight the Congressman's wife but made the Congressman's blood run cold. And again, of course, he struggled with the agonizing feeling that there was nothing—or, at any rate, very little—that he could do. He determined to do that little, however, such as it was, though he was careful to keep his face impassive and his intention secret.

"Now zip me," Lady Maudulayne said, "and tell me how I look."

"I am always delighted when you take these intimate little chores away from Southgate and let me do them," Claude Maudulayne said. "It makes for a fragrant memory of youthful domesticity, even if she does resent it. There, you're zipped. Carry on."

"And tell me how I look, I said."

"Ravishing," the British Ambassador replied. "How else?"

"I want to," Kitty said. "For all our relatives of palm and pine, black, white, yellow, green, blue, red—"

"Wrong color," Lord Maudulayne said cheerfully. "Anything else, but not red. Is Tashikov coming?"

"Oh, yes. Madame called, personally, and we exchanged heavy pleasantries. I try not to let my mind work too fast for those people, but sometimes I can't help it."

"Well," her husband said, "you let it work as fast as you like on your level, because I can assure you theirs are going like lightning on *their* level. I rather thought he'd come, since he didn't get asked to the White House."

"I must say I do admire the President," Kitty said, adjusting two enormous jade earrings and giving her face a final pat with an enormous powder puff. "He does have spunk, you know?"

"The old boy puts his foot in it sometimes, but most of the time he does very well, in my estimation. He's still feeling his way, in many respects."

"Do you suppose it was just because he insulted Terry that Terry went to South Carolina and did what he did?"

Claude Maudulayne shrugged.

"Who knows why Terry does anything? Except that his motives are never as noble as one would gather if one believed all one heard and read about him at this particular moment."

"But it was rather brave, you know. You must admit that. He might have been killed."

"Cowards don't often kill, and most of these mobs seem to be composed of cowards. Still, he was taking a chance, I'll grant you. It's certainly got the wind up all the Africans and Asians at the UN."

"Which takes some of the pressure off us," his wife said with some satisfaction; and then added with a characteristic fairness, "How heartless politics is, really, particularly international politics. Somebody's misfortune is always somebody's good news, isn't it?"

"Yes, I must admit that I look forward with some interest to Orrin's expression when they get here. I told him in New York that this clever young man meant trouble for both of us, and I think he was inclined to think it was just typical British worry about the colonials, don't you know. I'm afraid they take a somewhat patronizing attitude toward our little problems at times. Which," he added with a wry honesty, "we reciprocate in full."

"I don't really see how this can affect them directly, though, do you? After all, the resolution is still directed against us, and this hasn't helped it any."

"No," Lord Maudulayne said ruefully, "from our standpoint, it has not. But they may get hurt by the backlash. Anything like this does them fearful damage all over the world. And this is such a particularly vicious way to turn the screw. I'm surprised none of our black friends thought of it before."

"You have to hand it to our honored guest," Lady Maudulayne said as she gave him a silver pump and extended her right foot, balancing herself with a finger on his shoulder. "He has a certain ingenuity about him."

"Oh, in his own twisted way, he's a genius," Lord Maudulayne said, putting on the shoe and reaching for the other. "His school record indicates that. But I wonder a little, on this. It's such a pat weapon that can be used so many ways. I wonder if he had help."

"Tashikov?"

"Felix."

"It's the same thing, isn't it?"

"I wouldn't want to say that about a distinguished colleague. Anyway, I'm not sure."

"Who's ever sure, until they turn up in Moscow being interviewed for television?"

"That's the last place Patsy Jason's husband will ever turn up, of that you can be sure . . . No, I think we're off base, and we mustn't ever say it. It's only a hunch."

"I have learned over the years, my dear," Lady Maudulayne said, "that when you and I arrive independently at the same hunch, it is more often than not the right one."

Lord Maudulayne smiled.

"How true. But we must just bury this thought, I think, and not even bring it to the surface of our minds, where it might show to some perceptive eye."

"But we mustn't throw it away altogether," Kitty said. "Please, let's not throw it away altogether."

Her husband grinned.

"How could we? . . . When do we fade gracefully away to the White House like Arabs in the night and leave our guests to drink themselves into a stupor on Her Majesty's liquor?"

"I think we'll stick it to seven. I really think most of them will be gone by then. I'm closing the bar at six-thirty."

"Very forethoughted."

"Thank you. Now, once more," she said, pausing at the door to turn gracefully and face him. "How do I look?"

"No lovelier than when I saw you that first day at Crale," her husband said gravely. She blushed with pleasure.

"What would I have ever done without you?" she asked softly.

"Fortunately," the British Ambassador said, "that is a question whose answer the Lord did not require either of us to find out."

In the public rooms, beneath the portraits of Sovereign current, Sovereigns past, assorted Hanovers, Windsors, Tudors, and Stuarts, they greeted their guest with suitable ceremony as he entered with his host and hostess of the night. The M'Bulu, gorgeous in fresh robes, bowed graciously to Kitty, shook hands with a pleased smile with the Ambassador, and took his position in the receiving line with a graceful dignity. The Hamiltons, seeming a little tense to the Maudulaynes, chatted briefly and then went on in to refreshments. The crush followed fast upon them and steadily increased for an hour as the Ambassador and his lady and the heir to Gorotoland fell automatically into the accustomed routine of "So nice to see you, Miss Mumble—*Mrs*. Mumble, sorry—Lady Maudulayne, Mrs. Mumble—So nice to see you, Mr. Mumble—Sorry, Mr. Murmur—Mr. Murmur, Your Royal Highness." In time this slacked off, the last dazzling smile had been exchanged, the last bone-crushing handshake endured, the last vigorously vague politeness expressed with suitable cordiality. The line was over and "The guests, thank God, are on their own," as the Ambassador remarked.

"You can't help being friends after going through an experience like that together," Lady Maudulayne said. "Why don't you come into the study for a moment and have a private drink, Your Highness? Then we can Circulate. I trust you hear my capital C."

"I do," Terrible Terry said with a friendly laugh. "Indeed I do. But you must call me Terry. Everyone does."

"I'm flattered," Kitty said, slipping her arm through his. "Heavens! How far up there are you?"

"Far enough," the M'Bulu said. "Possibly," he added with a teasing little smile as they entered the study and closed the door behind them, "His Lordship thinks I am too far up, right now."

"Not at all, old chap," the Ambassador said briskly. "You got there by your own efforts. Who am I to cavil? After all, one doesn't criticize Mount Everest for being where it is. Why criticize the M'Bulu for being where he is? I assume you're taking Scotch."

"As a good Britisher," Terry said with a smile, "how could I take anything else? I do like ice, though. Americanized to that extent."

"Quite Americanized, I'd say," Kitty told him. "Goodness, how exciting it all is! I think you were fearfully brave."

"I felt it was the least I could do," the M'Bulu said modestly.

"It was so clever of you to think of it. I don't see how ever you did."

"Oh, it was my idea," Terry said quickly. "It was my idea, right enough."

"Did you think I was implying it wasn't?" Kitty asked with a merry laugh. "Goodness, I'm not that stupid. I hope I know shrewdness when I see it, by this time."

"If so," Terry said with a little bow, "it must be because like recognizes like."

"Now I know why you were such a smash in London," she said. "Not only clever, but flattering as well. The only reason I mentioned it," she added, looking him straight in the eye with a candid smile, "is because there has been some talk going 'round that Felix Labaiya put you up to it."

"Now, why," the M'Bulu demanded slowly, a trifle too slowly she felt, "would Felix Labaiya want to do a thing like that?"

"I don't know. But you know how rumors start in this town."

"Felix had nothing to do with it," he said firmly. "It was quite my own idea." A dark scowl banished his customary smile for a second. "I think these are the great hypocrites, here. I think it is time someone showed them up."

"And how neatly it all fits in with your resolution at the UN," Lord Maudulayne said politely. "It couldn't have been better if someone had planned it that way."

"I planned it that way," Terry said, again with the dark scowl. Then his expression changed to one of growing amusement. "That Felix, though, I will tell you. He is an imaginative fellow, that one. I think it will be some time before the world discovers all the surprises of which he is capable." And, as though overcome by some vast secret joke, he threw back his head and gave his shout of delighted laughter.

"He came up with one surprise sufficient for us in your Gorotoland resolution," Lord Maudulayne remarked. The M'Bulu shrugged.

"It was inevitable."

"And now you are sure it will pass," Kitty said. He shrugged again.

"With the vote in First Committee, and now this? Inevitable."

"You are very sure of yourself, too. Another reason for popularity, I suppose."

"Oh, well," he said, and he said it with a deliberately patronizing tone that he hoped would get through the armor of these two self-possessed and charming people before him, "why should you worry if you lose us? You have so much real estate."

But they disappointed him, for Kitty laughed and the Ambassador chuckled.

"How simple and wonderful life is when you look at it simply and wonderfully," Kitty observed. "And now I think we really must go and circulate. Everyone will be wondering and waiting. It is always fatal in Washington to let people wonder and wait. Their imaginations are prompted to supply so many explanations that don't exist. Will you escort me, please?"

"Gladly," Terry said. "I have enjoyed our talk."

"We, too," Lord Maudulayne said. "We must do it again one of these days."

"When I return as head of independent Gorotoland."

"A year from now, then," his host said cheerfully.

"Oh, much sooner," Terry said. Kitty laughed and linked her arm through his.

"So determined, too," she said. "Heads up, backs straight, eyes forward, and here we go!"

And with a style that was recognizable wherever one came upon it around the world, the Ambassador and his lady went forth to meet their guests as pleasant and imperturbable as the day was long. For just a moment, struck and a little awed by their self-control, and remembering the misty isle of his education and adolescence, their guest had a sudden poignant vision of a thousand gallant banners going by, passing into history, never to return. But only for a moment: because for him, as for all the other M'Bulus of this world, black, brown, yellow, and white, it was really a matter of the greatest inconsequence whether the homeland of his hosts was successful or unsuccessful, hurt or not hurt, whether it retreated graciously or scrambled home in awkward disarray, whether history treated it fairly or unfairly. He couldn't really, Terrible Terry told himself as he dismissed his memories and strode forward to Circulate with a capital C, care less.

And there they came, the Secretary of State thought as the oaken doors swung open and the colorful trio advanced upon them, Mother Britain and her little changeling child—except that it was not quite certain, given the M'Bulu's pleased expression and the tiniest line of tension around Kitty's lips, who was shepherding whom. It was a tough problem for them, he thought sympathetically, forgetting for a second that it was a tough problem for his own country as well. As if to prevent any such illusory lapses, the Indian Ambassador approached and reminded him.

"Mr. Secretary," he said with a polite hiss, "and everyone's beloved, Mrs. Knox. How delightful to see you here at this delightful reception for our young friend."

"It's nice to see you too, Mr. Ambassador," Beth said. "We were hoping you would be able to come down from the UN for the festivities."

"I was able to get away," Krishna Khaleel said importantly, "but only just. We had a meeting of the Asian-African states this afternoon, you know, concerning the—the unfortunate episode in South Carolina yesterday, and it lasted for some time."

"Oh?" Orrin said. "And how does that concern the Afro-Asian states?"

"The Asian-African states are concerned by everything that touches upon the question of color. It is one of the major things that divide the world, of course. Sometimes it makes for a shade of difference in the way various states approach various matters. *Our* shade," he said, and laughed merrily. "What a pun!"

"You slay me as always, K.K.," the Secretary told him. "And what was the final purport of your conference?"

The Indian Ambassador looked grave.

"We were very disturbed, of course. It was even proposed by some of our hotheads, like Mali and Ghana, that we should adopt an informal resolution condemning you. But the wiser heads prevailed."

"I know yours was one of them," Beth said with a comfortable assurance that brought a flattered smile from the Indian Ambassador. "You lend such stability to the proceedings up there."

"I will admit," Krishna Khaleel said, "that it was basically my suggestion that was adopted. This was: to let it pass, in view of the quick amends, as it were, being made by the President, and by you, Orrin. I said you were obviously embarrassed by what had happened, and that, given sufficient goodwill and tolerance on all sides, everything could be straightened out to the satisfaction of all those who, appreciating honest efforts to correct wrong, as it were, would be willing to give the benefit of the doubt, as it were, to those who made the efforts. And, of course, applaud the corrections once made, as it were."

"I appreciate that, as it were," Orrin Knox said. "Of course, really, I don't see where anybody at the UN has any right to be concerned about it at all. It seems to me it's a matter between us and Terry."

"Oh, at the UN we concern ourselves about *everything!*" K.K. said with a laugh. "You know that, Orrin."

"I do indeed. Well, thank you, K.K., I appreciate it very much. I hope he's happy with what we're doing for him, even if it does make us look slightly ridiculous now, after Harley's initial adamant stand at his press conference."

"But that is the great charm of it, my dear friend! For many of us, it is delightful to see you slightly ridiculous. And, of course, it does you no harm, really. We admire you for having the courage to reverse an untenable position, even if under pressure, and pay proper attention to one of the world's great young leaders."

"One of the world's great young leaders shouldn't be complaining now," the Secretary said. "I had him and the Foreign Relations Committee of the Senate and the Foreign Affairs Committee of the House to lunch at the Department this noon. And now this. And then the White House dinner. Almost everybody came to the luncheon, including Congressman Jawbone Swarthman of South Carolina, and I'm glad he did, because that kept everything extremely polite and absolutely noncontroversial. But I think it flattered Terry's ego, which I suspect is monumental."

"Monumental," Krishna Khaleel agreed. "But perhaps necessary to rise to power in Africa. Things are so chaotic there."

"What will you do when he becomes independent and drives all the Indians out of Gorotoland, K.K.?" the Secretary asked with some relish. "Give him a state dinner in New Delhi?"

"I should hope," the Indian Ambassador said stiffly, "that he would not desire to pursue so unfriendly a course. If he does, then"—he shook his head—"who knows? I would hope we should be able to understand his motivations."

"I'm sure that will make everything all right with your people. As long as they understand his motivations. And of course you can probably always get a loan from us to help you resettle them in India."

"We will simply continue to hope," Krishna Khaleel said firmly, "that he does no such things. Excuse me, now; there is the Ambassador of Panama and I must say hello to him. I shall see you at the White House later, and then at the UN next week, Orrin?"

"I think I'll stay down here for a few days, unless there's something quite urgent to be attended to up there."

"Oh," the Indian Ambassador said, and a veiled expression came and went swiftly in his eyes. "Oh, I see."

"You did say there would be nothing from the Asian-African bloc, didn't you, Mr. Ambassador?" Beth asked. K.K. nodded.

"I did say that. And now excuse me. The Ambassador of Panama, as I said." And with a smile and a bow he was off across the room to a little group that included Felix and Patsy Labaiya, Bob Leffingwell, LeGage Shelby, and a couple of attachés from the Embassy of Sierra Leone.

"You know what I think?" Beth said, and her husband nodded.

"You think K.K. was telling me that Felix is cooking up something and I'd better get back up there. But what can Felix possibly cook up? He's busy with his Gorotoland resolution, and this thing will blow over shortly. Anyway, Hal's there, and there's nothing the UN can do. They have no jurisdiction."

"Does that matter? I think something else, too. I think we'd better follow K.K. right over."

"I'd rather talk to Claude and Kitty," the Secretary said, "but I expect you're right . . . Well, Felix," he said as they arrived on the other side of the room and the group, a little self-consciously and awkwardly, opened out to include them, "I hear you're cooking up a little surprise for us." He was rewarded by a startled glance from the Panamanian Ambassador, but it was instantly obliterated by his usual smooth and self-contained smile.

"Washington!" he said. "How the town talks! I can't possibly imagine what it could be."

"Neither can I," Orrin said with a cheerful smile, "so I thought I'd ask." He looked candidly about the group, K.K., Patsy, Bob Leffingwell, LeGage, each presenting his own version of innocence. "Nothing?" he asked, looking from eye to eye as they all shook their heads with expressions of puzzled amusement. "Well, this new job must be making me both suspicious and gullible. I could have sworn there was something to it. But since you all reassure me, I'll put my suspicions to bed. Bob, how have you been?"

"Very well, thank you, Orrin," Bob Leffingwell said with just the right degree of noncommittal courtesy. Their meetings had been few since the Senate battle over his appointment as Secretary of State, and he and the man who had beaten him had not gone out of their way to make contact. Many eyes in the room were upon them, and there was no point in more than the most casual cordiality. But Orrin could not resist a dig at Patsy, who looked slightly nonplussed, for once.

"Have you signed him up to manage Ted's campaign yet? I hear that's in the wind, too."

"Why," she began hurriedly, "I don't know what—" and then in midsentence decided to change course. "Why, yes," she said with a candid smile, "we'd certainly love to have him if he'd come, but you know HOW HE IS. There are times when he's ABSOLUTELY IMPOSSIBLE."

"Yes, I know," the Secretary said, and was pleased to note that this prompt agreement with its overtones of past controversy flustered her too, though Bob Leffingwell didn't turn a hair. "Where is Ted? Did he go right back to California?"

"He's flying out at seven-thirty," Patsy said, and added with a satisfaction of her own, "He has a special appointment with the President at six-thirty, you know. The President asked him to stop by and discuss matters of interest to the party before he went back."

"That's nice," Orrin said. "I'm glad he's keeping in touch with us."

"Yes," she said, "isn't it nice that the President feels he can rely upon HIM for advice in these difficult days."

He laughed.

"Patsy, you're priceless. Good luck if you decide to go with them, Bob. I intend to do everything I can to make it difficult for Ted to get the nomination, of course. Life won't be dull."

"I'm sure he intends to reciprocate," Bob Leffingwell said. "It should be a lively few months."

"I'm not worried," Orrin said with a calm he did not entirely feel, but which he knew would irritate them and which was also politically necessary. "Felix, I'll see you at the UN soon, I suppose. Your resolution comes up for a vote on—"

"Tuesday, isn't it?" the Ambassador of Panama said, looking at K.K. for confirmation. "Barring," he added with a pleasant smile, "unforeseen developments."

"Will you be coming up for it, Mr. Secretary?" LeGage asked. "I'm going back myself after the President's dinner tonight, if there's anything you want me to tell Hal Fry—"

"I don't know yet whether I'll be there or not. Nothing for Hal at the moment, but I'll let you know if anything develops. You've been busy, I see— all these pickets out front. Will you picket the White House too? That will be nice."

"It wasn't my doing," LeGage said earnestly. "That was the local office's idea."

"Someday," the Secretary said, "you will have to decide where your loyalties really lie, 'Gage. If you aren't happy with U.S. policies, maybe you'd better get off the delegation."

LeGage looked both abashed and defiant.

"Only one man can remove me," he said sullenly, "and he hasn't."

"Of course not," Patsy Labaiya said indignantly. "OF COURSE NOT. After all, isn't this a FREE COUNTRY? Whatever do you mean, Orrin, trying to intimidate a perfectly honest expression of support for the bravest man we've had visit us in YEARS. You ought to be ashamed not to be speaking out for Terry yourself. My brother did."

"Sometimes I think," the Secretary snapped, "that your brother doesn't do anything else but speak out for people. But I suppose it all makes for votes, and that's all that matters, isn't it?"

"There are times," Patsy said angrily, "when that IS all that matters. Such as next year at the polls. YOU'LL find out."

For a startled moment they all stood suspended, amazed by their own emotions, paralyzed by the abrupt personal turn of the conversation. Orrin and Patsy stared at one another blankly, K.K. looked terribly anxious and upset, LeGage appeared startled and alarmed. Felix had a secret little smile that did not quite conceal the wary speculation in his eyes as he looked at the

Secretary, Bob Leffingwell was impassive, Beth Knox concerned. Into their tense little circle came their hostess with a no-nonsense air.

"I've been watching all you indignant people for several minutes," she said cheerfully, "as has everyone else, of course, and I think it's quite time that you broke it up and got drunk, or something. The bar's going to close in ten minutes, and that's fair warning to all. Felix, come talk to me about the UN, and Patsy, go and rescue Terry from the Norwegian Ambassadress. I'm sure he doesn't want to hear any more about fishing rights in the North Sea."

"Good for you, Kitty," Beth said with a humorous relief as the moment broke and they scattered quickly and a little sheepishly in obedience to their hostess' command. "I was wondering how to rescue this bull in a china shop from his indiscretions. The way to do it, obviously, was just to be a bull in a china shop oneself. Or cow, rather. But that doesn't sound very charming, does it?" She chuckled as Kitty gave her arm an affectionate squeeze and moved off to other guests. "Come along, Mr. Secretary. You've spread enough diplomatic sweetness and light for one reception."

For a moment her husband continued to look stubborn; then he grinned suddenly.

"Alas," he said, "where is that 'New Orrin Knox' I've been reading about? Patsy sounds off and, right away, there's the old one, snarling away. How can you stand being married to such an incorrigible?"

"It's never bothered me in the least, except that now and again I still manage to be surprised at the inadvertent moments you choose to let it go." She smiled. "However, I think it's about time Patsy got told off on that subject, and who more fitting to do it?"

"That's what I thought. It'll be all over Washington by the time we reach the White House tonight, but who gives a damn?"

"Not you, obviously. And I don't think it was such a bad idea to remind Felix that you can be hard to handle if pushed too far."

"You don't like Felix very well, do you?"

"No," she said, looking across the room, where their hostess was now engaged in lively conversation with the Panamanian Ambassador. "And I don't think Kitty does, either."

Her husband grunted.

"That's good enough for me. If you two are suspicious, there must be something wrong."

"I can't get it out of my head that what happened in Charleston wasn't all coincidence. Why don't you ask Cullee? Terry's staying with him, and he might have an inkling."

He nodded.

"I will, when we get to 1600."

But later at the White House, in the most hurried of murmured conversations as the guests went into the East Room for the concert after dinner, the Congressman proved both evasive and uneasy. This was not like Cullee, and the Secretary puzzled over it for some time—until he heard from him much later that night in a call at home, in fact.

And now, Terry told himself with a mounting excitement, he was coming to the climax of his visit to the great United States. He had shown them up in the eyes of all the world, and here they were honoring him with a state dinner at the White House, just as he had demanded. Their bumbling President had insulted him, and he had taken his vengeance in a way from which they would not soon recover in the minds and hearts of all the earth's colored peoples. Now they were humbling themselves before him, the M'Bulu of Mbuele, the heir to Gorotoland, because they had no choice. Ah, you are proud, he told them fiercely inside his mind as the Embassy limousine with its standards fluttering slowed for the West Gate, carefully found its way through several hundred DEFY picketers with placards waving, and turned into the long curving drive to the White House portico: but I am prouder. And I have made you do as I said; I, Terry.

"This is such a lovely house," said Kitty beside him. "I always so enjoy coming here."

"Yes," he said, looking with an exaggerated approval at the Marines in dress uniform who lined the drive, rigid at attention at regular intervals. He gave a patronizing little laugh. "They do things well on their formal occasions. But, of course, not as well as you. No one does them as well as you."

"Thanks, old boy," Lord Maudulayne said. "It's always nice to have your commendation, no matter how minor the point. It's so rare that it's doubly appreciated. We must bring you up the Mall with the Queen behind the Horse Guards and the Household Cavalry, next time you're in London."

"You may, at that," the M'Bulu said cheerfully. "You just may, at that."

"Everything's going very well for you, isn't it," the British Ambassador said. "Good show all around. U.K. on the run, U.S. in wild confusion, UN bowing and scraping—the world's going well for Terry. Right?"

"I cannot complain about it. But should it not go well for one, when one has justice on one's side?"

"It should," Lord Maudulayne agreed with a dryness that was not lost upon his companion. "It should."

"Possibly there are varying degrees of justice," the M'Bulu said quickly. "Possibly there is more on one side than on the other."

"There's hardly time to get into a philosophic discussion of that right now, old fellow," the Ambassador said as the car rolled to a gentle halt and one of the President's military aides stepped smartly down the steps to open the door. "Even if we could possibly compose our differing points of view, which I doubt. Here we are. Enjoy your glory."

"I shall," Terrible Terry said with a rather savage smile. "You may be sure I shall."

"You know," the President said in a puzzled tone as he finished knotting his white tie in the master bedroom on the third floor, "that Ted Jason's an odd fellow. I don't know why he wanted to come and see me. I couldn't very well refuse when he asked, but it was a very peculiar conversation."

"What's that, dear?" Lucille said politely from the bathroom, and he raised his voice and repeated, "A very odd conversation!"

"Yes, it is," she said pleasantly. "You seem to be talking to yourself. I can't get the drift of it."

"Well, come out here," he said, rather more loudly than he intended, "and perhaps you will. I said it was an odd conversation I had with Ted Jason. Governor Jason. Governor—"

"I know," she said, bustling into the room as she always did, plump and pink and soft and cuddlesome. ("I *do* love Mrs. H.," one society reporter had recently cooed to another just before they proceeded to rip Mrs. H. to tatters. "She always looks like a marshmallow dipped in peppermint sauce. So *sweet*." There had been a knowing laugh and they had plunged at once into a savage dissection of the First Lady.) "I know exactly who Governor Jason is, dear, so don't shout. He has an odd family, too."

"He may be the next President of the United States, so perhaps you should be more respectful."

"I know who the next President of the United States is going to be," she said comfortably. "Here, do let me straighten that tie; you can never seem to get it quite at the right angle."

"And who's that?" he demanded, submitting patiently.

"You," she said, pushing and tugging and patting and whisking with little clucking noises of dismay and finally of approval. "I've never had the slightest doubt of it."

"Ha!" he said with a scornful snort. "You haven't?"

"No, dear. Now, do try to be nice to this funny young man who's coming—"

"I'm on record in ten dozen places," the President pointed out reasonably, "as saying I won't run. And I'll be nice to this funny young man."

"Oh, I know what you say," she agreed, handing him a pin and an enormous lavender orchid corsage, "but that doesn't make any difference. Who else could it be?"

"I can think of two, out of two hundred and fifty million," he said, obediently pinning the corsage for her. She gave a deprecating little smile and dismissed the idea.

"Neither Ted nor Orrin," she said placidly, "could possibly do it half as well as you do. And the country likes you so. Why should it want anyone else? And how could anyone else get it unless you withdrew? And you aren't going to withdraw."

"But I *have* withdrawn," he said with a helpless laugh.

"Yes, dear, but of course nobody believes you for one minute."

"Now, look," he said, "you and I have been married for forty-one years. Do I lie, or do I tell the truth?"

She looked quite shocked.

"Oh, you tell the truth. At least, you think it's the truth at the time."

"It *is* the truth!"

"Yes, dear. Now tell me how I look?"

"I am not going to run for President of the United States!"

"Fifteen months from now, on January twentieth, Harley M. Hudson of Michigan will be sworn in for his first elected term as President. I don't know why you make such a fuss about it." She dimpled suddenly and, stretching on tiptoes, kissed the end of his nose. "After all, I wouldn't feel safe with anyone else. That's why I married you."

He chuckled and relaxed.

"It was mutual. But you must learn to have more faith in the public statements of your elected officials."

"You'll see. How do I look?"

"Oh, no, I won't. *You'll* see. You look just like the girl I married. How do I look? I have to impress that young whippersnapper with the majesty of the office."

"Don't try," she advised. "You're always so much more impressive when you don't try. He'll be impressed enough."

"I don't know," he said grimly. "I think after Charleston the only thing he's impressed with is Terence Ajkaje."

"Do you think Ted Jason put him up to it?"

"Either Ted or Felix Labaiya. Ted was very smooth on the subject, of course. He gave me that statesman's glance with the silver hair gleaming and told me in several thousand well-rounded evasive words how much he regretted the episode but also, of course, how much he regretted that we were vulnerable to such a thing. And how much he regretted, too, that I had given Terry the original snub that might have made him feel so vindictive. He wasn't *saying* it had, he gave me to understand; it just *might* have."

"Don't you think he would have done it anyway?" she asked with a shrewdness the society reporters would not have given her credit for. "Don't you think he planned to do it when he went down there?"

"I don't doubt it for a minute. But of course you couldn't convince the world of that now. I'd like to know for sure who put him up to it, though. It would illuminate some things."

"It was really very brave of him, all things considered."

"Oh, it was," he agreed. "I don't deny that for a minute. Bravery springs from many causes, though—not always as noble as the world likes to think."

"Will it die down, do you think?"

"Oh, yes. All this fuss over him here ought to smooth his ruffled feathers. And Tommy Davis' injunction concerning the school itself will stand until the full Court can get to it, so that situation will move along. With more unhappiness on both sides, no doubt; but at least it will move, which is the important thing."

"Then it's up to us to give him a very pleasant evening and send him back to the UN happy."

"That's right. Maybe it will show the Africans and Asians we aren't so bad, after all."

"It's going to take a lot more than that," she said. He sighed, and nodded. "I'm afraid so."

There was a knock on the door and the naval aide put his head inside.

"His Royal Highness is here, Mr. President."

"Very well," the President said. "Take him to the Blue Room and we'll be right down."

And now they were all caught up in the stylized formality of a state dinner at the White House, as the long line of arriving limousines began to turn off Pennsylvania Avenue in steady procession, rolling at regular intervals of a minute or two under the portico to discharge their passengers. The Hamiltons were among the first arrivals; Bob and Dolly Munson followed soon after with the Secretary of State and Mrs. Knox; other Cabinet members and their wives came after; the French Ambassador and Celestine Barre and other members of the diplomatic corps, with a heavy emphasis on Africa and Asia: Krishna Khaleel, the Pakistani Ambassador and his wife, the Ambassadors and Ambassadresses of Guinea, Ghana, Sudan, Libya, Congo Brazzaville, Congo Leopoldville, the United Arab Republic, Morocco, Tanganyika, Kenya, Nigeria, Mali, Uganda, Liberia, Ethiopia, many in their colorful native costumes. Justice Davis of the Supreme Court arrived with the editorial director of the Washington *Post*; Senator Cooley, looking grumpy and as though it were much against his better judgment, in the company of his South Carolina colleague, Chairman J. B. Swarthman of the House Foreign Affairs Committee; other members of the Foreign Relations and Foreign Affairs committees. The Chief Justice and three other members of the Supreme Court, and their wives, came next; the editor of the Washington *Daily News*; several owners of the Washington *Evening Star*; assorted society editors; columnists and correspondents; several of television's most noted commentators. A State Department protocol officer, standing unobtrusively just inside the door, was pleased to find that he could place a check mark after every name on the list of expected guests. He was not surprised. The President's sudden decision to entertain the M'Bulu had blasted twenty-three scheduled dinner parties, including Dolly Munson's, which it replaced, but nobody minded. When the White House beckoned, one came if one were alive, inside the country, and outside an institution.

Thus it was that there had arrived by special messenger at noon the day before, at exactly 52 homes housing 38 couples and 14 single persons, the chaste white card, 4½ by 5½ inches, bearing top center the chaste, small Presidential seal in gold and beneath it in flowing script the information that the President and Mrs. Hudson requested the pleasure of the company of Mr. and Mrs. Mumble (or Mr. Murmur, as the case might be), at dinner on Saturday at eight o'clock. Attached to each card was a smaller white card, bearing in the same calligraphy the advisory, "White tie"; a name-pass to be surrendered at the West Gate; and a slip of paper, this also in script but obviously mimeographed, reading, "On the occasion of the visit of His Royal Highness the M'Bulu of Mbuele."

Armed with these bona fides, the guests arrived; were greeted by uniformed aides who waited in the entrance hall where the red-coated Marine

Band, nestled in a sea of potted palms, played welcoming light-opera airs; and were escorted to a small table down the hall, where each received an envelope with the name of his or her dinner partner. Then they were shown a large, detailed outline of the M-shaped table, with appropriate indications of the seats they would occupy, and were then led to the massive gold, white, and blue expanse of the East Room; deposited in a chatting, steadily-growing line; and told politely but firmly to stay put until further notice.

At eight twenty-nine, all guests having arrived, the Air Force Band, stationed in a corner of the East Room, struck up "Hail to the Chief" and the President, the First Lady, and their guest of honor, having passed the time in the Blue Room in innocuous chatter which touched on nothing any of them was thinking about, appeared at the door. "Hail to the Chief" concluded, there was a long roll on the drums, and with a flourish the band plunged into something else that brought a start of recognition and then much humor down the line. For a moment the M'Bulu looked puzzled; but the tune sounded familiar, and with a sudden start the former graduate student of Harvard realized what it was. He glanced quickly at his host and was startled to find that for just a second the President gave him the slightest of winks. With a sudden broad grin, he returned it; and so, to the strains of "When the Saints Go Marching In," played with solid relish by the band, the glittering assemblage passed through the receiving line ("Miss Mumble, Mr. President—sorry, Mrs. Mumble—Mr. Murmur, Your Royal Highness") through the Green Room, the Blue Room, the Red Room, and so to the State Dining Room, where the hungry throng fell at last upon the lavish repast.

There, seated at the table covered with gleaming damask and decorated with masses of chrysanthemums and autumn leaves, dining off the White House gold service in a setting of fabulous beauty, it was not too easy for the guests to exchange the thoughts that many of them had concerning the intriguing series of events that had brought the kindly if sometimes awkward President to this implicit and gorgeous apology to the dashing young giant who sat beside him like a piece of midnight swathed in gold and green. Yet there was evident in the glances of the Africans and Asians a subtle but deep-seated satisfaction, a lively sense of the humiliation of their host and his country which thrilled them all, no matter what their other differences and antagonisms might be. On this they were all agreed, and it gave them a certain powerful unity of attitude, made even stronger because it was not matched in the remainder of the company. Senator Cooley might feel angry and resentful (he had carefully been placed between Celestine Barre and Dolly Munson, who did their best to soothe him), and some others might also have no doubts of where they stood, but in the more complex and conscientious minds of many at that pleasant board, not including LeGage Shelby but certainly including Cullee Hamilton, there were doubts and worries, shame for what had happened in Charleston, shame for what it symbolized, angry and conflicting emotions about it, and also, in the hearts and minds of many, a desperate attempt to try to find some fair ground on which all disputing claims and all opposing prejudices could be composed and led to work together toward constructive solution. None of this, however —the smug, superior, supercilious hatred or the troubled, uncertain attempt to be fair—broke through the surface of that distinguished assemblage, whose members talked merrily of this and that as they ate their way steadily through Sea Food Marguery, Broiled *Filet Mignon,* and assorted side dishes, in an atmosphere inwardly electric with racial tensions and outwardly bland with the necessary suppression of true emotion that so often characterizes the formal occasions of Washington officialdom.

Down upon them from the marble mantel over the fireplace looked the graven words of the second President, John Adams, to his wife Abigail:

"I pray heaven to bestow the best of blessings on This House and on all that shall hereafter inhabit it. May none but wise and honest men ever rule under this roof."

In a world John Adams never knew and perhaps could not have understood, the man who ruled there now, doing his best to be wise and honest, chatted pleasantly with his difficult guest; but the blessings upon This House that night were troubled and unclear, and there was no certainty anywhere in such savage times that wisdom and honesty would be enough to protect John Adams' successor and the hopeful people who looked to him to lead them safely through the wilderness of envy and deceit in which they found themselves confused and wandering.

In an hour's time, after the last wine had been downed, the last Baked Alaska gulped away, the President rose and toasted his guest in a brief and formalized statement, graciously noncommittal. His guest responded in the same terms and the company lifted glasses to them both. Then the guests separated, the ladies to the Blue Room for coffee, liqueur, and gossip, the men to the Red Room for gossip, liqueur, and coffee. Half an hour passed in this customary ritual, and then the gathering regrouped to return to the East Room, there to sit in gold-leafed chairs and listen to forty-five minutes of piano-playing by one of the nation's mop-haired virtuosos, flown down from New York especially for the occasion.

During the somewhat informal procession to the East Room, the Secretary of State was observed to murmur hastily to the Congressman from California, who shook his head and seemed embarrassed; the junior Senator from California, Raymond Robert Smith, was observed to hover nervously around Governor Jason's sister, Patsy Labaiya, and the Ambassador of Panama; Le-Gage Shelby could be observed in happily animated conversation with the Ambassador of Guinea; Mr. Justice Davis and the senior Senator from South Carolina were observed to be pointedly not speaking to one another; and the French Ambassador was observed to stroll arm-in-arm toward the concert with the Ambassador of Ghana while his wife offered a wide-eyed and respectful audience to the evidently profound comments of the Ambassador of Cameroun.

And so presently, after the virtuoso had performed, and with a winsome smile and a toss of his rambling locks had vouchsafed one brief encore, the President once more arose and with a smile indicated to his guests that their evening at 1600 Pennsylvania was over. He murmured something to his guest of honor, who smiled and apparently agreed, and nodded to the Secretary of State, who shortly thereafter sent his wife home with the Munsons and lingered behind casually. Fifteen minutes later, so skilled and practiced were the White House staff and the military aides at this routine, the last guest had been coated, carred, and carried away. The bands departed, the cleaning crews went busily to work dismantling the table in the state dining room and waxing the East Room, the First Lady said good night and disappeared to the family quarters on the third floor, and in his study on the second the President faced his two remaining guests with a relaxed and comfortable air.

"Sit down for a moment, Your Highness," he said, doing the same in a deep leather armchair that he drew up facing the M'Bulu, while Orrin perched on a corner of the Presidential desk. "I won't keep you for a minute, but I wanted to know if you were satisfied with the evening here."

The M'Bulu smiled and spread his palms with his charming shrug.

"I cannot complain of a single thing. The company was magnificent, the food was superb, the hospitality was all that one associates with America." He could not resist a little laugh that somehow sounded more spiteful than amused. "Some parts of America, that is."

"Yes," the President said. "Well. We hope that unhappy memory will soon be banished from your mind."

"The kindness shown me in Washington will surely do much to achieve that objective," Terry agreed.

"I want you to know also," the President said, so easily and matter-of-factly that it hardly appeared he was apologizing at all, "that I am sorry they misinterpreted me at my press conference. I probably should have made a formal apology at once, but you know how it is. One assumes certain obviously understandable errors can be forgiven by men of reasonable goodwill."

"Yes," Terry said politely, his amicable expression changing a little. A silence fell, during which the Secretary was on the point of shooting out an explosive, "Well?" But he restrained himself, and after a moment the President resumed.

"We can assume, then," he said gently, "that you don't hold a grudge against the United States?"

The M'Bulu gave his merriest laugh.

"Oh, heavens! Mr. President, I could not be happier!"

"And this is the end of it, as far as you're concerned?" Orrin asked. Again there was the rollicking amusement.

"Mr. Secretary, this is the end! . . . Of course," he added, more soberly, "I do think that—well, there are some things in your country that are not perfect. I could wish they were better."

"Yes," the President said gravely. "You have helped to emphasize them to the whole world, possibly at real risk to your own life, and you have a right to criticize us for them. But we work at it, my impatient young friend. We work at it all the time, and it gets better all the time."

"Not very fast," Terry remarked.

"About as fast as a democratic society can move."

"Then perhaps a democratic society is not the answer to the world's problems," the M'Bulu said quickly.

The President nodded.

"Yes, that's the obvious comment. So narrow it overlooks a great many things having to do with the freedom and dignity of the individual—but obvious."

"Are rotten eggs and tomatoes part of freedom and dignity?" Terrible Terry inquired, and now he was not smiling at all. "Is trying to win a great victory over little children part of freedom and dignity?"

"Not dignity, no," the President said. "Surely not. But freedom, yes. Now," he went on, as the M'Bulu made as if to interrupt, "I may condemn certain practices in your country—we, for instance, abolished slavery here well over a hundred years ago, and it has been a great many years, and then only under the greatest of desperation, that one of us ate another—but that does not stop the United States from supporting independence for Gorotoland, as we expect to do this coming week at the United Nations. We believe you can correct these evils, which some might say were signs of a barbarous and savage and unworthy country, if you are given sufficient tolerance and help and the freedom to solve your problems within their own context. Would you say that was a tolerant, fair-minded attitude, or would you not?"

For a long moment they stared at one another, until the M'Bulu's eyes finally dropped and he shrugged.

"I would say it is typical of the United States."

"Is it fair?" the President persisted. His guest gave a sudden laugh and, as always when pressed, an evasive answer.

"Fair, fair! Freedom! Dignity! Such words! All I know is that I have had a delightful evening with charming hosts, and now I must go back to the Hamiltons and get my rest before returning to New York tomorrow."

"And there are no shenanigans planned for the UN?" Orrin Knox inquired. Again the M'Bulu gave a laugh, startled this time.

"She—nan—i—gans?" he repeated carefully, sounding not at all like a former graduate student at Harvard. "A wonderful word, whose meaning I can guess. No, Mr. Secretary," he said with a flourish, "I do not think any she—nan—i—gans."

"Is that a promise?" Orrin asked, and Terrible Terry looked at him with a playful blankness.

"I have nothing in mind but to go back to New York, make my speech to the Assembly, and hope for the best when the vote is taken."

For a long moment in his turn, the Secretary stared at him, and this time with a bland innocence he stared back and his eyes did not drop.

"Good," the President said comfortably. "Then we part friends. Let me see you down. Staying with the Hamiltons, you said?" For a second his eyes met Orrin's and looked away again, but not before the Secretary had responded with the slightest of nods. "Cullee's a fine Congressman, a fine

American. Orrin, wait just a minute and I'll be right back. I want to talk to you about an invitation I got from Peru today to visit down there."

But when he had seen his guest safely off in a White House limousine and returned to the comfortable study, minus his predecessor's coin collection but otherwise the same masculine leather-filled room it had been as long as he could remember it, the Secretary had nothing to report on Cullee.

"He won't tell me anything. His wife didn't even want to tell him I was calling, and then he was very guarded, possibly because she was there. Something's going on."

"You mean you didn't believe our distinguished visitor?" the President asked dryly.

The Secretary snorted. "Not a word. No more did you."

"That's right," the President said thoughtfully. "Not a one."

But that was not the way they heard it at the other end of Sixteenth Street.

"Oh, you should have seen them, the two stupid fools," said Terrible Terry, sprawled in the Hamiltons' biggest armchair. "They believed it all. No shenanigans at the UN, said the great Orrin Knox, that fool! You don't hold a grudge against the United States, said the great President. How much of an idiot can a man be! I fooled them! I *fooled* them!"

"Did you?" Cullee said. "I'm sure you should be very proud of that."

"Why shouldn't he be?" Sue-Dan demanded in a tone so sharp that Maudie, bringing in coffee on a tray, stopped short and gave her an exaggerated stare. "And stop staring at me, old woman! Bring that coffee in here, and get out!"

"You've no call to speak to Maudie like that," the Congressman said with an angry sharpness of his own.

"I'll speak to Maudie any way I—" she began, but he interrupted.

"You'll speak to Maudie like a lady. She *is* a lady, even if you're not. A fine Senator's wife you'll be!"

"Senator's wife!" she said scornfully, as Maudie set down the tray, gave her an insolent look, and flounced out. "*That's* a chicken that'll be a long time coming out of the egg. Go on, Terry; I want to hear about it even if this brave boy doesn't. His friend Mr. Knox has already been on the phone trying to spy on you."

"Oh?" said the M'Bulu, all trace of amicability suddenly gone from his face, a dangerous quietness replacing it. "How was that?"

"He called from the White House," the Congressman said with a patient calm he did not feel, "to tell me you were on your way, that's all."

"That's what *he* says," Sue-Dan observed with a sardonic little smile. "That's what you say, Cullee."

"All *right*, suppose he did want to know what was being planned. And suppose I told him. What could you do about it, big boy? Or you either, little gal?"

"Did you tell him—" Terry began, leaning forward tensely in his chair, but Cullee held up a hand.

"Oh, no," he said in a tone of tired disgust. "I didn't tell any of your precious secrets. I don't think it'll matter much to us, anyway."

"Who's us, Cullee?" his wife asked softly. "Who's 'us'?"

" 'Us' is the United States. That's the country I belong to. Who do you belong to, Sue-Dan?"

"I belong to you, Cullee," she said sarcastically. Then her tone hardened. "I also belong to the colored race. Terry and me, we belong to the colored race. We wouldn't expect you to understand that, Cullee."

"Are 'Gage's boys and girls still outside?" he asked, ignoring her thrust, though a deep rage at its unfairness welled in his heart; and, going to the window, he drew the draperies and looked out.

The street was quiet at last; the group of DEFY picketers that had been in front of the house all day with big banners proclaiming "TERRY THE COLORED HERO" and "AFRICA WILL FREE AMERICA" was gone. He let the draperies fall back.

"I guess he's called them off."

"They'll be back," she said with satisfaction. "They'll be back everywhere they're needed, until the job is done."

"I don't think Cullee cares about the job," Terry said tauntingly. "He just cares about standing in well with the white man. He doesn't want to get involved in anything messy."

"When are you going back to your own country?" the Congressman asked levelly. His guest laughed.

"Are you tired of me already, old Cullee? Well, I guess *they* are too. When I get my vote, I'll go. You can tell your friend the Secretary, if he's interested."

"Tell him yourself. You fool him so well."

"Well," the M'Bulu said, "let me put it to you this way: Who do they think they are? All they've done to the colored people all these years, and then they think if they issue a pretty invitation and put on a pretty party and the President pats you on the head and says, My boy, be nice, you'll be nice. Why, hell and damnation!" he exclaimed with his guttural British precision. "Who do they think they are? Who do they think *we* are?"

"Go to bed, Terry," Sue-Dan said, finishing her coffee, getting up, and starting for the stairs. "He doesn't care. You're talking to a stone wall when you talk to Cullee."

"Stone walls get broken down," the M'Bulu observed harshly. His host with a great effort controlled his impulse to shout back in anger.

"Yes, Terry," he said softly. "Go on to bed. You're tired and you tire me. We'll have breakfast at eight and I'll take you to the plane."

"Don't bother," the M'Bulu said with a grin. "I'll whistle to Claude Maudulayne and he'll send an Embassy car 'round."

"Good night, then," the Congressman said quietly, and after a moment's hesitation his guest arose, picked up his robes from the sofa where he had flung them when he got in from the White House, and started slowly after Sue-Dan.

"You coming, Cullee?" she asked from the top of the stairs.

"Why?"

She laughed.

"Suit yourself. Good night, Terry. Be sure you stay in your own bed."

The M'Bulu threw back his head with a shout of amusement.

"I would love not to, but I am afraid old Cullee would not permit it."

"You're right," the Congressman said with a last halfhearted attempt to be more amiable. "Hospitality doesn't extend to offering wives in this country. It's against the rules. Not that Sue-Dan," he added under his breath with a twist of agony in his heart, "wouldn't enjoy it."

He picked up a magazine and dropped aimlessly into the armchair, one leg over its arm, as Maudie came back in to get the coffee tray.

"Don't like him," she said grumpily, lowering her voice just enough so that it was inaudible beyond the living room. "Don't like her. Think I'd best go."

"Oh, Maudie," he said in genuine alarm, "don't do that. I have to have somebody around here I can talk to."

"Who he think *he* is, coming to this country and messing things up?" she demanded indignantly. "We gettin' along down that road without 'no-'count African trash showin' us what to do. We don't need African trash."

"You go to bed, too, Maudie," he said. "Maybe we'll all feel better in the morning."

"He's trouble," she said as she started for the kitchen. "He's Mr. T. for Trouble. T for Terry and Terry for Trouble." She repeated it like a litany as she went out and left him alone in the softly-lighted, luxurious room. "T for Terry and Terry for Trouble. Yes, *sir*."

And so at last, he thought, as he looked about the empty room of this house which used to hold such happiness for him and recently was holding so little, he was alone to think about things for the first time in three days. He had been presented quite an issue by this dashing visitor; this hero of the front pages, the air waves, and the television cameras; this bright, self-appointed symbol of the colored man's hopes and the UN's problems. T for Terry and Terry for Trouble: it was certainly true enough for him.

And doubly so, of course, because, in a sense that he had been vividly aware of ever since he won election to the House, he was indeed trapped between the two races. His every instinct as a Negro had cried out to accept Terry's taunting challenge to go with him to Henry Middleton School; after the limousine had driven away from "Harmony," he had stood in the bedroom with hands clenched and said to himself over and over in an agonized whisper, "I should be there. I should be there." Yet at the same time he had known with an equally agonized certainty that he could not be.

There was herein a conflict so fundamental and yet so subtle that he knew very well that it could never be understood by the great majority of his people. It was a conflict on the practical political level, and, since he was a decent and steady man who felt a great responsibility to his country and a great concern for her welfare, it was on yet another, much higher, much more racking level. The practical aspects of it were easy enough to grasp; Sue-Dan, much as she wanted to be a Senator's wife, was still capable of accusing him of being afraid to participate so dramatically in the desegregation struggle because it might antagonize his white electorate in California. And this was true. He didn't like to admit it to himself, but he had to: it was true. He was to some degree bound by the knowledge that even in California he could arouse antagonisms that would be fatal to his public career if he went ahead as fast and as blatantly in that area as LeGage, for instance, was always wanting him to do.

'Gage and Sue-Dan, he thought with a sigh; there was a pair for a man to contend with. Both wanted him to be what he was, his race's finest representative in the national government; both wanted him to advance to the Senate; and yet neither could resist constantly needling him to take actions so violent in the area of race that they would inevitably destroy his public career, topple him from the House, and make of the Senate a blasted dream.

Well: he wasn't the only man in public life who was torn many ways by many things, and he probably shouldn't let it bother him too much. And perhaps it wouldn't, were it not compounded by the other factor: an ability not given to many of his people to place their problem in perspective, to stand back and judge their needs against the over-all necessities of the United States, hard pressed and under fire everywhere, in this most disorderly and irresponsible of centuries.

Never before, he imagined, had humanity been so completely frivolous about its own survival. In a sort of gargantuan joke on everybody, the fabric of a stable world society was ripped and torn on every hand, reason and restraint were tossed to the wind, decency and truth were hurled in history's waste can, things that were declared to be things that were not, things that were not solemnly hailed as things that were. "Freedom!" they cried, and destroyed freedom in its name. "Progress!" they shouted, and scurried back as fast as they could scramble to the dark night of dictatorship and the death of the mind. And here was one little colored boy, trying to make sense of it all; one little colored boy, he thought grimly, who had been more than well-treated by his white countrymen and therefore felt himself under obligation to be responsible when he approached the matter of the beloved country they shared together.

Did this make him, then, a "white man's pet," as LeGage would have it? Because he wouldn't walk with Terry through obscene women to take a little girl to school, because he wouldn't engage in the easy slurs of the white man that were such a staple of daily conversation among so many of his people, because he tried to be objective—a desperately difficult thing to do, in this age of organized intolerance of the other fellow's point of view?

Well, maybe. But he could not honestly believe it. He had some concept of himself better and higher than that. He remembered what his mother had said, shortly before her death, when he was first elected to the House.

"You goin' there to be a servant to the country," she had said with the intensity of the dying, staring at him out of the enormous dark eyes in the wasting face. "You be a good one."

Be a good one. It was an injunction he had always done his best to follow, even now when his wife, his friend, everything, and everyone were conspiring to make it as difficult as possible.

Be a good one.

He got up with a sudden air of decision, crossed the room to the telephone, dialed a number, and said softly to the voice that answered—drowsily, for it was past midnight—"Mr. Secretary?"

From another telephone high in the Waldorf-Astoria in New York there came a muffled, questioning sound fifteen minutes later. The acting head of the United States delegation to the UN was also struggling awake.

"I'm sorry, Hal," Orrin Knox said. "I didn't want to wake you, but it seemed best. Cullee Hamilton just called to tell me what Felix has in mind. Are you awake?"

"Yes," Senator Fry said, obviously making an effort to be instantly bright and receptive and apparently achieving it. "Go right ahead. I'm listening."

Two minutes later he objected, "But we can stand that, can't we? It may be a little embarrassing, but—"

"Any other time," the Secretary agreed, "it would be embarrassing, but we could probably get it quietly killed in committee, or beaten if it had to go to a vote. But with this business of Terry to compound it, it could really do us great damage—very great damage—all over the world. Particularly in the way it's going to be offered, which ties it in with the other matter. We really may not be able to beat it, with the Afro-Asians as excited as they are . . . I just called Patsy and woke her up, which I must say I enjoyed doing because of a little argument earlier in the evening that I'll tell you about when I see you, and she said Felix was on the Pennsylvania Railroad sleeper to New York. She was a little vague, I suspect deliberately, as to where and when you could reach him tomorrow, but I'd like you to see him if you possibly can. Tell him that if he will hold off on this, I'll begin serious talks with him at once on that Panama matter he's been after. He'll know the one."

"Is it important enough to head him off on this?" Hal Fry asked in some surprise. "What is it, cession of the Canal?"

"No, but in that area. So will you see him, please?"

There was a momentary hesitation and the Secretary caught it up at once.

"What's the matter?"

"Nothing."

"Come on, now, what?"

"Well, it's just that—it's my day to go up the Hudson, you know? I haven't been able to get there in a couple of weeks, and I felt I should. Not that it makes any difference," Hal Fry said with a sadness so deep it made the

Secretary want to cry, "but I think I should. However, under the circumstances—"

"No," Orrin said, "you go. What time will you be back?"

"Oh, about three, I suppose."

"Well, all right. But do see Felix then for sure, O.K.? Because it could be quite vital. The stakes are suddenly much higher all around than they have been. I'm counting on you."

"Sure thing. When will you be coming up?"

"I guess Monday morning, now. I hadn't planned to, but there it is. The world doesn't stand still for plans, nowadays. Now go back to sleep and get some more rest. You need it."

"I took it easy today; I feel much better. And Orrin—thanks about tomorrow."

"Certainly. You know you're very welcome. Just be sure and see Felix when you get back."

"Right."

12

The day was glorious as he turned off West Seventy-second Street onto Riverside Drive and drove north toward the George Washington Bridge. The sky was bright with the exaggerated blue of autumn, a very few clearly defined clouds drifted white above the New Jersey Palisades, a lone river steamer plowed slowly up the wind-whipped channel of the Hudson, and close to the churning gray water the sea gulls dipped and swung. Not many cars were on the Drive at ten o'clock on this beautiful Sunday morning, and he drove with the feeling, sometimes unexpectedly granted even in the city of New York, that he was master of the universe. It was a feeling he would have enjoyed any other time, but today, as always on these visits that now extended back over so many years, he felt only a sadness so deep he wondered if he would ever recover from the burden. Each time, of course, he did, or thought he did, but each new time the pain returned as crushing as before.

This, however, was something he must try not to think about too much, even though the years did not lessen it as years were supposed to do. One could adjust to certain things, but one could never really accept them; the aching protest remained, no matter how dutifully one made obeisance to the Lord's unfathomable will. It was so unjust, so unnecessary, so *unfair*—but he must stop that. It never solved anything, helped anything, or got him anywhere in his endless argument with a destiny that had turned out to be much darker than he had ever dreamed it would be when he first embarked upon it.

Not, of course, that the world was aware, save in the most casual way, of the void that lay beneath his outwardly successful career. "If, now and again, the senior Senator from West Virginia seems gripped by a melancholy beyond that normally brought by the endless contentions of men at the United Nations," *Time* had said in its cover story on him three months ago, "he perhaps has reason." There had been the briefest of comments, a genuinely kind reference, as though it were something the magazine had to include but did not relish, to his personal tragedy. Back home, it was rarely mentioned, seldom thought of, hardly known. His constituents, and many of his friends, had only a vague notion that there was something unhappy there. Fortunately his fundamental good nature and likable character were such that few really remembered and understood and felt the kind of sympathy that was, in itself, a pain.

For this, in all honesty, he was grateful, for he did not know for sure whether he could bear what he had to bear if it were the object of a constantly expressed general commiseration. There were things it was best that society not notice too much; some doors it was best, by mutual agreement, to keep closed. This was one of them. Nothing could be done about it, and endless expressions of sorrow could only make more difficult a burden that at no time was easy. He was grateful to society for forgetting. It did not help him forget, of course, but it made his remembering a little easier.

And so as usual, he told himself with a bitter self-sarcasm as he swung over the massive bridge to the Palisades Parkway and started the scenic run above the river toward West Point and Newburgh and his destination not far beyond, he had once again worked himself into the perfect frame of mind for it. Why did he always do this? Why could he not achieve the serenity of acceptance that he had sought in vain to achieve over the empty years? Why, why, why? . . . Well: he knew the answer to that, right enough. Because it was the sort of thing no man could accept serenely, unless he was a saint or until he was dead.

Best think about the UN, he decided hastily; that was certainly problem enough to fill any man's mind for the remainder of the ride. He had watched it feeding on its own tensions in the past three days, the endless self-cannibalizing of ideas, intentions, motivations, hopes, fears, objectives, ambitions, speculation, gossip, that went on all the time but always stepped up to an exaggerated pace whenever some new, unusual event occurred in the world to provoke it. What had begun as an unfortunate but probably harmless comedy of errors in the President's inadvertent press conference remark and his first reaction to the M'Bulu's visit had been transformed abruptly by the latter's dramatic gesture in South Carolina into something far more dangerous and troublesome. And now Felix Labaiya was stepping in to make it even worse. And behind Felix, he supposed, either as a direct party in interest or just for the hell of it, was the Soviet Union.

And yet why, he challenged himself abruptly, should he so quickly assume that the Soviets had anything to do with it? Wasn't he being quite unjust to Felix, who after all had never given any overt cause for such suspicions? Of course there was gossip about him in the corridors and the Lounge, but, then, there was gossip about everyone on some count or other. No one had ever caught Felix out in anything that could be attributed beyond question to Soviet influence. Why should one assume now, just because something was embarrassing to the United States, that Soviet influence was calling the tune? Might not Felix honestly feel this way? Many delegates did, particularly among the newer states. Why shouldn't Felix arrive independently at the same judgment?

Furthermore, the assumption of Communist influence was too pat. Like many a United States delegate, Hal's first impulse on being assigned to the United Nations had been to assume, for a while, that Communist malevolence was behind everything hostile to the United States. It did not take him long to perceive that while the malevolence existed, it did not encompass every antagonism, or inspire every hostility, to his country and the West. If the West weren't vulnerable on so many points, he was honest enough to admit, it wouldn't suffer attack on so many points. If his own country weren't vulnerable, it wouldn't now be such a sitting duck for the double-barreled assault of the Ambassador of Panama and the heir to Gorotoland.

Thus his thoughts went as the river grew narrower and more lovely above West Point and the sharp outlines of earlier morning gave way to the gentling haze of the day's growing warmth. And then abruptly he was unable to fill his mind with the subject any longer, for now he was nearing his objective and the time had come to brace himself once more for other things.

He passed through Newburgh, turned off Highway 9-W to the river, came in sight of it rolling magnificently to his right, came to the well-remembered clump of woods, the small neat gates, the small unobtrusive sign: Oak Lawn. He turned in and began the winding approach, his breath beginning to come shorter as it always did despite his angriest efforts to keep it steady, his heart beginning to pound hurtfully. Had it been easier when she—before the day he had come home and found—but that, too, he did not want to think of, though he inevitably did. He supposed her presence used to help somehow, though, looking back, it seemed to him that it had always been the closest thing to hell that he would ever know on earth.

And then he was at the parking lot, carefully placing his car alongside the others—some modest and empty, others, not so modest, with chauffeurs waiting—and was on his way up the familiar walk to the familiar door. He was greeted with the hushed, respectful tones that were standard courtesy here, escorted down the long, waxed corridors, taken through the big sun porch overlooking the river, left to walk out alone upon the lawn. Fifty feet away, sitting by himself on a rattan chair in the brilliant sunlight, he saw a strikingly handsome boy of nineteen, his eyes looking far away, intent on something no other eyes would ever see, beyond the river.

"Jimmy!" Hal Fry called, his voice high and near breaking, as it always was at this moment, however he tried to keep it normal. "Hi, Jimmy!"

The boy turned in his slow way, that to a stranger might appear thoughtful, and gave the gravely beautiful smile that illuminated his face with a kindness beyond comprehension. There came an expression of friendly and all-embracing greeting, though Senator Fry knew that he had not recognized him now for many years, would never recognize him again, did not have the slightest realization of who he was or the slightest memory that he had ever been there before.

With a little half-sob in his throat he tried to keep his smile steady and reassuring as he went forward through the gorgeous morning to greet his son.

Three hours later, after the half-touched luncheon, the agonizing gestures toward coherent, consecutive conversation, the farewell attempt to impart, as if a raised voice and desperate reiteration could do it, some memory of this visit, some anticipation of the next, he was on the road back down to New York, driving slowly in the thickening afternoon traffic. He was trying hard, but without too much success, to control the crying in his heart as he remembered the politely puzzled smile; the kindly, considerate concern, utterly genuine yet terrifyingly impersonal; the regret at his going that was already forgotten by the time he had walked twenty steps. For a moment his eyes blinded with tears and he lost sight of the road. If Jimmy had not been so attractive a boy, if he had been ugly or malformed, if it had not been so easy to see all the wonderful things he would have been if only—if only—

He told himself with a great effort of the will, aided by the angry cries of a group of college kids roaring by, too close, in a convertible with the top down, that he must snap out of it or run the risk of endangering his own life and that of others on the highway with him. His own he did not particularly care about at this moment, but he could not be so irresponsible toward others. It seemed as though half the population was out taking advantage of the last golden days of fall, young couples, old people, solitary drivers, families with children, gay groups of happy folk. No doubt in sheer healthy exuberance twenty or thirty of them would have smashed each other up and be dead by nightfall, but it was not his task to add to the toll if he could help it.

So by concentrating carefully on his driving and steadily, fiercely, determinedly pushing into the back of his mind the contrast between his personal problem and the heartbreaking beauties of the lovely day, he safely negotiated 9-W, got back on the Palisades Parkway, came eventually again to the George Washington Bridge and the crossing to the city. It was five o'clock; the early dusk was beginning to fall; the river glinted like molten brass as it stretched away south on his right. Wrapped in a mixture of sunset, fog, and haze, their mystery and magic increased by the twilight, the towers of Manhattan shot up in jumbled confusion against the sky. Like no other city, he thought: no other city. In many buildings the lights were already beginning to come on; across on the Palisades as he went down Riverside Drive the neon signs of amusement parks and grocery products added their twinkling glitter. Like a ruined caravel, the wreck of the copper sunset sank in low black clouds and night had come.

And now he must find Felix, he told himself with a feeling of guilt. The visit had taken longer than he had intended; he should have cut it short and come back sooner—but how could he? How could he? They had told him long ago there was no hope, but how could one not have hope? Perhaps the next question, the next carefully joking comment, the very next attempt to arouse interest—and suddenly the polite smile would become really perceptive, the eyes turn suddenly from impersonal kindness to genuine understanding, the softly slurred words become suddenly clear and filled with the urgency of the great intelligence that had once been there. Perhaps, perhaps, perhaps—dear God, was it not worth hoping for? And how could one hurry, when the chance might be just around the corner?

But there he was again, he told himself as he drew alongside another car at the intersection of Forty-sixth and Fifth, and he must not, *he must not.* Ahead beyond the canyoned buildings he could see in his mind's eye the tall bulk of the Secretariat looming, lit here and there where cleaning women worked slowly through, readying it for the new week, or where in some isolated office someone worked for the world, even on Sunday. And so did he, and he must make up for lost time now.

He realized with a mild start of surprise that the car next to him was moving forward, even though the stop light was still red; the car behind him honked impatiently, so evidently the signal had become stuck. He moved out across Fifth, cautiously at first and then more surely as he realized the cross-traffic had stopped. This struck him as odd until he was almost to Third Avenue. Then he remembered that the signal light he had seen as red had been at the bottom of the signal post, not at the top; and red—real red—of course was at the top. For the first time a strange little prickle of fear ran along his scalp. "There it is again," he said aloud in a surprised voice; and added, as though it could be brought back to sense by a matter-of-fact tone, "That's *damned* peculiar."

And so it was; but as he drove on across Second and First and into the garage beneath the Secretariat and left his car—he found it simpler and cheaper to leave it there and cab back and forth to the Waldorf—he felt nothing further. His vision was quite all right again; he experienced only the natural tiredness to be expected from the emotional strain of the visit and the physical strain of the drive; he was, on the whole, rested and lively and alert. As he started toward the elevator he noticed a familiar limousine in its place near his and, on an impulse, turned toward the attendant, a pleasant-faced boy from Malaya who was studying law at Columbia.

"Is the S.-G. in the building?" he asked in some surprise. The boy nodded.

"He came in about an hour ago with Ambassador Labaiya of Panama. They went right on up to his office, I believe. Señor Labaiya came back down and got his car about ten minutes ago."

"Thank you." He hesitated a moment; it might make it difficult to find Felix later, but he felt he really should talk to the Secretary-General. "Maybe I'll run up, too, just to say hello."

"Yes, sir. Do you want me to call and tell him you're coming?"

"No, thanks. I'll just go up."

"All right, sir."

On the thirty-eighth floor he found two secretaries on duty, an air of unusual bustle. In some alarm he asked for the Secretary-General and was shown in almost immediately.

"Senator Fry," the Secretary-General said, rising and coming forward with a friendly smile that seemed to Hal to hold considerable concern. "Do sit down. My secretary has been trying to reach you at the Waldorf."

"Yes, I've been out of town. I just got back." He decided on the direct approach, and the knowledge that Felix had just been here fortified it. "What can you tell me about the Panamanian resolution?"

His host looked startled.

"So you've heard about it, then?" Hal Fry, who had learned long ago in West Virginia politics that it was sometimes best to feign a knowledge one did not possess, said nothing. The S.-G. sighed.

"He was just here, you know. Perhaps if you had come ten minutes earlier, it might have been possible to talk the matter over and work out something less damaging. I am sorry."

"So am I," Hal said, and he was, as he suddenly began to realize how narrowly he might have missed the chance to save his country the trouble that now would almost certainly plague her here in the UN. "Do you have a copy I can see?"

"It's being mimeographed for distribution to the delegations," the Secretary-General said. "I would like to show it to you, but—" he smiled. "You know the delicate technicalities of my position. I can't play favorites. Everyone should have it by about 8 P.M., I should think."

"It's bad, though." The S.-G. nodded.

"It is, as our critics of the organization often say, just words. But—very hurtful words. And very damaging, in the context of these times and the circumstances that prompted its introduction."

"Is it a new resolution or an amendment? Because if it's a new one, then maybe we can stop it before it gets to the floor of the Assembly . . ." His voice trailed away at the S.-G.'s expression. "Damn it! Somebody very clever has been at work on this thing."

The Secretary-General looked tired.

"Very clever indeed. Felix is clever. Terry is clever. Their friends are clever. I am the object of their cleverness a dozen times a day. I know they are clever."

"What do you think the reaction will be?" Hal Fry asked, a growing dismay in his heart as the full import of his missing Felix began to bear in upon him. Probably it wouldn't have made any difference, probably Felix was determined upon it, probably he was beginning to torture himself unnecessarily—and yet. Yet it could have been just the thing needed to head Felix off, a quiet talk with this patient and thoughtful man here in this office that had seen so many would-be crises smoothly compromised away before they could burst into the open in the hectic atmosphere of notoriety, prejudice, and exacerbated attitudes on the floors below.

"The reaction will be about as you anticipate it in many areas," the Secretary-General said.

"We may need your help," Senator Fry said simply, and his host nodded. "I am always being accused of betraying my own colored race," he said with a grim humor, "but I don't mind it, by now. My good offices are always available in the interests of compromising differences. I shall do what I can, of course, within the limitations of the Charter."

"Well, that's something," Hal Fry said with a certain bitter jocularity. His host smiled.

"I would hope so. I like to think I am of some value in this house. Would you like me to call Felix and see if I can get him back right now? It might be we could still—"

But even as he reached for the phone in response to Hal's nod, it rang under his hand. He lifted it and listened, shook his head at the Senator with an expression of annoyance, and finally said, "Yes, Mr. Ambassador. It will be done. . . . That was Tashikov. He has heard that the Ambassador of Panama has an amendment to his resolution on Gorotoland and he wants it translated into Byelorussian. This will prevent distribution until at least midnight and, of course, foreclose any counteractivities until tomorrow. He obviously knows what it says, so there's no point in recalling it now. Felix couldn't if he wanted to."

"Which he does not," Senator Fry said.

"Again, I am sorry. Ten minutes' time, and—"

"Well, we'll just have to see it through. It won't be easy, but we've no choice, apparently."

"Good luck," the Secretary-General said.

"We'll need it," Hal Fry said. "That's for sure."

A few minutes later at the Waldorf he called Orrin in Washington and told him what had happened, apologizing bitterly for his own delay in returning to the city. The Secretary assured him that he was quite certain it wouldn't have made any difference at all, that Felix was apparently operating on a broader plan than they had either of them imagined him to be, and that even if a meeting had been held in the Secretary-General's office, the chances of a compromise would have been nil.

"I do believe this," Orrin said, "so I don't want you to worry about it for a moment. How was the boy?"

"The same."

"In good health, though."

"Oh, yes," Hal Fry said with a terrible bitterness. "My son will live forever. He won't have a mind, but he'll be in good health." He made a strangled sound. "My God, Orrin, how does the Lord let such things happen?"

"Now, Hal," the Secretary said firmly, "stop it. That won't do any good, and you know it. I want you to find Lafe and go to delegation headquarters at once and start making plans for a reply tomorrow. Do you hear me? That's an order."

"Yes . . . Yes, I guess that's best for me."

"It's best for the country. I want us prepared tomorrow. I'll be flying up at 9 A.M. I want everything ready."

"All right," Senator Fry agreed, obviously forcing himself to be business-like, and succeeding. "I guess it's the least I can do, after messing it up the way I have."

"And stop *that*, too! I'm not kidding when I say it wouldn't have made any difference. You're just letting it upset you because you were already upset by your trip up the river. It wouldn't have made any difference. Now, damn it, get that through your head!"

"Yes, Orrin," Hal Fry said humbly. "You're a kind man and I'll try not to let you down again."

And although the Secretary once more reassured him, with all the indignant force at his command, and although he presently returned to the conclusion himself that it probably wouldn't have made any difference even if he had seen Felix, he could not escape the guilty feeling that he had failed Orrin, failed the President, failed the country by staying too long in the golden day with the handsome boy who did not know him. He realized that his state of depression was making him feel this way, but he couldn't help it. He *did* feel this way, and that was all that mattered.

13

"Mrs. Vhadu Labba of India, please," said the heavy voice of the busty blonde at the phone desk. "Mrs. Vhadu Labba of India, please call the Delegates' Lounge . . . Dr. Ranashah of Iran, please . . . Ambassador Labaiya of Panama, please . . . Lord Maudulayne of the U.K. . . ."

And now, as always in the hours preceding a crucial meeting of the Assembly or the Security Council—in other words, almost every day—the United Nations hummed with gossip and speculation from top to bottom and one end to the other. Word of the new turn of events—sped by a speculative story from the New York *Times'* UN correspondent under the headline "U.S. FEARS U.N. MOVE ON TERRY"—had given the organization its newest sensation. "It looks as though Uncle Sam is in for it," a member of the Canadian delegation had remarked, not without relish, to a member of the delegation of Pakistan; and, typically, their cheerful agreement was being echoed, to greater or lesser degree, in many other conversations now going on in the lounges, the corridors, the eating places and conference rooms of the world's mansion. Its inhabitants, disregarding the admonition to those who live in glass houses, rarely let pass a chance to throw stones at one another and now were having a high old time of it.

Thus the North Lounge was even noisier than usual on this morning of Felix Labaiya's latest *démarche* in The Problem of Gorotoland, now broadened by the M'Bulu's dramatic bravery in South Carolina and about to be broadened much further by the Panamanian Ambassador's decision to seize upon the pattern of events and turn it to his own purposes. The support for his doing this was loud and vigorous in many sections of the room, and it was already apparent as the two senatorial members of the American delegation came in that many of the smaller states were already beginning to make up their minds in the matter, and not in a way favorable to the United States.

"Well, buddy," Lafe Smith said with an appraising glance up and down the Lounge, "it sounds as though Felix has our work cut out for us, doesn't it? You can always tell when somebody shakes this beehive. The buzz gets deafening."

"Yes," Hal Fry agreed as they walked along toward the snack bar at the other end, greeting fellow delegates on the way, nodding to friends, creating a stir by their passage. "I expect the *Times'* story is pretty well correct, too." He was feeling better and more like himself this morning. A sleep of deep exhaustion had worked its benison during the night.

"Oh, yes, I think so. I had breakfast with my friend from Gabon and he's apparently seen the amendment, which is being floated about by the Communists to everybody but us, of course. It's not very complimentary, I'm afraid."

"One thing I will say for the UN," Hal Fry remarked. "It has succeeded in raising the power of words to a level never before achieved in human history. We go forth and do battle over phraseology in this place with all the fierce determination of the Greeks at Thermopylae. And behind the words, of course, the greater part of three billion people around the globe who have so little knowledge and education that they'll believe the first word that reaches them and go into the streets and do battle just on the strength of it. That's why these resolutions are so important, for all that they're 'just words,' as the critics like to say."

Senator Smith sighed as they reached the snack bar and ordered coffee.

"Yes. I could wish we weren't quite so vulnerable to certain acts by certain people in certain areas, but—there it is. We are. I'm just surprised it hasn't happened before. Where's the hero of the hour, by the way?"

"Terry? I don't know. He's staying at the St. Regis. I tried to reach him there around nine, but he's already left. Probably leading a pep rally in the Afro-Asian bloc."

"Secretary Knox of the United States, please," the young lady at the telephone desk said. "Secretary Knox, please call the Delegates' Lounge."

"Speaking of heroes," Lafe said, "where is he? I thought he was due in this morning."

"He's coming. He called me a little while ago. Harley wanted him to stop by the White House before he came up, so he's delayed a bit. But he'll be here."

"Let's go find a table by the window," Lafe suggested, "and see who gathers 'round."

"All right," Hal said, and they started back out into the main part of the crowded room, carefully balancing their coffee cups as they went. "Oh-oh!" Hal tossed over his shoulder. "Do you see who I see?"

"I do indeed. Suppose we do the gathering."

"An excellent idea," Hal agreed as they moved toward a sofa, occupied, and two empty chairs around a coffee table by the enormous wall of windows facing up the East River. "Good morning, gentlemen. Is this summit private, or can anybody join?"

"By all means, Hal," Raoul Barre said pleasantly, ignoring the increased hum of comment that swept the room as the two Americans sat down. "I'm sure we have no secrets from you."

"Felix does," Senator Fry said. "Don't you, Felix?"

The Ambassador of Panama gave his dry little self-contained smile and looked up from stirring his coffee with a bland expression.

"My dear Hal, only the necessities of having my amendment translated into Byelorussian, of all God-forsaken things, prevents it from being in your hands right now."

"That was a very thoughtful move, on someone's part," Hal observed. "It preserves the element of surprise. At least for us. Apparently everybody else has seen a copy."

"Oh, I think not," Felix Labaiya said calmly. "Plenty of rumors, speculation in the *Times*—the usual stuff. But actual copies, no, I don't think so. After all," he said with a sudden pleasant smile, "I don't mean to be crude about this. I'm only doing what, regretfully, seems necessary to salvage United States honor in the eyes of the world. No one should be more willing to support me than your delegation, Hal, as a matter of fact."

"I assume your motives are of the most noble," Hal Fry said, "because I think it would look rather odd if the brother-in-law of the Governor of California led a world crusade against the Governor's country. The Governor's country might not like it when it came time to go to the polls."

"I married into a very understanding family," the Ambassador of Panama said calmly. "I think my motivations will be quite clear to everyone when I speak this afternoon."

"I hope so, because they baffle nearly everyone now."

"Oh, I don't believe so, Hal," Raoul Barre said. "Not everyone. I think vast sections of Africa and Asia understand them very well. After all," he said with a sardonic little smile, "it is as simple as black and white."

"And what color is France trying to be?" Lafe Smith inquired. "Gray?"

"France believes in an intelligent adaptability," her Ambassador said with some impatience. "We have many friends, good friends, in Africa. We do not intend to lose them. Surely you can understand that."

"Yes, I understand. It's all very practical."

"I should hope so," the French Ambassador said. "It is good to have a bridge between the two worlds, is it not? Possibly we can be of great assistance to you. Felix does not object if we try."

"We are not prepared to compromise on this amendment," Senator Fry said. "You both understand that, of course."

Raoul Barre shrugged.

"Sometimes events conspire to make compromise seem more desirable toward the end than it does at the beginning. Surely two Senators do not have to be told that."

"Two Senators who have the votes," Hal Fry said with more show of confidence than he felt, "don't have to be told anything."

Felix Labaiya smiled.

"When the roll is called, we shall see on votes."

"Well," Hal Fry said, finishing his coffee and standing up, "that's true enough. Are you speaking before Terry or after?"

"Possibly, after. I may permit him to prepare the psychological climate."

"Trust him for that," Lafe said. Felix Labaiya laughed.

"I do."

The day's plenary session of the General Assembly, scheduled to begin at 10 A.M., was, as usual, gradually pulling itself together in the Assembly Hall shortly before eleven. The Ambassador of the Netherlands, this year's Assembly President, sat in his seat at the center of the high desk on the podium looking patiently about the enormous blue-and-tan room, a tidy little rolypoly man whose pink cheeks, white hair, and blue twinkling eyes gave him a deceptive appearance of jolly Santa Claus, belied by his brisk gaveling and firm rulings when his colleagues, as often happened, became obstreperous. At his right sat the Secretary-General, his fine head and thoughtful face in repose as he, too, waited patiently for the delegations to take their places. The S.-G.'s principal deputy, a lean, grizzled American who moved about with an air of intense and impatient energy that gave him the aspect of a greyhound on leash, had not yet appeared on the podium to take his seat at the President's left.

On the floor of the huge concave bowl of a room—a room which, with its insistent pastels, its stark fluorescent lights, its garish fried-egg murals by Léger, its general air of being too bright, too harsh, too demanding, too loudly noisy in its décor, might almost have been designed deliberately to murder thought—increasing numbers of delegates were beginning to move to their seats at the long, gleaming wooden tables, like so many writing shelves in some gigantic schoolroom, that served as desks. In the radio, television, and translation booths, set high in the walls on both sides of the chamber, reporters, technicians, and members of the Secretariat could be observed chatting and gossiping behind the glass. The public and press galleries, banked up in sharply rising rows of seats at the end of the room opposite the podium, were rapidly filling. A constant stream of people passed back and forth through the aisles that divide the sections of seats on the floor, stopping to chat, to say hello, to greet one another with vigorous handshakes, to exchange hasty gossip and comment.

In all this colorful thronging assemblage of the nations, it could be seen that on this day more Africans than usual were wearing their native costumes, apparently by way of emphasizing that they were Africans—something the Ghanaians and Guineans often did but others were not so diligent about. Today bright robes and togas, vivid caps and sashes, could be seen dotted profusely about the room, standing out brilliantly against the sober Western business suits of the other delegations. This did not pass without comment, nor did the entrance of the major figures in the drama of the day: the Ambassador of Panama entering with the Ambassador of France; the British Ambassador and the Indian Ambassador, approaching from opposite ends of the aisle that divides the floor at the back from the first rows of the press gallery, stopping to greet one another with elaborate cordiality; the Soviet Ambassador, hurrying in with the Ambassador of Cuba, nodding brusquely to the head of the American delegation, who nodded as brusquely back. There was much questioning, particularly in the press gallery, where many correspondents were scanning the floor with binoculars, concerning the whereabouts of the M'Bulu. He had not yet appeared, and his absence served to increase the interest in the vast chamber, where many sought his giant figure.

There was an unusual air of drama and excitement about the Assembly this day. High at the back of the public galleries the blue-uniformed guards glanced at one another nervously, for one never knew when some well-organized disturbance might break out.

At three minutes to eleven the President rapped his gavel smartly and announced in his brisk broken English, "The plenary session of the General Assembly is now in session and the delegates will please be in order. The pending business is the draft resolution submitted by Panama on The Problem of Gorotoland. The Chair calls upon the distinguished delegate of Panama, Ambassador Labaiya, to speak to his resolution."

Far over at the right of the chamber, from his delegation's place next to Paraguay, Felix Labaiya could be seen, as heads turned and voices hushed, rising and moving down the aisle toward the podium. In a moment he had walked up the steps to the speaker's stand, bowed to the President, and turned back to face the attentive assemblage, many of whose members were adjusting earphones and settling back to listen.

"Mr. President," he said, choosing to speak in English rather than Spanish (many delegates took their earphones off again), "I should like to defer my statement in order that the Assembly may first hear a brief statement by a distinguished visitor to the United Nations who, we hope, will soon join us as a member in his own right, His Royal Highness the M'Bulu of Mbuele. I realize that it is somewhat irregular, Mr. President ("When did that ever stop the UN?" Lafe Smith whispered to Claude Maudulayne, over on the left where the U.S. and U.K. delegations sat side by side), but this was announced last week and I believe has the general approval of most of the delegations. I would hope that neither the United Kingdom nor the United States would object." He paused with pointed politeness for a moment; both the delegations concerned sat impassive, and after a moment he went smoothly on. "Then, Mr. President, I now invite the Assembly's courtesy and attention for our distinguished visitor, His Royal Highness the M'Bulu."

There was a burst of applause as he returned to his seat, and for a minute or two the room hummed again with gossip and comment as the podium remained empty. In the pause the Secretary-General's American deputy, who could be seen by the nearer delegations to be looking angry and disturbed, came from the President's private room directly behind the wall that backs the podium, took his seat, and whispered across to the President and the S.-G. For a moment their heads were together, and just as they broke away again, the other two men startled and bothered too, there was a mounting commotion over on the left side, where delegates could see the door of the room behind the podium. It was followed in seconds by a sudden gasp from all around the hall.

The M'Bulu appeared and walked with his stately tread to the lectern, clad in the robes he had worn in Charleston, spattered and bedraggled from head to foot with rotten tomatoes, rotten eggs, streaks of mud and dirt.

For a long moment the gasp that had greeted his appearance was succeeded by silence; and then Ghana and Guinea were on their feet applauding, the rest of the African and Asian delegations were beginning to stand, from the Communist bloc came raucous bangings and thumpings on desks, a little group of Negroes in the public galleries suddenly unfurled the red and black banners of DEFY and began screaming unintelligible things, the enormous chamber was suddenly filled with a storm of sound. One by one the smaller nations, the so-called neutrals, the uncommitted states, all the peoples around the world who for one reason or another had cause to applaud anyone who would defy the great powers of the West, stood and applauded too. Very few delegations, in fact, remained seated and silent. All those who did were white, and many of their members looked desperately troubled and upset.

"Oh, brother," Lafe Smith said softly to his colleague, "this is serious."

"Yes," said Hal Fry grimly. "Indeed it is."

For several moments the television cameras roved about the chamber, catching the United States and United Kingdom delegations looking soured and isolated in a sea of standing, applauding delegates, bringing the impassive face of the M'Bulu, head erect, eyes straight ahead, repeatedly before the viewers, lingering with loving attention on his spattered robes, while the press reporters stood in their gallery and scribbled hasty notes. Then with a sure instinct for timing Terry brought the tableau to a close by raising a long left arm. A quick hush fell, and into it he said one slow and powerful word that renewed pandemonium:

"Free—dom!"

Immediately the roar of sound welled up again as the chant was repeated from all across the floor:

"Free—dom! Free—dom! Free—dom!"

The Africans were in a frenzy, the Asians wildly excited, the Communists, for once, in the presence of a showman better than they were. The President of the Assembly, his rosy cheeks purpling, his blue eyes popping, pounded and pounded and pounded his gavel, his shouts for order drowned out in the rhythmic chant that filled the Hall and drove out thought and sensation with its hypnotic reiteration.

That, too, Terry permitted to run on just long enough. Then he raised both arms and, with a vigorous down-sweeping gesture, steadily repeated, commanded silence. Gradually the noise subsided; an excited, buzzing, rustling quiet began to fall. Experienced diplomats, who a second before had been shouting with the rest, turned to one another amazed that they had done so, shaken by the impact of the most basic emotions set loose. A spent silence descended upon the chamber. Into it the heir to Gorotoland began speaking with a slow and powerful deliberation.

"Mr. President! My friends of the United Kingdom! (Raucous laughter from many delegations.) My friends of the United States! (Cheers, applause, laughter, harsh, ironic, menacing.) My friends of Africa and freedom-loving peoples everywhere. (Great applause and shouts.) Where I have been, you know. What I did, you have heard about. What happened to me, you see." He paused, stilling a rising murmur of boos, and then spat out his words: "Do you think it worthy of the home of the brave and the land of the free?"

(Wild shouts of "No! No! Free–*dom!* Death to the Americans! America the slavers!" Communist desk-banging, shrill screams and shouts from the demonstrators of DEFY in the public galleries.) Terrible Terry went gravely on.

"Will you give me freedom?" he demanded, and a great shout of "Yes!" replied.

He nodded with a fierce satisfaction. Then his expression changed back to one of grave and sober contemplation.

"Mr. President," he said slowly, and a real hush fell at the note of gravely chiding sorrow in his voice. "It seems to me that it is time for this great organization of the world to take official notice of the desperate social conditions within the United States of America. It is time for all people who truly love freedom—who truly seek right and justice for humanity—who cry out when oppression and cruelty occur anywhere in the world—to make it clear to the United States that the world will no longer tolerate such barbaric practices as exist in this country behind the façade of democracy. It is an empty democracy, Mr. President! Look at me! This is the kind of democracy it is!"

And he stepped away from the rostrum and forward to the edge of the platform, so that all could see him full-length, spattered and smeared with the colorful mementos of the ladies of Charleston. An uneasy mixture of applause and murmurs rose from the floor, and many delegates looked nervously toward the United States, for this was suddenly a truly serious thing the M'Bulu was doing and many were not sure how fully they dared support it.

He stepped back to the rostrum and for a long moment looked out upon them in somber contemplation.

"Mr. President, I have no doubt that all of you, my friends of the freedom-loving countries, will overwhelmingly approve independence for Gorotoland.

That is fairly easy. That does not take real bravery. That is a matter of simple justice.

"I ask you this, however: Will you also be brave enough to condemn a nation whose ideals and actions are so far apart—who commits such crimes against innocent human beings *simply because they are not white?*

"Will you also be brave enough to censure the United States and demand that it conform to the high and noble ideals of the United Nations?

"That will be your true test, my friends.

"I urge you to think well upon it!"

And, drawing himself once more to his utmost height, he bowed gravely to the Assembly, turned and bowed gravely to the apoplectic little President on the raised dais above him, stalked slowly back to the private room behind the dais, and disappeared.

For several minutes the Assembly sat dazed, as if drunk from so much powerful emotion, shaken by the enormity of the challenge thus openly flung at last at America. Many of the delegates had felt these things for many years. Many of them had wished to do something about it. None had dared. Now Terry had. The shock of it was so powerful that, it appeared, not even the Americans themselves could think of an answer. It could be seen that angry whispered conversations were going on within the delegation, and many heads now turned to see; it was expected that momentarily either Senator Fry or Senator Smith would exercise the "right of reply" and come forward to respond to the harsh criticism of their country. But the moment passed. ("We've got to say something," Lafe hissed angrily. "I said wait until Felix is through!" Hal Fry hissed back, and for a long moment they openly glared at one another, until Lafe's eyes dropped and he shrugged and slumped back in his chair.)

Presently in a shaking voice the President said into the uneasy tension:

"The Chair now recognizes the distinguished delegate of Panama to finish explaining his resolution."

"Mr. President," Felix Labaiya said with the small, neat, self-contained precision that characterized his person, his attitude, his thinking, and his voice, "I shall not detain the Assembly long, for I know we wish to proceed speedily to debate, and perhaps to vote upon, this resolution. The resolution itself was circulated to all delegations two weeks ago. It has been overwhelmingly approved by First Committee, and it does not need further explanation from me. I hope, and I expect, that it will be approved here, too, so that the United Nations, through the General Assembly, may proceed swiftly to bring Gorotoland into the independent partnership of free nations.

"But, Mr. President," he said, and something in his voice made many sit forward intently in their seats, those who did not speak English holding their earphones tightly to their ears to receive translation, "the task will not be complete if that is all we do in this resolution. A grave event, a display of great courage and kindness, followed by a vicious insult to both human decency and to the representative of another country, has occurred on the soil of the host nation to the United Nations. True, the insult has been condemned by officials of that country; but the deeper insult, to humanity, to human dignity, to peoples of differing racial backgrounds, to the United Nations, to *you*—has not been expiated. Nor can it be, the delegation of Panama believes, until the United Nations comes to the assistance of the wayward country and aids its officials, by a great expression of world opinion, to rid their society of its greatest evil, the evil of racial discrimination. Therefore, Mr. President, the delegation of Panama proposes, and herewith formally adds to its resolution on The Problem of Gorotoland, the following amendment:

"Whereas, the distinguished representative of Gorotoland, acting in the greatest traditions of human freedom and decency, has been savagely attacked in a city of the United States of America; and,

"Whereas, this attack grew directly from policies of racial discrimination in the United States of America, which decent men everywhere deplore and condemn; and,

"Whereas, the continued existence of these policies in the United States tends to place the United States in direct violation of the principles of the Charter of the United Nations and therefore casts grave doubts upon the qualifications of the United States to continue as a member of this body"— there were gasps of surprise from many places across the floor, but he went on with unperturbed self-possession—

"Now, therefore, be it resolved that this resolution is hereby amended to direct the Security Council, acting on behalf of the United Nations, to make an immediate investigation of racial practices in the United States, looking toward the ending of such racial practices, and offering the full assistance of the United Nations in this task so that the United States may truly conform to the principles of the Charter and be fully worthy of membership in this great body."

He paused and the room almost visibly palpitated with the swirling thoughts of all the silent delegates.

"Mr. President, that is the amended language of my resolution. I commend it to your early and favorable consideration. Simple justice and the imperatives of history demand it. Let us meet the demand and thus, in friendly spirit, help the great Republic of the West to show forth to the world, once more unsullied, the banner of freedom she raised in the presence of mankind in 1776."

And he turned, bowed to the President, descended the steps of the rostrum, and resumed his seat beside Paraguay as the room burst into an explosion of talk and argument, silenced almost as soon as it began by Senator Fry of the United States, rising in his place and waving toward the Chair.

"The Chair recognizes the distinguished delegate of the United States," the President said in a quivering voice, "to exercise the right to reply—?"

"Point of order, Mr. President," Hal Fry shouted, and the President amended hastily, "On a point of order," as Hal came forward down the aisle while galleries and delegates strained to see him and a tense silence fell once more upon the room.

"Now, Mr. President," he said, "the United States has heard, with a patience far greater than these two performances here this morning have warranted, vicious attacks upon itself. The United States has made, it feels, full apologies and amends for what occurred to His Royal Highness in Charleston. The United States does not feel that—"

But there was a commotion on the floor, and the Soviet Ambassador was on his feet, also crying, "Point of order!"

"The distinguished delegate of the Soviet Union desires recognition on a point of order," the President said, and Tashikov came forward as Senator Fry stepped down and took a temporary seat at the side.

"Mr. President," Vasily Tashikov said angrily, and delegates all over the room adjusted their earphones and switched hurriedly to the Russian translation, "the point of order is that under Rule 73 of the General Assembly, points of order are not debatable. The distinguished delegate of the United States is attempting to debate his point of order. Therefore, he himself is out of order."

And he returned to his chair amid scattered applause as Hal Fry stepped back to the podium and started to speak. The President silenced him with his gavel.

"On the point of order raised by the distinguished delegate of the Soviet Union," he said, "the Chair feels that the point is well taken and that the distinguished delegate of the United States should state his point of order without debate."

There was a burst of clapping from many of the Afro-Asian bloc, and the Senator from West Virginia, wishing he did not feel suddenly so tired in this moment of crisis, bowed to the Chair.

"Very well, Mr. President," he said, and his voice dragged a little for a second in a way that made Lafe Smith down in the delegation look suddenly intent; but then he went on, strongly as usual. "Very well. The point of order of the United States is that this amendment is not germane to the resolution seeking independence for Gorotoland and therefore is out of order at this time."

"My God," the London *Daily Express* whispered with audible savagery in the press gallery, "how phony can you get?" The New York *Post* nodded and chuckled, but the New York *Times* looked quite annoyed.

The President, the Secretary-General, and the Deputy consulted together for a moment while the Assembly stirred restlessly below. Then the President spoke.

"It is the opinion of the Chair that the point of order is not well taken under the rules of the Assembly, and therefore the point of order is overruled."

"We appeal the ruling, Mr. President," Hal Fry said.

"The United States has appealed the ruling of the Chair," the President announced. "Under the rules, the appeal must be put immediately to a vote without debate, and accordingly the voting will now begin." He reached in his little box and drew a name. "A vote Yes will uphold the point of order and defeat the ruling; a vote No will uphold the ruling and defeat the point of order. The voting will begin with Turkey."

"Yes."

"Uganda."

"No."

"Ukrainian S.S.R."

"*Nyet.*"

"U.S.S.R."

"*Nyet.*"

"United Arab Republic."

"No."

"United Kingdom."

"Yes."

"United States."

"Yes."

"Upper Volta."

"*Abstention.*"

"Uruguay."

"*Abstención.*"

Ten minutes later, most of the Afro-Asian bloc having lined up against the United States, Portugal and South Africa having done the same in voices full of spite, much of Latin America and Europe having abstained, the President spoke.

"The vote on the appeal is 38 Yes, 43 No, 32 abstentions, remainder absent, and the appeal is defeated. The distinguished delegate of the United States."

"Don't tell me he's going to try something else!" *Paris-Match* exclaimed in the press gallery. "Hope springs eternal," said the *Christian Science Monitor* with an uncomfortable little laugh.

"Very well, Mr. President," Hal Fry said, "I move to adjourn debate on the item under Rule 76."

"The Chair, under Rule 76, will grant five minutes each to two speakers for the motion and two against." There was a movement on the floor, several messengers went to the podium, the President finally rapped his gavel.

"The Chair will recognize the United Kingdom and Cameroun speaking in favor of the motion, Ghana and Guinea speaking against. The distinguished delegate of the United Kingdom."

"Mr. President," Lord Maudulayne said with a measured imperturbability, "it is not the purpose of the United Kingdom to inflame further passions which have already been inflamed enough here this morning. As the target of the original draft resolution proposed by the distinguished delegate of

Panama, it might be presumed to be of assistance to the United Kingdom for the issue of Gorotoland to be confused by the introduction of what can only appear to us to be an extraneous matter.

"However, while the United Kingdom makes no brief for anything that may happen in another country—and also is not quite so anxious as some to appoint itself guardian of others' morals—we nonetheless agree with the distinguished delegate of the United States that this is entirely aside from the central issue of immediate independence for Gorotoland. We do not think this house should confuse the issue by permitting itself to be dragged into debate on a matter which is something for the United States to solve, in her own way, within her own borders. Great progress has been made in the United States toward solution of this problem ("Not very damned much!" a DEFY demonstrator in the gallery shouted, and a guard started hastily toward his seat), and there is every sign that the progress will continue. It is not our purpose here in the United Nations—it is not our right—to presume to interfere in this process through the channels of world public opinion that we can mobilize here. We must be judicious, tolerant, and fair. Otherwise the United Nations descends to mere name-calling and sinks in the sea of its own passions. We support the motion of the United States to end debate on this item."

"The distinguished delegate of Ghana," the President said, and the delegate, clad in his gorgeous native robes, strode angrily to the podium and began furiously speaking, so excited that the words tumbled out in a torrent and he forgot to bow to the Chair.

"Mr. President! The distinguished delegate of the United Kingdom says we must be fair to the United States. Was the United States fair to the M'Bulu? Was that fairness, Mr. President—the rotten eggs and rotten tomatoes and dirt we have seen here? I ask you, Mr. President! Does anyone call that fairness?"

He paused and a shout of "No!" rose from many delegations.

"Mr. President! Ghana urges you to vote against ending debate on this matter. Ghana urges you to condemn the United States, just as you would condemn any other power, be it big or little, that so violates human decency. That is what the United Nations is for, Mr. President—that all should be judged equally, on the same basis, whether they be big or little. Let us remember the Charter, Mr. President! Let us be true to the United Nations! Let us continue debate, and vote, on this tragic issue!"

"The distinguished delegate of Cameroun," the President said patiently, and another Negro in robes walked down the aisle as the Ghanaian came up, brushing past him with an expression of contempt and not speaking.

"Mr. President," the delegate of Cameroun began in liquid French, and earphones went on all over the room and dials were hastily switched to the French translation, "we are hearing great speeches here today. We are hearing great emotional appeals here today. People are banging desks and displaying dirty clothes"—a startled sound, followed by hisses, responded to this—"and appealing to the Charter of the United Nations.

"Is everything perfect in Ghana, Mr. President, I would ask my distinguished colleague? Do democracy and liberty shine down upon its sons and daughters, Mr. President—or only upon a few of them? Mr. President, sometimes it is well to catch the mouse in one's own house before sending the cat to catch the neighbor's.

"I do not make any defense, Mr. President, of certain unhappy things in the United States of America. God knows any man of color who visits New York is aware that they exist. But, Mr. President, I do pay tribute to the sincere attempts of the United States to work out this problem, and to do it peaceably and constructively within her own borders.

"Within her own borders—that is it, Mr. President. Ask yourselves: Where would you like the United Nations to investigate next? In your country? Where does it stop, Mr. President?

"Mr. President, the issue of independence for Gorotoland is clear-cut. On that my delegation stands with our brothers of Africa. But do not confuse it, I beg you, with internal affairs of the United States which are no concern of this honorable Assembly."

The President rapped his gavel to silence the mixed boos and applause that followed, announced the distinguished delegate of Guinea, and once again two Africans met in mid-aisle and ignored one another as the lithe young delegate from Guinea strode to the podium.

"Mr. President," he said slowly, also in French, "the distinguished delegate of Cameroun, as usual, is very much of an expert on emotional appeals. He shows us how it is done, Mr. President, and no doubt we are the better instructed for it.

"But, Mr. President, my delegation does not feel that these emotional appeals of the delegate of Cameroun are sufficient to meet the grave issue now before this house. A grave insult has been given a great African by the United States of America; and, Mr. President, do not let us hide the sequence of events. The insult was tendered first by the President of the United States. Only then, following his lead, was it tendered by the people of the United States, those miserable people in South Carolina.

"They have insulted all of us of colored blood, Mr. President. That is the issue here. For too long this hypocritical pretense has been allowed to go on, here under the very nose of the United Nations. It is not just what happened in South Carolina. It is a long miserable record of discrimination, cruelty, unfairness, unkindness. I ask you, my fellow delegates: Which of you whose skin is not white is free to go anywhere he pleases in the United States? Which of you who is not white feels himself treated with full equality as a human being in the United States? Not one, Mr. President! Not one! Mr. President, the delegation of Guinea joins Ghana in urging you to vote against adjourning debate on this item. History is watching us, Mr. President! We must act!"

There was loud approval as he strode down from the rostrum and back up the aisle to his seat, and as it began to subside there was a new stirring of interest and turning of heads as a commotion broke out around the American delegation. "There's Knox," the London *Observer* said with some excitement. "Now things ought to start moving." "Moving where?" the *Daily Express* asked scornfully. "They're up against a blank wall. They're not going anywhere."

And so, indeed, it seemed to the Secretary at first glance as Senator Fry and Senator Smith and the other delegation members rapidly filled him in on what had occurred prior to his arrival. "Possibly I took the wrong tack, Orrin," Hal began, "but I thought—" "Absolutely right," the Secretary said. "The least we could do is try it out. And maybe the vote will go all right this time."

This hope, however, proved empty. The President, announcing that, Rule 76 having been complied with, it was now in order to vote, reached into his little box, drew a name, and announced that vote on the motion to adjourn debate would begin with Ceylon.

"No."

"Chad."

"*Oui.*"

"Chile."

"*Abstención.*"

"China."

"Yes."

"Colombia."

"*Abstención.*"

"Congo Brazzaville."

"*Oui.*"

"Congo Leopoldville."

"*Non.*"

"Costa Rica."

"No."

"Cuba."

"No."

"Cyprus."

"No."

"Czechoslovakia."

"No."

"Dahomey."

"*Non.*"

"Denmark."

"Yes."

"On the motion to adjourn debate on this item," the President announced in due course, "the motion is 47 Yes, 50 No, 17 abstentions, others absent, and the motion is defeated."

"Mr. President!" Orrin Knox shouted from his chair in the U.S. delegation, and a buzz of excitement spread over the chamber. "Mr. President!"

"The distinguished delegate of the United States, Secretary Knox," the

President said, and the Secretary moved forward purposefully to the rostrum, bowed to the President, and turned to the Assembly.

"Be good, Orrin boy," Lafe Smith said, half aloud, and Hal Fry said, "He will be."

In the oratorical manner he had perfected long ago in the Senate, the Secretary of State stared out impassively upon the vast chamber, now silent awaiting his words. Then he began in a level, deliberate tone.

"Mr. President, we are witnessing here today an attempt to make the private business of the United States the public business of the United Nations."

There was a little resentful stir, but he went on calmly to take them by surprise with his next remark.

"In some respects, this may be justified.

"It is true that an unfortunate incident occurred in South Carolina. It is true that the President of the United States did not leap at once to entertain one who is not the head of an independent state.

"It is also true, Mr. President, that the President was acting entirely within the bounds of standard diplomatic procedure. It is also true that the problems of South Carolina would not have become the problem of the M'Bulu of Mbuele had His Royal Highness not seen fit to involve himself deliberately in them.

"No one asked him to intervene in the internal affairs of the United States or the sovereign state of South Carolina, Mr. President. We have not presumed to interfere with the way he treats his colored people. Why should he interfere with us?"

"He isn't the United States!" someone shouted from somewhere in the gallery, and the President hastily rapped for order. The guards once more shifted nervously at their stations.

"No, indeed," the Secretary said sardonically. "No, indeed he is not the United States. And I will grant you," he said, more solemnly, "there does rest upon the United States an obligation, springing both from our history going back to the American Revolution and from the restraints that world responsibility should place upon those of us who have it, a duty to maintain for herself a standard of conduct worthy of her, irrespective of what others may do.

"I do not pretend, Mr. President, that the United States, in the sequence of events of the past three days, has been entirely blameless or has lived up entirely to that personal standard which the President and the overwhelming majority of Americans desire to maintain. But we try, Mr. President; we are trying to improve the situation, to bring the Negro to full citizenship, to extend to all Americans everywhere regardless of color the blessings conferred by our Revolution.

"Against that background, I must respectfully say to this honorable house that agitating the matter here can only inflame the situation within our borders." (On the floor the Ambassador of South Africa caught, with a wink, the eye of the Ambassador of Portugal, who smiled without amusement and nodded.)

"Mr. President, none of this means, of course, that I would wish to detract from or decry the personal bravery of His Royal Highness in doing what he did. But there are two kinds of bravery, Mr. President. There is the bravery of the dramatic gesture, isolated in time and carrying with it no responsibility to stay around and help take care of the consequences; and there is the bravery of those who must live with the problem from day to day and somehow, God willing, eventually work it out in a way that will be fair and just to all. His Highness has had his little moment, Mr. President, and I would not try to say that it was not a brave moment, for it was. But the United States of America and her people must, in this area, deal not with moments but with years; and that requires of us, over the long haul, a much greater bravery than that of one who dips in and out of the situation for whatever it may be worth to him in temporary headlines.

"Mr. President, we have made formal apologies to the M'Bulu. He does not seem to be happy with them, but that represents a lack of restraint on his part, Mr. President. It does not represent a lack of grace on ours.

"Mr. President, I move to adjourn the meeting."

At once there was a surge of exclamation and protest from some delegations, scattered applause from others, a little dutiful desk-banging by the Communists, a flurry in the press and public galleries. The Secretary's motion, if approved, would have the effect of terminating further consideration of both the amendment and the original resolution on Gorotoland. It was not subject to debate, but it was immediately obvious that, in typical United Nations fashion, the outcome was not going to be the open-and-shut conclusion he proposed.

Indeed he knew, and his Senate colleagues suspected as much, that he did not really intend it to be. With the instinct of an experienced parliamentarian, he had sensed that a change was under way in the assemblage before him. Restraint was not always a United Nations characteristic when one of the great powers of the West was on the run, but the emotional impact of the M'Bulu's speech was fading, second thoughts were beginning to intrude, self-interest, that great modifier of ideals and passions, was beginning to operate. The United States still provided two-thirds of the UN budget; at least two-thirds of the organization's members were still dependent, in one way or another, upon United States friendship and financial assistance. The mood might return to vengeance in enough delegations to swing the final vote, but there was a sudden realization that it might be well to delay that vote and think about it for a while. The realization had produced one of those moments that come so often in the Congress in Washington, when opposing forces reach the exact point of meeting head on and then suddenly understand that a crushing victory by either might have very serious consequences. It was a cause for reappraisal, reconsideration, and regrouping. Orrin had recognized it as such and changed tactics accordingly.

Although it was somewhat irregular under the easily flexed rules of the

Assembly, it was with a general feeling of relief that its members heard the delegate from Ghana once more seek recognition, and the President grant it, while Orrin stepped temporarily aside.

"Mr. President," Ghana said, "I am wondering if the distinguished delegate of the United States would be willing to change his motion to a motion to suspend the meeting on this item to a day certain. The distinguished delegate," he said with the first note of humor in an angry day, "is in a more favored position than most delegations: he can give himself his own instructions. Others may wish to consult with their home governments. Would he consider such a modification?"

"Mr. President," Orrin said, stepping back to the rostrum, "what does the distinguished delegate of Ghana have in mind?"

"I would leave that to the wisdom of the distinguished Secretary and the judgment of this Assembly," Ghana said smoothly, and stepped down.

Again there was a silence as Orrin stood at the rostrum, obviously thinking it out, though perhaps not quite at such length as he made them believe. Finally he spoke with a thoughtful slowness.

"Well, Mr. President, this is all rather irregular, and I should, all things considered, prefer a vote at once on my motion to adjourn. However, in view of the suggestion of the distinguished delegate of Ghana, which is typical of his thoughtful approach to this matter—("Oh, brother," Lafe murmured to Hal Fry)—I might be willing to modify my suggestion to suspend to next Monday, a week from today."

There was an immediate commotion from the general direction of the U.S.S.R., and—shouting "Point of order! Point of order!"—Vasily Tashikov could be seen hurrying down the aisle to the platform. The delegate from Ghana went back to his seat, the Secretary of State turned away to a seat at the side without speaking to the Soviet Ambassador, earphones went on, dials were spun to the Russian channel. The President said patiently, "The distinguished delegate of the Soviet Union is recognized for a point of order."

"The point of order, Mr. President," Tashikov said angrily, "is that we are here proposing to let the guilty man decide the terms of his own sentencing. We are proposing to let the criminal decide when he shall be hanged. This is not the purpose of the United Nations, Mr. President—"

"Now, Mr. President!" the Secretary of State cried with equal anger, steaming back up the steps in a show of rage that made the Soviet Ambassador step hastily back from the rostrum, "the distinguished Soviet delegate is himself out of order to use such terms about a fellow member of the United Nations. How dare he call the United States a criminal, Mr. President, he whose nation has on its hands the blood of many millions of innocent people, and in whose graveyard rest the carcasses of so many once-free states?"

"Point of order, Mr. President!" Tashikov shouted, while his colleagues in the Communist bloc dutifully pounded their desks and pandemonium again began to sweep across the chamber. Into it the President furiously banged his gavel and, with some instinct of perception that enabled him to catch the slightest of movements in areas from which help might come, cried out with great relief, "The delegate of France seeks recognition. The distinguished delegate of France is recognized!"

"Mr. President," Raoul Barre said calmly as both the delegate of the U.S.A. and the delegate of the U.S.S.R. resumed their seats, stalking stiffly down separate aisles to rejoin their delegations, "I shall not inflame this discussion further but will only say that I have been in consultation with other members of the French Community and other nations, and it seems to us that a reasonable compromise in this matter would be to amend the last motion of the distinguished delegate of the United States to read suspension until Thursday. It is now Monday, and that will allow for the balance of today, Tuesday, Wednesday, and Thursday until 10 A.M. for members to consult their governments and each other. Surely that should be sufficient to satisfy all parties concerned. I therefore make that formal motion, Mr. President, as a substitute for the last motion of the delegate of the United States."

"All those in favor of the motion of the delegate of France please signify by raising their hands," said the President with a relieved promptness that, as Hal murmured to Lafe, would have been at home on Capitol Hill. "All those opposed. Apparently a large majority is in favor of the motion as modified by the distinguished delegate of France, and this plenary session on this item is now suspended until 10 A.M. on Thursday."

Back in the Delegates' Lounge after the Assembly Hall had emptied, the world now really abuzz with sensation, the United States for the first time really on the defensive in the United Nations and on her most vulnerable point at that, the Secretary of State awaited with a number of emotions the arrival of the French Ambassador, with whom he had arranged a hasty date for lunch. Presently from the swirling crowd the dapper figure of Raoul Barre appeared and came forward. Orrin shook hands with some warmth.

"I want to thank you. I think that was exactly what had to be done, at that point."

Raoul nodded.

"Yes, it seemed to me so. As soon as Ghana began to give ground, it was obvious they all wanted a compromise. I don't know, though, how effectively they can be held off later on."

"No," the Secretary said, somewhat gloomily. "Nor do I. But we must do our best. Come along and tell me about the French Community. I gather we may be able to hold them."

The French Ambassador shook his head soberly.

"I do not know at this point. It will take some shrewd diplomacy and much hard work, but possibly you can beat it."

"Possibly!" Orrin Knox said. "We've got to beat it."

But whether they could or not he did not at the moment know, a doubt increased by the number of bland and noncommittal greetings he received as they proceeded to the elevator and up to the Delegates' Dining Room on the fourth floor. Only one greeting was quite unequivocal. As they stepped off the elevator and stopped by the reservations desk to get their table number, a small figure at the Secretary's elbow stepped back a pace and held out his hand. Orrin turned to find himself greeting the Portuguese Ambassador.

"Congratulations, Mr. Secretary," he said with an ironic politeness. "Now you know how it feels."

And to that, the French Ambassador noted with a small inward smile as he took the Secretary's arm and pulled him away, Orrin for once had no rejoinder.

So the word went out across the seas and to all the nations that the United States of America had this day been publicly attacked and humiliated before the world and might very well find herself, in three days' time, formally condemned for social practices which to a majority of the world's inhabitants had long seemed deserving of condemnation. That she had been making earnest attempts for many years to right the wrongs, that Administration after Administration in Washington had done its best to speed the process, that decent folk of both races in South and North alike were working together patiently in a fearfully difficult situation, made no difference now. It was not an age in which men were disposed to stop and think, or be objective or fair, even had they the knowledge and the decency to do so. It was an age to take advantage of every weakness, and there were many now who were ready to move in for the kill, if kill there were to be.

In steadily mounting crescendo the babble of opinion crashed across the world as afternoon wore into night. Lights burned late in many delegations. International cables and telephone lines were jammed. DEFY's picketers paraded two hundred strong outside the UN. A constant stream of delegates ascended to the thirty-eighth floor to see the Secretary-General. In Washington men pondered how best to defend their country, or take advantage of her, and in New York the *Times* advertising department got a call to delay the "FAIR PLAY FOR GOROTOLAND" ad, because its sponsors wished to revise it in view of late events. All across the broad reaches of America the citizenry reacted with annoyance or anger or bitterness or shame, according to individual attitude and inclination.

At the St. Regis in New York the delegation of Yugoslavia gave a dinner-dance and the M'Bulu of Mbuele partied long and happily into the night.

Two

FELIX LABAIYA'S BOOK

This week's principal contributor to "The Talk of the Town" inserted a piece of paper in his typewriter and wrote with a glowing satisfaction (for it had been a truly thrilling interview):

"*Terry*

"We had a talk a couple of days ago [he informed *The New Yorker's* readers with a cozy warmth] with the M'Bulu of Mbuele, the vigorous young African leader who has thrown the United Nations and the United States into one of the biggest uproars they have known in years. We found him at the St. Regis, a charming and attractive six-feet-seven known to friends as Terry, not at all abashed by the fuss he had caused from Charleston to China (Red, that is).

"We thought of a panther as we watched him pace up and down the room, for that is the impression he gives: overwhelming virility, powerful masculine force, sleek and trigger-quick control. We found him, like ourselves, more amused than bothered by events of recent days in which he has played so heroic a part. He was also not at all averse to giving us a candid picture of how an intelligent, freedom-loving African has come to achieve leadership in his continent's struggle to achieve full status in the world.

" 'From my earliest days, I think,' he said with a faraway look in his eyes, pausing in his pacing long enough to sit beside us on the couch for a moment before leaping up to pace again, 'I have been dedicated to the fight for freedom. Britain encouraged forces of oppression in my country which had to be beaten before Gorotoland could be free. Some of these were very close to the throne. I enlisted in that battle at an early age.'

"We told him we had heard that there had been some dynastic difficulties for a time in his progressive and prosperous land. He smiled, though a little somberly, we thought, and made a charming gesture with his hands.

" 'The fight for freedom is never easy,' he told us. 'Sometimes it requires heroic measures of us all. Do you not think so?'

"We said we did, and asked him if he thought Gorotoland was now well on its way to a deserved freedom at last. At once a happy gleam came into his eyes.

" 'It is almost literally a matter of days, now,' he said confidently. 'I think the world's freedom-loving peoples will join us in our battle. The outcome is inevitable.'

"He broke off abruptly to go to the window and greet a couple of pigeons which had alighted there to eat the crumbs he had put out. We liked the way he talked to the pigeons: at once tender, encouraging and manly. The pigeons cooed, and flew away.

" 'Of course you understand,' he went on, coming back to sit beside us again, 'that Britain is now resorting to almost hysterical measures to block our independence. Every charge is being used against us—slavery, human sacrifice, cannibalism, Communism'—he grinned, so infectiously that we could not help grinning back—'there is nothing too inflammatory. But it won't work. It is old hat, and it won't work.'

"We asked him how it had felt to defy a hate-filled mob when he used his great prestige to help a frightened little Negro girl start integration at a white school in Charleston, South Carolina, last week. He gave an answer that, we thought, was typical of him, touching in its modesty, noble in its innate and instinctive dignity.

" 'Something like that is not easy, of course,' he told us earnestly, 'but when the imperatives of history speak, one answers, even in your great country. One cannot blame the past for being the past, but one must have the courage to march unfrightened into the future. If one's cause is just, one must inevitably triumph.' He smiled, and shook his head reflectively. 'Still,' he confessed with a touching candor, 'I cannot say it was easy.'

"We told him we thought a great many Americans admired his courage and supported him fully in what he had done.

" 'That moves me deeply,' he assured us, 'because there are certain hysterical people in your country, too. Even here they see Communism under every bed, and circulate stories around the United Nations that it was all a—your expression is "a put-up job," I think.'

"We assured him *we* did not believe it, and he smiled gratefully.

" 'After all,' he said, 'I really did risk my own life. It is foolish to think I would do a thing like that unless I really believed in it, is it not?'

"We told him we couldn't agree more."

This week's principal contributor ripped the sheet from his typewriter and sent it along to be edited with a pleased little sigh. It had been a thrilling interview, the M'Bulu so big and black and handsome, his knee scarcely an inch from the principal contributor's, his long, prehensile fingers occasionally exerting a gentle pressure upon that intimate appendage by way of emphasis. The whole thing had been so—so *democratic*, somehow.

This week's principal contributor, who mercifully had not seen the sardonic smile with which the M'Bulu studied his departure, told himself that he had rarely met so magnificent a personality, felt so immediate and electric a sense of understanding intimacy with another human being. He only hoped he could make *The New Yorker's* readers feel it. God knew *he* had.

For Felix Labaiya, as his chauffeured limousine drove up and deposited him at the Delegates' Entrance on First Avenue, there was no such mood of fun-and-games. His interests lay elsewhere, for one thing, and for another he was far too self-contained and practical a soul to waste his time in unnecessary fawning on an adventurer whom he assessed accurately, and dismissed, for what he was. An intensive three days lay ahead for the Ambassador of Panama, a prospect which neither displeased nor intimidated him.

Felix was used to hard work and, in a diplomatic context, thoroughly enjoyed both its challenges and its demands.

The task was made easier by a secret excitement, a glow of triumph every bit as great as any felt by Terrible Terry in his brightest moments of glory. Felix had the Colossus of the North fairly hooked, and he did not see at the moment how the Colossus proposed to escape.

So enormous were the implications of this fact, so astounding its ultimate possibilities in the world, that he had to stop and remind himself every few moments that he had actually brought it off: brought it off, or helped to bring it off. He was not sure at exactly what moment the idea of the M'Bulu's dramatic assault upon the citadels of Charleston had coalesced, or whether he or Terry could take the ultimate credit. Somewhere in the course of their private talks at "Harmony" there had been mention of Justice Davis' ruling on the Middleton School appeal; there had been a reference to occasions in the past when African diplomats traveling in the South had been insulted; and then a sudden, apparently simultaneous moment of illumination in which Felix had said with a quick excitement, "Perhaps you could—" only to be interrupted by the M'Bulu's suddenly eager, "Possibly I could—" And then, in great secrecy and mounting excitement, encouraged by LeGage Shelby, whom they had taken immediately into their confidence, they had become committed. LeGage had slipped away as soon as the Jason Foundation luncheon ended to find the necessary child and arrange with her parents to have her ready at the proper time; Felix had suggested casually to his in-laws that it might be well for them to leave the house to the M'Bulu and be far away as soon as possible; and they had known him well enough to take his advice and, without haste but with tasteful dispatch, depart. Terry had been left to plan his moment, hampered only by the unexpected self-invited presence of Cullee Hamilton. But that, as it turned out, had been no handicap. Perhaps, in the sense of ultimate pressures which could be brought to bear upon the Congressman when his fellow Negroes began really to understand that he had left it to a foreigner to make one of the most dramatic gestures ever made in the South against segregation, it would turn out to be a very useful weapon indeed.

And so it had come about, just as they had discussed it in the cool high-ceilinged rooms where the proud planters of the past had sown with graceful self-righteousness a harvest more terrible than they knew. It lent an extra spice to the game—for him and, he knew, for both LeGage and Terry—that the idea should have come to them at "Harmony." It was somehow fitting that it should be so, and that there, where so many proud people had lived their carefree, unthinking lives, preparation should be made to humble pride.

Pride: how he hated their pride, the arrogant ones, the bland ones, the crude, the powerful, the mightily supreme ones, the creators and oppressors of his country who used weapons of money and influence and thoughtless superiority more cruel than any weapon of shot or steel. He turned now and stared at their flag, snapping in a freshening breeze as an early hint of the winter to come gusted up First Avenue; it flew among more than a hundred others, yet for him it blotted out all else. To lower it figuratively here, he was attempting; to lower it literally where it still flew in his own land, he must. For Felix Labaiya-Sofra, born to be an oligarch of Panama but somehow diverted to purposes he deemed more noble and worthy than that, nothing in the world was more important than this fierce desire which had been a part of him as long as he could remember.

That it had been so deep an aspect of his being for so long could probably, he supposed, be traced to his grandfather, since it had effectively skipped his father; or perhaps, for that very reason, it could be traced to his father. His father he thought of now with a customary contempt as he passed between the blue canvas windbreaks that shelter the walk to the Delegates' Entrance, nodded absently to the guard on duty, and passed within the tall glass doors. Luis Labaiya was a dutiful servant of the Yanquis; no one had ever been able successfully to accuse him of not being that. Any independence he might once have felt had disappeared long ago in the necessity to do well in business, to hold and increase the vast salt and mineral deposits left him by Don Jorge, to double his patrimony ten times over by a shrewd policy of co-operating with the owners of the Canal, running their errands, flattering their egos, supplementing and easing the exercise of their power with the ubiquitous contribution of his own. Old-timers in the Canal Zone looked back to his occupancy of La Presidencia with a nostalgia they did not feel for some who had resided there. "We never had this trouble when Louie Labaiya was in," they sometimes told one another in tones of exasperated reminiscence. Times had changed since Louie, and nowhere was it more evident than in the person of his son.

That this surprised and disappointed Louie, he had made quite clear before he had died eight years ago. That it would not have disappointed his fierce old grandfather, Felix was certain. The ghostly presence of Don Jorge was with him still, aided, it is true, by the actual presence of Donna Anna, now in her ninety-seventh year and still commanding the family with a wraithlike vigor that no one dared challenge, at least to her face; but more alive and vigorous by far was the spirit of the indomitable man who had seized a fortune for himself in gold near El Real and salt at Gulfo de Parita; who had led revolutions against Colombia, conspired with the agent of the hero of San Juan Hill to bring Panama to birth in the jungles of the Isthmus—and then lived to see the victory turn bitter as his erstwhile allies proved to be as firmly insistent on complete control of the Canal as he himself would have been in their place. This was not an irony he could appreciate, however. There had been in his proud and rigid mind the dream that, having used the Yanquis, he could throw them out. It did not work that way; nor could it possibly have done so in the face of the national imperatives that had prompted the United States to build the Canal in the first place. Don Jorge had served in a government or two, then been quietly forced out at the insistence of the American military governor of the Canal, who regarded him, accurately, as a troublemaker. Angry and embittered, he had retired to

Boquete near the foot of the volcano Chiriqui, built himself an enormous home overlooking the valley, and proceeded to brood in an arrogant and ominous loneliness symbolized in the name he gave his house: La Suerte, which stood for *La suerte está echada,* or, The die is cast.

But, like many such gestures in the annals of man, this one, too, proved to be more defiant than prophetic—at least, in the days of Don Jorge. Yanqui presence brought Yanqui money and Yanqui trade, a commerce that rapidly and inevitably tied the oligarchic families of Panama to the lead-strings of the United States. Like most Latin American nations, the new republic consisted of a thin layer of wealth on top and a great drop down to the illiterate, impoverished mestizos below. Inevitably, in the immemorial fashion in which wealth adheres to wealth, an economic cohesion of interest took place among the leading families. Inevitably, Don Jorge's son, coming to maturity in the years of growing prosperity and stability at the top, found himself increasingly unmoved by his father's grim attempts to keep alive the fanatic flames of the past. By the time the world turned toward its second great convulsion and it became necessary to greater states than Panama that it should be absolutely reliable with no chance of waverings or uncertainties, Luis Labaiya was of an age and temperament to accept without hesitations or qualms of conscience the obvious intention in several powerful cities far away that he should be one of those chosen to do the job of holding the Caribbean that had to be done.

Shortly before his election to the Presidency, however, there had been one sharp, embittered interview at La Suerte whose impact had never faded from the mind of Don Jorge's youthful grandson, then just coming to an age in which the defiances of the past are easier to understand than the compliances of the present. The old man had commanded them to come together to his lair at the foot of Chiriqui—for lair it seemed, then, with its stone ramblings, brooding vistas, heavily-furnished, darkly-shuttered rooms, and general air of somber retreat—and there had given his son the harsh ultimatum that he was not to accept the Chief Magistracy on the conditions of good behavior implicit in every official and unofficial American approach on the subject. Luis Labaiya, by then sufficiently self-assured in his own personality to be no longer overawed by his father, and already committed to the certainty of coming power, had ventured to reply, not with the equivocal politeness he should perhaps have used, but with a bluntness that had astounded and aroused his father.

Even now, as he walked across the marbled floor of the Delegates' Lobby and prepared to take the escalator down to Conference Room 9 in the basement where he had been invited to speak to the African states, Don Jorge's grandson could see as vividly as though the old man were before him this moment the expression of utter disbelief and anger that had rushed across his grandfather's face. For a moment he had thought Don Jorge would literally have a stroke, as he alternately flushed and paled, flushed and paled, while his breath came in hurtful gasps, harshly and almost out of control. When he had finally mastered himself to the point of coherent speech, he did not address his son at all. Instead, he ignored him as though he were not there and, turning to his grandson, in a whisper whose intensity rang in Felix' ears to this day, repeated two words: "*Remember me! Remember me!*"

And so he had, the Ambassador of Panama thought grimly as he bowed with his polite, self-contained, closed-off smile to a member of the Polish delegation, passing him alongside on the up-escalator. He was convinced that he knew the sense in which Don Jorge had meant it: Remember me—remember Panama—remember the revolutions and all the bright banners flying—remember to hate the Yanquis—remember the dream of "the Canal to us!"—remember there is still tomorrow—remember not to forget! All these things were symbolized for him by his grandfather, and it was with a bitter anger and contempt for his father that he had followed him, shaken, white-faced, silent but still unyielding, out of the gloomy doors of La Suerte, down the rutted, winding hill road through the crowding jungle, and so presently back across the Isthmus to Panama City and Luis Labaiya's destiny.

And now they were both dead, the bitter old man and the defiant younger, and he, Felix, was male head of the family and embarked upon purposes that one of them, at least, would have approved, even though the other would not. He too had had his interview with his father, then on his death-bed with cancer, and it too had been a bitter one. In his own eyes Luis Labaiya had served the cause of freedom and justice well in the Second World War, conducted the Presidency with a decent regard for his country-men, shown an enlightened attitude toward education and social reform, moved surprisingly far from the selfish pattern of the Latin *patron*. But these things were not sufficient for his son, as they were not sufficient for an increasing number of Panamanians, swiftly becoming sick with what the Americans, looking across the street from the Zone, were coming to refer to scathingly as "the Canal disease."

"Whatever Louie's faults," they told one another, and they thought he had some, "at least he didn't have the Canal disease."

But Louie's son, and more and more of his countrymen every day, certainly did.

The truth of the matter—that the Americans had dreamed, planned, financed, built, and maintained the world waterway with a justice much fairer to Panama than many of her citizens would ever admit; that they genuinely did regard the Canal as an international trust that they must administer honorably and well, and that they had done so beyond challenge by impartial judgment—these were as nothing in the face of the emotional obsession that settled upon the surrounding republic. To this obsession it was easy for Felix, prepared by his grandfather's whispered admonition which he knew he would carry for life, to succumb. He had followed the traditional pattern of wealth in Latin America, it is true, and gone north to get his education in the United States; but in a very real sense this was done in much the same spirit in which Terence Ajkaje had done it—to scout the enemy's defenses. He had returned to break the traditional pattern by taking post-graduate studies at the University of Panama, just beginning to open to underprivileged Panamanians of his own generation the promise that they, too, could acquire the knowledge that might, in time, give them the strength to move the world.

In time—but there was no time. The world was spinning ever faster, and those who would move it must seize the fleeting chance and tip it while they could. Companions and projects his father only dimly suspected began to concern Felix Labaiya; not until Felix, by then a two-term Deputy in the National Assembly, joined Aquilino Boyd to help lead the march on the Canal Zone on Independence Day, November 3, 1959, did his father realize that Don Jorge and not himself had won the battle for his son. And by then it was too late for Luis Labaiya to win him back, though he tried.

Again there was the call to come to La Suerte, by now remodeled, modernized, made bright with Yanqui paints and Yanqui prints, only Donna Anna's quarters far in the left wing preserved, as they had always been, in dingy splendor. There was even a swimming pool, now, and on long weekends lively groups of friends, quite often including members of the Canal Zone staff, the military governor and his lady, and other American residents as well as wealthy Panamanians, would travel the still-difficult two hundred miles out to frolic and disport. Near the end of his father's life, Felix began to introduce a new element to these parties, one that increasingly embarrassed Luis Labaiya: angry students from the University, young scholars and professors, youthful journalists, occasionally a stranger or two from overseas, visitors full of positive opinions and instantaneous contention who rapidly disrupted the easygoing air of the *estancia* and turned previously relaxed gatherings into battlegrounds of argumentative tension. It was not long before Luis' friends, particularly his American friends, began to find other things to do upon receipt of invitations to come to La Suerte. Urged on by increasing anxiety for his son and unexpected word from his doctors that he was engaged in a physical battle he could not win, the ex-President made one last attempt to persuade a moderation that Felix was no longer prepared to accept save as a deliberate means to an end. In his heart he had already left moderation far behind.

The Ambassador sighed deeply now, an unconscious commentary on the gap between generations that he was not even aware of, as he thought of that second confrontation between father and son at La Suerte. As he had entered the high-ceilinged bedroom with its view down the valley, glanced at the wasted hands lying on the coverlet, and looked into the desperate eyes with a feeling of pain that he could not conceal, he had known a sudden resurgence of the love for his father that he had felt long ago as a child and had almost forgotten since in their increasingly bitter political arguments. A sudden vivid memory of a young and handsome Luis Labaiya riding a horse down jungle roads with a self-assured and self-confident swagger flashed into his mind; it was all he could do to suppress a sob. But his father's opening words had ended the moment at once and instantly reestablished the insurmountable barrier between them.

"The principal reason I do not wish to die," he had said in the husky whisper that was all the cancer still permitted him, "is that I fear for my son."

With a great effort Felix retained his self-control and replied with a calmness he did not feel.

"I am sorry for that," he said gravely. "Sorry that I have disappointed you and sorry that you are worried for me. Neither has been necessary."

"You have made it necessary. It has not been my doing."

Felix realized that his nails were biting into his palms; the sensation was sharp enough to conquer his impulse to cry out in anger. Instead he retreated to the cold precision to which he always retreated when his purposes, his ideas, or his emotions were under attack from any source.

"It has been the doing of the times. The world has moved from what it was. It is simply that I have moved with it. As," he continued when his father's ravaged hands made a movement of protest, "Panama too is moving with it. And will continue to move."

"It is not impossible," Luis said, "that another Labaiya may someday sit in *La Presidencia*. I should like to feel before I go that you would govern with honor."

"What is honor?" Felix asked bitterly. "To bow to the Yanquis? To be their colony? To let them operate our Canal and rake off its profits into their own fat pockets? There are some who have considered that honor. Not I."

"My son, you talk in slogans, not in facts," Luis said with a painful slowness. "They built the Canal. They do not run it at a profit. They do not keep from us anything which is rightfully ours."

"Is La Suerte's land ours?" Felix demanded harshly. "Do we love La Suerte? So is Panama's land ours, and so do I love Panama."

"And I do not?" Luis demanded with a ghostly but equal harshness. "La Suerte is nothing to me, Panama is nothing to me? You talk like a child and a fool."

"And yet I am neither," Felix said coldly. "And many grown men who are neither agree with me. And the day is coming when all Panama and all the world will agree with me. And then the enemy will be gone, and we will be left in peace to prosper as God intended."

"The enemy! You are beyond intelligence to use such terms. My friends are not 'the enemy'!"

"Your friends are not my friends," Felix snapped.

"My son is not my son," his father said, and turned on his side with an infinite weariness.

"Father—" Felix began, but there was no sign of relaxation in the rigid back beneath the coverlet. Automatically he satisfied himself that the cloth still moved, faintly but regularly, with breathing, and then turned away and walked out on the terrace of La Suerte and stood for a long time, his eyes blinded by tears that shut off the valley of his childhood and growing-up, the jungle and mountains and tropical vistas of his dearly beloved home. But his back was rigid too, and no more than his father's did it give sign of yielding. It was the last time he cried for anyone, and he would have died himself rather than have his father know that it had been for him.

Two weeks later Luis Labaiya was dead, the funeral was over, the business of readjusting was done, Felix was head of the family, now dwindled to himself, and his mother, and Donna Anna, huddling together in the old wing of the house in a protest, silent but inescapable, as strong as his father's. So be it, then. He was alone; he had always been alone; he would be alone. And when he was through, the world would know that in Felix Labaiya-Sofra it had a man who achieved what he set out to do.

Perhaps it was this quality more than any other that had really brought about his marriage to Patsy Jason. Some spark, not of fire but of the cold blue light that burns in certain people, had leaped between them when they met in Washington. He had been there as counselor of embassy first, a tentative and cautious offering from the current government in Panama—an offering that said, in effect, Here is your chance. We shall see if you will continue down the road you are going or be Louie Labaiya's son. It had occurred to him in the bitter days following his father's death that obviously his best advantage lay in appearing to be the latter and giving them to understand that he was not bidding them farewell forever. He had gracefully eased himself away from the more publicly obstreperous companions of his radical days and begun to assume, not too slowly, not too fast, the necessary mantle of conformity.

"I knew that when Louie died and he understood the full responsibilities of his position, Felix would be all right," they told one another comfortably in the Zone. The enemy had even been invited back to La Suerte, and presently it seemed as though nothing at all had changed and that the House of Labaiya was again what it had been under his father, a pillar of Panama, one of the principal rocks upon which to rest the curious relationship between the Giant of the North and its tiny brother of the Isthmus.

There had come in due course the invitation to go to Washington, and he had accepted it eagerly, for there was still much that he wanted to know about the Americans on their home ground. In the gleaming white capital, which he reached in an autumn season much like the present with the leaves turning and the air soft and a gentle wistfulness in the busy atmosphere, he had moved at once into a position of prominence in the diplomatic corps. "Panama Sends an Eligible Young Bachelor," the *Evening Star* reported in a personality sketch in its society pages shortly after his arrival. "Pat and Perle and Dolly and Polly are all going to be after the new counselor of the Embassy of Panama," the article had begun, "for he is everything a hostess' heart could desire. Young, handsome, and dashing, he reportedly has a reputation in his homeland for being a great one with the ladies. So, watch out girls!" And the girls, of course, instead of watching out, had flung themselves at his head with a gay abandon that amused, if it did not particularly impress, the eligible young bachelor from Panama.

Like most Latins—indeed, like most foreigners of whatever nature—Felix was somewhat baffled by the American attitude toward sex, a practical function in his country that few people thought about twice. Either you got it or you didn't; if you did, fine, and if you didn't, well, *mañana* was another

day and more than one fish swam in the boundless sea. Bafflement soon
yielded to amusement, and a calm decision to make the most of it; before
very long he was living up to his reputation in a way that caused some de-
liciously excited gossip in Georgetown and other purlieus of the capital's
knowledgeable. This had been going on for six months when he met Patsy
Jason at a party at Dolly's. He was given to understand at once that this
was not to be a conquest as simple as the rest.

Why it shouldn't have been he was for a time puzzled to understand,
which was exactly the result intended, as he soon came to realize. His first
impulse was to dismiss it, but something about Patsy, with her striking dark
good looks, her outwardly vacuous chatter, and her inner certainties, seemed
to appeal directly to something in him.

"I think you're very cold-blooded," she had told him when she finally consented to being escorted to a ball at the beautiful main building of the Pan-
American Union at Seventeenth Street and Constitution Avenue.

"I have company in that," he responded with a rarely flashing smile.

"I know," she said with a giggle. "Aren't we WORTHLESS?"

But they both knew they weren't, of course. Few more intelligent people
lived in Washington; few more perceptive, ambitious, and shrewd; few whose
ultimate interests ran more nearly together. It was soon obvious to him that
Patsy's principal aim in life was to further the ambitions of her brother,
then serving as Undersecretary of Defense before returning to make his successful race for Governor of California. Ted had lost his first wife and had
not yet married the stunning Ceil who was now his second; Patsy, having
nothing else to do with her time and share of the family millions, was keeping house for him on Foxhall Road and serving as his hostess. Felix was
given to understand early that everything was subordinate to Ted, which of
course made it doubly flattering when it became increasingly obvious that
his own person and interests were assuming an equal, and soon a greater,
place in Patsy's life.

That this condition could not last, he was quite sure, but there were plenty
of reasons why he should take advantage of it while it did. They were both
extremely wealthy—although compared with the Jason millions, of course,
his own patrimony seemed relatively minor—both ambitious, both determined,
both inclined to be ruthless in going after what they wanted. They were also
completely at home in the world of national and international society and
politics in which they moved, aware of most of the subtle influences that
went into its operations, quick to see and act upon those things that could
be of use to them. "Those two *ought* to marry," the editorial director of the
Washington *Post* had commented to Justice Tommy Davis as they watched
the stunning couple circulate over the green lawns among the strawberry-
laden tables at the British Embassy's June garden party for the Queen. "They
were certainly made for this town."

They were made for something more, and both were aware of it. They
were made for power. The difficulty involved in differing nationalities was
not what it might have been in some other cases. The Jasons had interests

in Panama, as they had in most places around the world, and Felix in any event was apparently embarked upon a substantial period of residence in America. "When Ted is President of the United States and you're President of Panama," Patsy had remarked after the wedding with a mock ruefulness, "where will I be?" "You can commute," he had assured her with a pleasant smile, knowing that at that particular moment, probably the high point of their marriage as far as its emotional content was concerned, she would no more leave him than fly. But the day would come. When it did, it would be no problem. The marriage, he knew instinctively then, would go on regardless; have a brief season of passion now, then settle; and go on.

They had been married at the Washington Cathedral at an enormously popular and enormously attended ceremony ignored by the Archdiocese of Washington, since for political reasons of his own Felix had chosen to fall away from the Church and Patsy was not about to join. The newly-elected Governor Jason gave his sister away, *Life* and *Look* each gave the ceremony six pages, everybody who was anybody was there to give it blessing, and what one reporter referred to as "the treaty of mutual assistance between Jason and Labaiya" was duly consummated. Felix entered upon it hopeful that in time the Jason interests might be added to his own in pursuit of the purposes to which he knew his life to be dedicated.

What these were he never entirely told Patsy. She knew he was concerned about the Canal, that he felt, as he assured her quite truthfully most Panamanians did, a restless resentment of the relationship with the United States; but that he contemplated anything more she never suspected, for, after all, how could he? There was no way to achieve it, even if he did. His march with Aquilino Boyd on Independence Day 1959 had apparently been the high-water mark of Panamanian protest. Things had simmered since, but simmered, with a few relatively minor exceptions, quietly. Felix seemed increasingly removed from the inner turmoil of Panama as he moved on from counselor to Ambassador and went in due time from Washington to the United Nations.

The day might come when his dream of winning support from the Jasons would prove to be delusion—who could say what time would bring in the affairs of ambitious men?—but he would not have been human had he not made it the basis of an active hope. If Ted became President, would there not be a more reasonable attitude in the White House toward the aspirations of his brother-in-law's country, a concession that the changing pattern of world events made no longer suitable the continuance of so archaic and antiquated a relationship between sovereign states? He had never spelled this out to Governor Jason, who kept his own counsel even more completely than Felix did, if that were possible, and thereby was perhaps the only man living for whom the Panamanian Ambassador felt a secret, uneasy awe. But it would not be human not to hope: it would make things so much easier all around if it should turn out to be true.

In time, so bland and well-behaved did his son apparently become, it came to seem that Luis Labaiya had won after all. On quick trips back to

La Suerte he and Patsy entertained with a lavishness rarely seen in the Isthmus. In Panama, in Washington, and at the UN the Ambassador of Panama went about with a circumspect and equable air that presently erased many of the memories of whatever mood of rebellion may have shadowed his earlier years. These things were now attributed, if anyone thought of them at all, to youthful exuberance, a need to sow political wild oats, a tendency to substitute action for the sober appreciation of Panama's best interests that any sensible man of course must have. "He just had to kick up his heels," they said in the Zone. Felix smiled and went his way.

There came a time when heads as shrewd as his, constantly studying and analyzing and restudying and reanalyzing the complex of nations and personalities at the United Nations, came to the conclusion that there might be found in the Ambassador of Panama an ally worth having. A short but intensive courtship followed, in which Felix found himself wined and dined and flattered by Vasily Tashikov until, as he told himself dryly, it was running out his ears. To it all he responded with a bland pretense of gratification which apparently fooled and flattered the Soviets, for they began to turn to him increasingly on matters inimical to the West, seeking his advice, which he was always careful to keep noncommittal, and beseeching his active support, which he now and then began to give.

Potentially it could be a dangerous game, and he knew it. He must always bear in mind three things—the disapproval of the United States, the disapproval of his own government, and the disapproval, perhaps most important of all, of his wife and in-laws. The most he had been able to persuade his government to agree to had been an occasional abstention on a vote of interest to Washington. This had caused some raised eyebrows in the State Department, but the temper of the world was changing, a little show of independence was considered a good thing—"At least they can't say we run Panama," somebody remarked jocularly at a meeting of the Policy Planning Staff. "Anyway, not all the time," somebody else responded wryly—and nobody became too alarmed. Very cautiously and very carefully Felix felt his way, widening the area of his freedom of action little by little; a process of education, of human manipulation, of playing with opposing forces, which fascinated him. The only thing he regretted was that it was something he could not discuss with anyone, even his wife. He could never forget that the ultimate result might yet be some explosive conclusion that would blow all his careful fabrics asunder. It might also blow his marriage asunder. There was no point in hurrying the day, though he was prepared to face it if the necessities of his country brought it about.

For there was something else about Felix Labaiya that no one suspected, and that was the fierce depth of his love for Panama. There was simply no argument as to what was right or wrong where his country was concerned. He was astute enough, and perceptive enough, to understand that this motivation could apply with just as overwhelming a force to the Americans as well, and indeed to most of the peoples with whom he dealt in the house of nations in Turtle Bay. But in his own case it erased all arguments of fairness, all appeals to reason, all attempts to see the American point of view on this issue that so deeply concerned his country. His deepest, and in a sense his only, love was Panama, and it followed therefrom that nothing could possibly deflect him from the basic purpose that was his. A thousand memories linked him to the Isthmus, its vistas, mountains, seas, islands, plains. Here he had been born, grown up, been influenced by his grandfather and father, matured physically, mentally, politically. This was his land. How could there be justice toward those who controlled its most valuable asset? They could quote statistics at him forever, explain how fairly they were administering it, point out that the Panama Canal Company made no profits, explain that its commerce furnished one-sixth of Panama's income, place themselves on a high moral plane, and talk about guarding an international trust—and all this mattered no more to him than it did to the most ignorant mestizo in the streets. He held it as a matter of blind faith, as fierce and proud as that of Don Jorge, that the Canal was Panama's. It was mentally, indeed almost physically, impossible for him to acknowledge any competing argument.

But it was an age in which to be cautious, if you wished to achieve something more substantial than headlines; a time to plan secretly and long before moving; an era in which the crumbling forms of world society furnished great opportunities to those who held tenaciously to their own private desires and advanced them when the time was ripe. The world was at loose ends. A purposeless illogic afflicted even the most carefully laid plans and projects of those whose writ had once run over many continents and across many seas; an insensate destructiveness crippled the crafty programs of those who sought to supplant them. A weird lassitude lay upon the West, an outwardly vigorous yet essentially nihilistic energy upon the East. Under their shadow those who were small and careful and discreet might sometimes achieve their purposes.

They might also, when the chance came right, furnish the fulcrum upon which to turn the earth.

So he had done in The Problem of Gorotoland, raised now by Terence Ajkaje's visit to a Charleston school into an issue of such import that it might well weaken his life's adversary in very grave degree in the eyes of many states and peoples around the globe. At first the matter had occurred to him—or, again, possibly, occurred to the Soviet Ambassador; here too his memory was a little hazy as to who had first proposed it when they had discussed it over lunch two weeks ago—simply as a generalized attack upon the West, a matter that would embarrass Britain, possibly bring her into conflict with the United States, strengthen his own standing among the uncommitted nations, make him more of a voice to listen to in the councils of the world. His government had not been averse to this when he explained it to them. Freedom was a great thing to be for, and Panama could not lose by taking an active hand in the fight for it, particularly in Africa. He had been gratified by the overwhelming approval that had come to him both in the United Nations and across the world. Then had come the bonus of the M'Bulu's dramatic gesture, his devastating appearance before the General

Assembly, his stirring call to action that had so excited and inflamed the Afro-Asian states. Now the issue was grave indeed for the great Republic and he, Felix Labaiya, had cut out for him a task more important and more vital than any he had yet undertaken.

As things stood now, it would take a two-thirds vote by the General Assembly to ratify his resolution and its amendment. He thought with a contemptuous smile of the feeble and futile efforts of the United States to head off his amendment yesterday, the series of crushing votes by which its moves had been defeated. Despite the recovery by the Secretary of State, the sudden sober realization of a challenge breath-taking in its implications which had finally gripped the Assembly and brought about a delay at the last moment, he was not too worried as he approached the door of Conference Room 9.

Terrible Terry, flanked by the delegates of Ghana and Guinea, was coming toward him with hand outstretched. He was Don Felix grandson of Don Jorge, and a supreme confidence buoyed him up. He was trim, neat, self-contained, and determined in his small, dark person; trim, neat, self-confident, and determined in his shrewd dark mind. His country needed him and he had never failed her yet.

He stepped forward with his pleasant suggestion of smile and bowed politely as he saw the group of midnight faces looking up to his with an eager and expectant air.

2

Now there was another problem to solve, the President thought with an exasperated sigh: it never ended, the tangle of jackstraws that history dumped upon his desk each day for untangling. He was aware of his own responsibility in the turn events had taken, he regretted now the very human impulse that had made him dismiss so lightly Terrible Terry's request for full-scale red-carpet treatment, but he still could not regret or modify the basic judgment of the M'Bulu that had prompted it. The man whose ennobled visage stared forth from this morning's editorial cartoon, godlike in aspect and haloed by an aura of light labeled "Freedom," was still a devious little international adventurer, and the President knew not all the friendly press puffs in the world could change the fact. But, then, this was an age when the fact was not important. The legend was all that mattered.

This was not the first time, or, he suspected, the last, that certain journals around the country had gone to extraordinary lengths to confer their blessings upon such legends. He thought how nice it would be if someday the truth unvarnished emerged from certain editorial offices, but he had long ago concluded that it was not to be. Diligent and devoted reporters might record the truth as faithfully as competence and integrity enabled them, but inevitably editorial decision shifted the emphasis, shadowed the facts, threw everything subtly but completely out of focus, so that the hasty reader emerged with quite a different impression. And, of course, side by side with bland overinflation of favorites and bland denigration of opponents went high protestations of public morality, well-publicized speeches on freedom of the press, stern trumpetings against governmental censorship. Yet, he supposed, the editors responsible were quite able to convince themselves that they were honorable and consistent men.

He could not, however, spend too long a time considering this particular aspect of twentieth-century America, for the challenge presented at the United Nations was for the time being more overriding than anything else before him. As he approached his desk each day at 9 A.M., after eating a solitary breakfast of fruit juice, boiled egg, toast, and coffee while he watched television news broadcasts and scanned the six major morning newspapers, he did not always know which of the world's many constantly bleeding sores would be before him for immediate attention. No such uncertainty existed this day. Every top headline, every telecast, confirmed it. Somebody in London had held a copy of the *Daily Mirror* up before the cameras. "U.S. BROUGHT TO WORLD BAR," the headline read. He was vividly and unhappily aware that this was exactly the way it was being regarded over the greater part of the earth's surface.

In this difficult situation there were certain things he could do of an immediate nature, and indeed in his statement, apology, and state dinner for Terry he had already done some of them. Now he must turn to the practical aspects of world politics: check with the Development Loan Fund on certain applications from overseas, have Orrin talk to certain Ambassadors about projects they desired under the foreign aid program, hint to others concerning possible military expenditures, apply with polite but unflinching steadiness the diplomatic and financial pressures that lay at the hand of the President of the United States when the chips were down. He did not like to operate that way, he told himself ruefully, but he was becoming as adept at it as his predecessor had been. It was part of what might be called, ironically, Growing Up in the White House. Always in international politics, as in domestic, there came the moment when you were either going to see it through or run away. If you decided to see it through, which by and large had been the policy of most American Presidents, you accepted the means to achieve the objective. He had always been able to appreciate, as an intellectual exercise, the dedication to the country that dominated the actions and the attitudes of the occupant of 1600 Pennsylvania, but it was like any other great responsibility. Until you had it, you never really knew. Now he did.

He must get now, he decided, an inside picture of the situation at the UN and he must get it from the one man whom he deemed to be, at the moment, closest to the center of the hubbub and most familiar with all its ramifications. He pressed the buzzer which announced to the office wing of the White House that he was at his desk. His secretary entered and he asked her to locate LeGage Shelby.

"If he's in town, send him right on in when he comes. If he's in New

York, tell him to stand by and we'll set up a conference call. And get me Secretary Knox for the same time, if you will."

LeGage might not know all the answers, but he would know some of them; and there was another reason for talking to him, too.

There was beginning to take shape in the President's mind a solution for the problem of LeGage, prompted by the noisy picketings of DEFY in the last couple of days. Again he told himself ruefully, for he was not particularly proud of the fact, that he was becoming as hard-boiled as the best of them. And the best of them, he knew, had sooner or later found themselves forced to be very hard-boiled indeed.

"Sue-Dan," her husband said, and realized that his voice was already sounding too exasperated for an argument that had just begun, "I don't want you to do it."

She gave a mocking laugh that brought over the wire from Sixteenth Street to the Hill its full burden of destructive amusement.

"What's the matter, Cullee? You think it would upset your pet white folks back in the district if your wife expressed her honest feelings for a change? Think they might vote against you if your wife helped her own people? Somebody in the Hamilton family has to, Cullee. *You* don't."

"Now, see here—" he began, but his secretary had paused on her way to the door to fiddle with some papers and he spoke sharply to her, instead. "Is there something more?"

"No, sir," she said hastily and walked out, wiggling the little brown bottom he had often been conscious of before. The door closed with a defiant thud. Probably they were all listening on the other phones, anyway. It was getting so he couldn't trust a one of them.

"I don't understand you at all," he began over again, more patiently. "One time you say you want me to be Senator and the next minute you want to do something that would knock it all out. Where did you get this crazy idea, anyway?"

"I want you to be Senator all right, Cullee," she said, sincerely enough but unable to resist a dig immediately after. "I'm just holding the colored vote for you while you slide up to the white one . . . Terry called me about it." She gave a wicked little snicker. "He's a big man, that Terry."

"Where is he?" the Congressman demanded harshly. His wife laughed again.

"Up in New York. Don't worry, he's up in New York. Where I'm going to be when I help LeGage open the African Bureau."

"African Bureau!" he snorted. "That Mr. LeGage Shelby, he's getting awfully important. How about World Bureau and be done with it? Anyway, you're not going."

"Oh, yes, I am."

"Oh, no, you're not."

"Cullee," she said, her voice rising, "I say I'm going!"

"I know what you say," he told her with a fair show of indifference he did not feel. "Suppose Maudie and I can't get along without you, is that it? Well, maybe we can, Sue-Dan. Maybe we just can. Try it and see."

"Well," she said uncertainly. There was a pause. "Can't mess up any beds with old Maudie," she remarked, and the thought started her chuckling again.

"Try and be common, Sue-Dan," he suggested politely. "Maybe you can just make it."

"LeGage wants me up there to help him," she said sullenly. "Terry wants me."

"I'll bet. I'll bet he does. That's just why you're not going."

"'Gage says it's going to be the biggest thing DEFY ever did," she said stubbornly. "It's going to help Terry and all the other African states. It's going to link all us colored peoples together all over the world. 'Gage says maybe it will be the start of something really big for all of us."

"Seems to me you and LeGage and Terry been talking all morning. You been on the phone ever since I left? Get a lot of wind out of both those boys, once you turn the valve on. Anyway, they're just giving you a story. They just want you up there so they can use your name and mine and tie me into it."

"Why shouldn't you be tied into it?" she demanded excitedly. "*Ebony* and the *Defender* and the Pittsburgh *Courier* and everybody else been after you here in the past hour wanting to know why you're not in it. What am I supposed to tell them?"

"They've been after me here, too. Tell them what I do. Tell them I think I can accomplish more working through the office to which I've been elected than I can walking in parades and carrying cards. What good does that do, except make a fuss?"

"Maybe that's what the white man needs," she said somberly. "One big fuss."

"Don't doubt Terry and 'Gage are just the ones to start it, but I think it's best you stay clear."

"They've started it already. How can I stay clear? How can any Negro stay clear? It's the colored man's dawning, Cullee. Only cowards stay clear."

"Oh, sure. That's me. I see."

"All we've got to go on is what you do, Cullee," she said pointedly. "Or not, that is. Afraid fine words don't mean much any more. The world's bustin' up, Cullee. People want to know what you're doing, not what you're saying."

"It's right out in public," he said doggedly. "Everybody can see."

"They don't see. Can't see anything but poor old Cullee won't help Terry take a little girl to school in Charleston, won't help LeGage fight for rights in DEFY, won't help start the African Bureau—just wants to sit on the Hill and be a white man's lap dog. Anyway, LeGage says he wants to talk to you serious. He says you're courting real trouble, Cullee. He says he's really worried about you."

"Yeah, I know. Well, you tell him I'm real worried about him. Where is he, anyway? The White House wants him. Just called a little while back to see if I knew where he was."

"He's at Howard, lecturing on non-violence."

"Non-violence!" he said with an exaggerated air. "That's my boy, sure enough. I suppose the Dean's office will know where to reach him. I'll call the White House and tell them."

"There you go!" she said, suddenly shrewish. "Call the White House, run their errands, tattle on LeGage, be a nice little nigger and everybody says, That Great Cullee! Well, not me. Not many of your own people, either. You're going to get in mighty bad with your own folks, Cullee, if you don't watch out."

"Well," he said sharply, "you're going to get in twice as bad if you go running after tramps like Terry and LeGage, and that's for sure. You tell me you're not going to New York and any African Bureau, Sue-Dan. I want to hear it before I hang up."

"What'll you do if you don't hear it?" she inquired spitefully. "Can't rape me over the telephone about it, can you?"

"Maybe you'll see when I get home," he said ominously.

"Maybe I won't be here when you get home." His heart constricted with a painful suddenness, but he replied with a show of boredom that he hoped was convincing. "Stop talking foolish, little Sue-Dan. You'll be wanting to fly off to the moon with the expedition, next."

"Might be nice up there. At least there's Russians there, and they like us."

"So they say. So they say. But don't you forget, they're white too, if that's all you think about. They'll turn on you too, if that's your worry. You're not going to New York to any African Bureau, Sue-Dan."

"We'll see," she said mockingly. "We'll see. Call the White House, big man, and tattle on LeGage. They'll love you for that. But don't be surprised if your own folks don't like you."

"I'll call LeGage myself," he said sharply, "if he wants to talk to me so bad. Then we can call the White House."

"What's the matter, Cullee?" she asked wickedly. "You getting a little scared, maybe, finally?"

"I'll see you at home," he promised angrily. A sardonic little laugh came over the wire.

"Maybe you will. Maybe you won't."

The Secretary of State became aware that his wife was regarding him with an amused smile from across the table.

"These are the times, obviously, that try men's souls. Come back from wherever you are, Mr. Secretary, and finish up. You're late for work already and we can't let the world run on a minute more without you."

"Well," he said, still frowning, "I'm not so very far away. Charleston—Washington—the UN—Africa—"

"—China—Europe—Latin America— Quite a distance from the state of Illinois, anyway."

"How are things in the state of Illinois? Have you talked to the kids?"

"Constantly. Crystal is humming with incipient motherhood and Hal is working twice as hard as ever before in his law firm. I think things in the state of Illinois are coming along all right. At least they're all in one color scheme, anyway." She chuckled. "I couldn't resist that."

"None of us can resist it. It's in the times." He looked with a still-troubled frown at the girl who used to be Elizabeth Henry before she became Beth Knox, and used the nickname he always did in moments of stress. "Hank, how is this sad old world ever going to work its way out of the tangle it's gotten itself into?"

"How are *we* going to work ourselves out of the tangle *we've* gotten into? One tangle at a time, Mr. Secretary. That one's bad enough."

He sighed.

"Yes. I managed to delay matters yesterday, but I can't be up there all the time. I have things to do here. And in another couple of days they resume debate. In the meantime, we've got to come up with something satisfactory or face very serious consequences."

"You don't really think they'd approve that amendment, do you? I can't believe they would, when the chips are really down."

"Why not? They know we aren't going to withdraw, even if they do pass it. They also know we're going to go right on financing their operations and giving them the money they ask, in spite of everything." He made an annoyed sound. "You know the United States. We never get really mad at anybody."

"The world can thank its lucky stars for that. I wonder if the world knows it."

"They know it, but it doesn't prevent them from taking advantage of it all they can. No, this is a very serious matter and there's no point in minimizing it. Our African and Asian friends love to take a high moral position toward us; it doesn't matter if their own caste systems and tribal relationships are ten times as ruthless as anything we may do here. They have the bit in their teeth and they're running with it, right now. There's nothing they'd like better than to pass a resolution condemning us, and they're very close to the point of doing it. They don't quite dare, at this exact moment, but give Felix and the Russians and the rest of them a couple more days of intensive lobbying, and who knows?"

"And we've done all we can?"

He shrugged.

"Harley's apologized. I've apologized. Terry's had his party at the White House. The press has had its Roman holiday. The UN has had its speeches."

"And the Jasons won't call off Felix."

He laughed without much humor.

"I'll bet anything Ted would like to, right now. This is going a little farther than Ted ever contemplated, I think. But Felix is committed now, you see. He's gone so far he can't back down. Nobody can back down.

It's reached the stage where there's no way out for anybody but straight ahead."

"Perhaps we could tack with the wind instead of trying to sail straight into it."

He took a last gulp of coffee and put down the cup with an air that dismissed the idea.

"How?"

She smiled, the little amused twinkle she often got as she contemplated his headlong approach to obstacles and prepared to help him ease his way around them.

"Well," she said, "you just listen to me, Senator, and I'll give you my thoughts on the subject . . ."

After he had heard them, he grinned.

"You're the greatest little fixer, Hank." He picked up his brief case and kissed her good-by.

"This is a very serious matter," she reminded him with a smiling echo of his own words.

"I know it is," he called back as he started down the walk toward the waiting State Department limousine. "You don't have to convince me. You've just made a sale."

The director of the President's Commission on Administrative Reform, seated at his desk in the wonderful old gingerbread castle at Seventeenth Street and Pennsylvania Avenue known as the Executive Offices Building, was engaged in what he liked best: the smooth and efficient completion of an administrative task. There were times when Robert A. Leffingwell regretted, and regretted bitterly, the sequence of events that six months ago had persuaded him to lie to the Senate Foreign Relations Committee and thus forfeit his chance to be Secretary of State; but for the most part he had found hard work to be an antidote to the despair that otherwise might have gripped him with the contemplation of how willfully and arrogantly he had thrown away the high office he had so desperately wanted. Though he did not show it to the outward world, Bob Leffingwell had learned much from his experience.

He did not wear it on his sleeve, for he had never been a man to make his private thoughts public, but he had been humbled to a very considerable degree. Carried on by his desire to be Secretary of State and his furious anger at anyone who dared stand in the way, he had fought back desperately, lied to cover a foolish and utterly inconsequential flirtation with home-grown Communism buried deep in his past, even consented, indirectly but nonetheless culpably, in the sequence of events that had led to the suicide of Brigham Anderson. A sick horror had come to him over that tragic event, and although he had kept his banners flying to the end, he had known the moment he heard the news that it meant the end of his hopes. For the first time in his life, perhaps, he had faced himself fully. It was not a pretty picture at that particular moment, and although he had never once relaxed

his rigid self-control with anyone, even his wife, he had lain awake in the
night after his defeat by the Senate and acknowledged bitterly, over and over
again, "I deserved it. I deserved it." Then had come the President's unexpected decision to keep him in the government, an act of compassion and
mercy for which he would be forever grateful, and from that moment Bob
Leffingwell had been a different man. Different and, he liked to think, better.

It was true, of course, that he would not have been human had he not
accepted willingly the organized campaign of rehabilitation begun immediately by his journalistic supporters. He had written the articles requested,
granted the interviews, begun to move about again cautiously but effectively
in the world of the opinion-makers. But he was a subtle enough student of
the operations of a certain type of mind so that he realized that *of course*
he had to be rehabilitated: it was the only way that his supporters might
be rehabilitated too. They had been repudiated by the Senate along with
him, and it was even more necessary to their egos than it was to his that a
rationalization should be instantly found and a program be instantly begun
to blur and fuzz in the public mind the outlines of responsibility for what
had happened. He had to be rescued because they had to be rescued: it was
as simple as that. The sooner the public could be confused on the basic truth
of what had happened, the better for the reputations of all concerned. He
knew all that with a shrewd and sardonic understanding.

Except that there was a difference. His supporters were interested only in
saving his reputation to save their own. The President, to some degree out
of the needs of politics but even more out of the genuine kindness of his
own decent heart, had saved *him*. This imposed upon Robert A. Leffingwell
an obligation both to the President and himself that he had determined
never to betray. So it was that he picked up his telephone to learn, with a
sense of shock and an instant determination not to give a single inch on anything, that the Honorable Fred Van Ackerman, junior Senator from Wyoming, was in his outer office.

His first impulse was to say he was busy, but he knew Fred was too
shrewd and demanding to accept that. He told his secretary to send the
Senator in and braced himself for whatever this particularly unfortunate result of the electric franchise might have to say. As he might have known,
it was both devious and direct.

"Bob," the Senator from Wyoming said, shaking hands with an elaborate
vigor, "you're looking wonderful. And you're doing a wonderful job down
here, too. Everybody says so."

"Thank you, Fred." There was an awkward pause, into which Fred Van
Ackerman smiled without humor.

"Can't say the same for me, though, is that it?" He brushed aside Bob
Leffingwell's halfhearted gesture of denial and dropped into a chair with a
sudden dark scowl. "I'll get the bastards yet," he promised, apparently a reference to his Senate colleagues who had censured him for his part in black-
mailing Brigham Anderson. Abruptly he got up and went to the window,
snapped his fingers impatiently, and returned to his chair while Bob Leffing-

well waited, outwardly impassive but inwardly baffled by both the visit and the attitude. No doubt it would all come clear, he assured himself ironically, if one would only be patient.

"You probably feel as though a leper has come calling," Fred Van Ackerman suggested with a sudden sharp glance that brought from his host another mild gesture of protest and denial. The Senator laughed. "Don't worry, I'll try not to contaminate you too much. As a matter of fact, I've got an idea, Bob, and I want to talk to you about it."

"Your ideas are always interesting, Fred," Bob Leffingwell said warily, and covered the wariness with a laugh. "I don't think anyone can deny that!" But his guest was not amused.

"They'd *better* be interested. I can still cause a little trouble." He leaned forward, suddenly intent. "You know this mess we're in at the United Nations. I thought maybe you and I could get something out of it, if we cooperated. We've got a lot of scores to pay back."

"I'm not interested in paying back scores, Fred," Bob Leffingwell told him coldly. The Senator from Wyoming gave a skeptical snort.

"Hell, you're not, Bob. Everybody's interested in paying back scores. It's only human nature."

"I'm really not, so if that's why you're here, I'm afraid you've come to the wrong place. Perhaps we'd better stop the discussion—?"

"Now, listen to me, Bob," Fred Van Ackerman said angrily. "Don't go high and mighty. Everything is changing, in this world of ours, and the advantage is going to those who change with it. God damn it, that's a fact, and you know it."

"What's new from COMFORT, Fred?" Bob Leffingwell asked. "Are you still on their mailing list?"

At this reference to the mysterious organization, the Committee On Making Further Offers for a Russian Truce, that had sprung up overnight the previous spring and given him a nationwide sounding board from which to trumpet his slogan, "I would rather crawl to Moscow on my knees than die under an atom bomb," the junior Senator from Wyoming gave a sudden secretive smile.

"Yes, I'm still on their mailing list," he said in a spitefully mocking tone. "COMFORT's not dead, you know. It's just lying low for the time being until the country gets over its orgasm about that damned fool in the White House. Harley knew we were getting to be too strong for him, so he pulled that cheap stunt in Geneva. But we'll be back."

"I don't think it was any cheap stunt," Bob Leffingwell said sharply. "It was an act of great courage and I happen to believe it saved the country. I'm sorry I'm so mistaken about it, Fred."

"Oh, hell," Senator Van Ackerman said, with one of his baffling transitions. "We don't have to fight about it, Bob. After all, our interests are the same."

"I'm sorry. I think you're the one who's mistaken, Fred. Now if you'll forgive me, I really do have things to do—"

"Relax. Relax. I think you and I and the Jasons and COMFORT and the nigger politicians like LeCage Shelby and Cullee Hamilton can all make common cause on this dustup in the UN. That's what I'm here for. I think it's a great opportunity to co-ordinate all the elements in the country that want a truly progressive approach to world peace and a truly liberal outlook in world affairs. I think we can get terrific backing all over the country. It'll also give us a head start against Orrin in the campaign next year. We can carry it right on into the convention and give Ted Jason terrific backing for the nomination. It's a natural."

"I'm touched at your decision to include me in this great forward marching movement," Bob Leffingwell said, "but I think maybe I'll pass it up, Fred. I'm a little too busy right here."

"Now, listen, God damn it!" Fred Van Ackerman said. "I said don't get high and mighty with me, Bob, and I meant it. After all, you're not so pure, you know. I never lied under oath to a Senate committee."

"Only because you never had the opportunity, I suspect. Shall I call my secretary to show you out, or can you just run along by yourself?"

"I'm not going to get mad, Bob," the Senator from Wyoming assured him. "I'm just going to sit here and tell you what I have in mind, and then I'm going to ask whether you think it's worth talking to the Jasons about. I'll talk to the niggers if you'll talk to the Jasons."

"I haven't any in with the Jasons."

"The hell you haven't. Everybody knows you're going to manage Ted's campaign next year when he runs for President."

"Who said that? It's a lie, whoever it was."

"Patsy said it. Last night, at the Sulgrave Club. So you see, you'll have two reasons for talking with her. You can tell her she's a liar, and you can tell her what I have in mind. And that's this, Bob . . ."

And that, Bob Leffingwell told himself with a self-scarifying disgust after his crafty visitor had left, was what you got for becoming involved with that kind of riffraff in the first place. Fred would never let him forget that he had supported him for Secretary of State, never let him forget that there was a bond of blood—Brigham Anderson's blood—between them. He would always try to apply all the pressures he could, for whatever devious project he had in mind. It had been all the director of the President's Commission on Administrative Reform could do to refrain from chucking him out bodily.

Still and all, he had to admit, as he settled back down at his desk and picked up a sheaf of papers that now seemed less interesting than they had half an hour ago, there was a certain amount of merit in what Fred had in mind. Whether there was any merit in its over-all political applications to Ted Jason's cause was another matter; whether he himself should even get involved in Ted Jason's cause was another matter still. He knew without any equivocation whatsoever that he would not do so if the President showed the slightest signs of wanting to run again; but certainly he had no cause to feel loyalty to Orrin Knox and no cause to refrain from assisting anyone who could block *his* Presidential ambitions—no cause whatsoever. Harley was a different matter. If he wanted it, Bob Leffingwell would support him 100 per cent against Ted Jason or anybody.

And yet—what did Harley actually want? Did anybody know? And how long could everything wait upon his decision? How much could others afford to delay their own planning? Was the day not coming soon when the first rule of politics—Look to yourself—would begin to apply?

He gazed thoughtfully out the window at the White House, gleaming just across the street in the autumn sun, as he considered all these questions.

Then he lifted the receiver and asked his secretary to get him Señora Labaiya on Dumbarton Avenue.

The direct phone to the White House rang in the Secretary of State's ornate office, and in a moment he heard Harley's polite, "Yes, Orrin?"

"Mr. President, you wanted me. Sorry to check in late, but I got in late from New York last night and overslept a little."

The President sounded amused.

"So Beth told me."

"You mean you didn't have her wake me up, with the world going to hell in a handbasket? That showed admirable restraint."

"Maybe it just showed I'm one of those Presidents who's his own Secretary of State and doesn't need any help from anybody. You know the type."

"You verge on it, if I may say so."

The President laughed.

"There's enough for everybody. You weren't exactly idle yesterday."

"No. Nor today. Nor tomorrow. And tomorrow. And et cetera. That's a tough situation up there."

"I know. Did you get a chance to see our special envoy to the colored races, Mr. Shelby?"

"He was out somewhere organizing a demonstration at the time, I believe."

"I've asked him to drop in for lunch. At my desk, strictly informal. Just a chat between us boys. To find out how it looks through a glass, darkly, and also to put a stop once and for all to these demonstrations, if I can. I'd like you to join us, if you will."

"As a matter of fact, I've just been setting up a date of my own with Cullee Hamilton. Possibly I could bring him along? Or, on second thought—"

"Yes, I think that would be better. Let's get the picture on LeGage first, and then you can talk to Cullee alone afterwards. I think it might be better to approach them separately."

"I have plans for Cullee I'd like to talk to you about."

"So have I," the President said. "I told LeGage to come by at twelve-thirty. Why don't you come over at twelve?"

"Yes. I'll tell Cullee something unexpected has come up, which it has, and ask him to see me at three. I'm sure he won't mind."

"Good. Oh, by the way. Did the Lebanese Ambassador get to you the other day?"

"He wants to give you an ornamental rug for the White House. I told him we'd set it up someday soon when it's convenient for you."

"You mean somebody wants to give *us* something? Don't let that man get away!"

It was absolutely ridiculous to feel nervous about this, Patsy Labaiya told herself as Grayson swung the car into Sixteenth Street and headed north toward the Hamiltons', but she had to admit that she did. There had been something about her previous conversation with Sue-Dan that had left her distinctly uneasy. She had been given the feeling that she was patronizing the Congressman's wife and she *knew* she wasn't patronizing the Congressman's wife. Being forced into a position where she had to deny that she was patronizing the Congressman's wife was just too much; it was as though she were, in effect, being patronized herself. She knew instinctively that this was exactly what the little b–biddy had intended. It was just too much. Really, they were so ANNOYING, when they wanted to be. It was just too much.

But, she told herself with great self-control, she must remember Ted's purposes and the larger outlook and not let herself be distracted by emotional reactions. When you were engaged in great enterprises you could not afford to let yourself balk at some of the people you had to deal with. It was best to forget all that, if you could, and remember the ultimate objective. She took several deep breaths and decided to review the rather strange call she had received a few moments ago from Bob Leffingwell.

The gist of it, she felt, had been symbolized by the uncomfortable way in which he had circled around Fred Van Ackerman's idea. He had made it clear that he thought somebody should do it, but he had also made it very definite that he thought it would be a grave mistake if the Senator from Wyoming did. He had talked rather vaguely about "Fred's plans to try to take Ted and everybody else into camp with COMFORT," without being too specific about it, and had concluded with a mild objection to "reports I hear that you're about to take *me* into Ted's camp."

"Surely you don't object to that," she had said lightly, but with a definite little flare of anxiety about the answer, because it would be quite disappointing if he didn't fall in with her plans for Ted's campaign.

He had laughed, a little uncomfortably, and said, "That all depends on the President, doesn't it?"

"How long do we have to wait on *that* unknown quantity?" she demanded, and he had revealed his own feelings by agreeing, "Yes, I know, it does create problems, doesn't it?"

"Assuming *that's* decided the way we all hope, then can we count on you?"

He had laughed evasively and replied, "Suppose we wait until it is."

But there had been something in his tone that made her tell herself as she put down the phone, Very well, my boy, *you* can be had, and that's for sure. It had been a great relief, really, because he was such a good public servant and such a darling of certain groups in the country that were quite vital to a well-mounted Presidential campaign. His adherence would give

Ted's campaign organization a style and *élan* that it would otherwise lack. Not that he needed to go out of his way to get those groups, of course—they were such suckers for a cause anyway—but there was no doubt Bob Leffingwell would contribute something that few others could contribute. Particularly now that he was, you might say, chastened and humbled—and vulnerable—as a result of the fire he had lately passed through in the Senate. Patsy was not above applying the same screws Fred Van Ackerman had tried to, if the necessity arose. Bob Leffingwell six months ago would have been too intractable to have in a position of power in Ted's campaign. Bob Leffingwell now was not that kind of problem.

So that was all right. That left her husband, suddenly venturing into dangerous waters at the UN, and her pending luncheon guest. Patsy was baffled by Felix, not the first time this had happened in their life together, but now of an urgency and concern it had never been before because it too was threatening to impinge directly upon Ted's ambitions.

It was a ticklish matter, this business of having the brother-in-law of a potential candidate for President suddenly blossoming out as a front man of opposition to the United States. Patsy could accept it, partially, on the ground that it, too, was an appeal to the colored races, both foreign and domestic, along the same lines as the Foundation's luncheon for the M'Bulu in Charleston; but she wondered how much further it could go before it approached the point where the backlash of reaction from the country would begin to affect Ted. Of course the country had not really had time to react yet. It was still in a state of shock over yesterday's UN developments, and nobody knew what the final reaction would be.

She decided that she would leave this to Ted to decide. She had never known his political instinct to fail him yet, and so far he had voiced no protest either direct or indirect to her or to his brother-in-law. No doubt if he came to the conclusion that Felix's activities were jeopardizing his position he would take steps to stop him, both in direct confrontation and with pressures the family could bring to bear through certain channels in Panama. At the moment he had apparently decided to let it ride. So she would do the same, though with a determination to continue her probing of Felix's motivations. They were certainly unclear to her at the moment.

At any rate, what she had to suggest to Sue-Dan might very well prove the antidote. It might be just the thing to let them all have their cake and eat it too. Felix could make his gesture at the UN, the Jasons and their friends would make their gesture in Washington, and everybody concerned would emerge with enhanced political prestige among the Negroes, whose vote was so necessary to carry the big cities and the big states in a presidential campaign. Like Bob Leffingwell, she too regretted that it had been given to Fred Van Ackerman to have the idea, and she was as determined as Bob to keep that element away from Ted's campaign; but, as far as she was concerned, that was Fred's problem. He could look to himself. The Jasons owed him nothing and they certainly didn't need him. The simplest way was to appropriate his idea and have done with it. Upon the means for doing this she now concentrated, as Grayson brought the car to a halt and went to the door to escort Sue-Dan to her side.

"You look BEAUTIFUL, Sue-Dan," she said with great warmth, suppressing a start of dismay at the sheath of sheer red silk, the elbow-length red gloves, the enormous red hat that set off the clever little fox-face and the wide, sardonic eyes. They wouldn't be overlooked at City Tavern, Sue-Dan had made sure of that. Patsy's annoyance flared again, but she suppressed it. "How ever did you think of such a STUNNING outfit?"

"It just came to me," Sue-Dan said as she got in. "I thought it would be nice to eat in, at the Hot Shoppe. You're looking beautiful, too, Patsy."

"I told you the City Tavern," Patsy said, trying not to sound sharp. "Not the Hot Shoppe." Her guest's eyes widened.

"Oh, *did* you?" She gave a pleased smile. "Now, I think that will be really nice."

"I hope so," Patsy said stiffly as Grayson steered into Sixteenth Street and started back down toward the gracious club in Georgetown. God knew what the reaction would be when they arrived, but whatever it was, there was nothing to do now but brazen it out. She had intended to do so anyway, but not under quite such flamboyant circumstances. She had hoped it would be done quietly, not in this screaming, garish getup which she knew had been deliberately selected to embarrass her.

"I'm so glad you could come," she said hurriedly, lest her annoyance get the better of her. "I've wanted for so long to really get to know you, since our family fortunes, you might say, are so intermingled."

"Yes," Sue-Dan agreed politely. "You might say that."

"My brother, you know," Patsy explained, and cursed herself for explaining, "and your husband, and the Senate, and all."

"Yes, Cullee may try it," Sue-Dan agreed placidly, staring out the window at the racing brown leaves that skittered across the streets as they rode along. "I expect your brother would like his help."

"I think it would be mutual," Patsy snapped. Her guest smiled, wide-eyed.

"Well, I wouldn't know," she said judiciously, without commenting one way or the other. "It might."

"I think so," Patsy said coldly. Her tone became more confidential and amused. "What do you do with yourself here in Washington—between campaigns, I mean? Sew with the other Congressional ladies and attend teas, or what? Doesn't that life ever get boring for you?"

"Oh, no, ma'am," Sue-Dan said casually. "Mostly I picket schools and sit in at lunch counters and try to get in places where they don't want me." She gave a little offhand laugh. "You know how it is."

Patsy flushed and suddenly dropped all pretense.

"All right, Sue-Dan, if you want to be nasty, you go ahead and be nasty. But you're my guest for lunch and I expect you to behave decently while you're with me, do you understand? I don't want you to give me Eliza crossing the ice all the time we're together, O.K.? I've had enough of professional insolence in my day, and I'm not taking any more of it from you. Is that clear enough?"

For a moment they stared at one another with unconcealed hostility, until Sue-Dan broke it with a tone as sharp as her own.

"Me and my people have had about enough professional tolerance, too, Patsy, so *you* can stop that. Maybe Cullee needs your brother, maybe your brother needs him. I guess your brother needs most, or you wouldn't have invited me to lunch. Now, what is it you want?"

"It isn't just my brother right now," Patsy said more calmly, as the car neared the Tavern and she noted the limousine of the Senate Majority Leader, occupied by his wife and Beth Knox, and several other familiar cars in the line approaching the door. "It's this business with Terry up at the UN that ties in with it. There's something Cullee can do about it, if he will, that would help us all."

"Behind your husband's back?" Sue-Dan asked in frank surprise. "What does he think about that?"

"He doesn't know about it yet, and he isn't going to know about it until it's decided. All right?"

"All right," Sue-Dan agreed, "but it seems funny to me."

Let it, was what Patsy thought, but she only said, "I'll tell you about it while we eat. Come along."

She was aware of a little stir of surprise and commotion as they crossed the threshold and stepped into the lounge, filled with briskly talking ladies and their guests. She could see Beth Knox and Dolly Munson staring—well, *let* them; Ted would wipe that skeptical little smile from Beth's eyes before he finished with Orrin; and as for Dolly, who did she think *she* was: just a cheap millionairess who certainly wasn't in the Jasons' league—and with an imperious air she bore down upon the startled hostess.

"Two for Señora Labaiya," she said grandly. "I called yesterday."

"Yes," the hostess said, starting to stammer, "but—but—"

Patsy's hand closed on the hostess' arm so tightly that she winced.

"Listen to me," she hissed. "We are NOT going to have a scandal in this club. We are NOT going to have it in all the papers and all over the world that you wouldn't serve the Ambassadress of Panama and her guest, the wife of a United States Representative. Now take me to my table right *now*, do you understand me—right *now!*"

"Yes, Señora," the hostess said, looking terribly flustered and as though she might burst into tears. "Yes, of course."

"Well, well," Beth murmured to Dolly. "Life gets more and more interesting every day."

"So Bob tells me," Dolly said. "Sometimes I find I believe him."

"Now," the President said comfortably, pushing aside the tray, emptied of sandwiches and milk, "tell us all about the situation up there as it looks to you. You've been taking quite an active part, I understand."

"I want to explain that to you, Mr. President," LeGage Shelby said with an air of confidence he did not entirely feel.

"Please do," the President said politely, and Orrin Knox congratulated him silently for exactly the right tone of gracious intimidation the interview required.

"If you mean the demonstrations by DEFY," LeGage said with a disarming if rather nervous smile, "my people seemed to want them, and I feel that— well, I feel that it's a legitimate activity for the organization to undertake, under the circumstances."

"Even though it of course is interpreted around the world as being critical of your own government," the President suggested gently. The chairman of DEFY looked defiant but thought better of it.

"I think American citizens have a right to express their opinion, Mr. President," he said respectfully. "Isn't that so?"

"Oh, that's so. I'm not attempting to challenge that, certainly. I wonder a little sometimes, though, whether it might not be better for all of us in the long run if now and then we exercised a little restraint about it. It might look better in the eyes of the nations."

"Nobody expressed much restraint in Charleston," LeGage said with a sudden sharp intonation. The President nodded.

"No, I grant you that. But if you think I approved, or am happy about it, or am pleased at any time about the way the whole matter is progressing, then I think you do me an injustice. I'm doing what I can. Your government," he added with a deliberate emphasis, "is doing what it can. It isn't as though nobody's trying, LeGage."

"No," LeGage said, but grudgingly. "I guess not."

"What really happened, down there in Charleston?" Orrin asked suddenly. "Where did Terry get his advice on what to do? From you, or from Felix?"

A veiled expression briefly clouded the eyes of the chairman of DEFY, but a candid smile succeeded it at once.

"That Terry doesn't need anybody to tell him anything. He's so full of ideas he's buzzing."

"I wish he'd buzz in some other beehive," the Secretary said, and they all laughed. "So it was just sheer coincidence that he thought of how to attack us in the most damaging possible way at our most vulnerable point. You had nothing to do with it."

"It was his idea," LeGage said solemnly. "I swear it."

"What came after was your department, is that it?"

"We did what seemed to be our duty," LeGage said, with the sudden sharp edge in his voice again.

"What do you tell the African delegates about our position when you talk to them?" the President asked. "And how do they receive it? I've been curious about that."

"They're kind of edgy with me," LeGage admitted, "and I am with them. They don't ever forget I represent the United States."

"How do you represent the United States?" the President asked mildly. "That's what I'm really interested in."

LeGage smiled without particular amusement.

"Oh, is that it, Mr. President? I see. Have I been letting you down?"

"You'd know more about that than I would," the President said with an air of fatherly blandness. The chairman of DEFY looked annoyed, then shook his head with a laugh.

"I imagine it's hard for you to trust me, at that," he said with a blandness of his own, "considering how many opportunities there are for an American Negro to be critical of his country if he wants to be. But you can believe me, Mr. President. I follow the policy of this government when the delegation agrees on something. You can ask Senator Fry or Senator Smith. They know they can count on me."

The President studied him thoughtfully.

"What's going to happen on this amendment of Ambassador Labaiya's?"

"We may take a licking," LeGage said without hesitation.

"Why aren't you up there trying to persuade some of them to vote with us?" Orrin Knox asked abruptly. "Isn't that more important than organizing demonstrations down here?"

"In a way, you know," LeGage said, "the demonstrations can almost be taken as a sign of good faith on our part. It shows we're sorry for what happened."

"*I've* shown we're sorry for what happened," the President said with a sudden annoyance. "Why is it incumbent upon you to do anything about it?"

LeGage looked startled by his tone and, either genuinely or disingenuously —they could not be sure—seemed abashed.

"It's important," he said lamely. "It's a symbol of something."

"Something we can do without, I think," the Secretary of State told him. "Why don't you show him that communication, Mr. President? I doubt if he'll understand it any other way."

A glint of real dislike flared in the eyes of the chairman of DEFY, but he changed it hastily to one of noncommittal interest.

"What communication is that?"

"This," the President said, tossing a cabled dispatch across the desk to him. "Read it aloud and you'll see how it's sounding on all of the broadcasts of the world, right about now."

"Moscow," LeGage read with a puzzled smile that slowly vanished as he went along. "The chairman of the Council of Ministers today issued the following statement on events in the United States:

"The U.S.S.R. has witnessed with dismay and condemnation the shameful treatment by the United States Government and people of the noble fighter for democracy, the representative of the freedom-loving peoples of Africa, His Royal Highness the M'Bulu of Mbuele.

"The U.S.S.R. has noted the continuing hateful discrimination by the United States against all members of the colored races, including those within its own borders.

"The U.S.S.R. unreservedly condemns these actions by the government of the United States. It appeals to all freedom loving peoples everywhere, including those of the colored races within the United States, to take the strongest possible steps to oppose these actions of the government of the United States which are universally condemned by mankind.

"The U.S.S.R. applauds the vigorous protests by United States Negro groups against these shameful practices and assures them of its continuing and active support in their fight for freedom. It hopes these protests will continue.

"The U.S.S.R. unreservedly endorses the amended resolution of condemnation of the United States, introduced in the United Nations by the Ambassador of Panama, and pledges its full support to that resolution in the General Assembly."

There was silence as the chairman of DEFY finished reading.

"You see," the President said gently, "why it might be better if your organization refrained from anything too—obvious, for a few days."

LeGage Shelby looked startled, then angry.

"Are you telling me, Mr. President," he asked sharply, "that DEFY is taking orders from Moscow?" The President gave him an impassive look.

"Again, you would know more about that than I would. I am assuming not. I am assuming your good faith. I am also assuming what must be obvious to any intelligent man, that if you now have a big demonstration at the UN, it is going to appear to the world that you are doing so in response to this appeal from Moscow, which in any sane century would amount to a call to armed rebellion but in our times must be regarded as just one more annoying attempt to stir up trouble. But the fact remains, if you do it, the clear connection will be drawn throughout the world. It will be regarded in exactly the same light as the riots that are going on right now in a dozen capitals in Asia, Africa, and Latin America. The consequences to your own country—I might say the consequences to your own organization—could be quite disastrous under the circumstances. Are you sure you want to risk them?"

LeGage gave him a long and thoughtful look.

"Is that an order, Mr. President?"

"I don't like to put it on that basis. Let's just say it's a cautionary piece of advice to a man I know is intelligent enough to see its value."

"You're asking me to disappoint my people," LeGage said with a faraway expression in his eyes.

"Your people stand or fall with the United States, you know, LeGage," Orrin Knox said. "We can't be separated. You're Americans, too. We're all bound together, for better or worse."

The chairman of DEFY gave him a strange, anguished look.

"I wish we weren't," he whispered. The Secretary of State stared back. Finally he nodded.

"I know. We all might be happier if history hadn't worked out as it has. But, it has. And therefore it is up to us, as Americans co-operating together, to do the best we can with the situation as we find it in each generation and as it comes our time to deal with it. Examine your plans and see if they contribute to that end, LeGage. If they do," he said gravely, "go ahead."

"To that," the President observed, "I would say, Amen."

For a while they were silent, in the comfortable study where so many things had happened, so many men been tested, so many great decisions made. The Secretary of State, though he stared straight out the window at the Washington Monument, was aware of tensions increased, relaxed, increased, relaxed, in the room beside him. He said nothing, the President said nothing. Eventually LeGage gave a half-laugh.

"Well! Here it is almost 2 P.M. and I expect there's work to be done up there in New York, as you say. Best I catch a plane and get on up and get busy on that delegation. That's what you appointed me for, isn't it, Mr. President?"

"Good," the President said with an air of relieved pleasure, rising to shake hands. "I think that will be very helpful to us, LeGage. I appreciate it."

"Mr. Secretary," LeGage said, "when will you be coming up?"

"Probably for the debate Thursday. Thank you for your help, LeGage."

"Oh, well, as you say," the chairman of DEFY told him with a sudden, racy grin, "we're all bound together."

After he had been shown out and they were alone, the President looked at the Secretary of State.

"Did you believe it?"

"As with Terry, not one word."

"No more did I. Do you want to bring Cullee here this afternoon?"

"I think it might be better to see him alone. Not that you wouldn't be helpful, but—"

"As you think best. If you want to bring him here later, feel free."

"Thanks, Mr. President," Orrin said. "I'll be guided by how it goes."

He had no sooner returned to his office at State than his secretary gave him word that Bob Munson had called. He returned it at once, to the Majority Cloakroom of the Senate.

"Robert? What's going on in the cave of the winds?"

"I've managed to prolong your session for you, right enough," Senator Munson said. "Now we may never choke it off. Ray Smith is in full flight on the San Fernando water viaduct, Tom August for some reason has decided to get involved, Seab is snorting and pawing the ground with blue smoke seeping out around the edges of his galoshes, and everybody's having fun. But something even more interesting has now come up from Fragrant Freddy, our little pal. He's just braced me with an idea."

"Don't tell me," Orrin said. "Let me guess." When he had, accurately, he grunted.

"I hope you discouraged that." The Majority Leader laughed, rather grimly.

"I did my best, but you know Fred. Ever since we censured him he's been even more obstreperous than he was before. He figures he has nothing to lose any more."

"O.K., then, stall him off. If anybody's going to undertake what Fred proposes, I want Cullee Hamilton to do it. It's the only thing that makes sense under the circumstances."

"I don't think anybody should do it. How many more pounds of flesh is it proposed to exact from us over the M'Bulu, anyway?"

"I'd rather wield the knife myself than let others do it," Orrin Knox told him. The Majority Leader made an impatient sound.

"That won't be very popular here. You know how Seab will react, and he won't be the only one. I may react myself. I think it's time to put a stop to this nonsense."

"Of course you're aware of what's happening in New York."

"We're aware. Seab's telling us about it at this very moment. Can't you hear that roaring in the background? It isn't the wild sea waves calling, old buddy."

"I think this is best," the Secretary said firmly. "Stall Fred."

"Does the President agree with you?"

"Call and ask him. He isn't entirely convinced, but he's willing to give it a try."

"I think you're mistaken, Orrin. Sadly mistaken."

"You aren't fully aware of what we face in the world, I'm afraid."

"I must say *your* horizons have broadened considerably," Bob Munson remarked with some sarcasm.

"They have. I'm counting on you, Bob. I want this done, and I want Cullee to do it."

"Yes, Mr. President."

"Go to hell. But be sure you do as I ask, first."

"I don't like it."

"I don't like it, either. You don't think I'm happy about our choices in the world these days, do you? I have to make some of them, and it isn't fun. *This* isn't fun."

"I'll talk to Fred. I can't promise anything, though."

"Thank you. I'll talk to Cullee. Oh, and Bob: talk to Seab, too, will you?"

"I already have that planned."

Before he turned back to the items on his desk, the Secretary put in a call to the comfortable house in Spring Valley.

"I just thought you'd be interested to know," he said when Beth came on the line, "that there is another brilliant mind running in the same channel as yours. That fighting champion of right and justice, Fred Van Ackerman."

"Don't let him do it," she said with alarm. "That would ruin everything."

"Bob and I are heading him off at the pass. But it's ironic, isn't it, how great political instincts seem to see the same things at the same time?"

"I'm just surprised yours didn't."

"Oh, it did. I'd been thinking about it. You just confirmed me in my wisdom."

She laughed.

"That's a good story."

"True. Absolutely true."

"All right, Mr. Secretary. I suppose you'll write it in your memoirs and nobody will ever know the difference."

"You'll probably write them for me, so you can have it your own way in the end. Don't give up."

She laughed again.

"I never have. Good luck with Cullee."

"Thanks," he said soberly. "I'll need it."

In the pleasantly luxurious house out Sixteenth Street the door from the garage slammed shut behind the master with a forceful thud. He came into the living room and threw down his coat as Maudie entered from the kitchen.

"Always throwing things down," she said grumpily. "Always have to be throwing things down. Didn't your mammy ever tell you to hang things up?"

"She told me, but I'm a bad boy, Maudie. I've always been a real—bad— boy."

"So you say," she said skeptically. "So you say."

He laughed.

"Why, Maudie, I never said it before in my life. Because it just isn't true, old Maudie, it just isn't true." He made a pretense of leafing through the early edition of the *Evening Star*, then threw it down. "Where is she? Where's that wife of mine?"

"Spectin' some day to come home and she not be here? Well, she's not."

"Where is she?" he demanded, a sudden twist of fear giving his heart a painful squeeze.

"She called," Maudie said indifferently. "Rest easy. She just been out eatin' in high-class style with high-class ladies. That gal hasn't run away. *This* time . . . In fact," she added as a car drove up out front, "there she is now, I expect. I'll go hide."

"You don't have to do that, Maudie," he said with a laugh he tried to make casual, but of course she saw through it.

"We expecting tornadoes in this house," she observed. "That's the kind of weather we got nowadays. I'm going to go hide in the cellar."

"O.K. Then don't stand behind the door and listen."

"I don't listen!" she said with great indignation.

"Not much. I bet you keep notes."

"Make me quite a book if I did," she said as she went out. "Make me quite some reading book, I tell you."

He hurried to the window as the door closed behind her and peeked through the curtains. Sue-Dan had told him nothing about her luncheon date, and it was with considerable surprise and much curiosity that he saw his wife and Patsy Labaiya engaged in farewell talk beside Patsy's Rolls-Royce. He could tell from their respective stances that the conversation was stilted, uneasy, and based on a mutual dislike. But it concluded calmly enough, as conversations between those in Washington who dislike one another do often conclude, with an exchange of cordial smiles, fervent promises to meet again soon, a quick, warm handshake as quickly and warmly returned. Sue-Dan came toward the house, Patsy got into her car, and it purred grandly off. He leaped away from the window and dropped into his big armchair, grabbing the *Star* and pretending to be absorbed in it. He looked up with an air of casual interest when she came in, and her look of surprise changed to one of knowing amusement.

"Come home to check up, Cullee?" she asked, sinking with an instinctive animal grace into a well-posed picture of relaxed unconcern on the sofa. "Come home to find out if I'd run away and gone to New York?" She raised her arm languidly, looked at her watch, and let the arm drop back along the sofa's edge. "You're a little early. Plane doesn't leave until 4 P.M."

"You're not going," he said, with an air of calm dismissal that unfortunately wasn't quite calm enough.

"You're not going?" she mimicked, adding the question mark he had tried to conceal.

"No," he said with a real anger now, "you're not going. And I'm not going to sit here and argue with you about it. You're not going, period. I didn't come home to check up. I came home to get some reports I forgot to take this morning."

"I hope you found them," she said with elaborate politeness. "Anyway, I'm glad you're here, because I've got something to talk to you about. Something that may help you be a good colored man again."

"Something from Patsy Labaiya," he said with a quick suspicion. "I don't want any part of that one. You can have her. Incidentally," he said with an elaborate sarcasm of his own, "I trust you fine ladies had a hotsy-totsy luncheon. Where did you go—Joe's Drive-In?"

"We went to the City Tavern," she said with a genuine anger. "I'll have you know that's where we went!"

"Well, bless me! Where did they seat you, in the kitchen?"

"No! Not in the kitchen! We ate in the best part."

"Yes," he said, "I expect Patsy wouldn't be seen with you anywhere else but *the* best part. It might hurt Ted's chances if you weren't in *the* best part. Patsy would think of that."

"Patsy was all right! They wanted to make a fuss and Patsy wouldn't let them. Also, Patsy could have had it in all the papers if she wanted, and she didn't do that, either."

"Just let me look," he said, leafing through the *Star* to the society pages. He gave a little exclamation of triumph and was pleased to see that his wife looked startled and dismayed. "Listen to this: 'Patsy Jason Labaiya will never cease to shock and delight this town. Who else but Patsy would have thought of the idea of taking the wife of California's brilliant young Negro Congressman to the swank City Tavern for lunch? The gesture of tolerance and understanding was of the dramatic nature Washington loves, and it couldn't possibly be missed—particularly since pretty little Sue-Dan Hamilton was clad in a flaming red dress that was, to say the least, easy to spot amid more quietly dressed luncheon visitors, such as Mrs. Orrin Knox, wife of the Secretary of State, and Mrs. Robert D. Munson, wife of the Senate Majority Leader. We asked Patsy'—oh, listen to this, Sue-Dan—'We asked Patsy, while Sue-Dan was in the powder room (and that must have been a sensation, too!), whether her luncheon with Rep. Cullee Hamilton's wife had any political significance. The usually gracious Patsy refused to comment, but Washington doesn't need a refresher course in arithmetic to put two and two together and come up with six, or even seven!' . . . Oh, Miss Patsy wouldn't tell the papers. Miss Patsy's your friend. Miss Patsy and you, you're society, Miss Sue-Dan. And we've just got to keep it out of the papers."

"I know she didn't plan it like that," Sue-Dan said stubbornly. "It says she wouldn't comment, doesn't it?"

"Oh, yes. It also says you had a pretty red dress, too. It *sneers* you had a pretty red dress. Let me look at that pretty red dress, Sue-Dan. My, my, that *is* a pretty red dress!"

"All right!" she said stridently. "All right now, Cullee! I want you to listen to what we talked about at that luncheon, because that's a lot more important than all that white sneering, or yours either. You hear me? I want you to listen."

"Don't talk too long," he said, throwing down the *Star*. "I wouldn't want you to miss that plane."

"If I ever want to go," she flared out angrily, "I'll go. I won't miss the plane, either!"

He leaned back as far as he could in his chair, put his arms behind his head, sprawled his legs as far apart as they would go, and looked at her across them with an insolent expression.

"You just tell me what you and sweet old Patsy talked about. You just tell me all about it, little Sue-Dan."

When she had, he sat suddenly upright with a sour expression.

"I won't do it," he said flatly. "Damn it, I said I wouldn't be a stooge for the Jasons, and I won't. Can't I get that through your head?"

"Can't I get through your head this is how to help your own people?" she demanded. "They're all after you, Cullee—*Ebony*, and the *Defender*, and the *Afro-American*, and them. They're going to start writing nasty things about you, such as, Where was our big Congressman when that little gal wanted to go to school? Where was big brave cowardly Cullee when he let Terry carry the ball? They're going to begin asking some mighty sharp questions about you, Cullee. Then what?"

"I won't answer."

"Won't *answer!*" she gave a hoot of spiteful laughter. "Fat lot of good that's going to do—won't answer! Cullee, listen to me. Patsy's your friend—"

"Patsy's Ted's friend. I don't even think she's Felix's friend."

"Listen to me! Senator Van Ackerman wants to do this, and Patsy doesn't want him to. She wants you to. She told me so I could tell you so you could get the jump on him."

He made a disgusted movement of his mouth.

"She's afraid of Fred Van Ackerman because of that crowd he runs with. She also wants a black boy to do it. That's Patsy's game. She doesn't give a damn about anything but my color. Patsy wouldn't want me to do it if I was bright blue, Sue-Dan. You know that. Also, how come Patsy's such a great friend of yours, all of a sudden? I thought you didn't like Patsy so much. Lunch at City Tavern kind of gone to your head, has it, maybe?"

"Damn you!" she said bitterly. "I swear to God, Cullee, I'm trying to help you, but you don't want to be helped, do you? You just don't want anybody to help Mr. Old Know-It-All Cullee. Don't want to be Senator, don't want to be a fighter for your own people, don't want to do anything but just—just—"

"Just want to lie in bed and do things to you, Sue-Dan," he said with a sarcastically happy air he knew she hated. "That's really all I want to do; you know that, now."

"All right, stop making a joke of everything! That's all I say, stop making a joke! You'll push me too far some day, Cullee. Maybe right now." A sudden shrewish expression came into her eyes. "Maybe you gone a little too far already."

"Well," he said, as a car door banged out front and he went to the window to look out, "here comes your ticket to New York. Now you can both slam me around."

"Who's that?" she asked skeptically. "Terry, maybe?"

"His Royal Highness the Shelby of Shelby," he said, opening the door and bowing low with a flourish. "Do come in, Your Royal Highness Shelby of Shelby."

No answering gleam of amusement or good nature greeted him from the chairman of DEFY. LeGage came into the room as though going into battle, paced up and down a couple of times, and collapsed violently into a chair.

"God damn! If I haven't been given the old civics lecture on how to carry the flag!" A savage mockery came into his voice. "We're all in this together, us black and white folks, did you know that? We're all Americans, each of us, we really and truly are. If you don't believe it, just ask the President and Orrin Knox; they'll give you the word! We've got to behave real nice, because we all stand or fall together! So be nice, now, everybody, be nice! Makes white folks unhappy when you're not, because we all stand or fall together." He slapped the coffee table beside him with the flat of his hand. "God damn! That's all I can say—God damn!"

Cullee Hamilton studied him for a long moment with an expression of distaste.

"What's wrong with that, loud boy?" he asked finally. "It's true, isn't it?"

A look of genuine anger came into LeGage's eyes, and the Congressman expected another outburst. But his ex-roommate spoke with a softness more ominous than anger.

"Seems to me we've got to have an understanding about some things, Cullee. I think you need to be set straight on the way things are going."

"You try to tell him," Sue-Dan said spitefully. "I've been trying for the past week, but it's no good. He won't listen. He knows it all."

"I don't know it all," Cullee said. "I just know you're riding 'way out there on the risky edge and I don't intend to ride out there with you. That's all."

"What's the matter, friend?" LeGage asked scornfully. "Afraid you might lose some white votes or something? Listen! One of these days it won't matter how the white folks vote."

"Who are you," the Congressman asked, "the Prophet LeGage? All us Black Muslims about to hit the high road, are we? I'm glad you told me, Prophet. I didn't know."

"Maybe you haven't been getting the phone calls I've been getting," LeGage said softly, "but a lot of people are watching you, Cullee. They want DEFY to take out after you. The Muslims aren't any joke, either."

"Better stay clear of that crowd," Cullee said with equal softness. "Real bad business, that crowd. Wouldn't want you to get hurt playing with them, 'Gage."

"I don't want you to get hurt, either," LeGage said, "but I'm telling you, Cullee, you will be if you don't help out your own people. Everybody's wondering about you, right now. They want to know where you were when Terry went to that school, and why you aren't doing more now, and why you aren't helping DEFY—"

"I told him all that," Sue-Dan said. "I told him what to do, and he won't listen. He's too big for us. Don't argue with him, 'Gage. Let's go to New York."

"Damn it," Cullee said, "you're not going to New York. Now that's final."

"Wonder if final does as loud as final talks," she said airily. "You better get on back to the Hill, Mr. Congressman. Your people need you. Your white people, that is."

"I'm going in just a minute. First I want to ask this wild man one question. Why are you so all-fired excited just because the President and Orrin Knox say we're all one country? We are all one country. Bad or good, we've got to work it out here, haven't we? Or maybe you know something I don't know that makes it different. You leaving us, 'Gage? You going somewhere we don't know about? Tell me, boy!"

"All my life," LeGage said with a strange tone of lonely anger Cullee had never heard in his voice before, "I've been trying to play it your way, the way so many of us have tried to do in the past. I've been trying to get along with *them* on *their* terms. Even when I've led DEFY out picketing someplace, it's been to accomplish something in a way *they* could understand, so *they* would do something about it. Well"—he drew a deep breath—"well, maybe now I'm not going to do it like that, any more. Maybe I'm going to do it the way *we* think is right, for things *we* want, and let *them* sweat, for a change. Maybe I've just decided I've got to be true to what *I* think is best for us, not what *they* think." He paused somberly. "That's about it, Cullee. And maybe I think it's time for you to stop playing their way, and help us."

"And maybe I would," Cullee snapped with a sudden anger, "if maybe you weren't running after Terry like a sweet little lap dog, and if maybe you weren't messing around playing stooge for Felix Labaiya, and if maybe you weren't getting 'way out there where you can't tell the honest colored folks from the witch doctors. What do you want to do, 'Gage—tear the country apart? That's what Russia wants, for us all to fall to pieces fighting over race. They're working on it every day. You want to be lap dog for them, too? Get on out of this house, if that's it, because you're no friend of mine."

"I'd rather do what I think is right for my people," 'Gage said bitterly, "than try to ride both races the way you do, Cullee."

"Your people? Your people? I suppose you're trying to say they're not my people, too, is that it?"

"Then act like it," LeGage said with an angry desperation. "Damn it, act like it, that's all I say to you. Else I'm not a friend of yours, for sure, or you of me."

"Guess that makes it unanimous," the Congressman said coldly. "Best you run along now and be a stooge for Terry and the Commies and all that junk. I think we can get along without you in this house."

"My house too," Sue-Dan said sharply. "Maybe I want him here."

"He won't stay unless I ask him," Cullee said tauntingly. "He wants me to ask him, don't you, old roomy? Want Cullee to beg, right? Well, Cullee won't beg. So get on out."

"I want him to stay," Sue-Dan said as LeGage made an angry gesture of protest but did not move from his chair. "You stay, 'Gage. We can make some plans for New York, once we get this white man out of here." She gave a scornful laugh. "He'd pass right over, except he's so black."

"You going?" Cullee asked, feeling the old tension, the visceral clash of absolute wills, the excited combination of things, mental, emotional, physical, sexual, or what-have-you, that went back to Howard campus days. But he was unmoved and unshaken. He had always won in a showdown before, always. He was confident he would now.

Finally LeGage spoke.

"Think I'll stay," he said softly. The Congressman got up at once, stepped quickly to the closet, yanked his jacket off the hook, grabbed his overcoat, and turned to the door.

"O.K., I'll go. You be good to each other, now, hear? Mighty fine bed upstairs if you want to use it, 'Gage. That little gal's quite something when you get her in it. Be my guest."

"That isn't—" LeGage cried out, his face suddenly contorted with pain. "That isn't what I—"

"I don't care what you!" Cullee Hamilton shouted with an equal pain. "I just want to get away from both of you, that's all, from both of you!"

But of course he knew, as he hurried to the garage, jumped in the Lincoln, and started blindly off in it, that this was not what he wanted at all, really. Not at all. But how could he go down their road, which led nowhere? How could he abandon the only thing that made sense to him, which was to try to be a responsible ambassador between the races, since he had been given the great honor of election to the Congress? How could he betray his own people, when he had it in his hands to do them more good his way than LeGage ever could in his?

"Always ragging me," he said aloud as he turned into Sixteenth and started down across town to the State Department, "always ragging me!"

He caught a glimpse of his distraught face in the mirror and realized with a shock that his eyes were both miserably angry and filled with tears.

How many times, the Majority Leader wondered with an ironic inward sigh, had he faced that pugnacious, touseled old physiognomy across the desk, and how many times had he tried with all the desperate craft of a hard-pressed imagination to think of the right arguments with which to bring its owner around to what he desired? How many times had he succeeded, how many failed? He could no longer remember, the process had occurred so often during their long years of service together in the Senate. But one thing was certain: It was one of the things that had always made life interesting.

"Yes, sir," he said aloud, "it has that."

"What has what, Bob?" Senator Cooley inquired. "What are you talking to yourself about, Bob? Me?"

Senator Munson smiled.

"I was telling myself that trying to figure how to outfox you was one of the things that had always made life interesting for me here. Then I'd told myself, Yes, sir, it has that, and that's when you began eavesdropping."

"You always do it, Bob," the senior Senator from South Carolina assured him. "You—always—do it! I try to hold firm to my principles, but you talk me around every time."

"Unn-hunh," the Majority Leader said. "Well. This time I'm not so sure about that, Seab. This time I'm plumb scared."

"What do you have in mind, Bob?" Seab Cooley asked with growing interest, and the Majority Leader, because this time he had in mind something that would provoke his old friend as he knew few things could, continued to play it for chuckles.

"Oh, I thought you might like to be named Ambassador to Liberia. I thought maybe I could arrange it with the President, if you did."

"Way things are going over there in that continent right now, best not send anybody but a black man any place there, Bob. Nobody but a black man can even get ashore, Bob, more's the pity."

"It would be an interesting experiment, though; you have to admit that. Especially," he said, deciding to take the plunge, "since we need all the help we can get with that particular problem right now." The reaction was exactly as he expected.

"Not from me," Senator Cooley said firmly. "No, sir, Bob, not from me."

"Yes," the Majority Leader said. "I was afraid that might be your position, Seab. Nonetheless, I doubt if even the most optimistic observer would say everything was going right for us at the moment. You know the situation up there in the UN. Combined with the way the Russians are beating the propaganda drums about it, it's not a pretty spot to be in. Something drastic may be required, it seems to me."

"Somebody's put you up to something, Bob," Senator Cooley said. "Who is it, Bob, Orrin? And what does he want us to do, Bob, pay that little kinkajou twenty million dollars in sob-money? Is that it, Bob?"

The Majority Leader, confronted with the instinctive ability to guess close to the mark that comes to many an experienced veteran of politics, decided to play it straight.

"Yes, it's Orrin. And you're somewhere in his vicinity, though you're over-stating it a bit. He thinks it might be well for us to make some more formal amends than we've made so far. The form remains to be worked out. He wanted me to sound you out about it."

"Do you agree with him, Bob? You don't, do you, Bob? I can always tell when you don't agree with what you find yourself asked to do. Why don't those folks downtown ever leave you alone, Bob? Seems to me you've earned the right to be left alone, for a while."

Senator Munson smiled, a trifle bleakly, but his tone was comfortable enough.

"Now, don't try to pry me loose from my obligations, Seab. You know why I do these things. It's habit—it's custom—it's duty—it's my word. Nine times out of ten, it is also my honest conviction. Adding it all up, I really don't have too much choice."

"Except on the tenth time, Bob," Seab Cooley said softly. "And this is a tenth time. You know it is, Bob. We've humbled ourselves enough, in this instance. We have to have some national pride, Bob, no matter what."

"I agree with all you say, but Orrin makes a reasonably convincing case even so. You know Orrin's pride for this country, Seab, and if he can see it this way, possibly there's something in it."

"Orrin's a puzzle to me right now," Senator Cooley confessed. "I can't quite understand Orrin, at this moment. He's not the Orrin we knew in the Senate. He's weaker, it seems to me."

"Well, I don't know," Senator Munson said thoughtfully. "He's got a lot of new responsibilities now, and they change a man. I think he's trying to do the best job he can as Secretary of State, and sometimes you can't be as forceful as you'd like to be in that office. You have to pick your way more cautiously because the whole world depends on it, sometimes. It makes a man more hesitant, I'm afraid."

"Just so a man doesn't lose sight of what's really best for the country, Bob. That's what worries me about that office. I've seen them come and go, Bob, and you have too, and you know what can happen there, sometimes. A man can get to balancing so many things against so many other things that some-times all he does is balance. He never does really move America forward; he's too busy balancing, worrying about what this country's going to say or that country's going to think. Sometimes you have to go straight ahead and say damn them all, Bob. You know that."

"I don't really think there's much danger that Orrin Knox won't go straight ahead and say damn them all if he really feels it necessary, Seab. He hasn't changed that much."

"Then why doesn't he say it now, Bob? We've done enough. Is he playing for the colored vote, Bob? That's what I want to know. Maybe it's as simple as that."

"Yes, I've no doubt that will be the first thing some of our good friends of television, press, and radio will say if the background of it comes out, Seab. Orrin will be doing exactly what they want him to do, but that won't stop anybody from impugning his motives . . . I'm not going to deny Orrin is a politician sometimes—not as good as you, of course, Seab, but no slouch— but I think in this instance it's a little too pat to say that's the chief motivation. I think he really believes the situation in the world is delicate enough to warrant what he has in mind."

"It isn't that delicate in terms of real power," Senator Cooley remarked. "It's only that delicate in terms of what people think."

"And unfortunately," Bob Munson said, "that's the foundation the world seems to rest upon at the moment. That's what makes the conduct of foreign policy such a slippery, uncertain, frustrating, infuriating thing. Do one little thing that somebody somewhere—anybody, anywhere—doesn't like, and half the nations on the globe start cackling like a flock of silly geese. That's *their* foreign policy: don't do anything constructive yourself, just cackle at somebody else. That'll bring you headlines and television coverage and a big, dynamic international image. It's a heady thing for all these peoples that came late to the world's attention."

"Then why should we do it, Bob?" Senator Cooley asked softly. "Seems kind of silly to oblige them, doesn't it? Why don't we just forget whatever it is Orrin wants, Bob, and go on about our business?"

"Because I said I'd give Orrin a fair chance. I didn't promise I'd go along with him; in fact, I said I might not. But I said he'd have a fair chance with his idea. I want you to help me give him that chance, Seab."

"I didn't make him any promises," Senator Cooley said gently. "Now, you know I didn't, Bob. And of course you know the reality of it for me, Bob: I could no more be a party to humbling the United States to a colored man than I could commit murder, Bob. My people in South Carolina would never forgive me. Furthermore, there's something else about it, too. You've lived here on the edge of the South long enough, you've known enough Southerners to know, Bob. It isn't a matter of politics, with me. I *really believe* they aren't competent and capable, Bob. I *really believe* the only way is to treat them decently but keep them in their place. I've never knowingly hurt a colored man in my life, Bob, and I never will. But look at Africa, if I have to have justification. It's a tribal chaos pretending to be a civilization, Bob; dress it up all you like and say it isn't so, but it still is so . . ." He stared out the Majority Leader's window, down across the Mall to the Washington Monument and the rolling hills of Virginia lying russet and hazy in the autumn sun. "No, Bob," he said softly, "it isn't as though I have a choice. Each of us has to do as he believes. I've believed what I believe for seventy-six years, Bob. I can't change now."

"I know that, Seab," the Majority Leader said in a tired tone, unhappy and saddened for all the peoples of earth who appear always to have no choice but to meet head-on upon the battlefields of their lifelong beliefs, "and I respect it. But the times are against you, the world has changed. You'll only hurt yourself, and you won't win. I think I can promise you that. You won't win because you're wrong. Not just politically wrong, in the context of our times, but fundamentally, morally wrong. Give it up, Seab. Make your formal protest, but don't make a real fight of it. You'll only get terribly hurt, and you can't win."

"Bob," the senior Senator from South Carolina said gently, "I don't make formal protests. When I fight, I fight. There's honor in that, too, Bob, you know. That's my kind of honor. Grant me that, at least, Bob."

"I do, Seab," Senator Munson said sadly. "I do, but I wish—"

"I'm not a wisher, Bob," Senator Cooley said, getting slowly out of his chair and preparing to go. "That's the trouble with the world right now—too much wishing. I fight, Bob. I don't trim. You can tell Orrin."

"Yes," the Majority Leader said bleakly. "I'll tell Orrin."

In the luxurious penthouse atop the State Department Annex the Secretary awaited his three o'clock guest with some trepidation, uncertain exactly what tack to take to secure Cullee's agreement for the project he had in mind, aware of many of the delicate considerations that surrounded it, wondering whether Cullee would be able to see and seize the opportunity offered him to serve his country in time of need. Orders had been left that he be shown up to the privacy of the penthouse, away from the formal offices downstairs, out of the often stultifying atmosphere of the Department itself, which Orrin found oppressive and tried to avoid as much as possible in his conduct of affairs. But atmosphere, of whatever kind, could only do so much. The rest depended upon men. He wondered what would come of their discussion now.

His eyes traveled across the white blocks of government buildings, the Potomac, Virginia, the lovely tree-filled city, and came at last to the Capitol sitting far and dominant upon the Hill. He was not quite used to this perspective yet. He had looked down from there upon the city for so long, and now he must look up to it, instead. There was not only an obvious symbolism here, there was also a tactical problem. His ties to the Congress were so strong that they were an instinctive, implicit part of his being; yet here he was in a position where he must deal with it, not as one of its most powerful and commanding insiders, but as an emissary from the Executive Branch, forced to rely upon argument and persuasion to secure the support he once could secure just by being Orrin Knox, with all that meant in power, influence, and personal authority. Now he was an office, not a man: the Secretary of State. It separated him from the sources of his power, put up a barrier, silken but distinct, between his colleagues and himself, forced him to rely upon subtler persuasions and gentler arguments. He studied the distant building on the Hill with an expression of naked longing on his face so pronounced that some of it still lingered when the private elevator arrived with a gentle thud, the door opened, and his visitor stepped out.

"I still miss it," Orrin said frankly, gesturing toward it with a nod as he came forward to shake hands. He noted at once that Cullee looked upset about something but responded with a fair facsimile of a smile in spite of it.

"It misses you."

"Please sit down. I have in mind that you and I should turn the old dome on its top together."

At this the Congressman looked genuinely amused for a moment, and the Secretary was gratified to note that his face relaxed into slightly less rigid lines as a result of it.

"That might be fun. I haven't really done that, yet."

"This may be the time," the Secretary said with a smile. He wondered if his visitor's trouble was personal and decided to find out. "How have things been going with you since we talked the other night?"

He knew he was right, for an unhappy expression came into Cullee's eyes for a moment. But he managed to speak in a noncommittal tone.

"All right. And you?" He smiled a little and settled back cautiously into the chair on whose edge he had been resting. "Not so well, I guess."

The Secretary gave a ruefully humorous grin and shook his head.

"The problems do not decrease, in this job. They add six and multiply by ten, every hour on the hour. Terry and Felix have really posed us quite a little conundrum, between the two of them."

Cullee started to smile, but whatever was bothering him came to the surface before he finished and turned it into an unhappy frown.

"For me, too," he said in a low voice. He looked up with a startling expression of naked agony in his eyes and, moved by some impulse the Secretary did not understand but felt deeply flattered to arouse, apparently decided to confide in him completely. "They're going to cost me my wife before they're through."

Orrin Knox felt a start of surprise, but suppressed it.

"I am so sorry," he said carefully. "How can they do that?"

The Congressman looked at him steadily for a long moment, the pain still deep in his eyes. When he spoke it was with candor that overwhelmed the Secretary.

"I wish I could tell you," he whispered, "what it means to be black."

And what do you say to that, Orrin Knox asked himself crazily: I am so sorry?

"Perhaps," he said, still with great care, "I can't understand. But I shall try, if you want to tell me about it."

"It traps me," Cullee Hamilton said, staring out the window with eyes that obviously did not see the beautiful city or the beautiful day. "It catches me where I can't break out. I'm—what I am, and I'm not ashamed of it, either. God knows I'm not. *You* don't think," he asked with an almost pathetic wistfulness, "that I'm ashamed of it, do you?"

"Of course I don't," Orrin Knox said firmly. "And whoever thinks you are doesn't know you, of that I am sure."

"Maybe they don't," the Congressman said slowly. "Maybe that's the trouble. Maybe *she* doesn't. That's probably it." He stopped and seemed lost in thought for several moments. The Secretary didn't dare break in, didn't, in fact, dare to even move a little in his chair, though one leg was pinching painfully upon the other and he would have loved to uncross them. He remained very still and presently Cullee spoke again.

"You see, my wife and my friend—LeGage—they both think I'm a coward and a traitor to my people and—and everything else, I guess. They don't think I'm much good. They think I should have gone to that school with Terry, and they think I ought to be up there fussing around at the UN, and if they knew I'd ever called you about Felix's plans, they'd—they'd really hate me, I guess."

"They'll never know from me. You can trust me on that."

"Can I trust you?" the Congressman asked, again in a tortured whisper. "You're white." He looked startled and dismayed by his own statement. "I don't mean that," he said sadly. "I really don't mean that. But that's what it's like on the—the other side. I like to think I'm an American, and I'm proud of it, too; but millions of Americans feel like that about—us, you know. They don't trust us, just because we're black . . . Only now," he said with a scarifying bitterness, "I've got myself in a place where it isn't only white people who don't trust me. Black people don't either."

"Oh, now," Orrin Knox said lamely, feeling more inadequate than he ever had in his life about anything, so deep was the unhappiness before him and so impossible was it, he recognized honestly, for a white man to really alleviate it, "that isn't true. It just isn't true. I won't let you torture yourself like this, Cullee. You aren't being fair to yourself at all."

"LeGage tells me I'm riding both races. Maybe he's right. Maybe I should cut over and be one way or the other. But how can I, and be honest? *How can I?* I can't hate the way so many of them—listen to me," he said with anguish; "'them'—and it's my own people I'm talking about—the way so many of *us* can. I guess hate was left out of me. I guess that makes me really unfit for the world we live in. You've got to hate nowadays, or you aren't anything. I guess that's it."

"Don't," the Secretary said, with a pain of his own. "Please don't. I grant you we are trapped in a terrible time, Cullee, but we're all trapped; you're not the only one. And we can't afford to let it get us down—we simply cannot —or we really will be lost, and the world will be lost, too, to those who wish to murder it. You and I have got to fight that, Cullee. So help me, will you? I can't carry it alone."

At this appeal, in which Orrin had been unprepared for, and startled by, his own intensity, the Congressman seemed to relax a little. But it was several moments before he spoke, and the bitterness was still in his voice when he did.

"I'd like to, but they'd just say I was trying to get white votes for Senator, if I did."

"All right," Orrin Knox said, for now the way out of this emotional dead end suddenly came clear; "and do you know what they're going to say about me? That I'm just trying to get black votes for President, aren't they? So what do we do about it, you and I, sit around crying because they call us names and don't understand us, or go ahead and do what we know is right? You tell me. We start equal with our own people, Cullee, so you tell me what you'd like us to do. I'll follow your advice, and that's a promise."

Again he did not dare move as their eyes held for a moment that lengthened until a stillness sang in the room. The Congressman spoke at last in a low voice.

"What do you want *me* to do?"

"Good," Orrin said with a great relief, aware that he had been given a trust that imposed upon him an obligation forever, but unafraid to accept it because he knew he would not betray it. "What I have in mind is this. See if you agree; and if you have suggestions, tell me. O.K.?"

For the first time Cullee Hamilton looked at ease and untroubled.

"O.K.," he said with the start of a genuine smile. "We'll show 'em."

"We will that," said Orrin Knox.

So the day looked much brighter to the Congressman from California as he got his car from the reserved parking lot of the State Department and drove toward the Hill. He would call the office of the Legislative Counsel for help on drafting the resolution when he reached his office, but first he would call home and tell Sue-Dan what had been decided, and that would be all right. True, it was the same thing essentially that she had wanted him to do, and it might be a little hard to explain why he had refused her and agreed with Orrin Knox, but, then, why did she need to know about Orrin Knox at all? Why couldn't he just tell her he had agreed with her after thinking it over, and everything would be all right? In fact, that was what Orrin himself had suggested.

It was with a rising excitement that he checked in at the House floor and then went direct to the cloakroom to make the call. Maudie answered, and the day began to die.

"Is she there?" he asked quickly. There was a strange little silence at the other end, and panic gripped his heart. "Is she there, Maudie?"

"Not here," Maudie said mournfully. "Not here, really, this time."

"What do you mean?" he demanded harshly.

"She just not here, I'm telling you. She and that LeGage took off together directly you left."

"But I want to tell her something," he said stupidly, as though the logic of his call would bring her back.

"She said to tell you they see you at the UN, if you want to come. She said she expect you know where New York is and how to find it, if you care to get there. She said she doubts you will, but, anyway, you know."

"Was that all?" he asked, feeling sick.

"That's all. You coming home for dinner?"

"I don't know."

"Got to eat. Can't beat trouble on an empty stomach. Anyway, maybe you'll get her back."

"Oh, sure," he said dully. "Maybe."

"I'll have it ready. You come home, hear?"

"O.K.," he said automatically. "I'll come home."

He went through the rest of the afternoon like a robot, but he kept his promise to Orrin Knox. He called the Legislative Counsel and told them what he wanted on the resolution, and he called the Speaker and told him what he wanted to do about introducing it. Now it seemed even more important than before that he keep faith with the white man who trusted him. He was too shaken emotionally to be exactly sure why, but he knew it was.

3

His host on the early-morning television show had been suitably complimentary to Panama, suitably apologetic for the United States, suitably anxious to take upon his own country all the blame for whatever unpleasant consequences might have arisen from the visit of the M'Bulu. Now Felix was on his way back across the maze of midmorning Manhattan to the East River, congratulating himself that with the eager encouragement of his interviewer he had been permitted to state his case in the friendliest possible atmosphere to many millions of those whose nation he was doing his best to defeat. It had been an enjoyable and constructive session, and he was grateful that he had been given the opportunity.

Furthermore, he had been able to do it without telling any lies. His claims of growing support throughout the UN for his anti-American amendment were entirely true. His talk yesterday to the African bloc had gone exceedingly well—the delegates had been only too eager to hear his carefully worded statement and had furnished with their own excited shouts and loud endorsements the added degree of criticism and condemnation of the United States that he had been too circumspect and careful to enunciate himself.

From then on, the day had proceeded with great success.

By the end of it, in fact, he had also talked to some twenty delegations outside the African bloc and had received from fourteen of them, including India, assurances of firm and active support. Krishna Khaleel, for whom the Ambassador of Panama did not have much respect but who nevertheless was an excellent troublemaker in his own fluttering, circuitous way, had taken off like a rocket amid fervent and exclamatory expressions of approval for what Felix was attempting to do. Felix had glimpsed him from time to time throughout the day, bustling about the Delegates' Lounge, pacing importantly up and down the corridors buttonholing delegates and correspondents, spreading the word and flexing India's not inconsiderable muscles with the neutral states.

At one point Felix had watched Senator Fry attempt to delay this vigorous progress long enough for a talk, but he had noted with an amused gratification that K.K. would have none of it. Instead he had gone hurrying away leaving the chief United States delegate with an expression of frank annoyance on his face. Hal Fry did not yet look really worried about the situation, Felix saw, but he made him a silent promise that he soon would be. By day's end, when they exchanged polite and wary inconsequentials at a New Zealand delegation cocktail party held in the Delegates' Dining Room, it was obvious that he was.

"Have you got all the votes in the Fifth Ward lined up?" Hal had inquired with an offhand humor, and Felix had smiled with a genuine amusement.

"Fifth, Sixth, Seventh, and Eighth. I think we will win in a walk."

"Oh, I don't think so," Hal Fry said. "Nobody is going to win this one in a walk. We'll make you run for it."

"As you like," Felix Labaiya had said calmly. "I'm in training."

He had expected some humorously sharp rejoinder, but the Senator had seemed momentarily dismayed and distracted by something, and a puzzled, almost pained expression had briefly shadowed his eyes. One of the numerous little princes from Thailand had come up at that moment and drawn the Panamanian Ambassador away before the American could collect his thoughts and respond.

They were worried, he told himself fiercely as the cab swung off Forty-second into First and cruised swiftly up to the Delegates' Entrance. Oh, yes, they were worried, for all that their official attitude was a sort of annoyed impatience with all these bothersome little states. Their flag still flew proudly with the rest in the half-circle before the Secretariat, but the wind had died down and it did not snap so briskly as it had yesterday. He realized with a tiny smile at his own fancies that this was a childish symbolism, but in a fight like this even the slightest of omens was worth reliance for the encouragement it could give. He made up his mind that before the day was over they would have still further cause to be concerned.

In pursuit of this, he put in a call to U.S. delegation headquarters as soon as he reached the Lounge. The chairman of DEFY was in and at his desk.

"Why don't you come over for coffee in ten minutes?" Felix asked, and LeGage agreed at once.

"I want to talk to you anyway," he said in a significant tone, and the Panamanian Ambassador suggested, "Then perhaps the Lounge is too public—"

"Oh, no," LeGage said with a sudden violence Felix could not quite interpret, "I don't care if they see me. I just don't care!"

"Very well," Felix said impassively. "I shall expect you."

And what did that mean? he wondered, as he studied the day's *Journal of United Nations Proceedings* with its listing of all committee meetings, its items on the agenda, its announcement of today's plenary session on the latest fighting in unhappy Kenya. Patsy had told him rather vaguely that she had seen Sue-Dan, though she didn't say much about their conversation; there was the old friendship between LeGage and Sue-Dan's husband. Could LeGage, Sue-Dan, and Cullee be cooking up something? What was going on, he asked himself dryly, in the darker reaches of the North American continent? Anyway, it could only help to advance his plans, whatever it was. If it didn't fit into them immediately, he was confident he could talk LeGage around until it did.

There came into his mind with a sudden uneasiness, as he nodded to a sheik from Saudi Arabia and one of his fellow Latins from Guatemala, the thought of his brother-in-law. He still had heard nothing from Ted, nor, apparently, had Patsy. He could always tell when she had, even if she did not tell him directly. No such overtones had been in her voice when she called last night. Apparently Ted was not worried yet about the course he was pursuing, and so Patsy wasn't either. She would have TOLD him if she were. There was no doubt of that.

Still, he had to confess that he did feel a certain puzzlement at the Governor's aloofness, for there was no doubt that he himself was on risky ground, pushing close to the limits of what Ted could afford to be associated with and still run for President. At any moment the backlash might begin, there might be some reaction, in the Congress or elsewhere, that would prove embarrassing; and then he would receive the phone call he had half expected ever since he introduced his amendment on Monday. What choice he would make then between the alternative courses of action that would be clearly presented, he did not, at this moment, know with any certainty; except that he knew he would have to make one, and, whatever it might be, it would not be easy. La Suerte sprang suddenly to his mind, the long view down the valley from the terrace, Chiriqui high and challenging behind. Be careful, Yanqui, he said in his mind to the one Yanqui he was afraid of; don't push the grandson of Don Jorge too far.

But, he told himself with an instantly following impatience, Ted was a practical man. What Felix was doing could be justified on grounds of Panamanian internal politics; Ted could understand that. Felix was being circumspect in his language, leaving real anti-American bitterness to others. He told himself he was worrying too soon and worrying too much. His self-confidence, shaken only by one man and by him never for long, surged back as he glanced up and saw the lithe figure of the chairman of DEFY enter the Lounge and look about for him with a questioning air that quickly gave way to a secret and intimate smile as Felix waved from his vantage place in the corner by the magazine racks.

"You know," Lafe Smith said, casually shifting his position at a coffee table far down the room near the window so that he could watch this meeting between the Panamanian Ambassador and the American delegation's most unknown quantity, "I really think you have one of the most fascinating jobs in this whole organization. Don't you think so?"

His companion gave a nervous little titter—God, he told himself, what a titter; but then again, what ti— But he stopped that line of thinking and told himself that his job was to pay attention to business and not get too involved in the lighter side of life. Not at the moment, anyway. That could come later; roughly ten hours later, he thought, glancing at his watch, estimating the day and allowing a graceful interval for dinner before life could get down to fundamentals.

Fundamentals! he repeated with a bleakness that would have surprised his many friends and colleagues. Was the same old merry-go-round really to be classed as fundamental? He supposed it was, in the minds of those who had not been so endowed with easy access to it as he. For him, however, who always hoped, without success, to stumble upon something more kind and lasting, something really fundamental, the word did not seem to apply. Fundamental physically, maybe, but, after all, you said that much, and then what? There must be something else; at least, he told himself with a pathos he did not realize, at least he had read about it and some people, such as the Knoxes and the Munsons, seemed to have it. But somehow it never came to him. *Chasseur formidable* he might be, but that was the extent of it. You could only hang so many trophies on the wall, and after a while you got tired of going in the game room. And as for his quick-dying hope that he might find something more permanent in marriage, that was a laugh, he told himself darkly. That was a real laugh.

Maybe, though, that was justice. Maybe he was like the character in the story who went down the corridor of mirrors opening door after door, only to find more corridors and more mirrors forever and ever. Maybe he deserved so futile a reward for what was, essentially, so futile a pastime. Certainly he had not picked well when he had finally chosen. Anyone with an ounce of brains and perception, anyone without his conditioning, perhaps, would certainly have known that the willing little girl who had tripped away from his apartment after an all-night visit on the morning of the Leffingwell nomination six months ago would hardly be the type on which to base a lasting marriage. Anyone who wasn't so used to slipping away from apartments himself would have realized that his was not the only apartment she had slipped away from. Or would continue to slip away from, he thought sourly.

He wasn't sure which of them had reverted to type first, but after exhausting each other on a hectic honeymoon it hadn't taken them long. He had realized abruptly that he was monumentally bored, and so, apparently, had she. For a very brief period he had tried to keep up appearances for the sake of his reputation and the sake of his pride, for he knew Washington was waiting to indulge in much cruel laughter at his expense. Then he had decided that the best way to meet that problem was to start laughing first. A couple of weeks of being back on the prowl had accomplished it. Irene, whose pride was perhaps less justified but certainly as strong as his, had chosen to make a scene about it at "Vagaries," and Justice Tommy Davis, that silly old busybody, had watched and spread the word like a gabbling schoolgirl. This had probably been a good thing, though he had resented it at the time. There had been much joking in the cloakrooms, much knowing comment around the Senate; he realized that his pride had been saved, all right. It was only in his moments of deepest bitterness that he realized at what a cost, in lost hopes, lost dreams, in personal comfort and happiness apparently to be denied him forever.

And yet, he thought with a hopeless protest, what had he done to deserve it? Was it really justice? What had he ever done to hurt anybody? Possibly he had, here and there, though he had tried not to. As much as conscious care could prevent it, he had tried to be as kind as possible, to make it pleasant, to keep it light, to be sure that his partners understood that it was all in fun and not to be taken too seriously. It was true that there had been a few instances when women had taken him too seriously; it had been clinging and messy, but could that be blamed on him? He had never promised them anything, never offered his heart any more than was necessary to achieve his physical objective. Maybe that explained it, he thought forlornly with a rare flash of self-analysis; maybe he had never received anything because he had never given anything. But it wasn't that he meant to be hurtful to anybody, he told himself with a bewildered truthfulness. It was just that he meant to be kind.

"You are so *moody*," his companion said, and he came out of his reverie abruptly to realize that he wasn't paying attention to business at all, either national business or international business or, for that matter, monkey business. He was suddenly aware that Felix and LeGage seemed to be having a most serious discussion, LeGage apparently intrigued but reluctant about something, Felix apparently urging him on. And as for little Miss—or was it Mrs.?—he would have to find out sometime—Indonesia here, she gave signs of being puzzled by his inattention, and that, too, required active application.

"Not moody at all," he said with his engaging grin. "Just thinking about how fortunate I am to have so lovely and talented a companion this morning. And," he added, his voice dropping, "this evening."

"Oh," she said with a blush. "Oh. Now."

"How long," he asked, deciding that was enough of that for the time being, "have you worked in the Medical Service?"

"Two years. Since my husband started at Columbia."

"Oh," he said politely, telling himself with some amusement that that certainly answered *that*. "I didn't know he was going there."

"Oh, yes. He is studying medicine, too."

"And then you're going back to Indonesia and help your own people, is that it?"

She smiled with a soft certainty that pleased him.

"Oh, yes. There is much need, you know."

"I know. I think that's very worthy of you—a very nice thing to do. I admire you for it."

"Thank you," she said demurely.

"I wonder," he said, for Felix and LeGage were still talking, although LeGage appeared to be agreeing and he estimated the talk would not run much longer, "how we Americans shape up alongside the others, as you see us in your office? Are we more healthy, or less, or about average, would you say, or what?"

"Quite healthy, I would say," and added, with just a touch of irony, "headaches, nerves, upset stomachs—simple things. But you have so many remedies for that nature of ailment in this country that it is very simple to provide treatment."

"I think I'll bring Senator Fry in someday soon. He's been complaining of feeling a little peculiar, lately."

"He has already been in. Did he not tell you?"

"No," he said, rather blankly. "He did not. When?"

"Yesterday afternoon, quite late. He talked to one of the doctors for several minutes and the doctor had me give him a prescription to soothe his nerves."

"I hope that does it," Lafe Smith said, more concerned than he liked to admit.

"I hope so too. I think he is quite worried about it, although he does not let on."

"I am too," he said frankly. "Look, do me a favor, will you? Let me know when he comes in again, and if you hear the doctor say anything specific about what's wrong with him, let me know that, too. O.K.?"

She shook her head with a smile.

"I could not do that; it would not be ethical. Nurses are not allowed to do that, Senator. You know that, surely."

He nodded.

"I know that. On the other hand, this man is my friend and colleague, and the Secretary of State and I are worried about him. He may not tell us if anything serious should occur." He smiled. "I would have to have a friend who could tell me." He mimicked her tone gently. "You know that, surely."

"What makes you think something serious might occur?"

"Just say I have a hunch."

She nodded.

"So have I. So does he."

"How about the doctor?" Lafe said. She smiled.

"I heard him say nervous tension. It is such an easy answer to everything; so many of them use it when they are too lazy to think of anything else. If he returns, I will tell you."

"Thank you," he said. "And thank you," he said, for Felix was standing up and exchanging his final words with LeGage, "for coming to have coffee with me. I shall see you for dinner, then?"

She smiled quickly.

"Oh, yes."

"And what about your husband?"

"He will be on duty at Harkness Pavilion all night. He does that to make extra money for his studies."

"His success means a great deal to you, doesn't it?"

She nodded, without smiling. "To Indonesia also."

"Well," he said, "perhaps I too can contribute some money to help with his studies."

"It would be nice," she agreed. He laughed.

"And you say we're direct," he remarked, and this time she did smile, somewhere between humor and shyness.

"It is not as though I did not like you at all," she observed.

"Thank you. For the betterment of Indonesia, the cause of stability in the Far East, and greater peace and democracy in the world, I shall do my best."

She smiled in a way that provoked the old familiar excitement, the well-worn but ever-hopeful interest that never knows, poor fool, when it has had enough, and said demurely, "I too."

He walked her as far as the door, aware out of the corner of his eye that LeGage was still sitting, apparently in deep thought, where Felix had left him; bade her farewell with a genuine friendliness until the evening, and then turned back and stood as if irresolute in the center of the tide of delegates flowing in and out of the entrance to the Lounge. Quite by accident, or so it seemed, he wandered toward the magazine racks, still without seeing LeGage, idly picked up a copy of the *Times of India*, and looked about for a place to sit. He gave a start of recognition just as the chairman of DEFY finally looked up and did the same, and moved purposefully toward him even as LeGage gestured automatically to the neighboring seat.

"Hi," Lafe said easily, taking the chair with an air of relaxed leisure. "Been here long?"

"Not too long. How about yourself?"

"Just came in," Lafe said. LeGage reacted as he expected, with a grin and a knowing wink.

"Tell me you just came in! I saw you with that little cutie of yours just now. How do you do it, Lafe? I swear I wish I had all the contacts you have."

The Senator shrugged.

"I haven't so many. One at a time. That one's pretty nice, I grant you."

"I didn't know you liked our side of the bed," LeGage remarked, not offensively but in the tone of one genuinely discovering something he hadn't known.

"Didn't you?" Lafe said. If this was the way to LeGage's heart, he would play it to the hilt. "Why not? Of course I don't want you to tell Seab Cooley about it, now. He might not understand."

"Expect he would," LeGage said, scowling. "Expect lots of men down South would understand. At least I'll say for you, you're honest."

"I try to be," Lafe said. He assumed an air of man-to-man frankness, not patronizing, not prurient, just candidly matter-of-fact. "I like it on your side. There's a certain acceptance you don't get on mine, maybe. It's comforting."

"Give her my phone number when you get through," LeGage said with a self-conscious laugh. "She's right cute."

"I might at that," Lafe said, adding mentally, When I'm a hundred and five and ten feet tall, buster. "What brings you over this morning," he asked casually, "Fourth Committee?"

"No," LeGage said, rather evasively, his fellow delegate thought. "I just decided to come over and find out how things are going on Felix Labaiya's amendment."

"Good. And how are they?"

"I haven't had time to talk to anyone yet. I just got here."

Lafe gave him an amused glance.

"Sure, you and me both. We're a couple of bum liars, 'Gage. What did Felix say? Does he think it's coming along O.K.—for him, that is?"

"Oh," LeGage said with an elaborate disinterest. "Did you see us?"

"You weren't exactly hiding. What does he want you to do, help him line up votes against us?"

He was aware that his colleague was considering several answers, all evasive. Finally 'Gage turned toward him with a grin that did not, really, contain so much humor, Lafe thought.

"Why, sure. Sure, that's just it. Do you think I should, Lafe?"

The Senator from Iowa shrugged and became aware that the young lady at the telephone desk, who had not been able to break through his concentration heretofore, was now calling insistently in an apparently vain attempt to round up Mr. Jansen of Norway and Mr. Selim Bukawara of Malaya, please.

"Why, I don't know, 'Gage," he said. "I think it's a rather sad commentary if you really have to ask."

The chairman of DEFY gave a shrug and a deprecatory laugh which did not, however, ring entirely true to Lafe Smith.

"Shucks, you didn't think I meant that, did you, Lafe? Felix is too smart to make me a proposition like that. I'm too smart to consider it. Now, wouldn't I look silly going around behind my own country's back trying to help put her in a bad light?" He laughed abruptly and slapped his thigh. "That old man in the White House'd have my scalp so fast I couldn't say de–se–gre–gation, if I did that. Now isn't that right?"

O.K., friend, Lafe thought, if you want to be nasty; I expect we can all play that game.

"Might even happen so fast you couldn't say DEFY, 'Gage," he said pleasantly. "That would be even faster, wouldn't it?"

LeGage gave him a sudden sharp and ugly look, then concealed it immediately with a forced laugh—not quickly enough, however, to prevent the thought in Lafe's mind that something quite drastic must really be under way here.

"Now," he said, suddenly determined to get to the bottom of it, and no nonsense, "what does Felix want you to do, 'Gage? I wouldn't want you to got yourself in a bind that could hurt you, up here."

"You *wouldn't?*" LeGage said, and now nothing concealed the savage sarcasm in his voice and eyes. "You *wouldn't?* Well, isn't that kind of you, Senator Smith. I didn't know you cared. What makes you think I'll believe that you care one little tiny damn what happens to me?"

"All right," Lafe said indifferently. "Maybe I don't, if you want it that way. But I do care what happens to this country, and if you don't care, friend chairman, I think you're a damned fool, because it's just as much your neck as it is mine."

"Is it?" LeGage demanded, breathing heavily but trying to keep his voice down. "Is it, now? Maybe we'll see about that someday, Lafe. Maybe we'll just see."

In response Lafe spoke sharply and too fast, and his reply could not have been more infuriating had he deliberately planned it so.

"You're talking like a child. A sick child. You're off in some dream world someplace."

"I know," LeGage said softly. "Tell me we're all Americans together, why don't you?"

"You're going down a bad road, boy," Lafe said, and was aware of a sudden convulsive movement in the chair alongside.

"Don't 'boy' me," 'Gage whispered savagely, turning his face away from the room and pretending to study the telephone dial, so that no one but Lafe could see his angry, half-crying expression. "I hate that!"

"I didn't mean it the way you choose to take it," he said, equally low-voiced, equally absorbed in studying the dial. "I said it as I would to any of my friends, that's the way I talk, you know that. But I guess it wasn't to a friend, in this case. But watch out for yourself, that's all I can say. It's a dangerous game and we could all get hurt."

"I'll play it right," LeGage promised fiercely, still averting his face from the room. "You can be sure of that. I'll play it right!"

"I hope so for your sake," Lafe said, forcing himself to relax and turn back casually, nodding brightly to a Pakistani, bowing politely to the Italian Ambassador, noting with half a thought the little group of interested delegates surrounding the M'Bulu and Krishna Khaleel, far down the room near the bar. His eyes came back to the entrance and it took him several seconds to really focus on the figure that stood there, peering about in a slightly self-conscious but typically brash and arrogant fashion. It was a figure so out of place in this setting that for a moment he literally could not believe it was there. When he accepted the fact, he started to rise, but too late. The junior Senator from Wyoming had noted his movement and was upon them both before they could escape. There was one small bright note for Lafe: LeGage's face was as much a study as his own, and he could not believe there had been any prearrangement about this unexpected meeting.

"Well, if it isn't Iowa's gift to the motherhood of the whole wide world," Fred Van Ackerman said with the unctuous heartiness that always trembled on the edge of a sneer. "How's it going up here? Getting all you want?"

"Want some, Fred?" Lafe asked evenly. "I might have a little extra lying around that I could arrange for you, if you're hard up."

"I've got more important things to think about, thanks," Senator Van Ackerman said. "Such as this almighty mess old Half-Ass Harley has gotten us into right here in the UN. What are you doing about that, Lafe? Anything?"

"We're working on it," Lafe said, rather lamely. Fred Van Ackerman snorted.

"Well, that's good. I'm glad to know somebody is. Why don't you run along and let me talk to LeGage here? Maybe he has some practical ideas about what we ought to do."

"What brings you up here, Fred?" Lafe asked. "Is Washington getting to be too small an area for you to do damage in?"

The Senator from Wyoming gave him a sudden furious look but refrained from reply. Instead he sat down abruptly in the chair Lafe had just vacated and turned to LeGage as though no one else were there.

"I'd like to talk to the only sane man in the U.S. delegation. How's it going, boy?"

"Tell him, *boy*," Lafe said, turning on his heel. "Tell him, and have fun."

"I never know what that fornicating jackass means, half the time," Fred Van Ackerman remarked, shaking his head. "Do you?"

But LeGage only gave him a strange look, as though words failed him, and after a moment the junior Senator from Wyoming dismissed it.

"Now look here, boy," he said, leaning forward and clamping a hand on LeGage's arm, "I think you and I can do business on this. I've got some powerful friends in COMFORT, you know, and I think maybe all of us liberals can get together and—"

Another day, Hal Fry told himself as he looked across First Avenue at the green-and-white shaft of the Secretariat making its powerful statement against the autumn sun, another dollar. He had been up since six, reading the papers, studying reports, making vote-tallies as earnestly as though he were helping Bob Munson on some major issue in the Senate. It was a frustrating pastime, because every time he thought he had a nation accurately pegged, some other aspect of its self-interest would occur to him and he would have to move it into the doubtful column again. Even the powers that normally sided with the United States were doubtful now, so many were the passions aroused by the Labaiya amendment and so strong the subtle, corroding elements that colored the world's attitudes toward the great Republic of the West. It was in an atmosphere of uncertainty and confusion that the acting head of the American delegation moved forward now, aware that his country was surrounded on all sides by active enemies and shifty friends, aware that the world was in a turmoil from which nothing constructive or lasting ever seemed to emerge, aware that men advanced on the basis of their passions with the mind left far behind, aware that in this present era events such as those which were now developing were quite capable of producing consequences of a gravity and permanent destructiveness far beyond the consequences reasonable men might have the right, in some other, more rational age, to expect. He did not even know, for instance, what would come of the appointment he was about to have, here in his office in U.S. delegation headquarters. His only strength at the moment was that his visitors had come to him, not he to them. For what it was worth, this was some small indication of status, and he decided to make the most of it. But it took some doing to be outwardly cordial and calmly unconcerned as he prepared to greet the Ambassadors of Panama and India and their carefree companion, the dashing young heir to Gorotoland.

Even as he rose to do so, the problem was suddenly and terribly complicated by the strangest combination of physical sensations he had ever known. A sudden feeling of nausea, a terrible dizziness, a feeling as though a vise had clamped upon his chest and stomach, shooting pains down his arms and legs, a sudden strangled feeling in his windpipe, a sudden hazy fog in his eyes—he was so completely taken aback at this fantastic and unexpected onslaught that for a second he was terrified that he might fall forward across his desk with hand outstretched in a greeting never to be completed.

Apparently, however, none of this was visible on the surface at this moment. He was to be struck with the fearful irony of it in succeeding days, that apparently his color remained unchanged, his outward appearance normal, only his eyes, Lafe was to tell him later, showing any indication of strain, and that only to those who looked into them with a real perception.

Now, none of the three faces that he could see in a half-blurred haze showed concern or alarm. Evidently what was to him a major and terrifying experience was not communicated to them in any way. What to him seemed agonized minutes must be only the slightest of seconds as the wave of pain throughout his body seemed to build and then began gradually to recede. It was not like what he had ever heard of a heart attack, though the chest pain immediately suggested that conclusion. It was an utterly irrational and erratic onslaught upon his entire system for which he could not, as a layman, find explanation: except that he knew, suddenly and completely and finally, that he was very seriously ill.

All of this, so deeply shattering, so profoundly unsettling as well as painful, the psychological impact even greater than the torturing physical pain, took seconds. With a great and definite effort of the will, through sheer strength of character, relying on plain and simple guts of which he fortunately had a great many, he continued his greetings as casually as he could, talking through a screen of pain that gradually, but only gradually, eased throughout his body. Some impulse to duty, some feeling that the accustomed forms would pull him through, some basic determination not to fail his task in this crucial moment for his country, gave him the strength he needed. But it was with a tenuous and shaky control at best that he continued the greetings so harshly interrupted.

"Felix," he said, "K.K., Terry—please sit down. I can't tell you how honored I am by this distinguished trio. Which am I entertaining," he added with a desperate attempt to cling to his customary humor, "the Three Graces, the Three Fates, or the Three Blind Mice?"

But this, which they of course could not understand was a genuine necessity for him in his present state, was obviously the wrong thing to say to the two Ambassadors, for Felix gave only his small, tidy, unamused smile, and K.K. looked quite offended. Only the M'Bulu burst into ringing laughter as he deposited his towering form gracefully in a chair. In fact, Hal Fry noted through the screen of pain, he even clapped his hands a couple of times as though he were a delighted child with a new toy. This act of innocence was so stagy that the Senator, even in his agonizing physical discomfort, was at once put even more on guard than he was already.

"Senator," Terrible Terry declared, "you are always so witty. No matter what happens, we can count on you for laughs. It makes of the UN a happier place than it might otherwise be."

"That's very kind of you," Hal Fry said, as the pressures began to increase again throughout his body. "I try to spread what cheer I can in such troubled times. It seems the least I can do."

"Some of us," Krishna Khaleel said in a tone of starchy disapproval, "do not think the world is quite that funny, Hal."

"You're certainly doing *your* best to make it not so," he snapped, egged on by the rising pain which now was attacking him again in his chest, his stomach, his eyes, down his arms and legs, threatening to choke off his breath, savagely enfolding his body in a silent and terrible embrace. "I suppose you have some reason for it that seems logical to you."

"The logic is clear enough," the Indian Ambassador said coldly. "You surely did not think the United States could maintain its racial policies in the face of world disapproval forever."

"The United States is doing its best to straighten out its racial poli—" he began, but his voice died, with the pain, and even more, at this moment, in the face of the three archly knowing expressions that confronted him. What was the use, he managed to think through the silently frightful struggle going on within him, when the world would not believe? What was the point in honor and good faith and the government trying to better the conditions of its people, when no one gave you credit, or even credence? These minds were closed. The great majority of minds around the world were closed. The United States could talk forever, reasonably and with complete honesty, about what it was doing to improve the status of the Negro, and from around the world it would get back exactly this smug, superior, impenetrable, know-nothing smirk. So why, he wondered painfully, should anyone bother?

"How many votes have you got, Felix?" he asked, feeling dreadfully sick but managing by sheer will power to put a cold forcefulness in his voice. "Apparently we might as well get down to brass tacks. You haven't got enough yet, have you?"

A sudden extra-agonizing twist of pain shot through his entire body. *My God*, he thought, *what is the matter with me?*

"Do you think I should admit it if I did not have the votes?" Felix asked calmly. "Certainly I should not. Prove it, if you think I do not have enough."

"I can't prove you haven't, any more than you can prove you have," he said with a painful slowness that to them apparently only sounded deliberate. "I just don't think you do. You don't think you do, either. So what is the purpose of this call? To try to bluff the United States into something? What do you take us for?"

The pain was gone, abruptly, from his stomach and chest; now an almost unbearable ache was in his arms and legs, and he felt as though he could not draw another breath, although, slowly and carefully, he did.

"Well, Hal," the Indian Ambassador said with a stuffy annoyance, "I must say you are not making it easy. I must say we did not expect to find such intransigence, Hal, nor such, one might even say, as it were, hostility."

"My as it were hostility is in good shape, K.K.," he said, again with what they apparently took to be a thoughtful slowness, though it was in reality an outward sign of the desperate struggle he seemed to be waging with his own body. "How else am I supposed to react, as though you were offering me rubies and roses? Now," he said with another effort of will that put a show of challenging vigor in his voice, "I want to know what the purpose of this call is. I have a lot of things to do, including a luncheon date, and I can't afford to spend all morning with you three, delightful though your company is."

"Are you feeling all right, Hal?" the Indian Ambassador asked, apparently really looking at him for the first time. He drew himself up in his chair and managed a firm smile.

"I'm feeling fine." The smile faded, because he could not hold it longer against the devils who were now re-entering his chest, turning their screws upon his stomach, shooting the waves of terrible dizziness into his head; but this his guests evidently did not perceive, and he covered it by a renewed tone of coldness. "I'm just annoyed by this attempt at flimflammery, that's all."

"We had not thought to find you in such a mood," Felix Labaiya said quietly. "We had thought to find you in a mood to listen to reason."

"In a mood to turn tail and run, is that it?" he managed with a sharpness aggravated by the bewildering sensations running through him. "That is not the American mood, Felix, even though you sometimes find it difficult to understand what that mood is. Perhaps your in-laws aren't a good example."

"My in-laws," the Panamanian Ambassador said with equal sharpness, "are neither here nor there. They understand my position."

"Do they?" he said, still able almost by instinct that could function without him to use the weapon he knew would trouble Felix most. "Better check with the Governor. I'm not so sure."

"He hasn't said anything," Felix said quickly.

"I haven't seen the wire-service clips this morning," Hal Fry said with a fair show of indifference, and the pain receded sufficiently so that he could come back to the everyday world long enough to feel a slight satisfaction that the opening had developed so naturally. He pressed the buzzer on his desk with a show of vigor. "My secretary will bring them in, and we'll see."

"There will be nothing there," Felix said firmly.

The pain was back, but through it he forced himself to give the answer he knew had to be made.

"There will be nothing there about the United States retreating, either," he said as they waited for the girl. "So there we are. Having a good time in America, Terry?"

"Senator," the M'Bulu said genially, "now you are trying to divert us. It will not work. The situation here in the United Nations has reached a point where diversions and evasions and side issues no longer hold the attention of the world. We are approaching a showdown, Senator. What will you do?"

"That is the question," Krishna Khaleel agreed. "What will you do?"

"Why do anything," he asked with a fair show of calmness, though someone was now working on the small of his back with a pair of forceps, "except continue to do what we are doing, which is to persuade the General Assembly of the validity of our position? There's only one way to decide it now, isn't there, and that's to have a vote and see who wins. Unless, of course, you intend to withdraw your amendment, Felix. That might speed things along considerably."

The Panamanian Ambassador looked at him with a strange expression, as though he considered him to be verging on insanity.

"I shall never withdraw it," he said coldly. Hal Fry shrugged, though the motion seemed to cost him a new set of pains searing up through his shoulders. *Is there no end to it?* his mind demanded; and for the time being, at least, his body answered, No.

"Therefore we must meet it as best we can, in the only way open to us," he said carefully. "You aren't afraid of losing the vote, are you, Felix? Perhaps that's what behind this little visitation."

"I think we are losing sight of our purpose in coming here," the M'Bulu said with a graceful laugh. "We have let the conversation carry us afield. We are really here in the best interests of the United States, Senator. We think there is a commendable way out for you."

Now it was back in his eyes again, a blurring haze that suddenly turned reddish; this upset him more than anything yet, for it harked back to his recent troubles of the weekend. But again he forced himself to remain still and outwardly calm.

"It would not be so difficult, Hal," the Indian Ambassador said earnestly. "It would, indeed, make all your friends and supporters around the world regard you with genuine pride and affection. It would be a simple exercise of restraint and dignity, Hal, of understanding what the tides of history are in this world of ours. It is not so much to ask of a truly great power."

"And what would that be," he asked, as the red light began to fade a little, "join in supporting the amendment? Surely," he said with an enforced levity that cost him greatly, "you can think of something more original than that, K.K.!"

"Nothing would be more becoming to a power of the stature the United States considers herself to have," the Panamanian Ambassador said with a smooth insolence that Hal Fry was too sick to counter. "Why should you object?"

"It would be such a simple solution," Terrible Terry said encouragingly. "Then we could all forget this unhappy wrangle and turn together toward new eras of peace and understanding!"

"I'm glad the world seems that simple to you," Senator Fry said, the pain swiftly receding all over his body for no reason he could see or understand. "And what would we get out of such an action?"

"Honor," said Felix Labaiya.

"Integrity," said Krishna Khaleel.

"The applause of the whole wide world, Senator; I can assure you of that; the applause of the whole wide world!" said the M'Bulu.

"Otherwise," Felix said soberly, "we must continue to line up the votes that can only result in a most humiliating condemnation of the United States in the eyes of the whole world. Surely you do not want that for your country."

"It would be terrible for you, Hal," K.K. assured him. "You cannot imagine the endless repercussions that a defeat on such an issue would have for you throughout the world."

"Oh, yes," Hal Fry said grimly, for both subject matter and pain were again conspiring, the pain once more racking his body with a savage capriciousness, now here, now there, now everywhere, "we can imagine. That is why we intend that it will not happen."

"Then you must do as we ask," the M'Bulu said happily. "There is no other solution."

"We shall see," Hal Fry said, wondering furiously through his fluctuating agony where his secretary was with the long yellow clips of copy paper from the two wire-service tickers in the outer office. He reached over and pushed the buzzer again with a hurried, impatient air, and this time the girl did hurry in with the streamers in her hands.

"Excuse me," he said, beginning with a great effort at casualness to riffle through them for the item he hoped desperately was there—for now, in his own physical pain and their organized onslaught against his country, it suddenly seemed fearfully important that it be there. "I want to find Ted Jason's statement in here for you, Felix."

"There is no statement," the Panamanian Ambassador said with an uneasy anger. "He would have talked to me first."

"Possibly," Hal Fry said calmly, "or possibly not. Let me see: 'Governor Edward Jason of California said today—' But, no, that isn't it; he's making some statement on Mexican wetbacks." In an instant the pain was gone entirely, and in his relief he resorted again to irony. "But don't give up, Felix. There are three more sheets." Now where in the hell is it, he asked himself with a growing impatience, diverted momentarily from the inexplicable things occurring in his body. Orrin had called him an hour ago; surely the plan had gone well. "Why, here it is," he said in a relieved tone of voice.

"Ted's statement?" the Panamanian Ambassador asked, and for once he did not seem to be quite the cool and collected customer he liked to have the world think he was.

"Why, no," Hal said with satisfaction; "Cullee Hamilton's resolution."

"What's old Cullee done?" the M'Bulu asked with the beginning of a smile which indicated that he would not be surprised to find the Congressman attempting to checkmate him.

Hal Fry started to read it aloud, but suddenly his private pack of devils was back again, exercising their marksmanship against his chest and lower body, sending the horrible waves of dizziness through his head, blurring his sight again, closing off his esophagus.

"Why don't you read it aloud, K.K.?" he managed to suggest before the kaleidoscopic sensations became too severe for him to talk. "It may change things somewhat."

"Well," the Indian Ambassador said nervously in his precise, clipped English; "well, let me see . . .

" 'Representative Cullee Hamilton, California's Negro Congressman, today introduced a joint Congressional resolution expressing the official apologies of the United States Government to the M'Bulu of Mbuele for the "danger and personal humiliation" he suffered while escorting a colored child to school last week in Charleston, S.C.

" 'The resolution authorizes a grant of $10,000,000 to the African prince to use as he sees fit for the "advancement and improvement" of the people of his native Gorotoland, and it also promises him the use of United States technical advisers in furthering any project he may wish to undertake along those lines.

" 'The resolution also declares it to be the sense of the Congress that the United States should "move with increased rapidity to improve the conditions of its Negro population at all levels." It pledges the "full co-operation" of Congress in achieving this aim.

" 'There were immediate indications that the resolution may have tough sledding in both houses of Congress. Experienced observers felt that its greatest difficulty will come in the Senate.

" 'There, the resolution was attacked soon after its introduction by Senator Seabright B. Cooley of South Carolina, who charged that it was a "put-up job."

"'Rep. Hamilton, the Senator said, was "acting as water boy for the political ambitions of Orrin Knox" (Secretary of State Orrin Knox) in introducing the resolution.'"

Well, that figures, Hal Fry thought through his pain as the Indian Ambassador finished reading and a little silence fell. Finally Krishna Khaleel shrugged elaborately.

"Well, what does it mean, eh? Just words. Just a resolution in the Congress. It does not affect us here, Hal. Surely you do not think it affects us here."

"Felix knows," Hal Fry said with a casual air that cost him much, for the agonizing sensations again were everywhere throughout his body. "Don't you, Felix?"

"I know it means a very difficult project for the Congress," the Panamanian Ambassador said tersely.

"You know it means the turning point here," Hal Fry said.

"If it goes through there."

"It will."

"We shall see," said Felix Labaiya.

"Well!" the M'Bulu exclaimed with a cheerful laugh, rising to his full height and draping his robes carefully about him as he prepared to leave. "So old Cullee fooled us all. What do you know."

After they had gone, after he had made farewells which seemed and sounded to him terribly shaky but which they in their annoyance and frustration apparently did not notice as such, the Senator from West Virginia sat for what must have been many minutes at his desk as the waves of pain came and went, came and went. Gradually they began to subside, and presently the time arrived when he was able to conclude instinctively that the terrible storm which had swept through his body was beginning to die away.

My God, my God, he repeated to himself in a sick and frightened bafflement, *what is it?* And later, with a grim determination, *Whatever it is, I've got to keep going; I've simply got to.* And finally, almost too much to bear now, prompted by the thought of a handsome boy sitting in the sun far up the Hudson, the agonized cry: *If you could only be here to help me, Jimmy. If we could only help each other.*

But they could not; and after a few more minutes, during which his vision gradually returned to normal and the dizziness slowly subsided so that he could stand up without fear of falling, he rose shakily, squared his shoulders, took a deep breath, and prepared to go across the street to the UN.

Perhaps forcing himself to conduct his normal business would provide surcease; perhaps there would come the blessed calming of customary things. But he knew as he stepped out of U.S. delegation headquarters and started, feeling steadily better now, across First Avenue to the Secretariat Building, that things were not the same.

Perhaps, he recognized with a terrifying honesty, they could never be the same again. In the space of half an hour fear had come to live with him, and he did not know, now, when, if ever, it might depart.

"Señor Varilla of Ecuador, please," the young lady at the telephone desk said with a bored intonation. "Mr. Takasura of Japan . . . Mr. Ben Said of Morocco, please . . ."

"So you see, boy," Fred Van Ackerman concluded expansively, "that's the way it shapes up. All of us want to get together and put over the real liberal viewpoint, and you're just the man to do it. DEFY's got to front this thing; it's the only move that makes sense. The Jasons are interested, COMFORT will come in on it, and I suspect the New York *Post* and the Washington *Post* and all that crowd will give us all the support they can, and that's plenty. But it's up to you to start it moving, right?"

"I don't know," LeGage said slowly. "I just don't know. I'm not so sure I want to run with that bunch on this."

"Why not?" the Senator from Wyoming demanded sharply. "Aren't we good enough for you? Why, see here, boy, that's the best support you could possibly ask for. It'll give us a chance to show up Knox and some of these other phonies who seem to think they can grab the liberal cause for their own political advantage. Nothing like the genuine article, now, is there?"

"I wouldn't know," LeGage said with a trace of sullenness. "Folks I represent aren't quite so concerned about labels as you seem to be. They're more concerned with results."

"Results!" Fred Van Ackerman said. "Results! God damn, 'Gage boy, you just stick with me and you'll see results!"

"Yes, I know," LeGage said like a flash. "You got resulted right into a censure motion, seems like I recall."

"Bastards!" Fred Van Ackerman said with a brooding emphasis. "I'll get them yet, see if I don't. That's why it makes so much sense for us to get together, boy. You people and I, we both want revenge. We've both had a dirty deal."

LeGage was silent for a moment at the colossal arrogance of this, but spoke finally in a soft voice.

"Oh? You think it's equal?"

"You're damned right I do," Senator Van Ackerman said. "Look now," he said with a sudden urgency, gripping LeGage's arm again, though the chairman of DEFY tried, too late, to move it out of reach, "how about it, now, boy? Just give the word and we'll start getting things organized any way you say. Under your orders, if you like, too, O.K.?"

"I want to think about it. I don't want to be rushed."

"Let me call you at 2 P.M.," Fred said. "If you want to call me earlier, I'll be at the St. Regis, or you can leave word at the delegation." An expression of spiteful satisfaction came into his eyes. "Most of 'em hate my guts, but I'm still United States Senator and they have to deal with me whether they like it or not."

"Why are you so hot to get involved in this thing, Senator?" LeGage inquired quizzically. "I don't remember you being such a big wheeler and dealer on the race issue up to now."

"It's in the times," Fred said quickly. "It's in the times. Nobody can escape it, if he wants to be a good servant to the country and help the cause of true liberalism. Why, God damn, we'll take the ball away from Knox and that old fuddy-duddy in the White House so fast they won't know what hit them!"

"We will?" LeGage said with a dryness that escaped the junior Senator from Wyoming. "I see."

"Remember what I said now, boy! We're all counting on you. I'll see you later, now, understand?"

"I understand," LeGage said, as Fred jumped up restlessly and moved off with a final wave.

"Good!" he said in farewell. "I knew we could count on you."

That LeGage, he told himself as he left the Lounge through the strolling delegates with his restless, questing air of always looking for some personal certainty and security he would never find, was a good boy. Personally he, Fred, could take them or leave them alone, preferably the latter, but in a fight like this you needed all the help you could get. LeGage was a damned good boy, for a nigger. LeGage, he told himself, could be quite an asset. Yes, indeedy, quite an asset.

As for the chairman of DEFY, it was with a sick distaste and anger that he watched the Senator depart. Except for Felix, it seemed to him, he got the same treatment from all the whites, and most annoying of all was this arrogant no-good who did so much fancy spouting about being a liberal. Him and his damned labels, LeGage thought bitterly. Of all the phonies! He could feel Fred's personal distaste for him oozing through every phony word, and he returned it a hundredfold for Fred and all his phony friends. "Been patronized enough for one day," he muttered with a fearful scowl that seriously alarmed a lady member of the British delegation, sitting nearby. "Just been patronized enough for one day."

Thus he was in a more than receptive mood when the Ambassador of Panama approached a few minutes later with the news of Cullee's resolution and the fruitless talk with Hal Fry. For a short time he was taken aback and abashed by Cullee's action—although it gave him a moment of savage pleasure when he thought of Fred Van Ackerman's boasted plans and how dismayed he would be when he found Cullee had beaten him to this phase of them—but the more he turned over in his mind what Cullee had done, the more he became convinced that it was just what Seab Cooley said: a put-up job for Orrin Knox. "Never thought I'd agree with that old man," he remarked with an unamused laugh; but his bitter suspicions and jealousies persuaded him. And the angrier he grew, with a deep, emotional, personal anger that was just something between Cullee and him that nobody else could understand, at this betrayal by his ex-roommate and this attempt to take the spotlight away from him in the eyes of the whites and his own people.

There came a point when he jumped up, startling Felix with his abruptness.

"See you later," he said. "I've got things to do."

Felix gave him a quick smile.

"I hope so. Then you'll—"

"I'll see you later," LeGage repeated impatiently.

"Good," Felix said with satisfaction.

But the chairman of DEFY did not hear him as he hurried out with his loping, pantherlike gait. His mind was filled now with just one thought, bitter and shrouded in an agonized unhappiness, and it was driving him on in a way he could not have imagined until it happened. He knew there was just one thing to do now, and he was on his way to do it.

The Ambassador of Panama remained seated in the Lounge for a few minutes, nodding politely to other delegates as they passed, pretending to read La Prensa, reviewing the morning, appraising events. He was under no illusions about the potency of Cullee Hamilton's resolution in this present context. It would, if successful, be a serious and probably fatal blow to his own amendment here, for the United States then would be able to argue that it was making more than ample apologies to Terry and also moving in good faith to set its own house in order. But the "if successful" was a powerful qualification that encouraged optimism. He had had occasion many times in Washington to observe the ponderous grindings of the Congressional machine, and he was not worried that it could produce action on the Hamilton resolution overnight. Certainly it could not do so by Thursday, when the General Assembly would resume debate on his amendment here.

He was forced to admit, however, that the development did make his own task more difficult. A gesture had been made, now, and much propaganda could be manufactured from it, even if it died in committee in the House and never came to the floor at all. He also suspected that Seab Cooley was correct, and that this was, among other things, a shrewd move by Orrin Knox to bring Cullee into his political camp and thereby weaken Ted Jason in California and at least partially negate his appeal to the Negro vote. Thank God, he told himself with a grim satisfaction, that certain powerful newspapers were so down on Orrin. That would take care of that, he hoped, imagining the knowing editorials, the harsh cartoons, the savage imputations of motive and character that would now be unleashed upon the Secretary.

And thank God, too, that he had been given the inspiration to find the lever that would finally tip the wavering LeGage in the direction he wanted him to go.

"I do think it is a real pity," he had said thoughtfully, "when you two are such deep friends, to discover that he would introduce his resolution for Orrin Knox, when he wouldn't do it for you." A startled and embittered expression had leaped into LeGage's eyes as this thought took hold, and in an instant's time he had reached his decision, jumped up, and hurried away, bound upon the errand Felix had been trying for twenty-four hours to persuade him to undertake.

As for his own over-all problem here, he did not think the Hamilton resolution made his chances so very much worse. It wouldn't be as easy as it had started out to be, but he could manage. Oh, yes, he thought with a calm confidence as he rose and prepared to meet the Soviet Ambassador for lunch and convey the invitation he had been asked to convey, Felix Labaiya-Sofra could manage. And would.

"It isn't as though we don't want you to succeed in whatever it is you want to do, old chap," Lord Maudulayne remarked as he stared about the Delegates' Dining Room with a speculative expression, "but of course you understand that it does pose a delicate problem for us."

"Well, I wouldn't expect you to do anything really forceful and affirmative," Hal Fry said with some sarcasm, for by now he was feeling much himself again; the mysterious pain was almost gone, only a very faint echo still twinging his arms and shoulders. "That wouldn't be in character, would it? Isn't the British policy Ruminate and Retreat? I thought that was it."

Raoul Barre chuckled.

"You are beginning to sound like Orrin, who doesn't sound like Orrin any more. It is like old times."

"And also somewhat unjustified, I think," Claude Maudulayne said mildly. "We have problems in the Commonwealth that make a cautious policy advisable. We do what we can."

"The handicap hasn't disturbed you on Gorotoland's independence," Hal remarked. "You're standing firm on that, Commonwealth or no."

"We have given our word," the British Ambassador said in a tone that canceled argument. "That is a different matter."

"But chivvying the United States is fair fun for all, is that it?"

"You forget," Raoul said with an ironic blandness, "that the Commonwealth is now black. So, of course, is the French community. A majority of both are of a color different from our own; there is, as our friend K.K. is fond of pointing out, a shade of difference in what we are now and what we used to be. It makes it less easy to move, here in this assemblage of organized argumentation."

"You French don't think much of it," Senator Fry said. "Why do you let yourself be swayed by it in this instance?"

"It is not the United Nations which sways us," the French Ambassador said with a shrug. "It is the community. But since the community is within the United Nations, we must of necessity give thought to what the community desires in the United Nations. And so with the Commonwealth. If you will forgive me for stating it with a harsh candor, what they both desire at the moment is the scalp of the United States. Unfortunately by a curious combination of mischance and miscalculation, compounded by the astute Terry and others, you have given them the opportunity to attempt it. It is most regrettable but, I am afraid, unavoidable."

"However, of course," Lord Maudulayne said thoughtfully, "we want to do all we can to work out a reasonable accommodation of views on this difficult issue. It is not as though we really wanted to leave you in the lurch, old boy. That would hardly be fair. Nor would it be consistent with what

Her Majesty's Government believe to be the best long-range interests of the Commonwealth, the United Nations, or the world."

"Thanks so much," Hal Fry said. "How do you propose to go about it, by doing nothing?"

"We are not 'doing nothing,'" the British Ambassador said. "Both of us have had numerous conversations in the past forty-eight hours, as I assume you have too."

"Don't add up to much, do they?" Hal Fry said. "Not much ground for accommodation, is there? At least I can't find any discernible pattern, except dislike for us and a great evasiveness every time I try to pin somebody down on how his delegation is going to vote."

"It is not clear yet at all," Raoul Barre said. "All is mysterious and hazy and full of hints. Dark faces materialize out of dark clouds, murmur dark words and depart, leaving us in darkness. I would not say at this moment that the outcome is certain either way. Therefore, I think you should make every attempt to appear with Tashikov this afternoon when he addresses the Afro-Asian group. I think it might prove very profitable for your cause, at this particular stage of events."

"I didn't know they were meeting or that he was going to appear," Hal said blankly. "They've kept it very quiet from the U.S. delegation, I'll say that for them."

"I suspect your Mr. Shelby has known right along, but his position is, shall we say, somewhat equivocal at best at this moment. However, it is the fact. At 3 P.M., in Conference Room 4, I believe. I think you should be there."

"That's obvious, if you can tell me how to go about it. I doubt if I could barge in uninvited." Possibly because he was suddenly very concerned with this new development, or so he told himself, he began to feel a slight pain, somewhere in his body, gently ominous and insistent, making his heart contract with apprehension; but there was no time to give in to it now, even if it became ten times worse. He hurried on, hoping that if he ignored it, it would go away. "Perhaps you can arrange an invitation for me through the community or the Commonwealth. Maybe if Cameroun or Sierra Leone, or somebody relatively responsible, could ask me—" But he was aware of a silent but definite hesitation on the part of his two old friends of the diplomatic corps.

"Well, you see," Lord Maudulayne said carefully, "if it were something that was to happen tomorrow, possibly, or next week, it would be possible perhaps to arrange something without any undue show of haste. But, as it is, only two hours away—well, I think that would seem too definitely like rushing it, would it not?"

"We mustn't rush anything," Hal Fry said with an annoyance beginning to be increased by the fact that ignoring his devil wasn't working; the pain was now rising steadily, insistently, with a terrible softness like some fearful flood up through his body. "That's for sure. That wouldn't look right, now, would it?"

"Really, old chap," the British Ambassador said, "I don't think it would. I think your best gambit now is to be dignified and not beg too much, you know. I think if they get the idea you are running around frantically seeking their favors, the reaction will be contempt."

"Is it ever anything else?" Senator Fry asked. "I have yet to see it, if it is."

"I still think it would be best to wait for an invitation, rather than ask," Claude Maudulayne said. "If it comes, it comes. If it doesn't, well—"

"We cannot afford to wait," Hal Fry said in the same tone, prompted by anger and pain combined. "My country is under direct attack. We must act in any way we can to defend ourselves here. I'd like to be calm and stately and British and pretend the foxes eating at our vitals aren't really there, but I'm afraid the world doesn't allow of it any more." He paused and stared for a long moment, through vision now beginning ever so slightly but surely to blur, at the crowded dining room, the avid and interested faces of the nations, more than a few casting covert but attentive glances toward their table as they talked. "Very well. I shall simply appear, if that is the only thing possible."

"Suppose they just ignore you and let you sit there?" Raoul Barre asked softly. "Such cruelty is not unknown to them, you know. In fact, they delight in it when the victim is a white man. Alas, our ancestors sowed a fearful harvest for us to reap; but I do not think we should volunteer to speed the gleaning any more rapidly than we have to. No," he said with a sudden decisiveness. "Such an event would be just one more humiliation for your country. You do not want to run the chance of it. I would suggest you talk to the Secretary-General. In the meantime, I shall talk to Cameroun and Senegal. One way or the other, perhaps something may be arranged by three o'clock."

"I should of course expect to do what I could too," Claude Maudulayne said, somewhat stiffly. "I just felt that it should not be too precipitous and undignified. All of these elements must be kept firmly in mind in dealing with them. There is a matter of face, and it is not to be ignored if one would succeed in attaining one's objectives."

"All right, Claude," Hal said, more calmly, for the pain, in what he was already beginning to recognize as its own capricious pattern, was suddenly lessening, though the blurring of vision remained about the same. "I know you mean to be helpful, insofar as your own interests permit." He sighed and shook his head with a tired little smile. "I'm sorry I sounded so impatient. Got too much on my mind right now, I guess . . . Are we through?"

"Yes," Raoul Barre said. "Where will you be in the next two hours?"

"You can reach me through the delegation," he said, the blurring too beginning to disappear. "I'll be checking in with them from time to time." At the elevator he turned to Lord Maudulayne with some of his usual humor. "Ask London whether they'll swap us a No vote on Corotoland for a No vote on the amendment, Claude. Maybe we can work out a deal."

"If the world were only that simple nowadays," the British Ambassador remarked.

"I'm told it used to be," Senator Fry said.

"Never again," said Raoul Barre.

If he held himself very carefully and walked very quietly, he assured himself as he entered the elevator that would take him to the thirty-eighth floor, everything would be all right and he would continue to feel steadily better. And of course at once, suddenly, powerfully, the pain was back in his body. He gave an audible gasp and leaned back against the wall of the car. The sweet-faced Italian girl at the controls turned at once with an expression of concern.

"You are not well, Senator?" she asked in a softly worried voice. He attempted a smile, which came out crazily, he knew; but by a great effort of will, he made his voice sound reasonably calm.

"I—don't quite know. I've never felt anything like it before."

"Shall I take you back down to the doctor?" He shook his head.

"No. I have an appointment with the Secretary-General and—don't—want—to—miss—it."

"But if you are sick—" she protested. Again he shook his head.

"It will pass," he said between clenched teeth, the old pat line coming wildly into his head as he fought, with eyes blurring and the terrible sick dizziness surging through his head in waves, to remain standing: *Even this shall pass away*. But would it? Dear God, would it?

"Well," she said doubtfully, slowing the car while she thought what to do. He managed to gesture with one hand.

"Please—keep—on—up. Really, I'll be—all right."

"Is it heart? My father—"

"I don't know," he said, and as abruptly as they had come the terrible cramping pains through his stomach and chest began to recede a little. "I don't think so." He pulled out a handkerchief and wiped his face in an automatic gesture, though he knew there was no sweat upon it for all his intense inward struggle. "I don't know," he said more strongly, "but I don't really believe so. If it were heart, and I felt that badly," he added with an attempt at a smile that went pretty well, because he was already beginning to feel in control of himself again, "I'd be dead by now, I'm sure of that. It just—comes and goes."

"Well," she said with a brisk decision, "we won't pick anybody else up." She smiled as they shot by waiting lights. "They won't like it, but we will take you straight to the S.-G."

"Thank you," he said, as the blurring, reddish in tinge and fuzzy around the edges, began to clear up a little while the car leaped upward. "UN Express."

"That's us," she agreed with a smile, still worried but relaxing a little as he seemed to be feeling better. The waves of dizziness, too, were becoming less; he might now be able to walk down the corridor to the S.-G.'s office without falling down. But it was with a very cautious feeling of holding himself tightly together, or putting one foot very carefully after the other, or not moving too suddenly or changing direction too fast, of balancing with great care this delicate bowl of jelly that seemed to be moving around the top of his head, that he gave her a shaky farewell smile and stepped out.

"I'll be all right. Don't worry. I'm feeling much better already."

"I hope so, Senator. Please don't take chances. We must all keep ourselves in good health here at the UN, for the world's sake, must we not?"

"If I can be as good a delegate as you are an elevator operator," he said, "the world needn't worry, I guess."

He was rewarded by a blush of pleasure and a sweet, though still concerned, smile as the door closed. Whoo–ee, he whispered to himself, do I feel like the devil.

But he was considerably better than he had been five minutes ago, he knew that, as he gave his name to the guard at the reception desk and was shown down the long corridor to the chaste office with its beautiful view off over Brooklyn. The principal thing that bothered him now, of course, that had bothered him ever since this morning and would continue to bother him until he licked it or it licked him, was that he was now more vividly aware than ever that at any moment, at any time of day or night, under any conditions, without rhyme or reason or provocation deliberate or inadvertent, he might find himself without warning in the grip of his private demon.

Again, apparently, none of this showed on the surface, for the Secretary-General rose to greet him with no indication that he was conscious that all was not well with his visitor. He gestured gracefully to a chair and then returned to his own behind the desk with an air of grave politeness and, the American thought, a touch of genuine weariness. That his impression was not false the S.-G. made clear after a moment during which he leaned his chin on the tips of his long narrow fingers and stared thoughtfully out at the lazily drifting autumn day.

"So it is not going well for the United States," he said finally, with what seemed a trace of sadness, "and now you are here to ask me for help." He sighed. "I wish it were possible for me to help you, but it is not."

"Well," Hal Fry said, wishing he were in better shape to combat this unexpected attack, for such in its indirect fashion he thought it might be, "I am sorry you feel that way, Mr. Secretary-General. I had hoped you wouldn't foreclose us altogether from your good offices. Especially since the request I have is a rather minor one, all things considered."

The Secretary-General smiled, rather wanly, Hal thought.

"Is there such a thing as a minor request these days at the United Nations? Is not everything expected and required to revolve around the central power struggle in the world? I sometimes find that a competing request for paper clips can be turned into a major battleground between East and West. What, then, is 'minor'?"

"Very well," Hal said, wishing that the reeling room would settle down, the vise, still pressing gently against his back, be relaxed even further, but knowing he must go forward henceforth regardless of how he might feel inside his besieged body, "perhaps it is not so minor. The Afro-Asian group is meeting at 3 P.M. They have invited the Soviet Ambassador to address them. I want them to invite me also. Arrange it for me, will you, please?"

The S.-G. looked at him for a moment from dark, impassive eyes with an expression of knowledge that seemed to invite some further comment; but the Senator decided he had best make none until he got an answer. It did not surprise him when it came.

"I am afraid that you enter there upon an area where I am even more completely foreclosed from assisting you."

"You knew, though, of course, about the invitation to Tashikov." The Secretary-General gave the smallest of confirmatory nods. "And it was impossible for you, even, then, to suggest to whoever told you, 'Perhaps it would be reasonable also to invite the head of the American delegation'?"

"Tashikov told me," the S.-G. said, "and it was not possible to make such a suggestion to him." He looked far away across Brooklyn and spoke in the same weary, almost wistful tone. "Even if it had come from one of the delegations concerned, I should not have been able to make such a suggestion. You underestimate how deeply emotions are stirred on this issue."

"Your own, too, I take it," Senator Fry said sharply, feeling physically crippled and psychologically on the defensive, a combination that gave him little room for grace. The S.-G.'s gaze swung slowly back to his and held it for a moment before he gave a slow, unhappy shrug.

"I can go far in denying Africa in the pursuit of my duties, and then I can go no farther. After all, Senator—" he paused and spread his hands wide before him on the desk, staring down at them with an expression in which pride and sorrow were inextricably mixed, "your answer is in my skin . . . Is that not true?"

Hal Fry nodded, feeling suddenly burdened with the sorrows of the world, resting so heavily upon the backs of poor mankind that it often seemed they could never be removed, making of his own physical worries, at least for the moment, something small and insignificant.

"That is true. I suppose that when all is said and done you have no choice, really."

"There are areas in which men do not have choices," the Secretary-General said softly, "though sometimes they can go quite far beyond those areas by pretending to themselves that they do. But there always comes the ultimate moment when the truth catches up. It has with me, on this. Certainly I do not wish to hurt the United States, indeed, without her where would the United Nations be, where would any small state be; but neither can I help her too openly." He sighed again. "No one could, white or black, in the present situation. The colored races of the world are so aroused that any attempt at intervention, even the most reasonable and sensible, would only antagonize them still further. I repeat, you do not realize how explosive the tensions are on this issue here in this house."

"Oh, yes, I realize," Senator Fry said unhappily. "The signs are clear enough. But the United States cannot afford to let itself be frozen out of the discussion of it, either. It is a matter of necessity that we talk to our opponents. It is a matter of simple fairness."

"Many of them do not equate the United States with fairness on the issue of race," the S.-G. said softly. "Why should they be fair to the United States?"

To this the acting chief of the American delegation had, for the moment, no answer; here too was the blank wall of disbelief that would admit of no qualification, the rigid refusal to acknowledge any moderating facts that would upset a pattern of thinking too comfortably direct and simple to permit of the difficulties of reasoned argument. But he made one last attempt.

"Mr. Secretary-General, do you really believe that the United States is doing nothing to better its racial conditions? Do you really, honestly, on the basis of your own intelligence and observation, think we have made no gains worthy of respect and consideration? I cannot believe you are so blind or so willfully intolerant."

The S.-G. did not look at him, nor did he answer. He only spread his hands wide again upon his desk and stared down at them with the same expression of sorrow and pride, possessed of an unchallengeable sad dignity of its own.

"All right," Hal Fry said, standing up. "I won't take any more of your time. The least we have a right to expect is that you will not intervene against us. We shall expect you to be neutral, and we shall hold you to account if you are not."

The Secretary-General looked up with a sadly ironic little smile.

"As I told the Secretary of State the other evening, neutrality is all I am permitted. I am a man with many masters, and none will allow me to move an inch beyond my golden cage."

"If that is all you can do, then God help the United Nations."

"I wonder if He will," the S.-G. said with the same combination of sadness and irony. "Yes, Senator, I sometimes wonder if He will."

On which cheerful note, Hal Fry told himself as he descended to the Delegates' Lounge in a different elevator so that he would not have to pretend to his little Italian friend that the pain, now steadily getting worse, was getting better, he had been wise to terminate a conversation that had obviously reached its end. Though it had not been confirmed in so many words, he did have the feeling that he had secured the S.-G.'s neutrality, and that was worth a great deal, for his active intervention could be very effective and damaging in the present situation. But he had certainly not secured his active help, and that could be almost as effective and damaging.

It was therefore with some relief that he heard his name called as he entered the Lounge and, turning, saw approaching one of the smooth and supercilious young men of the Ghanaian delegation.

"Senator," he said without preamble, "I have been authorized to tell you that the Afro-Asian bloc is meeting at 3 P.M. in Conference Room 4, and if you would wish to address us at that time, we should be pleased. We have extended the same invitation to the Soviet Ambassador."

"Oh," Hal said, with a smile that he hoped did not look too relieved, "did Lord Maudulayne talk to you?"

"I believe the invitation was suggested by Ambassador Labaiya," the Ghanaian said, and now it was Hal's task to refrain from looking too surprised.

"That was kind of him," he said gravely. "And kind of you all. I shall be there."

"That will be delightful," the Ghanaian said in a tone that edged insolence but just managed to stop this side of it. "We shall be expecting you."

And that, Senator Fry told himself, was a puzzler. What was Felix doing, being nice to him? He decided that he must be on guard—always on guard, ever on guard. Could suspicion and mistrust ever stop, in this antiseptic temple to man's undying hope and unchanging nature? Maybe, but he did not expect to live to see the day.

Or live at all, he told himself with a wryly desperate humor, as the terrible dizziness began to come back again in waves through his head. It was about two-thirty and he had just enough time to see the doctor. He found a phone, requested and received an immediate appointment, and took the elevator back up to the Medical Service on the fifth floor.

"Tour 27," Miss Burma (East) said into the microphone at the guides' desk in the Main Concourse on the ground floor. "All persons holding tickets marked 27, will you go to the glass doors, please . . ." She cupped a hand over the mouthpiece and added to Miss Viet Nam (South), "Will they never stop coming, these idiots, these schoolgirls and schoolboys, these goggle-eyed tourists?"

Overhearing this explosion, prompted by the steady stream of visitors that had been flowing past the desk ever since 9 A.M., Miss Malaya (North) and Miss Thailand (West) moved in closer with ironic and understanding smiles.

"But they are so innocent," Miss Malaya (North) said with a knowing little laugh. "They *believe* in it."

"I am glad someone does," said Miss Thailand (West). "I don't know whether *they* do," she added, with an upward gesture in the general direction of the General Assembly Hall.

"How could anyone not believe in it?" inquired Miss Viet Nam (South) blandly, "when all of us here have seen such remarkable proofs of it? It has saved half of my country—and half of your country—and half of your country—and half of *your* country—and who knows where all this half-ing will end? No one can say it has not accomplished much, this half-ing!"

"Now you are being bitter," remarked Miss Burma (East). "This has been agreed by the great powers and thus all have been satisfied. In Moscow this half-ing has been a triumph of communism and in Washington it has been a triumph of democracy, and so everyone has been happy."

"Except that Moscow has been happiest of all," said Miss Malaya (North), and they all laughed with a knowing air, like a group of little cymbals tinkling away with a polite scorn in the echoing concourse.

"You do not believe, then," said Miss Thailand (West), "that it has really been a triumph for the democracies, this half-ing? Washington has told us so. Do you not believe Washington?"

"I do not even half-believe Washington," said Miss Viet Nam (South), and they all laughed merrily again.

"We must back to business," Miss Malaya (North) pointed out with a show of mock firmness. "Tour 28," she said sharply into the microphone. "All who hold tickets marked 28, please go to the glass doors."

"Look at them!" she added with her hand over the mouthpiece. "Just look!"

"Many of those who are waiting to go in Conference Room 4 are black, I notice," Miss Burma (East) observed. "An unusual number, I would say."

"I suppose they are interested in the Labaiya amendment," said Miss Thailand (West). "It probably brings them."

"It seems to me an unusual number, all black, though," said Miss Burma (East).

"Perhaps it has to do with the Asian-African conference," suggested Miss Viet Nam (South).

"You may be half-right," Miss Malaya (North) remarked, and again they all tinkled away most merrily. "But it does seem an unusual number."

"You say," the little owl-eyed man asked him with a pompously solemn and all-knowing air, "that these new attacks began this morning? The prescription I gave you the other day has had no effect?"

"Evidently not," Hal Fry said. "As I told you, over the past few days I've been noticing odd little things—an occasional reddish blurring of vision, principally."

"And this of course has been related directly to the increasing difficulties of the United States here in the United Nations," the little owl-eyed man suggested smoothly. Hal Fry gave an impatient laugh.

"Oh, come on, Doctor. Let's don't tell me about nervous tension again. I haven't been under any pressures from that."

"Sometimes we are under pressures of which we are not aware."

"Yes," Hal Fry said skeptically. "Well, I know what the pressures are here, and I'm fully aware of them, because they are considerable. But they aren't causing these spells."

"I see. Could you describe them again?"

"I've just described them. I'm having one right now, and I've told you about it. What are you trying to do, trip me up?"

The little owl-eyed man shrugged.

"Well, if you won't help yourself," he said with an unmoved smugness, "I'm afraid I can't help you."

"Now, look," Hal Fry said, trying to keep his temper, which was not easy, for his eyes were blurring again and the combination of dizziness and cramps through his stomach and upper body was shortening his breath, accelerating his heart, and making it difficult for him to talk clearly, "I know they considered you the brightest boy in your class at N.Y.U.—"

"They did, as a matter of fact," the little owl-eyed man said calmly.

"—and I know this has given you a lifelong license to be positive about everything, but I am telling you this business is like nothing on land or sea. It's completely erratic the way it comes and goes. It just doesn't make sense. It bears no relation to tension, or lack of it, or anything else. Hadn't you better give me some serious tests and try to find out what it is?"

"I am quite sure tests wouldn't show anything more than we know right now as a result of the preliminary check the other day," the little owl-eyed man said serenely, "but eventually, if it persists, we shall give you some and then you will see."

"*If* it persists! I can tell you it shows no signs of diminishing."

"It came abruptly; it may go with equal abruptness, once the tensions are removed."

"Damn it," Hal Fry said angrily, "it isn't due to tension!"

"You are raising your voice," the little owl-eyed man pointed out reasonably. "It is always a sign of some inner disturbance."

"You're damned right it is," Hal Fry snapped, the agony now rising fearfully through his body. "I'm disturbed by you, because you won't listen to what's wrong with me."

"I've been listening," the little owl-eyed man informed him. "All right," he said, scribbling a prescription on a piece of paper. "Have the dispensary fill this; take two at bedtime and one before each meal. And see if that doesn't correct your nervous tension."

"But it isn't nervous tension," Hal Fry said, more quietly. "Look," he added curiously, "aren't you just interested, as a doctor, in what these symptoms mean? I should think you'd like to find out from a scientific standpoint, if nothing else."

"We live in a difficult world," the little owl-eyed man said. "I see nothing here that doesn't fit the classic pattern. Take those, and if they don't help, come back. I'm always glad to talk to you. That's what we're here for."

"If I had anything to do with it," Senator Fry said sharply, "you wouldn't be here." The little owl-eyed man permitted himself the smallest of smug and knowing smiles.

"That too fits the pattern. Fortunately, you do not. Don't worry too much about the country's difficulties," he called as the Senator rose and started out the door, narrowly missing a collision with a pretty little nurse from some Asian country. "Everything will work out all right."

That's what you think, you supercilious son of a bitch, Senator Fry replied silently, but there was no further point in arguing with this one. He walked out, slowly and carefully, for fear that he might fall if he walked too fast. How he would get through the next hour, he did not at this moment know, but he did know one thing: He must.

"I say," said the London *Daily Telegraph* with a pleasant relish as they sat in the press section of Conference Room 4 and watched the big double horseshoe of seats fill up with black and brown, "do you expect they'll roast Senator Fry over a slow fire or put him out to the ants?"

"Good show any way they do it," the Manchester *Guardian* said. "Imagine the smarmy nerve of barging in here uninvited."

"Oh, he was invited," the *Telegraph* said. "Ghana invited him, I understand."

"I guess they thought it would be a dull day without a little fun," the *Guardian* said with a chuckle. "This is one time when the Yanks get told off right where they live, I'll lay odds."

"Couldn't happen to a nicer country," the London *Daily Mail* remarked with a jovial acid, sliding into a seat alongside and peering casually over the crowded chamber. "Always heartening to see the good receive what they deserve."

"I know," the *Daily Express* agreed with a chuckle. "It encourages one's faith in the instinctive abilities of backward peoples to do the right thing, given sufficient education and information."

"Uncle Sam has educated them this time, all right," the *Guardian* said. "Where's friend Terry?"

"There he is," the *Telegraph* said, "just coming in over there with Tashikov."

"Tashikov gets around, doesn't he?" the *Daily Mail* observed.

"I must say he's had everything handed him on a silver platter this time," the *Evening Standard* said.

"It's all so stupid," the *Telegraph* said. "Why don't the damned Americans ever grow up? It embarrasses all of us, having to drag them along with this racial albatross 'round their necks."

"Come now, old boy," the *Sunday Observer* said from the row behind. "Would you want your daughter to marry a nigra?"

"Have a bloody good time of it if she did, from what I hear," the *Daily Mail* said with a laugh. "Looks like we're drawing a good house today."

"I can't tell," the *Guardian* said. "It's dark in here."

And so it was, for as the seats on the floor began to fill up, delegates coming in and greeting one another effusively, the air of tension quickening as more and more entered, it was apparent that the gathering was almost entirely colored, partially Asian but much more Negro. Here and there a white face stood out with startling vividness, but even in the press section the whites were far outnumbered, and in the public galleries the audience appeared to be almost entirely Negro. It was indeed dark in here; nor was it entirely a matter of pigmentation. There was something about the manner in which the delegates greeted one another, about the self-important swaggerings of the Ghanaians and Guineans and the rest, about the overpowering attitude of look-at-us-we're-wonderful, that finally prompted the *Telegraph* to murmur to the *Express*, "Bottom dog on top ride mighty high."

"On *our* backs, buster," the *Express,* with less levity and a certain grimness, murmured back.

On the floor, however, all was happiness and harmony as the gathering grew. The M'Bulu of Mbuele, obviously in his element, could be seen passing from delegation to delegation, bowing, shaking hands, waving gaily to friends and acquaintances. At his side, equally cordial, equally ubiquitous, the Ambassadors of India and the Soviet Union also passed among the crowd. Off to one side the Ambassador of Panama could be noted, deep in conversation with Nigeria and Ceylon as the clock neared three and the babble of talk and greeting mounted. Causing a great stir of excitement, the acting head of the American delegation entered the room just before three, appearing to be a little slow, a little tired, a little preoccupied; but he shook hands with the delegate of Mali, in the chair, with a good show of cordiality and then took a seat in a chair at the front of the room and looked about with an expression that seemed calm if somewhat preoccupied.

Promptly at three, the delegate of Mali rapped his gavel and announced, "Unlike the habit of some other gatherings at the United Nations, this one will start on time!"

There was a ripple of appreciative laughter and a round of applause begun by Terrible Terry. When it died the chairman looked first at Senator Fry, on his right hand, and Vasily Tashikov, on his left.

"We are honored today," he said, "by the presence of the distinguished delegates of the United States and the Union of Soviet Socialist Republics, whom we have invited to address us on the subject of the amendment offered to his resolution by the distinguished delegate of Panama."

Again there was a burst of applause, and in response to it Felix stood and bowed gravely, his eyes meeting those of the Senator from West Virginia without expression.

"The first speaker," Mali said, "will be the distinguished delegate of the United States."

There was a scattering of applause, coldly correct, exactly measured, as Senator Fry rose to speak. He had hoped he would be called last, he had hoped for a little more time in which to let the latest storm abate in his body; but he was captive of the situation, as indeed were they all, and there was nothing for it but to go ahead. He was aware that Lafe had entered at the back of the room and was standing against the wall staring at him as though he would will strength into him by his look; and in a way, Hal realized gratefully, he did. He took a deep breath, leaned forward to the microphone in front of his chair, and began.

"Mr. Chairman, distinguished delegates: I wish to thank you for inviting me to address this important conference today, particularly since the subject of your discussion is one in which the United States of course is intimately concerned." There was a little ripple of sarcastic laughter, and a sudden anger strengthened his voice. "The United States is not ashamed of the actions which it has taken, as a government, to improve the conditions of the Negro race within its borders. The United States has done far more in actual accomplishment than most of those who attack the United States have achieved with words. The United States is not here to make apologies to anyone for its conduct as a government."

There was an angry stir across the floor, a scattering of boos and hisses from the galleries; tension gripped the room as fiercely as his private demon was gripping his body. God, give me strength, he said in a silent inward prayer; let me get through this. I must, I must.

"No, Mr. Chairman," he repeated slowly, "the United States is not here to make apologies to anyone for its conduct as a government. But it is here to make apologies and to make suitable restitution—as a government, though it is not guilty as a government—for the actions of some of its private citizens, acting in their private capacity.

"Although my government cannot always control these actions, or be on hand on every occasion to prevent them from getting out of hand, still it is willing to consider itself responsible in a larger sense and to take appropriate steps—just as the government of some other country, for instance, may be responsible for the murder of some of its tribesmen, or another government may be responsible for maintaining a class of slaves known as 'untouchables.' My government is willing, with honor, to accept its responsibilities in this regard.

"However, Mr. Chairman," he said, and he was forced by the ravening pain to slow down for a moment, so much so that a little stir of interest moved through his audience until he took a deep breath and forced himself on forcefully enough so that the interest subsided, "the United States does not believe that any good purpose would be served by holding it up to world calumny here in the United Nations." He was aware of the slightest of movements from Vasily Tashikov, a hand going slowly up to his forehead, but did not think of it for more than a second, telling himself wryly out of his own pain that perhaps Vasily had headaches too.

"The United States, believing that its record as a government is a good one in the racial field, believing that it is moving through certain important channels in Washington to make full amends both to His Royal Highness the M'Bulu and to its own Negro citizens, therefore believes that it would be most unwise and indeed unfriendly for the General Assembly—"

He was aware that Tashikov's hand had come down again, and even as he saw the quick, commanding movement with which it descended, some instinct, some sixth or eighth or tenth sense, told him through his terrible discomfort what was going to happen, so that his own voice rose even as other voices began to rise in wild banshee shoutings from the public galleries —"to take the action proposed by Ambassador Labaiya!"

"To hell with the United States!" a voice bellowed from the galleries. "Murderers! Damned bigots! Racial assassins!" screamed another. A surging, shouting mob began to pour down the aisle toward the floor as the delegates turned and watched. But there was about their watching the impassive aspect of those who had known all along what to expect, and as he remained at his seat while the UN guards fought with halfhearted energy to hold the well-organized mob, Senator Fry understood, with a sick sadness compounded by the raging fires of his sick body, why he had been invited at the last moment to address the Afro-Asian conference.

For almost twenty minutes—long enough so that all the television cameras and still photographers and news reporters and radio commentators could snap their pictures and make their breathless broadcasts and secure their eager interviews—the mob continued to shout its obscenities and scream its insults from the galleries. It was clear enough at once that despite its initial surge toward the floor, this had not been its purpose. The purpose was headlines, and swiftly and efficiently they were achieved.

There was time, as the riot went on, to distinguish certain participants, some of them very famous and widely known in both the white and colored worlds: the chairman of DEFY, shouting obscenities crazily with the rest; the pretty little wife of the Congressman from California, screaming like a fishwife in the intervals between her posings for the cameras and her hasty interviews with the lady correspondents covering the UN; the famous male calypso singer, hating the white man but loving his money, whose Cadillac was waiting for him outside; the famous female blues singer, sick to death inside her sharp-featured little head with all her twisted hatreds of her native land; and even, quite out of place, looking incongruous but screaming and shouting with the rest, a few strange and wild-eyed whites carrying COMFORT banners, a few unwashed unfortunates up from the Village, and even a few of the more far-out and fantastic denizens of the literary, theatrical, academic, and journalistic worlds. All in all, Hal Fry thought with a tired disbelief when the shouting finally died and the mob was cleared out, it was one of the most conglomerate collections of human trash ever assembled in one place for one purpose. And the purpose, obviously, had been fully achieved.

"Mr. Chairman," he said, when the delegate of Mali had secured order at last and the other delegates were once more waiting attentively, many with little ironic smiles and knowing looks at one another, "I think the United States has nothing more to say on this matter at this time. You have seen the nature of the opposition. We would prefer to think it does not represent the spirit and judgment of your distinguished conference."

And feeling dizzy and weak, his condition certainly not improved by the tensions of the scene, he sat down.

"The distinguished delegate of the Soviet Union," the chairman said calmly.

"Mr. Chairman," Vasily Tashikov said smoothly, "the distinguished delegate of the United States said you have seen the nature of the opposition. I say you have seen the nature of the emotions aroused by the inexcusable racial policies of his government. Nothing I could add would make the point any stronger, gentlemen. The amendment of the distinguished Ambassador of Panama never seemed more worthy than it does at this moment after this brave, noble protest by freedom-loving elements in the United States, provoked by the racial policies of their own government. Mr. Chairman, I shall save further comments for the debate that resumes in the General Assembly on Thursday."

"Is there further discussion?" the chairman asked politely, and Hal Fry in his mind said savagely, of course not, you've all of you achieved what you came here today to achieve. "Then," said the chairman blandly, "this conference is adjourned subject to call of the Chair."

Around the world there sped the word of a new United States humiliation, and on radio and television and in the newspapers the sensation was great and the commentaries profound. Men of goodwill were sickened and disheartened; men of ill will gloated and told one another happily that their cause had been advanced. The dilemma of the beleaguered Republic was flung once again in the world's face, tossed in it, pushed in it, rubbed in it, so that by nightfall the psychological climate in which America must perforce operate in meeting the challenge of the Labaiya amendment had deteriorated to a new low.

Only one decisive act emerged from it all out of Washington as the night came on: a statement from the White House press office.

"The President," it said, "is pleased to announce the appointment of the Honorable Cullee Hamilton, Congressman from California, to the seat on the United States delegation held until 4 P.M. today by Mr. LeGage Shelby.

"Mr. Shelby's resignation from the delegation was requested, and received, by the President."

4

And now LeGage was off on collision course, and so was his own wife, and it was a cold day for a wounded heart as the Congressman from California dressed slowly in his empty bedroom and prepared to depart for the Hill and the first day of action on his resolution of apology and recompense to Terrible Terry and his own people in the United States. Understandably, he had slept very little, watching with a sad fascination until late into the night the televised recapitulations of the riot at the UN, the supplemental riots in twenty obedient capitals around the world, the interviews with Sue-Dan and the chairman of DEFY as they were encouraged to denounce their countrymen and mouth a sullen insolence toward their government. Both spoke with a self-conscious, exaggeratedly hostile air, as though they were afraid some one might talk them out of it if they stopped to listen, and he got the curious impression from both that they were really talking to him and to no one else.

Well: if so, they could talk a long day in hell, he thought bitterly as he descended the stairs to greet Maudie and eat his lonely breakfast. And so could all the other black bigots in the world, including the one who had called him shortly after midnight and breathed heavily into his ear for several moments before saying in a stagily ominous voice, "The Prophet is watching you." He had told the voice immediately and with great explicitness what it could do to the Prophet; it had appeared taken aback by the harsh anger of his tone, and hung up. But he expected there would be more of the same, both anonymous and in the open, and he told himself grimly that he was prepared for it. He was sick and saddened by what might well prove to be the permanent loss of his wife and his friend, but he wasn't so sick and saddened that he couldn't fight back. It hadn't really hit him quite as hard, in fact, as he had thought it might in his advance imaginings.

You picked the wrong man if you think you can scare Cullee, he told whoever-he-might-be with a silent wrath. Old Cullee doesn't scare.

Nor, he thought with an equal grimness, does old Cullee fall for all these oily questions from the press in the middle of the night, either. They had all called him, AP, UPI, the Washington *Post*, the New York *Post*, the New York *Times*, the New York *Herald Tribune*, the Chicago *Tribune*, *Ebony*, *Jet*, the *Afro-American*, the Pittsburgh *Courier*, the *Defender*, the Atlanta *Daily World*, and the rest. Had he known Sue-Dan was planning to do what she did? No comment. Oh, then he didn't know, was that it? No comment. Oh, then he did know? Well, if he didn't know, did he approve? No comment. Oh, then he didn't approve? Was he going to see her when he was in New York? What about his resolution now? What did he think of LeGage's actions? Hadn't he been under pressure to participate himself? Why hadn't he participated himself? Oh, no comment?

That, they implied, sounded damned fishy to them, and, they indicated strongly, they were going to use his silence as the basis for all kinds of speculation, since he was going to be so damned stubborn about it. One or two from his own race even told him what they thought of him, before they hung up. He was, he gathered, an Uncle Tom, a white man's nigger, a stooge, a patsy, a traitor to his people. It was a pleasant burden to carry with him into a bed whose emptiness complicated his unhappiness further by arousing a fiercely anguished desire that no one was there to satisfy.

But it would take more than that to break old Cullee, he repeated to himself as he entered the dining room. By God, it would.

"My sakes," Maudie said tartly, "here come Storm Cloud No. 1. Stop fighting the whole world and sit down and eat your breakfast. Won't do you any good to hate on thin air. Need something more than that to back it up."

"I don't hate anybody, Maudie," he said, observing the banner headlines in the Washington *Post*, the glaring front-page picture of Sue-Dan and LeGage struggling with a couple of UN guards, the terse little box insert informing the capital that "Rep. Cullee Hamilton, the man who wasn't there at yesterday's UN riot, refused comment at his Washington home tonight on developments involving his wife, Sue-Dan, and LeGage Shelby, the man he has succeeded on the United States UN delegation." The day's editorial cartoon showed a gallant group of giant glamorized blacks, stately, statuesque, overwhelmingly noble and righteous, rising accusingly out of an enormous gallery to look down upon a tiny Uncle Sam staring up in startled disarray.

"Nobody here but us Americans," the caption said.

"You know, Maudie," he said as he bit into his toast with a savage emphasis, "white folks baffle me sometimes."

"Baffle me, too, but I stopped trying to guess 'em fifty years ago. Won't do you no good, believe me. Don't think they know what they doin' themselves, half the time. Best not to trust 'em, either, you got any such ideas."

"What ideas?"

"You and that Orrin Knox and the President. I heard about it."

"Maudie," he said mockingly, "you've been peeking. Wasn't anybody supposed to know about that."

"Whole wide world knows. They say you stoogin' for Orrin Knox."

"So they say," he agreed with an airiness he did not entirely feel. She sniffed.

"Needn't get smart about it. Gettin' smart cost you a wife. Not that she's worth keepin', seems to me."

"I don't care what it seems to you," he said sharply. "You keep your opinions of my wife to yourself, hear? Also your opinions about my being smart. I'm not being smart. I'm doing what I think I have to do for the United States of America, that's all."

"What the United States of America do for you?" she demanded. He snorted.

"Got me in Congress making enough money to support one loudmouthed old woman who isn't worth what I pay her. That's what."

"Humph," she said, trying to sound angry but ending up in spite of herself in a chuckle that gurgled into a laugh. "Guess that ain't much. Bet my grandpappy do better than that as a slave."

"O.K.," he said, for the first time since yesterday afternoon feeling amused and a little relaxed, "you just think about this as Cullee's Castle, fine old plantation down in Georgia, and see how you make out. Don't bother me about food money, that's all. Just raise your own 'taters and corn down there in the pasture and don't bother me, that's all I ask of you, Maudie."

"Feed you on fatback and hominy," she said. "Be lucky you get that. What you going to do now about all this?"

"All what?"

"Her and him. Orrin Knox and them. All this stuff you tearing yourself to pieces about. All this mess you mixed up in."

"Why, I don't know," he said, finishing his coffee and getting ready to depart. "I expect I'll just play it by ear and see how it goes, Maudie. I've got me a resolution that's going to take some doing to get through the Congress. I expect that'll keep me busy for a day or two, wouldn't you say?"

"Going up to New York with all them high-flyin' Africans too? Understand you're a mighty important man now, up there at the UN, well as here in Congress. How you going to ride all your horses at once, you ever think of that?"

"I've thought of it. I'll tell you in a couple of weeks."

"Be down in the pasture with my corn and 'taters when you want me. Also be here when you come home. That's important too, I think, have somebody here when you come home."

"It is," he said gratefully. "Guess I won't sell old Maudie, after all. She's too good a slave to sell."

"Get on, now," she said, shooing him out the door. "You goin' smilin'; now you come back smilin', you hear?"

"Yes, ma'am," he said. "I'll try."

But he was not at all sure that he could; nor did he anticipate that the day's events would put him in a much better mood, even though he knew that much of a decisive nature would probably occur on his resolution before he again parked his car at the house off Sixteenth Street.

"But, my dear boy," the querulous, familiar old voice said swiftly over the telephone, "I don't really think we can afford to go along with this pretense by Orrin that he doesn't have a political interest in this. It's so blatant, my dear boy. So fearfully blatant. I think no true liberal can afford to ignore his obvious motivation, even if it is tending toward a constructive result."

The executive director of the Washington *Post* sighed a heavy sigh that was promptly taken up at the other end of the line.

"Now what's the matter?" Justice Davis asked sharply. "Have I offended you in some way? You must tell me if I have. I'm only trying to be helpful, you know. I'm only trying to assist the liberal cause."

"Yes, Mr. Justice," the executive director of the *Post* said patiently. "I'm sure we all appreciate your efforts and welcome your support."

"Well, then," Tommy Davis said triumphantly, "don't sigh at me when I'm being helpful. It makes me feel unwelcome. I don't like it."

"I'm sorry. What do you want us to do about Orrin?"

"What were you planning to do?" Mr. Justice Davis shot back promptly. The executive director of the *Post* shook his head in a puzzled fashion that he was glad the Justice could not see. The Justice, for all that he had gone into a spell of deep depression following the tragic outcome of his involvement in the attempt to bring Brigham Anderson into line on the Leffingwell nomination six months ago, had snapped back with remarkable vigor in the past few weeks. Now he was his old self again, lecturing his colleagues on the Supreme Court, fighting publicly with the Chief Justice, advising the *Post* and anyone else who would listen on how to conduct the affairs of the world. He was one of the few major participants in the crucible of the Leffingwell business who seemed to have come through it with an unshaken certainty in his own righteousness. The executive director of the *Post* suspected that a good deal of this was on the surface and that underneath the busy little Justice still felt moments of horrified doubt and unhappiness about Senator Anderson's suicide; but for the practical purposes of the working day, he seemed to be quite himself again. The executive director of the *Post* wished the same could be said for everyone who had been involved. Certainly *he* had been badly shaken by the experience, and he still was.

"My dear boy," Tommy Davis chided from the other end of the line, "stop brooding and answer my question. What are you planning to do about Orrin?"

"Probably the same thing you would do in the same position. Let him have it."

"Right between the eyes, I hope," Justice Davis said with some spite. "The utter gall of attempting to appropriate the liberal position on the racial issue! How dare he, my dear boy; really, how dare he?"

"He didn't get where he is by reticence."

"Who does he think he's fooling?"

"No one, when we get through with him, I trust."

The Justice made a pleased little encouraging sound.

"Good! I am so glad to hear you say that, my dear boy. Frankly, I was beginning to wonder about you lately."

"Oh? How's that?"

"It has seemed to me that your devotion to the liberal position has been somewhat—tentative—in the last six months. I don't think the paper has been swinging as hard as it should on some of these clear-cut issues."

"Since when has there been a clear-cut issue?" the executive director of the Post inquired. "I don't recall one, of late."

"Never admit it, my dear boy!" Justice Davis ordered. "No true believer can afford to admit that there might be two sides to a question. That destroys our whole position. It lets Them get the advantage. Surely I don't have to tell the Post that, with all your fine record along those lines!"

"We appreciate your compliments, Tommy," the executive director said dryly. "But right now there is a rather delicate problem involved. How do we handle Cullee Hamilton, for instance? What do we do about LeGage Shelby? Is Orrin really involved the way we think, or isn't he? After all, we only have Seab Cooley's word to go on. I never thought we'd rely on Seab to justify our position on anything."

"Never hesitate!" the Justice said sternly. "Never doubt! And why worry whether it's Seab or someone else? It suits the purpose, doesn't it? Anyway, we both know it's true, whoever says it. Orrin Knox has only one motivation in this, only one. He wants the Presidency, he'll do anything to get it, this is only one more phase of it, and he's got to be stopped, my dear boy. He's simply got to be stopped!"

"I agree with you there. But it seems to me we have to proceed with some care, considering our traditional position on racial matters and the fact that Cullee is so directly involved."

"If there's anything I despise," the Justice said sharply, "it's these Negroes who play the white man's game. Really!"

"You seem to approve of some of them," the executive director said mildly.

"Why wasn't he down there in Charleston doing the only proper thing any self-respecting Negro could do after I handed down my injunction? The law of it was on my side; not even Charleston's attorneys challenge that. He should have leaped at the chance to follow through. Instead he left it to a foreigner! Prince Terry had to do it for him. I should think he'd be ashamed!"

"Maybe he is. Maybe that's why he's decided to take this action in the Congress now."

"Only because Orrin put him up to it," the Justice said triumphantly. "So there we are again, back to Orrin."

"Yes. Back to Orrin."

"Do let him have it," Tommy Davis urged. "Write the editorial yourself, and let him have it. Anything that can stop him from becoming President is all to the good, my dear boy, you know that. In the face of stopping Orrin, all else pales. It really does, my dear boy. Furthermore, most of the press seems to think so, too. I hear there have been several editorials already pointing out the truth about this."

"You get around, don't you?"

"I have my spies," the Justice said with satisfaction. "What's next in Charleston, by the way?"

"They're coming back with another appeal tomorrow, but I won't entertain it. The injunction stands until the whole thing comes up to us from below through the regular court channels again. It will take some time."

"Well," the executive director said, "I'll see what can be done about Orrin from here."

"I know you'll think of a way to separate him from Cullee."

"Even though we agree entirely with what he and Cullee are trying to do?"

"You can do it, my boy!" Tommy Davis said with great confidence. "The *Post* knows how!"

But the world this morning, the executive director thought with a sigh as the bustling little voice went off the wire, was not so simple a proposition as that. Indeed, it was becoming less and less simple as time went by. Old certainties were being shaken, the old righteous—and self-righteous—positions were being challenged by the rush of events. The world was no longer the happy, open-and-shut proposition it used to appear to be when viewed through a certain highly-publicized angle of the ideological eyeglass; the comfortable assumptions that had once been accepted without question, the pleasantly rigid certainties that formed so comforting a foundation for a shaky universe were no longer so valid. The smugly arrogant denials of intelligence and honor to one's opponents, which had for so long characterized certain notable companions in the cause, were shattered now a dozen times a day upon the hard rocks of a world in disarray.

Now it was no longer enough to cry with a high, ringing certainty, "This is their position, down with it! This is our position, up with it!" There was too much inter-blending, too much commingling, too much of the one in the other. Now the United States had been brought to a position of peril all around the globe, and on both sides, he knew with an unhappy inner honesty, men must share equal blame for it.

But of course it would never do to admit it. On that point the Justice was always and eternally right. The slightest concession to fairness and They, as Tommy called them, would indeed swarm over you. The comfortable slogans, the automatic thinking, the shielding, protective certainties that did away with the necessity for unsettling objectivity and did so much to make the world seem secure—they might be withering away in your mind and heart, you might even be subject to a certain genuine terror now as you realized how much you might have shared, however idealistically, in bringing your country to her present desperate position—but it would never do to admit it in public. That would indeed be abandoning the life-line; that would indeed be throwing away the anchor. That would demand a courage and a character that were really too much to ask in times like these.

He pulled his typewriter toward him with an impatient yank and felt the gradual, warming surcease of doubt, the reassuring, womb-like return of certainty, as his practiced fingers began to fly over the keys:

"Despite our solid endorsement and support of the purposes of the resolution offered by Rep. Cullee Hamilton in the House yesterday, we cannot overlook the strong suspicion that it may, in essence, be nothing more than a stalking-horse for Secretary of State Orrin Knox in his incessant—and interminable—campaign to win the Presidency.

"We do not blame Rep. Hamilton for being taken in by the shrewd ambitions of a practiced politician. Inexperience is no man's fault, and we wish his resolution well.

"Even so, we cannot escape the conclusion that . . ."

And so, the President thought as he walked slowly along the arcade beside the Rose Garden toward his office in the gentle air, one faced decisions and one made them, sometimes wisely, sometimes well, more often, perhaps, with uncertainty and doubt and a prayer that subsequent events might prove them to be right. He had wanted LeGage off the delegation and Cullee on, he had given LeGage enough rope, and it had come about as he had planned. Now it remained to be seen whether this was the right course, when all was said and done.

Apparently, thanks to Orrin and his missionary work with the Congressman from California, it was. The resolution had gone into the House hopper as planned, the change in the delegation had caught the critics between wind and water—for, of course, it was difficult for them, even though supporting the chairman of DEFY, to condemn his replacement with another Negro of Cullee's stature. There was a subtlety of distinction between the two men too great to explain to the public, so the critics must perforce go along with it. The new line, of course, would be an attack upon Orrin while attempting to salvage what Cullee had done. He had heard it already on the morning news roundups, not too blatant, not too harsh, just a casual turn of phrase, a bland implication that planted the seed of suspicion in the public mind about the Secretary's motives and Cullee's co-operation with them. By nightfall the weed would be flourishing, and at 11 P.M. when the final big television newscasts were delivered to the country, the whole thing would be solidly rooted in the form it would have forever after in all the media of communication—as the crafty plan of a shrewd politician using the legitimate aspirations of the Negro race and the international needs of the United States to advance his own ambitions.

Well: certainly he would not deny that Orrin was a politician, or that he wanted to be President. By the same token, he was aware and had always been of a deeper motivation, a fiercer and more genuine dedication. It had not been so easy for the Senator from Illinois to leave the forum of his power and move downtown to the State Department in the wake of the defeat of Robert A. Leffingwell. He had done it, basically, for just one reason: because he, the President, had asked him to. It had been for the President the quickest and most efficient way out of the immediate political dilemma, and it had also been the chance to bring into his Administration in its principal office a man whose character, loyalty, and devotion he had seen tested on many occasions. He had never regretted that decision—he did not know, truthfully, what he would do without Orrin's counsel in the many moments of terrible challenge that he had to face in this era when no man knew with certainty whether the free world would go under, or survive.

For Orrin himself, it had been a period of testing and change, a time of reassessment and reappraisal of many policies most vigorously defended and many beliefs most vigorously held.

Six months ago in the Senate, for instance, the President could not conceive of Orrin Knox being a party to what was, in effect, a major apology by the United States to a minor African dignitary—even though that apology was also a greater apology, of much deeper and more serious import, to its own Negro citizens. Even knowing these implications, he doubted that Orrin would have supported it; or at least, he would not have supported it at first, but would, in his characteristic fashion, have proposed many qualifications and provisos before it was modified enough to suit him. Now Orrin as Secretary of State had initiated a clear-cut proposal that the United States say to the whole world, "We were wrong," and extend the admission even further, to its own citizens of the colored race.

He himself had regarded this project with some misgivings, particularly the language offering further apologies to the M'Bulu and the offer of $10,000,-000 to help Gorotoland. He did not like the idea of further apologies to Africa's irresponsible glamor boy; nor did he think it entirely wise to offer aid to an area which was, after all, still under the British Crown. There had been no official reaction as yet from London, but he could imagine that this was only a temporary hesitation as to the best means of expressing displeasure. It was, in fact, quite irregular—assuming this was an age in which regularity of procedure meant anything any more, which it was not—and perhaps if Orrin had consulted with him more fully before working out the resolution with Cullee, he might have suggested some more diplomatic way to go about it.

But he had, in this instance, made the initial decision to back Orrin's judgment. Therefore, he was prepared to go along with the result. Orrin was in charge of this, and he would support him to the hilt.

So much for that, he told himself as he paused for a moment at the side door to his office and looked across the immaculate lawn and stately trees to the line of tourists beyond the distant iron fence, waiting to tour the public rooms of the White House. When would the weather turn? he wondered suddenly. The long warm autumns of Washington sometimes changed in an hour, driven away by the scudding winds and heavy-laden clouds that blew in from the Middle West across the Shenandoah and the Blue Ridge, or pushed down over New York and New England from Canada. He shivered in anticipation, though the prospect before him still was warm and lovely.

Winter was coming—perhaps the winter of the world was coming. Who could tell?

He turned and went in to face his secretary's waiting face and lifted pencil, the calls to be made and received, the decisions to be studied and rendered, the endless round of problems, the unceasing challenge of the days.

High on the beautiful terrace of the State Department Annex overlooking Washington, the Secretary was entertaining many of the same thoughts as he walked slowly up and down, all alone, in the thinning autumn sun. He had not even bothered to stop in his office but had come directly up in his private elevator to the eighth floor, gone through the enormous empty state dining room, drab and dejected as all dining rooms are in the cold light of morning, and out onto the tiled esplanade with its gorgeous view over the Potomac, Virginia, and the pleasant reaches of the city stretching to the Capitol on his left. Toward this last he turned now, walking as far as he could, to the Twenty-first Street end of the terrace, until he faced full-on the distant building, dominant and gleaming on the Hill.

Below him in all the conglomeration of concrete-and-glass caverns known as State and New State, the life of his department moved along on its appointed rounds, some of its work a genuine contribution to the betterment of the world, some a precise and precious exercise in dead-endism that furnished jobs and position to people who would be lost with real responsibilities and so clung with a frantic tenacity to what they had.

At least 50 per cent of the department's laborings, he told himself with a melancholy irony, was devoted to the science of how to make mountains out of molehills that didn't matter, and molehills out of mountains that did. Bright young men, growing somewhat gray and elderly now, educated in the years after the Second World War to accept the idea of their country as not-quite-best, labored with a suave and practiced skill to gloss over the anguish of unnecessary decline. Experienced in the glib rationalization of failure, the smooth acceptance of defeat, they found cogent arguments and reasonable explanations for each new default of will on the part of their government and could always be found hovering at the elbows of those officials, like himself, who still held firm to some vision of America more fitting and more worthy than that. There they smoothly offered their on-the-other-hands and their let's-look-at-it-from-their-point-of-views and their but-of-course-you-must-realize-the-people-won't-support-its. Meanwhile the Communist tide rolled on, explained and rationalized, possibly, but not stopped.

Yet somehow there still emerged at times, through all the red tape and flagging determination and conflicting egos, some thread of reasonably consistent policy, sometimes forceful and effective, sometimes far out of contact with the harsh realities of the struggle for naked power going on in the world. Secretaries and Under Secretaries came and went, but as in the Pentagon, which he could see squat and powerful across the river, few ever exercised any real influence upon the day-to-day operations of their departments. There was a strength in institution far beyond the power of men to change, however determined and forceful they might be. He or the President could determine upon a policy, but somewhere along the channels of fiercely jealous authority beneath his feet it would run aground, be snagged upon some incompetent clerk or devious official, be changed and modified and turned into something quite different by the time it reached the knowledge of the world. It was a wonder to him that foreign policy ever got made at all, so many were the administrative pitfalls that awaited it at every turn; and he sometimes did not find it surprising that the information on which high officials must of necessity base their decisions should come to them in a form dangerously inconsistent with the facts, and the nation's desperate needs in the light of those facts.

This he had come into office determined to correct, but he could not say that in six months' time he had been able to do much about it. He wondered if he would ever have that feeling of sure control here that he used to have in the distant Capitol now tantalizing him in the misty morning. Probably not: probably he too would sooner or later settle for what most Secretaries, of whatever department, sooner or later settled for. He too, in time, perhaps, would say the hell with it, forget about the administrative operations of the department where so many worthy hopes were smoothly talked away, and concentrate instead upon the trips, the speeches, the attempts to sway Congress, the big, dramatic gestures that might win men's minds and appeal to their beliefs in a threatened time. Perhaps he too would abandon the rest and live almost entirely in the hope and determination that eventually he in his turn might move to 1600 Pennsylvania and make his own attempt to change the terrifying pattern of drift and frustration.

Except that this, too, was in a sense self-defeating, for unless a man could be sure that his orders were being carried out, what in the long run could he be sure of? And in a Cabinet department of thirty-nine thousand employees, or an Executive Branch of three million, if it came to that, how could he possibly know what was being faithfully carried out, what was being lost in paper shuffling, and what was being deliberately thwarted by those who preferred the death of the mind to the disciplines of remaining free?

For the moment, he was relieved that the battle had moved back to the arena with which he was most familiar. It gleamed whitely before him, lately scrubbed and sand-blasted so that every pillar, arch, and window stood forth clear and sharp. There was his challenge and his problem at the moment, and he studied it with an appraising gaze and a million memories as he thought of the personalities and pressures revolving within.

The idea which he and Beth had arrived at almost simultaneously by different paths of reasoning was now before the Congress, thanks to the co-operation of Cullee Hamilton, with a sponsorship that made it much less vulnerable than it might have been as a frankly-sponsored Administration project or as something with the wild backing of Fred Van Ackerman. It was true that he had passed the idea along to Cullee during their talk here in the Department, but the Congressman had contributed his own definite ideas and some of the language. He had expressed great contempt for Terry, but the $10,000,000 grant to Gorotoland had been his idea, and so, of course, had been the pledge of increased speed in improving the conditions of his race within the United States.

Orrin had been wary of the tone of this final section of the resolution, but Cullee had said simply that anything less would satisfy neither world opinion nor American Negro opinion. In fact, he had said finally, he would not introduce the resolution at all unless that language were in.

The Secretary had been forced to yield, though he had deemed it his duty to explain to Cullee exactly the problems he was inviting for himself.

"Do you think Seab Cooley and the rest of them would like it any better if it was milder?" Cullee asked. "I don't. I think they'd be against it under any conditions. So we might as well make it honest and let them shout."

"They'll shout all right," Orrin had said. "They may kill it in the Senate, too, if they shout long enough."

"Let them, if they want to make the United States look even worse than it does already."

"We don't want that to happen."

"We don't," Cullee agreed. "Maybe they'd better think of how the United States looks to the world, for a change."

"Seab won't think you're such a fine young man, I'm afraid," the Secretary said with a touch of irony. The Congressman, whose air of self-possession and control had renewed itself steadily as they talked, had shot him a quizzical look.

"Comes a time when the old ways change. It's only a miracle he's lasted this long."

"Try not to hurt him too much," Orrin said, beginning the remark with a continuation of irony but surprised to find that he really meant it, and startled that he should actually be asking charity for Seab Cooley from anyone, let alone a Negro. Cullee apparently considered it equally fantastic, for he gave a skeptical laugh.

"Times change, but I don't think they've changed that much. I think you'd better ask him to go easy on me, not the other way around. I'll be lucky to get out with my scalp before he's through with me."

But he had insisted on this strong language in the resolution even so, and the result had been that it was fully as much his project as it was Orrin's. The Secretary, remembering the closed-off, stubborn look and the ultimatum he had received when Cullee thought he wasn't going to have his own way, was moved to smile as he thought of the broadcast implications that the Congressman was his stooge. He knew better than most that Cullee wasn't anybody's stooge. He only hoped that Cullee wouldn't let himself be shaken by assertions that he was, though of course certain professional guardians of the conscience of mankind would do their best to drive a wedge between himself and Cullee if they could.

Essentially, though, this was not his major worry as he stared across the lovely city at the great Capitol floating against the autumn sky upon its russet hill. For all that some strange little unexpected quirk of sentiment or foreboding enabled him to imagine Seab as weak, the man they had to beat was of course the senior Senator from South Carolina. The Secretary thought he could get the Speaker's support, he knew he had Bob Munson's, but Seab he would have to beat because there could be no compromise on this for Seab, for Cullee, or for him. Particularly since Seab had already thrown down the gauntlet in his attack upon Orrin in the Senate yesterday and in his remarks in his talk with Bob, which Bob, as instructed, had faithfully passed along.

He and Seab had come, perhaps finally, to a parting of the ways, and he realized it with a real regret, remembering the many legislative battles they had fought together, the many long years of their association and close friendship in the Senate, the way they had stood together only six months ago on the nomination of Bob Leffingwell.

But politics was politics, people were people, the needs of the country and the imperatives of the age wrought their own iron changes upon men. Yesterday's companion was today's opponent, and Seab would have to take a licking. There was simply no alternative now, though he would try to make it as painless as possible for the old man. Seab had done great things in his day, and in many ways had served his country well; he had the right to a graceful defeat, and, if Orrin could manage, he would have it.

Of all the people who might have been surprised and amused to learn of these wistful musings of the Secretary of State as he left the terrace and the lovely city and the Capitol upon its hill and went down to his office on the floor below, the one who would have been most amused was at that moment making his way slowly, with his trudging, sloping gait, along the corridors of the Old Senate Office Building on the way to his private hideaway in the Capitol to do some telephoning.

Angered he would have been, first, possibly, but then truly and honestly amused; for it would not have occurred to the senior Senator from South Carolina at this early stage of it that he had much to worry about in this nonsense being generated in the House by Cullee Hamilton. He had endured this kind of thing before, the little gnats had nibbled him, as he liked

to put it, but he had always overcome them. And, he was calmly certain
at this moment, he would overcome them now.

Not, of course, that it was going to be a breeze. He was too old and experienced a warrior to minimize either his opposition or the problem posed
by it. Just as he sensed the changes in his own state that threatened his
Senate seat after all these long and controversial decades, so he sensed the
changes in the world that would make of this a battle as fierce and unyielding as any his fierce and unyielding old heart had ever had to carry
him through. The bearing of the one upon the other was direct and inescapable: He could no more afford to have it said in South Carolina that he
had allowed Cullee's resolution to pass the Senate than he could accept in his
own mind a condition of affairs in which Cullee's resolution made either
sense or justice. He could not permit the one; he could not conceive of the
other. There was nothing for Seabright B. Cooley to do but go full steam
ahead, damn the torpedoes, and confound his enemies if he possibly could.

That this would automatically bring down upon his head all the outraged
condemnations of those who had, unsuccessfully, condemned him before, he
was fully aware. As a matter of fact, he told himself as he poked the elevator
button with a Senator's impatient three rings and the car obediently shot up
from the basement to get him and take him down to the subway cars, he
couldn't care less. He had taken the measure of that sleazy crowd time and
time again, and he was quite confident he could take it now, especially since
he had already thrown it a bone in his speech in the Senate yesterday.

Seab was rather proud of that speech as he thought back upon it, for it
had brought the issue foursquare before South Carolina, the Senate, and the
country even before it had really had time to get started in the House. And
it had served to give notice to the President, and to Orrin as well, that they
hadn't fooled him one little bit by getting a nice young darky to do their
work for them. He had made the situation clear to his own people and he
had also picked up an extra dividend from the liberal crowd by doing exactly
what they loved, which was to flush Orrin out in the open and pin his ears
back. If in the process he had virtually ignored the author of the resolution,
that was both political strategy and native instinct.

He was not about to admit that a colored man could have been clever
enough to think of anything like that, even an intelligent colored man like
young Cullee. He had meant it when he had asked Orrin to convey the word
that he wished the Congressman well; but there were limits to what he could
imagine as the intelligence behind Cullee's dignified and well-spoken exterior.

Thus the concentration on Orrin and the President, and the careful avoid-
ance of Cullee's name in his speech yesterday. And thus, too, the bitter
scorn Seab had poured upon the Administration for its apparent intention
to bow to the worldwide clamor of what he had chosen to delineate, in
another of the impromptu inspirations that often won him appreciative
laughter and sometimes won him votes, as "all the little tarbabies of this
world, Mr. President, all the little tarbabies of this world."

There was involved here what seemed to him, as he had said to Orrin on their ride back to the Sheraton-Park after he had dined at the Knoxes', a fundamental issue involving the stature and prestige of the United States. There was involved, further, a fundamental and most vital issue as to whether the world was to conduct itself with a reasonable orderliness or fly completely off axis, as it always seemed to be on the verge of doing in this hodgepodge, helter-skelter century. If every little black man who cared to raise a holler could grab the attention of the nations and make great states bow and scrape before them, where was it all to end? Certainly not in any conclusion that he as a white man, or even as a self-respecting citizen of what he liked to think was still a self-respecting nation, could contemplate with casual calm.

He had said something of this in the chamber yesterday. He intended to say much more before the debate was over. He was quite sure he would have powerful and active support. Despite Harley's dramatic doings at Geneva, with all their still-proliferating consequences, the general trend in the world, so far as the United States was concerned, was down. The country had never really stopped sliding since the end of the Second World War, in spite of an occasional dramatic event that seemed to be staying the tide, and not all the impulsive pyrotechnics of Truman, the placid drifting of Eisenhower, the sometimes erratic empirics of Kennedy and Harley's predecessor, or the stubborn courage of Harley himself, had seemed to reverse the trend. The country was approaching a time, Seab firmly believed, indeed had long been in it, when taking a stand was really becoming the most important thing in the world for America and her allies to do: a stand, no matter what, as long as it *was* a stand.

The senior Senator from South Carolina, who like the great majority of the earth's peoples sensed things almost more with his viscera than with his brains, was firmly of the opinion that what was giving the Communists the globe was not any such "historical imperative" as the Communists liked to prate about. What was giving them the globe was in major part a lack of guts on the part of the free world. The cowardice of the West was the Communists' secret weapon, not any fancy talk about history: such was the opinion of Senator Cooley and, he suspected, the opinion of all those silent millions around the world who understood, directly and simply and without endless agonized rationalization, that the race goes to the swift and the battle to the strong, that nothing succeeds like success, and that to the victors belong the spoils.

For him, conditioned as he was by his background and his upbringing, and aware as he was that the issue about to come before the Congress was involved basically with the issue of color, this was as good a place for the country to take a stand as any; and he was grimly prepared to do his best to persuade it to. He had told Bob yesterday that it was ridiculous to prolong the session of Congress over such a matter, but Bob repeated that he had promised Orrin and suspected the Speaker had too, and so they would have to see it through.

So be it, then; they would have to see it through. He, Seabright B. Cooley, would see it through. He walked scowling through the Senate Library on the gallery floor without a word to anyone, startling the clerks and page boys who watched him pass; made his way through the labyrinthine corridors and gangways behind the Library to his private office; and opened the door and went in, closing it securely behind him.

Then he dialed a number on the Capitol code and leaned back in his chair, staring far down the Mall to the Washington Monument and the Lincoln Memorial as he said with a drowsy amicability about as innocent as a rattlesnake on the coil, "Jawbone? Is that you, Jawbone? This is Seab, over here. How's things going with that nice colored boy's resolution?"

He could not, had he known it, have chosen a worse moment to call the chairman of the House Foreign Affairs Committee, for that nice colored boy was even now sitting across the desk from Representative J. B. ("Jawbone") Swarthman of South Carolina with an expression polite but firm on his face and along his jaw a line that indicated a mood averse to nonsense. J. B. Swarthman was not a man to be intimidated by niggers, as he had just told himself scarcely a minute ago, but he had always liked Cullee, he was indeed a nice colored boy, he was—well, to use the phrase certain white men used when they felt they had to excuse themselves for making exceptions, Cullee was different.

This did not make things easy for Jawbone as he lifted the receiver and heard the voice of his senior Senator, the man who had sponsored his career many years ago and to whom he owed most of his political preferment and advancement. It was with a nervousness that Seab could clearly sense that he cried out, "Hey, there, Senator, how you be over there?"

"I said how are you over there," Seab Cooley reminded him gently. "Leave me out of it for a minute, now. What's the matter, you not alone?"

"Why, sure, I'm alone, Senator," Jawbone lied magnificently, giving Cullee a broad wink and smile that produced from him a baffled expression. "What can I do for you, sir?"

"You sure you're alone, now, Jawbone," Senator Cooley said softly. "You sure, now."

"Why—why, sure thing, Senator!" the chairman of Foreign Affairs cried heartily. "You know I am, now!"

"I don't know any such of a thing," Seab Cooley said quickly. "In fact, I suspect he's sitting right there with you at this very minute. Is he now? Is he now, Jawbone? Tell me that, now!"

"Now, Senator," Representative Swarthman said, an injured tone coming into his voice, "you know I wouldn't lie to you! Now, I wouldn't lie to you, hear?"

"I'm sure of that," Senator Cooley said comfortably. "That's why you're going to tell me yes, he is there. Isn't that right, Jawbone?"

"Well," the chairman of Foreign Affairs said, crumpling suddenly but retaining his injured dignity, "maybe he is and maybe he isn't. Anyway, I'm not going to tell him what you say, am I?"

"I want you to," Senator Cooley said. "I want you to tell him I said you aren't going to pass that resolution through your committee. That's right, now, isn't it?"

"Senator," Representative Swarthman said in unhappy protest, aware that his colleague from California was stirring uneasily in his chair, "I can't tell him that, Senator. Not yet, anyway."

"It's true, isn't it?" Seab Cooley demanded sharply. "You not telling me it isn't true now, are you, Jawbone? The man who dandled you on his knee when you weren't any bigger than a tadpole? The man who helped you run for Congress 'way back there when you weren't more than a boy in knee breeches, hardly; the man who's helped you through thick and thin for forty years? Now, you're not telling Seab Cooley you're going to pass that resolution through your committee, are you? What are our folks in South Carolina going to say about that, Jawbone?" He paused and a thoughtful menace came clearly into his voice. "What am I going to say about that, when one who has been like a son to me turns upon his father?"

"Oh, now, Senator," Representative Swarthman said in anguish. "Now, Senator, you hadn't ought to talk to me like that, Senator. I'll do my best for you, you know that; I always do, don't I? Well, then!"

"If what he wants is for you to kill my resolution in committee," Cullee said suddenly from across the desk, "I don't think you can do it. I really don't think you can."

"No, now," Jawbone said hurriedly, "it isn't that at all, now."

"What did he say?" Senator Cooley demanded. "Is he putting up a fight, Jawbone? Tell him right out, now. Take your hand off that mouthpiece and tell him right out so I can hear. Do it, now!"

"Senator," Congressman Swarthman said, beginning to sweat profusely, "don't be hard on me, Senator. It isn't easy over here. I think we can work it out—"

"Not with my assistance," Congressman Hamilton said flatly. "Tell him he can't bluff you. Tell him you haven't got the votes. It's the truth, isn't it?"

"I don't know whether it is or not," Jawbone objected hastily. "I've got to check around—"

"He's telling you you don't have the votes, now, isn't he?" Seab Cooley demanded. "Don't you listen to him, Jawbone. Tell him right out that you aren't going to do it. You hear me? Tell him right out!"

"Senator," Representative Swarthman said lamely, "please let me work it out, Senator. It isn't so easy."

"You can't work it out," Cullee said coldly. "It's going through."

"You get rid of him," Senator Cooley directed, "and then you call me back when you can talk, Jawbone."

"Well—" the chairman of Foreign Affairs said doubtfully.

"I'm counting on you, Jawbone," Senator Cooley said ominously. "You know I'm counting on you, now. You understand that, don't you, Jawbone?"

"Yes, sir, I understand that," Representative Swarthman said limply.

"And you can work it out right for me?"

"Well, perhaps— I'll have to call you back, Senator."

"I'm counting on you, hear? I'd be most fearfully disappointed if I found I couldn't count on you, Jawbone."

"Yes, sir," Representative Swarthman said feebly, replacing the receiver as though it had bitten him, which in effect it had. "Yes, sir. Whew!" He pulled a wildly decorated bandanna handkerchief out of his pocket and wiped his forehead with it as he turned to Cullee with an attempt at a placating smile. "He's a great one to tell you what to do, is the old Senator."

"I think the committee should meet this afternoon and send the resolution to the floor so we can work on it tomorrow or Monday," Cullee Hamilton said. "The whole world's watching, and I think we ought to move fast."

"Well, now," Jawbone said with a nervous smile, "that would be moving *pretty* fast, wouldn't it? I mean, you understand basically I'm sympathetic— or anyway," he corrected himself hastily, "I see why you feel you have to do it, Cullee, but you know how things go around here. That would be setting some kind of speed record; you know that, don't you?"

"It's time the United States set a few speed records on this," Congressman Hamilton said bluntly. "Everybody else is."

"Well, I just don't know whether we can round up the committee for this afternoon. That's all."

"We can get a quorum if we try. I'll help the staff call the other members, if you like."

"Oh, no," Jawbone said hastily. "Oh, no, now. I'll have the girls do it. Don't you bother your head about it. I don't want you to do that."

"And we'll meet this afternoon, then. Two o'clock, would that be a good time?"

"I don't rightly know, now!" Jawbone protested. "Don't rush me, Cullee. I—why, I expect I'd have to see the Speaker before I could call a committee meeting that sudden."

"Good idea," Cullee said, getting up promptly. "I think I'll go see him myself."

"Oh, *no*, now," Representative Swarthman cried desperately. "Now, don't you go bothering the Speaker, there! We'll work it out, Cullee. We'll work it out, that's for sure!"

"I'm sure we will," Congressman Hamilton said politely, "but, just for the hell of it, I think I'll see him anyway."

Why was it, the chairman of Foreign Affairs Committee demanded of himself as the door closed firmly behind his visitor and his final protest died on his lips, that things like this always happened to him? Why was it that he always seemed to be getting himself caught in the middle between the strong personalities that dominated the Capitol? Now Seab was on the rampage, and Cullee was equally determined, and the Speaker would come into it, and pretty soon the reporters would get hold of it, and oh, *God*. He groaned aloud as he sat at his desk nervously picking his fingers and waiting for the next blow from an unfair fate.

It wasn't that he didn't do his best to be a good Congressman; he did take the Foreign Affairs chairmanship seriously and do his best even though he had originally wanted the Agriculture Committee chairmanship and it had only been political chance and seniority that had put him in charge of Foreign Affairs. Sometimes it baffled him completely, but he tried to do his best, even though he could never escape that silly nickname the press had conferred upon him long ago, for all that he had brazened it out by adopting it for his own and using it on all his literature and stationery. "Jawbone," indeed! What could anybody expect, with a silly fool tag like that? It was bound to affect a man forever, particularly here on the Hill where the derisive chuckle always lay just below the surface of the buddy-buddy laugh.

"Jawbone!" Well, he wasn't sorry he had made that speech criticizing Franklin Roosevelt back there in 1938, even if some wag in the Press Gallery had seen fit to remark that F.D.R., having been attacked with everything else, was now being belabored by the jawbone of an ass. The comment had spread like lightning through the Capitol—Seab had even called from the Senate side an hour later and joshed him about it—and by next day the wire-service reporters were beginning to refer to him in their dispatches as "Rep. J. B. ('Jawbone') Swarthman." The nickname at first had been deleted by their editors downtown, but after a week or so it was agreed by informal consensus that it should be left in, and before long he was "Jawbone" to everybody. Good old Jawbone, hearty and easygoing, who had jawboned his way into a seemingly endless series of re-elections to the House, aided every step of the way by the paternal interest of the senior Senator from South Carolina, who had always said he had one member of the state's House delegation that he could really depend upon. Not that Seab's support of Jawbone's re-election had been necessary at any time in the past decade, but the old man still thought it was. Seab still thought he could call up the chairman of Foreign Affairs—a position of some power and dignity, by God, after all—and talk to him as though he were still a fledgling Congressman hardly dry behind the ears. Well, he couldn't any more, Representative Swarthman told himself indignantly. Seab was slipping and he knew it, and now he was just casting about desperately for an issue and thought he could cash in all his I.O.U.'s at once to get Jawbone to help him out.

Jawbone wasn't so sure about that, though; he wasn't at all sure about it, this time. No more than Seab could he afford to be caught off base by his people on the racial question, but leastways he had a little flexibility to move around in. Like Seab, he had supported a lot of progressive and liberal things, T.V.A., R.E.A., the school lunch program, the foreign aid program, the aid-to-education program, and so on. He wasn't any stick-in-the-mud, and his people knew it and understood it and re-elected him for it, as long as he didn't get too cozy with the northerners on the matter of civil rights and mixing of the races. And he wasn't under any illusions about the way the issue affected the standing of the United States in the eyes of the world, either; he had been to too many international gatherings and talked to too many foreign diplomats during his time on the committee, and particularly during his chairmanship, to have any doubts about that. It was a hell of a problem for the country, and he as chairman of Foreign Affairs was right on the front line of it—caught in the middle again, he told himself with a sigh, between what he realized in his mind were the needs of his country and knew in his being were the instinctive and adamantine beliefs of his constituency.

So here was this resolution by Cullee Hamilton, with Seab taking out after it on the one hand and Cullee pressing hard on the other. He would have to vote against it, or maybe be out of the city on business, or something, but he didn't really see how he could avoid letting it come to a vote in committee, or how he could stop it if it did. Even if he wanted to, which he wasn't at all sure he did, there was the situation Cullee had accurately perceived: Jawbone very likely didn't have the votes.

But how was he to work his way out of the situation gracefully?

And would anybody give him time to do so?

Although he jumped as though shot when the jangle of the telephone abruptly broke in upon this uncomfortable reverie, he was not really surprised in the least that the answer to this last question should be No.

The Speaker had been having a little talk with young Cullee, the Speaker said, and before that a little talk with Orrin Knox; and he just thought mebbe Jawbone had better call his committee together this afternoon early and take a vote on that resolution. If he, Jawbone, wanted to vote against it, why, everybody could understand that, but as long as Cullee had the votes to bring it to the floor—the Speaker had already nailed that down for sure with a few phone calls to other members of the committee—why, better go ahead and get it over with. Especially since that would look good at the United Nations, which was the main reason for having a resolution, anyway.

At least, that was what the Speaker thought about it, and did he, Jawbone, agree?

Well, then, if he did, maybe they could meet at 2 P.M. and take care of it. All right?

"All right," Representative Swarthman said wanly, and the Speaker, who had not achieved his position of great power and influence in the Congress without knowing men and what troubled them, asked casually, "Would you like me to call Seab and explain it to him? I'd be glad to."

"I would," the chairman of Foreign Affairs said fervently. "Yes, sir, Bill, I *would*."

"Leave it to me," the Speaker said.

But apparently the Speaker's persuasions were no more effective than anyone else's, for no sooner had the House Foreign Affairs Committee decided, shortly before 3 P.M., to send the Hamilton Resolution to the floor with a favoring report, than the President Pro Tempore was on his feet in the

Senate denouncing the "inchy, squinchy, little bitty vote of 15–13" by which the House committee rendered its verdict.

The speech was one of Seab's most effective, filled with pyrotechnics and raising just those questions of national integrity and voluntary self-abasement that disturbed all who contemplated honestly the full implications of the issue. Much as they hated to give him the attention and the prominence, many influential voices in the communications world found themselves forced to do so on the evening news reports. Enough of his ideas on Orrin Knox agreed with theirs so that they could not have avoided comment upon his speech if they wished to give the country what they regarded as the proper impression; and this, of course, they did.

Thus as the nation had a pre-dinner drink and listened, certain ideas got another boost, just as the Senator from South Carolina had hoped they would: a question concerning the good faith of the Secretary of State; a vague feeling that the Speaker and the Majority Leader were helping him put something over; a certain skeptical, half-amused, half-pitying attitude toward the Congressman from California, encouraged in the Negro community by some of its most influential voices; a further mistrust of the Ambassador of Panama, already deep because of his amendment at the UN; the first beginnings of an uneasy wonderment about his brother-in-law, the Governor of California, singled out for special attack by Senator Cooley in his recapitulation of events in Charleston.

Away at his leisurely tree-shaded capital in the West, the Governor began to sense the national reaction to this somewhere around 10 P.M., Pacific Time, and very soon thereafter a conference call had been set up between Sacramento, Washington, and New York. It was 1 A.M. at the St. Regis, and in his carefully soundproofed, tightly-shuttered room (he was extraordinarily sensitive to light, and though he slept well in his native mountains he was often jarred awake by the most casual of nocturnal city sounds) the Ambassador of Panama came instantly alert from a fragile, uneasy sleep when the phone rang.

"Yes?" he said in some alarm, not knowing whether he was to be told of war, revolution in Panama that could mean either triumph or dismissal, or some other event suitable for disturbance in the late hours. When he heard his wife's voice he relaxed a little, though some sharpness remained in his tone as he asked, "What's the matter? Are you ill?"

"N–o," she said, which for some reason disturbed him even more.

"It's Ted, then. Is he all right?"

"I'm fine, thank you," his brother-in-law replied, and he came immediately to a tense attention, for this might well be the conversation he had expected for the past three days.

"That's good," he said carefully. "Are you in Washington?"

"No, Sacramento. This is a conference call. Pat's in Washington."

This diminutive of the diminutive for his sister's name was not often used by the Governor, and something about it gave Felix to understand that this indeed was a family matter of some importance.

"I see," he said slowly. "To what do I owe the honor at this ungodly hour?"

"Oh, a lot of things," Ted Jason said with an easy laugh. "Seab Cooley. Cullee Hamilton. Orrin Knox. A resolution in the House. An amendment at the UN—all sorts of things."

"I wanted to ask about that resolution in the House," Felix said quickly, deciding it might be best to go on the offensive. "Who do you suppose put him up to it, Patsy?"

"Well," she said, "I did. Or, anyway, I tried to. Apparently Orrin beat me to it."

"How did you do that?" he asked evenly, though his heart was beginning to beat furiously at this surprising news of what he could only regard as betrayal. "Better yet, *why* did you do it?"

"I thought perhaps—it would be best. I talked to Sue-Dan Hamilton about it, but apparently she and Cullee are at outs at the moment, so he must have listened to Orrin instead."

"But you knew what it might do to my amendment!" he said angrily. "You knew it would give them a chance to try to weasel out of it—"

"I believe she thought it might be well for us to have an out, Felix," his brother-in-law said smoothly. "For us Americans, you know, it's 'we' who want a chance to get out of it, not 'them.' *We're* 'us.'"

"I suppose it was your idea all along," Felix said bitterly.

"No, it wasn't, but I must say I agree with it. I feel perhaps you've gone a little far in this matter, Felix. I'm rather puzzled about it, so I thought I'd call and find out. I had no idea in Charleston that this was what you had in mind. Nor," he added in a tone that always separated the Jasons at moments of crisis from the rest of the world, "did my sister."

"It doesn't matter that I had no idea what *my wife* had in mind, I suppose," Felix Labaiya said in the same bitter tone.

"I can't see that it has any particular bearing," the Governor said pleasantly as the wire from Washington remained silent.

"Well—" Felix began, and then he too fell silent. An expensive moment passed without comment from anyone on either side of the continent.

"It was just that I felt that you might like an easy way out yourself, darling," Patsy said finally. "After all, you've made your point, I think. And it is beginning to embarrass Ted quite a bit, thanks to that old fool Seab Cooley and some other people, and—well, I just thought it would be best if we tidied everything up. Not that I thought ORRIN would be the one to beat me to it," she added with a little laugh that was so lighthearted and unconcerned that it infuriated her husband. "REALLY, that man!"

"Of course," Felix said, holding his temper with great difficulty and trying to sound equally unconcerned, "you realize that I am completely surprised to learn that Ted is embarrassed about anything in connection with this. I thought Ted was happy with the luncheon and with the way things were going. Certainly he never told me any differently."

"I'm telling you now," the Governor said, still pleasantly. "I do think you're out on a limb, Felix. It's one thing for us all to express indignation and criticism when something goes wrong in the racial area, and it's another to attempt an outright international humiliation of the United States of America. Obviously I can't afford to go along with that, even if I felt like it. Which," he added with some sarcasm, "contrary to what you sometimes hear about the Jasons, I do not."

"I regard my amendment as inevitable," the Ambassador of Panama said stubbornly. His wife made a startled, skeptical sound.

"Oh, now, darling. Surely it wasn't inevitable. It needn't have happened at all if you hadn't introduced it. Surely THAT'S obvious."

"Someone would have if I hadn't," Felix said, still stubbornly. His brother-in-law took him up on it at once.

"Why did you feel it had to be you? What made you feel you had to step into the middle of a situation highly difficult and embarrassing for the United States? Did someone ask you to?"

"No one asked me to," Felix said evenly, though at great cost. "You both seem to forget that I am the author of the resolution on Gorotoland—"

"That's a puzzle, too," Ted Jason said, "but no matter."

"—and obviously it was logical for me to be the one to add the amendment."

"Oh, the amendment was prepared by someone else and they just wanted the right man to introduce it?"

"The amendment was prepared by me," Felix Labaiya said sharply. "What are you accusing me of, Ted?"

"He isn't accusing you of anything, really," Patsy said. "We're just puzzled, that's all."

"I want him to tell me what he's accusing me of," Felix repeated angrily, his heart pounding with an agonizing rhythm.

"I'm not accusing you of anything," the Governor said calmly, "except what you accuse yourself of by all this defensiveness."

"Defensiveness, my God!" the Ambassador of Panama exclaimed. "When you both call up and jump all over me together? I am not supposed to be defensive? Maybe Jasons are that inhuman, but I am not!"

"Now, now!" Patsy said with a curious mixture of alarm and mockery. "Attacking the family is the cardinal sin, you know. EVERYTHING else, but don't attack the family!"

"That's right," her brother said, sounding not at all amused. "What's gotten into you lately, Felix? It seems to me you're moving into a very strange and equivocal area of late. Have the Russians promised you the Canal, maybe, or something like that?"

"The Russians," the Panamanian Ambassador said in a voice he made carefully level, "haven't promised me anything except support for my amendment. Which is more than the United States has done. I talked to Hal Fry and he wouldn't budge an inch. I told him it would look much better if the United States made an honest apology than if it tried to fight the inevitable tide of the times, which would mean taking a major defeat."

"When did you become devoted to the doctrine of inevitability?" Governor Jason inquired. "And basically, Felix," he went on in the blunt tone he adopted when he was getting down to cases, "since when did you take it upon yourself to lead the pack against the United States? We don't like that, I may say."

"Is this the national 'we' or the family 'we'?" Felix couldn't resist snapping, though he knew it would arouse the Governor. He didn't care, Ted was too insufferably smug and self-righteous about all this. "You do not seem to have any qualms about attacking your own government if you think it can win you a few extra votes with the blacks. You just look at it as I do," he suggested bitterly. "I want to impress the blacks too. That's the only thing that makes sense these days in the United Nations or the United States, as you apparently very well know. After all, you need Cullee in California, don't you? You need him in the entire country."

"If you think my motivations are as simple as that," Ted Jason said with an odd little laugh that indicated more loneliness than he perhaps knew, "then I think you know me as little as everyone else does." His sister made a little protesting sound but he ignored it. "Now, I'm not going to argue it with you further. Your position in this is highly embarrassing to me and my sister. A resolution has been introduced in the Congress, at whoever's instigation, and it provides an excellent solution for all of us. I think you would be wise to take advantage of it."

Felix snorted, for suddenly he felt that he had his fearsome brother-in-law on the run, that maybe he had the measure of this Yanqui as he had all the rest. A certain exhilarating excitement filled his heart, which was pumping hard now, not in contemplation of anything unpleasant, but rather in contemplation of his own indomitable invincibility.

"How could I take advantage of it?" he demanded. "The only way to do that would be to withdraw my amendment, and things have gone much too far here at the UN for me to do that. And even if I did, someone else would reintroduce it at once."

"Let someone else," Ted said coldly. "At least it would not be Patsy Jason's husband."

"Or Ted Jason's brother-in-law," Felix shot back. The Governor snorted in his turn.

"What do you gain by that? I'm not denying it to you. I repeat, though, you are childish if you think that is my only motivation." He asked a question so abruptly that it took Felix' breath away. "Do you love Panama, Felix?"

"I must assume that is a rational question," Felix said finally. "What do you think?"

"So do I love the United States," Governor Jason said. "There is some motivation here more worthy than how do we appeal to the blacks, you know . . ."

A little silence fell and into it Patsy finally spoke.

"I really think it would be best if you should withdraw your amendment, darling. You can say that since the United States seems to be moving toward a more reasonable position through Cullee's resolution, you don't feel it necessary to press the matter at the UN. Then we can all join in backing Cullee, without any side issues."

"You have it all thought out, don't you?" her husband asked. "What is Panama, what am I, 'side issues'? You have some loyalty to me, you know," he said, even though he knew that of course if she did it was far outdistanced by her loyalty to her brother and her own country. But she laughed in her exaggerated way.

"Of COURSE I do! That's why I don't want to see you going off by yourself down this—this strange road. It IS strange now, you must admit that!"

"Let me ask you, Ted," he said bluntly. "Do you think I'm a Communist?"

"That is an area where assumption is useless and appearance a lie," the Governor replied promptly. "I think you are being foolish. What the reason is, who knows? No one will ever hear me say you are."

"Of course not," Felix agreed. "No candidate for President could admit he had a brother-in-law who—"

"That is right," Ted said crisply. "If that is all you want to see involved here, and all you know of me, very well, we'll put it on that cheap basis. I can't afford to have you be a Communist or have you play the Communist game because it would hurt my chances. Reduce it to that level, if you want, and it is still valid. I don't like what you are trying to do to my country and I want you to stop. Is that clear enough for you?"

"We really do feel, darling—" Patsy began, but Felix interrupted her.

"What is the use of talking? The amendment is in. It remains in. If you want to criticize it, Ted, go ahead. But surely you can understand that when a man becomes committed to something, he cannot back down. Furthermore, I do not believe the United States is so perfect in all this. I do not believe her record on race is so beautiful that she deserves to escape scot-free with the world's blessing."

"No more do I," Ted Jason said, "but I believe she is trying, and I believe she is constantly improving. I believe in criticizing her on home ground, when she needs it. I don't believe in trying to make her an international scapegoat."

"There, I am afraid," Felix said coldly, "you will not find much agreement in the UN."

"Very well," Ted said, reverting to his earlier pleasant tone. "Patsy, I guess he's your problem. I've tried."

"Oh, dear," Patsy said. "I DO think you are making SUCH a mistake, Felix."

"I am sorry," he said firmly. "A man must do what he must."

"Yes," Ted agreed. "He must."

"Do take care of yourself, darling," Patsy said. "I worry about you so."

"I will," Felix said. "Come up to New York, if you like."

"Perhaps—next week," she said vaguely. "I want to see what happens on Cullee's resolution."

"It will be academic," Felix said. "My amendment will pass tomorrow. But don't come, if you don't feel you should be near me when it does."

"Oh," she said, still vaguely, "it isn't that."

"Of course it is," Ted Jason said pleasantly from California. "Good night, now, Felix. I think we understand each other, all around."

"I'm sorry," the Ambassador of Panama said, "but—"

"A man must do what he must," Ted said. "I know. Good night, Patsy."

"Good night," she said absently. "Good night to you too, darling. DO take care of yourself."

"Yes, yes," Felix said impatiently. "I said I will."

But as he put down the receiver, snapped off the light, and resumed the uneasy search for fugitive sleep, he did not feel a certainty as calm as he hoped he had displayed to his wife and her brother. He was taking a gamble that might or might not work out, placing everything on this throw of the dice, betting that he had enough votes in the General Assembly to put his amendment through tomorrow, betting that once it went through Ted might criticize it but the family would not risk a divorce or cast him off or give substance to any personal scandal while Ted was seeking the nomination. Therefore he must be very careful from now on. He must make his stated motivations clear for the record. He must follow in the concluding stages exactly the pattern he had followed up to now, expressing an attitude more regretful than condemnatory toward the United States, enunciating only a friend's wistful chiding to bring a recalcitrant associate back to the paths of virtue. None of his own personal emotions must show. "When Ted is President of the United States and you are President of Panama," Patsy had said lightly long ago, "we'll give you the Canal." Nothing else held him to the Jasons now, but that was a tie so strong that he could not afford to break it too soon. He would weaken the United States all he could here in the UN, but he was in no position yet to risk an open break.

He did not think he had in the conversation just concluded, even though each of them had grown short and hostile at times. The Jasons weren't free agents, either, when you looked at it realistically. Their tie was to the convention and nomination next year. Of course they wanted Cullee's resolution, what could fit in better with their plans? But his last thought as he finally sank into a restless dozing was that they also wanted to avoid a family scandal, they also wanted to profit, if they could, from the good opinion of the colored races everywhere, and so they would hesitate for a long time before bringing about any open break with the man who was moving so forcefully to secure that good opinion here. They would hesitate at least long enough for him to put through his amendment tomorrow in the General Assembly and then it would be so politically advantageous for them that they could not afford to pull away, he told himself as he, the grandson of Don Jorge, dropped finally to sleep.

A sleep denied, had he but known it, to the Congressman from California, who lay in his lonely bed in the house off Sixteenth Street and wondered over and over again whether he was not in reality being an utter fool, an idiot, a pawn of politics, the stooge and white man's nigger that loud voices in both races were so kindly telling him he was. The press had been after him for comment ever since Seab's speech, and some of them, dissatisfied with his stock answer—"I believe the vote in the House Foreign Affairs Committee speaks for itself. I wouldn't want to make any comment on any other aspect of the situation at this time"—had made it quite clear what they thought of him for introducing the resolution in the first place. He had remarked to Maudie at dinner, more puzzled, really, than angered, that "sometimes it seems as though nobody wants anything done in this country unless it can be done exactly their way. If you won't play with them, they won't give you any credit for anything."

It baffled, but it also hurt; and there came a time, after he had heard the skeptical sarcasm in enough reportorial voices and seen and heard enough television and radio commentaries assailing his good faith and denouncing his gullibility, when he had almost begun to believe it.

"They can ride you pretty hard," he had conceded glumly just before he went up to bed. "You can almost believe it, if you listen to them long enough."

Maudie had told him not to listen and not to worry, but even she seemed a little shaken by it all. Her own earlier skepticism about "Orrin Knox and them" had given way to a fierce loyalty in his support, but even so, he could see the speculation in her eyes in unguarded moments.

"Don't you desert me, Maudie," he had finally said with a rueful laugh. "Don't know as I could get along at all, if you left me."

"I won't leave you," she promised, "as long as you're doing right. As long as you're doing right, I won't leave you."

But it was clear enough that the qualification was very real in her mind, and that she would be the judge if she felt the time had ever come.

Now as he lay in his bed and thought of himself and his wife and his friend, of the M'Bulu and Felix and Orrin and the President and everyone else involved in the tragic issue of race in this, its latest twisted turning, he wondered if it would ever make sense and if they would ever come out right on the other side—not just the other side of this immediate tangle, but the other side of the whole business. This was only one little phase of it, one little facet, thrown up into the headlines, transformed into a world scandal by the plans and ambitions of many states and individuals. Yet it went on every minute of every day in a thousand and one variations, from nervous college kids sitting at drugstore lunch counters to scared little children and howling mobs at schools to the cruelest kind of intellectual snubbing at New York cocktail parties where members of his race were invited for the publicity value of their skins, only to be insufferably patronized as human beings once they got there. So many things, so many things, hurtful, unhappy, unjust, unbearable—the miseries of it all, as his mother used to say mournfully on the rare occasions when she let it get through her defenses, the miseries of it all!

And for him, at this moment, in this time, on this immediate problem, miseries even deeper and more profound. Miseries of an empty bed when you needed your wife and she wasn't there; miseries of a friend closer than a brother, gone and maybe not to come back; miseries of doing what you thought was right, but who knew, maybe for the wrong reasons, maybe just for ambition when all was said and done; miseries of stepping out front and trying to do a job and being made the target for every snide and sneering two-bit nothing in both races as a result; miseries of wondering whether you could trust a white man, any white man; miseries of wondering whether you had indeed been a sucker and a stooge for one particular white man; miseries of wondering whether he would stand by you or let you down; miseries of wondering whether you might really be selling him your birthright, as some said; miseries of wondering if you might not end up with the contempt of both races for trying to help them both—miseries of being black and in a position where you couldn't avoid your responsibilities. Miseries of being an American and trying somehow to see your way clear to helping the country you loved solve, with liberty and justice for all, her deepest unhappiness and most rending agony.

He gave his body a sudden, furious twist across the bed, buried his face in the pillows, smelled Sue-Dan; and of course that did nothing to help; it only made it worse. Where was she in New York, and what was she doing? Probably with her family; he could probably rest easy that she wasn't with someone else. Or could he? It wouldn't be LeGage; he trusted LeGage there implicitly, whatever else might go wrong between them; but it could always be the M'Bulu. Terrible Terry would be flying her around town with all his pretty robes flapping, giving her a big old time with all those fancy Africans at the UN, putting on a big show, being the great royal hero who had America on the run.

Yes, it could be Terry, she would probably like that, she was getting bored with *him*, he wasn't a sufficiently vigorous hater of the white man to suit her, maybe she was with Terry right this minute, reaching for him the way she did for—

"No!" he cried aloud in anguish, whipping upon his back so that he lay full asprawl. "No," he whimpered more quietly so as not to wake Maudie. "Oh, *no*."

For a long time he lay so, really thinking very little, images blurred and incoherent passing through his mind, jealous, sexual, fearfully painful, consciously masochistic as he removed himself from his memories and placed a triumphantly grinning Terry in them. The time came when this produced a physical reaction, agonizing, excruciating, rending, and easeful, all in one. He remained where he was, breathing heavily, as it passed and left his body limp; and little by little rational thought returned, and he began to think again about the road he had chosen and where it might lead him, and how he might best pass along it with credit to his country, his people, and himself.

There recurred to him presently his conversation with the Secretary of State, the tone of voice in which Orrin had called him from Spring Valley shortly after midnight and told him what he and the President had been discussing. At first the Secretary's approach had been cordial but cautious; it was obvious that he was worried that Seab's speech and all the other attacks upon them both might have shaken Cullee badly. Cullee's initial hesitation had shown him he was right to be worried. Characteristically Orrin had wasted no time in coming to grips with it.

"How about it? Are you really worried about what they say? Do you want to back out? You can, you know, if it really bothers you. That would bring criticism too, but we'd help you ride it out."

At first, a little overwhelmed by this direct and unadorned approach, he had hesitated.

"Go ahead and tell me," Orrin had said. "The only way we can get along together on this is to have all our cards on the table. If you really think you're being my stooge or I've conned you into something, say so. It won't be true, but if you think so, it might as well be. Do you?"

"N–o," he had said at last. "At least—I don't think so."

"I have ambitions too, you know," the Secretary of State had said bluntly. "Maybe I'm just using you for all you're worth. Maybe my only motive is to line up the colored vote to help win that nomination. You'd be a powerful asset if I had you on my side. Of course you know that. Better think about it carefully," he said with an irony entering his tone. "I may be a bad and evil white man, out to use you all I can."

The Congressman had gotten a glimmer at that point of why it was that Orrin Knox had gone so far in the public life of the country, for this direct-ness and candor gave him a major psychological advantage even as it placed others at a disadvantage. Cullee couldn't really say, "Yes, I distrust you," even if he did, for Orrin had set the question in a psychological framework that would have permitted him to dismiss such an answer with a sardonic comment that would have left him with the advantage still.

If one were in any doubt of him at all, one was naturally disposed by this candor to be less doubtful of him, to trust him more and come further toward his position. So Cullee had responded with something of a matching irony.

"Maybe I'm out to use *you*. Maybe I could use your support in my race for Senator just as much as you could use mine for President."

"Oh, you *are* going to run, then," Orrin said. He added, "I'm very pleased for you," and sounded it.

"I'm not sure yet," Cullee said, already regretting the impulse.

"Nor am I," the Secretary responded promptly. "Let's let the good word stop right here, in both cases. But about this other, now—are you all right? I want you to feel completely satisfied in your own mind. That's the only way it can possibly work."

Cullee hesitated again, so long that he thought Orrin would break in; but for once the Secretary exercised great restraint and said nothing. Finally the Congressman spoke slowly.

"I—think so. That's all I can say right now; I—think so. You'll understand."

"Yes," Orrin Knox said, rather bleakly. "I guess I do. Well, then, assuming we can proceed on that basis, here's what the President and I think would be the best thing to do—"

Cullee had listened alertly to their plan of action, suggested a couple of minor modifications, and finally agreed to it.

"Promise me one thing," Orrin had said just before saying good night. "If you begin to doubt, later on—if you feel you can't trust me, or the pressure gets too great for you from your own people or mine—don't hesitate. I'd rather have you out of it altogether than dragging along reluctantly. Then I couldn't trust you, and right now I do implicitly."

And that, of course, was another effective facet of Orrin, the unqualified conferral of trust, once he had made up his mind about someone.

"You can trust me," Cullee had said. "If I decide to let you down, I'll let you know in plenty of time."

"I believe you," Orrin said. "Good night."

"Good night," he said, feeling absurdly warmed by this, which of course, he told himself dryly a little later, was exactly what Orrin intended him to be.

5

"It isn't as though this were some bloody picnic, after all," the London *Daily Express* said sharply. "Why isn't Knox here? Why does he leave it in the hands of a second-rater like Fry when his country is about to take a licking?"

"Maybe he doesn't want to sit here and face it," the Manchester *Guardian* suggested. "Too much for the Knox pride, possibly. How about that?" he demanded of the New York *Times* as they went down the private back press stairs and came out into the Chamber to see before them the garish blue-and-tan amphitheater of the Assembly Hall, its half-moons of shining wooden desks with their cold neon lights beginning to fill with delegates and staff as the hour neared eleven and the time approached to begin final debate on Felix Labaiya's amendment.

"I don't know," the *Times* said slowly. "Anyway, I'm not sure I agree with all your assumptions. Fry isn't a second-rater and Knox isn't afraid to take what he has to take. It could be, you know, that he isn't here because he doesn't think the United States is going to take a licking."

"Don't you?" the London *Evening Standard* demanded. The *Times* shrugged.

"Your count's as good as mine, pal. What have you found?"

"Not very bloody much," the *Daily Express* confessed. "But everything I have found looks bad for Uncle Sammy."

"There isn't much margin either way, I'd say," the Chicago *Tribune* said.

"I'd say the breaks are going to us. After all, he needs two-thirds, you know. At the moment, he just ain't got it."

"Hope goeth before a fall, old boy," the *Daily Express* remarked. "Look at Tashikov coming in, down there. Does he look like a man who's about to take a defeat?"

"Look at Hal Fry coming in down there," the Chicago *Tribune* said promptly. "Does he look like a man about to take a defeat?"

"Why bother to look at either one of them?" the *Evening Standard* inquired. "Go and search among our darker brethren, if ye would find the truth. I must say K.K. looks happy. Ghana looks happy. Guinea looks happy. All God's chillun look mighty, mighty happy. I'd say that's a better indication than the boys on the front line, wouldn't you?"

"How's the gallery today, by the way? Ready to riot?"

"Doesn't look it," the *Evening Standard* said slowly as they all turned around to stare up intently at the tourist groups with their guides, the housewives from Mamaroneck and Glens Falls, the businessmen from Milwaukee and Phoenix, the earnest dark faces that filled the greater part of the galleries.

"That raises an interesting point," the *Guardian* remarked. "How do you see a thundercloud at night? I mean, supposing they were there, among all those nice serious darkies from the ladies' sewing circles and the Men's Study and Poker Leagues? How would you know?"

"That's what the guards wonder, I'm sure," the *Express* said. "Did you see how carefully they've been checking them in? You'd think it was a garden party at the Palace."

"Here comes Felix," the *Standard* said as they all turned back and resumed their study of the floor. "I see he and Hal are going through the motions. We ought to be getting under way pretty soon."

Below them in the long left aisle running down to the distant green marble rostrum, the acting head of the American delegation and the Ambassador of Panama were indeed going through the motions, though it was, in Hal Fry's case, even more of a burden than it would have been otherwise. He had spent a troubled night, waking suddenly to heavy waves of dizziness and unexplained cramps through his stomach and back, his breath short and his heart palpitating painfully, drifting off again into a blurred, hazy world between sleep and waking that had given him very little rest. Orrin had called at eight with the plan for the day, and that had ruined the only period of really restful sleep he had been able to achieve. He had only picked at breakfast, feeling nauseated and weak, and it had been by another effort of sheer will—God, if the world only knew what a stout character I have! he had told himself wryly—that he had been able to get to U.S. delegation headquarters and go through the motions of getting ready for the debate.

Lafe had dropped in early, looking fresh as a rose, though the Lord knew where he had unfurled his petals the night before, and had immediately begun to question him on his health. That hadn't helped much, either.

"I hear you went back to the doctor," he said accusingly, and Senator Fry shook his head.

"I suppose she tells you everything I do," he said. Lafe smiled.

"Enough to keep me informed. I hear it's still nervous tension."

"That's the pet medical fad of the century, yes. There's a certain type of doctor that would be lost without it."

"How is it this morning?"

"I didn't have a very good night. Or eat a very good breakfast. But I'm feeling a little better now."

"Think you'll make it for the debate all right?"

"I've got to make it for the debate. Orrin isn't coming up, so—"

"How's that? I thought sure he'd be here, especially since you aren't feeling so well—"

"He doesn't know exactly how I'm feeling," Hal Fry said firmly. "And I don't want you to tell him, understand?"

"I'll see."

"Please now, Lafe. Please."

The junior Senator from Iowa stared at him thoughtfully.

"All right. Up to a point. But you can't go on very long like this, buddy."

"Do I look that bad?"

"You look pretty good, as a matter of fact. Except your eyes, which don't look good, to me, anyway. Others might not notice, but I know you so well I can tell."

"Lafe," he said suddenly. "There's one thing that troubles me"—he gave a wry half-laugh—"among many other things, but"—he sobered again instantly—"this one most of all."

"If I can help," Lafe said simply, "you know I will."

"You know about my son," Hal said. The Senator from Iowa nodded slowly.

"You've never told me, but Orrin did, once."

"If anything should happen to me," Senator Fry said with a sudden bleakness that wrung his colleague's heart, "what would happen to him? I've left him provided for, of course, but—he needs company."

"Does he?" Lafe asked quietly, with a compassion that robbed it of hurt. "Are you sure?"

"I've got to think so," Hal Fry whispered. "I've just got to think so. I have to have—some hope, Lafe, even when they tell me there isn't any."

"Well, in the first place, I don't believe for one minute that there is any reason at all for you to think you aren't going to snap out of this, whatever it is. But in the second place, assuming worst came to worst and everything bad happened, you can rest easy about your son. I promise you he'll have company. I'll go and see him myself, regularly, as long as I'm in Washington. And when they finally kick me out of the Senate"—he grinned a little—"I probably won't go home anyway, but if I do, I'll try to get him moved somewhere where I can see him regularly. How's that, good enough?"

I mustn't cry, Hal Fry told himself desperately, but in spite of himself his eyes filled with tears.

"You're—very kind," he said. Lafe gave a strange smile in which bitterness and irony and protest were mingled.

"Oh, I have one or two small virtues. Nobody thinks so, but I do."

"You—have a great many," Hal Fry said. He added quickly, for now the physical pain was beginning to return strongly again, complicating and multiplying the emotional, and he did not think he could continue much longer without breaking down altogether and making a real spectacle of himself, "His name's Jimmy."

"Jimmy," Lafe repeated gravely. "I'll remember."

"Thank you," Hal Fry said humbly. "Thank you."

"Yes," Lafe said. "Now," he went on with a sudden briskness that deliberately broke the mood, "if you're not feeling up to it, I want you to let me do the talking today, O.K.?"

"I'm all right," Senator Fry protested, but his colleague went on in the same no-nonsense tone.

"We'll go over and get started as usual, but the minute you don't feel up to it, you let me know and I'll take over. I want you to promise, now. It's great to be heroic, but there comes a time to be sensible."

"I have my duty to do," Hal Fry protested with as much vigor as he could muster. "I can't let the country down, just because I've got the screaming williwaws."

"It's my country too," Lafe said with a smile. "Now, no nonsense, buddy. I mean it. The minute you need help, you sing out. I'm going to be watching you, so don't try to pull any fast ones."

"Yes, Big Brother," he said through the reddish screen that was beginning to come between him and the world. Lafe grinned.

"Good. I'm going to go answer my Senate mail now. I'll see you over on the floor about ten to eleven."

And now here they were in the Assembly Hall, and Lafe was indeed watching him as he stood nearby exchanging suave insincerities with the smug young delegate of Kenya. He himself, feeling somewhat better now, though still with a strange clamping tightness in his chest and throat and still with the strange feeling that he might fall if he walked or moved or turned too fast, was doing the same thing with the Ambassador of Panama. Felix looked, he thought, rather the worse for wear himself, this morning.

"Got it all sewed up, I suppose," he suggested, and Felix smiled his small, tight smile.

"I have reason to feel confident."

"That's good. I wish we all had that privilege."

"You do not, then," the Ambassador said with a polite quickness. The Senator from West Virginia managed to smile through his physical difficulties with what appeared to be a comfortable humor.

"Oh, it isn't that I don't think we're in good shape. It's just that I learned in the Senate years ago that it doesn't do to be too sure of anything before a vote."

"I have received many pledges of support," Felix Labaiya said.

"I too. Some rather surprising ones, in fact."

"Oh?"

"Oh, yes."

"Well, you will excuse me. I have to talk to the Indian Ambassador."

"You may have the pleasure," Hal Fry said, seeing that worthy at the moment far across the chamber talking to two gorgeously robed Nigerians and a sheik from Mauritania. "Give him my love."

"He will be pleased," Felix said with a dry little smile.

"I'm sure," Senator Fry said with a reasonably cheerful grin. "Meanwhile," he added as he saw a figure equally colorful come down the aisle in stately progress, "I shall talk to Terry."

"Senator," the M'Bulu said, holding out an enormous hand and engulfing Hal's cordially within it. "How pleasant it is to see you this morning."

"And you. I've been hearing all sorts of interesting things about you. And reading about you. And seeing you on television. You've been a busy man recently, haven't you?"

Terrible Terry smiled, a complacent, self-satisfied expression, and looked about the hall, now abustle with arriving delegates. The roly-poly little President from the Netherlands had taken his seat at the dais beneath the map of the world, and the Secretary-General had just come in and assumed his place alongside. It would not be long now before the opening gavel would fall.

"Yes, I have been rather occupied, you know. Today—Tonight—Meet the Press—Face the Nation—White Paper—UN Report—Accent—Impact—Shock —Smash—Challenge—Answer—Question—NBC, ABC, CBS, Mutual—parties, rallies, Madison Square Garden—" He gave an elaborate sigh, and adjusted the drape over one arm. "You know the routine."

"It is boring, isn't it?" Senator Fry agreed in a tone that prompted a sudden sharp glance from his towering companion. But Terry had the grace to laugh, a lighthearted, happy sound that indicated complete confidence in the outcome.

"Oh, yes, but necessary if one is to mobilize American public opinion behind an anti-American cause. One needs to appear on all those programs if one wishes to win sufficient publicity in this country to really defeat your government's purposes. It is really, still, quite powerful, you know."

"Oh, is it?" Hal Fry inquired over the distractions of some little man who was kneading the small of his back with a pair of iron calipers. "I wasn't so sure."

The M'Bulu looked, for a second, quite thoughtful.

"I think we have you beaten," he said candidly, "but one is not always sure a battle is over until the last man is dead."

"That's been my experience too," Senator Fry said with as much show of cheerfulness as he could manage.

"Well," the M'Bulu said abruptly, but with a charming smile, "I must go and confer with some of my African colleagues concerning the debate." He held out his hand again with an elaborate ceremony that was not lost upon all the many delegates and members of the press who were watching. "May the best country win."

"I hope so. I have great faith in the innate good sense of mankind."

"Oh, I too," Terry said earnestly as he turned away and started toward waiting Ghana and Mali. "I too."

At the seats to his left where the British delegation sat, Hal Fry could see the Ambassador coming in, trailed by the pink-cheeked, scrubbed-faced female secretaries and the stringy, bland-eyed, hair-askew male members of his staff. Lord Maudulayne himself looked chipper and alert, and it was with a cordial smile that he worked his way behind the row of chairs and came along to a seat beside the Senator at the dividing point between the two delegations.

"Good morning, good morning," he said cheerfully. "You look ready for anything, old boy. I hope you're feeling well."

"Fine, thank you," Hal Fry said, though it was a lie. "And you?"

"I could be better if I thought a few more votes were solid," Claude confessed. "But, even so, I don't feel too badly."

"Have you decided what to do on the Labaiya amendment?"

The British Ambassador nodded.

"I think so."

"Don't move too fast. There may be late developments."

"Oh?" Claude said with real interest. "Will Orrin descend in his chariot on a beam of light to show us all the way? Or even Harley, perhaps? It will have to be something pretty good to turn this mob. Or, rather, I should hasten to add, this distinguished gathering of distinguished delegates at this distinguished world organization."

"It may be effective," Senator Fry said. "We can only hope. Anyway, I expect there will be quite a little debate. I don't believe the outcome is at all certain yet."

"Nor do I. I must say getting your Congressman Hamilton to introduce his resolution was a clever move. It's had quite a bit of impact here, though I doubt it's enough. Possibly if there were time for him to get it through Congress—except, to be honest, does anybody think he can? Nobody thinks so here."

"I don't know. It won't be easy. On the other hand, the stakes are high and, I would hope, as fully understood there as they are here. Of course you know we were about to adjourn for the year when all this blew up, and having to stay on won't improve tempers. But, we'll see."

"It would be a satisfactory solution for many of us, I think," Lord Maudulayne said. "There are a lot of people who don't really want a head-on collision with the United States but feel they have no choice on this issue."

"All we can do is try," Hal Fry said.

But as the President of the Assembly rapped his gavel and declared the plenary session opened, he knew it was an uphill battle at best that confronted his country. The normal tension of a major UN vote was increased today by an extra excitement, a certain vindictive assurance on the part of many delegates hostile to the United States that was palpable in the air. There was a certain look about many of the Africans that could not be mistaken—a smug certainty, a superior knowledge of what was going to happen. Hal told himself sternly that he must remember tolerance, difficult though it was in the face of intolerance.

"The first speaker on the agenda for today," the little Netherlander said, "is the distinguished delegate of Panama, author of the amendment which is now before the Assembly for action under terms of the agreement reached on Monday last. The distinguished Ambassador of Panama."

"Mr. President," Felix Labaiya said, "it is not my purpose to delay this august body in its desire to reach a speedy vote on this amendment. All delegations are familiar with the amendment. It has received the support of many powerful states and peoples. It is offered, Mr. President, not in hostile criticism but as a friendly encouragement to one of the leaders of our world to truly show us an example of democracy and justice in action. Not in anger, Mr. President, but in sorrow and pity, and also in hope, do we ask the United States to live up to her highest ideals. We hope this expression of world opinion may help her to do so."

"It's nice to have so kind and devoted a friend," Lafe whispered to Hal Fry as Felix turned, bowed low to the President, and walked, with a smooth sense of what was fitting and effective in present circumstances, back up the aisle to Panama's seat beside Pakistan, shaking eager dark hands held out to him as he went.

Hal Fry wanted to say something humorous in return, but a sudden onslaught of dizziness prevented it and he only said, "Yes," lamely. Lafe at once looked concerned.

"Are you all right?"

"O.K.," Hal managed to say, and turned back with a show of impatience toward the podium as the President announced, "The distinguished delegate of the Soviet Union," and Vasily Tashikov strode purposefully to the platform, his gray head bobbing as he walked along with his plowing, determined gait.

"You're sure?" Lafe demanded.

"I'm sure," he said angrily, though he felt as though some giant were twisting his insides about in capricious jocularity.

"All right," Lafe said doubtfully as they put on their earphones and turned the dials to the Russian channel. "But no games, now."

"Mr. President," the Soviet Ambassador said, "the Soviet Union does not desire to prolong this debate, either. The Soviet Union thinks the issue here is very clear. Freedom-loving peoples everywhere understand it. It was not enough to have Little Rock, Mr. President." (He said it with a heavy sarcasm faithfully parroted by the translator.) "It was not enough to have Birmingham and Montgomery, Alabama. It was not enough to deny to African diplomats the courtesies of their station in Washington and force them to live in pigpens and hovels, Mr. President." ("You ought to see some of those $100,000 pigpens," Lafe Smith whispered to Lord Maudulayne, who nodded.) "It was not enough to have all the shameful incidents which have demonstrated to the world for so long exactly what is this great American democracy we hear so much about all the time, Mr. President, from those who would rather talk than perform. Now we must have an attack upon a great leader of Africa, combined with a noble attempt to keep a little girl from going to school.

"Mr. President," he said, and his tone became even heavier with sarcasm, for on this issue the Communist states had found the lever to wipe out much of the psychological gains of the President's action in Geneva, "is this the nation that presumes to tell the world that it ought to lead us to salvation? Is this the great democracy that thinks it is so much better than everyone else? Can it be, Mr. President, that this country that believes so fervently in freedom and justice actually needs to be admonished by this great world body? Oh, Mr. President, what a spectacle! What a sad commentary, Mr. President!

"Can it be," he asked with a fleering slowness, "that this great country is not so perfect, after all? Can it be that its pretensions have finally been exposed for what they are? Can it be that the great United States of America stands condemned before all of humanity?

"It is so, Mr. President. And for the first time, thanks to the fine amendment of the distinguished Ambassador of Panama, the world can at last render judgment on these pretenders. The world now has the opportunity to condemn these murderers of freedom, these mockers of justice and decency, *these worthless people who hate you simply because you are black!*

"Do they deserve mercy, Mr. President? No, they do not. Do they deserve justice, Mr. President? Ah, yes, that they do deserve. That they cannot escape. They must not escape it, Mr. President. The world's freedom-loving peoples demand the punishment of these guilty ones, Mr. President. All whose skins are white and who love justice demand it, Mr. President. All whose skins are not white demand it. It is time to end this hypocrisy once and for all and say to the United States, You are guilty and you are condemned!"

There was a wild burst of applause from many delegations and from the public galleries as he concluded, bowed abruptly to the President, and walked quickly to his seat, ignoring the congratulatory hands held out to him along the aisle.

"The United States—" the President began. "Did the United States wish—?" he said uncertainly.

There was an immediate buzz of interest across the chamber as delegates and spectators craned to see the United States delegation. It could be seen that Senator Fry and Senator Smith seemed to be in an intent and serious discussion, concluded when Senator Fry was seen to nod, a momentary expression of what appeared to be sadness on his face—yet what could he be sad about? Senator Smith was seen to lean back in his chair with an air of satisfaction that seemed to say, "That's better!" as a crew-cut young State

Department aide to the delegation walked hurriedly down the aisle to the podium and whispered in the President's ear.

"The United States of America," the President said, "originally requested permission to speak at this time, but now has requested a delay temporarily. The Chair accordingly recognizes the next speaker on the list, the distinguished Ambassador of France."

"Now what was that all about?" the *Daily Mail* demanded. "International Row Splits U. S. Delegation; Lafe Smith Favors Blacks?"

"It wouldn't be the first time, so they tell me," the *Daily Express* said with a raucous chuckle.

"Mr. President," Raoul Barre said in his firm and graceful voice as many dials at many seats were switched rapidly to the French translation, "it is true, as the distinguished delegate of the Soviet Union has just reminded us, that this is the first time this body has had a chance to decide whether or not to condemn the United States. The United States is thus a newcomer to an area where the Soviet Union has been before. It is not surprising, therefore, that this should be a novelty and a matter for comment to the Soviet Union." (There was a little desk-banging at this, but he went calmly on.)

"Mr. President, it is not the purpose of my delegation to point the finger of scorn at anyone. We cannot defend certain practices in the United States. No more can we defend certain practices in the Soviet Union. We think there must be some consideration given to the matter of intent, to steps being taken to correct certain situations, to action within the United States on these matters. In short, we think attention of this distinguished assembly should be drawn to a resolution now pending before the House of Representatives of the Congress of the United States."

There was more desk-banging, a little mocking laughter from Ghana, Mali, Kenya, and the U.A.R. Raoul Barre ignored it.

"My delegation believes, and at an appropriate time later in the debate will offer a motion to the effect, that this debate should be adjourned until action has been completed by the Congress on the resolution now before it."

"Well, there's a neat out for you chaps," the *Guardian* murmured to the New York *Herald Tribune* as the French Ambassador stepped down and returned to his seat amid a stir of buzz and argument all across the chamber.

"Who do you suppose put him up to it?" the *Evening Standard* inquired.

"Nobody 'put him up to it,'" the New York *Times* said a little testily. "Hal Fry talked to him yesterday; I do know that. Maybe it came out of that."

"Well," the *Daily Express* said skeptically. "Maybe. It sounds like just what the French would do in a situation like this."

"What's that?" the Chicago *Tribune* asked dryly. "Try to find a civilized way out? I should hope so."

"Wait a minute," the *Christian Science Monitor* said hurriedly. "What's Kenya up to?"

"What are they always up to?" the Chicago *Trib* said with a shrug.

"Mr. President," the youthful delegate of Kenya said in the clipped British accents with which two-thirds of the world's colored dignitaries poured forth their scorn upon the white man, "the distinguished delegate of France says we should wait until there is action in the United States Congress upon a certain resolution. Well, Mr. President, let us consider this resolution for a moment. Who is its author, Mr. President? One who presumes to call himself a spokesman of the Negro race, Mr. President. Did we nominate him, Mr. President? Did we appoint him spokesman of the Negro race?"

He paused dramatically, and shouts of "No!" came dutifully up from many delegations.

"He is self-nominated, Mr. President. He is self-appointed. Or, rather, I should say, he was nominated and appointed by his white masters to run their errands for them. That is the truth of it, Mr. President!"

"Oh, God," Lafe murmured with a groan. "Do you think he'll have the nerve after that?"

"If he doesn't," Hal Fry said sharply, though he now felt so terribly weak and dizzy that it was all he could do to remain seated upright, "I shall have to."

"No, you won't," Lafe said angrily. "Now, damn it, no nonsense, Hal. I mean it."

"We'll see," Hal Fry said weakly. "We'll see."

"Mr. President," the youthful delegate of Kenya said smoothly, "it is with pity and shame that we should look upon this poor fellow as he tries to do the job of his white masters. They want him to turn aside our justifiable wrath in this Assembly, Mr. President. They want him to offer us a little stick to distract us, as though we were dogs who would be made to chase after distractions. They want him to offer us a little stick, but"—his voice suddenly rose sharply—"to our dearly beloved friend from Gorotoland they offered big sticks, and stones, and rotten eggs, and dirt and shame, just as they offer it to their own colored people in their own land, Mr. President!"

There were shouts of "Down with the United States! Shame, shame!" The delegate of Kenya held up his hand for silence.

"Mr. President, does this little fellow who has given up his birthright to do the job of his white masters really believe that we can be diverted from the just rendering of judgment upon the United States for her shameful racial practices? Do he and his white masters really think so little of our intelligence and understanding? Shame, indeed, Mr. President! Shame indeed upon this little black lackey and his white masters! They know their resolution cannot pass the Congress of the United States, dominated and controlled as it is by Senators and Congressmen from the Southern states. They know it is an empty gesture. Do they take us for fools, Mr. President? Does this renegade from the Negro race really think we are so stupid? Has he become that much of a white man?

"Mr. President," he said, into the angry mutterings he had aroused from many sections of the great assemblage, "this is a futile and empty gesture, and everyone knows it. We know it. The proposers know it. The Ambassador of France knows it.

"The only matter before this Assembly is the amendment of the distinguished Ambassador of Panama. We are not concerned with some will-o'-the-wisp created by a black lackey, in some other gathering in a country whose attitude on race is all too well known to us. We are concerned only with the amendment of the Ambassador of Panama. Let us vote on it, Mr. President. *Now!*"

And, as many delegates stood and gave him a standing ovation, he strode with an air of unassailable righteousness back up the aisle to his seat.

There occurred then several moments of vagueness and uncertainty at the podium. Again it could be seen that there was discussion in the U.S. delegation; again the crew-cut young State Department aide hurried to whisper to the President. The Secretary-General was observed to leave his chair and go behind the wall in back of the podium to his private waiting room, hidden from the Assembly. In a moment he was back, shaking his head. Again there was frantic conferring at the rostrum, further hasty conferring in the U.S. delegation.

"I'm going up to him," Hal Fry said grimly through the whirling haze before his eyes.

"You're staying right here!" Lafe said in his ear. "Just try to stand up. You can't do it."

"Yes, I ca—" Hal Fry said; but the words died, for he couldn't. He sat back with a helpless expression. "I'm too dizzy," he whispered.

"You sit right here," Lafe said quickly. "If you want to be helped out, the others will take you. If you can stick it, I'll take you myself after he speaks."

"I'll stick," Hal said, with an attempt at a smile that hurt his colleague to see. "That's the least I can do."

"Good," Lafe said. "Don't move."

And he jumped up and strode down the aisle toward the podium, causing a renewed and livelier buzz as delegates, press, and visitors craned eagerly to see him go. He too stopped briefly to confer with the President and the S.-G., and then turned away to start toward the S.-G.'s private room. With an abrupt air of decision, as though he had finally made some commitment in his own mind, the Secretary-General rose suddenly and followed after. He caught up with the Senator and they disappeared together behind the wall that bore upon it the map of a troubled planet.

For several minutes, as the excitement and speculation increased and the whirr of buzz and gossip mounted, there was no further action at the dais. Then the S.-G. returned to his seat, impassive but with a certain indefinable air of relief. The Senator from Iowa followed and conferred quickly with the President.

"If the Assembly will be in order," the President said, "the United States of America will now address the Assembly. The distinguished representative of the United States."

"Mr. President," Lafe Smith said, "much has been made here today of a resolution in the United States Congress. Much has been said about the character and integrity of its author. In our country, when a man is attacked he has a right to speak back and explain his actions and his purposes. In this Assembly a man should have the same right. It is my honor to present to this worthy gathering a man I am proud to claim as a fellow American, a fellow worker on my delegation, and a colleague in the Congress of the United States, the distinguished Representative from the State of California, the Honorable Cullee Hamilton."

"Oh, brother," the New York *Post* snapped. "Of all the cheap stunts!"

"Nothing like desperation to bring out the good old American corn, is there?" the *Daily Express* agreed.

"You mean we're not supposed to defend ourselves but just let all the rest of you bastards walk all over us?" the New York *Herald Tribune* inquired with a sudden angry glint in his eyes. But the *Express'* answer, if any, was lost in the noise and confusion from floor and galleries as the Congressman from California appeared from behind the map-wall and walked slowly forward to take his position, with a little bow to the President, at the rostrum. Lafe Smith hurried back up the aisle to take his seat beside Senator Fry, and the room quieted down.

Of his thoughts at that moment, no single one stood forth with any clarity of outline in Cullee's mind as he waited for the hum and stir to subside. He was not, indeed, really conscious of the room; a moment which under other circumstances might have been a proud one for him was instead a blur in which he found himself concentrating desperately on the task of holding himself steady and planning his opening remarks. He was not conscious that someone from over in the direction of the delegation of Mali shouted "Traitor!" or that the Soviet Union and its satellites were banging their desks or that others from Africa were booing or that the uproar was met and matched with counternoise of applause and approval from many other delegations. Nor could he perceive in the public gallery his wife and his friend, or note that they seemed to scrunch down a little lower in their seats, as though for fear he might see them.

He could not have seen them at that distance, even had he known they were there; and at this moment they and all else were crowded from his mind by the sheer necessity to remain standing and not keel over, to open his mouth and let something intelligible come out. One tiny thing he did notice as he glanced down at his hands gripping the lectern: he was holding it so tightly that his knuckles were white. White! There's an irony for you, he thought, in his first glimmer of coherence since Lafe's voice had dragged him forward, through a great unhappy confusion, to face the world. With it came another thought: This is like the House. Pretend it's the House. You've done that so often, it's easy; pretend it's the House—and presently, in what seemed a flick of time to those who watched but an eternity to him, he found that he was able to draw a deep breath and, through the gradually subsiding uproar, begin.

"Mr. Speaker—" he said, and caught himself as there came a quick reaction of laughter, partly hostile but predominantly friendly; and, encouraged by it, he corrected himself and, increasingly assured, managed to speak with a gradual return of his usual even dignity.

"Mr. President: I suppose I could waste your time, and mine, by indulging in personalities with other delegates who have spoken here. I just don't know what good it would do. If you want to think badly of me, I can't stop you. If you want to be decent to me, I will thank you. It's your decision, and I can't see that calling names is going to help anybody decide about it."

He paused, and there was a ripple of approval across the room, most of it from Western delegations but some, too, from the Africans and Asians.

"There is one thing I think you should know," he said quietly. "I happen to be an American, and I happen to be proud of it. And if I can love my country in spite of all the things some of my fellow Americans have done to my people, then I don't see what gives some of you the right to be so smart and self-righteous about attacking her."

"I don't know, I don't know," Lafe said in a worried tone, but Hal Fry, now in one of those sudden capricious quirks of his private demon, feeling much better, said, "No, he's right. He knows how to talk to them."

"Quite a fuss has been made here," Cullee went on, and now he had them listening intently, "because I introduced a resolution. A lot of people wanted me to introduce this resolution, and they weren't all white, either. Some of them were people who are attacking me now because of it. Some people say I did it because the Administration wanted me to. Of course I talked to the Administration about it. It involves foreign policy and some important matters for my country. Why wouldn't I talk to the Administration? I'd be a pretty poor Congressman if I didn't, I think." There was a little murmur of approval and agreement, and no competing desk-banging, this time.

"Well. So I introduced a resolution. You all know what it does. It expresses the apologies of the Congress to my good friend from Gorotoland there, His Royal Highness the M'Bulu. My wife and I"—for just a second his voice got a little thin, but only a couple of people in the galleries noticed it as he hurried on—"my wife and I have been in Terry's home. He has been in my home. Not with all *his* wives," he added with a sudden impulse of humor that proved to be correct, for there was a wave of appreciative laughter over the hall, "but, anyway, *he* has. I was with him in Charleston." The laughter died abruptly and he talked right into the silence as he knew he must. "I advised him against doing what he did there"—a scattering of boos came up—"because I happen to believe there are more effective ways to handle it, and I have a responsibility to work for them peaceably in the Congress of the United States. But, he went ahead. That was his privilege. Because he did, many things have happened, including my being here right now.

"So. Something had to be done, I thought, to express officially our apologies in the Congress, and also to give aid to his country which, we all hope, will very rapidly be set free of its colonial status to Britain. And I also thought the Congress should pledge itself officially to move even faster in the area of race relations than it has in the past."

At this there was skeptical laughter here and there over the floor, and he responded sharply.

"You think it *hasn't* done anything in the past? Brothers, you need to read up a bit. You need to get smart about what's going on in this country, and I don't mean just in Little Rock or Alabama or Charleston or any other place the distinguished delegate of the Soviet Union can think of. He's white too, remember. And his Chinese friends are yellow. I'd think a lot about letting them take over Africa, if I were you."

There was violent desk-banging and some shouts of protest from the Soviet delegation. He ignored them and went on.

"My job is in the Congress, and that's where I work for my people. Terry has his ways; I have mine. I guess the Ambassador of Panama"—he said sarcastically—"and his wife—and his brother-in-law, the Governor of California who would like to be President—and all their friends and relations have their own ways, too." He paused and then added dryly, "Perhaps I'm mistaken, but I think they're white, too. At least they were last time I looked." There was a sudden delighted shout of laughter from many delegations.

"You know he's got to do it this way," Hal responded to Lafe's quizzical expression. "It's the only way that will work."

"So there was a white amendment introduced up here. And there's a colored resolution introduced down there. And you want to vote on the white one because the way things are set up you can't vote on the colored one. But I tell you something, my friends, it's the colored one that really means something, because that's the one that carries the money for Gorotoland and that's the one that puts the Congress on record to do more about our race problems at home. When we vote in the Congress, things happen. I think you ought to give us a chance to do it.

"I'm not going to pretend to you that it's going to be easy, because it isn't. We've got some tough fighters on the other side. They may win. I don't think they will, but it could be. You've got to give us the chance, though. I can tell you one thing for sure, my resolution never will get through if you pass this amendment here today. I'd withdraw it right now if that happened. It would be beaten anyway, if that happened. And that isn't the only reason I'd withdraw it. I'd withdraw it because I have some pride for my country.

"And there would go our apologies to Terry. And there would go the money for Gorotoland. And there would go the chance to make a recommendation on race matters in the United States that would really mean something.

"I think," he said with a sudden harsh sarcasm, "that those things are a lot more important than a lot of name-calling here by fancy highbinders who don't know what they're talking about when they talk about the United States of America!"

There was a sullen murmuring, and he shouted with a sudden anger, "All right, look at *me!* I'm the United States of America! I'm black and I'm the United States of America! How about that, dear friends of the United Nations who know so much! How about that? . . .

"Mr. President," he said more quietly into the abrupt silence that greeted his explosion, "I want to make a motion on behalf of the United States delegation, of which I have the honor to be a member.

"I move that the debate on this amendment be adjourned until the Congress of the United States has concluded legislative action on my resolution."

At this there was an instant uproar, shouts of "Point of order! Point of order!" from the Soviet delegation and the Ambassador of Panama. The little Dutchman in the Chair conferred nervously with the Secretary-General, then hastily recognized Felix Labaiya, who walked hurriedly to the podium without speaking to Cullee, turned, and faced the restless Assembly.

"Mr. President," he said coldly, "I move under Rule 79 of the General Assembly that the meeting be suspended."

"Mr. President—" Cullee began angrily, stepping forward, but the President forestalled him with a hasty gavel.

"Under Rule 79," he said, "the motion of the distinguished delegate of Panama takes precedence over all other motions and must be voted upon immediately without debate. All those in favor will signify by show of hands—"

"Roll call, Mr. President!" Vasily Tashikov shouted. "Roll call!"

"A roll call is requested," the President said. The Secretary-General reached into the box, drew a name, passed it to him.

"The voting will begin with Iceland," he said.

"No," said Iceland.

"India."

"Yes."

"Indonesia."

"Yes."

"Iran."

"Yes."

"Iraq."

"Yes."

"Ireland."

"No."

"Israel."

"No."

"Italy."

"No."

"Ivory Coast."

"No."

"Jamaica."

"Yes."

"Japan."

"No."

Fifteen minutes later a tense waiting silence descended on the hall as one of the tellers at the table at the foot of the podium brought the results to the S.-G., who passed them to the President.

"On this motion," the President said, "the vote is 55 Yes, 59 No, 6 abstentions, remainder absent. The motion is defeated and the vote recurs on the motion of the distinguished delegate of the United States. Under Rule 76 there may be two speakers for and two against. Does any delegation desire to speak in favor of the motion?"

"God damn it!" Lafe whispered furiously to Hal. "Let's get on with it!"

And this, for once, appeared to be the judgment of the Assembly. Both sides were apparently afraid to talk any longer, for fear the tenuous margin of victory—But for whom? No one could be sure—would be lost. A desperate tension gripped the hall as the President slowly repeated, "The vote recurs on the motion of the distinguished delegate of the United States to adjourn debate on this item until the Congress of the United States has completed action on the delegate's resolution. All those in favor—"

"Mr. President!" Felix Labaiya shouted out in angry interruption, rising and hurrying with his quick stride to the podium as they all turned to watch and exclaim at this new turn of events. "Mr. President, I have a modification to propose to the motion of the delegate of the United States. I demand to be heard!"

"The delegate of Panama will be heard," the President said in a tone at once surprised and placating. "The delegate will state his modification."

"Mr. President," Felix said, and he was sure he was speaking firmly enough so that they could not realize the intense agitation that gripped him in the wake of the failure of his previous motion, "Mr. President, there must be *some* sense exercised here. There must be some working of the will of this house upon those who would thwart the decencies of mankind. The motion of the delegate of the United States is an open-end proposition that could delay this forever, Mr. President!" (There were shouts of "True! True!" from Kenya and Mali.) "Under this motion the Congress of the United States could dally and dawdle for weeks or even months without acting on the delegate's resolution of apology. The Congress could even adjourn and go home without acting at all, under the pretext that it would take up the resolution at its next session in January, Mr. President, which would mean that *we* would be unable to act on my amendment here until our own next session, a year from now.

"Is this the kind of justice the Assembly desires, Mr. President?" he shouted indignantly, more openly emotional than he customarily preferred to be. "Is this the kind of mockery we want to have made of our United Nations procedures?"

A great shout of "No!" welled up from many places across the floor, and he nodded with an abrupt, violent gesture of satisfaction, as much as to say, All right, then!

"Mr. President, I move that the motion of the delegate of the United

States be modified to adjourn this debate to a day certain. I move that the motion read to adjourn debate to one week from today."

"That tears it!" Lafe whispered as a roar of approval came up, but Hal Fry only whispered hurriedly, "Wait and see."

At the podium the Congressman from California came forward again to the lectern, an expression of contempt on his face as the Ambassador of Panama stepped back.

"Mr. President," he said, "this is highly irregular. This modification is not in writing as Assembly rules provide; it is not formally before the delegations—"

"Stop stalling, white man!" someone shouted from the general direction of Kenya, and a look of blind anger came for a moment over his face; but he mastered it.

"But, Mr. President," he said with a grating emphasis, "the United States of America is not afraid of a little pip-squeak parliamentary trick like this one. I know, Mr. President, that we should all bow down to the great Ambassador of Panama, who loves the United States so, and whose wife and brother-in-law the great Governor of California love the United States so, and to all the rest of them. But my delegation is not about to do it."

"Don't be too smart," Lafe urged him in a worried whisper, "or you'll turn them all against us." As if he had heard this inaudible admonition far down in the sea of faces before him, Cullee's tone changed back abruptly to one of reason, at a cost only he knew, for his knuckles again were white with strain where they gripped the lectern.

"Now, Mr. President, if anybody here is making a mockery of anybody's procedures, it is the Ambassador of Panama. He knows the Congress in all probability cannot complete action in one week. No, Mr. President," he said as a ripple of sarcastic laughter ran through many delegations, "it is no more reasonable than to expect this Assembly or your own legislatures to move with equal speed on something. Men need time to digest and consider a thing of this importance. The Assembly knows that. The Ambassador knows that." He paused, and so volatile was the group before him that they immediately quieted and followed his next words with a growing murmur of approval. "I will say, however, that I do believe the Ambassador has a point. I will grant you that I did not think through the full import of my motion. Some time limit may well be perfectly reasonable, and I am willing to accept it."

"Oh, brother," the London *Daily Mirror* whispered to the London *Evening Standard.* "How graceful can you get when you're eating crow?"

"Jim Crow?" the *Standard* inquired with a pleasant relish. "Who knows?"

"But I am only willing to accept it within the reasonable limits of what men can accomplish in the parliamentary procedures of a free body, Mr. President. I will modify my amendment to read that debate be adjourned to two weeks from today. I so move."

"Mr. President," Felix Labaiya said, coming forward again as Cullee stepped back, and again ignoring him, "the delegate of the United States gives an appearance of reasonableness here. But Mr. President, how much longer must the world accept the excuse that his country is unable to move fast but must drag along—and drag along—and drag along—on these racial matters? How much time does a nation want? It is more than a hundred years since the slaves were set free, Mr. President, and how free are they today? I say the United States has had enough time, Mr. President! I say we should stop being patient, here in this United Nations, with those who flaunt the will of mankind on this great issue that concerns the whole world so deeply. I say if the United States intends to act in good faith, *let her act.*

"If the delegate of the United States will not accept my modification, Mr. President, I shall *move* that his motion be amended to read one week, and I shall ask for a vote of this Assembly to force the modification."

"Does the distinguished delegate of the United States wish to speak further to the question of modification of his motion?" the President inquired into the buzzing, rustling, whispering, gossiping silence that fell. Cullee stepped forward, and down in the American delegation Lafe Smith said, "Come on, Cullee baby, we're praying for you. Nobody can help you now. Do it right!" And again Hal Fry, enwrapped in erratic and wandering pain, managed to say encouragingly, "He will. He will."

In this, perhaps the moment of greatest responsibility he had ever known, there shot through the mind of the Congressman from California as he stood again at the lectern, the fearful thought that at this moment in time, at this particular juncture of history, in this very place, right here and now, the fate of the United States in the United Nations literally rested in the hands of just one man. The moment would pass at once, seized or lost, turned to advantage or allowed to slip away forever—and all on the basis of what that one man did, right here and now. Instantly with the thought there came the additional one: I can't think about that or I'll be lost; and so, with a silent prayer that his colleagues of the Congress would back him up in what he was about to do, he spoke briefly and to the point and in the only way that was now possible, given the angry restlessness in the vast throng watching him intently from the floor. Anything else, and the debate would obviously go on, to who knew what ultimate conclusion for his country.

"Very well, Mr. President," he said with a quiet gravity into the fiercely attentive hush that came to the assemblage as he spoke, "the United States is not afraid to accept the challenge put forward by the Ambassador of Panama." There was a little raucous laughter, a few catcalls, but he finished calmly. "I move that debate on this amendment be adjourned to one week from today to permit the Congress of the United States to consider my resolution now before it."

"The Assembly has heard the modified motion," the President said hastily before anyone else could interrupt. "All those in favor—"

"Roll call!" shouted someone from Ghana, all alone in the silence, and the

President nodded obediently. The Secretary-General drew the name; the President received it.

"The voting will begin with Cuba."

"*No!*" shouted Cuba.

"Cyprus."

"No."

"Czechoslovakia."

"No."

"Dahomey."

"Yes"—and there was a sudden intake of breath across the hall.

"Denmark."

"Yes."

"Dominican Republic."

"No."

"Ecuador."

"*Sí.*"

"El Salvador."

"*Sí.*"

"Ethiopia."

"No."

"Federation of Malaya."

"Yes."

"Finland."

"Yes."

"France."

"*Oui.*"

"Gabon."

"*Oui*"—and again the explosive hiss, countered immediately as Ghana shouted "No!"

And once again as the roll call neared completion with China, Yes, Colombia, *Sí,* Congo Brazzaville, *Oui,* Congo Leopoldville, *Non,* Costa Rica, *Sí,* the tension rose and the silence became almost unbearable. With Costa Rica's vote the tension broke and there was an immediate buzz and stir all across the great room as many delegations began to tot up their tally sheets.

"On the motion of the distinguished delegate of the United States to adjourn debate on the amendment of the distinguished delegate of Panama to one week from today," the President announced, "the vote is 50 Yes, 49 No, 21 abstentions, remainder absent. The motion is adopted and debate on this item is adjourned to one week from today.

"If there is no further business to come before today's plenary session," he added quickly, "the Assembly will stand adjourned until 10 A.M. Monday, at which time we shall have before us the resolution of the Soviet Union relative to attempts by forces in the island of Luzon in the Philippines to break free from the central government."

"Now," Lafe said as they walked off the floor together, "I think you're going back to the Waldorf and lie down, my boy, and I think that as soon as I can make arrangements, you're going in the hospital for some really thorough tests."

"That's ridiculous," Hal Fry said, for he was now feeling much better and in truth it did seem ridiculous. "Just ridiculous. I'm feeling fine. No kidding," he said, as his colleague looked skeptical. "I am." He smiled. "I'll race you to the Delegates' Lounge."

"You will in a pig's eye. Come on, now. I want to see you back to the hotel. And really, now, Hal—"

"I'll be all right, I said. I really *am* feeling much better."

"I want your solemn promise," Lafe said as they started down the stairs to the Delegates' Entrance on the ground floor. "One more spell like today's, and you go in for tests and no nonsense. Promise?"

"Oh, for heaven's sake," Hal Fry began, but his colleague gave him a squeeze of the arm for emphasis that made him wince.

"Promise, I said."

"Well. I'll think about it."

"You'll do it," Lafe said.

"Yes, Daddy," Hal Fry said. "I'll do it."

"All right. That's better. I wonder if we should wait for Cullee."

"I think he's having lunch with the S.-G."

"That should be interesting."

"Quite."

Before lunch, however, there was the inevitable visit to the Delegates' Lounge, and as he entered it, talking to the Secretary-General with a politeness that had not yet yielded to comfortable familiarity, the Congressman from California wished with an agonizing wrench at his heart that he had not come. Across the room, framed in the windows, backed by the East River in the autumn sun, he saw the four people he would most have preferred not to see. Simultaneously they saw him. The M'Bulu gave him an ironic smile and bow, Felix a blank stare; LeGage looked at him with a strange expression filled with pain and anger, and Sue-Dan appeared tense and ostentatiously uncaring. His own thoughts were such a mixture of things that he started to nod but found that this hurt so much that he had to stop and look away.

The Secretary-General, apparently not noticing, though Cullee suspected he noticed very well, took his arm in a kindly fashion and turned him away toward the center of the room.

"Here is someone you should meet," he said, "even though you seem to be opposed today. I am sure that on other issues of interest to Africa you will soon find yourselves in agreement."

But even as he started to make the introduction his voice died, for the smug young delegate of Kenya was obviously having none of it.

"This is what I think," he announced loudly, so that conversation stopped all around and many eyes turned to see, "of American stooges."

And with elaborate care he spat upon the rug at the feet of the Congressman from California.

"Miss Sadu-Selim of the U.A.R.," said the young lady at the telephone desk. "Señor Alvarez of Mexico . . . Mr. Abdul Kassim of Iran, please call the Delegates' Lounge . . ."

Three

CULLEE HAMILTON'S BOOK

And so in the course of the Almighty's unpredictable unravelings of the puzzles He sets for men, the fearsome burden of the world's troubles had come to rest for a time upon the shoulders of the Congressman from California; and as he stood in the Delegates' Lounge and watched the sputum of the terribly, terribly self-righteous young man from Kenya stain slowly into the green rug at his feet, he held desperately to just one thought: Thank God they're broad shoulders—thank God they're broad. He knew he had to hold to some such thought and think very hard of nothing else, for otherwise, despite the gently restraining hand of the Secretary-General on his arm, he would draw back an enormous fist and in a lightning insensate reaction the smug young man from Kenya would be suddenly and sadly damaged and put out of commission for quite some time. And that, of course, would be exactly the kind of scandal the smug young man from Kenya and all his friends and encouragers were hoping for.

So instead Cullee remained for a long moment with his head lowered and in his eyes a gleam of such contempt that the young man from Kenya, for all his brash arrogance, was frightened and abashed and presently turned away with an uneasy, self-conscious shrug that somehow did not look at all as brave and scornful as he intended. Nonetheless, the fact of his contemptuous action remained; and after a moment the talk began around them again, with an extra excitement and liveliness now in the wake of this new unanswered affront to the United States. In a moment the whole Lounge was buzzing with it. Nearby a group of reporters buzzed with it too, and it would not be long before the whole wide world would buzz. Of such noble items was the story of mankind composed in this sad, chaotic age.

"I think perhaps we had best go up to lunch, now," the Secretary-General said calmly at his side, and after a moment he allowed himself to be turned away and led out of the huge room where Rumor was king and Gossip prime minister. As they left he caught one more glimpse of the quartet by the window, out of the corner of his eye and hardly in focus, but clearly enough so that even as he deliberately tried not to look he could see again the sardonic smile of the M'Bulu, the little air of satisfaction on the Panamanian Ambassador's face, LeGage's strained and embittered expression, the self-consciously scornful look of his wife. Don't be so show-offy, little Sue-Dan, he told her silently: don't be so show-offy or your big man will— Only that wasn't true, he caught himself up blankly: her big man wouldn't do anything at all, the way things stood now. And he did not know when they would change, or if they would.

It was therefore in a closed-off unhappy world of his own, lost in his thoughts and barely able to be civil, that he permitted himself to be taken over the soft carpets to the elevator and so up to the fourth floor to the Delegates'

Dining Room. In the elevator, as they stepped in, the Indian Ambassador was talking rapidly to the delegate of Ghana; before they fell abruptly silent, K.K.'s "an obvious piece of smarmy political lollygagging in the hopes he can get to the Senate" came clearly to his ears. He started to swing about angrily, but again the S.-G.'s firm pressure on his arm prompted a more sensible reaction. He turned slowly and nodded with an air of cold dignity. K.K. returned it briskly, but Ghana gave him only the barest of nods. You black bastard, he thought with a sardonic contempt, haven't you heard we're all brothers? Ghana must have gotten the message, because he returned an angry frown. Cullee turned back and faced front, feeling somewhat better.

In the dining room, conscious that many eyes were giving him the outwardly casual, quickly appraising examination reserved for those who have power by those who are jealous of it, he made some desultory attempt at small talk with the S.-G. which did not move very smoothly, despite that gentleman's long practice in the exchange of necessary nothings with his unruly colleagues. Finally the Congressman put down his knife and fork and turned to the older man with an air of troubled intensity.

"How do you stand it?" he demanded. The Secretary-General looked surprised for a moment, and Cullee went on in a bitter tone: "Being patronized by the blacks, I mean. You expect it from the whites, but how do you stand it from your own people?"

"You say my own people," the S.-G. said with an air of weary discontent. "You sound like the whites do, listing us all together. My own people are the Nigerians. They don't patronize me. The rest of Africa—" He shrugged. "At this stage, all we seem to be able to do is despise one another. It is fashionable to blame the colonialists for this, but I am not so sure it is not inherent in us. Perhaps it is our fatal flaw, being hostile and suspicious and unkind toward one another."

"They do a powerful lot of talking about brotherhood," Cullee said, aware that dark ears nearby were straining to hear and hoping they would, "but I don't see much of it lying around this place. Don't they understand I'm trying to work it out in the Congress in the best way it can be worked out?"

"They're impatient," the S.-G. said. "You have to understand—"

"Yes, I understand," Cullee said shortly. "I understand what an easy excuse that is for riding roughshod over every decent and practical way of doing things. It's all very well for these Fancy Dans from outback to do a lot of talking, but it's another thing for them to achieve anything with all their talk. It isn't that simple."

"To many of them, it is."

"Then they're never going to get anywhere. They're always going to be disappointed."

"And you aren't disappointed?" the Secretary-General asked gently. "I had rather thought you were, in many things."

"Why should I be?" Cullee demanded harshly, picking up his fork and resuming his meal. "I'm doing all right for a Negro, in my country."

"If that is the ultimate in aspiration that a Negro can have," the S.-G. agreed, "then I grant you, you should be well content."

And why indeed should he not be, the Congressman thought angrily as he found himself suddenly involved in the storm of doubt, self-doubt, doubt of purpose, doubt of country, doubt of ultimate aim and achievement, that he knew the older man had deliberately tried to force him into. Well: it wasn't hard. Old Cullee didn't need much of a push to get to brooding. It was part of a nature that had always given him troubles that were hard enough to bear when the world was leaving him alone, let alone when it was not.

There came to his mind, in one of those journeyings back that come so often when the heart is hard pressed by events, the sleepy little street in the sleepy little town in South Carolina where he had been born; not too far, as he learned many years later, from Seab Cooley's Barnwell. Of all the facts in the universe, that at the time was among the remotest, though it would eventually become a joking point and also, in some curious way that he had expressed to Orrin Knox the other night in Washington, a small sentimental link between himself and the fierce old Senator. It was a link neither had ever mentioned to the other, except in an occasional indirect exchange of compliments, as through the Secretary of State; but it was there, if they needed it. For all the defensive insistence of the South that its residents "understood one another," in some infinitely subtle, infinitely complex and indescribable way, they did. They "talked the same language," particularly in time of need. If he ever needed the Senator's help, the Congressman had always felt, he could get it, and vice versa. Until now, when he knew they would meet on the battleground of the one issue upon which, he felt fearfully, neither he nor Seab nor their respective peoples might be able to really help each other, desperately imperative though it was for them and their country that they do so in this confused and tragic time.

All of this, however, was far from the little world of the little boy who was born in Lena, S.C. to a field-hand father and a housemaid mother, striving with only a fair success to maintain some shred of stability in a hand-to-mouth existence for themselves and the five children Providence saw fit to give them in quick succession. His father had died when Cullee was eight, killed in a tractor accident on the broad acres of some big house. Cullee remembered him only as a towering, sweating, absent-minded, almost illiterate presence who in his concluding years took to drink with increasing frequency and ferocity, until toward the end his mother would bar the door of their cabin at night and send her children secretly away to hide with neighbors while she faced her husband alone. But she always did face him; that was one of the major things her children always remembered, and would remember until they died: she always did. The tenacity of character in that gaunt little body amazed them then when they half understood it and amazed them even more now that they appreciated it to the full. Sometimes she suffered beatings for her courage, but more often there was only a brooding silence that gripped the household after she had faced their father down, nursed him through a day or two of oblivion, and then called them home to resume their family living. Once in the midst of this, when the parents still were barely speaking to one another and a fearful hush lay upon the household, his father had suddenly lain his head on the table and started to cry.

"You so good," he said finally in a wondering voice, as though if she weren't it would be so much easier for him, as of course it would. "You so good." His mother had said nothing, but her oldest boy had agreed, in silence and with a fierce, protective love that blazed in him still. She was indeed; and to some degree everything he had done and was doing and would continue to do was an attempt to make up to her for the hard life she had been forced to lead in those early years.

Out of that life, of course, had come one Congressman, two doctors, a professor, and the happily married wife of one of the nation's rising young electronics scientists; so that much more than a casual flame burned in that indomitable heart. What had they all received from their father, aside from physical size, the Congressman often wondered in succeeding years; possibly some capacity for endurance and for pain, some streak of sensitivity beneath it all that had prompted him to realize the nature of the woman his life had run beside. Perhaps what he gave them was symbolized by whatever it was that had brought that harsh, hopeless, unhappy admission of her superiority on that long-ago night. Life did not explain these things, and who could say? His children tried to be fair to him in their own minds, but there was no doubt where their loyalty lay. "In the jargon, of course," his youngest brother had remarked after medical school had given him the jargon, "you know we're all of us definitely mother-oriented. But after all," he added with a cheerful grin, "what else could we be, under the circumstances?"

Under the circumstances, they all knew now, it was their mother who pushed them, with a fierce pride that drove none of them harder than it did herself, onto the paths they were all successfully to pursue. She had always kept herself neat; she had always reiterated over and over to them that they must keep themselves neat; she had emphasized diligence and courtesy and "respect for your betters"; she had drummed into them thrift and respectability and "all the other homely old virtues that nobody gives a damn about in this day and age," as his next-to-youngest brother had remarked with a bitter-edged irony not long ago. And it was true. She had been determined, with a determination almost frightening in its intensity, that they should amount to something, that they should make their place in the world, that they should all of them rise higher than any of their forebears ever had in a society which could concede them many things but would only rarely forgive them the fact that they were black.

To their mother this had seemed the preordained way of things, and to her generation, hearing the approaching drums of protest but too tradition-bound to answer them, the Negro's "place" was approximately what a good many of their white countrymen, North and South, thought it was. For Cullee and his brothers and sister this was not so easy to accept. "You made us too proud," he had told her once when she was protesting in considerable alarm his unsuccessful attempt to enter the University of South Carolina. "You made us too proud to take all this stuff. Don't blame us if we act like you taught us."

"Like I taught you?" she had demanded, arguing with every line of her taut little figure, as she always did. "You aren't acting like I taught you. You're getting 'way above yourself, Cullee. You're going to fall."

"Above myself?" he had cried in a sudden, harsh anger. "Where's that? Who's above me and what's above myself? Not anybody! Isn't anybody in this world better than Cullee Hamilton. Not anybody!"

But it was not, of course, that simple, and he realized it early. The carefully circumscribed world in which Negroes lived, the servilely defensive mechanisms by which they were able to maintain their tenuous position in a white society and preserve to themselves in the midst of it some semblance of personal identity and independence, were impressed upon him, as upon all his race, as soon as he was able to perceive that there was a world outside the narrow limits bounded by the cabin, the neighbors, his father's sadness, and his mother's courage. The quivering attention to the white man's mood, the desperate readiness to subordinate one's own wishes to his, the constant planning so that he would not be offended and would not become either too fond of you or too hostile toward you, the endless rearranging of one's life to suit his arbitrary rules for governing your conduct—all of these were soon, too soon, a part of his growing up. Something as simple as going to the bathroom became a major issue when you were in town with your mother. There were only one or two widely separated places where you could go, and very early you learned that on shopping days you mustn't drink too much water in the morning because you wouldn't be able to urinate, unless you used back alleys, which your mother's pride wouldn't permit you to do, until you got home again. And you sat in certain places in buses and streetcars, and you entered only certain doors that were marked for you, and you attempted to walk down the street in an inconspicuous manner, and you learned not to listen to what the white man was saying, unless of course you were supposed to hear, in which case you learned to laugh just a little too loudly and just a little too heartily to reassure him that yassuh, boss, he was indeed the Lord of Creation and you his admiring vassal, constantly surprised anew by his wisdom and his all-knowing superiority and his ineffable and incomparable wit.

He hated it, the whole artificial contraption, the whole strange, awkward, childishly inhuman forcing of life out of its normal pattern to suit the whole strange, awkward, childishly inhuman concept of the relation of the races that dominated the society of the South. It therefore came to him as a great shock when he discovered that, for all the pious speeches and the noble pretenses that flooded the printed page and the troubled channels of the air, essentially the same concept also dominated the society of the North.

It was a while, however, before this became a major factor in his life, for first there came the growing up, the going to grammar and high school, the gradual but definite realization that he and his brothers and sister had been favored with an intelligence and drive far beyond the level that kept so many of their contemporaries content to remain within the agreed-upon boundaries that separated the white and colored worlds. Ironically, the very fact that they were superior drew the white man's approval and help. "I wonder what would have happened to us if we hadn't become fashionable?" his sister had mused wryly once, and he had responded quickly, "Just the same thing." But they were honest enough to acknowledge that they weren't so sure. At least it wouldn't have been quite as easy as it turned out to be, thanks to their mother's pride, their own ability, and the desire of the white man to ease his conscience with a few good examples to point to.

By the time he entered high school, "Kate Hamilton and her kids" had become the favorite project of half a dozen white families. This guaranteed them ample clothing, hand-me-down but substantial; enough food, often home-cooked and hand-delivered; more than enough housework for his mother, and, as they came along to working age, enough for all of them to make a modest but solid living, to purchase a small house in the colored section of town, to begin to live a life that was, by Negro standards, prosperous and good. Along with many other purposes, this served also the possibly subconscious but nonetheless powerful psychological need of those who gave them assistance. "I swear I can't put up with some of these shiftless niggers," they would say, sometimes in the Hamiltons' hearing. "But Kate Hamilton and her kids are different. It's a pleasure to do for them. Now, if they were all like that—"

If they were all like that, he suspected, the situation would still be exactly the same; but it did not seem to him that the family should refuse the help so kindly given, whatever the motivation. In this his brothers and sister concurred, though for a time his mother's pride was sufficiently hurt by what she regarded essentially as being patronized that she was inclined to be grudging and prickly in her acceptance of it. Those who gave assistance would have been horrified to be told that they were being patronizing, for to them it was a perfectly genuine expression of kindness between the races. In time his mother came to accept it as such and not worry about its subtler aspects. Kate Hamilton and her kids prospered and learned much about the delicate art of being successfully black in a white man's world.

For Cullee and his mother there had been no such dramatic confrontation with the gods as had been granted Terence Ajkaje and his mother on a storm-rocked night far away in Africa; yet at roughly the same time in their respective lives there had come to the Hamiltons, too, the conviction that there was waiting for the oldest son a destiny rather more special than that reserved for most of his contemporaries.

The direction this was to take did not become apparent until he had graduated with high honors from high school and decided to go to Columbia University, far away in the magic North. This decision he made and adhered to despite the urgings of the president of the bank where he had been handyman that he stay there and try eventually to work up to clerk. Somehow this did not seem quite the future for his obvious intelligence, at least in his own mind.

"You're a smart boy; it's a good life," his employer had said. "You can't expect much better down here."

"Maybe I'm not going to stay down here," he had said.

"You won't like it up there," his employer predicted. "You'll make more money and they'll make over you some, maybe, but they won't understand you. You won't be with your friends."

"I'll take my chances," he said.

"The bank'll be here," his employer said. "Come back when you've had enough of it."

"I'll never come back," he had said flatly; and, of course, he never had, except to get his mother and take her to California when events conspired to send him West.

When he first entered Columbia, however, he would have been astonished had anyone told him that California would become, in time, a major factor in his existence. The thing that filled his mind then was the wonder of being out of the South, of being in the North, of being in a society where nobody gave a damn about your skin and only judged you for what you were.

This kindly illusion lasted roughly three months, during which he was given quite a rush by many of his white classmates and the self-consciously tolerant groups to which they belonged. How self-conscious, he did not realize at first, but it was not long before he began to be aware that for all their outward camaraderie there was a subtle shade of difference, invisible but unmistakable, tenuous as fog but hurtful as acid, that separated him from his newly found white friends. His colored friends told him with raucous sarcasm that he was being a fool, that it had all happened to them too, that just because he was big and good-looking and obviously bright he was being patronized, as they had been, to help white pretensions preen and white consciences rest easy.

"You just wait," one of them said, a star athlete as Cullee seemed likely to be. "One of these days you'll get the final tribute. Some one of these white babes will go to bed with you and you'll think, by God, now I've arrived, she really likes me. But don't kid yourself. She likes black skin and the chance to tell her pals how democratic she is. But as for *you*, she couldn't care less."

And when it happened, exactly as his friend had predicted, he tried desperately to convince himself that it wasn't as empty as that. But he knew with a withering certainty in his heart that it was.

For a time the shock of finding in the North the matching side of the coin his race found in the South—made, if anything, more unbearable because it was so damnably patronizing and so utterly false in its pretensions of humanity and tolerance that always evaporated instantly at the slightest attempt to establish any sort of genuine interdependence—was enough to throw him into a mental and emotional turmoil that sadly jeopardized his private stability and scholastic record. He did not do well in his year at

Columbia, basically because he had hoped for so much from the North and found so little. You could take New York with all its phonies and blow it off the map, he concluded bitterly after the tenth or fifteenth or twentieth hectic all-night party on Morningside Heights at which blowsy, hairy, be-spectacled girls and blowsy, hairy, bespectacled boys proclaimed at the top of their lungs through a haze of cigarette smoke and cheap liquor how much they loved humanity, particularly its blacker sections. They didn't love any-body but themselves, he decided, and they wouldn't give him or any other Negro the time of day if it didn't bolster their fearfully insecure egos to do so. He was sick of the lot and ready to try being black again by the time the scholastic year ended. He had reached the conclusion that he could not escape his race, and, furthermore, did not want to.

There were various colored colleges available to go to, but a growing interest in politics and government led him inevitably to Howard University in Washington. His mother had given him, among other things, a tempera-ment that did not believe in taking things lying down, and confronted as he was by the tragic tangle of black-white relationships in his country, it was basic to his character that he should start looking about for ways to contribute what he could to its solution. The chances for a Negro in politics were slim at best, but three were serving in the Congress when he came to Washing-ton, and it was part of his nature that he should begin to think, secretly and not always daring to admit it fully to himself, that someday he might follow the same road. It seemed to him that the trend was in the times, that the steady spread of the franchise to the Negro in all but the most stubborn areas of the South, together with the rising economic level of his race, made it within the grasp of possibility in his lifetime. He had not been on campus two days before he met someone else who felt the same and, with an urgent candor that surprised and delighted him, said as much with an impatient enthusiasm that made him want to get out and start running for office at once.

Most of the people who are destined to mean the most to a life enter it without any special fanfare, and so it had been in this instance. He had been standing in line before one of the registration desks awaiting his turn when a tall, rangy figure had come alongside and asked abruptly if it could borrow a pencil. Hardly even bothering to turn his head, he had smiled and automatically said yes. "You might at least look at me," the rangy figure had said, holding out a hand with a demanding air. "I'm LeGage Shelby." "O.K.," he had said with a grin, shaking the hand and giving its owner a startled, amused glance, "I'm Cullee Hamilton." "Get through registering and let's have lunch," 'Gage had said, and he had nodded, feeling flattered and also interested. Once years later he had asked LeGage how he happened to come up to him so abruptly that morning and 'Gage had shrugged. "Who ever knows what draws people to one another?" he said. "You looked like a good guy." He grinned. "I guess I must have too. You didn't say no when I asked you to lunch."

As a matter of fact, he thought moodily now, finishing his dessert and exchanging some meaningless remark with the Secretary-General as they waited for the bill, he had rarely said no to LeGage on anything thereafter. By nightfall, after a continuing talk that had ranged over every conceivable subject that could occupy two adolescent minds, they had decided to room together and dedicate themselves, in tandem, to the improvement of the Negro race. It had not taken them long to admit to each other that this was their secret aim in life, and it had not taken LeGage long to translate it into the practical terms that Cullee himself had already begun to think about. "I think you should go into politics and I should manage you," 'Gage had said abruptly. "With my brains and your beauty, we couldn't lose." "Thanks so much," Cullee smiled. "We'll see who contributes what, but anyway, it sounds like a good idea to me."

If only, he reflected now, things ever worked out as simply as they began. The two of them had gone into politics, right enough, but life had carried them down far different paths, and the two idealists who had roomed together at Howard could hardly bear now to look at one another in the Delegates' Lounge. Well: it wasn't his fault. He had remained true to what he believed in; he knew that. And the thing that made it hurt, of course, was that LeGage had too.

For the first two years of their friendship, they had studied and talked and lived together with a singleness of purpose that overrode and nullified the basic tensions that almost immediately began to flare between them. "You're only going to manage my political career," he had remarked abruptly one day a month or so after they had found lodgings near the campus, "not my whole life." The issue had been minor, something about which drawer of a bureau was to hold whose items of clothing, but the argument which had occurred had been out of all proportion and had shaken them both. LeGage had finally apologized profusely, there had been much earnest talk about ultimate purpose and standing-together-in-the-white-man's-world and all the rest of it, but their friendship had never been entirely easy from then on. LeGage usually precipitated their arguments; LeGage usually apologized and implored him successfully to abandon his frequent threats to move out; but a constant tolerant forgiveness on his part never seemed to change the pattern. "Why don't you just take it easy?" he had finally suggested. "Can't you rest comfortable unless we're fighting?"

But LeGage, as he came to realize, was not one to rest comfortable about anything, and in time their arguments became more serious as Cullee built up an increasingly brilliant academic record in history and government and became an increasingly popular campus figure, active in student politics as president of the junior class, active in athletics as a track man with a growing national reputation. LeGage had no flair for athletics or the casual popularity of student politics, though his academic record matched Cullee's and in some areas surpassed it. His flair was for a more profound sort of politics, more serious and potentially more dangerous. The rising tide of Negro impatience in the decades following the Second World War gave LeGage what he thought was to be his personal key to the future. The day came in senior year when he expressed it aloud to his roommate.

"You may be a Congressman, boy," he had declared expansively, "but me, I'm going to be one of those who make Congressmen move around."

"I'll be expecting to hear from you, then," Cullee had said, and LeGage had said, "You will," in a tone of such absolute conviction that his roommate found it a little chilling. He was not surprised to receive, a year after they had graduated and he had gone on to the University of California at Berkeley for his law degree, a triumphant letter from LeGage concerning the founding of his "Defenders of Equality For You." DEFY sounded like LeGage, he thought then, uneasily; and it might mean a great deal more trouble than good.

In their concluding months at Howard, however, the steadily differing directions they were taking did not concern him as actively as it was to do later, because he had other things on his mind. The principal one, and it often seemed the only one, went by the name of Sue-Dan Proctor, and he was as helpless in the face of it as though he had no character or will of his own.

This entrance into his life did have its own particular kind of fanfare, blaring across a hundred yards of campus, filling the universe with a sudden insistent sound, upsetting his vision, shattering his thoughts, striking instantly into his heart, demanding and securing a hold upon his being that he neither wanted nor expected, then, to ever break. The perfect figure with its promise of everything his powerful body desired at that particular moment of its development—at that particular moment, now and forever, he was very much afraid—wiped out the world and filled it up again with the most powerful obsession he had ever known, all in the two minutes it took him to see her, move toward her, intercept her casual, flaunting walk across campus and blurt out an invitation to have a cup of coffee at the student union. "Why," she said, an amused smile lighting up the clever little fox-face with its enormous dark eyes and slightly too large forehead, "I don't mind if I do."

That time, too, there had been an all-day-and-into-the-night conversation that had ranged over everything conceivable, but that time, of course, there was a desperate sexual urgency that put it within ten minutes on a plane from which it had never shifted since. The body and mind of Sue-Dan Proctor—"I'd like to spell it S–U–D–A–N, just for kicks," she had told him with an ironic little smile, "but I might as well be honest. It's Sue for my mammy and Dan for my daddy, and I guess that's plenty good enough for me"—had everything Cullee wanted, and in two weeks' time he had taken possession of them—or, rather, as he soon came to realize, they had taken possession of him.

Physically, he and Sue-Dan consumed each other, and for the rest he was content enough that she had a shrewd and perceptive mind, a quick intelligence, a concern for him and his ambitions that, while always a little more detached and realistic than he might have liked, was nonetheless single-minded in its devotion to his welfare. "You ought to go into politics," she had said, almost as early in their relationship as LeGage had, and quite independently of him. "I have a friend who thinks that, too," he had said; "my roommate, in fact. I'd like you to meet him." He had approached this confrontation of the two people he already suspected were to be, with his mother, the most important in his life, with a nervousness that literally had him sweating when he introduced them. But he need have had no worries; they hit it off at once, liked each other cordially but, he sensed with relief, impersonally, and seemed to be completely agreed on him and his future. He felt that he was in the hands of two faithful friends, not one. The only thing that disturbed him in the slightest was the fact that Sue-Dan seemed to agree rather more with LeGage's impatience on racial matters than with the moderation that was already beginning to characterize his own approach. She did not, however, choose to make an issue of it then, and in fact got rather short with 'Gage when he remarked, "This boy thinks our best bet is to walk instead of run." "He'll get there walking," Sue-Dan had said sharply, "and maybe before you."

All that, however, was a long time ago; and as he and the Secretary-General left the Delegates' Dining Room, past the ever-watchful battery of eyes, he thought with a sigh that as walking had become more difficult and running more popular, so had his relationship with both of them begun to deteriorate. In those days Sue-Dan must have thought she and 'Gage could bring him around; the growing waspishness that had become so characteristic in recent years had only come when she realized this was not to be. And at first, of course, he had followed their lead and attempted to proceed along a line of protest more violent than maturity and a growing judgment of political and social factors in mid-century America later convinced him to be sound.

They were married four months after they met, and shortly before graduation, sitting around with 'Gage and the placid girl he had decided to marry, the subject of where Cullee should go from there had inevitably come up. He was about to graduate with high honors in political science, he had decided that law was the best road to politics. A record-breaking triumph in the recent Olympics had put his face on the cover of *Life* and given him something of a national name, and it was with some care that he was considering the matter.

"You come from South Carolina," 'Gage said. "Why don't you go to law school at the University there?"

"Are you crazy?" he had demanded. "This is here and now, boy; it isn't Judgment Day."

"Why not?" 'Gage had said calmly. "At least it'll make a terrific row when they turn you down, and that'll help the cause."

"It will, Cullee," Sue-Dan had said. "You'll be a hero. My hero!" she added, with an ironic little laugh that he didn't know whether to take as a compliment or an affront, and so ignored.

His initial reaction had been one of profound doubt and misgiving. At the University of South Carolina he would of course be rejected automatically because of race. Then he would have to reapply somewhere else with a consequent loss of time and expenditure of effort. It all seemed pointless to him, except, as LeGage said, for "the cause," and he was already growing leery of LeGage and his causes. Immediately after graduation he had taken Sue-Dan home to Lena to meet his family and was pleasantly surprised to find that his mother at first seemed to like her. This peaceful interval did not last long. They had been home two days when his sister asked what he planned to do next, and the serenity of the visit came abruptly to an end. "He's going to go to law school at the University of South Carolina," Sue-Dan said promptly, and the roof fell in.

Six hours later, after an argument that had raged back and forth before, during, and after dinner, he had been forced to take his wife and leave the house, still hearing as they went the bitter protests of his mother, the uneasy comments of his brothers and sister, the shrilly angry defiance of Sue-Dan. "You're all stick-in-the-muds," she finally said bitterly. "The world has moved on and you're being left behind. Can't you see that, you're being left behind!"

"We've been honorable people all our lives," his mother shot back, "and I hope Cullee isn't going to let you change that."

The estrangement thus begun had lasted six months, during which he had allowed himself to be persuaded by his wife and LeGage to go ahead with their plans for him. 'Gage was full of ideas about getting publicity, and in that time of national emphasis upon civil rights, publicity was not hard to come by. Feeling an inner reluctance but allowing himself to be carried along by their enthusiasm, he had presented his application to the University law school in person: the picture of it being flung back in his face by the registrar appeared on every front page in the country. "Appeal it," LeGage said, and so he did, to the president of the University and the board of regents. "S.C. LAW SCHOOL ADAMANT ON NEGRO TRACK STAR," the headlines said, and again against his better judgment, he permitted himself to be interviewed on national television programs and presented on national networks. LeGage was wildly excited by the uproar that had been created, and Sue-Dan looked at him with an unusual respect. Without telling anyone but his mother, whom he telephoned secretly one night at the height of the controversy, he applied by telegram to the University of California at Berkeley, and in short order—in fact, for there was an eye for publicity in Berkeley, too, within nine hours after his final rejection by South Carolina—the University announced that he had been accepted. His life went West, and he knew instinctively that it would never return to the uneasy and unhappy regions where it had begun.

Why he should have chosen California, he did not entirely know; some impression of a greater tolerance, some thought that with a racial background composed of Spanish, English, Chinese, Japanese, Mexican, and Negro there would be a greater acceptance, was probably at the base of it. Like most dreams, this too suffered the attritions of time and fact and reality, but on the whole he found the atmosphere less restrictive than the South, less hypocritical than New York, and generally more conducive to feeling like a human being than he had found it anywhere else in his troubled land. Sue-Dan, also, seemed to settle in, to be more content, and the fact that LeGage was far away, off in Chicago organizing DEFY, contributed its share, too, to the growing serenity he felt about his life and career. His brothers and sister followed him West within a year. At the end of two they had persuaded his mother to sell the house in Lena, had purchased another, much more substantial, in Oakland, and were committed to a new life in a new place. The quarrel over his application to South Carolina died when the incident died, and in sum it seemed to have left him with increased respect from his family, increased respect from his wife, and a certain aura attached to his name nationally that could be, as LeGage wrote him earnestly several times, put to good use when he decided to go actively into politics.

His desire to do this never slackened, though by the time he finished law school as one of the top five of his class he was very well aware that even in California this would not be easy. The thought of returning to New York, much as he hated its frantic cocktail-hour insincerities, occurred to him briefly; so did Chicago. The availability of those two black ghettos as a foundation for a political career was, superficially, enough to overcome his dislike for them. But something deeper made him reject this relatively easy way out. Somewhere in himself, even in the unpleasantness of the episode in South Carolina, he had found the strength to begin to understand the two sides of the puzzle in which he had been trapped by the accident of birth. Away from LeGage's constant hammering, it occurred to him suddenly one day that so had all his countrymen been trapped, of whatever color. It was the start of wisdom.

For this, as for so many things in a character thoughtful and determined, he had his mother to thank; some basic common sense in her, some steady and fair-minded way of looking at things even when they were at their most hurtful, had been passed along to him in their long talks about the situation. She was the only one he could talk to calmly about it: LeGage was too angry and Sue-Dan too sarcastic. It was his mother who helped him restore the balance. He had grown so sick at the self-interested hypocrisy he found in so many that it took him a good while—aided by his mother's reasonable reminders—to realize that along the way he had also known quite a large number of kind and decent white people, as disturbed as he was about their mutual problem, genuinely interested, genuinely democratic, truly tolerant because it never occurred to them to think that being decent to fellow human beings was something upon which they should preen themselves. Good white friends on the track team, others that he studied with, some he had known socially, several professors, the white doctor who gave them with infinite kindness the news that Sue-Dan would never be able to have children, even his employer 'way back at the bank in Lena who had done his best to be helpful according to his lights—there were quite a lot, when he stopped to think about it. And in time, fortunately while he was still young enough to profit from the process, he did.

Looked at in this light, the white world emerged to him as less of an endlessly forbidding dead weight hanging over his world and more of a problem that might, with time and patience and sufficient goodwill and tolerance on both sides, be solved in a peaceable and mutually helpful way. The conclusion led inevitably to a reappraisal of his own race, to a rethinking of many of the scornful, angry, spiteful conversations that he had heard at other all-night parties on Morningside Heights, in Harlem, at Howard, and in Berkeley.

"Why, man, isn't one of 'em gives a good God damn about you . . . You can find 'em north, you can find 'em south, you can find 'em east, west, and outer space, and they all want the same thing, to keep us down . . . Hell, they wouldn't give us the time of day if they didn't have to, and where they don't have to, they don't . . . In their minds they're all Simon Legrees and we're all Uncle Toms. What makes you think you can talk sense to *them?*"

So many voices, so many spiteful, scornful comments, so much impatience, so much anger. That, too, he found he had grown sick of as he passed out of adolescence and into maturity. Not for him, he came to realize, the incessant sick hatred of the whites; not for him the pathetic, self-conscious, self-defeating downgrading of the Negro heritage in America; not for him the fearful self-despising that left so many of his friends, particularly in the younger generation, adrift in limbo between the white world they hated but tried to mimic, and the black world they despised but could not escape. "It seems to me the whites are human beings, just like us," he had written LeGage during this period of reappraisal, and LeGage had written back an angrily scathing letter in which he said it wasn't so, and who did Cullee think he was, Pollyanna? But he concluded, silently and doggedly, again discussing it only with his mother because he found Sue-Dan to be as scornful as LeGage of his efforts to be fair, that it *was* so, and he was not Pollyanna: he was only Cullee Hamilton, who had some vision of his country, confused like everybody's but nonetheless strong in him, who thought he might someday be able to help.

Why he, as a Negro, should have this feeling about the country, he did not altogether know. "What has the country ever done for you?" one of his colored friends at Columbia had sneered; and the attempt to find a coherent answer had ended in vague generalities and the scornful mockery of his friend. Yet somehow it had come to him: nothing that could be expressed very clearly, nothing that was very well defined, just the feeling that here in this America men had been given something very precious, that birth had given it to him too, and that somewhere under the drab and the dross and the sad betrayals of the dream that far too many men permitted and far too many men enjoyed, there was a reality and a loveliness that nothing could besmirch and nothing take away, unless its own people took it away by their impatience, their mutual intolerance, and their inability to remain true to what they had. He did not propose to be one of those who threw away

America. Others might, but the guilt would not rest on him. Of that he was determined.

When he graduated with such high honors from law school, the way to make his contribution began to open up for him. He received offers from seven law firms, three of them Negro, four of them white. One was in Atlanta, two in New York, two in Chicago, one in San Francisco, and one in Los Angeles. He dismissed the South, New York, and Chicago, and narrowed his choice to San Francisco and Los Angeles. Much as he loved San Francisco, shining whitely on her hills, it seemed to him that the opportunities for ultimately entering politics were better in the raucously sprawling world of Southern California than they were in the beautiful city by the Bay. He and Sue-Dan gave up their apartment, packed their few belongings, said good-by to the family, and started down Highway 101. Controversy waited for them at the end of it, and once again national headlines swirled around his name.

This, however, came a little later, after he had put in a good year with the law firm, after he had learned a little more that white people weren't all bad. Then they decided to buy a house in the San Fernando Valley. "For a quiet guy who doesn't go around trying to stir up trouble," LeGage wrote him in a triumphantly crowing letter, "you sure do make a stir, boy. We're coming out to help you."

But the help of DEFY was exactly what he did not want in the hectic two weeks during which his prospective white neighbors held indignation meetings, sent him threatening letters, dumped garbage on the lawn of the house he wanted to buy, and made stout statements to the papers that their dignified community "would not be permitted to become a haven for those who are unable to find homes elsewhere." Fortunately for him—very fortunately—the head of his law firm was a courtly old gentleman who had principles and believed in living up to them, so that there was no reprisal at work, though he learned later the attempt had been made. By dint of a fearful argument with LeGage, who was supported by a scared and vitriolic Sue-Dan, he had managed to stop the picketing, the protests, and the fiery statements that his roommate wanted to initiate. Instead he had acted with great dignity under great provocation from both sides of the issue, confined his public remarks to the single statement that he hoped common decency and mutual goodwill could bring the situation to a successful conclusion, and asked respectfully that he be allowed to address a meeting of the householders who apparently feared him so.

This he was urged to do by four of them who also had principles, and who came to him openly and assured him of their support. They too engaged in fearful arguments, pointing out to their angry neighbors that the whole country and indeed the whole world were watching, asking if the swarm of reporters, cameramen, and television commentators who had immediately descended to record this new sensation involving the name of Cullee Hamilton were to send forth to the world a portrait of a community so devoid of simple fairness that it would not even let a man state his case. Sober second thoughts began to supersede the first hysterical reaction, and the night came when he stood up in a crowded room and faced his first hostile audience.

Nothing he would ever do again, he felt in that hour of crushing tension, would make upon him the fearful demands those opening moments did. Yet by now he had acquired much character, much strength and steadiness. It was with a relative calmness that he made his little talk.

It was not long. He said that he knew many of them were very upset, as he was too; that he had not intended to cause any such uproar when he bought the house; that he was a college graduate, as was his wife, and they were good citizens who would be, he thought, good neighbors; that he knew this dispute was a symbol of something that gravely troubled the country as a whole, but that somehow the strength and goodwill must be found to work it out if the country was not to be fatally injured. He said that he and his wife would contribute their strength and goodwill if his listeners would contribute theirs; that he had made his purchase in good faith; that he intended to be a good neighbor to them and he hoped that they, as his fellow citizens of a country they all loved, would be the same to him. He was not truculent and he did not truckle; he was himself, earnest and simple and direct and honest; and they gave him a hand, at first slow and reluctant, that turned into a standing ovation before they were through. The millennium had not come, but some small flag of goodwill had been raised against the darkness of the times. A week later, relieved, under no illusions, but aware that he had asked for, and been given, the chance to prove that he meant what he said, he and Sue-Dan moved in. The press, sensation over, went away. The world settled back into place.

Inevitably, however, it did not settle back into the same place; and now, as he expressed his thanks for lunch and said good-by to the Secretary-General, he marveled at how quickly the shift had led him into the paths he had wished for so long to follow.

Within a month there had come an invitation to join the local committee of his political party; within two he was beginning to make appearances around the Congressional district; at the end of a year he was being mentioned, at first half humorously but then with an increasing seriousness, as a possibility to run against the incumbent Congressman of the opposite party. Many things motivated the sudden rush he received: the desire to make amends, the desire to use his prominence, the desire to build up a candidate against the sitting Congressman, even, as he honestly admitted, something of the same desire to claim tolerance by going through its motions that had so disgusted him with New York. He perceived all this with an instinctive cynicism which did not, however, leave him embittered as it might have LeGage or Sue-Dan. So motivations were mixed and perhaps not always as noble as they were claimed to be on the surface: so what? Were his own always unalloyed? Were anybody's? He did not think so at twenty-nine as he began to ready himself mentally and emotionally to take the major step, for a Negro, of running for Congress in a district overwhelmingly white. He would take support as it came, he decided. His own purposes and what he thought he could do for the two races were sufficiently important so that he could afford to be a little hurt if some people didn't love him for himself alone. He didn't love them for themselves alone, either, he was honest enough to acknowledge to himself; he loved them for their ability to help him get where he wanted to go, to the Congress of the United States.

The announcement that he would run brought the immediate and inevitable response that he had expected. Once again the hordes of the communications world descended upon him. In the election that year, no single campaign for House or Senate received the attention and publicity his did all across the nation. His opponent complained bitterly, but there were ways of taking care of that. The opponent was photographed at ridiculous angles, his voice emerged strangely high-pitched and squeaky from the television screen, the lighting and makeup made him look ill, the reportorial panels before which he appeared were ten times more hostile and severe in their questioning of him than they ever were of Cullee. On election night Cullee was elected by a majority of 30,000 votes. His wife ended a wildly exultant bout of love-making at 3 A.M. with a sardonic little laugh. "You know what that election was?" she said. "That was a bad conscience speaking. How long do you think that kind of support is going to last?"

This comment, so typical of the shrewd candor and casual cruelty that he had come to realize were paramount in her personality, had terminated the love-making, the exultation, and the state of euphoria in which he had been able to convince himself for a few short hours that he was really a symbol of a new era in race relations; but it was a good thing for him, and in time he came to thank her for it. It did not make him bitter, as she perhaps hoped it would, or make him uncertain and unsteady, as seemed to be an increasingly dominant purpose of hers; what it did was to make him more determined than ever to live up to the responsibility he had been given and so to conduct himself that the support that had been conferred with a bad conscience would be transmuted to a support grounded firmly in appreciation, gratitude, and respect.

Here, too, he was strengthened by his mother, descending with a valiant tenacity into the long horror of a terminal cancer discovered three months before his election. Her admonition that he was "going there to be a servant to the public—you be a good one" had increased, if increase were needed, his determination to do just that.

And in this aim, he thought he could honestly say now as he walked slowly along the green carpet, drawn back to the Delegates' Lounge by some impulse he understood very well but was helpless to fight however he despised it, he had been successful. There was a tolerance toward the newcomer in the Congress, he found, which smoothed the way for those who were able, diligent, devoted to their duties, and not too obviously concerned with the promotion of their own political advantage; and there was a disposition in the district, too, to give him a chance to prove himself now that he was in office. Neither he nor the voters knew exactly what they had on election night. By the end of his first term, both did. He had served them well, and they returned him by a much enlarged majority for a second term, and, two years later, for a third.

In the machinery of the House, composed with such subtlety of the rules men make for their own guidance and the human skill and error with which they uphold or evade them, he early found an enjoyable and effective place. There was a certain look-at-us-we're-being-tolerant air about the way his party's leadership pushed him forward, but the gruff common sense of the Speaker made it quite clear to him that if he had not measured up as a man this would have been forgotten as soon as suitable political profit had been secured. The Speaker, he made clear, would "go along with this kind of nonsense" just so far and no farther; he ran his dominion with an iron hand, and his bowings to political necessity were grudging and dispensed with as soon as possible. He apparently liked Cullee personally, with a genuine affection, and Cullee was pleased and flattered to accept a beneficence that he knew to be neither hypocritical nor self-interested. You always knew where you stood with the Speaker, which was why he was so powerful and mighty a man. Cullee, as he often found occasion to realize with thanks, stood very well.

So it was that he was appointed at the start of his first term to the Foreign Affairs Committee, one of three freshmen so honored; and so it was that he soon became a member of the Speaker's little group of favored young men, one of those who was selected to propose important bills, make crucial motions, offer major amendments, make major speeches. He realized that some of the same practical considerations that go into many a sudden surge to prominence in the House had gone into his own: he was black, the Administration wanted to appeal to the newly emergent states of Africa and Asia, it would be advisable to put him on Foreign Affairs, it would be advisable to give him a lot of publicity and use him as a spokesman on racial issues—and so on. Of such shrewd considerations, compounded of the thoughts and plans and purposes of powerful men in powerful places, is many a successful career composed, in Washington. But some, selected arbitrarily for honors on some such political basis as race, fail to measure up. Some take the ball and run with it. He did.

The encouragement he received imposed upon him, as he had explained to Orrin Knox, a major obligation to be responsible. It had come to mean something, to be Cullee Hamilton. He was conscious every day of the burden it imposed upon him to be decent and honorable, as one of the few Negroes so favored by his countrymen. He had enough pride of race and enough belief in the Constitution of the United States to regard this as his right; but in the deeper sense in which any man of integrity, black or white, approaches the honor of public office conferred freely by his fellow citizens, he knew also that it was a privilege, and one that he must always do his best to live up to.

Two things only troubled the foundations of his world, and they were of course the two things that meant the most and the two, he knew now as he once more entered the Delegates' Lounge and sensed the little excited flurry of looks and whispers that greeted his entry, he would either have to set right or do without in the crisis growing from the visit of Terence Ajkaje to the United States. One was his relationship with LeGage Shelby and the other was his marriage to Sue-Dan.

With LeGage his friendship over the years had undergone subtle but definite changes as he had gone down one road and his brilliant, impatient roommate had gone down another. 'Gage had moved more and more toward the violent elements in the Negro struggle for full equality in the United States—never, until now, far enough to lose contact with the middle ground that Cullee instinctively felt to be the indispensable foundation for the leadership LeGage was gradually building up with his incessant speechmaking, article-writing and statement-issuing, but farther than Cullee ever was ready to follow him. This of course had only increased the tensions of their close but uneasy personal relationship. Patiently over the years Cullee had taken upon himself the burden of being kind, of being patient, of assuming the blame for misunderstandings and making the excuses for angry arguments growing out of differing natures and a different approach. It never occurred to him that LeGage, in some terribly grinding way that 'Gage had lightly and quite to his own surprise admitted to Felix Labaiya, had always felt a fearful inferiority toward him. Cullee was too direct to be subtle in his personal relationships, and because he approached everyone on the same level of friendly courtesy, he would have been astounded to know the full extent of LeGage's jealousies. He knew there were some, but he assumed them to spring only from the fact that he had achieved in public office the recognition that LeGage professed to want for him, but perhaps did not, entirely. The deeper psychological twistings of his roommate's nature he neither perceived nor could have fully understood had he perceived them. Thus he did not really understand their ability to make him at times so unhappy. A feeling of baffled hurt was the extent of his reaction; but that was more than enough to keep him in a state of tension concerning LeGage that was as bothersome in its own way as LeGage's constant state of tension about him.

On the political plane, of course, the differences were sharper, the basic arguments clearer, the clashes harsher and more open. Right now they were at their peak in the wake of his decision to accept Orrin Knox's suggestion, to introduce his resolution of apology to Terry, to adopt the role of Administration advocate on a basis of moderation that LeGage was moving rapidly away from as his own impatience found its answer in the rising impatience of the younger Negro generation in the United States. In a very real sense, Cullee knew, he was risking his position with his own race by continuing to pursue a policy of moderation. It was not a fair charge, but one that could be given a glaze of superficial plausibility—and superficial plausibility was all it took to sway many minds in this careless age—that his moderation sprang not from his own nature but from a desire to appease and preserve his white base of support in his plans for political advancement. He knew this was not the case, he was pretty sure LeGage knew it, but he was coming to understand that LeGage had reached a point at which he was beginning to take leave of fairness, was beginning to abandon justice, was beginning to sacrifice their friendship to his own ambitions and the ravenous demands of his followers.

This could mean only that one or the other of them must change his position, or their friendship with all its memories and shared ideals would be gone forever. He did not honestly see how he could change his, however bleak and lonely this certainty made him feel.

Sue-Dan—Sue-Dan was another matter. He had been obsessed with her the day they met; he would, he suspected, be obsessed with her to the day he died. She always had one advantage, he had often thought bitterly as she had sided increasingly with LeGage in their running battles over race: she could always spread her legs, and he'd come running. At first this had been wonderful, and in the opening years of their marriage he had felt humbly grateful that he had found a wife who could give him such satisfaction. Two bodies did not always go together that completely; theirs did, and it was a great happiness. But there came a time when he realized that this was jeopardizing his independence, sapping his determination, suborning his integrity. Their arguments did not end in conclusions, but in sex; and that was no ending. Increasingly Sue-Dan, like LeGage, had attempted to control and dominate his thinking, persuade him to change his views, lead him in directions a stubborn steadiness told him he should not go; and she had a weapon LeGage did not have, and used it as coolly and calculatingly as she knew how.

But Cullee Hamilton, thank God, had more to him than that. Increasingly in these recent years sex had not been enough to bring him to her way of thinking, and as she began to realize it she had begun to react with the waspish carping that had become noticeably sharper in the days since Terry had decided to escort a little girl to school. He felt that she was still devoted to his personal advancement, and the idea of being the wife of the first Negro Senator since Reconstruction appealed to her own pride and self-esteem; but she could not resist the acid comment, the extra dig, the debilitating, weakening, dismaying comment that sought to find in destruction of a competing ego the dominion that could not be found in love. And still his body ached for her, whatever she did, whatever she said. He despised himself for it, hated himself for it, told himself he was a weakling and a fool—and still came back.

Except that now he did not know whether he would come back; and the bleakness and loneliness he felt at the prospect of losing LeGage's friendship was as nothing compared with the bleakness and loneliness he felt at the prospect of losing Sue-Dan. Yet it had come at last to the issue, and he felt that here no more than there could he make the final sacrifice of integrity that was demanded of him.

And so once again, as on the day a week ago when he had stood in the Senate and hardly known what was going on because he was so deeply involved in thinking about his personal problems, he found himself adrift on the angry sea of turmoil and emotional upset that always seemed to surround those two people. As long as he had known them both, it occurred to him with a sudden deeply wounding bitterness, they had never given him peace of heart or mind. And yet they expected him to put up with them, and forgive them, and subordinate his own purposes and personality to theirs, and not expect much of anything in return except the chance to serve them and say, Yes, 'Gage, and Yes, Sue-Dan, and never keep an ounce of pride and independence for poor old Cullee.

Well, poor old Cullee this time had other fish to fry. Poor old Cullee had about decided that it was time to cut loose from both of them and their ideas on what to do about race, and how to humiliate the white man, and all the rest of it. Their whole approach was sick, sad, pathetic, and self-defeating, and he as a member of the Congress of the United States knew it even if they didn't.

And yet—and yet. So steady was his temperament and so fair his nature that even to them he could not be unjust. Maybe they were right after all. Maybe all those who said you had to resort to violent measures or live forever under the white man's intolerant and self-interested domination were correct. They weren't living under it any more in most of Africa. Why should they live under it any more in America, where men were supposed to be created equal and have an equal chance to make good on their own merits? Why should they tolerate any more, in this chaotic twentieth century, the sort of nonsense that said the color of a man's skin had anything to do with his essential worth? Wasn't he really, perhaps, being just an Uncle Tom, a white man's stooge, a middle-of-the-roader trying to maintain an impossible position even as the road was washing away from under him? Wasn't he really, perhaps, being just a pawn of white man's politics with his resolution and his attempts to be fair and his foolish desire for integrity? Why did he think he had all the answers, and Sue-Dan and 'Gage were so wrong?

And why did he think, he told himself with the deepest self-scarification of all, why did he think that he could fool himself into thinking that his confusion had any other basis than it did? Why did he think he could deny to himself what was really gnawing at his heart, the bonds of friendship and the chains of love? LeGage, for all his tiresome jealousies and difficult hypersensitivities, was his oldest, nearest friend, closer to him than a brother. Sue-Dan, for all her sarcastic and cutting attitudes, was his wife, after whose body he lusted as hotly as he ever had. Even now as he looked about the room for the faces he knew instinctively he would not find, he felt the stirring in his thighs that always began at the sight of her, the sound of her, the smell of her, the thought of her. It didn't matter what she said or what she did; she had him where he was most helpless and he couldn't seem to do anything about it. And in a different sense, though nearly as commanding, he was held in the ties of youth and memory and gallant dreams and shared ideals to LeGage.

Had his wife and his friend been in the room at that moment, and had they been capable of the imagination and perception to approach him with the face of love, he would have withdrawn his resolution, abandoned his fight for moderation, perhaps become as intolerant and impatient as they. But they were gone, and although they did not know it, their moment to recapture him was also gone.

And yet—and yet he missed them both with such a terrible hunger and unhappiness that he did not know, at that moment, whether he would have the strength to continue on his middle road when the moment came, as come it must, to make the final decision and bid them final farewell.

It was no wonder, therefore, that he showed a blank and unseeing visage to the hostile, sneering eyes of Ghana and Guinea, the skeptical glances of Brazil and Ceylon, the quizzical examinations of India and the U.A.R. as he turned blindly and left the noisy Lounge to start his personal search for honor without betrayal and integrity with love.

2

"You understand, of course," the little owl-eyed man said in his dark green office in the Medical Service on the fifth floor of the Secretariat, "that seizures of this type are quite frequently caused by some deep-seated psychosomatic—"

"I understand," Hal Fry interrupted bluntly from behind the screen of pain that seemed to be separating him from the world, "that we've been all over that before, and there's nothing to it. How many times do I have to tell you that it isn't overwork, it isn't tiredness, it isn't my love life—"

"Have you got any?" the little man interrupted quickly. "Are you sure you've told me all you want to tell me, in that area?"

"I don't want to tell you a damned thing. And I don't think I have, either."

"Ah, I thought there was something you were ashamed of. You wouldn't have been trying so hard to conceal it, if there weren't."

"What in the *hell* have I been trying to conceal? You haven't asked me and I haven't told you. I don't see that it has any bearing—"

"Come, come, of course it has a bearing. Our sexual lives have a bearing on everything we do. Yours does. Mine does. Everybody's d—"

"Are you married?" Hal Fry demanded abruptly. The little man gave a sudden blink.

"Yes."

"Happily?"

"We're temporarily separated," the little man said stiffly, "but that's neither here nor th—"

"Ah," Senator Fry said, though the terrible dizziness was back in his head and he didn't know how many more seconds he would be able to maintain this whimsy without fainting, "that accounts for your nervous manner, then."

"What nervous manner?" the little man demanded sharply. "I haven't a nerv— Now, see here," he said coldly. "Suppose you stop playing games and let's get on with this. Obviously you're suffering from some sort of sexual maladjustment. How do you and your wife react to one another during coitus?"

"We don't react at all," Hal Fry said, and a sudden little expression of pain, unassociated with the pain now ravaging his chest and abdomen, came into his eyes. His inquisitor perceived it with a triumphant cry.

"So! You don't react at all! And you're trying to tell me you don't have a sexual prob—"

"My wife died ten years ago," Hal Fry said. "Assuming it's any of your business."

"Well," the little owl-eyed man said. "Well. I'm sorry. Then obviously you're reacting from a lack of sexual outlet. Do you have a mistress?"

"No, I don't have a mistress! How much longer is this nonsense going to go on?"

"Now, see here. You came to me. I didn't come to you. If you have a problem and want my help, well and good. If not, there's nothing I can do and we might as well stop wasting each other's time."

"You're supposed to diagnose medical ailments," Hal Fry said bitterly, "not parrot all this guff that has no bearing."

"It has a bearing. A history of a marriage that was basically unhappy, followed by a long period of widowerhood without adequate outlet—"

"Who said my marriage was basically unhappy? And what do you know about my outlets?"

"I can tell," the little man said, not without a trace of smugness. "Was it happy?"

"Why should I tell you?"

"Ah," the little man said with satisfaction. "You see, I was right. And the shame of whatever it was you did that made it unhappy, followed by ten years of abstinence or unsatisfactory temporary liaisons, has finally culminated in a psychosomatic physical reaction that is—"

"Now, see here," Senator Fry said, "I wish you'd stop talking all this damned nonsense and try to find out what is really wrong with me. Right at this moment I can barely see you—my vision seems to have some sort of red shadow over it—and I have terrible cramps in my stomach and my head feels like the devil and I think if I had to walk across the room I'd fall flat on my face from weakness. And raking up my past won't help."

"It was an unhappy past, then," the little owl-eyed man said softly, staring at him with a wide-eyed candor. "The pattern is quite classic. The unhappy marriage, the guilt complex, the years of regret and frustration, all leading up to a psychiatric collapse of one sort or another. You have children?" he demanded abruptly.

"Why should I tell you anything?" Hal Fry asked through the agonizing vise that had clamped itself abruptly on his chest. "I have a son."

"How old is he?"

"Nineteen."

"Is he with you?"

"He's nearby."

"In school?"

"No."

"Oh," the little man said with a quick, pouncing softness. "In an institution?"

"Why should I tell you anything?"

"I see," the little man said, nodding thoughtfully. "Yes, that would explain it. The marriage made unhappy by the mentally defective child, the guilt feeling, the bitterness, the early death of the wife, the years of trying to find something to fill the emptiness, the futile searching for activities to occupy a life—"

"Look," Hal Fry said savagely, "I am a Senator of the United States. If you don't think that's enough to occupy a life, you're crazy. I don't have time to turn around, I have so much to occupy my life. So what does that do to your silly theories?"

"Look inside yourself," the little man said softly. "Study your own reactions. Analyze your own sickness. You'll see. Then come back and we will see what we can do about it together."

"I wouldn't come back to you if I were dying." The little man smiled, a calm, superior smile.

"You're not dying. You're just very much confused. A week from now, two weeks, a day maybe, you'll be back telling me I'm right."

"But I am *not well*," Hal Fry said desperately, for now all his symptoms seemed to be attacking him at once and he literally did not know whether he could stand up and walk. "I have duties and responsibilities I must fulfill. I must get well. You are being no help to me at all."

"I have been the greatest help to you that any man could be, for I have given you the key to unlock your own illness. You will thank me for it before long. Wait and see."

"I'm sick," Senator Fry repeated hopelessly, "and I must get well."

"You *are* sick," the little man agreed, "and you *will* get well. If you want to."

"I think," Hal said, managing to rise and surprised to find that he could move, slowly and carefully but without falling, toward the door, "that you are insane. I think you are insane from an insufferable arrogance of intellect and pride that will not let you make an honest diagnosis, because you know that if you tried to, you couldn't."

"Patients often get abusive when they are forced to face themselves." The little owl-eyed man turned away indifferently to the papers on his desk. "Come back and see me when you are ready to get well."

"I'll die before I come back to you."

"You won't die. Come back when you are ready."

And that, Hal Fry thought as he walked with an unsteady determination out of the office, past the pretty little Indonesian nurse who smiled sympathetically to him as he went, and down the corridor to the elevator, was about the best you could expect from these overtrained, oversexed, and overtheorized doctors who tried to read into everybody else their own sick frustrations. All the little man had accomplished was to instill the seed of doubt, to unnerve him, to rake up the past and make him feel even unhappier than he already was, to weaken and sap his strength of will and fortitude of character at a point at which he was coming rapidly to the conclusion that strength of will and fortitude of character were about all he had left to go on.

"I *am* sick," he repeated in a stubborn whisper as he waited for the elevator to take him down to First Committee and the debate over Indonesia's threat to Australian New Guinea, "and I *must* get well."

But whether he would, and whether strength of will and fortitude of character would be enough to permit him to carry on his responsibilities here in the crucial days before the final vote on Felix Labaiya's amendment, he did not know. Yet he determined one thing as he stood there waiting. From this point forward, insofar as will and character could assist him, he would make no further admissions to anyone that he was feeling sick, he would do nothing to indicate to the world that he was not fully capable of discharging his duties in this time of crisis for his country, he would carry on to the best of his ability in the way in which he was needed.

He did not know what was wrong with him, but he knew it was something far more fundamental than N.Y.U.'s brightest student could possibly be direct and uncomplicated enough to perceive. Maybe by thinking very hard about the tasks ahead he could persuade himself and his body by a sheer feat of will that it was not so.

He took a deep breath, squared his shoulders, and stepped into the elevator, a set smile on his lips and his eyes straight ahead as the machine shot downward to First Committee.

South upon the Potomac, where men were as concerned as anywhere about the day's debate in the General Assembly and the fate of Cullee Hamilton's resolution in the Congress of the United States, the senior Senator from South Carolina was thinking at a furious rate as he presided, apparently half asleep, over an afternoon session of the Senate Appropriations Committee. Justice Department witnesses were before the committee, and Seab Cooley was listening with an ominous benevolence as the Attorney General made an earnest appeal for additional funds to finance the assignment of special United States marshals "in case of emergency." The phrase brought the reaction everyone had been awaiting from the chairman.

"Now, Mr. Attorney General," he said gently, stirring awake and giving the witness a shrewd glance from his hooded old eyes, "would you tell the committee, are these emergencies you *discover*, or emergencies you *create*?"

"Emergencies that come to us for solution, Mr. Chairman," the Attorney General said, rather tartly. "I don't believe it is our policy to go out of our way to create emergencies unnecessarily."

"You don't believe it is your policy to go out of your way to create emergencies unnecessarily."

"No, sir."

"No, sir. No, sir. Well, I'm glad to hear that." He smiled blandly and the sudden tension that had come upon the alert young men of the Attorney General's staff eased somewhat. "You may proceed, Mr. Attorney General."

"Oops!" whispered the Dallas *News* to the Los Angeles *Times* at the press table. "Thought we were going to have a story there, for a second."

"Seab's just going through the motions," the *Times* whispered back. "I don't think his heart is in it today."

And, if truth were known, this press table analysis of the chairman's rather absent-minded manner was correct. His heart was not in it. In fact, his heart felt tired, and old, and, quite uncharacteristically, discouraged.

It was not like Seabright B. Cooley, who had smitten his enemies hip and thigh when they attacked him in Gath and fell upon him in Ashkelon, to feel put upon and bothered by the world, but today he did. He had been following certain matters very closely, without saying anything to anyone about it, and just before the committee session began he had stopped by the paperstand near the public elevators at the entrance to the Senate side of the Capitol and dropped in his coin for the late edition of the Washington *Daily News*. "CULLEE HOLDS FINGER IN UN DIKE," the paper had announced with its customary cheerful insouciance. "WINS DELAY FOR US TO SPANK OURSELVES."

This rather carefree analysis of the debate and vote in the General Assembly was in fact, as often with the *News*, rather closer to the realities and the Washington reaction than many people cared to admit. "Of all the damned things," Bill Kanaho had snorted, stopping by to read over Seab's shoulder. "Why in hell should we be humbling ourselves again?" Seab had nodded and made a mental note of the name of Hawaii's senior Senator as one who, despite his racial background, might be a tried and trusted ally in the bitter struggle that would ensue when Cullee's resolution reached the Senate— if it reached the Senate. But of that the senior Senator from South Carolina had few illusions and little doubt. The cards were stacked in the House, and everything his spies over there told him only served to emphasize the fact. It was now Saturday afternoon, and present plans were to bring the resolution to the House floor on Monday and ram it through under a tight limitation of debate that could bring a decision by nightfall.

This situation was, of course, attributable principally to the one man to whom such bursts of legislative speed in the House were almost always attributable. The Speaker, who moved in obvious and powerful ways his wonders to perform, had followed up his success in bringing the resolution out of the Foreign Affairs Committee yesterday on a 15–13 vote by arranging for the House Rules Committee to meet later this afternoon and approve the debate rule for Monday. Even with the parliamentary delaying tactics permissible under House rules, this would probably mean a final vote not later than 9 or 10 P.M.; assuming, of course, that the narrow vote in the Foreign Affairs Committee did not accurately reflect the divided sentiment in the House, and assuming also that Seab's southern friends would not stand together. If the South remained solid and the House was as divided as the Foreign Affairs vote indicated, then the resolution might be stopped in the chamber of its birth and Seab would not have to fight it in the Senate.

Of this pleasant and desirable outcome, however, he was not at all positive as he heard, with just enough attention to make the Attorney General nervous, that hard-working official's concluding paragraphs. Jawbone Swarthman had shown toward the Speaker the same qualities of malleable timidity that had made Seab sponsor his political career in the first place; the only trouble was that this time he had shown them toward the Speaker instead of toward his senior Senator, and this defection had left Seab feeling like a parent stabbed by his own child. Jawbone had called him right away, of course, apologizing profusely, and had explained that his decision to vote with the majority to bring the Hamilton resolution out of committee had simply been due to "pressures over here that you understand, Senator, sure you do." Seab had said dryly that he did, but that he had a few pressures himself to exert against Jawbone in South Carolina and perhaps it was time he did so. For the first time this threat had not produced its customary result. Jawbone had said merely, "Yes, well, you know how it is, Senator," and this vague response had been more alarming to Senator Cooley than any amount of open defiance. It had indicated quite clearly that Representative Swarthman, too, thought he was slipping and was no longer quite so afraid of his vengeance as he had always been heretofore. Of course Jawbone had assured him, sure now, sure now, that he would oppose the Hamilton resolution when it reached the floor of the House.

"You don't think I'd let that little old resolution get through the House, now, do you, Senator?" he had demanded indignantly. "Speaker wanted it out of committee, so I let it get out, but you sure enough don't think I'd stand for that kind of nonsense on the floor, do you?"

"Will you speak against it?" Senator Cooley had asked quickly, and Representative Swarthman had replied without a moment's hesitation, "Got to, Senator. Got to!" But whether he would if the Speaker got sufficiently threatening, Senator Cooley was not at all sure. Jawbone might just do what he had done before at crucial moments, duck out home and not come back until it was all over.

And of course behind the Speaker stood the President and Orrin Knox, playing their game of global politics and try-to-please-everybody which, as he had told Orrin the night he had eaten dinner at his house, simply could not work in the face of all the fantastic and unending pressures confronting the United States. He had not heard from the Secretary since he had attacked him and set in motion the wave of press condemnation of Cullee as the stooge for Orrin's political ambitions, and he told himself with a grim little smile now that he wasn't about to make the first move. Orrin could beat him in the House, if he got the Speaker and everybody else lined up, but he would have a tougher time of it in the Senate and he knew it.

Even so, the Senator from South Carolina was uneasy and disturbed. He was seventy-six and the winds of time were blowing about him. Added to them now were the winds of change in a hurrying, heedless century. He did not know whether he could withstand the two of them together.

"That was a powerfully moving statement, Mr. Attorney General," he said with a sleepy sarcasm. "We will try to take all you say into account when we put our grubby little hands upon your bill."

"I think," the President said as the early sunfall of autumn began to sift across the White House lawn and throw a golden light into his oval office, "that the best thing is to make them a simple offer without any strings attached. Export-Import Bank can do it, or the Bank for International Development. Or I may even be able to lay my hands on a couple of million somewhere in the Defense Department budget. The important thing is to get to them fast."

"Without strings attached," Bob Munson echoed rather dryly. The President smiled.

"Well, only one, of course—that Felix withdraw his amendment and behave."

"Mr. President," Orrin Knox said with some irony, "you are not trying to tell us that the President of the United States is resorting to international bribery. How shocking."

"The President of the United States is doing his best to protect the United States," the President said calmly. "It is a duty he has."

"And one that Felix won't be moved by in this instance, I'll bet," Senator Munson said. "I'm afraid there's something deeper there that can't be bought off with a gift of a few millions."

"I agree," the President said. "But, after all, Felix isn't the government of Panama."

"Yet," the Secretary of State said. He frowned. "I wonder if it would do any good to talk to Patsy."

"Assuming there is anything left of that marriage," the President said, "perhaps so. But is there? Lucille tells me there isn't."

"The feminine grapevine," Senator Munson said, "is something beyond the comprehension of mere man. Dolly tells me the same thing. Senator Bessie Adams tells me the same thing. No doubt Beth tells you, too, Orrin. But there are still plenty of reasons why Felix wouldn't want it to collapse just now. He isn't President of Panama, and he needs the Jason family for a while yet. God help us when he becomes so, however."

"He will," the President said. "Of that I am convinced. In the meantime, as long as a reasonable man sits in *La Presidencia*, we've got a chance to stop this present monkey business."

"Perhaps we can also dislodge Felix," Orrin said, "or at least set back his timetable a while. Suppose I ask Hal Fry to make the offer direct to him at the UN and meanwhile let his government know about it in an informal way. Then if he turns it down he should get a reaction from home. It might give him pause."

"Of course," the President said thoughtfully, "he must have the support of his government in offering his amendment or he wouldn't offer it."

"I don't think so," Orrin said. "He occupies a rather peculiar semi-independent position down there because of his father. He's been excused a great deal already because of Louie, and the same tolerance apparently extends to what he does at the UN—up to a point. Maybe we can arrange for this to be the point."

"I hope so," the President said. "Maybe we can also offer something along the lines of giving Panama more say on the Canal Board. That might be more appealing than money."

"He's obsessed with the Canal, of course," Orrin said, "and of course so are they all. It may make it difficult to create a division, but at least we'll try. I'll talk to Hal."

"Good," Senator Munson said. "Meanwhile, back at the Capitol, there is the little matter of passing Cullee Hamilton's resolution. I understand the Speaker has the skids greased in the House, but you know the Senate. Those who grease skids in that great body sometimes find themselves sliding down ass-over-teakettle while those who were supposed to slide stand on the sidelines and give out with the merry heehaw. Sentiment is very divided on my side of the Hill, however smoothly Bill's machine may be operating."

"I'm not so sure it is," the Secretary of State said. "The reports I get are of considerable uncertainty there, too. It's going to be a very close vote, I think, and that of course will encourage all the skittish in the Senate. You have your work cut out for you once again, dear Robert."

"Great," the Majority Leader told him. "Dolly and I were supposed to be boarding the *Leonardo da Vinci* this morning to sail for lovely Italy and the golden isles of Greece. Here I am in Washington, plotting crafty stratagems. There ought to be a law."

"I'd veto it if there were," the President said with his comfortable smile. "Another week of work won't hurt anybody, even if it has been a long session. The problems of the world don't diminish."

"Lord, no," Bob Munson said. "How reliable is young Cullee, Orrin?"

"He has troubles. I believe his wife and LeGage Shelby and a lot of his own press and people are after him for not being radical enough. And for being a stooge of the Secretary of State, in Seab's handy phrase."

"Can he stand the gaff, do you think?" the President asked. "It's my impression he will, but one never knows when the pressure grows."

"It will test him," Orrin said. "But he's been tested before."

"Not like this, though," Bob Munson said. "It's different when your own people turn against you."

"Well, of course, a great many of them won't," Orrin said. "It's only the noisier elements who will. He can assess that for what it's worth. We're all going to have to bolster him up, however, both when he's up there and when he's down here for that House vote on Monday."

"Talk to Hal about that, too," the President suggested. "How is Hal?"

"I don't quite know," the Secretary of State said thoughtfully. "It's hard to tell. Lafe thinks he has something seriously wrong with him, and I think he does too. But the doctor he's gone to at the UN can't seem to find anything."

"Maybe just overwork. Should we send him on vacation for a while?"

"I don't think he'd go. He conceives it to be his duty to stay there. I expect it would do more damage to take him off than to leave him on."

"It's a tough time. We've got to be able to rely on him."

"I trust him to tell me when he needs a rest," Orrin said. "When he tells me, I'll relieve him. You know Hal's problems. It's the least we can do."

"All right. I'll trust you to trust him. Just keep an eye on it, though."

"Lafe is," the Secretary of State said. "I've put him on a special detail . . . And speaking of Seab, Bob—"

"Ah, yes," the Majority Leader said, "speaking of Seab." He sighed and shook his head soberly. "Our old friend may be about to meet his Waterloo. The times are against him. The world is against him. Right is against him. I'll try to protect him as much as I can, but—"

"I think we all should," the President said with equal soberness. "Fifty years of service to the country demands some kindness and respect, whatever you may think of him on individual issues."

"Imagine!" the Secretary said in a bemused tone. "Who ever thought we'd have to talk about protecting Seab?"

"It will come to us all," the Majority Leader said softly. "May we have friends so loyal when the time arrives."

"I wish I were certain we were doing the right thing in this resolution," the President said slowly. "But I find out in this job that one is never certain of anything. There are always a dozen sides to it, so you make up your mind as best you can and go ahead. You can't stand still."

"The curse of our times," said the Secretary of State. "The compulsion to move. Just move, it doesn't matter where, as long as you keep moving. There's no time to plan, to study, to think things through. The world whirls too fast, and if you don't stay on the merry-go-round, you get thrown off."

"I wonder if they're as uncertain in Moscow," the Majority Leader said.

The President smiled.

"There is a gap between those of us who are responsible to an electorate and those who are responsible to no one but themselves. But I live in the faith that judgment will be rendered upon them in due course."

"So do we all," said Orrin Knox. "I'll talk to Hal."

"Do that," the President said. "Give my love to Seab, Bob. In fact, tell him I'd like to see him, if he cares to come down."

"Better call him yourself," the Majority Leader suggested. "He's not much of a one for liking intermediaries, at his age."

"I'll wait until the chips are really down," the President said, "and then maybe I will. Meantime, Orrin, you take care of Felix."

"I'll try," the Secretary of State said as they rose to go, "but it won't be easy

. . . Are you all right?" he asked, with a sudden shrewd glance at the President. The latter sighed.

"I'm a little sad about the world. But that's a chronic condition. Aren't we all?"

For the Ambassador of Panama, as evening deepened into night and Manhattan came ablaze, there were no such philosophic musings, for indeed he had no time for them in the wake of the Assembly vote to delay consideration of his amendment pending Congressional action on the Hamilton Resolution. He had been astounded by the vote, because four days of intensive politicking in the corridors, the lounges, and delegation headquarters of the United Nations had persuaded him that he had a sufficient margin of support to block any such delaying tactics. Now he was tagged with at least a partial failure, and he was too experienced a student of men and events not to know that the partial failure, barring some sharp reversal or effective change of position, was heading toward a total failure when the Assembly cast its final judgment on his amendment.

As things stood now, two-thirds would be necessary to pass it, and no two-thirds had been on his side on the question of delay. Delay usually brought attrition rather than accretion when the issue was as controversial and close-fought as this. Of the possibilities he was considering to reverse the trend, the simplest and most effective would be for Cullee Hamilton to abandon his own resolution in the Congress and join in the condemnation of his country which seemed to come so easily to so many American Negroes. How it could come easily to Cullee after his statements in the Assembly, however, Felix could not see, unless there were pressures of some major kind brought to bear. And what they were, he could not perceive, except the obvious ones of Sue-Dan and LeGage and the general hullabaloo of the radical Negro groups and press, encouraged and inflamed by certain white groups and commentators.

Certainly, he thought with a frown on his small, neat features, the pressures did not include persuasion from Felix's brother-in-law. Cullee's speech had certainly indicated a growing impatience with the Governor and his family, even though there was so far no comparable indication that Ted Jason was becoming impatient with him. Ted still hoped, Felix reflected with some scorn, that he could win Cullee's support for his Presidential ambitions despite Cullee's apparent inclination to side with Orrin Knox. At least the Congressman had volunteered to act as errand boy for the Secretary's resolution, and that was sign enough that he was inclining toward him in the nomination battle that loomed next year. But Ted still hoped, apparently, and perhaps he was right to. In the politics of the great Republic, Felix had observed, time wrought startling changes, and many men who said this thing this day were found tomorrow to be saying something else.

So he had perhaps best not worry too much about Governor Jason and concentrate instead on how to encourage the other pressures that might bring Cullee around. At the same time, he must also intensify his efforts within the UN, where some who had assured him blandly of their support before the roll was called had been found among the opposition when they cast their votes. Brazil, for instance, attempting as usual to prove to the world that she was independent of absolutely everybody. And Colombia, possibly afraid of him and what he might do if he became—when he became—President of Panama.

Of course Washington had not been idle, either, in the days preceding the vote. There had been sudden approval of certain long-pending international loans, conferences between the Secretary of State and, in some cases, the President himself and certain Ambassadors. Promises had been made, admonitions delivered, assistance proffered or withheld. He would say for Orrin Knox and the outwardly bumbling Executive who sat at 1600 Pennsylvania that they had not been willing to let the issue go by default. Some very shrewd international politics had been played; and, fortified by the activities of the delegation here in New York, what he had believed to be his own solid majority had been turned into a successful, if narrow, one for them.

Now, he supposed in bitter anticipation, he could expect another conference call from the Jason family, another suggestion, twice as strong, that he be content with having made his record and not pursue the matter further. Well: he had much more of a record to make, and he was not going to abandon it now. That final vote—win, lose, or draw—on his amendment was necessary to his future, and he would not be deflected from his purpose for one minute by anybody.

He made up his mind, as he finished dressing for dinner and began turning over the names of favorite restaurants where he might eat before going on to the dance being given in the Delegates' Dining Room by the delegation of Nigeria, that he would give further and intensive thought to one or two other ideas which might yet put a new and more favorable complexion on things before the issue was finally decided. Felix, grandson of Jorge, was not through yet.

He was giving his room a last glance before leaving, a determined expression on his darkly handsome face, when the phone rang and he received, much to his surprise, an invitation from the acting head of the United States delegation to have dinner at Chateaubriand before going on to the dance at the UN. With a tight little ironic smile on his lips and a quizzical little light in his eyes as he spoke quickly into the telephone, he told Hal Fry that Yes, he'd be delighted.

The drinks came, the food came, the wine came, the coffee came. And when, Felix asked himself impatiently, are we going to get down to business? His host, he decided, looked tense and somewhat strained, and there crossed his mind the rumor in the Delegates' Lounge that Senator Fry was unwell. He decided to put an end to shadowboxing and ask, for whatever it might be worth in throwing his opponent off balance.

"How are you feeling, Hal? You don't look so well, lately. I hope it's nothing serious."

"Just a little overwork, probably," Senator Fry said, and by the effort of will that he found necessary sooner or later in all conversations now, he managed to sound sufficiently unconcerned. "You've kept us on the jump so much these last few days that I've hardly had time to take a nap. We hope," he said with a reasonably comfortable smile, "that you have reached your high-water mark and will now recede."

"I am not prepared to admit that yet," Felix said stiffly.

"No, I wouldn't," Senator Fry agreed. "Poor strategy. But if you have to, I am authorized by my government to make the event more palatable."

"We do not want American bribes," the Ambassador of Panama said in the same tone. "Do you have any realization of how much ground you have lost by trying to buy off votes here in the UN?"

"Apparently not enough for you to beat us," Hal Fry said tartly. His companion frowned.

"We haven't voted on the amendment yet. We shall see."

"Indeed we shall," Hal said with an equal coldness, wondering if the nausea he felt would permit him to conclude the conversation with dignity. "In the meantime, my government is prepared to offer yours a loan of two million dollars and—just wait, Felix, don't give me that superior smile of yours until you hear it all—give Panama vice-chairmanship of the military government of the Canal and additional representation on the board of directors of the Canal Company. In return you will withdraw your amendment here."

For several minutes the Ambassador of Panama remained silent, a frown on his face and thoughts darting visibly behind his dark eyes. Then he looked up with an air of scornful puzzlement.

"Why are you doing this? It's like shooting a mosquito with a shotgun. The concessions are out of all proportion to the issue. Why is it this important to you?"

Senator Fry made an impatient movement.

"Oh, come off it, Felix. The last thing in the world that you do well is be ingenuous. Why is it so important to you? Why is it so important to the Soviet Union? Why is it so important to Africa and Asia? You tell me. If it is that important to all of you to attack the United States, then it is that important to the United States to fight back. So don't give me any of that 'why is it so important' guff. It doesn't become you."

"It is only an amendment in the United Nations," Felix said sardonically, "where all men do is talk. Why should that be of such great concern to your great country? Surely a few words passed here will have no effect upon the course of world events or the success of the United States in the working out of her noble destiny."

"In some other world, no," Hal Fry said, taking a swallow of brandy and feeling it burn on down into the chaos in his insides. "In any rational world, where the UN acted responsibly upon the matters before it, no. But this is not such a world. So it matters. The offer is being communicated to your government also, but we are giving you the first refusal."

"That is a childish move," the Ambassador said angrily. "Do you really think you can embarrass me by that?"

"It is our hope," Hal Fry said calmly. "What do you hear from Ted and Patsy? Backing you 100 per cent, I'll bet."

A strange, bleak expression came over the handsome face across the table, and when the Ambassador of Panama spoke it was in a strange, remote voice.

"Does anyone really think that I can be deflected from my purposes in this world? How little you all know me. How very little."

"I am sorry," Hal Fry said gravely. "I did not realize. I shall get the word to my government and yours right away. And we shall beat you on your amendment."

"Why would I care?" Felix asked in the same odd tone. "The record is what matters to me in this, not the result. And do not be too confident. Cullee Hamilton's resolution is not through the Congress yet. And who knows how firmly Cullee will stand?" He stood up abruptly. "I shall tell my government myself. Thank you for the dinner."

"Tell Patsy and Ted, too," Senator Fry suggested, but he doubted the Ambassador heard as he walked with blind swiftness across the lavish room to get his hat and coat.

So much for that, he thought as he paid the bill and walked out into the sharpening autumn night. He had not had any hope for the idea, nor had Orrin when he called. It had just been worth a try on the outside chance that Felix might respond. But the Panamanian Ambassador, he realized, was farther gone down his lonely road than any of them had guessed.

And, of course, despite Hal's confident air, Felix was entirely right on one thing: Cullee's resolution was not through Congress yet, and unless it did go through Felix might still secure the condemnation of the United States that in this weird, unbuttoned age could mean so much incalculable and far-reaching damage in the eyes of the world.

At the corner waiting for a cab, he noticed again the strange reddish tinge over the signal lights and hesitated to move, not knowing whether the light was with him or against him. Dear God, he thought as a sudden pain shot through his chest and a wave of dizziness swept over his body, help me, help me, help me.

And somehow, he must still find, if he could in the night city whose life rushed by him on all sides, the Congressman from California, whom none of them had seen since early afternoon, and let him know he still had friends. Orrin thought this might be necessary in the wake of the bitternesses aroused by the day's debate, and he thought so too, particularly after Felix's final, equivocal warning. If, that is, the Lord permitted him to stay on his feet. He was not at all sure that He would, as he stood there hesitating.

"Botten-booden-dooden-daddy," the enormous Negro on the drums said into the microphone at his elbow with a bored and drooling emphasis. "Botten-booden-dooden-daddy-*doo*."

And botten-booden to you too, you silly bastard, Cullee Hamilton thought wearily through the haze that filled the little room off 138th Street and Lexington. Just botten booden-dooden right up your—

"Now, honey," the girl at his elbow told him with her silly laugh, "you stop that old thinking, now. You just stop. All you done ever since we met is just think and think and think and *think*. What's the matter with you, anyway?"

"I like to think," he said. "Did you ever try it?"

"Honey, you shouldn't ought to talk to me like that," his companion said in an aggrieved tone. "Of course I think. Now and then, when I'm not"— she gave a shriek of laughter that passed unnoticed in the general gabble and babble of drunken voices all around—"well, *you* know."

"No, I don't," he said. "When you're not what?"

"Botten-booten-dooden-daddy—*oh*," the drummer remarked mournfully. "Ba-dooten-bodden-dooten-*do!*"

"When I'm not making love to *you!*" she cried with a happy laugh.

"Why, you sweet thing," he said. "I didn't realize you had that in mind *at* all."

"Oh, *you!*" she screamed. "I bet you're just terrific."

"I manage," he said. "How about another drink?"

"I shouldn't," she said. "I just shouldn't, now. I won't be good for *any-thing*. Just not *anything*."

"I will," he said. "It makes me better. Hey, waiter! Two more here!"

"I hear you," the waiter said sullenly. "Who you think you are, King Kong?"

"Just get it," he said indifferently. "Get it for a lost man on a dark, dark night."

"Honey," his companion said, "you're a mystery to me, just a plain mystery. What is it—your wife cheating on you?"

"She may be, for all I know," he said, staring about the hectic little room with its hectic black faces crowded into every square inch, black bodies elbowing one another at tiny tables or standing crowded together along the walls. "Why should we worry about that?"

"We shouldn't," she cried. "We shouldn't! Let her go, Big Joe, let her go. Like the song says."

"That's right," he said. "There's a song for everything and everything for a song."

"Gimme that glass," she said, reaching for it and letting her arm trail across his chest. "You could give me the creeps, honey, if I let you. But I won't. We're going to be happy and forget all about everything."

"I'm sure," he said. "I'm sure of that. We'll creep right into bed and be happy. But don't forget H. J. Res. 23."

"What's that?" she asked. "Some new kind of medicine for the itch?"

"My itch," he said. "House Joint Resolution 23. But don't worry about it."

"Who are you, anyway, honey?" she said. "You great, big, handsome, mixed-up man?"

"Ba-botten-botten-dooden-do-doot," the drummer said with a significant emphasis. "Do-doot-botten."

"I'm Mr. A. Nonymous," he said. "Representative A. Nonymous. I'm the Prophet Cullee, going to lead you out of bondage. Don't you want to be led?"

"Honey," she said, "I just live around the corner. Why don't you forget all that and come along home with me?"

"Oh, I intend to," he said. "Just let me finish this drink and then we'll go and I'll forget all about it. I tried to find them, anyway, and I couldn't. Her folks claimed they didn't know where she was. I don't believe them, but the hell with them, anyway. All I want is you."

"Good," she said in a relieved tone. "You just come along now, and we won't think about *anything*."

"Ba-dooten," the drummer said as they went out. "Ba-dooten-dooten-dooten-*dooo*."

"I have an hour," he said five minutes later, just around the corner, "and then I have to go and be with a lot of very important people. *Very—important—people*."

"An hour's enough."

"That's it," he said a little later. "That's it, sister, that's *it*."

"That's *it*," said the junior Senator from Iowa gently. "That's *it*, thank you, thank you, thank you." He left his body where it was, propped his head up on his left hand, and looked down at her face close to his with his engaging boyish smile. "I am impressed with the advantages of Indonesian culture."

"You talk so much," she said, accepting a light for her cigarette. "Why do you always talk so much?"

"I am a man of worldly affairs, with many important things on my mind. It makes me garrulous. I'm sorry if it bothers you."

"Oh, no. It is just part of you, I suppose. As long as you are not nervous."

"Do I act nervous?" he asked in some surprise. "I was not aware of it."

"You act very—practiced. Perhaps nervous is not the word."

"I should hope not."

"Unhappy," she said, and his right hand, traveling slowly over her body, stopped abruptly.

"Oh. Are you a psychiatrist, too?"

"I am sorry."

"No, seriously. You have a point, possibly. If you think so, pursue it."

"It would only make you more unhappy."

"If there's anything I abominate," he said, with a grin between amusement and genuine annoyance, "it's these damned half-finished conversations with people I'm in bed with. It's no time to be cryptic, but sooner or later everybody tries to be. It's most annoying, really."

"I am very wrong," she said gravely. "You are very happy. Not even in Indonesia, land of happy people, is there anyone so happy."

He laughed and his right hand began again its slow, insistent traveling, up and down, and over and around, and back and forth, and up and down.

"You win," he said. "I lose . . . Is this all right?"

"Very nice," she said, pressing closer into the curve of his chest and arm. "Your friend the Senator Fry was in again today."

"Oh? He didn't tell me he was going to the doctor, although I urged him to. He was feeling very badly during the plenary session."

"He looked strained. I do not think he finds the doctor very satisfactory."

"Perhaps he should see someone else."

"I think so. That doctor is—" She gave the tiniest of chuckles, deep in her throat. "He is nervous, too, I think."

"Good God," he said with a humorous sound of protest. "Don't tell me you're going to compare us. I haven't seen him, but I can imagine: horn-rimmed glasses, big intense eyes, hairy arms, a squat body, a smug expression, a degree from Columbia or N.Y.U., and a sex life as messed up as Gaius Caligula's. Absolutely sure, of course, that he knows what's wrong with everybody else. I don't think that's what Hal needs right now."

"Nor I. I was talking to my husband about him this afternoon—"

"Ah, yes, your husband. The hope of Indonesian medicine in another couple of years."

"I think so," she said gravely. "He has an idea."

"Sometimes ideas from intelligent young men are helpful," he said with equal dignity. "And what," he said in a lighter tone, moving his hand a little faster, a little more delicately, not so roughly, frolicking it over her body as though it had a life of its own, "does Indonesia's white hope think it is?"

His hand stopped as abruptly as though paralyzed when she told him. He took in his breath in a sharp gasp and goose-pimples broke out on his body. She kissed him gently on the nipple.

"I know," she said softly. "It is terrifying and tragic, if true."

"But—" he said stupidly.

"My husband is quite positive, though of course, as in most medicine, it is simply a guess. But the idea came to him last week, I believe at once when I first mentioned the Senator to him. Since then he has been reading and investigating. I told you he is taking his internship at Harkness Pavilion. There are several cases there and he has been talking to their doctors. It mimics many things, of course, but certain basic details seem to fit."

"But wouldn't any doctor—" he began, and she shook her head against his arm.

"It mimics many things," she repeated, and smiled a little. "Even a hairy graduate of NYU could be fooled."

"Especially if he were already convinced it was something else and too arrogant to admit the possibility it might be what it is," he said bitterly.

"My husband is not arrogant," she said. "He thinks that may be what it is."

"I think I shall like your husband, when we meet. And apparently we soon will. My God," he added abruptly in a stricken tone. "Poor Hal. Poor Hal, poor Hal!"

"Of course we are not yet sure. Perhaps tests will show differently. There is one that is infallible. My husband thinks he should have it."

"But how can we get him to take it? He refuses to admit he's sick enough to go into the hospital for a full examination."

"You are his friend," she said simply. "Tell him to."

"He won't listen to me—" She put a finger on his lips.

"If you tell him as though you really mean it, he will listen. He is very fond of you, you know. He will listen."

"Yes. He must. My God, what a thing."

"Do not think of it now," she said gently. "It will be too much to bear, for a little while. Think of other things, and later you can be ready to think of it again." She turned toward him and took his hand in hers. "Do this," she said. "And this—and I will do this—"

"Yes," he said in a grateful whisper. "Yes. That's it. That's *it*."

"That's *it*," Terrible Terry said to the admiring ring of multicolored faces that surrounded him. "That's exactly why it's so impossible for the United States to stand in the path of history saying No. No one can say No to history. History says Yes."

"History says Yes," agreed the righteous young man from Kenya, with a portentous and self-conscious air. "We are history's Yes-sayers."

In the Delegates' Dining Room, chairs and tables removed, ceiling and pillars draped and decorated, lights aglow and floor thronged for the dance given by the delegation of Nigeria, there seemed to be at the moment more talking than dancing. Many little groups like the M'Bulu's stood about engaged in earnest conversation, broken by occasional outbursts of laughter at some particularly devastating sally at the expense of the Western powers. Here and there a few dancing couples, clad in the colorful robes of their native tribes, moved gracefully to the strains of the orchestra playing at one end of the room. The windows were thrown open onto the great concrete esplanade overlooking the East River, and across the dark hurrying water the lights of Brooklyn cast their gleaming patterns in the crisp yet gentle night. It was in one of the open apertures that the heir to Gorotoland stood now, holding court for a dozen faces ranging in color from blackest black to tannest tan. Upon them all at this particular moment there was an expression of reverent agreement.

"After all," Terry said, "it is not as though an ambitious American politician can speak for the colored races of the world. Some of your delegations today seemed to vote in the belief that his empty gesture is sufficient to salve the stern consciences of our peoples as they look upon this hypocritical democracy and say to it, in the thunderclap of the ages, 'Set your own house in order!' My friends, do not be persuaded down that garden path."

"Hear, hear!" said the righteous young man from Kenya. "I say, hear, hear!"

"So do I," said a young lady from Pakistan. "I, too, say, 'Hear, hear!'"

"Then," the M'Bulu said with a confiding air and a sweeping gesture around the room, "go forth and talk to our brethren. Tell them the fight has just begun. Tell them we need votes for a week from today. Tell them the downtrodden of the earth look to them to do the noble thing . . . Excuse me," he said abruptly. "I see some people I must talk to. Uhuru!"

"Yes, uhuru," said the young lady from Pakistan. "Indeed, uhuru."

As quickly as Terrible Terry had the Ambassador of Panama observed the chairman of DEFY and the wife of the Congressman from California enter and stand uncertainly near the door, and as quickly did he disengage himself from two members of the Canadian delegation and bear down upon them. Starting from somewhat nearer, he arrived a second sooner and was already bending low to kiss Sue-Dan's hand as the stately figure of the M'Bulu approached, bringing with him the eyes of the room as surely as though he were carrying a banner. A little buzz of talk immediately sprang up, and there was a general drawing-away around them. It was thus, separate and apart and standing much as they had been earlier in the day in the Delegates' Lounge, that Cullee Hamilton saw them as he entered the room a second later and looked about for familiar faces. Those that immediately blotted out the rest of the room were all too familiar and for several seconds looked at one another with strange, tense expressions that were not lost upon the rapidly growing gathering.

"Well!" said the M'Bulu finally with a merry laugh that rang clearly through the room, "here comes the hero of the hour! Cullee, dear friend, do come and join us here in this delightful concourse of the nations!"

"I don't want to talk to you," the Congressman said, coming close but so filled with conflicting feelings that he was not conscious of how he got there. "I want to talk to these two people."

"Oh, let him talk," Sue-Dan said with a laugh that was pitched a little too high and sounded a little too strained. "He never hurt anybody just talking. Did you, Cullee?"

"What kind of a person are you?" the Congressman asked bitterly. "I told you not to come to New York. Where have you been?"

"None of your business."

"I really don't see that it is, either," Felix said in a tone of calculated indifference. "Surely when someone wants to come to New York—" But he was stopped by the Congressman's hand, enormous and painfully tight, upon his arm.

"Listen, you," Cullee said with an ominous quiet. "This is my wife. Understand? I know you don't give a damn where your wife is or what she's doing, but I care about mine. So why don't you just run along before I tell Ted Jason on you?"

"Take your hands off me," Felix said with a cold dignity, turning pale. "You are making a public spectacle of us all. Possibly that suits your cheap sense of the dramatic, but it doesn't help your own cause any—"

"And don't lecture me on my cause, either," the Congressman said in the same ominous voice, emphasizing it with a sudden jerk on the Ambassador's arm, while all around eyes widened and voices gasped and excitement grew. "At least it's a cause I'm not ashamed of. How do you feel about yours?"

"I am not ashamed, either," Felix said harshly. "I am proud of anything that can promise justice to your cruel and stupid country."

"Maybe you don't know what people here think about you, Cullee," Le-Gage suggested. "Maybe you better find out, before you get so big-man about everything."

"Big man, big man," Sue-Dan said with a biting little laugh. "Where's Big Man now?"

"They think enough of me so they voted for me today," the Congressman said with a stubborn anger. Terrible Terry gave again his merry laugh.

"They think enough of American money, American bribes, American promises. But they don't think much of America when it comes to race. When are you going to get intelligent and side with your own color, Cullee? You can't be so very happy, playing at being a white man."

"That's what he's always wanted to be," LeGage said bitterly.

"Do you want me to hit you right here and now?" Cullee demanded, but it was not his ex-roommate, strained and unhappy and watching him with an expression of pain and mistrust, who gave him answer.

"Hit us all, why don't you?" Sue-Dan said with a shrill little laugh that rang through the now-silent room. "That would look fine, wouldn't it? But I tell you this, Cullee"—and suddenly the little fox-face looked harsh and vicious with the burden of its emotions—"if you do, I won't *ever* come back to you . . . Not ever. I mean it, Cullee. You just try it and see."

"You don't plan to come back, anyway," he said in an agonized whisper, for suddenly he was entirely convinced that it was true. "You wouldn't come back, whatever I did . . . Would you?" he added uncertainly, in a tone that robbed him abruptly of all force, so wavering and uneasy was it. She seized upon it with a laugh both scornful and triumphant.

"Let's see what you do for your own people awhile, Cullee. Let's see how you act with your white friends down there in Congress. Then we see whether I come back or not. That's how we find out."

"I've got to do what I think is right for everybody," he said in an almost inaudible voice while they watched him closely and without the mercy that might otherwise have made them turn away from his anguished face and tortured eyes. "For everybody. Not just—us."

For a long moment, no one gave answer. Then the M'Bulu bowed low.

"Obviously," he said in his clipped tones, "we are in the presence of an upright and moral man who cannot be swayed by the appeals that move ordinary mortals. I would suggest that we leave him to think about it. Sue-Dan, may I have the honor to dance with you?"

"*My* honor," she said, moving into his arms with a smile that she made deliberately as intimate and suggestive as she could.

"If you will excuse us, Cullee," the M'Bulu said, and they swept away onto the deserted floor as the orchestra came abruptly to life and the gathering in all its glittering gossip began to stir and shift with the patterns of casual association that had been temporarily frozen by the tense tableau at its center.

"You are a fool," Felix Labaiya said in a cold voice. "You are a fool and you are losing everything. Did you hear me?" he said sharply. "I said you are a—"

"I heard you," Cullee Hamilton said dully. "Go away."

"Very well," the Ambassador said scornfully. "Beware the dancers, or they will knock you down."

And he turned abruptly away, leaving only the chairman of DEFY to proffer whatever assistance, or further condemnation, he might feel moved to contribute.

"Cullee—" he said, starting to lay a tentative hand on the Congressman's arm. "Cullee, let me—"

"You too," the Congressman said, unseeing. "Go away."

"I—" LeGage began helplessly, but his ex-roommate looked at him with so anguished an expression that his voice died away.

"Ah, God!" Cullee whispered harshly. "Just—go—*away*."

"All right, Cullee," 'Gage said hastily in a shaken voice. "I will."

Somehow after that the Congressman from California managed to get from the center of the room, where he was indeed becoming an object of interference as well as derision to the gaily clad multitude that swirled about him, to one of the open windows. He looked back across the room for his wife and the M'Bulu, but everything blurred, he could not see them, his head was filled with the incessant pounding beat of the orchestra, growing more reckless and insistent as the dancers swayed faster to it. He turned with a harsh little noise of protest in his throat and walked out onto the esplanade, moving blindly along it north in the direction of Beekman Place until the sounds of Nigeria's party became absorbed and lost in the night clamor of Manhattan to his left and the swift coursing of the river below to his right.

Finally he stopped and, with hands rigid upon the railing, stood staring at the water and the lights of Brooklyn across the way. "Pepsi-Cola," Brooklyn said brightly; "Sunshine Biscuits." The commercial messages of a civilization that offered little comfort for the mind and little surcease for the heart came emphatically to him over the dark channel. He sighed profoundly even as he realized with a start that he was no longer alone. Someone was approaching along the dark walkway from the distant Dining Room.

"Yes?" he said sharply, drawing himself up in readiness, not knowing what casual or not-so-casual intruder might have slipped passed the guards to invade the night precincts of the UN. But a comfortable laugh came back and he relaxed as he recognized it.

"Don't shoot," the junior Senator from Iowa said easily. "It's me."

"Hi," Cullee said, a cool defensiveness in his tone. "What can I do for you?"

"First of all," Lafe Smith said, "you can take that chip off your shoulder and throw it in the river. I'm not here to fight with you. Unlike some."

"Oh. You saw."

"Who didn't?" Lafe said, the match for a cigarette momentarily lighting his shrewdly amiable face. "The whole wide world, in my estimation. I wouldn't let it bother me, though, if I were you."

"You wouldn't?" Cullee said with a bitter irony. "That's easy to say."

"Easy to do, too, if you know which direction you're going, and why," Lafe said. "Or so," he added thoughtfully as "Sunshine Biscuits" blinked at him cheerfully from across the river, "I have usually found."

"You make it sound so simple," Cullee said, still bitterly. "It isn't so simple when you're black."

"I grant you that," Lafe said gravely. "I'm not discounting that; I'm not crazy. I'm also not without a heart. I didn't see much sign in there that anybody you were talking to had one."

"They—I don't think they meant to be mean," Cullee said lamely. "They don't know what they want."

"Oh, I think they do. I think they know very well; whether mistakenly or not, at least they know. It seems to me that the problem is whether you know. Do you?"

For a moment his companion gave no answer, staring out across the river, a dark, silent bulk looming head and shoulders above the Senator from Iowa. Then he gave again the deep sigh he had uttered at the start of their conversation.

"I don't know," he said in a muffled voice. "I just don't know."

"I thought as much, which is why I came out. I thought maybe I could help, and I thought also that you should know that everything is set for your resolution to come up in the House on Monday. Orrin called about half an hour ago to say that the Speaker had arranged for a special Rules Committee meeting late this afternoon. They broke about half an hour ago after approving a six-hour debate rule on Monday. So you're on your way. If that pleases you."

"I don't know, now—I just don't know."

"It still isn't too late to back out, of course," Lafe remarked matter-of-factly. "House rules will permit you to withdraw the resolution if you want to, won't they?"

"Yes, they will."

"Why don't you, if it bothers you so?" the Senator suggested, still with an impersonal logic in his voice. "Then you'd be in the clear, without all this bother and unhappiness. Wouldn't that be the simplest thing to do?"

His companion made a peculiar sound, between a sigh and a harsh, unamused laugh.

"What's Old Doc Smith trying to do?" he asked. "Give me shock therapy and get me really confused? You know damned well nobody down there wants me to withdraw that resolution."

"Seab does," Lafe Smith said. "A lot of people do. Wouldn't it be best for you to do what they want?" A blunt sarcasm came into his voice. "Why take a beating for the white man?"

Again his companion was silent, and when he finally spoke it was in a tone that made the Senator think that possibly, just possibly, he was gaining ground in what he had come out on the esplanade to attempt.

"What are you trying to do? Make me mad enough to fight?"

"You don't need that," Lafe said quietly. "If you decide to fight, it will be a matter of judgment and not of emotion."

"That's right," Cullee agreed, promptly enough so that Lafe could tell he was flattered. "I don't do things just because I'm mad."

"Everybody knows that, which is why some people want to make you mad, in the hope it will throw you off balance and then you really won't know what to do. Have they succeeded?"

But once again his companion seemed to retreat into some inner area of silence that the intruder could not penetrate without an invitation and a road map.

"I don't know," he said again, finally. "I just don't know."

"Well, I won't try to persuade you. You're a rational man, you know all the considerations involved; you are, I know, as concerned as we all are about what is best for the country. I trust you. Will you shake hands on it?"

"If you like," Cullee said. He gave again the heavy sigh as he complied. "I'll do my best. I'll do what I can."

"You have to work it out," Lafe said. "If you need us, call us." He smiled. "We won't call you. Good night, Cullee."

"Good night, Lafe. I appreciate your friendship."

"You have it. I feel we're all in this together."

"That's what I think too," the Congressman agreed in a bleak voice. "But it isn't so easy to tell some people that."

He turned again to his brooding over the water, his hands once more rigid on the railing, his arms stretched as tautly as though he were trying to force the iron itself to speak. Brooklyn continued to call cheerfully to him across the silent river; at his back the voice of Manhattan said urgent things in a tense, unintelligible roar. Maybe it all added up to something; maybe there was to be found in it somewhere an answer to his hurt, unhappy people and his hurt, unhappy land; but if so it escaped him right then. Perhaps he could come to it later, perhaps the way would be clear sometime, at the end of all this weary road. He smiled, without amusement as he thought of what Le-Gage's reaction would be to the weary road, that mournful concept out of a past LeGage and his like tried to pretend had never existed. How they loved to display their self-conscious scorn for the Negro past, these Fancy Dans who weren't worthy to lick the boots of those who had endured slavery and come through it with faith and human decency intact. He uttered a growl of contempt and distaste that broke harshly into the night. Once more he found he had company, as the Soviet Ambassador spoke, so close to his elbow that he jumped.

"You are unhappy," Vasily Tashikov said. "The white man's world is using you like a puppet, the black man's world threatens to spew you out, and you are all alone to shiver in the winds of history's reckoning. It is very sad."

"What do you want?" the Congressman demanded, turning so abruptly that he almost bumped into the slight form beside him. He would say for its owner's control that he did not yield an inch. Instead, he asked impassively, "It is true, is it not?"

"What if it is?" Cullee said with a bitter scorn. "What of it? Is that supposed to make me a patsy for you?"

"I am a little hazy on that expression," the Soviet Ambassador said, "but I suppose it means the same as stooge. Make *you* a stooge for *me*," he remarked thoughtfully. "How crude."

"Why don't you go back in there and leave me alone?" the Congressman demanded bluntly. "I have nothing for you, or you for me."

"Nobody has anything for you," the Soviet Ambassador said with a certain dreamy inevitability in his tone. "Neither the white man who uses you nor the black man who despises you. Poor Congressman Hamilton! It is a sad world he lives in."

"Will you leave me alone?" Cullee demanded again. But the Ambassador remained at his side, a small, tenacious leech.

"Look, you," he said, in the same gently inexorable tone. "How can you possibly defend a dying bourgeois imperialism in the face of your own people? The Negro is humiliated in the South, despised in the North, forced to remain in second-class citizenship east, west, and all over. And you try to defend his oppressors! You run their errands! You argue their cause! You introduce their resolutions and play their vicious game! For shame, Congressman Hamilton. For shame!"

"Ah—" Cullee began, but the Ambassador cut him off.

"Really, how *can* you defend them? What earthly justice is there in the Negro's condition in this great empty land of pretense? Just tell me, as a flat proposition, *what sense does it make?*"

And to this, of course, because there was no rational answer but only an answer of faith that progress had been made and would continue to be made hereafter, because there was not so much, when all was said and done, that could be pointed to with the unassailable logic demanded by his inquisitor and the watching world, the Congressman from California did not, for several minutes, give answer. When he did, it was in a slow, uncertain voice in which the dogged stubbornness had dwindled to a trace.

"All I know is, we're better off than we used to be," he said, suddenly unclenching his hands from the rail and rubbing his eyes in a desperately tired fashion, "and we're going to be better yet. If America can just keep working at it, we'll be better yet. That's all I know."

"If," the Ambassador said scornfully. "If, if, if! This feeble, rotten country, this joke of a democracy! Do you have the simplest privileges of a white man's pet dog? Would he let *you* come in and lie by the fire on a winter night? Why, of course not. And the whole world knows it, my friend. The whole world."

"All I know—" Cullee began again, in infinite weariness, but the Ambassador was on it at once.

"Justify it. Look at it from any angle you like and say it makes sense. I defy you to do so. And here, on the other hand, are all the new free states of Africa, standing forth in their liberty and independence. Nearly two centuries of America and the American Negro hasn't got as much as the free Negro of Africa achieves in two years. How they are laughing at you, my friend, as you attempt to defend the United States imperialist oppressors. It is no wonder the delegate of Kenya spits and your wife has left you. It is no wonder you are the laughingstock of this whole UN."

But at this there was some indication that the Soviet Ambassador might have gone too far, for abruptly he found himself grasped by the coat-front and lifted off the ground so that he dangled half strangled like a puppet on a string, his feet jerking ignominiously, a harsh, gasping breath just managing to emerge from between his frantically opened lips.

"You see that water?" the Congressman asked softly, holding Vasily Tashikov out over it so that it slipped away darkly beneath his feet into horrible distances foul with horrible deeds, awash with the sickness of the horrible great city in the horrible black night. "I could drop you in it right this minute and nobody would know, Mr. Ambassador. Nobody at all would know until you floated up somewhere down in New Jersey, maybe, or they found you half eaten by the crabs. Assuming any crab would stoop to eat you. Assuming that!" And with a sudden half-cry of inarticulate rage the Congressman shook the Ambassador until his teeth rattled and his breath came ever shorter from his rapidly purpling lips.

"Now," he said, lifting him abruptly back over the railing and slamming him down on his feet so hard it was a wonder it did not break his ankles, "get away from me, you twisting bastard, always twisting everything up, and leave my country alone. Go on away and tell it to somebody else. Just get away and leave us alone. I don't ever want to speak to you again."

For a long moment the Soviet Ambassador struggled, with long, hoarse gasps for air, to regain his breath, teetering back and forth on his heels like a far-gone drunk, his face gradually sorting itself out into some semblance of cohesion. When he finally spoke, it was in a painful wheeze. The words came clearly nonetheless.

"You can silence me . . . but you . . . can't . . . silence . . . what I say. It doesn't . . . make sense. It doesn't . . . make sense! It doesn't . . . make sense!"

"Go on!" Cullee Hamilton cried, aware that in the distance from the brightly lighted doors of the Delegates' Dining Room a guard was coming on the run. "Go on!"

"Yes," the Soviet Ambassador said, still with difficulty, brushing away the guard's helping hands and frantic questions with a furiously impatient air,

"I will go on, and we will beat you, silly dupe of the imperialist oppressors, and your evil country too."

Some time later—how much he did not know for sure, though the music was diminishing, in the distant Dining Room and in the lighted arches of the windows fewer and fewer figures could be discerned, the night wind was growing colder, and it must be nearing midnight—he came gradually out of the depths of unthinking, unfeeling, unmoving where he had remained since the hated figure of his opponent had disappeared, still fuming, with the still-worried guard, into the darkness. And there, he suspected, he too should go, having given way to anger, having revealed his own terrible unease, having laid bare the terrible choices that could not be rationalized in a world clamoring for certainties and viciously eager to condemn the middle ground. Into the night he should go and there find—what? More liquor, and what good would that do? More sex, and how permanent an answer would that provide? There were many ways to run away from thinking and self-knowledge in the Borough of Manhattan, but he had discovered one thing, somewhere along the years, and that was the truth of what his mother had said one time when he had done something naughty as a child and threatened loudly to run away from home if he got licked for it. "You can run and run and run," she had said, "'way down that long dark street, and at the end of it you know what you still going to find? Yourself, little boy, that's what. Yourself."

True enough, he thought now; always true, of course, for everybody; and yet somewhere there must be an answer to the confusions of Cullee Hamilton, caught between the races, his wife probably in bed this very moment with the triumphant M'Bulu, his dearest friend turned away from him in hopelessness, facing all alone on the United Nations esplanade the plight of the decent man who tries to hold to a moderate course in the Century of Immoderates which will have none of it. He could talk to Orrin Knox or the President, but they would only repeat what they had said before, only try, like Lafe Smith, to bring him around and prod him along with their reverse psychology of whip-and-carrot and play-on-pride. He could seek out LeGage in the vast haunted city, but he would only repeat what he had said before, try to goad him into frenzy with scorn and sarcasm and the old, worn arguments about the white man's guilt. And how would that serve America, or point the way to decency, or bring to either race the benison of an end to hatred and the start of love?

Presently, a tall figure bulking large against the garish messages of Brooklyn across the water, silent and enwrapped and barely nodding to the guard who let him out onto First Avenue after midnight, he left the UN and started walking blindly across the island of Manhattan. There was one more he might talk to, and perhaps he could see him tomorrow; but that, he suspected, was just a stalling. Essentially, there was no outside help for it and no easy way out: there was just one little boy at the end of this long street, and that was himself. If Cullee Hamilton couldn't help Cullee Hamilton, then, sure enough, wasn't anybody who could.

3

"So you see," the Senator from West Virginia explained, on the broad green lawn in the soft sunny Sunday morning, under the kindly, sheltering tree, "we do the best we can, and once in a while—a *great* while—we seem to respond."

"But not very often," Lafe Smith said gently. "Not very often. If truth were known."

"If truth were known," Hal Fry said in a tortured whisper, "not once in the last five years."

"Yes," the Senator from Iowa said. "Jimmy," he went on after a moment in a conversational tone, "would you like me to bring you a present next time I come? I might be able to find something you'd like, down in New York."

There was a quick look, a smile of infinite warmth and kindness, and—nothing.

"It doesn't do any good," Senator Fry said in the same half-whisper. "It just never does any good."

"Somewhere there must be an answer. Somewhere there must be."

"Don't you think I've tried to find it?" Hal Fry asked sharply. "What do you think I've been doing all these years?"

"I know," Lafe said quickly. "Of course you have. I didn't mean it to sound like that . . . But, *somehow*, there must be a key."

"Why should I think so, any more than anyone else with the same—problem?" Senator Fry asked. "Lots of people never find the key because there just—isn't—anything—to unlock."

"But he looks so—"

"That's what kills me. If he only looked like an—an—"

"Don't say it!" Lafe said sharply. "Don't *say* it. You just torture yourself and it doesn't do any good. And maybe it isn't true. You have to hope."

"How long?" Hal Fry asked with a stricken look. "How long?"

For several minutes they said nothing, the handsome boy between them smiling graciously into the distance at something only he could see, the sound of softly muted voices coming to them from other groups under other trees, in the distance the sounds of a tennis game on a court below, hidden by the drop of hill to the Hudson. Finally Senator Fry stirred and slowly stood up.

"I think we'd better go. You've been very kind, but—this is enough."

"As you say. It's up to you."

"No, I really think we'd better." He looked down at his son, and for a moment the boy looked up, happy, serene, appearing to possess some other-worldly understanding that gave him again the heartbreaking expression of sympathy and kindness. His father leaned forward, kissed him on the forehead, and turned abruptly away.

"Good-by, Jimmy," Lafe Smith said. "I'll see you soon."

The handsome face turned toward him for a moment. An expression of fleeting regret came momentarily into the beautiful dark eyes, then was erased as instantly as it had come. Lafe too turned away, with a heavy heart and a rising tension through his body. His day's real task was just beginning.

How he would approach it, as they walked quickly back through the main buildings, he did not for the moment know. It was not until they reached the car that he decided that the direct approach was, as always, the best for him.

"Would you like me to drive?" he asked casually. "You probably don't feel like it right now, do you?"

"Why?" Hal demanded quickly. "Do I look sick?"

"A little. And understandably, I should think."

"I'm feeling pretty good this morning. Upset about him, of course, but then I always am. The other isn't so bad today. Maybe I'm finally turning the corner on it, whatever it was."

"I hope so," Lafe said slowly. "Give me the keys."

"You say that in a funny tone," Senator Fry said with a half-humorous but questioning smile. "What do you know that I don't know?"

"Give me the keys and get in. We'll talk about it."

"All right. I hope it makes more sense than that little know-it-all at the UN. It seems it's all a guilt complex because of—Jimmy."

"I wouldn't say so," Senator Smith said, easing the car smoothly into the Sunday-thronged parkway going south. "I have a friend," he added presently, "who thinks you ought to go in for a complete checkup and some real tests for a change, instead of all this oddball chatter that may only be wasting time."

"What do you mean, wasting time? It isn't that bad, is it?"

"Who knows?" Lafe said shortly. "If you won't go in for a checkup, who can tell?"

"Who is this friend of yours, anyway? Some blonde you found under a sofa—or on top of it—in one of the conference rooms in the Secretariat?"

"He's a young fellow who's interning at Harkness Pavilion. I had a long phone conversation with him Friday night after the Nigerian party."

"How did that go, by the way? I tried to get dressed and make it, but I really did feel lousy, as I phoned you. Did I miss anything?"

"You did. Everybody including his wife and LeGage Shelby jumped on Cullee Hamilton, and I don't know whether they succeeded or not. He was out on the esplanade later and I went out and talked to him, but I don't know whether I succeeded or not."

"Funny, I didn't see much in the papers about it."

"Oh, yes, it was in the *Times* this morning; he was the fifth paragraph, something about, 'It was reported meanwhile that Congressman Hamilton, under severe criticism and pressure from African Negroes and some American Negroes as well, might withdraw his resolution when the House meets tomorrow.' The *Daily News* also had an item, small but gory. 'Negro Congressman Rows With UN Africans at Dance,' I believe the headline said."

Hal Fry shook his head with a saddened expression.

"That's a shame. I hope he'll stand firm."

"I don't know. It's up to him. There's nothing we can do. Anyway, buster, don't change the subject. How about going in that hospital and getting that checkup?"

For a few moments his companion was silent as they drove along, maintaining a steady pace that cut the miles away under them as they sped toward the city. Then he sighed and spoke in a voice that suddenly sounded drained of all will and determination to fight back.

"I'm afraid to, Lafe. *I'm* afraid they'll really find something, too."

"Maybe not," the Senator from Iowa said. Then he added firmly, "But—maybe. In any event, wouldn't you like to know?"

"I've often wondered, as I suppose everyone does," the Senator from West Virginia said slowly. "I don't know whether I would or not. You see, I've had quite—quite a bit—to bear—in my life. I don't really know that I want to be told for sure that I've been singled out to bear more."

God, Lafe Smith inquired politely, how does one answer that one? Got any ideas? But through the dimness that blurred his vision for a moment he recognized that he must not voice any doubts, not give any quarter to weakness when strength was all that remained to see his colleague through whatever destiny was his. So he spoke in a matter-of-fact tone that disclosed no emotion other than courage for the working day.

"I don't think that it will come to that. But of course it *is* your decision, and perhaps I have no right to force you to it. Maybe it's best to leave it a mystery, if that's what you prefer."

"And go along half crippled when we face what we do in the United Nations?" Senator Fry said quickly, and then gave a sad smile. "You see? I answer my own question . . . When can they take me at Harkness Pavilion?"

"I'll call for you tomorrow morning and see," Lafe Smith said, speaking very carefully for fear he might sob or make some undignified sound or otherwise betray his emotions. "I think perhaps the sooner the better."

"Yes," said Hal Fry, staring unseeing at the fading autumn colors as they sped along, "I think perhaps so."

Moving briskly about the gleaming yellow kitchen at "Vagaries," supervising the final touches on the brunch, Dolly Munson thought with a worried little frown about her husband. For all that she had been in love with Bob for quite some time, it was not until their marriage that she had begun to realize the insistent, incessant demands of the Majority Leadership and the inevitable wearing effects it has upon those who hold it. There was a sort of subtle, steady attrition that began in January, when Congress convened and there came a brief burst of furious activity as Presidential requests reached the Hill and bills were introduced. There was then a temporary respite in February and March while committees met and members made speeches around the country as party organizations held banquets in honor of their respective political saints. Then, after the Easter recess, the pressure began to pile up and the grind was on. From then until final adjournment, Congress worked, and worked hard. And no one worked harder than the man in the Senate who must set the pace, help to pilot legislation through, thread his way amid the conflicting claims of a hundred imperious egos, and bring his colleagues safely to shore when the final gavel fell.

No one worked harder, although, she would admit, the Speaker probably worked as hard. But she wasn't married to the Speaker and he wasn't her responsibility. Bob was, and now as she gave the cook a final compliment, took off her apron, and prepared to go out on the terrace to greet her guests, she decided firmly that they really would travel after adjournment, maybe as far as Europe, as they had originally planned, maybe on around the world. The Majority Leader had earned the rest, in this lengthy session that had seen so many things occur in the United States and elsewhere, and she was determined he should have it. Particularly when it now appeared that the session would conclude in one fine fandango over the Hamilton resolution, the visit of Terrible Terry, and the ramifications thereof.

Without this situation, of course, there might well be a Sunday brunch today at "Vagaries," for it was a form of entertaining she particularly enjoyed, but it would not be one so directly concerned with the imperatives of politics, both domestic and international, and the difficulties of dealing with worldwide human emotions and opinion. The guest list on another occasion might include some, but not all, of the friends about to arrive at any moment now: Orrin and Beth, Claude and Kitty, Raoul and Celestine, the Speaker, the President and Lucille, Seab, and—an impulsive afterthought and one she hadn't quite had the nerve to tell Bob about—Patsy Labaiya. Only an episode like the present could bring them all to "Vagaries" on so intimate a basis at the same moment; and there was no telling what their informal proximity at this particular stage of it might produce. "We'll be thirteen, you realize," she had said gaily to Lucille, "and who can say what our luck may be?" The First Lady had given the gentle little laugh that so often preceded her most perceptive and unexpected thrusts. "If anyone can make it good, dear Dolly, you can," she had said, "but maybe even you will have difficulty, in times like these."

"The President brings his own luck. I'm counting on that to pull us through."

Surprisingly, Lucille had sighed, openly and with a frankness that surprised her hostess.

"Maybe so," she had said slowly. "If he doesn't get too discouraged."

"It's your job not to let him," Dolly said lightly, but the First Lady's mood was not so easily broken.

"I do my best, but a man can only stand so much of this world's accumulation of persistent ills."

"Surely there isn't any doubt that he can, is there?" Dolly had asked with some concern, and this had finally brought Lucille back to her normal softly tenacious optimism.

"Oh, no," she had said, much more cheerfully. "Don't take me seriously, and don't quote me. I married a good man. He won't fail us."

"Of course not," Dolly said in a tone of affectionate scolding. "Or his wife either."

But she had found it a disturbing little exchange, both then and in retrospect, and it was with considerable concern that she heard now the sounds of Presidential arrival in the driveway and came forward through the drawing room to meet her guests of honor. She was a little surprised to note that Harley looked as comfortably calm as ever and wondered fleetingly if Lucille hadn't been imagining things. The First Lady gave her a warning wink, and she linked her arm through the President's with a cheerful smile and led him to the terrace.

"Autumn is doing her best for you, Mr. President," she said, and he nodded in pleased agreement as his eyes swept over the terrace: the long table sparkling with white linen, silver, and glass; the beautifully tended lawn; the maples and elms, russet and gold in the gentle sunshine; the dreamy peace that lay upon the world.

"Lovely, lovely," he said. "Heartbreakingly lovely, in fact. In some ways I think autumn is Washington's loveliest season." His eyes darkened a little, more revealingly than he knew. "So perfect—and so transitory . . . But," he added, more briskly, "that sounds almost gloomy, and that isn't the way I ought to sound. Or have any reason to sound. Lovely season, and you loveliest of all, Dolly, as always. Where's my Majority Leader?"

"Greeting Orrin and Beth about now, I expect. Yes, here they come."

"Good," the President said. "It sounds like a fine little gathering."

And so, as it formed and proceeded along its way through the grapefruit, the consommé, the salad, and headed into the sole, the lamb roast, julienne potatoes and cinnamoned peas, it seemed to be. It was not until they came to the cherries jubilee and coffee that a more serious note was injected, and that by the Speaker, who finally leaned back in his chair and said in his calm and unhurried drawl, "Well, sir, looks like we're going to have an interesting day in the House tomorrow. Shaping up into a mighty interesting day." He chuckled. "Better come over and watch us, Seab. We might wind up doing something you won't like."

The senior Senator from South Carolina, peering down the table from where he sat between Celestine Barre and Beth Knox, wagged his head and smiled in a gently reproving way.

"Now, Bill, you know you hadn't ought to taunt me, Bill. You know it's not good for my health, at my age. How do you know I won't like what you do, Bill? How do you know that, now?"

"Because I expect we're going to pass Cullee's resolution," the Speaker said crisply, "And I don't expect you're going to like that, are you?"

"Passing the House," Senator Cooley said in the same tone of gentle reproof, "isn't passing the Senate. Now, Bob can tell you that, Bill. Passing the House isn't passing the Senate. Don't expect the Senate to be quite as easy to push around as your House, Bill. The Senate's a different matter. Bob can tell you that."

"Yes," the Majority Leader said, "Bob can tell you that, all right. It may not be so easy where Seab and I live."

"Isn't going to be easy where I live," the Speaker retorted, "but I'm telling you it's going to be done."

"Why, Bill?" Senator Cooley wanted to know. "Why, now? Did anybody ever stop to answer that, before we got ourselves all rushed into this tangle by a couple of colored boys? Not, mind you, that I dislike them—at least, I don't dislike ours, that Cullee, who's a fine boy. It's that foreign Yankee-Poo I don't like."

"Nanki-Poo, Seab," Orrin Knox corrected automatically. "Anyway, the allusion isn't pertinent. If you want to blame anybody for getting us into this, blame me. I'll take it."

"Who can logically blame any one individual for what happens in government?" the President suggested. "Or life, either, for that matter; so many factors go into a thing. Isn't that right, Seab?"

"Some people," the Senator from South Carolina said with an ominous emphasis, "are more responsible than others. Why!" he exclaimed, making Celestine jump, "if it hadn't been for you, Orrin, all this would have been brushed over and forgotten in two days' time. Now we've got the whole wide world pawing over our business. It's a crime and a crying shame, Orrin. And a fine position for a sovereign power to be in."

"Well," the Secretary of State said, his voice becoming tart in spite of his inward efforts to keep it calm, "if you think anything like this can be brushed over in two days without the world noticing it nowadays, Seab, I think you're a little behind the times. Isn't that right, Claude?"

"Don't bring *my* poor husband into it," Kitty Maudulayne said lightly. "He's got enough troubles as it is."

"I don't think Senator Cooley understands what we're up against up there in the United Nations," Lord Maudulayne said. "Or the M'Bulu's talent for dramatics, for that matter. He happens to be a very shrewd young man."

"And with plenty of shrewd young men elsewhere, including this country, to capitalize on it," the Secretary said. "LeGage Shelby, for instance. To say nothing of all the white crowd who go fawning around after him."

"And where does that leave your Cullee Hamilton?" Raoul Barre inquired in a dry tone. "Rather exposed, does it not?"

"Cullee's all right," the Speaker said. "Cullee knows what he's doing."

"Cullee's my dupe," Orrin Knox remarked. "At least so I hear from the President Pro Tem of the Senate and all his friends in the liberal press."

"Now, Orrin, you wouldn't deny me my little fun, now, would you, Orrin?" Senator Cooley said. "Anyway," he added pugnaciously, "I expect it's probably true."

"You know very well it isn't," the Secretary said. "But it's finally put you in bed with the Washington *Post*, anyway. A lifetime ambition has been real-ized by both of you."

"Orrin," Senator Cooley said with a puckish little twinkle, "you sound quite annoyed. Quite—annn—oyed. I'm surprised at you, Orrin, letting us liberals mortify you like that. Pshaw, Orrin!"

"I assume," Raoul Barre said politely, "that the Congress will pursue its plans to pass Mr. Hamilton's resolution? He will not appear in the House tomorrow and say it was all a foolish mistake? This might prove somewhat embarrassing to his country and to some of us who have devoted some time and effort to finding a formula with which his country might escape embar-rassment. Of course," he added with a mild sarcasm, "if his country thinks that the UN is sufficiently important to worry about in these matters."

"We do," the President said. "We know we differ with you on that, Raoul, but we do. So there we are, difficult and illusory and tenuous and full of headaches as the organization may be. We feel its potential is such that we have to support it."

"To say nothing of its ability to cause trouble in world opinion," the Secretary of State remarked. "It's the great Hyde Park Corner of all the world, and all the world's loudmouths use it to sound off."

"What is world opinion?" the French Ambassador inquired thoughtfully. "We will help you appease it, since you are a friend of ours, and that is what you seem to want to do. But what effect would it have if you did not appease it, and what good will it produce for you if you do? More fundamentally, *can* you? That is the question that occurs to us."

"That occurs to me too," Senator Cooley said dourly, accepting another cup of coffee from the maid who moved among them around the long white table in the kindly sun. "Can we, now, Orrin? And why should we try?"

"It doesn't seem to me that those questions are subject to debate any longer," the Majority Leader said, "if you will forgive me, Seab. Yes, I know you *will* debate them, and no doubt at length, but either you accept the neces-sary place of the UN in the scheme of things or you don't. We have, as the President says. So there we are."

"Oh, now, Bob," Senator Cooley said, "don't try to con me into anything right here at breakfast, Bob. You know the Senate will have to consider that boy Cullee's resolution most carefully, Bob. There are many aspects to it, many—aspects—to it. It will have to be most—carefully—considered."

"I suppose you'll delay it ALL you can," Patsy Labaiya said abruptly from down the table, and they all turned in some surprise at her tone, which was harsh and accusatory. "It will be JUST like you, Senator."

"Well, Patsy, dear," Beth Knox said comfortably, "what else would you expect him to do? He has a right to, if he feels like it."

"I suppose," Patsy said. "I suppose everyone will say, 'There's Senator Cooley saving the Old South again.' Well, not I. I hope you get beaten, Senator."

"I might wish the same for your husband at the United Nations, ma'am," the Senator from South Carolina said politely, "except that to do so might seem a little crude and unsociable. But I consider him no friend to the United States, ma'am, I will tell you that frankly."

"Well," Patsy said, flushing, "I don't have to comment on that, and I won't. It's his business. My family isn't involved."

"But how extraordinary, dear," Beth said pleasantly. "You're involved. I mean, he *is* your husband. Doesn't that involve your family?"

"Ted isn't involved!" Patsy snapped. "So don't try to make out that he is, Beth."

Beth nodded.

"No, I know we mustn't embarrass Ted. It's very important that Ted not be involved. Even so, one can't help feeling that he might perhaps repudiate what Felix is doing. It might help."

"Why don't YOU repudiate him, Orrin?" Patsy demanded. "Why don't YOU declare him *persona non grata* and send him home to Panama, if you're so worried about what he's doing? I don't see YOU taking any action."

"I don't want him to, yet," the President said mildly. "However," he added in a slightly sharper tone, "if I should decide so, Patsy, you can be sure it will be done without any regard to you or your family or anything but the best interests of the United States."

"Oh," Patsy said, studying him closely for a moment, obviously taken aback by his tone. "Well, of course, that's your privilege."

"It is. Meanwhile, I'm sure the whole country must be wondering a little, as Beth says, about why your brother hasn't made some comment. I think perhaps it would be well for him to do so."

"Is that an ORDER, Mr. President?" Patsy asked. He smiled and shrugged.

"Who am I to give orders to the Governor of California? It's just a thought I have. Bill, is that resolution really going through the House tomorrow?"

The Speaker nodded.

"Orrin and I have it pretty well in hand," he said with the comfortable assurance that always distinguished his approach to legislative crises. "May be a few of 'em jump the traces, but mostly it's pretty well in hand."

"If you will forgive me," Raoul Barre said, "I still think your problem is young Mr. Hamilton. He did not have a happy time of it Friday at the United Nations. He is also under fearful pressures from his own people. You may be preparing a battle whose hero will run away before the first shot is fired."

"Somebody else will introduce the resolution if he backs out," Orrin said. "We aren't without replacements, on this team."

"It won't be the same," the French Ambassador said. "You need his name and color if you are going to impress our somewhat erratic colleagues in Turtle Bay. That is obvious, certainly."

"Yes," the Secretary admitted somewhat glumly, "that is obvious, true enough. I wish I knew where he was, right now. I'd talk to him."

"I doubt if that would be wise," Lord Maudulayne said. "It is my impression he's been talked to, and at, enough. He has to work it out in his own way, it would seem to me. Not, of course, that it is any of my government's business, except that we would like to see that aspect of The Problem of Gorotoland solved as equably as possible for all concerned."

"You can't defeat Felix's basic resolution on immediate independence, can you?" Orrin asked, and the British Ambassador gave him a look of amused surprise.

"My dear fellow, not if you vote against us, no. And that, I take it, is what you intend to do."

"Whatever we intend to do," the President interjected with a pleasant smile, "it will not be announced at a brunch at Dolly's, no matter how charming and delightful a hostess she is."

"You're too kind, Mr. President," Dolly said. "I thought all kinds of historic things would happen here this morning. That's why I invited you all. Please go right ahead."

"I think we really must go right ahead and get back to the White House," Lucille Hudson said. "We have that reception at five for the President of Brazil, you know. We shall see you all there, of course. I do think, dear—"

"Yes, of course," the President said, quite as though he hadn't given her the signal. "I'm sorry to have held you all here as long as this, but it's such a beautiful day, and the company is so enjoyable, and one doesn't find these islands of peace as often as one would like, in these days." He rose and took Dolly's hand in his. "Good-by to you all, and we shall see you at the house later. Dolly and Robert, many thanks."

"It is always an honor," Dolly said. "Lucille, dear—"

"Our pleasure, Mr. President," the Majority Leader said. "I'll see you out."

There was a general stir, a getting-up and moving-about in the wake of their departure, and in it Beth could be heard saying clearly to Patsy, "We do hope there will be some news from Ted, Patsy, dear. And that it will be *good* news."

But Patsy's reply, if any, was lost in the general murmur of farewells and departing conversation, and it was only as they stood on the steps of "Vagaries" waiting for their car that the Secretary of State was able to remark to Beth with a chuckle, "You ought to be ashamed of yourself, you know, needling poor Patsy like that. How would you feel, trapped between husband and brother with the whole world watching?"

"I am mean, aren't I? But I expect Patsy will survive. She's never been *very* trapped between husband and brother. That marriage was always a convenience to both of them, I suspect, and now that Ted's ambitions are being threatened, I don't expect it to last much longer."

"Felix is playing a strange game, I must say," the Secretary said as the car arrived and they got in and swung down the curving drive to Albemarle Street. He frowned. "And I still wish I knew where Cullee was."

High in his apartment overlooking Manhattan, on the thirty-eighth floor of the Secretariat Building, the man who did know awaited his visitor with a curious mixture of anticipation, unease, and regret. The Secretary-General had been awakened at ten by the Congressman's muffled and unclear call, but out of it he had received the plain impression that he was somehow supposed to help remove a confusion that was obviously great. He was not sure that he could. In fact, he was almost certain he could not, and he wished now with a bleak unhappiness that Cullee Hamilton had decided to go elsewhere with his problem that perhaps had no real solution.

And still, of course, it was part of the S.-G.'s job to play host to such matters, to indulge in such conversations, to participate in the endless web of talk that was the United Nations, to help disturbed and passionate and impatient people thrash over and over and over the complexities of situations that never seemed to get either better or worse but stayed always at the same level of racking, pointless, immobile arguments that baffled and paralyzed the world. The only comfort, and it sometimes seemed small and cold, was the glib phrase so beloved of the Americans: "Well, as long as we're talking, we're not shooting." They weren't shooting, the S.-G. reflected, but while all of them talked, some of them also went right along with their imperialistic conquests.

At any rate, now he was faced with an issue that concerned not only his position but his race, and he told himself with the half-guilty feeling of relief that had become endemic in his months in office, that fortunately he had no authority whatever to offer anything but advice. There were occasions when he sharply regretted that his title carried with it no more real power than it did, but there were others when he was thankful that it was basically symbolic and he need not assume too many responsibilities for the unending ills of mankind. The Soviet-imposed impotence of the Secretary-Generalship sometimes proved to be, though a hindrance and a fretting for a strong man, a welcome, if possibly cowardly, relief for a weak one.

Which of the two he was, he had never faced up to squarely in all his life, he thought now, remembering the relatively easy course of events by which he had risen under the British to a place of top leadership in colonial Nigeria, risen even higher in free Nigeria, and then been chosen to break an East-West deadlock in the United Nations. He had been noticeably bright as a child, and something of the same favoring tutelage as that given Terence Ajkaje far away across the black continent had been given him in his time by their mutual masters. He too had gone to England, and spent his years at Oxford; he too had been trained to succeed eventually to independent power; and more smoothly and more surely than Gorotoland, Nigeria had achieved it, and he and colleagues similarly trained had been ready. In his land, too, there had been the jealousies and suspicions of tribe against tribe, the fierce clash of individual will and ambition; yet somehow the transition had been safely made and he himself had emerged on the world scene as a leading and responsible statesman of Africa. For a time he had helped Nigeria withstand both the temptations of a renascent tribalism from within and the incessant nagging ambitions of Ghana from without. Then the United Nations had threatened to founder on the selection of a new Secretary-General and his life had moved to a pinnacle he had never thought to occupy.

In all of it, he could see now, he had never really had a major testing that could tell him whether he was truly a strong man or one who might be not so strong. In the tribal testing of his youth, his entry into manhood, his exploits in hunting and warfare, he had been adjudged the bravest of the brave; but those were not always the terms in which the white man's world measured bravery. There were other, more subtle things that his education and experience in that world had only partially prepared him for. The concept of character, the belief that a man could be brave inside his heart and mind without outward physical proof of it, that in endurance and courage and the stubborn adherence to principle there was a profound and worthy strength, had taken him a long while to realize. It could not be seen, and in his civilization that which could not be seen could not be understood: it could only be feared. For a long time that had been his reaction to the white man's type of bravery, which could be so strong on occasion and yet be surrounded with agonies of thought and self-doubt that puzzled, when they did not greatly amuse, his kind.

But the more he had seen the white world, the more he had come to understand it, and to wonder if he could muster from within himself such reserves of character should the need arise. He had received news of his selection to be Secretary-General with utter astonishment when the word had reached him in Lagos, and he had come to New York afire with the idealism of this new position with all its potential to do good for all peoples, everywhere. His work on the delegation during two tours of duty prior to his selection had left him reasonably knowledgeable yet still with an abiding idealism concerning the organization. Disillusionment had come within a week after he moved to the thirty-eighth floor. The Soviet Ambassador had explained with brutal directness exactly how little the S.-G. was empowered, and expected, to do. His first reaction had been one of crushed protest, of retreat, of injured dignity and disapproving silence. Then he had wondered if that was the proper way to meet it. Possibly he should take a leaf from the British, and from others he had known over the years, and stubbornly and insistently assert his own position and the moral influence that went with it. Yet that would require a major effort of will and an unhesitating ability to challenge every Soviet deceit, defy every Soviet threat. That in turn required a courage and determination that might have been given to some of his predecessors, but had not been given to him.

There had come over him gradually a wistful acceptance of his attenuated and emasculated position. He had tried, he often told himself defensively. He had gone through the motions and made the necessary protests, and even, on one occasion or another, taken the lectern in the Assembly to make short and pointed statements in his own defense. But somehow his heart had not really been in it, he had been too uncertain of his position in the world. It had been too easy for the Communist bloc to undermine his morale and weaken his intention by their public attacks, their unremitting private pressure, their studious distillation of verbal poison through the corridors and committee rooms of the UN. They had perceived at once that he was uncertain, had congratulated themselves that they had made the right decision when they yielded to the British suggestion that he be chosen to break the deadlock, and had acted to make the most of it ever since. They had been determined to throw him off balance from the outset, they had succeeded, and they had never permitted him to recover. He was, if truth were known, a very sad man; sad as a public figure, and sad inside.

And now the Congressman from California wanted him to give fatherly advice and furnish a strength he knew he could not provide. Too many people looked to him for this kind of strength, too many ascended to the thirty-eighth floor hoping for comfort, reassurance, and leadership. Because he had a noble head and carried himself well and looked, in his black dignity, like the perfect image of the elder statesman, many went away convinced that in his vague comments and tentative suggestions they had found a genuine strength to help them. Orrin Knox had apparently felt so, but Orrin Knox, characteristically, had not really been looking for advice; he had known all along what he intended to do and had only been clearing it with headquarters. The S.-G. had been resentful of his own inability to offer more, yet glad he could do that much for the volatile Secretary of State. Cullee Hamilton was something else again. Cullee was one of his own, and he might well be searching for real comfort and real strength. It was with an inward sigh and an outward aspect of impassive graciousness that he rose as the Congressman was shown in and went forward to shake hands with a grave, dignified air.

"I'm sorry to bother you again," Cullee began awkwardly, "but I thought perhaps—well, I thought maybe you could help me see more clearly what I ought to do."

"Sit down," the Secretary-General said kindly, thinking that perhaps if his guest were harried enough he would not realize how inadequate was the comfort he would receive. The Congressman took a chair facing the great window and stared out across Manhattan with an unhappy expression.

"Now," the S.-G. suggested with a calm certainty in his voice, "tell me."

"Well, basically, I guess, I—I just want to know whether you think I am doing the right thing. In my resolution, and all. I guess it's as simple as that."

"Do *you* feel you are, my son?" the S.-G. inquired with a paternalism that startled the Congressman a little; but his expression instantly changed from skepticism to gratitude at the kindness in his host's voice.

"I think so," he said humbly, "but a lot of my own people—*our* own people," he said with a beseeching smile that made the Secretary-General feel even more hopeless, so futile yet so automatic was this assumption by many American Negroes that Africa was somehow superior in knowledge and perception to their own more advanced society—"*our* own people don't seem to think so. A lot of them seem to really hate me for it." He frowned unhappily and suddenly blurted in angry protest, "But what else can I do? Why can't they understand that? What else can I do, unless I want to stop trying to be fair altogether and join the whole pack of them in trying to tear down everything? What good does that do? Do they *know?*"

"They don't know," the Secretary-General said with an unhappiness of his own. "They don't have any standards by which they can know. It is that which makes it all so difficult."

"Then am I doing wrong? Am I expecting too much of them when I try to impose understanding on them? Should I just try to appease them and forget any obligations to my own country? That's what I don't know." He sighed. "I thought maybe you could tell me."

"I can tell you only to do what your conscience suggests," the S.-G. said. "Nothing else would suffice. Furthermore, you would listen to nothing else. Isn't that right?"

The Congressman gave him a tensely unhappy look.

"It isn't enough," he said, looking down at the slow-crawling Sunday afternoon traffic along First Avenue, far below. "It isn't enough. I've got to have answers. And there aren't any answers."

"That is right," the S.-G. said, and suddenly, surprisingly, found himself in the grip of a candor far greater than he had planned, so honest and so disturbed was the handsome face before him. "It is no more true for you than it is for me. I have no answers either, though I, too, would like to have them." He stood up and turned away, staring down also at the traffic, his hands clasped tightly behind his back. The conversation was not going as he had intended, but he found it impossible to stop the rush of words that hurried to his lips.

"When I was elected here, I expect there was no more idealistic man in the world concerning the United Nations. To think that I, a black man, had been chosen to serve this great assemblage which is, let us be truthful about it, still dominated in many ways by the white powers even though we Africans are granted our positions of influence in it. To think that I, from Lagos, Nigeria, had been chosen Secretary-General. To think of all the service I could render to humanity! My son, no one came here with higher hopes. No one was given more swiftly to understand that they were futile and childish and naïve and empty. Answers! I received answers, surely enough, I can tell you. Such answers as it sometimes nearly breaks my heart to realize. Better I were back in Lagos than in this mockery of an office. Better for the world. Better for me."

He paused, appalled to find himself so shaken with bitterness that for several moments he could not go on. Out of the corner of his eye he could see that his young visitor was watching him with a frightened awe, but he plunged on nonetheless.

"You ask me whether you are right or wrong. Who knows what is right and what is wrong in this topsy-turvy upside-down organization that could be so great if its members would only let it be! Look you! We send a little medicine here, we distribute a little food there, we give proof of what we could do if mankind would only devote as much attention to its own preservation as it does to its own destruction. And what does it all add up to, alongside the veto and the futile, empty debates? And the hatred that spills across the Assembly Hall and the Security Council Chamber between nation and nation and race and race? *You* want answers! How do you think it feels to be given a position of responsibility without power, honor without influence, pretense without privilege? The hope is so great here—and so small and shabby is the execution. And I, who have this title of Secretary-General, can do nothing. Nothing at all, nothing, nothing, nothing, nothing! What do you think of that, my young friend who wants answers?"

Cullee Hamilton, he realized, was on his feet too, and for several moments he did not reply. When he did, it was in a voice lower than the Secretary-General's but equally shaken.

"I'm sorry. I didn't realize. I guess things are difficult for all of us in these times. I'm sorry I took your time. I'm sorry."

"It is I who am sorry," the S.-G. said, "for giving way to an old man's lament. But you came to me for help, and I could not give it—and so I burdened you with my own unhappiness. It was not kind of me." He smiled sadly. "You see, I fail even in the small crises of life as I do in the big ones. Good luck to you. May all things come well of your own deciding."

"Yes," the Congressman said softly. "Of my own deciding. I guess that's really what it's going to have to be."

And there, the Secretary-General thought with a terrible self-bitterness as the door closed behind his visitor, goes another I have failed. Do the gods have no mercy for an old man in this sick, sad world that makes such fearful sport of us all?

Whether they did was not, at this moment, a matter that concerned the ancient figure that walked slowly along the deserted corridors of the Old Senate Office Building. He would not have expressed it that way, anyway, having a due respect for his own Lord but even more for his good right arm, and having learned in many a bitter legislative battle that when the crisis came it was not a matter of bemoaning fate or beseeching divine intervention but of getting in there and fighting. The thing that made *him* melancholy on this curiously unsettling Sunday was not his own weakness or the betrayal of the gods. It was simply a vague, unsettling restlessness and weariness unlike anything he had ever known before.

He felt, if truth were known, useless, and he was not fooling himself about it, even though he had tried to fool the others. Seabright B. Cooley, seventy-six, had nowhere at all to go when the brunch ended at Dolly's; and so, as he had on so many thousands of occasions in the past, he was returning to his office on the excuse of doing some work.

"No, thank you, Orrin," he had said, "no, thank you, Beth," when the Secretary and his lady had held out an olive branch and invited him home with them for the afternoon and dinner. "Got some work to do at the office. Got to get ready for young Cullee's resolution. Got to read up on all my precedents and rulings. Got to work."

But, with a strange bleakness that wasn't like him, he was admitting to himself now as he trudged along that this time he really had no work. He was just old Seab Cooley, feeling tired and beleaguered and unbefriended by the world.

This, he told himself as he met a guard and nodded a gruffly friendly hello, was a bad mood to be in and he must snap out of it. It was no mood in which to face either his age or the demands upon it that were being imposed by the visit of the M'Bulu and the events flowing therefrom. He needed to be in top form, shrewd and alert and perceptive and astute as he had always been; and these qualities were not strengthened, nor were they encouraged, by a self-pitying depression. He must stop being maudlin and begin to plan.

No sooner had he given himself this stern advice than he passed the door of the office that had belonged, six short months ago, to the senior Senator from Utah; and as he remembered his last visit to that office and what he had found there, the body of Brigham Anderson dead by his own hand, his resolve collapsed and the sorrow of the world swept over him redoubled. He didn't want to think of all that tragic tangle, but there it was again. Somehow, although it did not bear directly upon the present situation, many elements in the present situation could be traced back to it; and so he felt the same unhappy aura shadowing this present battle. Perhaps its conclusion would be equally sad for somebody. Perhaps, he acknowledged with a sudden constriction of his fierce old heart, for him.

For they really were against him now, the forces of the hurrying world and the intolerant, impatient twentieth century. They were not prepared to admit that he might be taking his stand on what he honestly believed, that he might be fighting from the citadel of a completely honest conviction. They only wanted to bring the citadel crashing down and him with it. And the measure of their determination was to be found in the savage anger with which they attacked him, and the ruthless way in which they sought to bring about his defeat.

Whether this applied to Orrin and Harley and Bob and the Speaker and young Cullee Hamilton, he could not honestly say. He rather suspected that they were moved, genuinely if mistakenly, by what they believed to be the imperatives of the age than they were by any personal vindictiveness. They didn't hate him, as some did—Fred Van Ackerman, for instance, who had good cause and was waiting for vengeance.

Nonetheless, they did oppose him, and that was what mattered. In other battles, he had been able to detach one or more from the phalanx that faced him and, by a skillful use of persuasion, pressure, and parliamentary maneuvering, put together an often winning combination. Now they were solidly aligned against him, and he did not know whether he could do so or not. Each for his own reasons was yielding to the appeals of political preferment in his approach to the racial issue. It did not make it easier to acknowledge, with a grimly ironic honesty, that to some degree, of course, he was too.

And yet, even though his stand was what his people in South Carolina and the South wanted him to take, he could not concede that his position was entirely political, or even in major part. By the same token, he could not quite believe that his more responsible opponents might be as fully convinced of the right of their position as he was of his. He could not quite see Orrin, with an eye on the White House; or the Jasons, with a similar ambition; or Cullee, with his desire to get to the Senate; or any of the rest, being as completely committed to a sincerely held position as he was.

That this might be a fundamental error, and one that weakened him as it led him to underestimate the depth of their conviction, he did not realize.

For, even if one were to grant all that, there was still the overriding importance of the international issue as it shaped up at the United Nations, and no American, he felt, could really be in doubt about it. Nothing could justify the apparent desire of his own government to assume the humiliation for itself in Congress instead of fighting the issue out in New York. He did not know what America was coming to, humbling herself in the face of the blacks and the Asians. He thought it was damnable nonsense to accept so abject a position.

One thing anyway, he recalled as he entered his silent office, tossed his coat on a chair, and began to leaf through a copy of Friday's *Congressional Record*, he had told Patsy Labaiya exactly what he thought of her and her scalawagging husband. Patsy had asked for it and he had let her have it. The thought was not enough to lift for long the melancholy that seemed to accompany him this day as he awaited Congress' decision on the Hamilton Resolution, but it did provide some little satisfaction. He would have more to say about the whole Jason family and their precious business when the Senate debate began.

When the Senate debate began—

His pleasure at this prospect was such that he did not realize for several moments that he was already, in effect, conceding House passage of Cullee's resolution and pinning his hopes of stopping it, once again, upon the complex and cantankerous body to which he had belonged for fifty roaring years.

He sighed, a heavy sound that grated strangely in the empty office, and turned with an automatic flicking of pages to the *Record's* voluminous story of the events of Friday last. He felt old—old and tired. But he would not have been Seab Cooley had he not presently lifted the telephone and dialed the familiar number that he so often called in the House in times of crisis, aware that its owner, like himself, was known for working on Sunday. Best give it the old school try anyway; best rally the troops on the eve of battle, shaky and equivocal though they had seemed to be a couple of days ago. Maybe today they were different.

"Jawbone?" he inquired gently. "This is Seab, Jawbone. How's everything shaping up over your way for that vote tomorrow? You not going to fail me now, are you, Jawbone, surely! Surely you're not!"

He had been away from the house off Sixteenth Street only three days, yet in some ways it seemed that he had been away forever. He looked at it as though he were seeing it for the first time, this handsome, comfortable home in this handsome, comfortable neighborhood. Was this fine house his? Did this belong to little Cullee Hamilton, from Lena, S.C.? How high you're getting, little Cullee Hamilton, he thought. How high and mighty in the world, little unhappy black boy from the swamps of the South. Little mixed-up child down a long dark street.

Well: not any more. Unhappy, maybe, but not lost and not mixed up, if not being lost and not being mixed up meant knowing what you intended to do. Not if it meant finally deciding something when you had spent three days going through the agonies of not deciding, with the whole wide world clawing your insides about it.

"Maudie!" he shouted as he went in. "Maudie! Hey, old woman Maudie! Your chick and child is home!"

Somewhere upstairs he heard her moving, and after a moment she came slowly down the stairs to the living room, where he was sprawled in his favorite chair, grinning happily.

"I hear you," she said tartly. "Guess I have two ears and an empty house to listen in. I hear you. Been hearing *about* you, now I *hear* you. Let me look and see if it's the same man."

"I haven't changed, have I?" he demanded, standing up and turning around elaborately. "Same me. Same simple little Cullee. Isn't that right, dear old homespun Maudie?" And he kissed her abruptly on the cheek.

"Hmphf," she observed, sitting down heavily on the sofa and looking him up and down. "Seems to me you're flying mighty high all of a sudden. What happened, they decide to give you the White House or make you king of the UN, or something? Must be something awful big."

"Nope," he said soberly, resuming his chair. "I just decided what I'm going to do, that's all. Any man can fly high when he knows that, Maudie. Any man."

"I been hearing all about it. You been in all the papers and on all the programs. Hasn't been anybody on earth last couple of days as important as Cullee Hamilton, seems like. I wondered about you. I wondered if it was setting with you all right. I worried about you."

"Thanks, Maudie," he said gratefully. "I expect you're about the only one who really did."

"Bet *she* didn't. You see her?"

"Didn't those programs tell you that, too? Yes, I saw her. Don't know whether she's coming back to this house or not, Maudie. Can't say as I expect you to cry about it."

"Oh, I'd like her back if it would make you happy. I'd always go someplace else if I couldn't stand it. Not so easy for you to go someplace else, maybe."

"No," he said quietly. "Not so easy. But, I'm not so sure I care, any more."

"Takes a while to get over that kind of caring. Easy to say, not so easy to do. You had dinner?"

"I'd like some."

"I'll fix it directly. So you're all happy now, is that it? Going to stay home now and sing and dance?"

He snorted.

"Now why're *you* riding me? Thought I could come home here to a friend. Now what?"

"Just wanted to be sure everything's all worked out."

"No," he said sharply, "I didn't say it was. I said I knew what I was going to do; I didn't say it was all worked out. It's a long way from that, but at least I know where *I'm* going. That's what matters to me, old Maudie."

"Matters to me, too. I was afraid all those fancy Africans and fancy Americans together would blow you right off the railroad. Best you do what seems right to you, I think, and let 'em holler. That's what *I* think."

He grinned.

"That's what I think, too. I'm glad to know I can count on *you*, Maudie."

"And don't get sassy. You be needing all the friends you can get before it's over, I expect."

"I'm going to win. I don't need friends."

"Everybody needs friends," she said sternly. "Don't you go talking like that or the Lord will punish you. Hear?"

"Yes, ma'am," he said meekly. "Get my dinner, Maudie. I want to feel like I'm home again."

"You're home."

For a moment after she had gone into the kitchen he remained sprawled in the big easy chair. Then he went to the telephone and dialed a number.

"Hi, Jawbone," he said easily. "This is Cullee. Is everything in shape for the vote tomorrow? How much of a margin are we going to win by?"

4

At precisely five minutes to noon, as was his invariable custom, the Speaker met the press. He had determined long ago that five minutes was exactly the proper time limit for his regular pre-session meeting with these industrious gentlemen and ladies—long enough to permit them to ask a sufficient number of questions so that they wouldn't feel cheated, short enough for him to easily ignore or quickly choke off anything that threatened to be embarrassing. Now as he looked around his ornate old gold-and-glass office just off the House floor and studied the group draped on sofas and chairs or standing against the wall or crowded up to his desk awaiting his word, he could sense that today they would have been difficult if they had had the time. He chuckled inwardly. They didn't, and he was ready for them.

"Mr. Speaker," the Houston *Chronicle* said with a straight face, "is it true that all us white folks are going to have to wear blackface from now on as part of this Hamilton Resolution?"

"You can wear what you like," the Speaker said promptly. "It's a free country."

"Mr. Speaker," the *Afro-American* said with an air that indicated he was not amused, "what are the chances of the Hamilton Resolution?"

"Good."

"Would you care to elaborate on that, Mr. Speaker?" the AP asked.

"Nope."

"We hear tell the vote's going to be awfully close," the New York *Times* observed.

"What you hear and what happens can be two different things."

"Can be," the *Times* agreed, unabashed. "Are they?"

"Said chances were good. They are good."

"Have you had any indication from Congressman Hamilton that he may withdraw his resolution?" UPI inquired. The Speaker grunted.

"Haven't talked to him. I think he would have talked to me if he had any such plan."

"Would you say your margin of victory will be comfortable, Mr. Speaker?" the Philadelphia *Bulletin* asked.

"Learned a long time ago," the Speaker said, looking at his most sagacious, homespun, and knowledgeably experienced, "that any margin that's for you is comfortable. Doesn't matter how big it is. It's only when it's against you that it's uncomfortable."

"Time!" his secretary said, and obediently, laughing at his concluding remark, the reporters trooped out. Always leave 'em laughing if he could, that was his motto, and he usually managed. He rose, squared his shoulders, and walked with a solid and determined dignity across the hall into the crowded Speaker's Lobby, and so through the elaborately etched swinging glass doors and into the great brown chamber of the House, filled with the buzz of arriving members and the mounting tension that always accompanies a major legislative battle.

And mounting tension it was, all right, at least for him, Representative Swarthman thought nervously as the convening bell sounded noon and the House dutifully stood and bowed to the Chaplain's prayer. By dint of rolling his eyes up as far as they would go beneath his lowered brows—which gave him a feeling of muscle strain and an incipient headache, as if he didn't have enough to think about—the chairman of the House Foreign Affairs Committee could observe the Speaker staring thoughtfully down upon him from the dais as the Chaplain droned on. It was all very well for Bill to look so Spirit of Liberty, Jawbone thought with an aggrieved annoyance; he didn't have to tote the burden of this day's battle. It wasn't his task to please everybody, something Jawbone knew very well couldn't be done even though he felt he had to attempt it.

Nor had he already had the difficult experience Jawbone had undergone last evening, of having to reassure Senator Cooley on the one hand and Congressman Hamilton ten minutes later that each was going to win. Reviewing those two conversations, coming so close upon one another, he didn't know how convincing he had been, and with a sort of nervous impatience he wasn't so sure that he cared any more. Actually he had been so busy listening to the overtones in the two voices that he hadn't been entirely aware of what he had said himself in his hurrying responses. Seab had apparently been his usual roaring, insistent self, but Representative Swarthman had thought he could detect a most unusual uncertainty underlying the stern old voice. It wasn't anything he could put his finger on, exactly, but somehow the Senator's heart just hadn't seemed to be in it. There had been the customary exhortations, admonitions, and gently delivered threats, but underneath there had been a subtle tiredness that was not at all like Seab. Of course, the old man was seventy-six and facing a hard campaign, and—there had come into his mind with a guilty excitement a thought he had never dared permit himself before. The old man *was* seventy-six, and he *did* face a hard campaign; the state *was* looking for somebody new, and might it not be that the time had finally come for a deserving Congressman to move forward and take his proper place in the upper house?

But not, he thought now with gloomy dismay, if the Congressman was going to let himself get trapped into the position of being too friendly to Negroes. He couldn't afford to have it said back home that he had put them ahead of his own people in this present tangle over the visit of the damned M'Bulu. When the showdown came, his loyalty after all was to South Carolina, in spite of what the Speaker obviously expected of him as he stared down while the Chaplain concluded and the Clerk began to run through a quorum call. He couldn't afford to run Cullee's errands too openly on this resolution, though he could of course understand why the Speaker and the Administration considered it so necessary. He just wished fervently he were somewhere else and didn't have the position he did as chairman of the Foreign Affairs Committee, which obliged him to take a leading role. He wished he weren't going to have to do what he knew he must for his own political survival. But there came a time when you had to think of your own future. It was all very well for the Speaker to look smug and above the battle. His future wasn't in question. It wasn't that simple for Jawbone Swarthman.

Nor, if truth were known, was it that simple for Cullee Hamilton as he slid into a seat just behind Jawbone and leaned forward to tap him on the shoulder. For all that he was sure in his own mind what he intended to do, the consequences were many and the ultimate effect upon his own career uncertain, and although his outward aspect was calm and determined, inwardly he was riding on courage and not much else. He didn't quite know what Jawbone was riding on, for his colleague from South Carolina jumped as though shot when he touched him and swung about with a wild-eyed expression that didn't focus for a moment. When it did, Jawbone gave a nervous and shamefaced laugh and tried to pass it off as a joke.

"Why, sure now! You scared me good, Cullee. You did, I swear. What do you mean, scaring your chairman like that, now!"

"Sorry. I didn't know you were so upset this morning, Jawbone."

"*Me?*" Representative Swarthman demanded. "*Me*, upset? Cullee, you never saw a calmer man in your life. I tell you that truly, not a calmer man. Why should I be upset?"

The Congressman from California shrugged, his eyes scanning the crowded floor and galleries.

"I don't know, I'm sure, especially after giving me that good prediction on the vote last night. I don't think we have anything to worry about, do we?"

"Well, now, Cullee," Jawbone said with an attempt at hearty assurance, "don't you worry your head about that, now."

"I said we didn't have to worry, didn't I?" Cullee said in a puzzled voice. "Or do we?"

"Well, sir," Representative Swarthman said, "it all depends on what you mean by worry—it all depends on what you—hey! What!" He swung back hurriedly and half-rose. "Is it time for me to get up yet?"

"Relax," Cullee said calmly, though he did not feel calm, for he was beginning to suspect that all this agitation concealed a far different approach to his resolution than Jawbone had indicated last night in his rambling and evasive telephone comments. "It won't be time for you to make your opening statement for the resolution for another ten minutes."

"I know," Jawbone said, a trifle wildly, "but I have other—I have to—well, look, now, Speaker's about to—the quorum's over, isn't it? The quorum's over!"

"Yes, the quorum's over, but what has that got to do with—"

"Mr. Speaker!" Jawbone cried, jumping to his feet just as the Speaker said, "A quorum is present. The Clerk will read the *Journal* of the last day's proceedings."

"Mr. Speaker!" Jawbone cried again. "Mr. Speaker, I demand that the *Journal* be read in full, Mr. Speaker. I do demand it, Mr. Speaker!"

There was a stir through the crowded chamber, for the reading of the *Journal* is customarily dispensed with, and is usually demanded only for purposes of parliamentary delay.

At the dais the Speaker looked both startled and gravely disapproving. His rejoinder came in a tone of sharp annoyance.

"All right, the gentleman from South Carolina has that privilege. You've demanded it, and you'll get it. The Clerk will read the *Journal* in full."

"Thank you, Mr. Speaker," Jawbone said hurriedly, and sat down, looking about defiantly over the floor as his colleagues studied him. Behind him the Congressman from California reached forward and tapped his shoulder again, this time not gently.

"What are you up to, Jawbone? You trying to sabotage things?"

"Why, no, sir," Representative Swarthman said. "No, sir, Cullee. I just intend to have a full and fair discussion here, that's all."

"So do I. With you, or without you."

"That's right," Jawbone agreed nervously, "but don't hold it against me now, Cullee. I have to do what my people want, just like you."

"But you promised me and you promised the Speaker—" Cullee whispered savagely.

"I never did! I never did. I'm not responsible for what you and the Speaker thought."

"Maybe you're not responsible for what we *thought*," the Congressman from California said as the Clerk began to drone through the *Journal* and more and more members began to leave the floor to get lunch, "but you're responsible for what we're going to think from now on. Did Seab Cooley put you up to this?"

"We discussed the situation, naturally. Sure we did. I wouldn't refuse to discuss it with my senior Senator. Would *you*, now! Would you!"

"All right," Cullee said in a tone of disgust. "All right, if I have to lick him, too, I'll do it."

"Mr. Speaker," Jawbone cried, jumping to his feet again. "Mr. Speaker, I make the point of order that a quorum is not present."

"Now what?" AP asked of UPI in the Press Gallery above. "Is he out to sabotage the whole thing?"

"Apparently," UPI said. "I think we're in for one of the House's great days."

"The Chair will count," the Speaker said testily as the Clerk stopped reading and blinked about the emptying floor. "Evidently the gentleman is correct and a quorum is not present. A call of the House is ordered."

Twenty minutes later, after the Clerk had run through the list of 435 members, the Speaker announced:

"On this roll call, 313 members having answered to their names, a quorum is present. Without objection, further proceedings under the call will be dispensed with."

"Mr. Speaker," Representative Swarthman cried, "I object."

"Mr. Speaker," Cullee Hamilton shouted, rising to his feet just behind him, "I *move* that further proceedings under the call be dispensed with."

"Mr. Speaker," Jawbone cried, "I move to lay *that* motion on the table."

"The Chair will state the question," the Speaker said in a tired voice as the galleries buzzed with increasing excitement, and absent members, apprised of developments by the lightning-fast corridor grapevine, began to hurry back onto the floor from dining rooms, cloakrooms, and hallways. "The gentleman from California moves that further proceedings under the call of the roll be dispensed with. The gentleman from South Carolina moves to lay that motion on the table. The question is on the motion offered by the gentleman from South Carolina to lay on the table the motion of the gentleman from California to dispense with further proceedings."

"Mr. Speaker," Jawbone shouted, "On that I demand the Yeas and Nays."

"Wheee," said the Detroit *News and Times*. "Ain't we got fun!"

Hands were lifted all across the chamber in response to Jawbone's demand, and the Speaker said, "The Yeas and Nays are ordered; the Clerk will call the roll," in an annoyed voice.

Twenty minutes after that, while the House stirred and fretted and gossiped with excitement, he announced:

"On this vote the Yeas are 136, the Nays are 245, and the motion to lay on the table is defeated. The question now is on ordering the previous question of the gentleman from California to dispense with further proceedings under the call of the roll."

"Mr. Speaker," Jawbone said firmly, "on that I demand the Yeas and Nays."

"You can have them," the Speaker said dryly as hands rose again across the chamber. "The Clerk will call the roll."

Half an hour later he announced:

"The Yeas are 249, the Nays 140, and the motion to order the previous question by the gentleman from California on dispensing with further proceedings under the call is approved."

"Now which call is that?" the Washington *Star* asked dryly of the New York *Herald Tribune*. "I've lost count."

"That's the call before the call before the call," the *Trib* told him. "'Way back there about an hour and a half ago."

"And we still haven't completed reading the *Journal*," the *Star* groaned. "Isn't Jawbone having fun!"

Whether he was or not it was impossible to tell from his expression, which was simultaneously harried, nervous, excited, and determined.

"The question now is on the motion itself, to dispense with further proceedings under the call," the Speaker said.

"I demand the Yeas and Nays on that motion, Mr. Speaker," Jawbone shouted, and behind him Cullee Hamilton, towering angrily, cried, "Mr. Speaker, how long is this farce going to continue?"

"I can understand the impatience of the gentleman from California," the Speaker said. "I can even," he added as a laugh swept across the chamber, "sympathize with it. Nonetheless, the gentleman from South Carolina is within his rights according to the rules of the House and we have no choice. The Clerk will call the roll."

Twenty-five minutes later the motion to dispense with proceedings under the previous call—the 'way back call, as the *Trib* called it—was approved 242–167. Representative Swarthman had now succeeded in delaying House consideration of the Hamilton Resolution two hours and fifteen minutes.

"The Clerk will continue the reading of the *Journal*," the Speaker said. The Clerk proceeded to do so for fifteen minutes, during which many members, many of them from the South, drifted casually off the floor.

At the committee table in the center of the Majority side, the gentleman from South Carolina and the gentleman from California ostentatiously did not speak to one another again, Jawbone hunched over, doodling on a copy of the Hamilton Resolution, Cullee slumped in his seat and glowering darkly upon the chamber. Presently Jawbone swung into action again.

"Mr. Speaker!" he cried, "I make the point of order that a quorum is not present."

"The gentleman is perceptive, astute, and omniscient," the Speaker said as Cullee rose to his feet. "He is also exactly correct, a quorum is not present."

"I move a call of the House, Mr. Speaker," Cullee said.

"The Clerk will call the roll," the Speaker said. Twenty-nine minutes later—"Lord," the *Wall Street Journal* remarked to the St. Louis *Post-Dispatch*, "aren't these jokers *ever* going to get down to business?"—the Speaker announced that 362 members had answered to their names, a quorum was present, and without objection further proceedings under the call would be dispensed with.

"Mr. Speaker," Jawbone cried, "I object to dispensing with further proceedings under the call."

"The gentleman has nothing to object to," the Speaker said. "This was on a point of no quorum. When I said we had a quorum, we were in business."

"But, Mr. Speaker—" Jawbone protested.

"Now, see here! I said we were in business and we *are* in business. Does the gentleman care to contest my ruling?"

"No, sir, but—" Jawbone began doggedly.

"The gentleman will have plenty to explain as it is," the Speaker remarked, causing a burst of laughter and applause from the now-crowded chamber. "The matter before the House is House Joint Resolution 23, introduced by the gentleman from California, and on this the House will resolve itself into the Committee of the Whole House on the State of the Union, unless my distinguished friend from South Carolina has something more to offer."

He paused, and Jawbone said hastily from his seat, "No, sir! No, sir!"

"The House must be thankful for small favors," the Speaker said. "Under the rule, debate is limited to six hours. Time *was* to have been divided equally between the chairman of the Foreign Affairs Committee, for the proponents, and the Minority Leader, for the opponents. However, I am wondering under these new circumstances which seem to have developed in the last couple of hours whether my good friend from South Carolina may not be having second thoughts about being a *proponent?*"

"Mr. Speaker," Representative Swarthman said into the amusement that followed, "if the Chair is agreeable and my good friend from California is agreeable—and the distinguished Minority Leader, I might say, is agreeable—it might be better if I were to control time for the opponents and the gentleman from California, Mr. Hamilton, were permitted to control time for the proponents."

"I expect that might be more sensible," the Speaker agreed, as the Minority Leader nodded and the House again burst into laughter. "A trifle irregular, maybe, but infinitely more sensible. Very well. The Chair will ask the gentleman from Michigan to preside as chairman of the Committee on the Whole House."

"The Chair recognizes the gentleman from California," the new presiding officer said as the Speaker came down off the dais and took a seat near the committee table.

"Well, what do you know?" AP muttered to UPI as they hurried out to file a "BULLETIN: Swarthman jumps traces, leads House revolt against Hamilton Resolution." "Maybe this thing isn't going through, after all."

"Could be," the UPI said. "Chalk one up for Seab Cooley."

"There's life in the old boy yet," AP agreed.

Thus hurtled unexpectedly into control of the battle for his own resolution, the Congressman from California found himself forced to think fast and think shrewdly as he left the committee table and came slowly down the aisle to turn and face his colleagues at the microphone-cluttered lectern in the well of the House. At first his hands gripped the edges of the lectern with an obvious tension, then relaxed until they lay quietly, long and supple, upon the old worn wood.

An unusual silence fell upon the House, and after a long moment he began to speak. This was not the General Assembly, temporarily dominated by those he considered intolerant and impatient half-illiterates from the bush who had to be addressed as though they were a revival meeting; this was his own House, his own colleagues of the American Congress. His tone was calmer, his words more polished and graceful, than they had been in New York.

"Mr. Chairman," he said, "I suppose the extraordinary performance we have witnessed just now on the part of my good friend from South Carolina is indicative of the attitude of some toward my resolution. As for me personally, he has left me in a surprising but not entirely unwelcome predicament. He has left me without a leader. Indeed, he has made *me* the leader. It is a responsibility I willingly accept."

There was a murmur of amusement and scattered applause. He permitted himself a smile and went on.

"Mr. Chairman, I will not attempt to fool anyone here by trying to maintain that this is not a very controversial matter. It is. I will not attempt to fool anyone here by trying to maintain that I like personally, or approve of the visitor from Africa who has caused all this uproar both here and in the United Nations. I have known Terence Ajkaje the M'Bulu of Mbuelo for quite some time. He is an obnoxious and self-interested fellow who fools few people in Africa and only the most naïvely and determinedly self-deluded here. But he is nonetheless a symbol, Mr. Chairman. It is as a symbol that we must consider him, and it is with a sense of national symbolism, I believe, that this House must address itself to the resolution now before it."

He paused and took a deep breath.

"I do not believe in keeping little children out of school." There was a stirring among Southern members, a sudden uneasy restlessness in the packed chamber before him, but he went firmly on. "I do not believe in medieval and inexcusable restrictions upon my race. I do not believe these things to be worthy of America in the eyes of the world. But, far more importantly, *I do not believe these things to be worthy of America in the judgment of her own heart*. Partly, if you like, I am concerned, as I think we all must be concerned, with America as the world sees her. Far more profoundly, I am concerned, as I think we all must be concerned, with America being true to herself.

"I am not one of those Negroes, Mr. Chairman, who tries to pretend that America has made no progress in the relations between the races. Nor am I one who condemns all of our southern friends, or who denies that many of them have tried and are trying, sincerely and genuinely, to help find decent solutions for a problem that sometimes seems almost insoluble. Nor do I maintain that all of my own people are perfect, or that all of us are ready for, or deserving of, the rights we are demanding.

"But, as with all things in this imperfect but, thank God, still-growing democracy, I believe a judgment finally has to be reached and a decision made on the basis of what seems best for all concerned. I think there comes a time when you have to stop balancing everything, or else you find yourself paralyzed forever between alternatives. There comes a time when judgment has to come down on the side of what is humanly and honorably and decently best—on the side of *what is right*. When I reach that point, I come down on the side of progress for my people and better treatment for my people and a full and fair exercise of their civil rights for my people. And for that, Mr. Chairman, I make no apologies."

There was again the uneasy stir from the floor. The Congressman from California went on in a quieter, more conversational tone.

"Into this situation, the M'Bulu, urged on by some who are not friends of the United States, saw fit to inject himself, for purposes of his own aggrandizement and to embarrass the United States. You all know what happened. You know what happened here, when this government, through the President and Secretary of State, sought to make amends. You know what happened at the United Nations, where the amends were summarily brushed aside and it was decided, by all those who are not friends of the United States, to make the most of it for no other purpose than simply to embarrass this country.

"You also know," he said somberly, "and I make no apologies for sounding immodest, because this is no time for false modesty—that I and I alone stopped the vote of censure against us in the General Assembly and secured a reprieve for us to consider the matter here."

"You and a few American dollars and some very fast diplomatic footwork," the Baltimore *Sun* murmured and the New Orleans *Times-Picayune* said, "He knows what he's doing. He'll come out all right."

"Now, Mr. Chairman," Cullee said, "what do we do with the time we have? We have before us my resolution, which I believe makes a fair redress to the M'Bulu for whatever he may have suffered. It also provides some genuine and needed assistance to his backward country of Gorotoland. I also believe it proves the good faith of this Congress and this government to the world. I think, and I believe other members of the U.S. delegation to the United Nations would bear me out if they were privileged to speak here, that it is the minimum that we can do and still expect the General Assembly to vote negatively on the move to censure the United States and interfere most drastically with our internal affairs.

"For all these reasons, Mr. Chairman, I urge the House to consider favorably H. J. Res. 23."

"In other words," the *Wall Street Journal* murmured to the Chicago *Tribune* as Cullee sat down amid strong and genuine applause from many of his colleagues, "it's a wonderful combination of altruism and self-interest." "At least we have the altruism along with the self-interest," the Chicago *Trib* responded. "Not every nation," he added cheerfully, "can make this claim."

"The gentleman from South Carolina is recognized for such time as he may desire," the Chair said, and the House settled back to hear the other side of it. Jawbone was ready for them.

"Mr. Chairman, my good friend, my very good friend from California has spoken eloquently on behalf of his resolution. Indeed he has. He has even been kind enough not to tell you that it was reported out by my committee by a vote of 15 to 13. He was even kind enough not to tell you that the chairman voted for it, under some persuasion from able gentlemen"—and he looked, with a puckish glance, at the Speaker, now sitting back among his colleagues on the majority side—"whose arguments seemed, temporarily at least, persuasive.

"Mr. Chairman, I want to confess right now that Jawbone Swarthman never made a bigger mistake in his life than to allow himself to be persuaded to vote for this little ole yellow-dog, tail-between-his-legs resolution. I was wrong, Mr. Chairman. I admit it freely, Mr. Chairman. How I could be so stupid, Mr. Chairman, escapes me. Except, as so many of my good friends kindly say, Jawbone *is* rather stupid, when you come right down to it.

"Well, sir, Mr. Chairman, no more! No, sir. Not on *this* resolution. Not on this let-the-world-kick-you resolution. No, sir, not on this little ole peewee look-at-us-aren't-we-humble resolution. That's not for Jawbone any more. I hope it won't be for this honorable House, either!"

For him, too, there came the burst of applause, the amiable congratulations to an old practitioner. They could always count on Jawbone for a good show and many of them were with him, anyway. It lent a warmth that Cullee had not received, and he was aware of it as he sat back at the committee table and listened attentively to his opponent.

"Now, Mr. Chairman, sir, my good friend from California chose to go off into matters concerning internal problems in this country and he chose to say his resolution and this annoying little old fellow from Africa were somehow related to those problems. Conversely, he chose to say that those problems were related to the United Nations and the rest of the world.

"Well, Mr. Chairman, could be. I don't deny every little Sneaky Pete in this whole wide world is out to get us, Mr. Chairman. That's common knowledge. What I want to know is, *When are we going to stand up like men and tell 'em they can't do it?* When are we going to stand up and tell 'em to go to hell, Mr. Chairman? When are we going—yes, now, Mr. Chairman, you needn't rap your gavel at me, I know that's unparliamentary language; and if there's any member of this House who never heard it or never used it, well, I apologize to that member, Mr. Chairman—but what I want to know is, Mr. Chairman, *When is it going to stop?* When are we going to act like *Americans,* Mr. Chairman?

"My good friend from California says if we pass his resolution humbling ourselves to this fly-by-night from the jungles of Africa, and if we give some money to his little ole bitty worthless country, the United Nations won't pass this amendment of censure offered by the great Ambassador of Panama who is a brother-in-law of the great Governor of California who aspires to such great things in this country. Well, now, I'm not against giving every little pinch of sand on the face of the globe just as many millions as it wants, Mr. Chairman, and I'm sure Gorotoland can be taken care of in the regular foreign aid program or some other means they'll think up down there at the White House. But supposing, Mr. Chairman, now just supposing we go ahead and pass this resolution and *then,* Mr. Chairman, suppose the United Nations goes right ahead and passes Señor Labaiya's amendment *anyway,* Mr. Chairman; then what? Can my good friend from California give me any assurance on that, Mr. Chairman? I pause for him to reply, Mr. Chairman, if he kindly will."

"Mr. Chairman," Cullee said, "certainly I cannot give any such assurance; nor can anyone. The chances are excellent that if we pass this resolution the Labaiya amendment will fail to receive the two-thirds vote it must have in the General Assembly to succeed. But I can't guarantee it; nobody can. I am interested in the honor of the United States, not in what somebody else may do."

"Well, now, Mr. Chairman," Jawbone said, "that doesn't sound like what the gentleman was telling us here a few moments ago. Then we were to trade our *honor* for the United Nations' agreement to refrain from telling us we were *dis*honorable, Mr. Chairman. Leastways, that's how ole Jawbone heard it. I'm interested in the honor of the United States, Mr. Chairman. I say there's only one way to uphold it, and that's to defeat this humiliating resolution and tell our delegation at the United Nations to fight it through up there; and if we get beaten, well, we get beaten. At least we won't have to be ashamed of ourselves. At least we'll be proud in our own hearts, and not have to feel that we're living on somebody else's sufferance if we act real sweet and humble and beat ourselves over the head to suit the Africans. That's *my* position, Mr. Chairman!"

And he sat down amid applause judged by the Press Gallery to be equal to, and possibly a shade greater, than that accorded the Congressman from California.

From that point the debate proceeded just about as expected. Cullee spoke briefly in rebuttal, Jawbone returned in re-rebuttal, other members of the Foreign Affairs Committee spoke briefly on one side or the other. The general debate ended around 8 P.M., and the time came for amendments. Three were offered, one by a Negro member from New York to expand the powers of the Civil Rights Commission, one by a white member from Mississippi to abolish the Civil Rights Commission, and one by a white member from Minnesota to establish an African Aid Fund to distribute aid to

Africa. All but the last were defeated by comfortable margins after short but
heated debates, and by 9 P.M. it began to appear that the final vote was approaching. The Committee of the Whole House on the State of the Union
dissolved back into the House, and once this parliamentary sleight-of-hand
was accomplished, the member who had been presiding as chairman of the
Committee on the Whole reported to the Speaker that the committee had
concluded discussion of H. J. Res. 23, and under agreement by both sides,
was ready to vote on one amendment—that of the gentleman from Minnesota—and the resolution itself.

The amendment of the gentleman from Minnesota lost 229–110, and the
Speaker announced:

"The vote now occurs on H. J. Res. 23. The Yeas and Nays are in order,
and the Clerk will call the roll."

"Mr. Aldridge!" the Clerk said in his pontifical tones, and when Mr. Aldridge said No, he repeated, "Nnnnnnnnn—oh."

"Mr. Althouse!"

"Yes."

"Yyyyyyyyyyyccccccc—sssss!"

And so the hour was here for his first testing, and in his seat at the committee table, keeping a penciled tally in disgruntled but re-established amity
with Jawbone, the Congressman from California felt tension tightening
through his body. See what you think of me now, little Sue-Dan, he thought,
and you, too, 'Gage, damn you. And you, fancy Terry, and you, sly little
Felix, and you, smart boy from Kenya, and you, tired old unhappy S.-G., and
all the rest of you smart, sneering blacks who don't know my country and
what it means and don't have the heart or the intelligence to understand even
if you did. Call me names now, damn you, and see if I care. I'm going to win
on this vote because I'm Cullee Hamilton of California and I don't give a
damn for any of you anyhow.

But it was not, as he had known, as easy as that. During the first roll call
Jawbone's excited intakes of breath as the tally seesawed back and forth
indicated well enough that it was a real battle.

"I told you!" the Congressman from South Carolina cried excitedly when
the first run-through ended and the vote stood 198 for the resolution, 199
against. "I told you!"

"Wait and see," Cullee said with a calmness he did not feel. Oh, God,
he prayed, don't let me down now; if I've done all this against the shouters of
my own race and failed, God help me— "Wait and see."

And presently, as the Clerk droned through the roll for the second time
and the absentees on the first call came forward to stand in the well of the
House and identify themselves to the Speaker and cast their votes, he began to sense that God had heard and helped, though not by very much.

The moment came when the last name had been called, the last member
had voted. A tense silence held the House, and though many knew from
tallies they had been keeping what the outcome was, there was still that

mysterious moment, stretching far back into history to the first awkward beginnings of Parliament itself, that always comes when men pause and await
the word of Mr. Speaker that makes it true.

"On this vote," he announced slowly into the hush, "the Yeas are 219, the
Nays are 214, and the resolution is passed."

"Ya-hoo!" shouted someone from over on the minority side, and with a
great explosive release of breath the House let go, men stood and began to
talk. Excitement welled up from the floor, the galleries, the busy regions of
the press. The word went out to the United Nations and around the world
that Cullee Hamilton had passed the first stage on his road to wherever it was
he felt he had to go.

And later that night, on all the radio and television programs, in all the
smooth and knowledgeable commentaries, his victory was recorded, his integrity was analyzed and there was endless speculation on what the outcome
would be when his resolution went on to the Senate and when, thereafter,
the United Nations returned again to its consideration of the Labaiya Amendment in the General Assembly.

Of the Congressman himself, much was seen that evening, always the same
shot, just off the floor, where the television cameras had caught him immediately following his victory, looking pleased and excited and saying defiantly, "This is the first battle. The second will come in the Senate, and
then we'll have won the war."

And following close upon this, a shot of the senior Senator from South
Carolina, saying coldly, "Mr. Hamilton has himself a fight in the Senate. In
the Senate we don't take American honor so lightly as they do in some
other places. No, sir, we—do—not."

And close upon that a brief clip of Terence Ajkaje, standing on the UN
Plaza with his gorgeous robes blowing about him against a backdrop of
Brooklyn, saying calmly in his most British accent, "It was an interesting
vote, but of course the United Nations must make its own decisions on
things irrespective of what purely local parliaments do, must it not?"

5

"Well, it worked," the Secretary of State remarked, dropping into a leather
armchair across from the mammoth desk in the oval office by the Rose Garden. The occupant of the chair on the other side of the desk responded with
an air of amusement that did not conceal the underlying tiredness that so often
shows through the outward urbanity of those who sit in that particular chair
at that particular desk.

"It worked for the House," the President said. "What will happen in our
old homestead the Senate may be another matter. Don't you agree?"

"We'll see," Orrin Knox said. "You look tired."

"Presidents always look tired. Presidents always are tired. But I had my
regular checkup last week and everything is in great shape, so they tell me.

I still plan to get away for some fishing as soon as we're safely past His Royal Highness the M'Bothersome M'Bulu. Have you talked to Cullee?"

"He called me at home last night, triumphant but not very happy underneath. His wife and LeGage have been giving him hell on this, as I told you. Riding this stooge-of-Orrin-Knox bit pretty heavily, I gather, plus stooge-of-the-white-man. It's quite a load for him to bear."

"But he's bearing it."

"He's good stuff." The Secretary frowned. "And he trusts me. I can't run out on him."

"I didn't know you were considering it," the President said in some surprise. Orrin made an impatient motion.

"I'm not. But—how do we let Seab down gently? That's what's bothering me now. How can we make any gesture to help him save face without Cullee thinking I'm betraying *him*? It's a problem."

"If Seab could come that close to beating us in the House," the President remarked, "I don't think I'd worry too much about saving his face in the Senate. He's doing all right."

"But he won't," the Secretary said flatly. "History's against him."

"Oh? I don't know that all the Senate agrees with that. I suppose you saw this story in the New York *Times* this morning"—he picked it up from the desk and put on his reading glasses—"'Southern Filibuster Threatened on M'Bulu Apology.' How about that?"

"Psychological warfare. Bob tells me the talk is in the air—it's always in the air, when they don't like something—but that's about all it is. It's so late in the session, and everybody wants to go home, and basically the resolution is relatively harmless from their point of view."

"Except in context of recent events," the President said. "How about that proviso on speeding progress in attaining civil rights? That's the sort of thing they'll normally fight tooth and nail, even if it's only an expression of intent."

"Well, I'm not saying they won't. Anybody who predicts the Senate is on dangerous ground. But I say it's rather less likely than more. Particularly since Seab is getting on and maybe doesn't really feel like expending the energy—or maybe doesn't have it to expend. Let's face it, our friend is getting old."

"I still say it didn't stop him in the House."

The Secretary made a scornful sound.

"With a weak sister like Jawbone Swarthman to work on? That didn't take much energy. I'll bet all Seab had to do was make a couple of phone calls and Jawbone was ready to fire on Sumter again. The Senate is another matter."

"The Senate," the President said somewhat ruefully, "is always another matter. I hope you're right. It will simplify things considerably if we can get it through the Senate in reasonable order."

"Possibly things will change at the UN, too," the Secretary said, "now that your friend the Governor of California has decided to get religion."

"Not necessarily my friend," the President said, "except"—he gave a mischievous smile—"as all you would-be Presidents are my friends. Apparently your putting the screws on Patsy at Dolly's brunch had some effect after all."

"*Your* putting them on. I'm sure that was what did it, when you made your little disapproving comment. So now we get this—" Orrin reached over and picked up the *Times* and read in a formal if mocking tone:

"'JASON CONDEMNS LABAIYA AMENDMENT IN UN . . . Governor Edward Jason of California today denounced a United Nations amendment attacking United States racial policies. The amendment was introduced by the Governor's brother-in-law, Felix Labaiya-Sofra, Ambassador of Panama.

"'Governor Jason in a statement issued through his office in Sacramento last night said that the Labaiya Amendment was "unnecessary and insulting" in view of action in Washington on a resolution introduced by Rep. Cullee Hamilton, also of California. Rep. Hamilton is a Negro.

"'The Hamilton Resolution was approved by the House last night by the narrow margin of 219–214. It apologizes to the M'Bulu of Mbuele, ruler of the British-held territory of Gorotoland in Africa, for an incident in which he was attacked in Charleston, S.C., when he intervened in school integration efforts in that city. It also pledges greater efforts by the United States to speed fuller civil rights for its Negro citizens.

"'Governor Jason said House passage of the resolution indicated approval by the Senate can be expected at an early date. He said this action by the Congress "obviates any need for an outside agency such as the United Nations to interfere in the domestic affairs of the United States."

"'The governor added that racial progress in this country "has brought the American Negro greater benefits, greater genuine freedom, and greater security than that achieved by Negroes anywhere else in the world." He paid particular tribute to Rep. Hamilton for his fight to assist Negro progress.

"'There was immediate speculation in Washington that the Governor's statement might have been prompted by fear that a too-close association with the anti-American views of his brother-in-law, Ambassador Labaiya, could hurt the governor's chances for the presidential nomination next year. His statement was regarded as a skillful attempt to disassociate himself from Sr. Labaiya while at the same time retaining the goodwill and support of America's Negro community.'"

The President chuckled.

"That last paragraph nails Ted to the mast, all right. I hope Cullee and the Negro community are suitably impressed."

"I don't know about the community," Orrin said, "but Cullee isn't. He attacked Ted in the UN debate, you know. I think those two are coming to a parting of the ways."

"One wants to be President and the other wants to be Senator," the President remarked. "When two ambitions are that strong and generally complementary, it takes more than a few candid remarks to make the parties hop out of bed. We shall see what we shall see as we draw nearer convention time . . .

What is the situation at the UN, assuming Felix ignores this, as I expect he will?"

"I expect he will, too," the Secretary said. "He's a strange boy, Felix. His ultimate ambitions include various things, such as becoming President of Panama and trying to boot us out of the Canal, I'm pretty sure. In the meantime, he will do what damage he can. Hal tells me things are holding pretty well, even though Felix did give him the cold shoulder when he tried out your idea of a loan and more representation on the Canal Company."

"I didn't expect anything from it, but it seemed worth the try. How is Hal?"

"Feeling better, apparently. So he tells me, anyway, and I checked later with Lafe, who said the same thing. I hope so. I hate to have him sick, and I would also hate to make a change in the delegation just as we come to a showdown on the Labaiya Amendment."

The President nodded.

"One change is enough for the moment. I only hope things are concluded in Congress on Cullee's resolution so that he can be back up there when the debate resumes on Friday. Why don't you have Bob sound out Seab about his plans? Maybe the three of you can work something out."

"I'm ahead of you. Bob and I are having lunch with him at one."

"And you have to let him down gently and still not let Cullee down at all. Good luck, my friend. That's a problem in diplomacy worthy of a Secretary of State."

"I'll do my best," Orrin said, rising. "Now I'll run along and leave you to the world's problems. I assume you've read over the message on Berlin and the report of the Eleven-Nation Nuclear Powers Commission—"

"Twelve as of yesterday. Don't forget South Africa."

"Right—and will let me know."

The President smiled.

"I shall. And what I recommend on the situation in Iran, and whether we should make any formal protest to India about the Prime Minister's statement, and whether it's worth trying to work things out with Indonesia, and if we should take further action on this new thing in Cuba. Also what to do about Guiana's latest, and whether or not to reply to the Soviet Union's newest charges. To say nothing of the things I have to decide today on the new expedition to the moon, extension of the draft, the construction of fifteen new Polaris submarines, whether to have the Secretary of Labor talk to Clete O'Donnell about his union's strike-threat at Cape Canaveral, the establishment of a new Titan launching base in Alaska, and the size of the standing army. Plus some odds and ends on unemployment, the medical bill, the possibility of an auto strike in Detroit, the possibility of a breakdown in steel negotiations, the problem of finding two new directors to fill vacancies on the Federal Power Commission, a proposal to extend Federal assistance to the program to clean up pollution in the Potomac River, and whether to authorize the Civil Service Commission to give government employees an extra day on Thanksgiving weekend." He shook his head with a rueful smile.

"And anything else that happens to come along as I sit here, defenseless and vulnerable, perfect target for all the bucks and all the problems that ultimately get passed along to this office, whose occupant has to know everything about everything because that's what his countrymen put him here for."

"You make it sound quite terrifying," the Secretary said, "but, in spite of looking tired, you seem to be thriving on it. So I shall remain ambitious, optimistic, undaunted, and unafraid."

"If poor old Harley can do it, I guess poor old Orrin can, is that it?" the President asked with a smile. "Well, who knows? Time will tell."

"Time and you. I expect to get a clear-cut answer from time long before I get one from you."

"It does you good to be uncertain about what I'll do," the President told him cheerfully. "It keeps you on your toes. Good luck with Seab."

"You're as cold-blooded as your predecessor," Orrin said with a grin, but not entirely in jest. The President looked amused.

"My secret weapon is that nobody but you suspects it. Check with me after lunch; I'll do what I can from here."

Now the time was approaching for him to face up to whatever it was that had, quite literally, been gnawing at his vitals, but even as he tried to prepare himself mentally to go into Harkness Pavilion later in the day, the senior Senator from West Virginia found himself interrupted by the crowding problems of the UN and the incessant carpings of his colleagues. That this was a good thing for his morale, in that it kept him occupied, he recognized; but as he sat in Special Political Committee and listened to the delegate of Guiana raise again the tired bugaboo of American economic imperialism, a sudden savage anger assailed him. He raised his hand, though the strange kneading pain was again working its way through his abdomen to his chest and breathing was painful.

"Is the distinguished delegate of Guiana aware," he asked, "that his country's policies have been so erratic of late that no new investments by United States companies have been attempted in the past three years? If this is American economic imperialism, Mr. Chairman, I would say the government of Guiana has found the perfect answer to it by being so unreliable that American capital doesn't dare venture in."

There was a murmur of amusement across the half-moon of seats in the brightly lighted room. The delegate of Guiana drew himself up to his full five-feet-one and glared at him.

"This is typical of United States flippancy, Mr. Chairman. It is impossible to discuss matters intelligently with the distinguished delegate from the United States when he is in that mood."

"Those who don't like the mood had better give some thought to not putting us in it," Hal Fry snapped. "Intelligent discussion begets intelligent discussion. Foolishness begets flippancy."

"Mr. Chairman," the delegate of Guiana said stiffly, "I shall proceed with my prepared statement. Not only is the United States guilty of gross economic imperialism, but even greater is her crime of—"

Hal Fry was aware of someone slipping quietly into the seat behind him. A narrow brown hand reached forward and closed gently on his right arm.

"You are very severe this morning, dear Hal," Krishna Khaleel murmured, leaning forward so that their whispered conversation would not disturb the rest. "What have we done to arouse this violent reaction from one who is normally so good-natured and equable?"

"I'm just tired of hypocrisy, K.K. Tired, tired, tired of it. People blandly ignoring the facts, people blandly saying things they know are not true. There comes a point beyond which decent men cannot stomach it. I'm sorry if that offends you. Your capacity is obviously greater than mine."

"Well, Hal," the Indian Ambassador said, "I can see you are in no mood for rational talk. Are you feeling all right?"

"Yes, I'm feeling all right!" Senator Fry whispered angrily, though a sudden excruciating pain suddenly shot clear up from his bowels to the top of his head and his eyes blurred the room for a second. With a great effort he made himself smile and speak more calmly. "What do you hear on the Labaiya Amendment? Has the House vote helped any?"

Krishna Khaleel shrugged elaborately.

"Who knows? Some say yes, some say no. It is all quite mysterious."

"And what do you say? That's what I want to know, accurate and objective observer that you are."

"I try to be, Hal," Krishna Khaleel said with dignity. "It is not always so easy when passions are inflamed as they are these days in world affairs, but I try to be."

"We all admire you for it. And so what about the House action?"

"It has been helpful," the Indian Ambassador said thoughtfully. "Yes, I would say it has. Whether helpful enough to change basic sentiments here, I do not, of course, know; nor can I say what the effect will be if the Senate follows suit."

"But there would be no doubt of the reaction if the Senate didn't."

"Oh, none whatsoever. None whatsoever. As it stands at the moment, of course, you are being given credit for a worthy, if somewhat belated and reluctant, attempt to behave like a decent and responsible power toward the colored people, your own and those of the world. We give you credit for trying. At the moment, that is. But . . ." He paused, and his eyes narrowed as they traveled over the crowded room with its kaleidoscope of faces and pigments. "We do not know, of course, what else will happen. It is still touch-and-go, if you like. Many of us wish you well. But we shall wait to see what it all means when you have finished."

"It's nice not to be patronized, K.K.," Senator Fry said with a cordial irony that apparently escaped the Indian Ambassador, for he replied only with a vaguely friendly smile. "You don't know how much we appreciate it. I should think we would have picked up several votes. I hear we have. And it would take two-thirds here to pass Felix's amendment, anyway. And there wasn't anything like that on his side on the vote against delaying debate. So I think we're in good shape."

"One never knows, does one? One never knows, in this world. I do hope your health is all right, my dear Hal. One hears such upsetting rumors in the Delegates' Lounge."

"That's about all one hears in the Delegates' Lounge," Senator Fry said tartly.

"But you are all right?" K.K. persisted, and Hal realized his expression must be more revealing than he knew.

"Fine, thank you, K.K. How about going out for a cup of coffee or something? Guiana's the last speaker and I don't think I'll bother to intervene again."

"I would love to, but unfortunately I have arranged to meet the M'Bulu for a brief talk in ten minutes." He hesitated. "If you would care to join us—?"

"No, thank you. Nice of you to be polite, but I wouldn't dream of it. Give him my love and bad wishes."

"Really, Hal," the Indian Ambassador said with some severity. "You *are* flippant, just as Guiana says you are."

"Purely defensive," Hal said, more truthfully than he would have liked to admit in view of the savage ringing dizziness that engulfed him. "See you later."

"Good luck at the hospital," K.K. said, and suddenly, solemnly, offered his hand.

"Who said I was going to the hospital?" Hal Fry asked sharply, even as he automatically returned the handshake.

"I wish you well, indeed, dear Hal," K.K. replied, his head averted as though he were genuinely affected, and Senator Fry thought he probably was. "Let me know if I can be helpful."

"Yes," Hal said still automatically. "I will."

Therefore his situation must be known to them all, he thought as he rose carefully and walked with what appeared to be a thoughtful slowness toward the door, careful not to give any appearance of haste that would prompt any wild-eyed assumptions that he was walking out on Guiana. He only hoped the word had not spread too far, otherwise it would quickly get back to Washington and there would be all sorts of bothersome complications at once. I don't want to make a federal case out of it, he told himself as he took the elevator to street level and started across the lobby past Zeus and Sputnik. I really don't.

At the door he paused, his eyes as always drawn upward to the silvered ball of the Netherlands swinging slowly on its steel wire, moving on its endless path, recording the swift, inexorable spinning of the globe.

"It is a privilege to live this day and tomorrow"; the inscription on the pedestal beneath the ball echoed in his mind.

God grant it me, he thought as he walked out upon the esplanade in the thin autumn sunshine and started across First Avenue toward U.S. head-quarters and the hospital that waited beyond, after he had put his office in order for the day. God grant it me.

"But, DARLING," his wife was saying over the telephone from Dumbarton Avenue in Washington, "you really can't BLAME Ted, now, can you? After all, he DID warn you. And so did I. It seems to me you really have no grounds for complaint at all. Really none at all."

"I suppose," said Felix coldly, "that this is all part of some arrangement he has worked out with the President to get his backing for the nomination next year." Patsy made an impatient sound at the other end of the wire.

"Now, that is absurd. SIMPLY absurd. Ted hasn't been in touch with the President at all since he left here last week. So how could he have 'worked out' any arrangement with that stuffy old man?"

"Possibly not," Felix said, "but I will wager you have." His wife hesitated for the slightest of seconds and then said thoughtfully, "It wasn't quite that way. I would say HE worked it out with ME. I don't know whether I told you we all had brunch at Dolly's on Sunday—"

"No. I'm sorry I wasn't down there to join you."

"Well, you have things to do there," Patsy said in a disinterested voice. "Anyway, he and Lucille were there—my GOODness, that woman is a frump—and Seab Cooley and I got into a little spat and the President had to jump in with both feet in his mouth as usual. But he did say he thought it was puzzling that Ted hadn't said something, and he did indicate that it might be well for him to do so."

"So you naturally accepted this as a command," Felix said with distaste, "and Ted naturally thought it was a warning. So he issued his statement."

"Why, of course. What else could he do, if he wants the President's support? Anyway, darling, I must say I'm not entirely in disagreement with him, you know."

"Oh, I know. Were you ever?"

"Oh, yes," she said cheerfully. "You know, I never told you, but he was most skeptical when I married you."

"Oh, was he. I could have expressed similar thoughts about him."

"How fortunate that everyone thought it best to be polite . . . Or was it?"

"Possibly not. Perhaps we should never have married at all."

"Who can ever tell what is best?" his wife asked in a vague tone.

"Exactly. Who?"

"Well, anyway, darling," Patsy said with a sudden briskness, "here we are, aren't we? So what happens now? Are you going to abandon your amendment in the UN? Are we going to get a divorce? What IS going to happen?"

"Nothing is going to happen except what is happening. We are proceeding under instructions from the General Assembly for a week's delay. Some of it is already gone. When the entirety is, we shall vote."

"You don't think the House action on Cullee's resolution has hurt you any?"

"What sort of action was it?" Felix asked scornfully. "A five-vote margin with almost the full House voting. What good does that do with opinion here in the UN? The full pressure of the Administration, and it only escaped defeat by five votes! That does not seem like a very strong sentiment in the Congress. And what effect will that have on the Senate? How will the precious resolution fare there? No, I would not say anything has hurt me, as you put it."

"Not even Ted," his wife remarked. He made a scornful sound.

"Not even Ted."

"Well, darling, I won't keep you any longer. I'm glad you called to ask about Ted. I'm glad *that* hasn't hurt. I'm glad all is going so well."

"Will you file for divorce, or shall I?" he asked bluntly, and was pleased to hear her startled gasp. But her response was calm and unperturbed.

"Let's don't rush things. It isn't anything that has to be decided right now."

"Very well, but tell Ted one thing for me. He has made his record, and we all perceive it. Now I would appreciate it if he would mind his own business and leave me to mine."

"But all of these businesses growing out of Terry's visit are so mixed up together," she said, "that how can any of us stay out of any of them?"

" 'And therefore,' " the M'Bulu concluded his quoting as he lay sprawled naked on his stomach on the disheveled bed, " 'it must be conceded that, however difficult the problems he has posed for the United States, the actions of the intelligent and idealistic young leader of Gorotoland while in this country have served as a worthy catalyst in the discussion of problems with which all Americans should be concerned.

" 'It may be that some may wish he had remained at home. But none can deny that, while here, his effect has been felt.'

"And *that*," he said in a tone of great satisfaction, "is what the New York *Times* thinks of *me*."

"Very powerful stuff," Sue-Dan observed dryly through the half-opened door of the bathroom. She surveyed herself full-length in the mirror on the door, gave her dress a tug, her hair a pat, and emerged to turn slowly about for his inspection. "How do I look, Terry? Better than those pretty gals in Molobangwe with goat butter in their hair?"

"Much better," the M'Bulu said, still in a tone of great satisfaction. He gave his sudden merry laugh. "At least in this country I know the butter is fresh."

"You're pretty fresh yourself," she observed, giving him an unimpressed surveillance that must have rankled, for under it he stirred uneasily and presently sat up.

"I don't wonder old Cullee got annoyed with you, if you looked at him like that. You didn't look like that half an hour ago."

"Half an hour ago is a long time, sometimes," she told him crisply. "How soon you got to be over there?"

"I told the New York press I'd meet them for coffee at ten. Want to go with me?"

"That would be a sensation, all right, but no, thanks. I think I'll have lunch with LeGage and then go shopping for a while."

"Better come with me," he said in a taunting tone. "Surely you don't care if Cullee knows."

"Cullee knows," she said flatly, taking one last turn before the mirror. "Does he care?" She shrugged.

"Who knows what Cullee thinks? He cares, but it won't change him." A shrewdly thoughtful and grudgingly complimentary expression crossed her sharp-featured little face. "He's got principles, that boy."

"Too bad you don't like him," Terrible Terry observed lightly. Her expression changed for a split second to one he could not interpret—angry, regretful, protesting, wistful, scornful, even, perhaps, hurt.

"Too bad you don't keep your opinions to yourself," she said shortly. "Isn't it time for you to get up and put on your pretty doodads for the white folks? They like you pretty."

"I *am* pretty," he said with a cheerful grin, rising slowly to stretch like some lithe and beautiful panther and then begin to put on undershirt and shorts, pants and socks and shirt, sober maroon tie and gray business suit. This completed, he went to the closet and took from their hook his gorgeous green and gold robes, inserted his arms in the sleeves, and, with a practiced gesture, swung the trailing sash swiftly across his chest and over his left shoulder, clapped on his little pillbox hat, and stood in full array before her.

"How is that?" he demanded. She gave a mocking imitation of being overwhelmed.

"My goodness to gracious Aunt Beulah, if you aren't the prettiest thing that ever hit New York. Guess a mere woman can't compete with you, Terry. Just as well I'm not going along, I expect; nobody'd look at *me* . . . What are you going to tell them?"

"Anything they want to hear," he said cheerfully. "Since they want to hear things critical of their own country, that's what I'll tell them. It isn't difficult, don't you know . . . What are you and LeGage going to talk about?"

"We thought we'd talk about Cullee. Do you mind?"

"No, I don't mind. It seems a little late, however."

"He can still drop his resolution," she said. "That wouldn't stop the Senate from acting, but it would make it easier for it to be beaten. Maybe," she said thoughtfully, "you and 'Gage should go down to Washington and see him."

"We can tell him what you'll do for him," Terry said with an impudent smile. "Maybe that will work."

"He knows. It hasn't seemed to lately. Anyway, who said that was any of your business, pretty?"

He threw back his head and laughed his merry laugh.

"I thought after last night that I was a member of the club. I'm sorry." She shrugged.

"Isn't any club. I just wanted to find out what those goat-grease gals in Molobangwe and all those little floozies at the UN see in you. You're not so much."

An expression of genuine anger shot across his face as he towered above her in his glittering apparel.

"Damned American," he said with a cold bitterness.

"Damned foreigner," she said indifferently. "'Spect you better run along, Terry. All your little press pals are waiting. Anyway," she added, opening the door, "I know LeGage is. So I'll see you later. Maybe."

"Have fun with Cullee," he said spitefully, following her out and closing the door with an angry slam.

"I always do," she said. The elevator came and they rode in silence to the lobby. She held out her hand in mock formality.

"Thank you for everything, Your Royal Highness." He gave his sunny smile, amicability abruptly restored.

"You, too. I don't envy old Cullee." He was pleased to see that this shot went home, for a look of resentment, oddly mixed with something that might possibly have been pain, came into her eyes.

"Go to hell," she whispered viciously. "Just go to hell."

He made a happy sound.

"I'm going to the UN. Ta, ta."

Far beyond the Mall, across the Lincoln Memorial and the Washington Monument and all the marbled buildings of the capital, the Majority Leader could see the hills of Virginia lying ablaze with autumn in the hazy sun. Soon now the weather would change; soon now, he thought with an ominous foreboding similar to the President's, all our weather may change and the final winter of the race come rushing on.

Often and often before he had experienced this feeling at times of crisis —the Congo, Berlin, Laos, Viet Nam, the convenient death of Dag Hammarskjold, the first Soviet moon shot, the conference last spring in Geneva, the endless parade of unnecessary evils forced upon the world by the indefatigable plotters of Moscow. Many a time he had looked out upon the beautiful city where confused and uncertain men of goodwill struggled to thwart the never-resting schemers who gambled daily with the life of humanity, and wondered how long a time was left in which to see the vista. Next year—next week—tomorrow—this afternoon—ten minutes from now—*now*? Sooner or later, he suspected, the Now would be here; the whole world's Now, when all the organized, efficient evil and all the struggling, uncertain good, and all the hopes and all the plans and all the craftiness and all the idealism and all the strange, unhappy mixture of bright dream and dark reality that went into human living would suddenly find their answer at last in two or three days and nights of great unearthly sound and illumination, of blast and heat and the crash of infinite thunders . . . and then silence, and no more. No more Washington, no more Moscow, no more Soviet Union, no more United States, no more functioning society anywhere, one vast ruin beyond the mind's ability to grasp, a gray and smoking graveyard adrift forever in the soundless caverns of the uncaring universe.

He shivered and told himself that this apocalyptic vision, which was the constant quiet companion of so many millions, must yet, somehow, be fended off by their combined common sense and abilities, their combined protests, their one great *NO!* to thwart and defeat the *NOW!* But in all honesty he could not tell himself that the chances for this were good. Surely, everyone said, no sane man would—but the decision did not rest with sane men.

In all this, everywhere was a battlefield, everything a battle. It did not matter, really, whether it came by clash of conventional arms in some jungle, in a propaganda lie spread around the globe, in a nuclear test, in a deliberately forced crisis in some entrapped city, in a showdown in the United Nations. Anywhere anyone was unhappy, anywhere anyone wanted to cry lie and distort the truth, the United States was on the defensive, and the truth, if it caught up at all, caught up too slowly to stop the steady corrosion of national reputation and international goodwill. Thus it all became important, in a situation in which the implacable intent was always to distort and always to tear down.

There could be, he had long ago decided, no dealing with such minds except on the flimsiest and most temporary of bases; and therefore there rested upon his own land the need to remain true to her principles, to walk honorably and do justice in the sight of the world. He had long felt a sad impatience with the flaccid cringing before some mysterious and undelimitable entity called "world opinion." He had always felt that the reason to do right was not because some illiterate savage in the swamps might think badly of you if you didn't, but simply because you owed it to yourself and your concept of yourself as a nation to do right. If you so acted, then goodwill and good reputation would follow.

Except, of course, that it did not, in this world torn apart by the ravenous ambitions of Communist imperialism and the headlong desire for independence of peoples who had the right to it, without the education or talent to make it work. Of the rights and wrongs of the latter he was aware, and on the whole he sympathized; but it was the former that posed the greater problem for his country. The only power history had ever known that was dedicated exclusively to increasing every tension, inflaming every difference, promoting every antagonism, destroying every chance for peace, did not need truth to further its campaigns. It needed only the prejudice, and the unhappiness, of others.

Thus it did not matter that British rioted against their Negro immigrants, that French preached *liberté* and practiced *inégalité*, that in India the Pious the most vicious forms of racial discrimination were practiced, or that in Africa itself black murdered black. These peoples did not wish to look in their own mirrors, and so they were only too willing to ease their consciences by following eagerly when the Soviet Union pointed the finger at the United States.

It was much nicer to forget all about what you were doing to the colored races yourselves and run happily off to thumb your nose at America. America was fair game. And America, he could not deny, at times deserved it.

The rights and wrongs of the present situation, whatever they may have been at any given moment in the past few days, were therefore utterly immaterial to the issue now. In a political sense they had gone down the drain the moment Terry took the little girl to school. All that mattered was that the United States, in the eyes of millions too impatient to be bothered with the facts and too ignorant to understand them if they could be bothered, had done something bad. There were the most real and imperative reasons for seeking to redress the balance.

Politically this was so, and in the deeper sense that he preferred to think of as his country's truest honor, it was also so. His native Michigan had its problems, Detroit was no shining example of harmony between the races, but this only served to emphasize the moral imperatives he considered binding upon him and upon the country. It was simply *not right* that the Negroes should be treated as they were in far too many places in America; and while the position of many of them had improved fantastically in recent decades, and while the whole emphasis of government had been upon improving their welfare even further, too much still remained to be done for either the country or the government to rest.

So he could not rest now, charged as he was with responsibility for getting the Administration's legislative program through the Senate. The slow and difficult processes of democracy, compounded of the disparate actions of individual men blending ultimately into some final, peaceably reached consensus, were in major degree his personal charge, at least insofar as the Senate was concerned. The margin in the House had been barely enough to pass Cullee's resolution, far from enough to justify any claim that the United States was wildly enthusiastic either about apologizing to the M'Bulu, who didn't deserve it, or increasing the tempo of help for her own colored citizens, who did. Could the Senate do any better?

He sighed, and immediately there came into his mind two people, one his wife, who was increasingly anxious that he bring the session to an end and get away for a greatly needed rest, and the other the senior Senator from South Carolina, once again the principal obstacle in the path of his legislative plans. He thought with a warm affection of Dolly, who now that she had him lawfully wedded and bedded at "Vagaries" hovered over him like a mother hen with one chick. It had been a long time since he had been surrounded by such solicitous and unceasing love, and he felt very grateful to her for it. There was imposed upon him, in return, the obligation to fall willingly into her plans, to agree to her constantly expressed desire and worry that he get away for a genuine rest, that he do something he had never had any particular urge to do, and join her in traveling abroad when the session was over.

When the session was over: that was the problem. He did not think at this moment that it would be more than another day or two, but Seab could always lead the South into filibuster. Except that he had the sense that Seab might just possibly not have the heart for it this time, that things had finally changed once and for all, that their old friend was aging rapidly and might at last be no longer able to summon his old vigor and valor. Furthermore, he did not think Seab had the votes. Many of their colleagues were skeptical of the resolution; few were under any illusions as to the worth of Terrible Terry or the ultimate intentions of the cabal that had flocked about him in this peculiar episode. Nonetheless, a majority, he was quite sure, were as convinced as he that the Congress must pass the resolution—some for practical reasons of world politics, some for reasons of idealism concerning America's national purposes, most for that combination of idealism and practicality that most honest men are willing to admit governs all their actions. It might not be large, but he was quite sure it would be a majority.

There remained only the problem of what to do about Seab, and here Senator Munson found himself in agreement with his two former colleagues at 1600 Pennsylvania Avenue and the State Department that some means must be found to let him down as gently as possible. It was not so easy to just say, To hell with old Seab Cooley; kick him in the teeth. He deserved better than that of his country and his colleagues, and the Senate, which could at times be a most surprisingly gentle and sentimental institution, would not, Bob Munson knew, either desire or tolerate too harsh a crushing of South Carolina's most famous son.

Nonetheless, the Hamilton Resolution had to go through, and it had to go through in a form strong enough so that it meant something. Any compromise with Seab could only be *pro forma,* the most modest of changes in language; and whether he would accept them or continue to oppose them remained an open question that was not so important as Seab might think.

Seab was going to lose because the times were against him and he had to lose. If worst came to worst, he, Bob Munson, would rally his support without compunction and vote the old man down.

But this harsh thought, prompted as it was by session-end tiredness and tension, was succeeded a moment later by another impulse, more tolerant and more kindly. He wondered, and all the possibilities of it suddenly brought a smile to his face, how Dolly would feel about it if he were to invite Seab to accompany them on the proposed trip to Italy she was talking about. It could be done without too much difficulty, separate staterooms, separate hotel rooms, but someone for the old man to travel with and someone for them to look after. Seab in the Forum was a thought that increased the smile considerably. Cicero would have trembled and Cato met his match if Seabritus Beus Cooleus had been around then.

The whole thing was a nice idea that pleased him, and he decided to talk to Dolly about it when he got home. His eyes still held the warm expression the thought imparted to them when Mary buzzed and told him over the intercom that Senator Cooley had arrived for lunch.

It was in no such tender mood that the senior Senator from South Carolina had left his own office in the Old Senate Office Building ten minutes before and begun to plod down the long marbled corridors toward the elevators, the subway, and the Majority Leader's hideaway in the inner recesses of the Capitol beyond. It had been scarcely half an hour since he had received one more of those increasingly numerous calls from South Carolina that were beginning to be a steady feature of his days.

The caller had been one of his oldest friends in Oconee County, and his message had been that he and some of the boys had been "doin' a little tawkin' about next year, you unastan, Sen'tuh, jes a little tawkin'," and the result of this tawkin' had been the conviction that well, now, it did look as though possibly it might be mighty tight for the Sen'tuh in the primaries next spring. The young Governor, he had *such* a good record, defyin' the Supreme Coht and the Fedril marshals and all, that it did look as though he was mighty pop'lar round 'bout. There seemed to be real serious tawk about maybe Seab, he might ought to think about retirin'. Not, his old friend in Oconee had added hastily, that any of his *real* friends thought he should; but then, you know, Sen'tuh, some yoh friends gettin' a wee bit old now, and it's this young crop makin' all the trouble. He jes wanted to pass this on, his old friend said, for whatever Seab wanted to do about it. Hissef, he concluded mournfully, he jes didn't know *what* he'd do in Seab's shoes.

This unsettling communication, which had recently been duplicated many times in calls and letters from all over the state, had deepened the melancholy that was threatening to become his constant companion. He knew very well what the situation was concerning the bright young Governor: he was attractive, intelligent, a powerful orator, and he was beginning to draw on sources of political and financial support that had heretofore been reserved to Senator Cooley alone. Furthermore, the new money in the state was backing him, and this included, for all their pious talk about the rights of man, the Jason family, whose interests and agents were many. In due course, not openly but in all the sectors where it counted, the word of this would be allowed to leak out. The young Governor might well be the one to put Ted Jason in nomination for President next year, and the hope would be that his support would bring with it many areas of the South restlessly doubtful about the Governor's position on the question of race.

"You all needn't worry what he *says* about it for the papers," the talk would go. "Jes' remember what he *did* for our boy in South Carolina." Thus Ted would be a liberal in the North, a conservative in the South, a brother to the Negro and a friend to the white, and all would be well on that particular front.

Well, Seab thought with a fighting humor, let him try it. First he had to beat Seab Cooley and then he had to beat Orrin Knox, and Orrin wasn't asleep at the switch either. Although he had exaggerated it for the press and had been delighted when they leaped to pick it up, Seab had not been kidding when he charged that Orrin's hand in Cullee's resolution had been inspired by his own political ambitions. He was only surprised that Cullee was letting him do it, and about his only satisfaction in the past twelve hours had been the way in which press, radio, and television had interwoven in their comments the recurring thought that the resolution was not basically a genuine expression of belief on Cullee's part but just a political tote bag for the ambitions of the Secretary of State.

He considered the idea of talking to Cullee about it himself, but abandoned it quickly. Any approach from him would only be regarded with the deepest suspicion, to say nothing of the fact that it might well be interpreted as a sign of weakness that would only encourage the Congressman in his stubbornness. He just couldn't bring himself to the point of putting himself even indirectly in the position of being supplicant to a colored boy, even as fine and steady a one as this. Where Seab came from, you just didn't consider anything like that.

Where he came from! There rushed flooding into his mind, with a pang so sharp it seemed to ravage his heart, the thought of his native state lying somnolent in the late-autumn sun, the low hills and valleys, the slow-moving rivers, the swamplands russet and dusty in the gentle haze. With it, as always, there came too the thought of "Roselands," of the Cashtons, Amy and Cornelia and their father the Colonel, of the long-ago loves and long-ago dreams that had taken a poor boy from Barnwell to the high and mighty eminence of member and major force in the Senate of the United States over so long a span of vigorous, violent, and controversy-ridden years.

How long a time it had been, the public life of Senator Seabright B. Cooley, and how diligently and at what great cost in energy and determination had he seen it through. How melancholy it was now to have to look back upon it and be forced to wonder, as all men sooner or later must, what it had added up to, what its ultimate meanings had been, how well it had been lived when placed against the background of its origin and its era. The era might be ending, new thoughts and new purposes might be moving beneath the surface of the South, but it was not in his mind or being to look back and say that he had failed his people, his country, or himself. I have served you well, he told Carolina and the Cashtons and the land he loved with all the fierce affection of a heart that did not have too many things to love; I have served you well. And it seemed to him that from all down the years there came back the approving answer, Yes, you have.

Why, then, must he face at seventy-six the strong possibility of repudiation at the polls, and, perhaps even more bitter, the thought of repudiation here in this Senate that was so much a part of him, on an issue upon which he knew a majority of his colleagues had serious reservations?

His mood did not brighten when he overtook Arly Richardson of Arkansas and John DeWilton of Vermont, as they boarded the subway car to the

Capitol, and learned from those two politically sensitive gentlemen that much of the initial Senate annoyance with the Hamilton Resolution was beginning to mellow under the persuasive arguments of the President and the Secretary of State, both of whom apparently had been very busy on the telephone in the last few hours.

"After all," Johnny DeWilton said with characteristic dryness, "what does a little resolution matter, among friends? If it will make the Hottentots happy, I can probably go along with it. I can't see it will make such difference one way or the other."

Arly Richardon was less inclined to be complacent, facing as he did in Arkansas much the same problem Seab faced in South Carolina, but even he indicated that it was so late in the session that he wouldn't want to do more than make a protest for the record and then vote against it.

"No filibuster for me this time," he said with a yawn. "If you want to, Seab, fire away. We'll all watch."

This was cold comfort, and no better was the indication a couple of minutes later from Alexander Chabot of Louisiana, dapper and elusive as always, that he, too, could not be counted upon for a filibuster.

"It's too late in the session, I'm too tired, and I want to go home. It isn't really that important, Seab."

"It is to me," Seab said bluntly, and Alec gave him his ironic sidelong glance and nodded.

"Maybe it would be for me, too, if I were up for re-election next year, but I've got four more years to go. By then Louisiana will have other things to worry about . . . Oh, I'll speak against it," he said in response to the look of dismay—could the old man really be that scared, Alec wondered unbelievingly—that showed for an instant on Senator Cooley's face. "But not a filibuster, Seab. Not this time."

The whole atmosphere had shifted subtly since the House completed action last night. The narrowness of the vote had not had at all the effect Seab had assumed it would have upon his colleagues. If anything, it had seemed to increase the feeling of many of them that they must give an even more emphatic endorsement to Cullee's resolution.

He found this particularly dismaying since the House vote represented a personal triumph that had satisfied him very well. He had not expected to beat the combination of Administration pressures arrayed against him, but to come within five votes of doing so had exceeded his most optimistic calculations. He had shown them he was a force to reckon with still, and while he had not beaten their precious resolution, at least he had come close enough to slow it down considerably. Or so, until he began to sense the mood of the Senate this morning, he had supposed.

His uncertainty gave a subtle but definite droop to his shoulders as he trudged along the corridors on his way to the Majority Leader's private office for lunch. It was with a startled disbelief as sudden as Alec Chabot's that the Secretary of State, coming along a few feet behind as Seab turned into the Senate Document Room on the gallery floor and started to walk through into the winding passageways beyond, realized that he was seeing a man who was old and tired as he had never, up to now, seen him old and tired before.

For himself, the Secretary of State also felt tired, if not so old. He wondered if it might not be true that all the leaders in all the countries felt tired in these savage days. He had a sudden vision of a little band of exhausted men, perched high in the superstructures of government above the vast uneasy mass of their fellow men below, all tired, all desperate, all uncertain, shouting wearily to one another across steadily widening chasms, gesturing halfheartedly through the rising mists with the terrible lassitude of those who have tried too much and failed too often, staggering together toward some ultimate and final disaster, dragging the helpless, bemused, and unhappy human race with them.

He sighed, a sudden, unexpected sound that startled a page boy darting past with a fistful of printed bills and resolutions, so that the youth said, "Hello, Mr. Secretary?" with a startled, questioning inflection. Don't ask me to make sense of it, Orrin Knox responded silently in his mind.

"How are you, Billy?" he asked cordially. "I hope school is going well."

"Just fine, thank you, sir." The boy flashed a smile and hurried off.

Would that I could say the same for the world you are about to grow up in, the Secretary said silently after him. Would that I could.

What had caused this sudden and, on the whole, uncharacteristic gloominess, he was not entirely sure unless it might be just the general burden of the world, insistent as it was in so many events, so many dark, unhappy things. His morning paper had contained the news of three murders, two rapes, a teen-age dope ring in Ohio, the figures to date on the year's traffic fatalities, a police scandal in Kansas City, a price-fixing conspiracy in one of the nation's major industries, a strike to secure an additional five minutes of coffee break at Cape Canaveral, the divorce of another of Hollywood's ideal couples, a revolutionary outbreak in Chile, another adamant statement from the Soviet Union, the attempted assassination of the Duke of Edinburgh on an official visit to Guiana, another attack on the United States at a "neutralist" meeting in Kuala Lumpur, a sudden and peculiar little riot in the M'Bulu's dusty capital of Molobangwe, another famine in Communist China, another crisis, another evil, another gray day on the downward slope of the twentieth century.

Perhaps humanity did not deserve to survive, he thought, so ravaged was it with hatred, so sadly bereft of love.

Well: that was no way to get done the jobs he had to do. He told himself that there might be time someday for such dank philosophizing, but it certainly was not now when he had so much on his mind and so many things that demanded his alert and unhesitating decision. To think too much about the evils of the world was to be hobbled by them, and this was not a luxury the Secretary of State could afford at the best of times, let alone in times as universally unrelieved as these.

In what some of his bright young underlings in the Department were wont to refer to as "the immediate sector," he thought he could feel reasonably well pleased with the course of events. Cullee's resolution had passed the House, and Cullee was apparently standing firm under the various pressures to which he was being subjected as a result of it. It was true, of course, that this morning's editorial cartoon had featured a docile Cullee on a chain held by the Secretary, the caption reading, "Ah wuhks for Massuh Knox," but Orrin's impression of the Congressman was that he would not be deflected by attacks as crude as that. Nor, he suspected, could he be swayed by the similar clamor out of New York, much of it directed along the same lines.

But now, having asked Cullee to take the gaff in this fashion, and Cullee having done so, the Secretary found himself faced with the possibility of having to ask him to accept a modification of his resolution that he would in all likelihood regard as a betrayal by a white man whom he really trusted. Cullee had decided to offer his resolution only because Orrin had convinced him of its merit and promised to stand by him. Now because of the stubborn old figure just turning the corner there ahead of him, Orrin might have to renege a little—not very much, but enough, given the hair-trigger sensitivity of black persuaded by white to take a position unpopular with many of his own people, to seriously embitter Cullee.

Seriously, and perhaps permanently; and the consequences of that the Secretary could not contemplate with any equanimity. He felt it to be vitally important to the welfare of the country that Cullee Hamilton should remain a moderate; he did not like to imagine the consequences if the Congressman became a fanatic on the race question. There were few enough with the vision to forgive the white man his many trespasses and perceive that in a joint devotion to the ultimate good of the whole nation lay the salvation of its uneasy parts. Not to forget, possibly—it would take many generations, if ever, for that—but at least to forgive, and to go on from there together to work things out on a moderate middle ground free from the shrill yammerings of radicals both right and left, both black and white.

Of equal importance with preserving Seab's dignity was preserving the dignity of Cullee Hamilton, and this he knew to be at the moment a much-battered though still powerful thing. The impression Orrin had of Cullee was of a very harassed and isolated individual who might, if he were not blessed with a strong character, give in. Such was only one of the many areas of havoc wrought by that high-riding, high-living, highbinding young character out of Africa, His Royal Highness the M'Bulu of Mbuele.

The thought of Terrible Terry, all six-feet-seven of him laughing away in his gorgeous robes, brought an expression of distaste to the Secretary's face as he made the final turn in the winding corridor and saw Senator Cooley entering the Majority Leader's hideaway down the hall ahead. He was quite a boy, was H.R.H. Terry, and Orrin Knox had a great respect for both his shrewdness and his inventive desire to do damage to the United States. Right now he was probably holding forth at the UN to some adoring circle of admirers, lambasting America for all he was worth. Was he, the Secretary wondered, aware of the strange little riot yesterday in Molobangwe and the thinly veiled hint in the early reports that it might in some way have been inspired by the left-leaning cousin he had appointed to run the country under his mother's regency while he was away? Possibly he was not laughing quite so happily after all; possibly the news would call him home. Or possibly it meant nothing. But to one accustomed now to listen with all senses alert to all the subtle noises that occurred around the globe, it seemed to the Secretary that there might be an indication of trouble ahead in Gorotoland, just as the recent British White Paper had predicted. He decided to ask for an immediate report from the African desk at the Department the moment he returned from lunch.

The thought of the UN, drifting in its rudderless and gossipy way through the endless shoals of international disaster, missing by some miracle this fatal Scylla, escaping by some marvel that terminal Charybdis, caused him annoyance too. He could agree with the Secretary-General that the social services of the organization were infinitely valuable and hopeful for humanity, and he could also agree on the marvelous potential—heartbreaking because so remote of realization—of the organization's political mechanism. But until its individual members arrived at some concept of law and reason and decent dealing with one another, the former would remain infinitesimal and the latter would remain beyond reach. And not all the pious, idealistic, eyes-closed exhortations of its earnest friends in the United States and elsewhere would change these somber facts.

Fine words could not make the UN better. Only the UN could make the UN better.

He was especially disturbed about it at the moment, because of his concern for the acting head of the delegation and the problems that a need for replacement would create at this particular time when so much depended upon continuity and vigor of leadership there. Whatever his analysis of its effectiveness as a political agency might be, the Secretary of State was well aware of the UN's character as a place where world opinion was free to run amuck. Some of its newer members had not liked the substitution of Cullee for LeGage—LeGage was more their type—and there had been much criticism in the Lounge and through the corridors and committee rooms and delegation headquarters. Some of this had been dutifully echoed by certain elements in the United States—LeGage had been invited to appear on a late-hours television show whose fey proprietor had wept copious verbal tears over his removal from the delegation—and all in all it had caused rather more of a fuss than seemed necessary.

"What business is it of theirs?" the President had demanded, and Orrin had remarked that everybody's business was everybody's business at the UN nowadays. For several reasons, therefore, he did not relish the prospect of having to make another sudden change in the delegation so soon upon the heels of the other, even though illness would of course furnish a valid excuse.

Whether this would be necessary, he did not know. Lafe, who had seemed quite alarmed about Hal Fry's health three or four days ago, had sounded more confident when he discussed it with him last night. "I think we're going to get it cleared up in a day or so," he had said, with an unconcern that didn't ring quite true. But Orrin had been unable to shake him with further questioning, and when he had spoken to Hal himself this morning there had been the same stout insistence that everything was coming along all right.

"You're sure," Orrin had said. "Because I don't want you to put on any heroics and then fail us when the pinch comes. I'd much rather you bowed out immediately than have you go along torturing yourself because of some concept of duty. I value it, and so does Harley, but your health is more important than anything else right now."

"Is it?" Hal had asked thoughtfully. "I wonder."

"We've got to feel we can depend on you," Orrin had said finally.

"You can."

So there it was. He assumed both Senators would come down to Washington for the vote on the Hamilton Resolution, whenever that might be, and he would have a chance to see for himself . . . whenever that might be. *That* depended, to a large extent, upon the determined old warrior who had just gone into Bob Munson's office ahead of him.

He was destined to lose—he *must* lose. Justly or unjustly, Seab was standing in the way of the racial juggernaut of the Twentieth Century. Justly or unjustly, it would roll over him if he would not moderate his views to accommodate its passage. There was an outside chance that he might perhaps be persuaded to do so. If not, there was nothing for it but to let the juggernaut roll.

Seab and Bob and himself—whatever the outcome was to be, they would in all probability decide it together in the next forty-five minutes. He was struck by the thought that once more the fate of a major legislative issue rested with these three friends who had worked with and against each other in so many, many legislative battles of the past. It was with an ironic but curiously gentle smile that he stepped forward into the Majority Leader's office to greet his two old colleagues and prepare to settle a major issue with them once again.

In the kitchen he could hear Maudie singing, and this sound, so foreign to his own once-more puzzled and uncertain mood, brought an extra edge of sharpness into his voice as he threw down his papers and flung off his coat and slumped with a strength-sapping tiredness into his seat at the dining-room table.

"Seems to me like you're having a high old time around here," he called out. "You got a boy friend out there, maybe?"

"Never mind my boy friends," she said, coming through the swinging door with a tray of sandwiches and soup. "Best you keep your mind on your own problems, I'd say. How come you home for lunch, anyhow?"

"I just wanted to be with you, Maudie. You're the only friend I've got right now. You know that."

"I expect that's truer than you like to think," she said, sitting down opposite and studying him thoughtfully, much as his mother used to do when he was embarked upon some course she wasn't entirely sure of but with which she wanted to help if she could. "They been giving you fits on this, haven't they? Seems like they don't know what they want. That's all right if you know what you want. Think you do?"

"Oh, sure," he said, fiddling with the soup without much appetite. "I want to pass my resolution and have my wife back and have everybody like me and be a hero to LeGage and all them and do my job at the UN and have the press like me and do what's best for my country and—isn't any limit on what I want, Old Maudie. Just a limit of getting there, that's all."

"You best forget that wife, and that LeGage, too. Neither one of 'em worth two spits on a dusty road. Likewise you best forget being a hero to everybody. You look in the mirror at night, if you can be a hero to that one when the sun comes down, that's all you got to worry about."

"And you, Maudie," he said, meaning to be light but sounding serious in spite of himself. "Got to worry about you, too."

She shrugged.

"Don't see me making any signs to move out, do you? I'll let you know when you stop being a hero to me. Won't be any mistake about that . . . What they cooking up?" He felt a sudden sinking sensation in his heart.

"Who?"

"Oh, that Secretary Knox and Senator Cooley and all. I been hearing all sorts of things on the TV just now."

"I didn't know you'd been keeping tabs on me. What did the TV say?"

"All about how they cooking up some change in your resolution. Seems it will get through the Senate sooner if they cut it back to make the white folks happy. I'm just wondering, that's all."

"I don't know anything about that," he said sharply. "They haven't mentioned anything like that to me."

"Wouldn't. Wouldn't 'til it's all done, would they? Might be you'd do something stop you being a hero to *them* if they told you too early."

"You think I'm a hero to them? You think I'm their pet, like LeGage and the *Post* and all them say? Is that what you really think? I'd like to know."

"Don't know. You say you doin' what's right, I guess you doin' what's right. I guess your white friends won't make you out a fool. Not if they think you worth anything at all."

"I guess they won't. I guess they'd better not. Anyway, Orrin Knox promised me—"

She made an impatient gesture.

"Promise on Sunday, cheat on Monday."

"Today's Tuesday. And Orrin Knox doesn't go back on his word."

"Well, that's good," she said, attracted by a sudden noise and peering outside. "That's good you got such faith in your white friends, because here come a couple of black ones going to give you a hard time. Nobody but Mr. LeGage Shelby and his big buddy, Mr. Fancy-Pants from Africa. Want me to serve 'em lunch?"

"Don't serve them anything," he said, a sudden tension constricting his heart and clamping down on his stomach so that he was unable to eat any more and shoved his chair back violently from the table. "Just don't serve 'em anything. If I ring, you come show them to the door, that's all."

"Oh, my. Going to throw them out in style, are we?"

"Going to throw them out, in style or not."

But for all that he meant it, and for all that he went to the door as though going into battle, it was not with any certainty of outcome that he flung the door wide and stared defiantly at the two who confronted him there. LeGage, his hand outstretched but not yet touching the bell, looked as tense and unhappy as he; Terrible Terry looked as though he were on the gayest of picnics. It was he who spoke first, sweeping in grandly as he did so.

"He is home, you see, LeGage, just as his office said he would be. Cullee, old chap, how are you?"

"My office doesn't lie," he snapped, though he wasn't sure of it lately. "What are you doing in Washington?"

"It's a free country, as my American friends are so fond of telling me," the M'Bulu said contentedly as he disposed his robes about him and sat down gracefully on the sofa. "I will have you know I have been invited down to attend a most smashing cocktail party here in honor of Justice Davis and myself. It isn't until tomorrow, though, so I thought I would accompany our mutual friend here in a visit upon you. You don't mind, I hope, dear old Cullee. You have a most charming home, empty though it is of the lady of the house."

"She'll be back," he said, as though the promise would be enough to produce her. The M'Bulu shrugged with an elaborate use of his hands-out, palms-up gesture. "Who knows? Indeed, dear Cullee, who knows?"

The Congressman looked at him with an expression in which contempt, jealousy, and pain were mingled, then whirled abruptly on LeGage, still standing uneasily by the door.

"Sit down," he ordered tersely. "What are you doing here with this jackass? What do you want of me?"

"I thought maybe we should have another talk, that's all," the chairman of DEFY said carefully, moving toward a chair. "You're getting pretty far out and away, these days. I thought maybe I could still bring you back."

"What's it to me what you think?" Cullee demanded. "And what do you mean, far out and away? We've been all over this ten million times; I told you what I was going to do and I'm doing it. What call have you got now, coming into my home and trying to chew me out?"

"You see?" Terry inquired of no one in particular. "I told you he would be difficult, LeGage. I told you it was a pointless errand, trying to bring old Cullee back to his own people. He's probably half white already, underneath those clothes. At any rate," he added with a sudden vicious tone, "I dare say his liver is."

"Do you want me to—" the Congressman began furiously, but restrained himself even as Terry said, "Oh, you couldn't," with an airy wave of the hand.

"I could, but I wouldn't want to dirty my hands with a piece of foreign trash like you. I said to you, LeGage, what do you want of me? Answer and get out."

"You know what they're going to do," his ex-roommate said, looking tense but determined. "They're going to water down your resolution so it won't mean anything anyway. Why in hell don't you get sensible and get back where you belong, with us? You're just a fool, all out there by yourself."

"I'm not all out here by myself! A lot of people are with me. Just because you and your bunch of fanatics want to mess up America, it doesn't mean a lot of good people don't believe in me."

"So modest, too," Terry remarked. "So very modest, our noble Congressman."

"Listen!" Cullee said. "What about things in your own back yard? What about things back home in dear old Molobangwe? Seems to me I heard about a riot over there yesterday. Maybe you better skitter back on home, you big pretty bug, and see what's going on in your own house. Maybe your cousin'll turn you out while you're over here telling us how to run our country. Ever think of that, Terry? Maybe you'd better!"

"Everything is under control," the M'Bulu said serenely. "Please be assured of that; everything is under control. Much as you'd like to see me destroyed, dear sweet Cullee."

"I'd like to see you strung up by the heels with your head in the pot. Maybe then we'd have some peace around here."

"You think that would do it?" Terry said with a sudden blazing harshness. "You think that would be sufficient to bring harmony to this great happy world so the blacks would love the whites and the whites would love the blacks and everything would be wonderful? Maybe I could offer to be a sacrifice if that would do it. But it won't, old Cullee, and you know it. It will take more than that, a lot more than that!"

"They're going to make a fool of you, Cullee," LeGage said softly. "They're going to get you fighting your own people and stooging for *them,* and all of a sudden some day you're going to wake up and find they've dropped you flat, and you won't have them and you won't have us. And where will you be then, I ask you . . . Look," he said, with a sudden agonized earnestness that shut the M'Bulu out of the room entirely and left just the two of them, arguing desperately as they used to do at Howard, as they had on so many angry, hopelessly entangled occasions in the past, "I don't want to see them hurt you, Cullee. I don't want to see you get separated from your own people. Orrin Knox is just going to use you and drop you; that's all they want is to have things their own way and have you to stooge for them . . . Please, Cullee," he said in an aching whisper. "Please come back."

"'Please Cullee, please come back,'" the Congressman said with a bitter mimicry that was curiously close to tears. "How you do sound, Mr. LeGage Shelby, dear old buddy and roommate of mine, how you do carry on! And what do you want from me, if it isn't to stooge for *you*? Tell me *I'm* far out and away! Where have you gone? A long way from where I used to know you, I can tell you that, a *long* way!"

For several minutes neither of them said anything more and the M'Bulu did not stir, so that there was in the room only their harsh excited breathing and a sense of loss become irrevocable. Finally Cullee spoke, in a lower and less agitated tone, frightening to LeGage in its dull air of finality.

"Now I think you better go. I trust Orrin Knox and I'm doing what I think is best. You want me to mess it up down here in Washington so you can get the whole world to stomp on us up there in the UN. Well, I think more of my country than that. I think I'm an American, 'Gage. I don't know what you are . . . As for you," he said to Terrible Terry with a contempt so withering that it penetrated even the bright defenses of that carefree soul, "I don't know what you are, either, and I don't care. So, now, get out. Get out. Both of you."

"Seems like you're always telling me to get out, lately," 'Gage Shelby said in a shaking voice. "All right, I'm going, but I want you to know—"

"Then go! Just shut up and go!"

LeGage stared at him with a strange intensity, his face torn by some terrible emotion Cullee could not understand or really see, so violent was the storm of his own feelings. Finally 'Gage spoke in a voice so choked it was almost a croak.

"You watch out, Cullee. Things are going to happen to you if you don't watch out. I warn you, things are going to—"

"Well!" Terrible Terry said lightly, rising to his feet. "I must say, how dramatic we all are, here in America. How—"

"Oh, for Christ's sake," Cullee Hamilton said, *"will you get out?"*

After they had, urged on by a tight-lipped Maudie who entered and said "Scat!" in a tone so intense that even the M'Bulu looked taken aback, he remained standing by the window staring out, one hand gripping the edge of the draperies, his forehead resting against the sash, the world seeming to spin away and away until he no longer felt any control of it.

It was in this detached and floating mood, in which all the world seemed unreal, all plans undone, nothing any longer important or imperative, that he became aware that a chauffeured limousine was drawing up before his door and saw descending from it the tall gray figure of the Secretary of State. Still moving as in a dream, he left the window and went slowly to let him in.

Here in these brisk asceptic corridors high on Morningside Heights there were no longer any of the assumptions of psychiatric prejudgment concerning the infinite complexities of the human mind. Here in Harkness Pavilion medicine meant business, and there was no nonsense in the way it went about it.

Thus Senator Fry found himself hurried briskly from doctor to doctor and test to test, this studied, that analyzed, efficient men and women skillfully reducing the human body and its functions to charts, graphs, and carefully organized reports. Once he remarked lightly—trying to cover the slashing pain in his chest—that he might be the medical mystery of the year.

"You won't be when we get through with you," the specialist who was checking his heart told him. But the electrocardiogram showed nothing, and the savage chest pains went on, and the specialist was not so confident when he said good-by and sent his patient on to the next station of his fateful journey.

By 3 P.M. he had been interviewed, tested, and examined for a dozen different things by a dozen different doctors. Conferences had been held, consultations had gone forward, a conclusion had been tentatively reached as one possibility after another was studied and eliminated. This he did not know. All he knew was that he felt an increasing sense of loneliness, a growing despair, for it seemed to him that he was traversing endless corridors, walking down endless hallways, looking into endless eyes that grew steadily more blurred and more impersonal as they discovered nothing, learned nothing, floundered deeper and deeper in the unfathomable mystery of the terrible storms that afflicted his body. In this sick blackness his heart cried out for his son, though he knew his son did not know him and could not help him, and for his friends, though he thought them uncaring and far away. He came to feel, though tended by many hands and the concern of many minds, utterly abandoned by the world. It was therefore with a rush of gratitude so profound it brought tears to his eyes that he entered the last of many neat white rooms and found waiting for him the junior Senator from Iowa and a young couple, apparently Indonesian, sitting with him on a wicker sofa.

"We thought we'd come and see the Pavilion's most distinguished patient," Lafe Smith said easily. "You remember this young lady from the doctor's office at the UN; and this is her husband, who is interning here. How have they been treating you?"

"Fairly gently," he said, managing a smile, "but with great thoroughness. I seem to have no secrets left—except, of course," and his smile turned sad, "the secret of what is wrong with me. That still seems to elude them."

"It won't for long," the boy said, flashing a comforting smile from his bronzed face. "They are pretty thorough here."

"I know that," Hal Fry said with a rueful humor. "Much better, I think, than the doctor your wife works for."

The girl smiled.

"He is not well himself, I think. Inside, not well. He is quite mixed up about many things. It might be better if he worked somewhere else, in some other profession."

"This is a young lady with definite opinions," Lafe said with a smile, "as you can tell."

"So I see. The two of you are going back to Indonesia when you complete your training, is that it?"

The boy nodded.

"We consider it a small, but perhaps worthwhile, contribution to our country. Doctors and nurses are needed so badly there."

"Will you have your own hospital eventually?" Hal asked in an interested tone, then abruptly reached out for a chair. At once the girl was at his side, holding his arm and helping him to sit down.

"We should like to," she said, returning to sit again, gravely, on the sofa. "It is a dream we have."

"I suspect you have a way of making your dreams come true," he said, managing a smile.

"Yes," Lafe said with humorous agreement. A little silence fell and finally Hal Fry broke it, as he realized he must.

"Now suppose you tell me what you know. I haven't been left all alone with you in this great big hospital just by chance. What is it?"

Across the face of the Senator from Iowa—When had he first seen that boyish visage, grinning at him across the Senate floor on its first day there? A long, long time ago, in some other world where things were right side up and one's body made sense—there passed a troubled frown. The young couple, Hal noted, were sitting very still. A terrible terror gripped his heart.

"What is it?" he demanded. "What is it?"

"Pretty much everything has been eliminated," Lafe said carefully, "except one thing that the blood count indicates, and for that they want to give you one further test to be sure. It involves an exploratory operation, probably tomorrow morning."

"Exploratory?" Senator Fry said, and the word seemed to hang like some ominous shadow above their heads.

"In a sense, yes," the girl said, "though not in the way you perhaps think. It does not involve a massive incision of the body."

"Only the sternum," the boy said. He gestured to it with a lean brown hand. "The breastbone. They test the marrow in it."

"What's that for?" Hal Fry said. A look of compassion that terrified him even more came into the eyes of the junior Senator from Iowa.

"My dear friend," Lafe said. "It is for leukemia."

And now, the Secretary of State told himself, he must embark upon one of the most difficult conversations of his life, and from it emerge, hopefully, with victory for Cullee and solace for Seab, a forward step for the United States domestically and a sign of good faith to the watching world. Quite a little assignment for a diplomat, as the President had remarked. He wondered if he could bring it off. Probably not, if his host's initial expression was any indication. The Congressman looked unhappy and hostile and curiously remote, as though he were simultaneously suffering from something and had lost interest in it.

"Cullee," Orrin Knox said, holding out his hand, "your office told me you were at home, so I took the liberty of coming here. I hope you don't mind."

"No," the Congressman said with an air of tired disinterest. "I don't mind."

"Good," the Secretary said, deliberately taking the chair he had noticed before to be his host's. Cullee gave no sign, but dropped dispirited on the sofa and put his hands behind his head with a tired, unhappy sigh.

"Are you all right?" Orrin asked. Cullee gave a small, unresponsive smile. "I guess so," he said, adding without insolence, "Are you?"

"As well as can be expected, I guess. The world being what it is."

"Yes," the Congressman said slowly. "Well"—and there was a spark of humor returning—"are you and I improving it?"

"Trying," Orrin Knox said. "Trying. Now we've got to get your resolution through the Senate and we'll have done all we can at this end of the line."

"Isn't it going through?" Cullee asked with a stirring of surprise. "I thought it was."

"I'm sure of it," Orrin said. The Congressman, he realized, was suddenly out of whatever doldrums he had been in and watchfully alert.

"You don't sound sure," he said sharply. "What's gone wrong?"

"I am sure. Nothing's gone wrong. We have the votes."

"Well, then—" The Congressman paused. "Maybe you'd better tell me what it is," he said with an ominous quietness.

The Secretary studied him for a moment, obviously debating what tack to take. Then he took a deep breath and what seemed a reasonable gamble and told the truth.

"Nothing really fundamental. I just don't want us to kill Seab Cooley while we're at it, that's all."

"How will it kill Seab Cooley?" Cullee asked scornfully. "That sounds too dramatic for me to swallow, Senator."

"It does sound dramatic, doesn't it? It could happen, though, if the resolution is so strong he feels he has to filibuster."

"Am I supposed to be concerned about that? Am I supposed to be concerned about an old man who has always supported the oppression of my people? Let him think about that while he's dying from a filibuster, if he wants to!"

"He's only done what his upbringing and training have taught him to do," Orrin said quietly, but his host only looked angrier and more excited.

"So have I! So have I! Now I'm supposed to go easy on that old man? You want me to go easy on the South, Senator? Don't make me laugh!"

"Laughing isn't what anybody is doing, at the moment," Orrin Knox said gravely. "We're trying to work this out—I'm trying to work it out—with victory for you and still not too much pain for him. That's all."

"No, you're not," Cullee Hamilton said bitterly. "You're trying to do exactly what 'Gage and Terry and all the rest have been warning me about. You're just using Seab Cooley as an excuse. You're afraid the resolution will offend too many people in the South, and that will hurt your chances for the nomination, and that's why you want me to water it down. That's what they told me and I said it wasn't so. I said I believed in Orrin Knox. My God! What a laugh!"

For a second all the Secretary's old angry impatience flared up within him, and it was all he could do to hold back some sharp and savagely stinging retort; but Orrin, as his colleagues had noted, was growing up, and so he managed, though not without an intense struggle, to suppress it. He looked at the Congressman with a calm and unflinching appraisal that made him drop his eyes and stare angrily at the floor. This accomplished, the Secretary spoke in a calm voice.

"If that were the best you could really think of me, then it would probably be wisest that I leave right now. I can't really believe, however, that your view of me is that shallow, however emotional you may be about it at the moment. There are reasons, my friend, for not driving too hard against a man who has been United States Senator for fifty years and served his country well in many battles on many fronts. You know them as well as I do. You wouldn't do it to the Speaker. No more would I want you to do it to Seab Cooley. Furthermore," and a certain tartness came back into his voice, "who said I wanted to water down your damned resolution? I haven't mentioned anything about it."

"You don't have to," the Congressman said in a quieter but still hostile tone. "I can see you coming. Anyway," he added with a sudden renewal of anger, "why play word games about it? What could I possibly change to please Seab Cooley that wouldn't destroy the whole meaning of it? He wouldn't be satisfied with anything less, and you know it. So what are we talking about?"

"We're talking about doing honor," Orrin Knox said, still with an edge in his voice, "—and I am going on the belief that you value the word—to a servant of this Republic who, whatever his faults in one area, has done well by his country in many others. That's what we're talking about. Are you with me?"

"I swear I don't see why I should be."

There was another angry silence, during which the Congressman in his turn stared at his guest. The Secretary's eyes did not drop, and presently Cullee spoke in a voice that yielded very little.

"I swear I don't see why I should be. He's done enough dishonor to my people so I don't see why I should honor him." A sudden bleak expression came into his eyes. "It's just like 'Gage said. He said I couldn't trust you."

"You know LeGage a thousand times better than I do," Orrin said, "but I don't think his views on me or any other white man are very conducive to a better understanding between the races. Now, do you, really?"

"At least he knows where he stands," Cullee Hamilton said bitterly. "That's more than I do, right this minute."

"No honest man knows where he stands exactly. Only approximately, and with a prayer to the Lord to forgive his errors, if he's wise. But that doesn't mean you can't see some things reasonably clearly, and one of them is that this eternal self-defeating suspicion of each other's motives isn't going to get any of us anywhere. Or does that sound like nonsense to you, too?"

"No," the Congressman said slowly, "it doesn't sound like nonsense." His face set into a stubborn scowl. "But I'm not about to soften things down for

Seab Cooley. Let him filibuster and be damned, as far as I'm concerned. He doesn't deserve any better from any Negro."

"Look: You don't even know yet what could be done. Why don't we just consider it for a minute as a couple of legislative technicians and see how it sounds? Here"—and he pulled a copy of H. J. Res. 23 out of his pocket and tossed it on the coffee table between them—"the only thing that might need to be changed is the last paragraph. We can let the rest of it stand, if it makes Terry happy."

"But not all of it, if it makes me happy? Why don't you leave me alone, Senator? It says it the way I want to say it." An ominous glint came again into his eyes. "You don't want me to chuck the whole thing, do you?"

"No, sir, I do not. The language now reads, 'It is also the sense of the Congress that the United States should move with even greater speed to improve the lot of its Negro citizens. The Congress pledges its full assistance in securing such greater speed. . . . How about 'should *give serious consideration to moving with greater speed*,' and so forth. Would that be agreeable to you?"

The Congressman shook his head, the stubborn, embittered expression still in his eyes.

"Even if it were, which it isn't, it wouldn't be to Seab Cooley."

"Bob Munson and I have just had lunch with Seab Cooley, and there is some reason to believe it might be."

"Then that's even more reason why I can't accept it, so that answers that."

"It doesn't answer anything," Orrin Knox said sharply. "Nothing. All he asks is a slight modification and the chance to make a speech against it, and then he'll have made his record and can get out of the way."

"And be re-elected in South Carolina and go on helping to suppress my people. No, thank you. And it isn't any 'slight modification,' as you very well know. 'Should move with even greater speed' is a long way from 'should give greater consideration to moving,' Senator. What do you take me for, a fool?"

"No, I don't take you for a fool!" the Secretary said angrily. "I take you for a man who has a reasonable kindness in his heart and might have the guts to show it, if he weren't too afraid of his own shadow. The President and I stand behind this, you know. We'll move, whatever the language says; you can be sure of that."

Cullee Hamilton shook his head.

"Not just my shadow, Senator," he said softly. "Lots of shadows, all black . . . I couldn't do it and feel right inside. God, you know that!" he said in an agonized voice. "How can you ask me to?"

"I don't know," the Secretary said, folding the resolution and putting it back in his pocket. "I don't know. Sentiment, I guess. Loyalty to an old friend. A foolish belief that things are best accomplished in this mixed-up land of ours when they are accomplished with the broadest general agreement and the least individual hurt. Some feeling that you might be able to understand, apparently mistaken. Some conception of a Cullee Hamilton who perhaps doesn't exist. Evidently," he said, and he got to his feet quickly, "I was wrong on all counts. Sorry to have bothered you. I guess all I did was send you back to the waiting arms of LeGage Shelby, right?"

"No," the Congressman said, "not quite that . . . Wait a minute." He gave a small, tired smile. "Maybe you've talked me around again."

"I don't want to do that," Orrin said, and then added with a sudden, engaging candor, "Of course I do, but not unless you can really see it."

"I might accept 'give serious and *affirmative* consideration to moving with greater speed,' and so on. But he'll have to come and ask me for it himself."

"Oh, well, then it's pointless. He never will."

"He must."

"He won't."

The Congressman shrugged and turned half-away.

"Very well. Then there won't be any changes—and if any are tried from the floor, I'll scream so loud they'll hear me around the world—and he can filibuster until he drops, as far as I'm concerned."

"You drive a hard bargain."

"It's the education we get. Will he come?"

"I'll call Bob, and we'll see what we can do. But I can't make any promises."

"Nor I."

But after the Secretary had left, quickly as an experienced politician does when he thinks he has an agreement, the momentary satisfaction Cullee had gained from this outwardly adamantine position faded rapidly.

There returned almost immediately his dismayed suspicions of Orrin Knox, the possibility that he might well be just a too-compliant pawn in the larger game of the Secretary's Presidential ambitions. The more he thought about it, the more his anger and dismay increased. Of course, the only possible position was the one he himself had followed right along. True enough, it would be easy to accept a modification in the Senate with the bland comment that, "I see no danger to my resolution; the modification is designed to accomplish the fundamental purpose; it is acceptable to me." But no one in the Congress would be under any illusions about the change in language, nor would the subtle and legalistic minds that hovered around the racial issue both domestically and in the United Nations. They would say Cullee Hamilton had sold out, and for what? Not even for his own political advantage, which some of them might be able to understand and forgive, but for the political advantage of Orrin Knox, which they could not understand and would not forgive.

But—on the other hand. There was the Secretary's desire, and the Congressman felt it to be quite genuine, to give Senator Cooley a face-saving way out, to protect an old friend and not let him be hurt too badly in reaching his accommodation with the inevitable. Cullee could see this. He didn't want to be mean to the old Senator just to be mean. He did, as Orrin had said, have "a reasonable kindness in his heart" and no desire to be harsh unless he had to.

Very well, then. Let the old man come to him, as he had suggested, and he would see. He might be able to give an inch if that would help Seab walk his rough last mile; and anyway, from what he heard, things were shaping up against Seab's re-election so strongly that a paper triumph on this small feature of the Hamilton Resolution wouldn't make much difference anyway. Perhaps he could afford to be generous, after all. Perhaps, as Maudie said, he should stop all this worrying and come back to the good opinion of the man in the mirror. On that basis, maybe he too could be gentle with Seab, as long as it didn't interfere with his basic purpose. Maybe he could.

It was therefore in a calmer and more reasonable mood that he heard the phone ring half an hour later and picked it up to be advised by an obviously surprised Orrin Knox that if he cared to drop in at Bob Munson's office around 5 P.M., a profitable discussion might be held. It would mean that not only Seab, but he, too, would have to come part way, but certainly no farther than he himself had suggested, and would that really be too much to ask? He was momentarily soured again and suspicious, but after a second agreed that yes, he would be there.

"After all," he said with just enough emphasis to make the point to the Secretary, "I have nothing to lose."

Orrin agreed, and the date was set.

Set for the senior Senator from South Carolina, too, and it was with a sense of growing triumph that he walked once more along the corridors of the Old Senate Office Building, once more rode the subway to the Senate side of the Capitol, once more trudged along with his rolling, barreling gait to the hideaway of the Majority Leader. He had made it quite clear at lunch that he might be willing to accept a compromise on the Hamilton Resolution, but only if that nice colored boy came to him; and now, apparently, he had. Bob Munson's call had been a little hazy on details, and at first Seab had objected stuffily that he didn't see why his own office wasn't a good enough place for the Congressman to come and have a talk; but then the Majority Leader had said something, rather vaguely, about "pride and personal touchiness—you know," and Senator Cooley had said yes, he knew. He had finally agreed, reluctantly but knowing he had the whip hand now and could afford to be generous, to meet Cullee on neutral ground, in Bob's office.

"After all, Bob," he had said with a happy feeling of triumph, "I have nothing to lose. You know that, Bob."

And Bob, a little hesitantly, had agreed, and the date was set.

So here he was, once more in command of a situation that had looked, for a little while, as though it might be difficult and perhaps disastrous. There had been moments in the past few days when he had actually wondered whether he could swing things his way once again, or whether the Cooley influence and the Cooley magic had finally failed. His own quick tally of known Senate opponents, probables and possibles, had convinced him that the outcome was entirely up in the air; but evidently there were things he didn't know about. Evidently Bob and Orrin and their young friend from California had found that the opposition was too strong for them, should the resolution be left as it stood. Evidently he was in better shape than he knew.

Evidently everything was going to be all right.

It was therefore in a relaxed and friendly mood, humming a little tune as he plowed along, that he came to the Majority Leader's office once again and, entering, found himself confronted by the three of them. They looked, as he could instantly see, rather ill at ease and not too happy about the way things were going.

"Now, then," he said expansively, for there was no need to keep everybody edgy, "it's nice to see you, Congressman, and you, too, again, Bob and Orrin. I hope the world is treating you well, now, Congressman, I truly do."

"Well enough, thank you, Senator," Cullee said evenly. "And you, sir, I hope."

"Oh, fine, thank you. Quite fine. Now, Orrin and Bob, why don't you—"

"We're just going, Seab," the Majority Leader said quickly. "Don't kick me out of my own office, now."

"Offered mine, Bob, but you said—"

"Yes, Seab, we appreciate your coming," Orrin Knox said hurriedly. "Come on, Bob, let's go down to the floor and see Tom August. I'd like to have him get this thing through Foreign Relations Committee tomorrow morning, if we can."

"Orrin still thinks he's running the Senate, Bob," Senator Cooley said with a lazy grin. "You just watch Orrin now, else he'll be running this old Senate again. Can't have that, Bob. No, sir, can't have that."

"I didn't do so badly, in my day," the Secretary said. "Cullee, thank you for coming. We'll see you both later."

"Yes," the Congressman said, in the same even tone.

After they had gone, he and the President Pro Tempore of the Senate remained for several minutes silent and constrained in the comfortable room littered with the photographs and political memorabilia of the Majority Leader's long career in Washington. Both seemed disposed to examine these, Cullee because he felt tense and nervous and at first uncertain how to proceed with the formidable old man before him, Seab Cooley because he felt disinclined under the circumstances to lord it over the boy but felt instead that he should give him a moment or two to calm down before Cullee began his inevitable offer of compromise. It was with some surprise therefore that he became aware that a great stillness, as palpable almost as Bob Munson's leather armchair, had come over the Congressman; and began to perceive, with the first flickering of alarm, that it was not the stillness of diffidence but the stillness of determination that had settled upon the handsome black face across the room. More quickly than he had intended, caught slightly off balance, not yet really worried, but puzzled, he broke the silence first.

"Well, sir," he said, intending to put the boy—or was it himself?—at ease, "why don't we sit down, now, and talk this over quietly?"

"Would you ask me to sit down if we were in South Carolina and not in Congress, Senator?" Cullee asked quickly, and it was not at all the sort of remark Seab Cooley had expected. It was not insolent, just curious: but it was not the type of curiosity he was used to from the dutifully genuflecting Negroes he knew in South Carolina. Not that they genuflected from fear of him, because he was very well liked by the colored race; he had done a great deal for them in his years in office, and they called him "the Old Senator" and were honestly fond of him. But—they just didn't question. At least the older ones didn't. The younger, he was uncomfortably aware, were beginning to talk like Cullee.

"Why," he said, "I expect I would ask you to sit down if we were in South Carolina. I'd invite any member of Congress to sit down in South Carolina and be honored to do it, sir. Honored to do it. Does that surprise you, now, Congressman? Is that a surprising thing?"

Cullee gave him a long look, his expression unfathomable. Then he gave an ironic little smile and shook his head.

"No, Senator, it doesn't surprise me that you'd invite any member of Congress to sit down in South Carolina. Please take the Majority Leader's chair, if you'd like. I'm going to try the sofa."

And with the casual grace of body that those who are athletes in youth never entirely lose, he turned away and let himself sink comfortably into it while the Senator from South Carolina, feeling oddly as though the interview were getting far out of hand, moved after a moment behind the big oak desk to sit in Bob Munson's chair. Again a silence fell.

"How soon do you think we'll be able to adjourn, Senator?" Cullee asked finally, and Seab recognized the remark for what it must be, an indirect opening to give the Congressman a chance to make his bid for compromise. This was better, and he decided to be as helpful as possible in moving the subject along.

"Well, sir," he said, "as soon as we can get finished with your resolution, I think. I think that's when, when we get finished up with that. And you know more about when that will be than I do, I expect. Isn't that correct?"

"Not I, Senator," the Congressman said with a smile whose import Senator Cooley could not determine. "I think that's up to you."

"Oh, sir?" Seab Cooley said in a less friendly voice. "And how is that, may I ask?"

"I understand you are ready to accept a compromise and drop your opposition. That ought to put it through the Senate tomorrow, shouldn't it? Then we *can* go home."

"I, sir?" Seab Cooley demanded, with an ominously rising inflection. "I compromise? Who said I would compromise? It is *you* who I am told will compromise, not I. That is why you are here, is it not?"

"No, sir," Cullee Hamilton said in a level tone. "I understood it was why you are here."

"But Bob told me—" Senator Cooley began. The Congressman interrupted.

"And Orrin told me."

Again there was silence, and now Cullee Hamilton realized he was seeing something that few men living had ever seen: uncertainty and dismay on the face of Seabright B. Cooley. Perhaps in his earliest days men had seen that—assuredly there were some far back who had—but it had been many and many a long year, the Congressman was sure, since the sight had been permitted anyone. Probably before he was born, he thought with a feeling both awed and sad; probably that long ago.

"Now, sir," the old man said with a careful softness that somehow seemed suddenly pathetic, "let me understand this. You thought *I* was giving in and I thought *you* were giving in. Appears to me somebody's mighty mixed up, Congressman."

"Yes, sir," Cullee said quietly. "I wonder which of us it is."

"My good friends gave me to believe you wanted to see me," Senator Cooley went on, still in the same careful way, "because you wanted to propose substantial changes in language that would help your resolution go through the Senate. Not that I'd stop opposing it, mind, but it wouldn't be so hard for me to let it go through, finally, if that was what the Administration really felt it must ask of us. But that wasn't the way you heard it."

"No, Senator, it wasn't. Not 'substantial.'"

"I wonder how I could have heard it that way?" Seab said thoughtfully, and the Congressman had the strange feeling that the old man was talking to himself and that he, Cullee, wasn't in the room at all as far as the Senator was concerned.

"I'm sure I don't know," he said.

"*You* heard that I was giving in, was that it?" Seab Cooley asked, and abruptly he was back in focus on his opponent, the sleepy old eyes examining him sharply from under their weathered lids, the pugnacious old jaw stuck out. Cullee nodded.

"Yes, sir," he said, not the "sir" demanded of color but the "sir" required by respect. "I was given to understand that you would filibuster against the resolution as it stands, but that a very minor change that would enable you to make a protest for the record and then yield gracefully would be satisfactory to you. I said that if you asked me for it I would probably be agreeable, and I thought that was why you were here."

"Ask a colored man?" Seab Cooley said, and Cullee knew that all chance of agreement was over. "*Ask* a colored man? Why, boy, what made you think that?"

"Because we have the votes to beat you," the Congressman said, trying hard to remain steady under the furious anger that suddenly surged in his heart, "and we will do so. With your co-operation or without it. That's why."

"*Ask* a colored man?" Senator Cooley repeated, and suddenly the Congressman's tight control snapped into open fury.

"Yes, *ask* a colored man! Why is that so difficult for you to understand, Senator? Day's coming when you and your kind will be asking colored men for a lot of things, don't you know that? At least," and sarcasm edged the anger, "I didn't require you to ask me in public. I gave you the chance to do it privately, though I knew it wouldn't do any good. I knew how you'd be. I just knew it."

"How can I be other than what I am?" Senator Cooley asked. "I was raised to think a certain way. I *do* think that way. Surely you don't expect me to change now. Surely not!"

"Yet you expect me to, Senator. I was raised in a certain way, too, and not the old way of always giving in when the white man says 'jump!' *I* don't jump, Senator. Can't you understand that?"

"I don't understand lots of things that go on nowadays," Seab Cooley said, and again for a moment there was the revelation of a tired and baffled old man, touching and disturbing to Cullee Hamilton even as he knew the interview could have only one outcome now. "I thought I could end my years in honor, not betrayed by my friends into begging from a colored boy. Even," he said with a small trace of smile, "as fine a one as I believe you to be."

"It isn't a matter of color any more, Senator, don't you see," Cullee told him, and almost in spite of himself his tone became gentler and more considerate. "It's a matter of who has the votes. And I have. Now, I will agree to one change in my resolution"—and he read it off from the piece of paper on which he and Orrin Knox had jotted it down—"and that is all. You can take it, make your speech for the record, if you like, and be defeated; or you can refuse it, filibuster, and be defeated. Your choice, Senator. Not mine."

"You still have the South in your voice a little," Seab Cooley said, apparently apropos of nothing but, as Cullee was quite aware, very much to the point of their conversation. "You from Georgia originally?"

"I came from Lena," the Congressman said, and the old man leaned forward quickly.

"Then you know what I have done for your race since I have been in Washington. Better schools, improved conditions, better housing, the school-lunch program—why," he said, and a genuine pride came into his voice—"I expect as chairman of the Senate Appropriations Committee I've helped to pass and pay for more things to help the Negroes than any other man in Congress. And they know it and they're grateful, too! Yes, sir, they know it and they are grateful. They know what it means to have a true friend in Washington to watch over them. They haven't forgotten all Seab Cooley's done!"

"I don't deny you've done a great deal for the colored race, Senator, and I don't deny that many other Southerners in Congress have done a great deal. But the thing you evidently can't see is that *it's all been so damned patronizing.* We want you to do things for us because you *like* us, not because you're 'watching over us'! Can't you ever understand that?"

"No, sir," Senator Cooley said with complete truthfulness, "I cannot."

"Then it *is* hopeless," Cullee Hamilton said dully. "It really is, not just this, but everything."

"I don't know what you mean by that," Seab Cooley said, "but if you mean you expect me to give in on this resolution just so you can flatter your own ego, you have another think coming. Yes, sir, another think. That's really what you want, isn't it, just to flatter your own ego that you made Seab Cooley beg? How are you any better than you claim we are, when you have a motive as shabby as that, Congressman? Tell me that, now!"

"I don't know," Cullee said in a tired voice. "Maybe I'm not. Maybe nobody's perfect. Maybe we're all mixed up in our motivations. Anyway, it doesn't matter, because I have the votes and the resolution's going through."

"I consider that entire last paragraph an insult to the United States and to all the fine white people who have tried to help the Negro all these years," Senator Cooley said. "But, sir, I sometimes think you're beyond help. Yes, sir, I sometimes think you're beyond help!"

"Maybe we're all beyond help, Senator," Congressman Hamilton said. "Maybe that's the secret history has waiting for us . . . Anyway, I said it doesn't matter, and it doesn't. I was willing to meet you halfway on a compromise, but you don't want it, so we'll have to go ahead as things are. Unless you want to change your mind right now."

"No, sir," Senator Cooley said. "It may defeat me, it may be the death of me, but I'll fight it through my way, because that's how I am. Yes, sir."

"I, too," said Cullee Hamilton. "So be it."

And when he called the Secretary of State down in the Majority cloak-room a few minutes later to tell him the result of the discussion, "So be it" was what Orrin said, too; and within half an hour the word was all over the Senate, seeping into the press, spilling over into radio and television, circulating through the corridors and the ever-chattering Lounge at the United Nations, carried around the globe, that the Senate would enter a no-compromise, no-holds-barred battle over the Hamilton Resolution on the morrow. The plan, said Chairman Tom August of Minnesota to the AP and UPI, was to approve the resolution in the Foreign Relations Committee in the morning, take it straight to the floor under a suspension of the rules, and pass it by nightfall.

"But what if Senator Cooley filibusters?" the reporters asked.

"So be it," said Tom August, who was not one to let a good phrase lie.

Both the Majority Leader and the Secretary of State took occasion during the evening to call the senior Senator from South Carolina, and both found him embittered by what he regarded as their betrayal and determined to filibuster if necessary to stop the resolution. Both apologized, both implored him to reconsider, both found him adamant. Both regretted it, but both were committed to the course they had chosen, and both, reluctantly but diligently, proceeded to push it forward.

Bob Munson began telephoning and firming up his votes. Orrin Knox did the same. By midnight they were sure they had enough to pass the resolution as it stood by a comfortable margin. Only one thing puzzled and disturbed the Secretary. When he tried to reach the Senate members of the U.S. delegation to the UN in New York, he was unable to; and when Bob Munson finally did get through to Lafe Smith around 1 A.M., he found him evasive and noncommittal as to whether he and Hal Fry could come down for the vote. Hal had gone to bed, tired out, Lafe said, and they would not know until tomorrow whether either one, or both, could make it.

In the meantime, Lafe said, everybody at the UN was vitally interested in the outcome of the Senate debate, and much that would occur subsequently in the house by the East River would hinge upon it.

"I know that," the Majority Leader said with some asperity. "Why do you suppose we're breaking our necks over this thing down here? We expect you and Hal to do the same up there as soon as we're finished here."

"We will," Lafe said calmly. "I think you can count on us both."

"I hope so," Bob Munson told him. "Orrin doesn't want to have to make any changes in the delegation at this late date."

"Orrin won't make any changes. If any changes are made—" He broke off. "Stop worrying. You do your job and we'll do ours, Robert, O.K.?"

"Well," the Majority Leader said, puzzled but perforce agreeable. "O.K."

6

The next day, just before noon, coming down the center aisle of the Senate to his desk and the circle of alert reporters who awaited him there he was still puzzled by this cryptic conversation with the Senator from Iowa. It was not the greatest of Bob Munson's worries, by any means; but it nagged away at a corner of his mind in a way that made him know he was going to come back to it later and get an explanation. Perhaps Orrin had one. He planned to come up to the Hill later in the afternoon, and possibly they could talk about it then.

In the meantime, here were his friends of the press.

"Bob," the *Wall Street Journal* said, "we hear Seab's going to filibuster. Are you ready for him?"

"My, my, the things you do hear," Senator Munson said, looking up at the rapidly filling galleries, many black faces among the white, an air of rustling, subdued excitement in the room. "He hasn't told me. Where'd you get that—from the New York *Times?*"

"We don't read each other except in the West Coast editions," the *Times* told him, "so that couldn't possibly be it. Anybody else going to go with the old boy on this, Bob, or will he be alone?"

"Really, I don't know what you're talking about. Seab may have a few things to say—it would be a strange day in the Senate if he didn't, on a major issue—but I expect when he's finished we'll go ahead and vote on the resolution."

"Without change?" asked AP.

"Without change."

"We thought there was some talk of a compromise with Cullee Hamilton—" UPI began. The Majority Leader smiled.

"There's always talk of compromise, around the Senate. These old walls are made of compromise. This old floor rests on compromise. The ceiling would fall if it weren't kept up by the steadily blowing breezes of compromise. But on this resolution—?" He shrugged and smiled across the aisle at Warren Strickland, the Minority Leader. "I haven't heard of any compromise, have you, Warren?"

"Not lately," Senator Strickland said. "Not since young Cullee laid down the law to Seab, anyway."

"How was that, Warren?" the New York *Herald Tribune* asked quickly. "We didn't hear about that one."

"Won't from me, either," Warren Strickland said cheerfully, turning away to riffle through his papers. "Anyway, Bob's right. No compromise is the ticket."

"You'll help Bob break a filibuster, then?" the Providence *Journal* inquired. Warren Strickland looked amused.

"Oh, we'll stick around. Interested. Intrigued. Curious to watch the sinuous legislative maneuvers of the Majority Leader. We always are."

"Thanks so much, pal," Bob Munson said. "If there is a filibuster, we will stay here until it is broken."

"The resolution is that important," the Washington Evening *Star* said thoughtfully.

"The Administration regards it as that important," Senator Munson said.

"How do *you* regard it, Senator?" the New York *Post* asked, off at the fringe of the group, and they realized from the special edge in his voice that he was not addressing the Majority Leader.

Down the aisle from the Majority cloakroom the senior Senator from South Carolina was slowly proceeding, head low and thoughtful upon his chest, eyes hooded and uncommunicative, an air of profound concentration about him, as though he were gathering strength for a battle, as indeed he was. Ignoring the New York *Post,* ignoring them all, he shook hands gravely with the Majority Leader, then walked slowly to the dais and assumed the Chair in his capacity as President Pro Tempore. There he slumped, apparently oblivious, while the galleries stirred at his entry and across the floor his colleagues murmured to one another.

"I said, do *you* regard it as important, Senator?" the New York *Post* asked again, the edge sharper in his voice, as they crowded around him at the dais. Senator Cooley gave him a bland look.

"Why, now, since that question comes from one of my stanchest editorial supporters in my argument with my good friend Orrin Knox—a supporter come a little later to the fold, but honest enough to acknowledge the error of its ways and be redeemed—why, sir, I will say to you that, yes, I regard it as important. Don't you?"

"Yes, I do," the New York *Post* said, standing his ground amid the amusement of his colleagues. "I think it is absolutely imperative that it be passed." His voice hardened. "Just as it stands, Senator."

"Well, sir," Senator Cooley said gently, "if you regard it as important enough that it's ab—so—lute—ly imperative that it be passed, then I'll just have to regard it as important enough that it's ab so—lute—ly imperative that it be defeated. Yes, sir, I will, now. Now that you've given me my cue, that is."

"What do you make of that 8–4 vote for the resolution in Foreign Relations Committee this morning, Senator?" the Memphis *Commercial Appeal* inquired. "Not exactly a wide margin in your favor, was it?"

"Well, sir, that just goes to show how prone you newspaper folk are to go running after what happens in committees. Yes, sir, it shows it. Now, when you get the Administration rampaging on something, and the President, bless his heart, working on all his old friends and colleagues up here, and Mr. Orrin Knox, our distinguished Secretary of State, huffing and puffing too, well, then, you've got a chance for a good vote in committee. A right smart vote in committee. *But*"—and his voice dropped significantly and he peered up with a sudden sharpness at the ring of faces hovering attentively around the dais—"that isn't the floor, ladies and gentlemen. That isn't the floor. No, sir, the floor's another matter."

"We haven't been able to find anyone who's willing to support you in a filibuster, Senator," the Los Angeles *Times* told him. "How about that?"

"How about it? I'll tell you how about it. Not everybody blabs his intentions to you fellows, that's how about it. I expect I won't be the only one talking before we're through. No, sir, I expect I won't. Others will be talking, too."

"Filibustering, Senator?" asked the UPI in a tone of noticeable skepticism.

"They'll be talking," Seab Cooley said.

"Actually, Senator," the St. Louis *Post-Dispatch* informed him, "we don't think anybody's going to help you. We think you're going to get licked and licked badly. It just doesn't seem to add up to anything else. What's your comment on that?"

"Young man," Senator Cooley said, "before you were born, people were counting Seabright B. Cooley out, and he wasn't out. Yes, sir, they were counting him out and he wasn't out. So maybe you all are counting him out too soon again. Could be."

"Could be, Senator," the P.-D. agreed as the warning bell rang at twelve noon and the Senate prepared to convene. "And again, could not."

And they turned and hurried off the floor, nodding and joking to one another, their hostility a palpable force he could feel as he stared out upon the chamber and rapped his gavel with a peremptory emphasis to open the session. They didn't like him and he didn't like them; and while it was far too late now ever to do anything about it, the weight of their mutual dislike did not make his task easier. The thought crossed his mind, as the Rev. Carney Birch snuffled through his wordy prayer, that life might have been easier had he not fought so hard over the years for the things he believed in. But had he not done so, of course, he would not have been Seab Cooley.

"Mr. President," Bob Munson said as Carney finished and Senate and galleries settled down to an attentive quiet, "I move that the reading of the *Journal* of yesterday's proceedings be dispensed with."

"Without objection, so ordered," Senator Cooley said. "The morning hour is now in order, and Senators may make such statements or insertions in the Congressional Record as they please, subject to the five-minute rule prevailing during this period."

"Now, why do you suppose Seab didn't have somebody demand that the journal be read?" the Boston *Globe* asked the Louisville *Courier-Journal* in the Press Gallery above. "I mean, that's one good way to start a filibuster—"

"Maybe he isn't going to filibuster," the *Courier-Journal* said. "It would be just like the old scamp to fool us all."

"He's got to filibuster, or be licked," the Charleston, South Carolina, *News and Courier* pointed out.

"*That* would be a tragedy," the Dallas *News* remarked, and they all, except the Charleston *News and Courier*, laughed.

"Mr. President," said Arly Richardson, on his feet with a New York *Times* editorial critical of the rivers and harbors bill with its appropriation for six dams in his state of Arkansas. The "morning hour" was under way.

An hour and forty-seven minutes later, the morning hour having been completed with only seven violations of the five-minute rule—Powell Hanson, speaking seventeen minutes on the need for more grain storage elevators in North Dakota, was the worst offender—Tom August rose and sought recognition from the Chair. It was now occupied by Murfee Andrews of Kentucky, to whom Seab had turned over the gavel half an hour after convening in order that he might resume his regular seat beside the Majority Leader. A silence settled over the galleries. On the floor, crowded with Senators who had hurried through lunch in order to return and be present for this moment, an extra edge of tension could be sensed in the murmured conversations, the behind-the-hand whisperings and over-the-desk exchanges as Senator August began, in his querulous, uncertain way, to call up H. J. Res. 23.

"Mr. President, I believe most Senators are familiar with the gist of this resolution, which was passed by the House yesterday. It apologizes to a distinguished visitor to this country, a leader of Africa who unfortunately got involved in a local controversy in one of our southern states—"

"Mr. President," Senator Cooley said ominously, "will the distinguished chairman of the Foreign Relations Committee yield? The Senator knows perfectly well that this black busybody injected himself deliberately into our school problems in South Carolina, does he not? No one asked the Emboohoo of Embewley to get involved, Mr. President. He involved himself."

"In any event, Mr. President," Tom August said nervously, "the fact remains that the M'Bulu of Mbuele was involved, with consequences, widely publicized, that we all know about. This episode, plus other—er—unfortunate aspects of his visit to this country, caused great criticism and hostility toward the United States at the United Nations, where our policy is based upon friendly relations with the so-called uncommitted nations." ("So-called is right," Johnny DeWilton of Vermont whispered to Blair Sykes of Texas, who laughed.) "Senators are aware that a resolution is pending before the General Assembly, offered by the Ambassador of Panama, to give immediate independence to the M'Bulu's country of Gorotoland. This resolution now has attached to it an amendment demanding a United Nations investigation of racial practices in the United States, carrying with it the threat of expulsion of the United States from the United Nations if those practices are not changed. Several days ago the General Assembly voted a one-week delay in consideration of that proposition, on the plea offered by a member of our UN delegation, the Honorable Cullee Hamilton, Congressman from California, that the Congress would pass his resolution here present.

"This resolution, as the Senate is aware, carries with it not only suitable indemnities to the M'Bulu and his country for any indignities he may have suffered but also a pledge by the Congress that the United States will move with increased speed to assure equal treatment to her Negro citizens.

"That, in essence, is the issue here. The resolution was passed by the House yesterday by a vote of 219 to 214. It was approved by the Foreign Relations Committee of the Senate this morning by a vote of 8 to 4. The rule states that such a resolution must lie over a day before it can be brought up for debate, but, Mr. President, because it is very late in the session and Senators are anxious to adjourn and return to their homes, and because of the vital nature of this issue ("And because of the General Assembly's one-week ultimatum," the Detroit *News and Times* said dryly in the Press Gallery above) I now ask unanimous consent that the rules be suspended to permit immediate consideration of H. J. Res. 23."

There was a whispering and a stirring over the floor as he concluded, and into it the senior Senator from Massachusetts, John Able Winthrop, rose and spoke in his dry, clipped way.

"Mr. President, reserving the right to object, I should like to comment briefly on what the distinguished Senator from Minnesota has just said. I am one of the four who voted against this resolution in committee this morning, because I do not believe in the United States humbling herself in the pursuit of some willful will-o'-the-wisp known as world opinion. I do not think this resolution will secure that opinion; nor do I think it will for one minute slow down those whose consistent policy is to besmirch and attack this country.

"It seems to me we can give goodies to the M'Bulu of Mbuele through other channels of the government, if we feel he must have them, and as for what we do for our own Negroes, that is our business, I submit to the Senate. I am proud of our record in recent decades and I think it is going forward with ever-increasing speed. I don't think we should put ourselves in the position of being pressured into a phony position just to appease the United Nations."

"It isn't appeasing the United Nations, Mr. President," Tom August said doggedly; "it is a matter of showing respect for world opinion—"

"I'll show respect for world opinion when world opinion shows itself worthy of respect and not before, I will say to my distinguished chairman. In any event, I don't see why we should rush this along, even if Senators are weary and worn and ready to take off for the boondocks. We can stay another twenty-four hours, if that's the regular order. I object to the unanimous consent request to suspend the rules, Mr. President."

"Mr. President," Bob Munson said, "I *move* that the rules be suspended and the Senate begin immediate consideration of H. J. Res. 23."

There was an immediate show of hands across the floor, and Murfee Andrews in the Chair said, "Evidently a sufficient number agree. The Clerk will call the roll."

"And still no big fireworks from Seab," the Denver *Post* said in a puzzled voice. "Don't tell me there isn't going to be any fight."

"Maybe saving his strength for the main issue," the New Orleans *Times-Picayune* suggested.

Whatever it was, there came no sign of protest save a loud "No!" from the President Pro Tempore as the clerk called the roll and the Senate voted 49–46 ("Too damned close," Bob Munson murmured to Stanley Danta of Connecticut, the Majority Whip, and Stanley nodded) to suspend the rules and begin immediate consideration of the Hamilton Resolution.

The vote concluded and duly announced by the Chair, now occupied by Verne Cramer of South Dakota so that Murfee Andrew could go out in the ornate Reception Room and receive a group of constituents from Kentucky, the tension abruptly heightened. It was observed that the First Lady had come into the Family Gallery, accompanied by the wife of the Secretary of State, the wife of the Majority Leader, the British Ambassadress, and the French Ambassadress; in the Diplomatic Gallery, wearing her usual brightly flowered dress and floppy hat, the Ambassadress of Panama came in alone and took a seat in the front row. There were immediate gesturings and beckonings and silently mouthed commands, and after a moment Patsy Labaiya left her seat in the Diplomatic Gallery and went around to join the Presidential group in the front row of the Family Gallery. Many little smiles and waves and intimate signs of greeting were tossed back and forth between its members and various members of the Senate, and in the public galleries tourists and other visitors were suitably thrilled by this atmosphere of Very Important Friends foregathered for a Very Important Occasion. The

Majority Leader secured the floor and began to speak in measured and thoughtful tones.

"Mr. President, I find myself in what is possibly a rather unique position as regards this resolution, in that I am for it for what many of its friends would probably consider the wrong reasons. Thus, Mr. President, I am not for it because I think the United States owes any apologies to one whose credentials are not of the best, either as a friend to this country or as a genuine friend to liberty in his native continent. I think I probably find myself in full agreement with the Senator from South Carolina concerning the episodes that have prompted all this furor.

"I also am not prepared to humble the United States or myself before a world opinion which in the first place is amorphous and indefinable, and in the second has shown itself in recent years capricious, arbitrary, and unfair in its judgments of this country and of many others whose principal crime seems to be the possession of white skin.

"I do not think white skin is automatically evil, Mr. President, any more than I think black skin is automatically noble. White skin has its errors to answer for to history, and black skin is rapidly building up a matching list of its own to keep white skin company. If we are to start matching error for error, I do not think that much of the past imperialism of the white race is any worse than the present irresponsible misuse of newfound freedom by much of the black race. Human nature is not improved automatically by a switch in pigmentation from one controlling group to another, Mr. President; it is improved by standards of education and integrity and forbearance and human decency which many of these newly independent peoples do not yet have. Until they do, it would more become them, as they joyfully murder and mistreat one another, to keep silent about the shortcomings of the white man. In any event, I do not think the white man should apologize unduly for what he has done in the past, when in the overwhelming portion of the former colonial areas he is doing his best to make amends and assist in bringing a freedom perhaps too big for many of its recipients to handle."

"Well, well," the New York *Daily News* murmured to the Seattle *Times*. "Our friend doesn't sound so very liberal on this one." "Damned equivocator!" offered the New York *Post*. "You can never tell where he stands on anything."

"But, Mr. President, all of that, to my mind, is beside the point to the central issue posed in this resolution; and that, as I see it, is the integrity—the *personal* integrity, you might say, if a whole nation can be said to have such a thing—of the United States of America." He paused and looked about at his attentively listening colleagues, the crowded galleries, the scribbling occupants of the Press Gallery, above the Chair.

"In my mind, Mr. President, as I think in the minds of most of us everywhere in this land, there is a concept of the country that I like to believe in; a concept, if you will, of what America is, of what she was intended to be, of what, God granting her strength and continued existence, she can become. Matched against that, Mr. President, I do not need the headline-hunting antics of a freebooter from Africa to tell me what my country ought to do. I know what she ought to do. As far as I am concerned, we do not need Terence Ajkaje, nor do we need the United Nations, to lecture us on the subject or to scourge us along the way.

"The United States, as a government and a people, should do all it can, as speedily as it can, to bring full equality to all its citizens of whatever color, not because somebody *demands* that it should, but simply because *it should*. Simply because it is part of the purpose of the United States. Simply because a nation founded on principles of equality and justice and dedicated to them must, unless it is to betray itself and so ultimately go down, strive to make those principles the daily foundation of its national life.

"We were given noble purposes by our founders to begin with, and, being human, we have often fallen short of them. But that does not mean that we have lost them, or that we should not continually and forever try to make them stronger and more effective in our national living. In the area of race relations, as in all other areas, we have an obligation, it seems to me, to do certain things for no other reason *than that they are right*.

"If we will so act, Mr. President, history may in the long run turn out to be kinder to us than we sometimes think, at this fearful juncture in mankind's affairs, that history is going to be.

"For this reason, I too, like the distinguished Senators from South Carolina and Massachusetts, am not impressed with what world opinion thinks about us, on this or any other matter. I do not regard world opinion as a valid reason for passing this, or any other, piece of legislation. I do regard as valid the just and honorable purposes for which America stands, however imperfectly. On that basis, I urge the passage of this resolution."

And, to a scattering of applause and some congratulatory murmurs, he sat down.

"Congratulations, darling," Kitty Maudulayne said to Dolly Munson in the Family Gallery, "I do think that was wonderful."

"He can do it, when he gets inspired," Dolly said, looking gratified. Patsy Labaiya leaned over and tapped her on the knee.

"Why doesn't HE run for President? Then Ted and Orrin could relax and Beth and I could stop meowing at each other like a COUPLE OF OLD CATS!"

"That's not a meow, it's a purr," Beth Knox said cheerfully, as Celestine Barre listened attentively between them. "Anyway, Harley's going to run again, so it's all academic. Isn't that right, Lucille?"

"Who knows?" the First Lady inquired, of no one in particular. "My dear, who knows? I *do* think Bob is terrific, though, don't you?"

"Yes," Dolly said, "but here comes Seab, girls, so hold your hats."

Below them on the floor there was a stirring and settling, a growing tension and anticipation. Beside Senator Munson, the rumpled figure of the President Pro Tempore rose slowly to its feet.

"Mr. President," Seab Cooley said softly, "I do want to congratulate the Majority Leader on a fine and patriotic address, worthy of delivery at anybody's Fourth of July picnic. I do not think, Mr. President, that any American could disagree with the basic thoughts presented in that fine address. It is only in the application that men may differ. For arguments concerning that, there perhaps will be other times than these closing hours of what has been a long and, in earlier months, a tragic session of this Senate." He paused and allowed the memory of the tragedy to come back briefly and touch them all.

"Mr. President," he went on, a little more strongly, "I know it is no oversight that the distinguished Majority Leader carefully refrained from going into the details of this resolution. No, sir, I know it was no accident that he did not discuss the events leading up to it, or the parallel events in the United Nations that have put this Congress, in both its houses, under fearful pressures to act, and act unwisely, in this matter. I know it was not mere inadvertence, Mr. President." His voice dropped to a gusty whisper. "It was deliberate, Mr. President. It was de–li–ber–ate! The distinguished Majority Leader did not *want* us to discuss what is behind it. He did not *want* us to consider the ramifications of it. He did not want us to talk about the humiliation of the United States implicit in this shabby resolution. No, sir, Mr. President," he cried, and his voice suddenly roared up angrily, "he did not want us to understand that we were being asked to humiliate our own country! Humiliation, Mr. President. That is what it is, humiliation!"

"Oh, hell," the Washington *Post* said in a bored whisper. "Does any sane man want to listen to that?" "Quite a few, apparently," said the *Wall Street Journal.* "Look at 'em."

And indeed the Senate was listening, and there were indications already that Seab might be gaining adherents. The Administration might have been busy, but it was apparent that there were still many troubled minds in the upper chamber. The President Pro Tempore sensed it with the instinct of many years of legislative battle and was heartened. He stood straighter at his desk and looked around the Senate with a searching glance as his voice gained vigor.

"Now, Mr. President, reduced to its essentials, what is the situation? There was introduced about a month ago in the United Nations a resolution by Felix Labaiya, Ambassador of Panama; I will not go into the question of Señor Labaiya's relatives by marriage, for we are all acutely aware of them." ("The old FRAUD!" Patsy whispered in the Family Gallery, and stuck out her tongue. There was a ripple of laughter, and Verne Cramer in the Chair rapped impatiently for order.) "The gist of this resolution, Mr. President, was to call for the immediate independence of the British protectorate of Gorotoland in Africa, home of strange practices and sinister rites and at least one kinky-haired kinkajou who shows the dangers of what happens when you educate some people. Mr. President, I shall not pass upon the merits of that. I understand the British are against it, having pledged independence a year hence and being orderly people who deem that period necessary for a smooth transition of power. I understand our Administration, urged on by one who lately sat among us, the distinguished Secretary of State, may be for it—ill-advisedly, as I believe; but, no matter.

"Following a big publicity fandango for His Royal Highness the Emboohoo of Embewley in my state of South Carolina—put on, I might say parenthetically, by the politically interested relatives by marriage of the Ambassador of Panama, including his brother-in-law, the great Governor of California—the Emboohoo decided to mix voluntarily and egregiously and inexcusably into the school integration problems of the city of Charleston. I do not know who put him up to this, Mr. President, though like many Senators I have my suspicions. Certainly they were not friends of the United States. The Ambassador was there; the Governor was there; others were there. At any rate, as a result of his intervention he received certain violent demonstrations of disapproval from citizens of that lovely city. I do not pass upon whether or not he deserved them, Mr. President. I just say he asked for them. Yes, sir, he certainly did ask for them. And—he—got them!

"Well, then, Mr. President. Next he went to the United Nations, up there in the great city of New York which does such a fine job of handling its own race relations and such a fine job of telling everybody else how to handle theirs, and he appeared before the General Assembly. And the Ambassador of Panama, related by marriage to certain distinguished Americans as he is, promptly introduced an amendment to his resolution calling upon the United Nations to investigate racial conditions in the United States, carrying with it the threat of expulsion of the United States from the United Nations unless certain racial laws and practices and traditions are not immediately changed."

The Senator from South Carolina paused and looked thoughtfully about the attentive chamber. A look of contempt came upon his shrewd old face and his voice sank to an intimate, almost conversational tone.

"Now, mark you, Mr. President, what the response was of the great Secretary of State and the fearless President, who six months ago in Geneva won the admiration of the world by his calm refusal to be intimidated by the threats of the Soviet Union. Did they denounce this so-called Labaiya Amendment for what it was, an inexcusable and fantastic insult to the United States? Did they condemn those who had at least indirectly instigated the shameful episode in Charleston—members of distinguished political families who now seek to weasel out of their responsibility? Did they uphold the dignity and self-respect of the United States in the face of this vicious attack upon it? No, sir, Mr. President, they did not. They crawled, Mr. President. They showed signs of timidity and fear. They apologized and they trembled and they said, Oh, dear me, what can we do to make you who hate us love us better? And out of their timidity and their fear and their lack of self-respect, Mr. President, they produced this strange resolution which is before us now.

"Do not beat us, United Nations! they cried. Do not condemn us, kindly little black brothers of the world! Do not be harsh toward us, dear Soviet Union and all your gentle friends! Look—we will do it ourselves! *We will do it ourselves!* Just leave us alone for a week and we will punish ourselves as severely as you like. And, Mr. President"—and his voice dropped again to its near-whisper, "do you know? That is exactly what they are trying to do. Yes, sir, Mr. President, *that is exactly what they are trying to do!*"

"Mr. President," Bob Munson said, "will the Senator yield?"

"No, sir, Mr. President!" Seab Cooley cried. "No, sir, I will not yield to the distinguished Majority Leader who is joining in this pathetic attempt to appease enemies of the United States who simply are not to be appeased, Mr. President. I notice that the Senator does not spend much time on the United Nations, Mr. President. He carefully avoids reference to it. He bases his reasons for his support of this resolution on his concept of the United States. But he knows that if it were not for the United Nations and its pack of addleheaded agitators, Mr. President, this resolution would not be before us at all. He thinks no more of that than many of us do, and so he carefully refrains from any endorsement of the United Nations.

"Is that not true, I ask the Majority Leader; and I will yield now for any clarification he may care to make."

"Mr. President," Bob Munson said, "I thank the Senator. I am not surprised that the Senator should have seized upon my omission of the United Nations as a launching-pad from which to fire his oratorical missiles. I certainly do not wish to have anyone draw the inference that I am against the United Nations, Mr. President, or that I do not think American adherence to it is valuable for us and necessary for the world. I simply meant that to my mind there is a reason more valid for us than what the United Nations thinks, and that is what we know we should do to be true to ourselves. I do not think we will find that if we are true to ourselves the United Nations will condemn us, Mr. President. On the contrary. But certainly I do not minimize the value of the United Nations, or of our adherence to it."

"Well," Senator Cooley replied. "I will say to the Senator that *I* minimize it, and so do a great many other Americans, and the number is growing, Mr. President, as we witness its irresponsibility and its readiness to condemn everything, erratically and lawlessly and without any reference to fairness or even common sense.

"The day will come, Mr. President, unless the United Nations changes *its* ways and acts more responsibly, when there is going to be a most searching re-examination here in this Congress and throughout this whole country as to whether the United States should remain in it. I will say that to the Senator, and such contortions as this shabby resolution of self-punishment are only speeding the day. I would suggest that he see that the word is carried back to the United Nations, since he loves it so."

"Wow!" the Indianapolis *News* said. "Are we ever getting bitter!" "There's a mood in the country," the Chicago *Sun-Times* said, "and it's growing." "I know, but this kind of talk is so—" the Indianapolis *News* protested. "It's growing," the *Sun-Times* repeated.

"So here we are, Mr. President," Seab Cooley said. "That is the situation. We have been blackjacked into this shabby resolution that comes over to us from the House, passed by the fantastically slim margin of five votes yesterday, and we are asked to pass it immediately lest somebody up there in the United Nations—some black somebody—be annoyed with us, Mr. President. Lest somebody say naughty words about us, Mr. President. Lest somebody call us bad names.

"Well, Mr. President, I am not so devoid and bereft of respect for my country or myself that I am ready to be pressured into this kind of self-humiliation, Mr. President. No, sir, I am not.

"Let the United Nations try to investigate us, Mr. President. I do not believe even so humble a fellow as my old friend the Secretary of State will let it in. Let the United Nations try to expel us, Mr. President—it had better watch out; we might be more than happy to go.

"I, too, say, like the distinguished Majority Leader—let us be true to ourselves! Let us do what we think is right! Let us reject this peculiar contortionist resolution and tell the United Nations to mind its own business. I beg of you, Senators, let us not wallow in self-humiliation. America deserves better than that from us."

And to their great surprise he started to sit down, as his junior colleague, H. Harper Graham of South Carolina, and a number of other Southerners began to rise. But the junior Senator from Iowa beat them to it and was granted recognition as Stanley Danta murmured to Bob Munson, "I didn't see Lafe come in," and the Majority Leader responded, "Neither did I, but thank God he's here. I wonder if Hal came with him. I could certainly use them both tonight." But he did not see the senior Senator from West Virginia. The Senate once more quieted down as Lafe Smith began to speak.

"Mr. President," he said, "I do not wish to interfere with what appears to be a well-concerted plan, under the experienced direction of the senior Senator from South Carolina, to take us into an extended discussion of this issue today." He smiled amicably. "I will not detain my eager southern colleagues more than a few minutes in their obvious desire to claim the floor and hold it, no doubt at some length, but I do want to say a word with regard to two subjects that seem of great interest and bearing here, namely the United Nations and world opinion. I have had some dealing with both in these last several weeks, as Senators know, and so perhaps you will be interested in what I have to report of them.

"Mr. President, I will grant anything and everything that anybody wants to say about the present and inherent weaknesses of the United Nations, except one thing: I will not grant that the world can get along without it at this present time in history. Imperfect as it is, erratic as it is, talkative and empty and futile as it is in so many respects, it still represents the only hope, *in actual being*, for the eventual development of a stable world community. At least, on the East River, men are talking together. At least, there, the smallest power can turn upon the greatest and state the truth—and it is not always we who are turned upon, Mr. President, and it is not always we who are criticized. I would say that the majority of the time it is, but not always; and the tides that affect the affairs of men are not eternal. They shift, Mr. President. The forum that condemns us now did not condemn us yesterday, and it may not condemn us tomorrow. The important thing to the world, and I believe to us, is that the forum be preserved, that it be kept in being, that its potential for good be strengthened in every way that is possible. And I say this, Mr. President, as one who went to the United Nations with very great reservations and a very deep skepticism about it.

"Now, Mr. President," he said, as Seab stirred uneasily and over on the Minority side Bessie Adams of Kansas started to rise and then thought better of it, "I repeat, I am not saying the United Nations is perfect; nor am I attempting to conceal its great and many defects. There are those in this country and elsewhere who attempt to do so, Mr. President, and in my judgment they are fools. Such willful self-delusion has no place in the cold gray world we live in today. But just as one can admit many defects in the democracy of the West and still end up believing it to be the only really decent and humanly hopeful system of government yet devised, so one can admit the many defects in the United Nations and still wind up thinking that the small spark of hope that flickers there is worth all the stupid and vicious misuse of its mechanisms that some of its members are guilty of."

"Mr. President," Senator Cooley inquired in a tired and skeptical tone, "is the Senator arguing that there is any guarantee that if we pass this resolution, the United Nations may not *still* pass its own resolution condemning us? Is he giving us assurance of that, pray tell?"

"Mr. President," Lafe said, "no man here can give that assurance. There are certain safeguards. This is a matter of substance, an 'important matter,' as the term is used in the General Assembly; therefore, a two-thirds vote is necessary to pass it. The Ambassador of Panama, I will say to all interested parties"—and he grinned faintly at Patsy Labaiya, leaning forward in the Family Gallery above—"does not have the two-thirds vote, at least at present counting. Nor is he even close to it. Therefore, there is that safeguard. But, Mr. President, even more importantly, there is the safeguard that if we act in good faith, surely it will be understood and accepted as such by the peoples of the world. Surely our purposes and our intentions will be honored, Mr. President. Surely our integrity will be recognized."

"The Senator has found this to be consistently the case in the United Nations, has he?" Seab asked. "Our good faith and integrity are always accepted and honored, are they? That is the Senator's argument, is it? Mr. President," he said with a wintry smile, "the Senator knows things we do not know."

"Now, Mr. President," Lafe said, and a certain asperity came into his voice, "the distinguished Senator from South Carolina persists in trying to turn this into a trial of the United Nations. It is not. It is a trial of us. I see over there on a sofa in the corner the distinguished author of this resolution pending before the Senate, my fellow member on our delegation to the United Nations, the able Congressman from California. I know he agrees with me, as do many other members of both houses of Congress who have served on the American delegation in the past, that in the area of world opinion, as it is represented and focused by the UN, there is indeed an unceasing war to gain and hold advantage. I will grant, and so will the author of the resolution, I am sure"—and he looked at Cullee, who nodded from where he sat even before he heard Lafe's thought—"that world opinion is a flimsy and fickle and often fantastically irresponsible thing. With some of the newer states in the organization, it bears no resemblance whatever to fairness or objectivity or honor. But that does not make it any less important, Mr. President. We are in the world, and we must listen to it and take it into account.

"Do we, as the Senator from South Carolina and to some degree, I gather, the Majority Leader, propose, go our own way and let world opinion like it or lump it, lucky if it likes it and possibly unlucky if it lumps it? Or do we combine doing what we think is right with what, in our terms of reference, we regard as 'a decent respect for the opinions of mankind'?

"I think we should do the latter, Mr. President, for this has been our historical pattern from our beginning. I think that I can speak for the distinguished author of his resolution"—and again Cullee nodded—"that he thinks so too. I know I can speak for the head of our delegation, our beloved friend from West Virginia"—and only the slightest change came over his voice, noticed and dismissed after a second's puzzlement by only a few—"who is in New York right now, preparing to carry the battle in the General Assembly after we have joined the House in passing the Hamilton Resolution." He paused and stared earnestly at his colleagues.

"It is the right thing for us to do, Mr. President. It is as simple as that. Let us do it."

There was a burst of applause from the galleries as he sat down, and Verne Cramer in the Chair rapped sternly for order.

"Visitors are here as guests of the Senate," he said crisply. "No demonstrations are permitted. One more, and the galleries will be cleared. The junior Senator from South Carolina."

"Mr. President," H. Harper Graham said with his dark-visaged scowl and somber air, "I invite the Senate to consider the actions of a worthless adventurer from Africa in my native city of Charleston as they apply to the traditional and historical relationship of the races in the southern states of this Union. Mr. President, I shall begin by—"

"Let's go have a cigarette," the Cincinnati *Enquirer* said as there was a general rising and stirring in the Press Gallery. "He's good for at least three hours." And, leaving a corporal's guard of two lonely wire-service men and the Charleston, South Carolina, *News and Courier*, they all trooped up the stairs and out to the gallery rooms beyond, where they would talk and gossip and pass the time of day until such time as Harper Graham should be through.

So passed the time until six o'clock, as Harper Graham finished and yielded the floor to Arly Richardson; as Arly Richardson concluded, after sharp and sarcastic set-tos with Ray Smith of California and Irving Steinman of New York; as Rhett Jackson and Douglas Brady Bliss of North Carolina engaged in a lengthy duet on the status of the Negro in their state; and as Lacey Pollard of Texas in his stately way went back through the legal precedents to show that there was no reason, really, why the Senate should be bound in any way by the opinions or actions of the United Nations. During all this time, the President Pro Tempore sat slumped and inactive at his desk, puzzling and eventually alarming the Majority Leader, who finally broke the ostentatious silence that had prevailed between them since the end of Seab's speech by jogging his colleague's elbow and demanding, "Are you all right? This isn't tiring you too much, is it?"

"Do you care?" Senator Cooley inquired in a distant voice that concerned Bob Munson even more. "Do you really care, now, Bob? Wouldn't it be better if I just dropped dead and then you could go ahead and pass that nice colored boy's resolution? Wouldn't that solve the problem for everybody?"

"Now, Seab," Senator Munson said with a rather nervous jocularity, "you're not going to drop dead until the rest of us are long underground, so stop saying things like that. I'm just worried about you. You seem so subdued and tired."

"I'm an old man, Bob," Senator Cooley said, and the Majority Leader realized with a sudden poignance that this was the first time he had ever heard Seab admit it. "I'm not as spry as I used to be. It isn't as easy as it once was to restrain my colleagues from taking a misguided action."

"You could have avoided it," Bob Munson started to point out, "if only you'd reached an agreement with Cullee—"

"You betrayed me on that, Bob," Senator Cooley said with a tired unhappiness that was more disturbing than any amount of his customary flamboyant anger would have been. "I trusted you, you and Orrin, and you betrayed me. I didn't like that, Bob. But it doesn't matter."

"Misunderstandings happen, Seab," Senator Munson said. "Maybe both Orrin and I were so hopeful we were getting you two to agree that we heard things in what you both said that weren't there. I'm sorry, and I know he is too. But don't you think you've said enough on this? You've made a good speech on the subject; now why don't you just let it stand at that? Your colleagues are doing a good job of making a record, and so have you. That's all you need back home, isn't it? Why not let it go?"

"When did I ever let anything go, Bob?" Senator Cooley asked wryly. "That's my trouble, isn't it? The Lord didn't make me to let things go. He made me to keep fighting. Especially against things I feel are wrong, Bob. And I do feel this resolution is wrong. You can argue it any way you like, Bob; I still feel it's wrong."

"What do you plan to do, then? Filibuster, later on?"

"I won't be alone, Bob, you can bet on that. I won't be alone."

"Seab," Bob Munson said gently, "I think you will be, and so do you. I've checked around, and aside from a few more brief speeches for the record, nobody wants to do anything more. Everybody wants to wind this thing up and adjourn the session, you know that. The resolution isn't important enough to warrant the kind of fight you want to make."

"Isn't important enough!" Senator Cooley said with a trace of his old doggedness. "I really think it's wrong to humble ourselves, Bob, leaving aside all else. I really do. Can't you understand that?"

"I understand it, but, Seab—you're not as young as you were. You really are old. I don't think you should filibuster tonight. I'm genuinely worried about it."

"I don't control the situation. You do, Bob. You aren't about to send the resolution back to committee, are you?"

"I can't drop it now, Seab," Bob Munson said. His colleague slumped back in his chair.

"No more can I, Bob," he said softly. "No more, then, can I."

There was an unhappy pause, during which, across the now half-empty chamber, Fred Van Ackerman engaged in a short and nasty exchange with Lacey Pollard. Finally the Majority Leader sighed.

"I'm sorry, Seab. I really am."

"Don't be," Senator Cooley said. "I expect I'll last, Bob. I expect I will."

But as he settled back into his seat, looking curiously alone, a sudden premonition shot through the Majority Leader's mind that he might not; and it was with a disturbed and uneasy feeling that he turned his seat over to Stanley Danta a few minutes later and prepared to go on downtown to the National Press Club to put in an appearance at the cocktail party being given by the Washington *Post* for Mr. Justice Davis and the M'Bulu of Mbuele. He regarded the affair with considerable skepticism, but he expected he should be there just to see who else was and what they had to say to one another, a motivation that impels attendance at many a Washington cocktail party and one that draws some of the most startling conglomerations together to exchange their thoughts upon the topics of the day.

He was not at all pleased to run into Fred Van Ackerman on the Senate steps and have him ask, quite unabashed, for a ride down in the Majority Leader's official limousine. Fred was going to the party too, it seemed, and after it was over he was going to come back and needle that old bastard Seab a little. Yes, sir, the junior Senator from Wyoming said with relish, he was going to make the old bastard sweat. Bob Munson told him that in that case he might have to help Seab filibuster, and said it with such conviction that his companion almost believed it. He could hear the wheels grinding around in that savage little mind all the way downtown and said nothing to disturb their whirring until they arrived at the door of the Press Club's noisily clamorous East Lounge, where Fred said tersely, "See you later!" "Assuredly," said Bob Munson coldly.

There was vengeance in the air, he realized, thinking back to Brigham Anderson's death and the censure motion against Fred, and somehow he must protect Seab against it. He was not so sure, as the roar of the room engulfed him, that he could.

"But, my dear fellow," Justice Davis was saying, over by the canapés, where a large and admiring group surrounded him and the towering M'Bulu, "what an extraordinary sequence of events brought you to power. And how nobly you have handled the responsibility. How nobly!"

"I have done my best," Terrible Terry said modestly. "Against," he added with a trace of annoyance, "what seemed at times considerable odds."

"I know," Tommy Davis said quickly. "Oh, I *know*. But you have surmounted every test so well. No one has been able to stop you. Not your enemies in your native land, not the British, not our own more—more *dismal*, shall we say"—there was an appreciative titter from all around—"fellow citizens. It has been a clear and shinning record of which all men of goodwill everywhere should be, and *are*, proud!"

"Hear, hear!" said the Ambassador of Cuba, and the Ambassador of Guiana said, "Oh, yes!"

"You are too kind," the M'Bulu said. "I may say that it is men like yourself in the Western world who prove to us who fight for freedom in Africa that there is hope for understanding and appreciation of what we are trying to do."

"What *are* you trying to do, Your Highness?" the counselor of the Australian Embassy inquired, but Terry gave him a startled and elaborately unyielding stare and continued unperturbed, as others drew slightly away from the counselor.

"I assure you, Mr. Justice, that we Africans deeply appreciate what you and others like you are doing here in this country to bring greater decency to the world. We only wish all whose skins are as dark as ours would work as vigorously as you, whose skin is not."

"I say, hear, *hear*," said the Ambassador of Ghana. "It *is* sticky," agreed the cultural attaché of the Embassy of Sierra Leone.

"You mean you disapprove of our distinguished Congressman and his resolution?" their host, the editorial director of the Washington *Post*, inquired with a chuckle as he approached the group in the company of Senator Van Ackerman. "Terry, how could you!"

"I could," the M'Bulu said, as they all laughed. "Oh, yes, I could. I do not think His Distinguished Distinction is a real friend to his own race. But he will not listen. Both his old friend, LeGage Shelby, and I tried to persuade him not to play the game our foes wish him to play. He has gone straightaway ahead."

"Perhaps Seab Cooley will stop him in the Senate," their host suggested. There was a snort from Senator Van Ackerman.

"Perhaps somebody," he said darkly, "will stop Seab Cooley in the Senate."

"We know you don't like Seab, Fred," their host said as everyone laughed, "but surely you don't approve of this tricky resolution, either. It's just a stalking-horse for Orrin Knox."

"I'll get to Orrin," Fred Van Ackerman promised. "One stupid fool at a time. As for the resolution, I guess I can go along with it."

"But surely you don't want to let your animosity toward Seab blind you to the meretricious nature of it," Justice Davis said earnestly. "Truly now, you must be objective, my dear boy, you simply *must*. It won't do to let yourself be blinded by prejudice, as They are."

"Oh, I don't know," Fred Van Ackerman said, giving him an insolent look. "What makes you think you're so perfect? I may support this resolution or I may not."

"But, my dear boy," Tommy Davis said in some dismay, "don't you see that it's—"

"I see a lot of things," Senator Van Ackerman said curtly. "Excuse me. I've got to get a refill."

"Goodness," Justice Davis said as Fred elbowed his way through the crowd which by now jammed the East Lounge of the Press Club to capacity and overflowed raucously into the ballroom beyond. "What an unpleasant young man."

"He is that," their host agreed with amusement. "But as long as he's out to get Seab and Orrin, maybe we can live with him. Look on the sunny side of things, why don't you, Tommy!"

"Well . . ." the Justice said doubtfully. Then he brightened, turning quickly to the silently watching M'Bulu. "Possibly," he said, "Senator Van Ackerman will succeed in killing the resolution while he is ki— That is," he amended hastily, "I don't mean to say while he is killing Senator Cooley, but—you know what I mean."

"I doubt it, Tommy," the Majority Leader said, coming up behind him so unexpectedly that the little Justice jumped and almost spilled his Gibson. "I doubt if anyone really knows what you mean, including yourself. How did you get involved in this strange affair?"

"It is not a strange affair," Justice Davis said with dignity. "It is a fine party, and the basic reason for it is that I expressed a desire to meet His Royal Highness the M'Bulu, whom I had not met, and our friend from the *Post*, here, very kindly arranged it."

"A small, private greeting," Senator Munson said, surveying the weaving figures, the rising voices, the reddening faces. He shook his head and blinked. They baffled him, but, then, they always had. He realized that the M'Bulu was watching him closely and, on a sudden impulse, smiled slightly and winked. The gorgeous figure towering opposite smiled back.

"What do *you* make of it?" Bob Munson asked, holding out his hand. "I'm Senator Munson, Majority Leader of the Senate. I don't believe we've had the pleasure."

"Call me Terry," the M'Bulu said, moving away from the group toward a position by one of the windows looking down upon the hurrying homeward crowds on F Street, twelve floors below. "What do I make of what?"

"All this," Bob Munson said. He nodded toward the roaring room, where many eyes were now turned toward them in somewhat woozy curiosity. "Here you are, doing your damndest to injure the United States, and here they are, doing you honor. Do you suppose it's just the free drinks?"

Terrible Terry shrugged.

"I think it might be better for the United States if it were. But, no: I think there is something else, and I must confess, just between ourselves, it baffles me, too. I think there is an element in your society that *enjoys* being insulted by foreigners. It is the only way I can explain it. And of course," he added with a grin of complete and happy cynicism, "who am I to complain of that?"

"Yes, I can see you're not about to. Well: I think we have you stopped."

"The Hamilton Resolution? I think the UN will want more than that. Anyway, it may not pass the Senate. You know more about that than I do."

"I'm not worried. It will be passed by midnight."

"Despite the old man Cooley? I hear he is powerful."

"He was," Senator Munson said. "In some ways he still is. But he has lost his magic."

"What?" the M'Bulu said in a startled tone. Then he smiled.

"In my country, old men really *do* have magic. But when they lose it"—his face hardened—"they are put out to die."

"They often are here, too," Bob Munson said. "But not this time," he added softly to himself. "Not if I can help it."

"What?" the M'Bulu said again.

"Nothing you would care about, or understand. When do you go back to Africa?" he asked politely. "I understand there's a small rebellion there you might have to worry about."

"What have you heard?" Terry demanded sharply, and abruptly all his easily confident aspect had disappeared. "What is new on that today?"

"Nothing," the Majority Leader said in a surprised tone. "I thought you were in touch—"

"I am," the M'Bulu said. "There is nothing to it. It is all over. I, Terence Ajkaje the M'Bulu, tell you so."

"Well, good for you, Terence Ajkaje the M'Bulu," Bob Munson said. Well, well, he thought; well, well. "Shall we drink to it?"

"Scotch and soda for me," the M'Bulu said, seizing one from a passing tray and drinking an enormous gulp straight down.

"It's nice you don't have to hurry back," Senator Munson said comfortably. "You'll be able to see this whole thing through then, won't you?"

"Perhaps," Terry said, staring straight ahead into some distance the Majority Leader could not see but which apparently needed the M'Bulu's most intense concentration. "I shall see."

"I hope so. We wouldn't want you to have to cut short your visit before all your triumphs are completed."

"Where is Justice Davis?" Terry asked abruptly. "He wanted to talk to me—"

"I'll find him for you," the Majority Leader said, looking about blandly at the circle of eager faces which was once more moving to surround them now that it was apparent their private talk was concluded. "Don't go away."

Now what particular chord do you suppose I hit there? he asked himself as he pushed his way slowly through the room, shaking hands and nodding greetings and calling out the casual small change of the Washington cocktail circuit. Granted that Terry might be worried more than the world knew about the strange little uprising yesterday in Molobangwe, still it was surprising he should reveal it to the newly met Majority Leader. He did not suppose the M'Bulu's inner feelings were often revealed to anyone, which was accurate; and he was at a loss to understand what sudden impulse or slipping of control had caused them to be revealed to him. He decided to tell Orrin when he saw him, for whatever it might be worth, as he moved on across the room, saw Tommy Davis and Fred Van Ackerman again talking in a corner, and was surprised and amused by the thought of how quickly these little collaborations and differences eddied and swirled in this hecticly self-conscious sector of American politics. More or less for the hell of it, he decided to join them, and was intrigued to see that Robert A. Leffingwell was doing the same from the other side of the room.

"Good evening, Bob," he said as their paths converged. The director of the President's Commission on Administrative Reform looked startled for a second, then held out his hand with a fair show of cordiality.

"Senator, how have you been? I haven't seen you in a long time."

"No," Senator Munson agreed. "How have you been? Keeping you busy over there in the Executive Branch, are they?"

"I seem to keep occupied," Bob Leffingwell said pleasantly. "You, too, I read in the papers."

"Always," the Majority Leader said. "Always. Although I think we're about to see the end tonight. For a while, anyway."

"Really going to adjourn, hm? In spite of my old friend from South Carolina," Bob Leffingwell said, and, despite the attempt at jocularity, too many old bitternesses from his long-standing feud with Seab Cooley got in the way and his eyes clouded with a reminiscent pain and anger.

"He can't win on this," Senator Munson said, ignoring it. "It's impossible."

"You've rounded up the votes, then, in your famously efficient fashion," Bob Leffingwell said, more relaxed. The Majority Leader shook his head.

"I don't really need them. The times are against Seab. He's got to lose. History says so."

"And you think it's a good thing."

"Yes, don't you?"

"I do," Bob Leffingwell said, "but I was wondering if you did."

"Yes," the Majority Leader said shortly. "I do. I can't say that I think *this* kind of thing is any help to the welfare of man and his nations, but the cocktail party is Washington's standard answer to everything, so I guess I'm alone in that."

"You're not," Bob Leffingwell told him. "I don't approve of this, myself. I only came because these people have been very loyal to me, over the years, so I thought I should put in an appearance. I agree with you this kind of fawning overemphasis on the Africans is no help. That surprises you."

"It does," the Majority Leader said, taking a hot crab-meat canapé from a passing tray. "You've changed."

"Oh, no," Bob Leffingwell said, taking one also. "I've been rather—over-emphasized—myself, thanks to some of my good friends. I have a lot of ideas that might seem startling. For instance: Just what is the game of that seven-foot calculating machine over there in his pretty robes? And why does some-one like Tommy Davis talk to someone like Fred Van Ackerman? Life has many little mysteries."

"Of which you are turning out to be one," Senator Munson said as the crowd swirled around them, louder, noisier, happier, and increasingly re-laxed. "What's Harley going to do next year? And are you going to work for Ted Jason?"

Bob Leffingwell looked amused.

"You have the right sequence. If Harley runs for re-election, I shall sup-port him actively. If he doesn't, I think I shall go with Ted. After all," he remarked quietly, "I owe Harley a great deal."

"Yes, you do." The Majority Leader gave him a direct, searching glance. "There are some who would be surprised at your capacity for loyalty."

"Are you one of them?"

"No, sir," Senator Munson said. Bob Leffingwell gave an ironic little nod.

"Good. I never knew exactly where I stood with you, during that fight."

"Nor will you ever know," the Majority Leader said, "during that fight. Now, too, you may have to guess."

Bob Leffingwell returned a direct and searching glance of his own. Then he smiled.

"I feel better. What do you suppose Tommy and Fred *are* cooking up?"

"They weren't speaking, half an hour ago. Let's find out . . ."

"I think that might be a good idea," Justice Davis was saying as they ap-proached. "Yes, I think it might."

"What's that, Tommy?" Senator Munson asked. "Fred going to blow up the Capitol or something?"

"Always laughing," Senator Van Ackerman said sourly. "Always joking, always happy. Why don't you run along, Bob? What we're talking about isn't any of your business."

"The last time you two had something to talk about," Senator Munson said in a sudden blaze of anger that startled them all, himself included, "a Senator died. I hope the talk isn't as evil this time."

He was aware that his voice had carried more than it should, for around them a little silence fell for a second before people resumed talking in a baffled, half-amused way, as though they were quite sure they couldn't have heard what they thought they had. Tommy Davis and Fred Van Ackerman were in no doubt, however. The Justice's face was completely white, the Senator's flushed with a scowling anger.

"I didn't talk to Brig—Brigham," Tommy Davis said in an agonized whis-per. "I never talked to him about—about anything, Bob. I swear I never did. I only talked to you."

Senator Van Ackerman gave an impatient shake of his head.

"And what did you do about it, Mr. Nobility?" he said in a savage voice, held low. "I don't recall that your part was so noble, except to censure me. Maybe that was noble."

With a great effort, Senator Munson kept his voice down, too; and over the great weariness that suddenly filled it he injected a quiet but implacable warning.

"I don't intend for you to bully Seab tonight, Fred. I just want you to understand that."

"What more can you do to me?" Fred Van Ackerman asked bitterly. "I've been censured; now what? You can't expel me if I insist that the rules be enforced. And they will be. I promise you that. . . . Now I'm going back. Don't let him scare you, Tommy. He talks, but it doesn't matter."

"I'd go too," the Justice said in a bleakly unhappy voice, "except I'm supposed to be a guest of honor." He shook his head in a dazed way. "Honor," he repeated, as if to himself. "Honor."

"I think I really must run along, too," Bob Leffingwell said quietly. "It was good to see you, Senator. Tommy, take care."

The Justice did not reply, and after a moment they turned away and left him. Several guests were approaching, and in a second he would be swept up again in their arch and woozy chatter; another second or two after that and he would be chattering away again himself, bright and cheery on the surface, whatever lay beneath.

"Anyway," Senator Munson said, "at least now I know it hit him."

Bob Leffingwell gave a harsh laugh, bleak and without amusement.

"Who didn't it hit?"

At the door they found their host from the *Post* and his towering star of the evening. The M'Bulu, serenity outwardly restored, looked down benignly, as they approached in the growing stream of departing guests.

"So delightful you could come, Senator. Now back to your duties, eh?"

"I'm afraid so. But it has been lovely. Simply lovely."

"I may see you later. I think I may come up and watch."

"I'm sure that would be very helpful," the Majority Leader said. The M'Bulu uttered his merry laugh, giving Bob Munson a slow look from half-closed, heavy-lidded eyes agleam with a sardonic mockery. "That is all I desire, really. To be helpful."

Senator Munson shrugged.

"Come up if you like," he said, though his calculations of the adverse effect of this upon the Hamilton Resolution belied the casual disinterest he displayed. "It's a free country."

"How true," Terry said cordially. "How true!"

Downstairs at the Fourteenth Street entrance to the National Press Building the Majority Leader said good-by to Bob Leffingwell.

"Don't you want to come up and watch too? It might be interesting, to see old friends tangle with—old friends."

"No, thanks," Bob Leffingwell said. "I'm staying out of the mainstream for a while. I'll come back next year, when we choose a President. And besides—what good does it do to add more unhappiness to unhappiness?"

"I'd like to agree and follow your example," the Majority Leader said, "but my job doesn't permit it. Good luck."

"To you, too," Bob Leffingwell said, and they shook hands with a warmth they had not shown to one another in many months.

Ahead of him as his chauffeur maneuvered the limousine right onto F Street, right again on Twelfth down to Pennsylvania, and then left along Pennsylvania to the Hill, he could see the Capitol looming white and serene against the evening sky.

The light that burns above the great dome when either house of Congress meets at night cast its beckoning signal to the beautiful city. The hour was half after seven and the night of the Hamilton Resolution was yet young.

7

In the chamber, there had occurred one of those breaks that come in a long debate when consensus is reached by many stomachs that it is time to be replenished. On the floor only a handful of Senators, all from the South, remained in respectful attendance upon Blair Sykes of Texas as he made his speech against the resolution. Downstairs in the Senators' private dining room every table was full and the talk was vigorous and lively. What the state of animation of all these distinguished people would be at 3 or 4 A.M. might be another matter, but for the moment everyone seemed to be in fine shape— not least the Secretary of State, who, after pausing to greet many old friends and former colleagues along the way, had finally reached a table in the corner and settled in with the junior Senator from Iowa and the Congressman from California to consume a club steak, salad, and coffee.

"How's it going?" he demanded, attacking the steak with energy and dispatch. "Seab given up yet?"

"I don't think so," Lafe Smith said. "He had a bite to eat a while back, and now he's lying down in the Majority cloakroom taking a little nap. But he's still on guard duty."

"Hasn't sued for peace to you, has he?" Orrin asked Cullee, and the Congressman smiled.

"No more offers. I expect our talk this afternoon finished that."

"Yes." The Secretary frowned. "Well, you understand Bob and I had to make the attempt. I'm sorry he misunderstood, but it probably wouldn't have made any difference."

"I don't think so," Cullee said. "If he did misunderstand," he added with a sudden glance at the Secretary; but the Secretary let it pass. "Do you think he'll really filibuster?"

"I wish not, but I'm afraid so. What do you hear around the floor?"

"I hear it's still O.K.," Lafe said.

"That was a good speech you made on the UN," the Secretary told him. "I've just been in the official reporters' room reading over the transcript of the debate so far. I think you said some necessary things."

"Thanks. I get awfully fed up sometimes, up there, but—" He shrugged. "What else is there? Except the final disaster?"

"If only enough of its members can believe that," Orrin Knox said, "maybe we can pull it through in spite of itself. And the world with it. . . . How's Hal?" he added abruptly. "Got any report yet?"

The junior Senator from Iowa gave a guilty little start which was not lost upon the Secretary, but covered it calmly.

"What?" he asked with an innocence that did not fool Orrin.

"He's in the hospital, isn't he? I can't reach him by phone."

"What makes you think that?" Lafe asked cautiously. His old friend and colleague gave him a knowing glance.

"He isn't here, and I can't reach him there. What's it all about?"

"He went in for a checkup, as I think you suggested. Or I did. Anyway, he'll be out tomorrow, I expect, and back on the job."

"You don't sound so sure."

"He'll make it," Lafe said, though he knew he was using "it" in the narrowest sense of the General Assembly debate. At least, he added to himself, I hope to God he'll make it; he'll die if he doesn't. Then the incongruity of that struck him, and he looked down hastily at his dessert and took an earnest bite.

"Well—" the Secretary said doubtfully. "No monkey business now, damn it. I don't care about the delegation, we can manage that, but I am seriously worried about his health. It would be just like him to do something quixotic."

"He has a very idealistic desire to serve," Lafe said. "Why don't you let him?"

Orrin Knox studied him shrewdly for a moment.

"Is it as bad as that?"

"Why don't you let him?" Lafe repeated, his expression yielding nothing.

"I'll be there," Cullee said. "I can help."

"So you can," Lafe said gratefully. "We'll manage, Orrin. Stop fussing like an old hen. It isn't as bad as you think."

"It's worse than I think," Orrin said. His colleague shrugged.

"So you say. Leave it alone."

"But—"

"Leave it alone, I said."

"Well," the Secretary said after a moment, "obviously I have no choice."

"I expect we should go back up to the floor," Cullee said. "I don't want to rush you, but—"

"Right," the Secretary said. "We don't want to miss the President Pro Tem. Or the M'Bulu of Mbuele. Or the First Lady. Or the Secretary of State. Or any other of these famous people here tonight."

And so, finally, the long night began in earnest. In the crowded chamber, with Family, Public, and Diplomatic Galleries filled to capacity and murmurous with interest, with the Press, Radio-TV, and Periodical Galleries jammed with watching newsmen and women alert and eager to send the word, and on the floor almost all Senators present and many standees from the House lined along the walls, George Carroll Townsend of Maryland completed a brief but heated condemnation of the Hamilton Resolution and sat down.

At once there was a commotion among the press. By leaning over the gallery rail and looking down, they could see that B. Gossett Cook of Virginia, in the Chair, had no other name on the list of speakers lying before him on the desk. For a moment he looked rather blankly at the Majority Leader, who in turn looked about quickly (as, above, the New York *Post* urged, "Put it to a vote while the old fool is out of the room! Put it to a vote!"). Then, not finding the one he sought, Bob Munson rose to his feet and, after a hasty admonition to Stanley Danta, began to address the Chair. Senator Danta walked quickly up the aisle to the cloakroom, disappearing through its swinging glass doors as the whispering increased across the big brown room.

"Mr. President," Senator Munson said slowly, "am I to understand that no further Senators wish to speak on the pending resolution prior to the vote?"

"The Chair," Gossett Cook said with a little smile, "perforce has to labor under that impression, he will say to the distinguished Majority Leader, in the absence of some indication to the contrary."

"Then I am to understand," Senator Munson repeated slowly, "that there is no one at all in this distinguished body who feels moved to—"

"Mr. President," Fred Van Ackerman said loudly, jumping to his feet. "Mr. President, I have something to say. Mr. President! Mr. President!"

"The Senator will address the Chair in proper order," Gossett Cook said with an asperity sudden and startling, for he was normally the most soft-spoken of men. "Does the Senator wish to ask the Majority Leader to yield? If so, let him ask."

"Mr. President," Senator Van Ackerman said with an elaborately insolent air, "will the distinguished Majority Leader yield to me?"

"For a question," Senator Munson tossed over his shoulder, continuing to look at the Chair.

"Very well, for a question. How much longer is the Senate going to stall around waiting for a senile old—"

"Mr. President!" the Majority Leader said angrily.

"Waiting for the Senator from South Carolina," Senator Van Ackerman amended smoothly as the galleries gasped. "I ask the Majority Leader if the final adjournment of this long and difficult session of Congress is going to be delayed just in order that Senator Cooley, who should be here right this minute if he wants to speak, may be sheltered and protected by the Majority Leader and this Senate?"

"The Senator from Wyoming," Senator Munson said, "will never live to see the day when he has friends who care enough for him to shelter and protect him. That is his misfortune. The senior Senator from South Carolina has, and I make no apologies to the Senate for it. If anyone else is impatient because

Senator Cooley has stepped off the floor momentarily and I am securing time for him to return so that he may speak his piece as fully and completely as he desires in this matter, let him join the Senator from Wyoming. I'll wait."

He turned and leaned against his desk, his back to the Chair, his eyes moving slowly, face by face, over the Senate. No one rose, no one moved. He turned back.

"Very well. Now, Mr. President—"

"Mr. President!" Fred Van Ackerman said. "If the Majority Leader is through with that old stunt, will he tell me why he feels it necessary to delay the work of this Senate? The Senator from South Carolina spoke earlier today. He's had his say on this. We know where he stands." An ugly rhythm came into his voice. "The Majority Leader isn't in any *doubt*, is he? The Majority Leader isn't *puzzled* about it, is he? The Majority Leader doesn't expect any *surprises* from the Senator from South Carolina, does he?"

"Mr. President," Bob Munson said, turning his back deliberately, "I shall not yield further to the Senator from Wyoming."

"You can't shut me up!" Fred Van Ackerman cried, his voice suddenly scaling upward in the snarling, unhealthy anger his colleagues knew only too well. "You can't shut me up, I will say to the Majority Leader! You censured me, but you can't take away my right as a United States Senator to say what I please! I will tell that to the Majority Leader; you can't take away my right to speak—"

"No more, I will say to the distinguished Senator from Wyoming," interrupted a familiar voice, and the Senate and galleries got a little release of tension as they turned and smiled to see the President Pro Tempore coming down the aisle, "and distinction, Mr. President, takes many forms—no more than he has a right to take away mine . . .

"Mr. President," he said, moving to his desk as Bob Munson sat down, "my apologies to the Senate for delaying this moment, and my thanks to it for not going on and passing me by. Thanks also to the Majority Leader for sending the Senator from Connecticut to wake me up. I was taking a little snooze, Mr. President, I will say candidly to my colleagues. I recommend it. It refreshes one for the tasks ahead."

"Mr. President," Senator Van Ackerman inquired, his quietness contrasting ominously with the laughter with which the Senate responded to Senator Cooley's last remark, "will the Senator from South Carolina yield to me?"

"I will," Seab Cooley said calmly, "if the Senator thinks he can contribute something."

"How old is the Senator?" Fred Van Ackerman asked cruelly, and there was a little gasp around the galleries and on the floor. For a full minute Seab remained silent, and even as he did so, something of the comfortable atmosphere in the room began to drain away as men were reminded that he was, indeed, very old.

"My age is a matter of public record," he said finally. "Assuming it has any bearing on the matter here."

"How is the Senator feeling?" Fred Van Ackerman pursued, like the school bully tormenting his victim.

"Very well in my body," Seab Cooley said slowly. "Even better in my mind. And in my heart, I will say to the Senator from Wyoming, better than he could ever feel, since to feel well there requires a decency he does not possess."

"Oh, good for you!" the First Lady murmured in the Family Gallery above. Patsy Labaiya sniffed, "What an old HAM," to Celestine Barre, who smiled in a noncommittal way.

"I won't respond to that," Fred Van Ackerman said coldly. "I will just ask the Senator if he thinks he will be feeling as well at four o'clock tomorrow morning as he feels right now?"

"I expect to," Senator Cooley said calmly.

"The Senator expects to," Fred Van Ackerman echoed with a broadly skeptical and completely humorless grimace. "I am sure we are all glad to hear it. I want the Senator to know that I intend to stay around and see it."

"I can't stop you," Seab Cooley said.

"No, you can't," Fred Van Ackerman agreed, as a page boy came from a side door carrying six books and a stack of papers which he placed carefully on the desk of the President Pro Tem. "No, sir, that's one thing you can't do. Stop me."

"Now, Mr. President," Seab Cooley began opening the first book with an outward appearance of calm, though his heart had begun to beat quite painfully, "I should like to begin my more thorough discussion of this resolution about the Emboohoo by describing for you the situation as regards the relations between the races in my state of South Carolina in 1865, immediately following the conclusion of the War Between the States. Senators will remember—"

And he was off, but not before Senator Munson and Senator Danta had conferred worriedly with each other about the obvious intentions of the junior Senator from Wyoming; not before Beth Knox had murmured to Dolly Munson, "Oh, dear, I hope this is going to turn out all right"; not before the Secretary of State had said to Cullee Hamilton, "Now you see the sort of thing we're up against over here; it isn't so simple," and Cullee had nodded gravely; and not before there began to come over the Press Gallery the conviction that its members might be about to witness and report on a most savage evening. Many of them had wished for years to see Seab Cooley brought low, but few indeed relished the prospect of watching the process. An uneasy, uncomfortable restlessness settled upon the chamber as the minutes went by and the filibuster began.

For the first three hours, however, everything proceeded according to pattern, and eventually all those who were concerned about what might happen, all those who feared it, all those who were eager for it, all those who didn't particularly care one way or the other, began to relax and think of other things they might better be doing—principally, bed. It was now nearing midnight, the day had been a long one. In the galleries and on the floor there was a noticeable thinning-out while the President Pro Tempore droned along, as he had in many filibusters before, carefully husbanding his energies and stretching out his store of thoughts to consume the greatest possible time with the least possible effort. In this he seemed to be succeeding as the two big clocks, one above the Chair and the other above the main door of the Senate, ticked slowly on.

Among his listeners, the reaction was about what might have been expected. In the Family Gallery the First Lady, temporarily worn out by the exhausting if customary social whirl imposed by the just-concluded visit of the President of Peru and the about-to-happen visit of the President of Brazil, said her good nights shortly after 11 P.M. With a little wave to the Majority Leader and to Senator Cooley, who paused and bowed low, she withdrew amid a flurry of whispered comment from the galleries. It had been a busy three days, the sort of thing she and the President had to undergo roughly every six weeks as one top-ranking dignitary or another came to Washington, and she hadn't been ashamed to tell Dolly and the others that she felt it. She wasn't as young as she used to be, said Lucille Hudson, and she had to take her sleep when she could find it, particularly with Brazil coming so fast on the heels of Peru.

She did hope, she made a point of telling Patsy Labaiya, that Seab would do a good job of his presentation, even though of course she didn't want him to succeed in killing the Hamilton Resolution. In her voice was the implication, sweetly and cordially transmitted, that she hoped he would light into both Patsy's husband and her brother and give them merry whatfor before he was done. Patsy could only grit her teeth and make the best of it, with a smile just this side of vinegar that delighted the other ladies. Shortly after Lucille left, Kitty Maudulayne and Celestine Barre confessed that, they too must run along, fascinating though it was to watch a filibuster. The group dwindled to three. After an awkward little moment of rearrangement that caused some amusement among the handful of Senators, then on the floor, Dolly found herself sitting between Beth and Patsy, a location, that caused her some amusement, too. But neither of her companions was quite in a mood to share her feeling. Beth's sense of humor, though excellent, wasn't quite broad enough to encompass the more satiric aspects of her husband's rivalry with Governor Jason. Patsy's sense of humor, on this as on all other subjects, was nonexistent. So they sat, listening with a determinedly diligent attention, while Dolly, a sort of no woman's land, sat between them, comfortable and amused.

Elsewhere in the chamber, others most directly involved in the matter of the Hamilton Resolution, the M'Bulu's visit, and all the various ramifications also whiled away the time in their various ways as the Senator from South Carolina went methodically on. While he traced the travail of his native state in Reconstruction days, the Secretary of State moved casually around the floor from friend to friend, sitting for a while to chat with this one, leaning over a desk to whisper in the ear of that one, returning eventually to resume his seat beside the Congressman from California on their sofa by the wall. There were still a few votes in doubt, and he was doing what he could to nail them down, even though his activities finally drew the sarcastic comment from Seab that "our dear old friend just can't seem to help meddlin', Mr. President, even though he has now moved far beyond us in his new and mighty position. No, sir, Mr. President, here he is meddlin' again!" Orrin had given Seab a cheerful look, and the Senator from South Carolina had permitted himself a slight, if somewhat grim, twinkle of amusement back. "Of course, now, Mr. President," he added, "our friend no longer has the privilege of speaking here, which must be fearfully frustrating to him. He was always such a talker nobody could get a word in edgewise when he was here. Guess he must just be homesick for all that talking now, Mr. President, that's why he's here." Orrin's amusement had broadened, and after a moment, with a shrug that conceded that he perhaps was out of order, he had returned to his seat beside Cullee and come forth to lobby no more.

His companion, outwardly amused by this byplay, was actually far away in his thoughts, off somewhere with his wife and his friend and all the aching problems of his present position and future plans. He had almost expected to see both Sue-Dan and LeGage at the session tonight, and once he had satisfied himself with furtively careful glances around the galleries that they were not, he had of course fallen to worrying about where they were. With the worry there had returned to his mind the bitter wrangle at his house that afternoon, and with that had come a sudden and increasingly disturbing memory of LeGage's final statement.

Cullee had not realized, in the heat of their argument, that this had been an actual bona fide threat, but now as he thought back over it while Seab droned along off in some other world, the realization began to come home to him with a genuine and alarming force. He had been too upset at the time to really take it in, and, further, it was beyond his own character, even under the impetus of such emotion, to desire real harm to anyone so close to him for so many years. He might threaten physical violence, and perhaps if provoked sufficiently would indeed knock 'Gage down, as he had done a couple of times in the fury of arguments long ago at Howard. But the mood always passed as soon as it came, he was always contrite and held no grudges, and, anyway, as he had remarked sheepishly on both occasions, "I didn't hit you very hard." "God, no," 'Gage had said with a forgiving grin. "I wouldn't be here now if you had." But all of this, Cullee knew now with a chilling certainty in his heart as he sat there in the Senate near midnight of Seab Cooley's filibuster, had no connection at all with the sick, strangled menace that had come to him in LeGage's choked and agonized voice that afternoon.

That boy he told himself with a frightened wonder—not frightened physically, for such fear wasn't in him, but frightened of what life did to people, which could be terrifying indeed—that boy is playing for keeps. And with some instinct that he couldn't have analyzed, but which brought him abruptly to his feet, startling the Secretary, he had hurried into the cloakroom and telephoned home.

"Are you all right, Maudie?" he had demanded when she came on the line, sleepy and disgruntled. "Is the house all right?"

"'Course I'm all right," she had remarked with considerable asperity. "Sound asleep until you started pestering me. What's the matter? Are *you* all right?"

"You're sure everything's all right around the house?" he persisted, and she retorted, "I said it was. What's the matter with you, I s—"

"You go look. I'll wait. You go check, will you, please?"

Grumping and complaining, she had left the phone and returned in five minutes.

"Everything's fine out here. You in the Senate?"

"Yes."

"Guess that's your trouble."

"Listen," he said. "Call me in the Majority cloakroom of the Senate if you need me for anything. Got that? Majority Cloakroom of the Senate."

"I got you. All I need is sleep, thank you."

"All right, Maudie. I'll be home after a while."

But despite her obvious impatience and the fact that everything was apparently in good shape at home, he had still returned uneasy to the chamber.

"Anything wrong?" Orrin had asked as he sat down, and the Congressman shook his head.

"Just remembered somebody I had to call. Not important."

"Good," the Secretary said, but Cullee had the feeling he hadn't fooled him much. He expected Orrin knew he had some new, deep worry to plague him; and so he had, an ominous and disturbing conviction that LeGage might be going 'way off base this time to do something of some unknown nature to him or his property. In spite of his attempts to appear unconcerned, the thought drew a frowning crease between his eyebrows which was quite obvious to Terrible Terry as he surveyed the scene from his seat in the front row of the Diplomatic Gallery above.

Twice already, as the hour neared midnight, the M'Bulu had been given the honor of mention from the floor as he sat, leaning slightly forward, looking amid his drabber seatmates in the galleries very much like what Cullee had called him that afternoon: a big pretty bug. Not one of the heavier, rounder bugs, but one of the long, thin, razor-beaked beetles of his native country, hard of shell and swift of foot, almost impossible to catch and requiring the application of direct force to eliminate. His primordially handsome face wore an expression of deep interest; he frowned thoughtfully or nodded smilingly or shook his head angrily as the Senator from South Carolina moved on from Reconstruction into the threadbare eighties and nineties and began to round the turn of the century with "the colored race in its proper place in society, the white race, Mr. President, watching over and guarding the colored with friendly care," and all things steady in the world of the South.

Midway in this recitation the President Pro Tem had suddenly interrupted his discourse to acknowledge the towering figure whose entry around 10 P.M. he had ostentatiously ignored.

"There he sits, Mr. President!" he had cried suddenly, startling the handful of Senators on the floor and the dwindling audience in the galleries. "There he sits, the foreign adventurer who came into my state and stuck his nose in where he didn't belong! There sits the Emboohoo making fun of this Senate now as we struggle with this inexcusable situation he has created, Mr. President! He should be booted out of this chamber and booted back to Africa, Mr. President. Courtesy is too good for him. He should be booted out!"

The Emboohoo had frozen into a look of the sternest disapproval for a moment and then, as he realized that the little hissing that broke out here and there in the galleries was not directed at him but at his ancient opponent, a pleased expression had come upon his face and he had bowed with a sardonic courtesy to Senator Cooley there below. The old man had turned his back upon him with a cold deliberation, and it was not until almost midnight that he had referred to him again.

"Mr. President," he had said somberly, and this time the Emboohoo's anticipatory smile faded fast as Senator Cooley went on, "certain distinguished visitors to this country may sit in the gallery and sneer at the Senate, but they would be better advised to look at what is happening in their own back yard, Mr. President. We read about riots, Mr. President. We read about troubles in the Emboohoo's country. Maybe instead of telling us what to do in America he ought to be back home telling his own people, Mr. President. Maybe they won't still be listening by the time he gets around to returning there. By which, Mr. President," he added dryly, "many of us here would no doubt be dreadfully saddened. Yes, sir, Mr. President. We would weep. Of that you may be sure."

And there, of course, though Terry congratulated himself that he had recovered with aplomb and turned to the galleries only a serene and self-confident countenance, the Senator from South Carolina with his instinct for the jugular had gone straight to the M'Bulu's. Terry was far more worried than he wished the world to know, and he had indicated as much to the Majority Leader at the Press Club earlier, with a sudden impulse of candor that he still couldn't understand himself, except that it must have welled up out of some fear far deeper than he realized. The reports from Molobangwe were confused and fragmentary at best, and as far as he had been able to ascertain through all the channels open to him, his mother was safe, his cousin was still loyal, the Council of Ministers still ruled the land in co-operation with them, and all was well. But there persisted the immediate interpretation of the riot that had come to him in many broadcasts and commentaries—that there might be behind it certain elements, more closely identified with his cousin than himself, anxious to give to the situation a more sinister aspect than the usual futile protests for freedom that occasionally agitated his dutiful subjects. He felt a gnawing uneasiness. He knew he must get back; he felt he should leave at once. His mother was old; he did not trust his cousin, for all that he had received all sorts of blood-pledges of fealty from him; the Council of Ministers was composed of weak and venal elders who bowed to each wind. He knew with an absolute certainty where he should be at this very moment—on a jet winging home, just as fast as he could go. No fear held him back, for the M'Bulu, like Cullee, had virtually no physical fear where he felt his duty to be involved; but there was the matter of the UN, the causes there going forward, most importantly freedom for Gorotoland but almost as important discredit for the United States, and he felt that he was also needed right where he was. It was a fearful tugging and hauling, and the decision was not made easier by the basic, almost animal concern for his rights in Gorotoland from which had sprung his inadvertent candor with Senator Munson.

He could, possibly, wait another week before returning, but he knew that was absolutely all. He was reasonably sure that things were under con-trol—the British had been moderately comforting when he had called Lord Maudulayne just before coming up to the Senate from the Statler, where he and LeGage had a room—and that was some comfort. It was only temporary, however.

"Everything in good shape so far as we know," the Ambassador had told him. "Although, of course," he had added cheerfully, "it really is hardly worth our time any more to care whether it is or not, is it? It may not be, of course, but to the best of our knowledge—" He had interrupted himself. "That is, we *think* it is. But, then—really, who knows? Why don't you nip off and find out, if you're really worried?"

And, having succeeded in increasing the worry, which was what he had intended to do, he had rung off with a cordial farewell. His equivocation did not fool the M'Bulu, who knew perfectly well that if there had been a real crisis in Gorotoland the British would have been there at once, in-dependence movement or no. At least, he thought they would. He would have felt offended, dismayed, insulted, and personally betrayed if he had thought the British would not come to his rescue. One counted on them to be there when one needed them, that was all. If one couldn't count on that in this world, what could one count on?

Catching a glimpse of the M'Bulu's face, which despite his efforts, did not altogether conceal the somber trend of his thoughts, the Majority Leader wondered briefly whether things were really as bad in Molobangwe as the expression might indicate, or whether it was some other facet of his many enterprises that had Terrible Terry worried. Bob Munson still was intrigued by their chat at the Press Club and had passed it along to Orrin Knox a while ago when he had wandered back to the sofa where the Secretary was watching the proceedings. Orrin had nodded.

"We don't know exactly what happened, but apparently it was indicative of something more serious than just the usual unrest over there."

"But you're still going to vote in the UN to give Gorotoland immediate independence," the Majority Leader had said with an ironic shake of the head. The Secretary had looked thoughtful and refrained from direct answer.

"It's a matter of balancing. Whether it's worth more to take the risk of offending the Afro-Asian states by assuring British control for a while longer or gamble on winning the friendship of the Afro-Asian states by helping to speed the British departure—"

"—and run the risk of Communist control of Gorotoland," Bob Munson said. Orrin Knox nodded.

"That's the sort of gamble the United States faces, these days."

"Don't overdo that balancing act," Senator Munson said. "We might all fall off the tightrope with a bang, someday."

"If we fall, I think it's quite likely to be with a bang," Orrin agreed with some grimness. "The condition of the world has made that almost a certainty."

But this comment, which had reawakened some of the gloom about world affairs that often seemed to fill his thoughts nowadays, was not enough to deflect the Majority Leader for long from his immediate task this night. He still had to see Seab safely through his filibuster to his inevitable defeat and, at the same time, make sure that the Senate completed all of its last-minute business so that it could adjourn as soon as it voted on the Hamilton Resolution.

The first part of this two-part project—to see Seab safely through—seemed to be coming along well so far, although Senator Munson was conscious of the fact that Senator Van Ackerman was staying close by and gave no signs of abandoning his earlier intention to harass Senator Cooley all he could. Fortunately there had been little opportunity so far—Fred had refrained from the obvious gambit of trying to debate with Seab, probably because he knew he would be chopped down if he did—but the time was coming when there would be opportunity, and the Majority Leader felt its approach with some uneasiness. He had agreed with Seab in a whispered conversation a couple of hours ago that when the old man grew tired and wanted a rest, he would yield to the Majority Leader, who in turn would yield to other Senators who wished to put their last items in the Congressional Record, make their last little speeches on matters of interest to the folks back home, and otherwise conclude the business of the session. Bob would then yield the floor back to Seab, who could proceed uninterrupted until such time as he decided to, or was forced by exhaustion to, conclude.

The only hitch in this was that Seab would need unanimous consent to yield to him, and he in turn would need unanimous consent to yield to someone else. All that was necessary to stop this was one objection, and the Majority Leader knew where it would come from.

It was becoming apparent, however, that the President Pro Tempore would soon need the respite. It was clear to everyone that he was beginning to feel the strain, even though there were still moments when his voice soared with something of its old power and when his sallies were as sharp and pointed as ever. The slow rate of speech with which he had started in order to pace himself was now even slower; his posture, determinedly erect and challenging to begin with, had gradually relaxed into a more and more stooped and sagging position. There were moments, now, when he leaned forward with both hands gripping his desk, a gesture which he attempted to associate with some particularly emphatic statement in his speech but which fooled no one.

"I think the old buffoon's beginning to rest," the *Reporter* murmured above in the thinned-out ranks of the Press Gallery, and the Chattanooga *Times* nodded.

"You don't speak for four hours straight at seventy-six without needing a little relief. I doubt if he can keep going much longer."

"Not without help," the *Reporter* agreed, and chuckled. "Maybe Fred Van Ackerman will help him."

To all those watching, the late-stayers in the galleries, the late-stayers in the press, the thirty or so Senators who remained on the floor while their colleagues napped or gossiped in the cloakrooms or had an occasional quick one in the Majority Leader's office, as was the traditional adjournment-night custom, Fred Van Ackerman was rapidly becoming the center of speculation as midnight came and went. If Fred was going to make any move at all, everyone agreed, it would probably be soon. Given Seab's obviously increasing tiredness, even his bitterest critics were not too anxious to see Fred go into action. There was a consequent feeling of relief, that perhaps it could all be worked out smoothly, when the Majority Leader rose in one of the President Pro Tempore's increasingly prolonged—and by now almost painful—pauses, and said quietly, "Mr. President, will the Senator yield to me?"

"For what purpose, Mr. President?" Senator Cooley inquired with a show of caution. "Is it a question, or—"

"I wondered, Mr. President, if the Senator would yield to me, without losing the floor, so that I might take care of a few last-minute housekeeping details that have to be completed in preparation for adjournment?"

"If the Senator will be brief," Senator Cooley said, "and in the understanding that I will not lose the floor."

"Very well, Mr. President," Senator Munson said. "Now, Mr. President—" he began in a matter-of-fact tone, but of course it didn't work.

"Wait a minute, Mr. President!" Fred Van Ackerman cried, suddenly leaping up from the book he had been reading with an ostentatious show of attention for the past two hours. "Wait a minute. Suppose the Majority Leader makes his request in proper form, Mr. President."

"Mr. President," Bob Munson said, "I ask unanimous consent that the Senator from South Carolina be permitted to yield to me without losing the floor."

"I object," said Fred Van Ackerman.

"Objection is heard," said Victor Ennis of California, in the Chair.

"Mr. President," the Majority Leader said, "I wonder if the Senator from

Wyoming has any conception of what he is doing here in this objection which I can only regard as dilatory, frivolous, and hostile to the efficient completion of the Senate's business on this adjournment night? This is not the act of one who wishes Senators to be able to complete their tasks and go home, Mr. President. It is the act of one who for some purpose of his own seeks deliberate delay. I wonder if the Senator would enlighten us as to what his purpose is?"

"I am deliberately delaying?" Fred Van Ackerman demanded in an exasperation almost ludicrous, as Senator Cooley sat slowly down with a watchful expression that did not quite conceal his physical relief. "I am keeping Senators from completing their tasks and going home, as the Majority Leader so pathetically describes? What is the Senator from South Carolina doing, Mr. President? I will tell the Majority Leader what my purpose is. The Senator from South Carolina wants to speak, Mr. President. I am helping him do it. I object to that unanimous consent request, Mr. President."

"The Senator has registered his objection once," Victor Ennis said. "That is enough."

"I do not want to have to make a motion that the Senator from South Carolina be permitted to yield to me without losing the floor, Mr. President," Bob Munson said, "but of course I can do it by motion."

"Go ahead," Fred Van Ackerman said indifferently. "The Senator doesn't have the votes. In fact," he said, looking scornfully around the floor, "he doesn't even have a quorum."

"Quorums can be gotten."

"Get one," Fred Van Ackerman offered. "It won't help any. Incidentally," he added sharply, "I believe it is against the rules for the Senator from South Carolina to sit down, Mr. President, as long as he has the floor. Is he giving up the floor, Mr. President?"

"The Senator is correct," Victor Ennis said reluctantly, as Senator Cooley got to his feet with an attempt at haste that looked somehow ungainly and awkward. "The Senator from South Carolina will remain standing as long as he retains the floor."

"And the Senator shouldn't lean against his desk, either, Mr. President," Fred Van Ackerman said. "That's the same as sitting."

"I ask unanimous consent, Mr. President," Lafe Smith said, jumping up, "that the Senator from South Carolina be permitted to lean against his desk when he so desires without losing the floor."

"I object," said Fred Van Ackerman.

"Mr. President—" Lafe began angrily, but Seab Cooley stopped him with a slow gesture of the hand.

"Mr. President," he said, fighting against the weariness that was now almost uncontrollable in his voice, "I thank my good friend from Ioway for his kind efforts in my behalf, but obviously they are no use at this particular moment. Possibly I can yield to other Senators if they wish to insert material in the Record—"

"Not by unanimous consent, Mr. President, and not while leaning against his desk," Senator Van Ackerman said with an emphatic relish. "The rules of the Senate are very important, as the Majority Leader has told me sometimes in his little lectures, and I think all of us should observe them. I intend to."

"Mr. President—" Lafe began again, but again Seab silenced him.

"No matter. No matter, I say to the Senator. I shall do what I can to accommodate other Senators, and if I am blocked the burden will be upon the junior Senator from Wyoming. We shall just have to see how it goes. Now, where was I, Mr. President—" And he looked slowly through the books and papers, now strewn across both his desk and that of Stanley Danta beside it, in a peering, nearsighted way that was more than a little pathetic. "I believe I was telling the Senate about the situation in the early years of this century, when the condition of the colored people in my state was—"

And in a plodding, still-slower fashion that made his old friends and colleagues wince as many of them drifted back to the floor, drawn by news of the developing situation, he resumed the thread of his discourse, stumbling often, now; pausing uncertainly from time to time, his figure looking even more crumpled and bent; beginning to wander a bit in what he was saying, the uses of deliberate delay long gone in the crushing realities of a growing, grinding, genuine exhaustion.

In this fashion 12:30 came, 1 A.M., 1:30, 2 A.M. Above in the galleries, refilling now as the news went out on late radio and TV programs that a good show was going on in the Senate, there was a growing excitement and gossip, and on the floor, where most of the Senators had now returned, there was a growing tension and dismay as men who had often opposed the President Pro Tempore but never really wished him ill watched the spectacle of his slow disintegration, like a great tree coming down at last after so many decades of standing fierce and straight above them all. Several attempted to interrupt and aid him by asking prolonged questions, but his answers were rambling and disconnected. Finally, impatiently, he made a gesture that he wanted no more interruptions, however kindly meant. Reluctantly they respected this; and the tree continued to fall.

"I wish he would STOP," Patsy Labaiya whispered furiously to Dolly Munson shortly after 2 A.M. as Seab's voice, husky and halting, sank finally to an almost inaudible mumble. "He's seventy-six and he OUGHT TO KNOW BETTER."

"He doesn't know how to quit," Dolly said unhappily. "It's an honorable trait."

"But not NOW. Lord knows I think the old fool is utterly wrong on this, but I'm NOT vindictive. I think he should STOP."

"I don't think he'll stop until the Lord tells him to," Beth Knox said.

"I don't want the Lord to tell him in front of ME," Patsy said.

"Neither do I," Beth said, "but if we want to stay, we've got to realize it may happen."

To her husband, still sitting on the sofa beside Cullee Hamilton, against the Senate wall, the same thought came with a renewed insistence a few moments later when his companion finally stirred uneasily and came out of the dark region of thought where he had seemed to be most of the evening.

"I wish he'd stop," Cullee said in a voice at once annoyed and concerned. "I never wanted him to kill himself. Can't we stop him?"

"I don't know how," Orrin said with an equal worry, "unless he gets so tired he's just got to stop. And I imagine that will be a while, yet."

"But he can hardly talk now," Cullee protested. "I wish he'd *stop*."

"I wonder—" the Secretary said. "I wonder if he'd believe it if I got a message for him from the President. Hold my seat," he directed, as though anyone would dream of taking it. "I'll go call him and see what I can do."

"He must be asleep by this time," Cullee said, but Orrin shook his head. "I think he's probably waiting for something like this. I'll be back in a minute."

There was by now, all through the body and heart and mind of the senior Senator from South Carolina, a bone-weariness so great that he literally did not know whether he could put one word after another to form consecutive sentences; and indeed, though he was too tired to realize it, there were increasing moments when he could not, when he would pause and grope for a thought and sometimes conclude with one considerably different from the one with which he had begun. His voice was now down to almost a whisper ("I can't hear what he's saying," the Dallas *News* complained at one point in the Press Gallery. "Be thankful for small favors," the Washington *Post* told him cheerfully), his eyes were smarting and burning, and a terrible weight seemed to be dragging on his arms and legs. His hands were trembling almost out of control and occasionally they would stray, apparently of their own volition, to the desk-top to give him a quickly furtive bracing—Senator Van Ackerman had been forced to call the Chair's attention to this five times in the past hour. In addition to everything else, he felt a terrible urge to urinate, which he was not certain he could control much longer. The room was beginning to disintegrate before his eyes, a grayness was creeping over everything; it seemed almost as though he were retreating into some private world a long way from the Senate. Only the instincts and habits of five decades kept him standing, kept him fumbling slowly, ever so slowly, through his papers, kept him talking on slowly, ever so slowly, in his steadily fading whisper. At 2:57 A.M. he made some almost incoherent reference to "*Journal* . . . yesterday," and the Majority Leader, feeling close to exhaustion himself from the strain of it all, promptly arose and asked unanimous consent that the Clerk be permitted to read the *Journal* of yesterday's proceedings without the Senator from South Carolina losing the floor.

"Mr. President," said Fred Van Ackerman, getting a little bleary-eyed himself but speaking with the strength of an implacable revenge and the advantage of better than thirty years over his opponent, "I object."

At 3:23 A.M., the whispering voice in the now almost completely silent chamber came to a halt, and as its owner stood slumped and exhausted, looking about him with a vague slowness that obviously did not perceive very much, Bob Munson leaned over and said in an urgent whisper, "For God's sake, Seab, give it up! You've done enough. Now quit it, damn it!" But after a prolonged, agonizing moment, during which everyone sat forward tensely, the terrible, touching whisper began again, "Now, Mr. President, I was telling the Senate—"

Ten minutes later, at 3:33, the Secretary of State was observed to return to the chamber with a piece of paper in his hand which he gave to the Congressman from California. Ignoring the immediate murmur that arose through the chamber as everyone turned to follow his movements, Cullee got up and, looking neither to right nor left, carried the paper down the aisle to the desk of the President Pro Tempore. Again the whisper stopped, and in the silence the old man could be seen, first looking vaguely then gradually focusing, upon the tall young figure before him. "What are you—what—" he began again in a baffled whisper, and Cullee whispered back, "For you, from the President." "Thank you, sir," Seab Cooley whispered slowly. "I do thank you, sir." But it was obvious as Cullee bowed and then returned, looking sad and stricken, to his seat beside the Secretary, that the message of the President was not going to be read by its recipient. He made the attempt, continuing to whisper something that even Bob Munson, leaning forward to glimpse Orrin's carefully large printing as it lay on the desk before them, could not understand; but it was obvious that the words did not penetrate. Then with a great, visible effort of will, Seab straightened his shoulders and opened another book and, although he clearly could no longer perceive its contents, whispered doggedly on.

At 4 A.M., still whispering, he reached for a glass of water, missed, and knocked it to the floor in such a way that its contents spilled across his books and papers. For several moments he stood looking down at them with an unseeing, almost stupid expression as Bob Munson mopped them off with his handkerchief, filled the glass with water from a pitcher brought hurriedly by a page, and held it out to him. He started to take it, but again he missed, and this time it fell to the carpet with a crash. A long, low sound of pity and consternation came from floor and galleries. After another agonizing pause, while they all waited breathlessly, the President Pro Tempore made another great, ponderously painful effort, and the racking whisper resumed.

At 4:13 A.M. ("Hot damn!" said the New York *Post*, glancing at his watch in the Press Gallery above, "I've won the pool!"), the slow, agonized, inaudible whisper again stopped altogether. The tension in the chamber suddenly shot up to an almost unbearable pitch, for this time it seemed obvious that the Senator from South Carolina could not possibly go on.

And this time, all those who thought so were correct. He had spoken more than eight hours at the age of seventy-six, and he could speak no more.

"Bob," he whispered, and he felt as though the fearsome effort of that one word would bring his death surely, on top of what he was feeling inside, "Bob—" And he held out a hand blindly toward the Majority Leader, who took it and, rising at once to his feet, assisted him to sit down, tremblingly and shakily and so abruptly that it looked like a collapse. In the Press Gallery several reporters rushed out to dart downstairs to be near the floor if he should have to be carried out, and everywhere across the chamber there came a release of talk and comment that Victor Ennis in the Chair finally had to silence with a heavy gavel.

"Mr. President," Bob Munson said in a voice touched with emotion, "the Senate has witnessed a gallant performance by a great public servant. Many of us do not agree with his position in this matter, but I think all who are generous of spirit, tolerant of mind, and loving of heart can accord him the honor and respect which are due him for all his many great years of service to our country. Mr. President, I move that the Senate now approve H. J. Res. 23, offered in the House by the distinguished Congressman from California. I request the Yeas and Nays."

"Evidently a sufficient number," Victor Ennis said, and it could be seen from the galleries that in one last gesture, the senior Senator from South Carolina raised his right hand a couple of inches before letting it fall back limply in his lap. It could also be seen that the Majority Leader waved commandingly to the junior Senator from Iowa, who got up and hurried to his desk; but the obvious intent of this was thwarted as the Senator from South Carolina shook his head ever so slightly and rejected the offer to help him off the floor. Lafe sat down uneasily in a seat nearby as the roll call began in the once more silent room, watching the President Pro Tempore with a concerned and compassionate stare.

"On this vote," Senator Ennis announced twenty minutes later, after there had come another dramatic pause when the Clerk reached Senator Cooley's name and a just barely audible "No" had been whispered, "the Yeas are 53, the Nays are 47, and House Joint Resolution 23 is approved."

In the ensuing half hour, while the last-minute articles were put in the Record, the last-minute speeches made, the business of the Senate concluded for another year, the President Pro Tempore sat silent and unmoving beside the Majority Leader. From the galleries his face looked gray and fallen-in upon itself, his body huddled and slack and curiously crumpled and small. Only once did he make a gesture, and that was to raise one hand with a painful slowness to his forehead, press for a moment, and then bring it down again; its violently agitated trembling was clearly visible to everyone. At one point the Majority Leader leaned over and asked with a deep concern, "Are you all right, Seab? Do you want to stay?" Very slowly the President Pro Tempore turned his head, and for a second a last gleam of irony touched his eyes. "I haven't missed an adjournment yet, Bob," he whispered with a painful slowness. "Don't . . . intend . . . to . . . miss . . . this one." The Majority Leader smiled hopefully, as though this comment presaged a quick recovery, but immediately the gleam had faded, the expression of recognition had disappeared, Senator Cooley had turned back to continue what was apparently going on inside himself, a terrible battle to remain where he was and not be taken from the floor in collapse. Lafe and several others who had gathered in seats nearby in case they were needed kept a watchful eye; but despite his obvious awful tiredness no one, even now, dared insist that Seabright B. Cooley leave the floor.

Above in the galleries the M'Bulu gathered himself gracefully together and, with a last faintly scornful look at the Senators below, departed the chamber. Beth Knox and Dolly Munson made their farewells to Patsy Labaiya and came downstairs to await their husbands in the Senators' Reception Room. Patsy, with a defiant little air, waved farewell to Ray Smith of California and went downstairs to find her chauffeur and be driven off through autumn-dark, still-sleeping Washington, silent and deserted in the cold little wind that was beginning to rise ahead of the dawn. On the floor Fred Van Ackerman, smugly pleased, gave one last contemptuous glance at his beaten opponent where he sat sunken and unresponsive, closed his book with an audibly satisfied snap, and left the floor. The Secretary of State, after asking the Majority Leader to tell Seab that he, Orrin, would come to see him later in the day, went out to find Beth and take her home. The Congressman from California, recipient of many congratulatory handshakes from Senators who had voted for his resolution, tried to accept them with a reasonable show of gratitude, though he did not really know, at that exact moment, how he felt about it. Certainly not gleeful, certainly not vindictive, and certainly not triumphant; just a sort of gray, flat, curiously uninvolved feeling—if anything, melancholy, uneasy, and sad. He had won, but he understood that, for him, many things were not yet over. Also, as soon as the vote was announced and he knew he had won, there had come a sharp recurrence of his earlier alarm. He would have called Maudie again, if it weren't so late. Perhaps the sound of her voice would give him anchor somewhere in the sea of inchoate reactions in which he seemed to be adrift. Perhaps it might. He didn't know.

But even as he had the thought he was informed that he would have the chance to find out. A page came quickly to his side from the Majority cloakroom.

"Sir," the boy said, "some lady who says she's your maid is on the phone. She wants you right away. She sounds real worried."

"Yes," Cullee said, hurrying forward even as his heart began to pound with a fearful constriction, "I'll be right there."

Shortly before 5 A.M., the Majority Leader, in accordance with tradition, announced to the Senate that he and the Minority Leader had transmitted to the President the information that the Senate had completed its business and had asked him if he had any further communications to make to it before it adjourned.

"The President said he had no further communications to make to the Senate at this time," Bob Munson said, "and, in accordance with the resolution of adjournment passed at 5:45 P.M. yesterday, I now move that the Senate stand adjourned sine die."

"Without objection," said Victor Ennis, "it is so ordered," and the long session that had seen the nomination of Robert A. Leffingwell, the death of Brigham Anderson, the Russian and American expeditions to the moon, the conference in Geneva, the visit of the M'Bulu, the Hamilton Resolution, and Seab Cooley's filibuster passed into history.

In the milling flurry of farewell handshakes, cordial wishes for good vacations, invitations to drop-in-if-you're-in-the-state, promises to see one another, and so on, that always turn the chamber into a noisy confusion after the last gavel falls, Bob Munson nodded to Lafe Smith, who came quickly to his side.

"Help me with this," the Majority Leader murmured, and together they turned to the President Pro Tempore, now a little more lively, a little more responsive, as many of his colleagues stopped by to shake his hand and congratulate him on a gallant fight.

"Seab," Senator Munson said, "Lafe and I want to see you home. May we?"

There was no answer for several seconds, and then Senator Cooley leaned forward, put both hands on his desk, and started to raise himself to his feet. Instinctively they started to help him, then as instinctively held back, as above in the Press Gallery the few remaining reporters paused to watch closely. But he fooled them all, he told himself inside his weary mind, he fooled them all and stood before them again, upright and on his feet and able, if slowly and cautiously, to move again.

"No, thank you, Bob," he whispered as they hovered close. "No, thank you, friend Lafe. I'll be all right . . . I'd . . . best . . . make it . . . my own way." A faint smile crossed his face. "That's . . . the only . . . way . . . I know."

"But," Lafe protested, "it won't be any bother, Seab, really. Let me get us a cab and I'll run you out to the hotel."

"I think . . . I'd like to take . . . a little walk . . . before I go home . . . thank you," Senator Cooley whispered. "I think fresh air . . . may be . . . what I need most . . . right now."

"Seab—" the Majority Leader said gravely, but the President Pro Tempore gave a little dismissing shake of his head.

"I'll manage, Bob. Don't . . . worry about . . . me . . . A little . . . fresh . . . air . . . and I'll be fine . . . If you could have . . . one of the boys . . . bring my coat from . . . the cloakroom—"

"I'll get it," Lafe said, and quickly did so as the galleries emptied and the floor thinned out, so that only a little handful of departing Senators and page boys remained to watch.

"Thank you," Senator Cooley whispered as Lafe helped him put it on. "Possibly you can help me . . . to the lavatory . . . if you will." Again a tiny show of humor crossed his ravaged face. "Wouldn't want to act . . . like a baby . . . right here on the floor . . . Bob . . . Wouldn't want . . . to . . . do . . . that."

"Sure thing," Lafe said, "and then we're going to see you home."

But after they had accompanied him as he walked with an awkward slowness but a still indomitable independence off the floor to the Senators' private toilet and there completed his painful but desperately necessary business, he still refused their offers. And finally, with a great reluctance, but unable to sway him and not quite daring to insist even in the face of his obvious absolute exhaustion, they bade him a deeply troubled good night at the entrance to the great terrace that runs around the West Front of the Capitol and looks down upon the town.

"Think . . . I'll . . . just . . . walk along here and then . . . down the Hill," he told them, still in the agonizing whisper. "I'll . . . feel more like . . . sleeping, after a little . . . fresh air."

And so the last they saw of him that night was his once powerful old figure, shrunken and worn, looking piteous and small in the folds of his heavy overcoat, starting out in the face of the wind, now quite cold and sharp as it whipped up from Virginia and the Potomac and the reaches of the storied streets below, to take his little walk before sleeping.

Silent and deserted still lay the boulevards of the sleeping capital as the Congressman from California sped home. Autumn's long-lingering night had not yet begun to fade, the east was still in darkness, in all the long run from the Hill to Sixteenth Street he saw only two taxicabs and a couple of early milk trucks. The City of Perfect Intentions and Imperfect Men would not begin to come fully awake for another hour or two. At the moment he had it virtually to himself, little Cullee Hamilton from Lena, S.C., as he drove home as fast as he dared, wondering fearfully in the wake of Maudie's frantic call what he would find this time at the end of his long, dark street.

There had been in her voice a genuine terror that had instantly called up its counterpart in him. She had been awakened by a noise downstairs, as though someone were furtively trying to pry a window; she had managed, with great courage, to get up and sneak down; had seen a figure, or possibly several, she was not sure in the darkness, outside the French doors in the dining room; and had screamed "Git!" with all the frantic vigor in her terrified voice. Then, trembling with fear, she had turned and fled back to the upstairs phone and called him, not knowing whether the intruders had obeyed her command. "Watch yourself," she had begged him when he cried out that he was coming home at once. "Watch yourself, hear!" He had grabbed his coat, flung himself down the stairs, raced back to the House garage to get his car, and gunned out and away so fast he had almost knocked down the guard who held the door open for him.

Now he was within three blocks of home, and it was only now, so instantaneous and automatic had been his reaction, and so violent and conflicting the many emotions of the evening which had left him, too, almost bereft of coherent and constructive thought, that it occurred to him that he should have had her call the police or have called them himself. But she had been too frightened to think of it, he had been too concerned with getting home to her immediately, and the chance had been lost. As he started to turn off into his side street a patrol car came swiftly down Sixteenth, and passed, so fast he hardly realized it was there until it shot by. Then he waved frantically and blew his horn with a long, steady, imperious blast. In his rearview mirror he could see the car slow, far down the empty street, and begin to hesitate. He completed his turn and came to the driveway, not knowing whether the police had understood his message or not, but knowing he could not wait to find out, for they might not have and he knew that the menace that awaited him itself would not wait.

There were no lights on in the house when he drove into the garage, and he wondered with a wild impatient anger why not. Instantly the explanation came to mind, and he grabbed a flashlight from the glove compartment and started out around the house. The fuse box stood open against the wall, its wires cut, the telephone wires, apparently an afterthought that had fortunately not come before Maudie's call, dangling useless too. A chill went up his back and with a sudden instinctive caution he snapped off the flashlight and ran, as silently as he could, a distance of some twenty feet along the hedge; stopped, yanked a brick out of the edging of the front garden, and tossed it across the yard, where it made a satisfyingly noisy crash in the rhododendrons; and then began stealthily to double back toward the house, moving with great care and the delicacy of footing he had learned in track.

From the house there came no sound, and he could only hope that Maudie was all right, probably hidden away under blankets and a mattress in the back closet. That was what he had told her to do, and some instinct told him that she had and that she was all right. But that was not sufficient to satisfy him now, nor was it enough to make him pause and await either the police or the dawn, whichever might come first. Along with his excitement another element was beginning to enter: He was beginning to get angry, with a fierce, blind anger that would not let him use the caution that another part of his mind told him he should. He was too mad: mad at LeGage, mad at Sue-Dan, mad at the world. An angry fury gripped him, a savage determination and desire to get whoever was running LeGage's errands, for he had no doubt that this was the aftermath of his ex-roommate's promise of violence. First he would get them, and then he would get LeGage; and only then, in some later, more peaceful world of sanity restored and calm returned, would he think of anything else.

Thus it was that after a moment, although he tried to move with silence and stealth, he found himself proceeding with more and more fury and less and less concealment. And thus it was, as he rounded the back corner of the house and moved forward like some restless panther to explore the cavern of darkness surrounding the tool shed, that he found himself suddenly jumped from behind, a flying tackle trapping his ankles and causing him to fall face forward, his arms pinned by desperate hands, four or five bodies flung down upon his as it thrashed with a violent desperation beneath their combined grunting, gasping weight.

In less than a minute of fiercely silent struggle he found himself trapped and held immobile despite the twistings of his powerful body; and then began the kicks, the blows, the terrible savage pains through his chest, his stomach, his testicles, his face, his arms and legs, his head, his whole convulsive frame. After five minutes, its thrashing began to lessen, and presently it subsided and gave no more response to the kicks and jabs of those who now did with him what they would. The last thing he heard as he sank into unconsciousness was the questioning note of a siren, a high welcoming scream from Maudie somewhere in the front of the house, the crashing, hurried departure of his tormentors; and then his mind mercifully abandoned the world and for some long time, down his long, dark street, he knew no more.

So the wind blew cold off Washington as the senior Senator from South Carolina moved slowly, ever so slowly, along the exposed stone terrace to the front of the Capitol toward the great descending flight of steps to the lower reaches of the Hill; and cold blew the wind of the world, though he knew it not. For him, the world did not seem cold at this particular moment, nor did it seem harsh and unforgiving, nor did it seem, indeed, at all like the world in which he had been living when he began his filibuster.

Curiously, as he started to negotiate the steps, teetering for a second and almost losing his balance on the first but then gripping the handrail and easing himself carefully down, one by one with a painful caution, the world seemed warm and shining and full of hope and promise, as it had when he first came to this city, so many, many years ago. He was exhausted to the point where he had passed beyond exhaustion, and at that moment he did not know for sure where he was or where he was going. In his own mind he was once again the idealistic young Congressman from Barnwell, living in a plain little room on S Street that he rented for $10 a week; and if he was going anywhere—and his mind, filled with vague scraps of thought and idle dreams, all muffled and confused and covered over with tiredness, was not sure—it was back to that little room. He realized vaguely that it was late, some big matter had concerned the Congress tonight, and he must get home to sleep before tomorrow's session. If his mind had any goal at all, that was it, as he inched slowly, ever so slowly, down the steps.

Back to the room on S Street, and next week, or in another ten days or so, when the session ended, back home to Barnwell and "Roselands" and Amy and Cornelia and the Colonel, and all the other familiar, friendly faces that were waiting for him there. There was a great future ahead for young Seab Cooley, and everybody knew it. They talked about it along Main Street and discussed it in the stores, and in many a stately home among the moss-hung oaks people knew with a calm satisfaction that they had done the right thing when they elected him to Congress. The years were bright and hopeful ahead, great things were moving in the world, the War to End Wars was coming to its victorious conclusion, and serene and untroubled the future lay ahead of mankind, awaiting only young and skillful hands to tap its bounties and give them to the great, beloved land.

At home dear friends, in Washington great hopes and a future as bright as any in the Congress. Only yesterday the Speaker had told someone, and the word had quickly come back to him, that "Seab Cooley has the brightest future of anybody here, right now. You mark my words, he won't go wrong. He's got too much to offer America."

And that was what he wanted to do, he told himself as he went slowly, ever so slowly, down the steps toward the little room on S Street: to honor his friends and be a credit to them, to bring glory to his native state and do great things for his country in the glowing years which awaited her in the coming golden era of a just and lasting peace.

So the world was not cold tonight, nor did he notice the wind as it blew from Virginia and the far reaches of the sleeping continent. He was young Seab Cooley, and he had so much to do, and no one could possibly be cold or unhappy or seared by loss of hope with such a future stretching ahead. As he reached the foot of the steps he turned back to pause and look up at the great white dome of the Capitol shining serene and steady above.

"Now," he whispered, as he saw it floating against the first faint flush of dawning in the east, "am I not serving you well, my dear country for whom the years hold so much? Will we not go on together to such wonderful greatness, you and I? And is not the world glorious in the morning?"

He watched the great dome for a moment and then, as he turned away, not noticing that his foot missed the last step and that he sprawled flat upon his back upon the grass, he asked the Lord one last silent question, whose little trace of arrogance amused him, for he thought the Lord would understand it, and forgive him:

Are You not pleased with Your servant Seabright? And is he not deserving of Your kindness?

He was not at all surprised, nor was he alarmed—rather he felt a peaceful, overwhelming gratitude as the world rose bright and shining and young and hopeful before him once again—when the Lord, as it seemed to him, reached down a giant hand a moment later to where he lay upon the grass, and tapped him gently on the forehead, and said, Yes.

Four
HAL FRY'S BOOK

Thus did the shade of difference work its way with the Congress of the United States in the wake of Terence Ajkaje's visit; and thus did it return to another forum where men contended even more fiercely and with even less charity toward one another.

Behind it in the cold dark morning in the beautiful city where a young man lay bloodied and an old man lay dead, it left the unanswered and possibly unanswerable question of whether their troubled peoples would ever find the love, the vision, and the mutual tolerance to justify all the hopes and sacrifices of both the races over so many years.

Ahead in the glistening house on the East River, it raised anew the question of whether a well-meaning, mixed-up, harried land would ever be granted the patience and the understanding to live true to her purposes in a world so determined to make sure that she should not.

In the mind of the man in Harkness Pavilion upon whom much of the immediate responsibility for finding an answer was now to devolve in the squabbling parliament of the nations, there was at this particular lonely hour a strange mixture of moods and emotions as he waited for dawn and the operation that would tell him whether or not he would be on earth much longer to worry about such matters. Now, after many sleepless periods as the bleak night dragged on, he was thinking, with a gleam of the irony he knew might soon be one of his few remaining defenses, of American advertising and what a balm it was for the beleaguered, what an easement for sore hearts and surcease for troubled souls.

Turning the dial of the transistor radio Lafe had brought him, in search of distraction as the haunted darkness of the silent hospital came gradually to life, he brought in successively a singing commercial for a stomach-acid remedy, a stern voice discussing sinus trouble, another describing the latest thing for backaches, yet another murmuring in hushed tones about bothersome situations in the lower colon. Interspersed with these came the frenzied adenoidal yodeling of some slackmouthed delinquent with a guitar, the wild, insane, animal caterwauling of the latest singing sensation; a quartet of precious voices of indeterminate gender racing up and down in strange abandon through the tattered remnants of a once-beautiful ballad of the early sixties; the mind-destroying clatter of the newest popular band.

Cozened, abjured, admonished, sung to, wailed at, pounded over the head with the outpourings both cultural and cloacal of his country's fantastic civilization, it occupied his mind for the moment to play a little game with what he heard.

Suppose all this were real: suppose, just once, that American advertising and the public American approach to things really got down to cases on what actually faced the country. Suppose the talents of Madison Avenue, the copywriters for the unctuous voices, the composers of the jolly jingles, the

writers of the idiot songs, really talked about the world as it actually was.
Would a great sobering, a great steadying-down, a great humbling, strengthening, virtue-restoring change come over the land, of the sort that must come
if it was to survive? Or would the output, still, be such things as:

"Is your digestive tract interfering with those homely little pleasures of
life that everyone should be free to enjoy? Does that 'certain feeling' mean
that *you* are missing out on easy regularity? Try Instant H.B.—*H-Bomb*.
With Instant H.B. all those pains will be forgotten. Your worries about
regularity will be ended once and for all—quickly—painlessly—so fast you
won't know it. Try Instant H.B. *It will take you out of this world.*"

Or, faced with a tussle in Congress over the defense budget, would there
pour forth upon the airwaves, suitably illustrated with cute little cartoon
figures on TV, some such rollicking advice as:

"Tell your boys on Capitol Hill:
"Pass that bill!
"Pass that bill!
"It's those Russians are the villains,
"That's why Uncle Sam needs billions. ('Pretty poor rhyme, Irving, but
    what the hell.')

"Write your Senator and Rep.:
"Come on, boys, get hep! *Get hep!*
"Give the President all he's wanting,
"Then we'll stop that Soviet flaunting.
"Let 'em have it with a will!
"Pass that bill!
"Pass that bill!"

In some such carefree fashion, no doubt, it would all emerge, if any
attempt were made to associate reality with the overlayer of thinking-twice-
removed that enveloped American society like a great bland fog. Somewhere
underneath it all was the troubled burden of the uneasy populace, faced
with challenges such as America had never faced; around their heads, in
their ears, in their eyes, in everything they saw or heard or read, a constant
din of frivolous inconsequence sought to persuade them that the newest fuel
system of the latest product of Detroit, to use but one obvious example,
really mattered more to them than the steady erosion of their national
position. In some protected upland far from the sludgy, slogging evil of their
enemies' advance—perhaps already, at least psychologically, taken out of this
world by the thought of Instant H.B.—they were invited to pretend together
that such concerns as this were actually of more importance than the destruction they faced as a nation if they did not somehow, and soon, find the
secret of survival.

And, of course, who could say with complete certainty that these things
were not important? At least they were to those who were directly concerned.
Indeed, what could be more important to a man in this world than facing

death from leukemia, if he had no inner strengths and no greater vision and no higher task to occupy his heart and mind than clocking the advances of his own illness? Would not he, too, listen desperately to jingles and pretend the world did not exist?

It was in that moment, brought back with a savage jolt to the particular reality he faced, that the senior Senator from West Virginia recognized anew the second of the two major strengths that were to support him in the days ahead. The first of course was his own character, whose nature he thought he knew about, but which now, obviously, was to be tested to limits far beyond what it had already endured; and the second was the spirit of dedication and service that had inspired his public career from the day it had begun thirty-odd years ago in the grubby little coal-mining town of Omar in West Virginia.

Here in the half-hopeful, half-hopeless arena of the United Nations that dedication had already increased steadily in the months past. Now under the spur of what might very likely be a terminal illness, it too would receive its ultimate testing. There came to him like a revelation the sudden thought that this was his jingle, this was his slogan, this was his way of submerging reality—by meeting it with what he believed to be the greatest reality of all, service to his country and to his fellow men of charity and goodwill, wherever they might be found, troubled and uncertain and needing help, upon the troubled globe.

At one point in the long night, when it had not seemed to him that he had slept at all—but when he suspected that he had, in nature's silent and secret way of restoring the body whether it wanted to be restored or not—there had come to him the searing question: restored for what? Restored so nature could play with it a little while longer before tossing it, ravaged and drained, onto the human scrap heap where cancer in one form or another had taken so many down the implacable centuries? It appeared to him in that dreadfully lonely moment that it must be so, though the operation that would confirm it beyond any doubt was still to come, and his mind still refused to accept the full impact of the possibility. Yet he knew the doctors must have little doubt, or they would not have permitted Lafe to prepare him; just as he realized with gratitude that only Lafe's assessment of his ability to endure it would have persuaded Lafe to secure their permission to prepare him. He could not yet abandon the outside hope, the one chance in ten thousand that they might be wrong and that the sternum-tap would prove it. But, to some degree already, there had come the beginning of acceptance, and with it, at first, a great despair.

In the grip of this, many hours of darkness had seemed to pass without beginning and without end, in a sort of terrible gray dream possessed of neither outline nor boundary into which he had retreated as an animal does when the world becomes too much for it. From time to time then, too, he had switched blindly over the radio dial, hardly knowing what came to him: the muted sounds of distant dance bands, softer and more harmonious in the night, the late-hour programs of orchestral music, the quieter regions of the air, broken now and again by news reports and the distant clashes of the hurrying world. Vaguely he had grasped that the Senate was locked in debate on the Hamilton Resolution, vaguely he had grasped the fact that Seab was filibustering. With a great ponderous tiredness, as though he were indeed struggling in a dream, he had wondered a little what would happen down there and what the reaction would be up here. Then his mind had slipped away again and lost itself in the contemplation of his own disaster, one more coming on top of those others he had suffered down the sad unhappy years.

Sad and unhappy and yet now, with the coming of dawn and the instinctive resurgence of heart and spirit that comes to all but the most utterly forsaken at the rising of the sun, seeming to have their own curious rewards and their own surprisingly rugged strengths. If they had not, he certainly would not have been able to entertain, in the midst of desolation, the casual parodies in which he had just engaged. His mind would have nowhere found the strength to continue to appraise the world with its own particular combination of goodwill, irony, and friendly determination. He would already have been driven well on the way to madness by the prospect lying before him. So there must have been a great deal for him in all those years, a great deal in all that strange parallelism in which a steadily rising public career had marched side by side with the steady blasting of his human hopes.

Not, of course, that any such peculiar destiny had seemed likely when it all began. Life had started hard for him, seventh child of a coal-mining father in West Virginia's chronically depressed regions, and at first it seemed unlikely that the future held anything more than a drab repetition of his father's life, better paid, perhaps, as the United Mine Workers gained ground under their fierce old president, but essentially as gray and unrelieved. Three of his four brothers had stayed in the mines and were there yet, officials of the union, doing moderately well but, because of some lack of character, some lack of the extra spark that permits men to rise above their peers, unable to break the pattern. He and his two sisters had escaped, they to marry and move away, he to make of himself something far beyond the wildest hopes of the two modest, hardworking, God-fearing souls who had given him life.

At first the potential showed itself only in an added brightness, an added quickness, an appealing and outgoing little personality that gave him a ready distinction in his family and among his playmates in the little town. Sometime in his fifth year a neighbor had taken the family's picture with an old box camera; a year later in kindergarten his teacher had similarly recorded the seven pupils in her class. Somewhere in his apartment in Washington he had them still, squirreled away in some buried box: out of both he smiled forth as though emblazoned, attracting the eye with his touseled hair and humorously intelligent eyes.

He had come across the two photographs scarcely a year ago and as soon as he had glimpsed them had known exactly what they were. He had thrust them back out of sight with a deep expression of pain in the eyes that once had laughed so merrily. But nothing could change what he had been then, or take from him the distinction of personality and character that had brought him up the long road to the United States Senate, carrying him through so much that others, less favored and so perhaps less singled out for the erratic chances of misfortune, had not been required to endure.

Through kindergarten, grammar school, and high school the curve of his life was steadily upward. A natural deference had swiftly been accorded him by others, strengthened by his school grades, which were good from the first, and by qualities of leadership that were early apparent. There came a time before long when he was deliberately singled out by his teachers for special attention and preferment; but before that he had singled himself out, not consciously or in any way immodestly or arrogantly, but just by being what he was. The sight of it delighted and humbled his parents, whose other children possessed sturdy characters but no particular distinction. In Little Hal, who early gave promise of being something far beyond what Big Hal had been, they felt that they had been selected for special blessing. Being deeply religious and having a household where prayer was the daily accompaniment of a hard life, they thanked the Lord for him and instilled in him an acceptance of the Lord's will that was to stand him in good stead later.

Somewhere during the years of his growing up there began to come into his mind and heart a desire to help people. Initially this expressed itself in things as small as assisting a beleaguered friend to study for an exam. Then, as he became more actively engaged in the social and political life of his school, a broader aspect began to appear. He began to realize, as more and more of his fellows looked to him for leadership in their activities and aid in their troubles, that he apparently possessed some aspect of character that encouraged confidence and trust, some extra element that enabled him to translate it into positive, affirmative good. Coming as he did from a religious household, this produced an almost inevitable progression in his thoughts. At first he was duly grateful to the Lord for conferring upon him the gift of kindness; and then he began to feel a conscious determination to perfect it and use it as best he could for those who turned to him in need. Finally he decided that he must use it even more actively, as a positive force to improve the condition of those around him and help them, if he could, to achieve a better life.

This process, a steadily growing development within him as he moved on from childhood into adolescence, represented a rare maturity of mind which he did not find expressed in very many of his contemporaries, bound as they were to the mine-scarred green hills of West Virginia. It was not surprising, and it too was probably inevitable, that by the time he was ready to enter college the meager life in which he and his family and friends grew up should have produced a deeply dedicated feeling that he must serve humanity itself, first as he found it here and then, if he were so favored, as he found it over a much wider area. He came to feel that with so much misery in the world, everyone who could help should help. If he had been given equipment a little better than most to bring to the task, then he should use it.

He realized, for he had a saving vein of self-humor and self-appraisal that kept him from taking himself too seriously, that it was very possible to become overly pompous about all this, and he soon learned not to express his feelings about it to anyone save his younger sister, Betty, who was the closest to him of any of his family. She possessed a sense of practical good humor as stable as his own, and when he told her of his dreams from time to time she encouraged him eagerly yet with a saving wit that helped to keep him from flying too far too fast. It was with her that he thrashed out such problems as whether he should become a great people's advocate, one of the world's great surgeons, a great journalist molding public opinion, another Gompers or Lewis fighting fiercely for labor, another Franklin Roosevelt gallantly riding the tides of social reform, a great research scientist finding at last the secret of cancer.

These were the games he and Betty played as they grew up in the grimy little town where poverty and disaster never slept, and it was not until their father was lost, just as Hal reached college age, in a mine disaster caused by the company's imperfect adherence to imperfect safety laws that it all coalesced into one fierce, burning desire to set things right in a sorry world through the channels of public service. The Great Depression had laid its turmoil upon the land, the New Deal was getting under way, "social service" was a phrase heard more and more frequently, and somewhere in the rushing surge of national activity he was sure there would be a place for him to give what he had. He went off to the University of West Virginia with his plan finally firm. He would study history, economics, political science, philosophy; get his degree and a teaching certificate in political science; participate as much as possible in the extracurricular life of the school; and eventually come home to the blackened valleys where disaster walked and give himself to service in whatever form it might open to him.

At the University in those turbulent years as things began to change from grimness to excitement, he soon found a place for himself among his fellows. His personality, already settling into the quietly humorous, quietly likable, steady, and down-to-earth pattern it would have for the rest of his life, attracted friends easily and soon gave him a special and well-established place in the life of the school. Of necessity he had to find work to help support himself, and before long was holding down three jobs, working as a waiter at the fraternity house to which he was pledged at the end of his freshman year, working in the stacks at the University library, working as campus correspondent for the Charleston *Gazette* and the Wheeling *News-Register*. In what remained of day and night, he followed the course of study he had set for himself, finding that he did well because his interests were engaged and he was pointing toward the life he wanted to lead. His grades in his first year were not sensational, for he did not have a sensational mind—his greater talents lay in the region of the heart—but his grades were good, and he was well satisfied with his progress as he assessed it when the year concluded. He had not yet found the time to engage in the extracurricular activities that he would have liked, but he hoped that this phase of his college career might open up in due course.

Toward the end of his sophomore year this began to come about, largely through his activities as campus correspondent, which brought him into contact with all the sources of social and political power on the campus. It was the work area he enjoyed best, and it soon made him a well-known and popular figure on campus. "For someone who doesn't hold office," one of his friends remarked, "you've got more influence than anybody I know." "Maybe I should hold office," Hal said. "Maybe you should," said his friend, and proceeded to set the wheels in motion.

A month later he was elected secretary of the junior class and a year later president of the senior class; but it was with no idea at all of entering active politics that he returned home upon graduation, got himself a job in the relief administration, and began the somber yet rewarding task of trying to restore some small flame of hope among hills and valleys where hope never burned very brightly at the best of times and had all but flickered out in these.

Thinking now of his college life through the mists of sedative-dulled pain and foreboding that swirled about him as a nurse rustled briskly in, snapped on lights that hurt his eyes, stuck a thermometer in his mouth, chivvied and chattered and thoroughly destroyed all chance of a return to even the most uneasy sleep, he felt that the experience had provided him with some book knowledge but more knowledge of people. It had also given him a wide assortment of friends with whom he had exchanged sympathy and understanding and loyalty and liking. He had not found a wife by the time he left college, though he had come close a couple of times; but he hoped that would come in due course.

Home among the hapless hills he worked for a couple of years, his cheerfully steady personality and stout heart proving exactly right for the task of helping the derelict and reassuring the frightened. So popular and well-liked did he become, in fact, that when he presently discovered some of the fraud and misuse of funds that plagued so many relief efforts in those days, it was almost impossible for his superiors to fire him, as they would have preferred to do rather than have him tell what he knew. Instead it was he, in effect, who fired them, for his former newspaper contacts stood him in good stead: he told his former employers, the stories hit the front pages, a major scandal broke upon his office. Out of it he emerged as apparently the only honest man among the five hurriedly slapped together from former officeholders, party hacks, and other political leftovers to assume the task of running relief in the area. Their concept had been to sprinkle the hills with greenbacks and funnel quite a few of them into their own pockets through an elaborate system of kickbacks. His concept had been to administer relief as honestly as he could without regard to personal advantage or political consideration.

When the scandal was over, he had been promoted to director of relief in his region, his powers greatly expanded, and over the state his name was suddenly well known and he was increasingly hailed as an honest and incorruptible man. Invitations to speak began to come to him; his ideas on things began to appear in the press. At twenty-six he was already on his way to becoming a major citizen of his crippled state, where the most appealing physical beauty was apt to walk side by side with the ugly ravages of industrialization and the grinding poverty of many of its citizens.

There occurred to him, since it seemed to be in so many minds including Betty's and his own, that this growing fame and popularity might well lead the way to a channel of service far wider and more effective than dispensing relief in the hills of West Virginia. It was an era when the national Administration in Washington inspired the young as it never had before or since. A logic so inevitable that he could hardly have avoided it urged upon him the idea that he should seek public office and use the influence it would bring him to assist in the task of righting the wrongs of an upset society.

At that moment, however, the political situation was such that he did not see open before him any of the state or national offices that he had made up his mind to try for. He also felt, for a large strain of practical common sense went along with his genuine idealism about it, that if he were to aim so high on the first flight out, he must strengthen his contacts with the party organization before venturing further. He decided to bide his time and in the interim turn to the teaching of political science. He found a job at Salem College, was highly popular with his students, accepted frequent invitations to speak around the state, continued to gain political strength for the next six years. Then the Congressman representing his home district died of a heart attack; a special election was scheduled; he announced his candidacy, took leave from his job for a month, conducted an intensive handshaking campaign through all the little hamlets and wide places in the road; won his primary and went on to win the general election without difficulty. At thirty-two he went to the House of Representatives, easygoing and friendly of personality, determined and idealistic of heart.

After a year and a half in office he resigned, as did a number of his colleagues, to go to war. By prior arrangement with the Governor, an elderly former Senator was appointed to hold his seat for him and did so without challenge for three and a half years, during which Hal Fry ranged far across the reaches of the Pacific as an officer in the Navy. His tour of duty was like that of so many others, long stretches of boredom, a few peaks of intense excitement as at Midway, for the most part the drab drudgery of war that men must endure in order that their nations may rise or fall, their villains be defeated, and their heroes come to glory. His nation had not fallen and he had not been a hero; but he had been one of the necessary parts of a necessary business, doing his job as he had in civilian life, with a relaxed and friendly competence that made him indispensable to the destroyer on which he ended the war as executive officer. He left the service with honor and commendation, and returned to resume the career of broader service upon which he had just been well embarked when a squadron of little planes came out of the dawn from Tokyo and rudely informed a naïve people that in the world they now lived in, life was real and life was earnest, indeed.

By now, in his mid-thirties, he was beginning to think that possibly he would not find the girl he wished to marry—or, if he found her, be fortunate enough to have her also wish to marry him. He had enjoyed a modest number of casual romances in the war, nothing very deep or very lasting, nothing that he felt he couldn't live without or that had brought him any shattering revelation of himself or any other. It was the time of life when the thought of permanent bachelorhood loses its horrors and begins to assume its attractions, and he started back to Washington, having been triumphantly re-elected to his old seat five months after leaving service, not at all averse to the idea that he might find his dedication to public service strengthened even more by the absence of family distractions. The figure of the bachelor politician married to his job was a common one—Seab Cooley was an example that had always intrigued and amused him—and who could say but what he would be the better public servant for it, if it turned out that way?

Two weeks after entertaining these smug thoughts, of course, he was wondering how he had ever been so stupid as to think he could possibly live without the girl he met on his first night back. Even now, though their bright beginning had gone steadily downward into darkness, he did not think he could have missed the experience of their being together and still consider his life to have been complete.

It had happened, as so many things do at the start of each new year in Washington, at the traditional Congressional Night Party given each January by the Women's National Press Club on the night of the day that Congress convenes. This particular year it had occurred on January 4, during one of those sudden heavy snowfalls that always surprise, dismay, and discombobulate the District of Columbia and its harried weather forecasters. The prediction had been "a little fog and drizzle but no danger of snow." As it turned out, while public business ceased, private enterprise closed down, and the citizenry crawled home in skidding, sliding, cursing traffic jams, a total of seven inches fell in the capital and up to nine inches in some places in nearby Maryland and Virginia.

That was not until nearly 3 A.M., however, and in the meantime the Congressional Night Party went forward undaunted at the Statler, its customary gaiety given an extra zing by the excitement of the snow and the enjoyable breakdown of the customary procedures of a mechanized society. Guests came in shaking snow off their coats, slapping their gloves, stamping their feet, cheeks aglow, eyes asparkle, shouting greetings happily as though they had come fifty miles across the ice behind a team of matched bays. Voices rose with a special liveliness and pleasure, drinks were downed at an even faster rate than usual, as all those of politics and press and diplomacy whose business is the business of the United States greeted one another joyously at the start of another Congressional session and the beginning of another new year.

In all this jovial throng, as Hal Fry worked his way slowly through the mob around the bar to ask for bourbon on the rocks, looking solid and dependable and even moderately handsome in his tuxedo, he was conscious of a tall dark girl just ahead of him, staring uncertainly about as though waiting for someone. He could not determine in that moment whether or not she was really beautiful, and having missed the opportunity to see her objectively then, he was never to recapture the chance. By the time he had come alongside, he had only a general but overwhelming impression of something warm and intelligent and desirable, something so appealing that he knew instantly he must have it if he possibly could. Among the minor talents of wartime was the talent one of his fellow officers had referred to as "scouting the terrain," and a minute of it convinced him that she was single, probably nice, and also, probably, in love. For one complacently resigned to bachelorhood this produced a surprising dismay for a moment. She said, "Can I help you?" in a tone that made him realize that his eyes must be showing an inordinate concern to prompt such a response. He smiled pleasantly and said, "No, thanks, I'm just trying to get a drink. Can I help you?" She too smiled and said, "No, thanks. I'm just trying to find an escort." "Well, good luck," he said, and she replied pleasantly. "Good luck to you, too."

The time would come when he would recall that indelible scene out of the sadness that ultimately came upon them and think that everything had been said right then, and that they really need never have gone any further, for that said it all. Can I help you? No, thanks. Well, good luck. Better that they had believed each other and let it go at that; but of course they did not; nor was he entirely sure even now, as there came a clatter of silverware and glasses in the corridor and the breakfast cart arrived to service the now wide-awake and humming ward, that it would have been better. In spite of everything, it might have been much worse, for there had been, for a time, a happiness that seemed to promise a lasting serenity and peace. At least they had that, whatever came later.

It took a while for this to develop, however, even though that first night brought them together much faster than he had at first thought possible. The escort did not appear, and as it happened the table where she sat was not very far from the one reserved by his hostess, the AP regional reporter who covered West Virginia. As the evening progressed through the lavish meal, the introduction of distinguished guests, the jocular speech by Senator Munson, the Senate Majority Leader, the jocular rebuttal by his opposite number, Senator Strickland, the Minority Leader, and finally the good nights and the farewell flourishes from the orchestra as the guests returned to the bar before taking off to struggle with the white world outside, he found himself looking far oftener than he intended toward her table. More frequently than not he found her looking back. When their eyes met for the fourth time, he shook his head with a smile and, blushing but game, she smiled back. It was inevitable that they should meet once more at the bar—"He didn't make it," he said, and she said, "No, he lives in Virginia and had to start home early to beat the storm—now I need a drink!"—and that after a nightcap he should ask where she lived and suggest that he see her home.

Her apartment was far up Connecticut Avenue, almost to Silver Spring, Maryland, and as they started out, tired but exhilarated by the party and the snow still falling gently upon the silent and almost-deserted city, it became an adventure that cut through temerities and hesitations that would otherwise have taken weeks to overcome. Twice his car skidded off the street into high-piled drifts. It took him half an hour to extricate it the first time, almost forty-five minutes the second. On the gradually ascending hills that mounted gracefully tier by tier from the center of town toward Maryland, he proceeded at a cautious pace of not more than ten miles an hour. It was almost 3 A.M. when they finally reached her door. It had taken them nearly three hours to cover a distance that in clear weather required no more than fifteen minutes at the most.

Inevitably, as they both realized by the time the journey ended, they would never again be just two people who had happened to meet at a Congressional Night Party. The tension, the excitement, the jokes and confidences and humorous morale-boosting with which they had lightened their tedious progress through the storm had put them on a basis of intimacy that would never be eradicated even if they never saw each other again. And of course they knew by the time it was over that they would certainly see each other again.

He had begun by telling her with a casual politeness something of his background and had ended by telling her with a sudden urgency his most intimate dreams and ambitions. He learned in turn that she came from a family in Wisconsin in many ways as conventional, modest, and religious as his own; that she worked as receptionist and office manager for a news bureau that serviced several of the larger newspapers in the upper Midwest; that she was twenty-nine and had been in Washington five years; and that she possessed an idealism about public service that came close to his own. They told each other silently something else, too, which was that underneath the increasingly serious conversation with which they accomplished their journey there lay the potential for the sort of understanding that informs and illuminates a lifetime.

At her apartment she said, "I live alone, but I'm certainly not going to be guilty of any nonsense about turning you out at this hour in this storm. There's a studio couch in the living room and you're welcome to it." She smiled. "I'll even get you breakfast."

For a second he had considered accepting, but it had seemed to him that this would have placed an essentially false emphasis upon a relationship that was, for all its storm-induced intimacies, only at its earliest stages. He felt it would be false to use the situation to seek further intimacies; it would also be false to feel that because of its forced nature further intimacies should not be sought—an involved masculine reaction that went through his mind in a flash and produced a grateful shake of the head.

"Thanks, but I'm staying at the University Club for the time being until I can find permanent diggings." He smiled. "It's only about two miles and five hours' journey downtown again, so I'll just run along, with thanks. But I will see you again?"

She nodded gravely.

"You will see me again."

"Soon?"

"Soon. Call me tomorrow afternoon—this afternoon—at work."

"Good . . . You know," he said, putting on his hat and coat and pausing at the door with a sudden impulse to candor that surprised him, "I was almost beginning to think that maybe I would never—"

"So was I. Perhaps we were both wrong."

"I hope so."

"I, too. Thank you for the ride home."

"Sleep well."

"Yes. You, too."

"Yes . . . Yes," he said with a sudden conviction. "I know I will."

But he did not, of course, for when he reached the club shortly after 5 A.M. and turned into bed exhausted, it took him another hour or so to drop off into a fitful sleep broken by the recurring thought, I won't sleep well until I sleep with you, I won't sleep well until I sleep with you, I won't sleep well until I—

After that, things moved swiftly along their inevitable path, and now as another nurse came in to give him a shot of B-12 in preparation for the operation soon to come, he felt no surprise, in retrospect, that the evening should have culminated so soon in their engagement and marriage. They did not need any lengthy period to confirm the certainty of each other conferred upon them by the snow. Their relationship remained chaste until they were married, and circumstances did not arrange—nor did they seek—another situation such as the night of their meeting. Somehow they both felt they did not need it, for they would be married so soon, and why mar it by the memory of something furtive and contrary to the upbringing of both of them? Or so he was given to understand her reasons to be; and since he could appreciate them easily, he did not press it but waited with a reasonable patience until the ceremony that would bring it all about.

This came three months after their meeting, on a day when the first intimations of Washington's lovely spring whipped scudding white clouds through the bright-blue air and the trees were misty with the first faint flushes of green. Many of his colleagues in the Congress attended, the newspapers both in the capital and in West Virginia gave it major play, *Life* and *Look* ran photographs, it was one of the big social events of the session. His parents, Betty, and two of his brothers were able to come on from West Virginia, Kay's parents and brother also made the trip from Wisconsin, and a week's honeymoon in Bermuda put the final seal on what appeared to be a thoroughly happy union.

And so, he thought now as his tired and frightened mind proved unable to keep away the haunting echoes of the past, it evidently was for a year or so. If there was a certain reticence, a certain holding-back, a certain withdrawal into some region where he could not follow, he put it down to background and upbringing rather than to basic character. If there accompanied it an already too-nervous insistence upon the outward form of things, an already too-harsh application of rigid standards of judgment to people and events, that too he thought could be traced to early training rather than any innate defect. He was a patient and loving man, and he told himself often in moments of puzzlement that it would just take a little time, a little understanding, a little extra generosity, and everything would be all right and as relaxed and comfortable as he had always hoped his marriage, if it came, would be.

That patience and understanding might be interpreted as a lack of interest and a lack of really genuine caring on his part never occurred to him. He would have been horrified and miserably unhappy to know that what he could not always recognize as reachings-out for comfort felt themselves rebuffed and thwarted by his calmly tolerant responses. The physical consummations which seemed awkward and unsatisfying in the days of their honeymoon got no better as he tried to understand and adapt himself to what was desired of him. But what was it? He could not be sure. Obviously not experimentation, for the slightest indication of it was always rejected with what seemed to be something close to terror; and not even the most conventional, for even his earnest attempts—which of course soon became too earnest and too self-conscious to be fair to either of them—seemed to produce only an empty half-satisfaction that was in many ways worse than no satisfaction at all.

"You know what?" he said finally, trying to be humorous and outgoing, but finding it, by then, a little difficult and strained. "I think we're both trying too hard, about everything. Maybe if we could just relax with each other, everything would go along all right."

She smiled.

"Maybe we need another snowstorm," she said, and he thought, with the ravaging unanswerable pain that comes when something is gone forever, If we had one, I wouldn't go home. That was my mistake. It would all be different if I hadn't gone home.

But even of that he was not sure, as the months went by and he began to conclude that it had been his fortune to marry a personality locked away in some impregnable fortress where he could not follow. She was so afraid of things—that was it, essentially, he decided. She was so afraid, and it was nothing he could really help her with, since it apparently grew from a childhood and character whose pattern had been frozen for life before he met her.

So he resigned himself, as many do, to doing as best he could with what he had. As far as the world knew she was pretty, attractive, intelligent, accomplished—a perfect partner and hostess for a rising young member of Congress, one of those wives, so often found in Washington, whose lives apparently are blended into, but actually only happen to run parallel with, those of their famous husbands. She was well-liked by other Congressional wives, saw to it that they received and returned the proper invitations, was very popular in West Virginia—what more, really, could a man want, save a truly loving and committed heart?

He decided that the best thing for him to do was concentrate on his career—he had become the dedicated bachelor public servant after all, he told himself wryly, if not quite in the sense he had earlier envisaged—and try not to think about what might have been. A Senatorship was opening up, he was by this time strong enough across the state to attempt it, and it began to seem that by devoting his thought and his energies to that he might block out the grinding ache of unhappiness that sometimes seemed to fill him so he could hardly breathe. The heart dies in many ways, some of them quieter than others, and he thought that if he could persuade his own to be concerned about other matters, its decease might not hurt him quite so much. He was well embarked upon this when she called him one morning at the Capitol to tell him that she had just been to the doctor and they were going to have a child.

This hope, too, he had almost abandoned in the three years of their marriage, and it took several minutes after she hung up for the knowledge to really penetrate. When it did, it was amazing how fast his heart came to life again. In ten minutes' time it was as though the dull ache and the grinding pain had never been. Now they could start over again in the light of the miracle of this new life; now everything would be all right once more; now the bad beginning could be forgotten and things could move on as wonderfully as he used to hope and expect. He went home happier than he had been since the early weeks of their marriage, determined to pour out such love and affection as would drive away the dark shadows that sometimes seemed to threaten, and never let them gather again.

For a little time it seemed to work. An old ease, an old friendliness, seemed to return to them in the early months of her pregnancy; the world once more was full of hope. His own enthusiasm for his son—for such he was convinced the baby would be—communicated itself to her, and she joined in excited, half-humorous plans that soon had the boy following him into the Senate and ultimately into the White House, with a show of amusement that persuaded him for a while that she was as eager and happy about the new arrival as he. He was shocked as he had rarely been when one day, in the midst of their joking, a shadow raced across her face and she suddenly said in a small, lost voice, "I am so frightened."

"But you mustn't be frightened," he had protested, fear instantly claiming his heart too. "It's something so happy and wonderful for us both. It will make everything all right again. You'll see," he promised fervently, as though words could work miracles where facts could not. "You'll see."

But she did not see; and from that moment his own happiness and confidence began to wane, strive desperately though he did to keep them at original pitch. Once having admitted her fears, she began to show an exaggerated, obsessive carefulness, a passion for self-protection that she said was for the baby but which he gradually became uneasily convinced was for herself alone. Try as he did to remain patient, this inevitably began to produce a growing irritation on his part, which showed itself in an exaggerated courtesy that he tried to keep humorous but which sometimes revealed the sharp edge of his anxiety underneath. Finally one day about three weeks before their child arrived this produced an unnecessary little incident that greatly frightened them both, though at the time it appeared that it did no real harm. Nor did it, he was often to think later, except as it contributed to the outward journey of a mind that he came to believe eventually must already have been well on its way.

They had been getting ready to go to the last social engagement they would attend before the baby came, a cocktail party given by nearby friends, and presently, dressed and starting on their way, they had locked the door and stood for a moment on the steps of the little house in Georgetown where they lived. There had been a freezing rain in the night, the steps were slick in a few places, and again a sudden wild look of fear had come into her face.

"I don't want to go. I'll fall."

"No, you won't," he said impatiently. "It's only a block and we'll be very careful. In fact," he added with an attempt at reminiscent humor, "we'll take three hours, if you like." But the attempt had failed, for there was no response as she stood there clinging to the iron railing, apparently stiff with fear.

"I can't," she whispered. "I can't, I just can't. Please don't make me! Oh, please don't!"

And suddenly she had begun to cry, making no attempt to stop the tears, letting them flow down her face as he stood there helplessly looking up at her, while across the street a bearded Georgetown type, clad in sport shirt and walking shorts despite the freezing weather, paused with his poodle to give them a curious glance.

"Very well," he said after a moment. "We can't stand here making a spectacle of ourselves. Let's go back in."

Impatiently he took her arm with a grip tighter than he intended, impatiently swung her around more quickly than he intended. She gave a gasp and half-stumbled, half-fell against the doorjamb where the railing joined it. The railing held and she swayed against it with an agonized little scream that terrified them both and brought a startled movement toward them from the watcher across the street.

"We're all right, thank you," Hal called, fumbling desperately to find his key. "It's just the ice. We're going in again."

The watcher looked relieved and nodded. Hal found his key, got the door open with a trembling hand, and took his wife inside. Half walking, half sagging as he supported her, she reached a chair and sat down, turning toward him eyes filled with terror that he realized hardly saw him at all.

"You've hurt him," she whispered. "You've hurt me. Oh, you've killed us both!"

"I haven't killed you," he said harshly. "For God's sake, snap out of it. It was only a little bump."

"You've killed us," she repeated, holding herself and rocking back and forth, "you've killed us!"

Later after the doctor had come and gone, given her a sedative and assured him that it was only nerves and that nothing had been damaged, he had sat downstairs alone for a long time wondering bleakly whether anything at all could be salvaged from the wreck of their lost affections. Out of his unhappy reverie there had come finally the conclusion that little could, that this portion of his life must be written off with as few regrets as possible or it would destroy him, and that henceforth he must concentrate on the child and devote to him the love, the care, and the hope that he might otherwise have shared with them both. His wife he would continue to love, in some sort of hopeless, distant corner of his mind where lost hopes lived, but aside from the necessary courtesies to keep the household together, he would withdraw the gift of his heart, which for reasons he would never really understand had not been received in the generous spirit in which it had been offered, and give it to his son.

Three weeks later the baby came, vigorous and healthy and holding promise of everything he had missed up to now. Only one thing marred the birth, which was difficult: the doctor, whose abilities he had regarded with considerable skepticism right along, but whom Kay had insisted upon on the recommendation of a friend of hers, had used forceps far more brutally than seemed necessary. The baby's skull at first was badly misshapen. But in a month it had filled out to a handsome normalcy, and with this initial worry gone and her son in her arms, Kay too seemed truly happy for the first time. Once again, so naïve and desperately ever-hopeful is the heart, he felt that the shadows had vanished and that once more there had come the chance that everything could still be all right.

At this point, too, the wider world impinged, for it would soon be time to reach a decision about running for the Senate. In the mood of pleasure with everything that came with his son's birth, obstacles sank into insignificance—they were not actually very many, so well thought of had he become by now in West Virginia—and the road seemed clear ahead. He called a press conference in his office in the Old House Office Building, announced his plans, and formally opened his campaign. Within a week a majority of the party's leaders in the state had endorsed him and he had received enough pledges of financial support to make the project economically possible. For the rest he intended to rely on the handshaking technique that had worked so well in his home district, a decision that consumed time but proved wise.

Four months later he had won the primary over the opposition of two of his fellow Congressmen and a former Governor, and in the general election that followed he won by a comfortable margin that sent him to the Senate secure in the support of his people at home, secure in the respect of his colleagues on the Hill, and secure, as it now seemed, in his own home.

There followed, while Jimmy grew steadily into an alert and beautiful child and domestic unease remained at a minimum in the light of his cheerfully bubbling presence, four years in which everything seemed to move onto an upland of great fulfillment and reward. He was well received in the Senate and within a short time had won a place of acceptance that gave promise of bigger honors and influence to come. He was not, as he himself recognized, one of the giants of the Senate, such as Orrin Knox or Seab Cooley; he did not possess the nature of the instinctive middleman of ideas and human interchange that had brought Bob Munson almost inevitably to the leadership; but he had a function to perform. He was one of what Stanley Danta once referred to as "the Young Reliables," the diligent, hardworking, straightforward, substantial men who brought to public service the devotion and the dedication, the balance and integrity without which the legislative processes of a free government cannot function.

As such, his road led upward. He was appointed to the Banking and Currency Committee and to Labor and Public Welfare, and began to apply himself to the problems that came before those two bodies. Because the problems were so intimately involved with the economic welfare of the country, and because he was so faithful in his devotion to them, it was not long before the Administration was using him to present its point of view and introduce its remedies. Some of these he questioned, and it was a tribute to his steadily strengthening position that he should have been called to the White House, that his views should have been carefully examined by its shrewd and forceful occupant, and that certain modifications which he suggested should then have been worked into the legislation bearing his name. He had early made clear that he would not give his name unless this were done, and his position was respected. The result was better and more workable legislation in several fields of vital economic import to the country. Toward the end of his first term, this had given him sufficient stature with his colleagues so that he was appointed to fill a vacancy on the committee on which Senators like to serve above all others, Foreign Relations.

So went his public career, on a rising arc, and few even of his closest friends suspected that at home the arc, after too brief a period of happiness, was going down again.

He could not at this moment, while two interns stopped by to question him on how he was feeling as the operation approached, put his finger on the exact point when the decline had begun. There was too much grayness over that period for him to single out any one instant and say: This was it. It was a general thing, the gradual awareness that Jimmy wasn't talking as quickly or as well as he should—though this was soon forgotten when he did begin, for then he chirped like a bright little cricket all day long and the ear could ignore an occasional oddly slurred word . . . the growing uneasiness that Jimmy was bumping into things a little too much and wasn't co-ordinating physically quite the way he should—though this too could be ignored in the obvious high intelligence of his mind and the quick perception of his mischievously laughing eyes . . . the occasional alarmed puzzlement when Jimmy had sudden little sleepy spells, for no apparent reason, and would sometimes come out of them "swallowing up," as he put it—but this did not happen more than once a month, and it too could be put aside in the doctor's comfortable assurance that it was "just some little virus, probably, and nothing to worry about."

Yet these things were not normal, and the pretense that they were could not be kept up forever. Before they knew it, he and Kay were meeting each other's eyes uneasily across the busy little blond head whose owner played unheeding at their feet. In both their minds worry came to live and tension and irritation began to develop from it and they headed toward some crisis on the subject whose nature and cause they did not know but could only await with silent and unexpressed foreboding.

To all outward appearances, and for 90 per cent of the time, their son was as cute and bright and handsome and lovable as any child they had ever seen. He was, in fact, precocious far beyond his years, and something of a tease as well, so that there were occasions when his parents could see that they might be faced before long with a real disciplinary problem if they did not exercise sufficiently firm control while they could. His way of doing it was to be pleasant, man-to-man, reasonably lenient, with a swat on the bottom when things threatened to get out of hand. Hers was a method of verbal injunction and threat which called on powers that deeply disturbed her husband and caused more than one sharp argument.

"I'll turn out the light in the bathroom if you don't keep quiet," she would call after the third request for a glass of water, "and then the goblins will get you." Or, "If you run outside when I'm not looking, there's a big black dog out there with green teeth and red eyes who will eat you up." And quite frequently, calling upon some dark memory of a churchgoing childhood in a tone of chilling severity that disturbed Hal most of all, "You'll have to be a good boy, now, or God will get mad at you."

It was this last that she used most often, and it was this that finally provoked a major blowup between them.

"What kind of God did you have in your house when you were growing up?" he demanded one day after Jimmy had been sent to his room with this admonition. "An Old Testament Jehovah? The one we had was a God of love who didn't hurt people; he helped them. And that's the kind I want in my home, not something to scare little boys with."

"He has to learn," she said defiantly.

"He has to learn, all right. But not like that. I don't want him afraid of God, or thinking he has to have a guilt complex about things, or something."

"He has to learn," she repeated stubbornly; and then, quite suddenly, she had begun to cry. "Anyway," she said in a bleak tone that frightened him badly, "I think God *is* mad at him—or mad at us—or mad at me—I don't know. *Why* isn't he like other children? Why does he have spells? Something's wrong with him, I know it is. He isn't right, Hal. He just—isn't—right!"

Because this brought into the open at last his own terror, he answered with a desperate anger that overwhelmed her arguments and drove her into a sobbing silence.

"I don't want you to threaten him with God again, do you hear me?" he had shouted at the end of it. "My son is going to be all right, and I don't want you to make him scared of God."

But they both knew that he was not all right, that Hal's use of "going to be" instead of "is" was tacit recognition of the fear that lived with them both, and that they were themselves scared of God and what He might have in store for them. Hal knew before six months had passed that she had been unable to break away from her obsession with it in her dealings with their son, for there came in due course the horrible afternoon when the boy went without warning into convulsions and, when Hal hurried into the house from the Hill, white-faced and terrified, returned to sentience long enough to look up wistfully and ask, "Daddy, why is God mad at me?" All but the formal shell of a marriage died forever in the look that passed between his parents at that moment, but there was no time then to talk about it.

The doctor came, an ambulance came, there were four days of recurring convulsions, increasingly heavy sedation, tests and studies and more tests and more studies, a black miasma of terror in which two strangers automatically went home together from Georgetown Hospital, automatically slept, automatically woke, got up and went back to Georgetown Hospital for another hopeless day, hardly speaking, hardly looking at one another, hardly conscious of each other's existence at all.

At the end of it, their son had lost twelve pounds and the power of speech; the bright, perceptive light was gone from eyes that no longer knew them or responded to the stimuli devised by patient but increasingly less hopeful doctors; and in a haunted house in Georgetown a bright little chirping cricket chirped no more.

Of this the doctor responsible for it said with an airily unctuous self-exculpation that the only thing he could think of was that the mother must have suffered some unusual blow or jar prior to birth. Other doctors said that it was more likely caused by scar tissue in the brain brought about by unnecessarily harsh use of forceps. But no one knew for sure, nor could anyone promise that it would ever be possible to restore Jimmy to what he had been before that afternoon. All they could do, they said, was try. For several more years, they did.

What happened then in the Georgetown house could perhaps have been easily predicted by the doctors, though they tried to impress upon both parents, together and separately, that they must not blame one another, that they must come together in love and helpfulness and give their child all the love they could in the hope that in some mysterious way unclear to doctors this might bring him back to them whole and laughing and complete. It had in some cases, they said, and it might in this: there were areas medicine did not know much about, and sometimes it happened that way. The important thing, they said to two people who sometimes seemed to have forgotten they had ever felt it for one another, was love.

For one of them the injunction carried weight, and perhaps it did for the other, too, or would have if it had not come too late. Hal Fry, drawing on some source of strength that he did not know he possessed, found himself swept by a powerful emotion in which pity and love were inextricably mixed, and in the first agonizing months as they tried with a desperate patience to arouse some spark of recognition in their silent son, he sought in every way he knew to comfort and sustain his wife. There were a few times, a few hours, perhaps only a few minutes, when this seemed to work, when she seemed to turn to him with a love and comfort to match his own; but they were fleeting and soon gone. There began to come a steady withdrawal, broken only by sudden surges of accusation and blame and a deep unfairness that wounded him terribly, though he tried to tell himself that she was not well, that it was understandable that she should be almost unbalanced by their tragedy, that she was not really responsible for what she said or thought, that she did, indeed, need all the love he could give her even though she did not seem to understand or value it. But, inevitably, love rebuked began to die again, and this time he did not think it would recover.

In all this he was forced to face his own responsibility, too, for there remained like an evil presence in the house the self-serving excuse of the guilty doctor that some unusual blow or jar prior to birth had done the damage. He did not know how many times, in sad and bitter arguments, they relived those fateful five minutes on the icy front steps, but it must have run into the hundreds as the months dragged by. Only rarely did he remark in his own defense that there was a theory, too, that it might have been injury during delivery, and that for this the doctor she had chosen over his objections was responsible. This produced always a reaction so frantically self-defensive that he realized before long that it must spring from a feeling of guilt as deep as his own. And so, held together by the necessities of their now-pathetic child, chained to one another in a bond of mutual guilt and accusation, they lived out those bitter years during which one medical remedy after another proved useless and there came to them bit by bit the realization that the situation would not change.

Somehow against this background at home he still managed to perform his public duties and continue to win the support of his colleagues and the approval of his constituents. Perhaps because the Lord had, really, left him no choice, he was forced to apply himself ever more faithfully to his work, strive ever harder to serve his country, apply and strengthen ever more fully the sense of dedication that had always been so paramount an element in his character. Once Bob Munson, watching him fall into a brown study at some committee meeting, had given his arm a squeeze and said, "I wish there was something we could do." But Hal had responded with a shake of the head and a smile that managed to be adequately confident. "I'm all right. I'm managing." And so he did, out of some well of strength within him which, fortunately, proved inexhaustible.

There came the time for him to file for re-election, and although Kay seemed to resent it, he was convinced that his only salvation, and perhaps the only salvation for them all, was for him to keep working as hard as he knew how. He threw himself into the campaign as into some nerve-deadening drug, spent six months replenishing his heart and strength by direct contact with the good people and the good earth of his native state, and was re-elected by a much larger majority than he had received in his first race for the Senate. His people obviously approved of him, and such whispered intimations of his family tragedy as filtered through to the hills and valleys only served to arouse greater sympathy and loyalty. He started his second term secure in everything except the love of his wife and the health of his child.

For several more years they kept Jimmy at home, while he grew steadily more handsome and more appealing in all except his eyes, which did not know them, and his mind, which did not respond. In time the doctors at Georgetown, still testing from time to time, still keeping a friendly interest, began to suggest tactfully that perhaps it was too much of a burden to keep the boy with them, that perhaps his presence was too terrible a reminder of what had happened and of what might have been. It was suggested that possibly they should find a home for him somewhere where he could receive constant care among his own kind. The cost, they said, would be substantial, but since—they added with a tactful gravity that did not prevent the words from devastating both parents—since it did not matter to him, perhaps it would be better for them.

There were such institutions near Washington, but after a number of inquiries they decided upon Oak Lawn, up the Hudson above New York City. Discreetly and sometimes from the most surprising sources, people whom they would never have suspected of having a similar problem, they received suggestions: Oak Lawn seemed to have more adherents than any in a radius of several hundred miles. After several visits, they decided to take Jimmy there at the start of his eighth year. It would be near enough for periodic visits, not close enough so that they would feel they must constantly visit, with all the pain and anguish that such a frequent routine would entail. Assured that he would be well and faithfully cared for, they left him sitting, smiling gently, in a chair upon the lawn and drove back down to Washington silent and hardly thinking in the terrible depression that came with the final crushing of all their hopes.

After that, the house in Georgetown seemed emptier and more haunted than ever, and within a month they had decided to sell it and move to an apartment in Arlington Towers, across the Potomac from the capital on the Virginia side. Three months after they did so he came home from a late session of the Senate to find that his wife had sought, and finally found, surcease from pain, an end to thinking, an end to grief and guilt and lack of loving, an end of everything that had apparently been too much for her to bear any longer.

Through the blank weeks that followed, a hiatus in his life whose details he had never quite been able to sort out, only the faithful and loving kindness of such friends as the Majority Leader, Stanley Danta, Orrin and Beth Knox, the Speaker, and his own family brought him through. His sister Betty left her family and came from Ohio, where she now lived, to stay with him for four months, supervising the immediate change of apartment to a suite at the Mayflower shared with widower Senator John Winthrop of Massachusetts, filling his life with comfort and care, urging, demanding, pushing, bullying him on to do his job and not stop to look back until such time as he might be able to do so without having it pull him under completely. Aided by Bob Munson and his colleagues in the Senate, who immediately found extra assignments for him to undertake—a trip with Powell Hanson of North Dakota and Bill Kanaho of Hawaii to an Interparliamentary Union meeting in Rio two weeks after Kay's death was one of them—he was subjected to an intensive therapy of affection and hard work that presently began to work its healing upon his shattered heart. It took time, but the day arrived when some of the constant sadness left his eyes, when he could smile again and mean it, when he even laughed now and then with something of his old ease and was able to offer once again his wryly good-natured comments on the world. This required more than a year, but when he emerged from it he had a new steadiness and certainty, a strength of character even greater than that he had possessed before.

Central to his recovery, though only his sister knew it, was the refuge they had been trained by their parents to turn to in time of need: the Lord Himself. The Lord had done strange things to him, and sometimes even now he could still reject the thought that it made any sense or possessed any justice; but for the most part the habit of prayer ingrained in him since childhood stood him in good stead when he needed it. There were occasions when only an unquestioning belief and acceptance could bring a man through what he had to face and alleviate the awful torments of the world. He turned to God because that was all there was left for him to turn to; and as often happens when men approach Him in that spirit at rock-bottom ebb of their dreams and hopes, God gave him comfort and sufficient strength to start the long road back.

Then he did indeed plunge into his work in the Senate with a devotion and dedication such as he had never known even in his most idealistic times. It was an age in which such dedication was welcome, for it was an age when his country was challenged everywhere by forces such as it had never encountered before, and when its survival demanded from each of its servants the utmost they were able to give. Having no longer anything to distract him or hold him back, with nothing now save an occasional visit to Oak Lawn to impede his concentration upon public affairs, he devoted himself increasingly to the work of the Foreign Relations Committee and the international activities with which it was concerned. His colleagues helped him in this, arranging for him to travel on the committee's business over most of the earth's surface. Downtown the President helped too, assigning him often to the special missions and international delegations on which the Senate always demanded representation and was usually given it by a White House still conscious, after so many years, of the sad precedent of what had happened after the First World War when the Senate was slighted at Versailles. Hal Fry was always available, always eager and ready to go. The youthful impulse to serve had been transmuted by time, experience, and suffering into the devout dedication of a mature and earnest man. "I feel safe when Hal is on the job," Harley Hudson's predecessor had explained once to Bob Munson as he sent Hal off to a meeting of the Organization of American States at Lima. "He has nothing to think about but the country, now, and, harsh though it is to say so, I think that's great for the country."

With his appointment to the American delegation to the United Nations he entered upon what soon became for him the most fascinating of all his experiences in the diplomatic field.

In the strange organization, conceived in such hope, delivered in such naïveté, growing to maturity in such headlong irresponsibility, he found that service to his country was more than a therapy, more than a dedication or a way of life that justified and alleviated other things. Service to the country was an absolute necessity that brooked of no slacking and allowed of no equivocation, that drove out thoughts of self-interest in the overriding imperatives of the nation's needs. There in that hectic assemblage he found fast sledding and a rough track. Principles upon which the United States was founded, decencies by which it had tried to live in its international dealings, were either unknown or not understood by many delegations. It did not matter that their own principles were often most peculiar, their claims to nationhood most flimsy, their outlook twisted and distorted fearfully by an unhappy past for which they were not to blame. What mattered was where they were *now,* and how they felt *now,* and he early realized that in this atmosphere the moral and political structures of the West could not long survive without the most loyal and diligent protection of those who sprang from them. "One nation, one vote." Though the nation might be a near-empty patch of desert or an island rising slowly from the primeval, the vote weighed just as heavily as those of the civilizations of centuries, though it could not be cast with the maturity of judgment or the perspective of history that centuries conferred.

There came to him as he watched the process in operation a concern and loving pity for his countrymen such as he had never known before. Observed from the vantage point of the United Nations, they seemed to him strangely lost and pathetic as they attempted to pretend that the realities that faced them were not what they were. There was among them, he could see, as they were reflected in the hostile eyes of many skeptical and envious faces, a desperate attempt to substitute words for deeds, a desperate urge to fling high-sounding phrases in the teeth of the gale of history that blew cruel and unforgiving upon the wistfully self-deluded of the Western world in the difficult passages of a violent century.

The endless passionate debates about "national purpose" that filled the newspapers, periodicals, and airwaves of his native land foundered on a hard rock that many Americans simply could not bring themselves to acknowledge: that they were up against a basically hostile climate manipulated by an opponent who had no *real* desire to get along with them.

This fact, so terrifying in its implications and so demanding of sacrifice and courage if the implications were fully acknowledged, was too much for most Americans—indeed for most Englishmen, or Frenchmen, or any other still-hopeful peoples of the West—to face. So they spun out the hurrying months and years of the enemy's brutal advance assuring one another that they must find a Purpose, while the one purpose that could possibly mean anything at all to themselves, their posterity, or the world—simple survival— was slowly but surely allowed to erode away.

Against that background the visit of the M'Bulu, with all its clever, damaging corollaries, had presented an issue as grave in many ways for his country as though the Cuban Communists had lobbed a rocket into Florida. Never before had the world dared to intervene so directly in the affairs of the United States, but he could see now that it had been inevitable for a long time. It had taken only the nerve and astuteness of Terrible Terry and his friends to bring about a challenge that had been in the making, in many envious hearts and bitter minds, for years. History had finally presented to America a reckoning that America, in far too many places within her borders, had invited and, in the world's judgment, deserved.

So it was now, as he fiddled once more with the radio dial to distract himself, that he felt a terrible protest in his heart against the God to Whom he had so often prayed, for having apparently abandoned him at a time when his duty and his desperate desire were to be active and on the job at the UN in these concluding stages of the problem presented by the M'Bulu. That was where he should be and that, he promised himself and the Lord with a defiant grimness, was where he was going to be until he dropped, if drop he must. It was the only thing—perhaps the last thing—that could give his life sense, and he did not intend to let anything deprive him of it as long as he could drive his body to house his spirit and carry it forward upon what he felt to be its mission.

There was a rap on the door, the entry of an intern and a couple of nurses with a wheelchair, which they pushed alongside his bed and asked him to get into. Even as he started to comply he paused and turned back, startled and dismayed, toward the radio.

"—found dead this morning by a policeman at the foot of the Capitol's West Front overlooking the city of Washington. Senator Cooley, seventy-six, had just completed an eight-and-a-half-hour filibuster on the resolution introduced by Representative Cullee Hamilton of California. The Senate passed the resolution following completion of Senator Cooley's filibuster.

"In a development that many observers believed might be connected with the death of the South Carolinian, Representative Hamilton himself was savagely beaten in the early hours of the morning by a group of unidentified men.

"Senator Cooley, President Pro Tempore of the Senate and for many years regarded as its most powerful single member, first came to Washington in—"

Oh, Seab! he thought with anguish: Cullee! What are they doing to us all?

And with a fierce determination that startled his young attendants as it flared across his face—I *will* help. God, I *must*.

2

The weather had changed at last, the wistful golden lingerings of autumn had come to an end. Fog and puffy, slate-gray clouds bearing promise of snow hung low upon the city and the river. A few tugs passed up and down the darkly churning channel, a few gulls, lonesome in the chilly air, swung dispiritedly over the water. The world looked cold, and it was.

In the overheated, overcrowded Lounge behind the two-story windows that framed this hostile scene of winter's encroaching desolation, the calls for Mr. Ahmed Khan of Pakistan, Señora Elena del Arbro of Chile, Mr. Grovious Bato of Yugoslavia, Mr. Bibbiyu Crubb-Shama of the Ivory Coast came sternly over the loudspeakers in the heavy tones of the young ladies, beginning to call a little more firmly, a little more stridently as the rising babble of the gathering delegates almost drowned out their voices. The plenary session on Kashmir was not scheduled to start until ten-thirty, but already the room was filling to capacity, its occupants concerned not only with the latest tensions of the uneasy subcontinent but also, and even more excitedly, with the action of the United States Senate last night and its intriguing and fascinating aftermaths, the death of Senator Cooley, the savage beating of Congressman Hamilton, the bubbling and all-important question of how the whole business would affect the Labaiya proposals when debate resumed in the plenary at 3 P.M. tomorrow.

Not the least of those who wondered, as he sat quietly off to one side, pretending to be absorbed in La Prensa but in reality carefully studying the stream of multicolored faces entering the Lounge, was the Ambassador of Panama himself.

For Felix Labaiya, the last couple of days had passed in the busy but essentially unsatisfying pastime of attempting to firm up the votes he had, attempting to acquire new ones, and attempting to keep alive in the press a steady flow of confident propaganda that would assist in all his purposes. He thought now that he had enough pledges to do what he wanted to do, but in this chattering and tricky atmosphere one could never be sure. One thought he had the commitment of some dusky delegation one moment, only to be led off down the garden path by a vague hint of withdrawn support a moment later. By rights, there should be no problem. He was dealing with the United States, a most vulnerable country on matters of race here in a United Nations that in recent years had been transformed into a temple of race, and yet—one could not be sure. They were, he suspected, just playing with him because he was white. He, too, ironically, was having trouble because of race. Yet he was almost certain that when the voting came he could count on very strong support, quite possibly enough to achieve his purpose—and this despite the fact that the Congress, surprisingly enough, had made good on Cullee Hamilton's promise and passed his resolution as he had said it would.

Contemplating the swirling crowd before him as more and more delegates came to the door, stood for a moment looking about for friends, and then moved on into the room to join the many little gossiping groups, he congratulated himself that patience and planning would place him in a position of commanding influence here despite his continuing questions and uncertainties about some delegations. The action of the Congress, he would give its members credit, had been more astute and perceptive of the realities here than he had believed possible; yet it was, after all, a gesture made under pressure. There had been enough things said during debate in both houses so that all he need do in the Assembly was quote certain excerpts from certain speeches in order to restore to their original hostility those delegates who might have been impressed by the final result in Washington. He did not think it posed so great a problem, particularly when what he proposed to do would of course arouse all but a few of the Afro-Asians to the point where they would very likely forget all their hesitations, if they had any, and rush to his support in the wild excitement of the moment.

So he thought his cause was in good condition as he prepared to put aside his newspaper and move down the long room to a chair by the window where he could see the gorgeous figure of the M'Bulu sitting alone with his back to the room, staring out moodily upon the wind-whipped waters of the winter-dark river. Don Felix, grandson of Don Jorge, master of La Suerte and oligarch of Panama of the new style, a long, long way from the old in these hurrying days of world upheaval, congratulated himself that he would yet win out over his country's enemies. They had achieved a shrewd maneuver with the Hamilton Resolution, but he told himself that it was hardly enough.

For the second time in twenty-four hours Terrible Terry was doing something he had almost never done in recent years: he was revealing to the world that he was seriously upset about something. It was not, in this case, a direct disclosure to another person, as it had been to Senator Munson in Washington. It was a more subtle, indirect uncovering, something about the set of his shoulders, the angle of his head, the half-defiant, half-angry, wholly tense way in which his elbows rested on the arms of his chair and his long fingers clasped themselves tightly together as he rested his chin upon them. He had deliberately turned his chair to the window so that his back was to the room, a move designed both to discourage interruption and to conceal from the avid eyes of the bustling throng the uneasy concern that filled his intelligent eyes and furrowed his massive forehead. He did not intend for the world to know that the heir to Gorotoland was gravely worried, and he did not know that the fact was clearly apparent to all who happened to glance, as many did, at his solitary figure by the window.

The assumption that sprang to most minds was of course correct: he was indeed upset about the odd little riot in Molobangwe, and upset about it now with a deep and steadily growing concern as he reviewed the details provided half an hour ago in a special report of the Resident, sent over to

him by messenger from Lord Maudulayne at British headquarters on Park
Avenue. Like Lafe Smith, with whom he had flown up on an early morning plane from Washington, he had decided to forego catching up on the
sleep he had lost during Senator Cooley's filibuster in order to get back at
once to the politicking of the UN as it approached the Labaiya debates.
Now he wished he had taken the time to get at least three or four hours
before facing this. He and Lafe had talked a little, quite inconsequentially,
and dozed a little, quite fitfully, on the quick flight up; such rest as he had
managed to achieve had been very brief and not very refreshing. Now he
felt tired and pestered by life and, for the first time in many years, not
quite so confident and sure of himself as was normal to his fierce pride
and monumental self-assurance.

Disclosed in the report from the Resident—accompanied by a cheerful
little note which said only, "Sounds a bit sticky, doesn't it? Have fun! M."
—was a pattern of activity that sent up many little warning signals to a
mind extremely jealous of its power and instantly suspicious of all attempts
to encroach upon it. The riot had begun in one of the outer compounds of
the town, had seemed to follow a predetermined route as it moved from hut
to hut in toward the palace, and had finally culminated in the ostentatious
flight of the Council of Elders to a nearby village. Dramatically his regent-
cousin had then appeared to quiet the mob, which had responded with a
suspicious speed, and then had recalled the Council of Elders, who had
given him great praise and tribute for his courageous handling of the hectic
situation. Acting, Terry was sure, under pressure, his mother too had added
her tributes, and the riot was over. At his cousin's request, everyone had
then joined in a wild public tribute to the M'Bulu and to his leadership of
Gorotoland's cause in the far-off United Nations. Apparently everything had
ended with the situation exactly as it was before: except that his cousin
had displayed to the world the fact that he could control the street mobs, the
Council, and Terry's mother. Otherwise, Terry told himself sardonically,
nothing at all was changed in Gorotoland.

The next step, he presumed, would be for his cousin, if he dared while
the British were still in control, to send him word that he might be better
off if he remained for a time in New York. Possibly he would be offered
the post of special representative at the United Nations, with the implicit
understanding that he had better not try to come home; possibly later he
would be found dead some morning on a New York street, his testicles cut
off and his body flecked with symbolic knifings signifying things to the
Goroto people that would be lost upon the Manhattan police. That was the
road, clearly, down which his cousin wanted him to proceed. The riot had
been simply a preliminary test to ascertain whether his cousin could get
away with it. Undoubtedly he had not been at all sure himself when he
had caused the riot to begin that he could manage it. There was the chance,
ever-present in volatile Africa, that the street mobs would get out of hand
and turn upon him—they could as easily murder him as follow him. And
the Council of Elders might not have been compliant enough to go along

with his plans; and Terry's mother might have exercised her still-great influence to thwart him; and it could have ended in the cousin's defeat and death and a completely unqualified triumph for Terry.

But it had not; and the reasons for this were ominous and probably as pointed as one sentence in the Resident's report intended them to be: "It seems clear on the basis of preliminary investigation that both outside funds and outside influence were present in the origins of this disturbance, and that Soviet and Chinese Communist agents, working secretly with the Co-Regent, were largely responsible for the pattern of events." Largely responsible for the fact that they and the Co-Regent had not succeeded, the M'Bulu knew with a strange mixture of humor and gratitude, was the fact that the M'Bulu had not yet achieved his aim of independence for Gorotoland and that consequently the British were still in control there.

As long as London remained in charge, neither his cousin nor the Communists would quite dare to overthrow him and his government entirely. The riot just served notice that they were getting ready. And of course they had timed it perfectly, after the British had issued their White Paper on Communism in Gorotoland, and after he himself had joined in heaping scorn upon it. Now who would believe him, if he attempted to turn about and say to the world, Yes, they were right? The West might, but Africa and Asia would only laugh.

What he had to decide right now, as he sat staring out upon the East River, was whether he should fly home immediately or whether he should chance staying until the final vote on Gorotoland's independence. He did not think any further attempt would be made to overthrow him until independence was guaranteed, and of course the vote here would not automatically produce it, even though he was sure the day would be greatly hastened, since the British would probably in their obliging way bow to the Assembly's will and begin to pack their bags. It would come soon enough, at any rate, so that he did not think he could afford to wait very long beyond the end of the debate. He might just be able to allow himself this extra day or two, but a shrewd judgment of men and events, coupled with an almost animal instinct for self-preservation, told him he could not tarry a day longer.

The one thing he would not do, given his heritage, brains, and ability, was concede the game without a contest and take the easy way out by seeking asylum in the West. Whatever else he might be, the 137th M'Bulu of Mbuele was not a coward, and there burned in him a ravenous pride and a fearsome desire to get his revenge upon those who had given him such a fright with the riot in Molobangwe.

He had just reached the decision to remain for the debate when the Ambassador of Panama interrupted his reverie and disclosed his new and intriguing plans; and as the M'Bulu contemplated them, his aspect gradually lost the forbidding air that had surrounded it for the past hour. He had decided to remain: very well, let them be hours passed happily in the confusion of his enemies, silly old Cullee lying all whacked up in Bethesda Naval Hospital, the foolish old United States that thought it could buy off the conscience of the world with a tricky resolution in a reluctant Congress, the hopelessly mixed-up British who thought they could tell the tide of history to wait a little while until they were graciously pleased to get out of its way.

They would be shown in due course, by such astute and farseeing men as himself, the Panamanian Ambassador, and all those others here in the United Nations who served the purposes of the future. He could not help a burst of gleeful laughter at the prospect, as his spirits returned completely to their customary cheerful ebullience. Even Felix, amused at the sound, forgot for a moment his characteristic intense, closed-off preoccupation with his own concerns and joined in heartily. Nearby many others, black and brown and yellow, saw them and chuckled in appreciation, not knowing the subject of their hilarity but knowing that it must augur well for the cause to which all of them were devoted.

It was thus that the junior Senator from Iowa saw them as he entered the Lounge, looking tired and worried, shortly before 11 A.M. The spectacle did not improve his somber mood.

He did not doubt that the Labaiya Amendment would be beaten now that the Hamilton Resolution had been passed, but it was impossible not to feel in the wake of all the unhappy events of the last twenty-four hours a sense of foreboding and misgiving that depressed him greatly. He knew, as an intellectual proposition, that this was not very sensible thinking, that only coincidence had made the outlook so depressing. But emotionally it was easy to fall into a somber mood.

Everything seemed to be going wrong.

Not, he repeated sternly to himself as he stood there looking about, drawing interested eyes and interested murmurs from the colorful crowd, that the United States really had anything to worry about now. Admittedly the attitude of the Congress had not been filled with a wild enthusiasm in either house, but it had passed the Hamilton Resolution and the country was now committed both to assisting Gorotoland and to moving even more earnestly in the direction of assisting its own colored population. The Assembly would have to feel a degree of vindictive unreason greater than any he had seen yet to insist on its own censure motion—particularly since it took two-thirds to pass, and particularly since the United States was still the principal foundation rock, financial and otherwise, upon which the United Nations rested. Both on the score of good faith and the score of its consistent dedication to the world organization, his country stood unassailable to any fair and honest appraisal.

Why, then, the uneasiness and the tendency to somber mood? Why the formless sense of impending unhappiness? Probably, he decided, for the reasons he had already thought of: his sorrow for Seab, his concern for Cullee, above all the tragic necessity of helping Hal Fry face what he had to face.

And yet, as the sole representative of the United States of America in the Delegates' Lounge of the United Nations at this moment, it was incumbent upon him to show a smiling and confident face to the gossiping nations that examined him so narrowly as he stood there. The sight of the M'Bulu and Felix and their jocular friends chortling away down the room did not disturb him, but they annoyed him, so carefree and unconcerned did they appear to be at such a time. Well, he told them in his mind as he forced his face into a pleasantly noncommittal expression by a determined effort of will, enjoy your little laugh, boys. We'll see who laughs last.

He was conscious of someone at his elbow, a dignified presence alongside. The Secretary-General held out his hand.

"Good morning, Senator. My congratulations on the action of the Senate. It has been well received here."

"Has it?" Lafe asked, shaking hands. "I wonder."

"Oh, yes. Somehow the tragic events attending upon it seem to have made it more acceptable. There is a certain"—the S.-G. hesitated and a curious expression, compounded of irony and a sad understanding, crossed his face—"a certain liking for blood, here. A death—a beating"—he gave a bitter little smile—"the passions they symbolize are taken as proofs that the United States is really concerned about this matter."

"My God. Was anyone in doubt?"

"Many. Many. After all, what was the response last week to the threatened action of the Assembly? It was to offer financial aid, or to withhold it, to couple the moral argument with the monetary whip—it seemed to many to be the standard American response. Now there is a feeling that America's heart is also engaged. It is felt it shows a certain—maturity, shall we say."

"Maturity!" Senator Smith said sharply, momentarily forgetting his duty to be amicable. "Good Lord, look who's talking! Maturity? It is very nice," he added more calmly, "not to be patronized. Maturity! Well, well."

"I am simply expressing the feeling as it comes to me," the Secretary-General said mildly. "I do not say it represents my own. I know what the United States has done in support of the United Nations over all these years. But this is the first time it has presented any proof that it is seriously anxious to improve the lot of its own colored people."

"The first time?" Lafe said, trying hard to keep his expression pleasant, but again finding it difficult. "What has my government been doing all these decades, if it has not been giving proofs to the world? We have given thousands of proofs to the world!"

"The new states are not aware of them, you see. It is only a very short time that they have been allowed to see the world beyond their borders. In that short time, many very well publicized events in America have shown them the other side of the coin. The mob that threw things at Terence Ajkaje symbolizes America to them. Or at least it did until now."

"And now, I suppose, all is harmony and they love us," Lafe said, "and we shall defeat the Labaiya Amendment by an overwhelming majority."

He was conscious of a little change in the S.-G.'s eyes, a veiled expression for a second.

"Won't we?" he asked quickly. "After all, it takes two-thirds."

"It is not my position to intervene in these matters," the S.-G. said, "unless requested."

"I'm requesting. What do you hear?"

"I should beware a wild majority," the S.-G. said cryptically. "I should also beware," he said with a relieved smile that showed how little he wished to talk, even guardedly, in so public a place, "of newspapermen trying to ferret out embarrassing things."

And he gave a little bow and faded gracefully away as the London *Evening Standard* and his colleagues moved in upon them.

"Good morning, Senator," the *Standard* said crisply. "How does the situation look to you now?"

"It looks as though I have an appointment across the street at U.S. headquarters," Lafe said easily, though his mind was racing furiously as a result of the Secretary-General's last remark.

"Come on, Lafe," the New York *Times* told him. "You can do better than that for us."

"Can I?" Lafe asked, a slightly acrid note coming into his voice. "How, pray tell?"

"Oh, just tell us how confident you are," the Chicago *Tribune* suggested. "How many hundreds of votes we have to spare in licking the Labaiya Amendment. And things like that."

"I'm not a vote-predicter, and I really do have to run along. Why don't you see me tomorrow? I'll know better what's going to happen then."

"That's no fun," the London *Daily Mail* said. "We'll all know then. We want to know now."

"Mmm-hmm. Well, excuse me, boys. Go see Terry and Felix down there. They'll talk."

"All right," the *Standard* said, suddenly annoyed. "We bloody well will."

"You bloody well do that," Lafe said, turning away. "See you later."

"What's going on here, anyway?" the New York *Herald Tribune* asked as they started purposefully down the Lounge toward the window where Felix and the M'Bulu were now holding forth to an admiring circle. "He didn't sound very happy."

Nor was he, as he got his hat and coat and hurried down the Delegates' Stairs to the Main Concourse and made his way out through the groups of students, the earnest ladies from Boston and Denver, the loudly talking tourists who crowded the low-ceilinged expanse awaiting their turn to tour the building. He was genuinely disturbed by the S.-G.'s obscure warning, for he thought he probably interpreted it rightly. He was also on his way to Harkness Pavilion to see his colleague. Neither item made him happy.

He paused briefly at the circular information desk and borrowed a phone to put in a call to Washington, completed it, and then hurried out past Zeus and Sputnik and the slowly swinging steel ball of the Netherlands to catch a cab and proceed north through the cluttered traffic of the frigid metropolis.

There had been an injection of procaine in the sternum. A few minutes after that, a needle had been inserted, suction had been applied, the needle had been handed to a nurse who carried it briskly away.

"Is that all there is to it?" he asked blankly. "Is that all that this elaborate preparation led up to?"

"That's it," the doctor said, smiling. The enormity of it struck him a heavy blow.

"It doesn't seem like much, for a death sentence," he said with an ironic bitterness. The doctor at once looked grave.

"It may not be that, but if it is—if it is—you will have to draw on all your resources—and I think you have them—to bear it. It will not be easy, but I think you can do it. That's my impression, anyway, from what I've read of you."

"Thank you," Hal Fry said, and in spite of the curious state of suspended feeling in which he seemed to be, a shadow of his customary humor came into his voice. "You're sure you can believe all you read in the papers?"

The doctor gave a sudden smile, as if surprised and pleased by this show of spirit, and Hal realized how anxious they must all be for him to carry it off well. You needn't worry, he reassured them in his mind. I've got promises to keep, and miles to go, before I sleep.

"I'm not sure I always do," the doctor said, "but from the little I've seen I'd say they were probably accurate about you. What's going to happen over there at the UN on this anti-American amendment?"

"It's going to be defeated tomorrow or the next day if I have anything to say about it," Hal Fry said. "And I will," he added with a sudden defiant grimness, for the general sedation he had been under for the past twelve hours was beginning to wear off.

"Tell me," he said. "If this is—what we think it is—what's the outlook?"

"It depends on the type. If it's the type preliminary tests seem to indicate, then the outcome will be"—the doctor hesitated—"relatively swift."

"How swift?"

"Forgive me. Two to three weeks. A month."

"But not the next couple of days, then," Hal said, feeling strangely relieved, as though the doctor had told him he had all the time in the world.

"Oh, no," the doctor said. "But—" he added, watching him closely, "you understand, Senator—swift."

"I understand. That doesn't matter, as long as I'll be all right for the next couple of days."

"You will," the doctor said, taking the cue without surprise and proceeding to discuss it matter-of-factly. "There will be some deterioration even in that time, but probably not enough to be noticeable to others. Especially if we keep you under sedation."

"I don't want to stay here," Senator Fry said sharply. "I've got to get back."

"But—" the doctor began, and paused at his patient's expression. "Very well. There's no reason why you shouldn't. When do you have to be there?"

"The debate starts at 3 P.M. tomorrow afternoon, and I ought to be there right now."

"Stay in today so we can give you some radiation, and then if you'll report back in tomorrow night and stay overnight so we can treat you some more, and check in each night as long as the debate goes on, we'll let you go in-between times. How's that? Fair enough?"

"I appreciate it," Hal Fry said. An agonizing spasm struck his chest. "There's just one thing—if there is some sedation that would stop some of these symptoms temporarily, could I have it?"

"We can give you some muscle relaxants and tranquilizers, if you like, to stop this pain from the nervous system that's giving you so much trouble. We don't want to load you up with too much, though, if you want to be active in the debate. But that's up to you. If you can stand it without too much sedation, it would be better for your reactions and general quickness. On the other hand, if it gets too intense—maybe you won't want to pay that price."

"Why don't you give them to me and let me be the judge? If I really have to use them, I will. But—I'll try not to."

"You're a brave man."

"I know. And what good has it ever done me?"

But that, he knew, was an understandable human bitterness, and the doctor dismissed it as such. Of course it had done him infinite good, carrying him through his marriage and its tragic conclusion, through Jimmy—Jimmy! Would there be time to go to Oak Lawn once more, and what would be the point, except sentimentality, if he did?—and now his courage must come to his aid again. And already it had, he realized as the brisk young nurses came in and helped him into his wheelchair, though he was perfectly able to walk and only a tiny bandage showed the site of the fateful intrusion into his marrow. He was beginning to come back already, at least in terms of humor and fighting heart.

That this pleased the doctor he made clear when he came in a little later to hand Hal a lab report and explain its notations of hemoglobin sharply down, white blood cells and lymphs sharply up, the presence of many mitotic immature cells.

"That's it?" Senator Fry asked, scanning it automatically as though it were a report on someone else. Somehow it seemed to be, so determined was his mind to raise a barrier of detachment that would see him through.

"That's it," the doctor said gravely. "Acute myelogenous leukemia, if you want to know the formal name of what's after you."

"Luke, meet Senator Fry," Hal said, leaning his head back on the pillow and looking into some far distance with an expression in which sadness and a tired philosophic humor were strangely combined. "Give me a couple of days, Luke," he said softly, "and then we'll go away somewhere together."

"You'll have them," the doctor promised, more moved than he wanted to show. "Harkness Pavilion's gift to the country will be to keep you in shape for that debate."

"Thank you," Hal Fry said, managing to smile a little. "I won't let Harkness Pavilion down. Or anybody else, for that matter."

"We know you won't," the doctor said. "We know . . . Look," he added gravely, "—you think this has hit you, but it hasn't, yet. Not really. The full impact hasn't come—it can't, at first; the mind won't let it. When it does, you call us immediately and we'll give you enough sedation to put you out completely for a while. All right?"

"And when I wake up, will you have taken it away?"

The doctor shook his head in sad acknowledgment.

"No. We won't have taken it away."

"O.K., then, I think I'll see it through without props . . . Anyway," he added with a defiant attempt at jauntiness, "I'm going to be so busy in the next few days that I won't have time to think about it."

"I hope so," the doctor said, "but we're here when you need us. Don't forget that."

"I won't, and I'm grateful . . . By the way, could you put out a statement, just to stop the gossip for a while? Just say I'm having a routine checkup and will be back at the UN tomorrow for the debate on the Labaiya proposals. I'd appreciate that."

"Right away," the doctor said. He held out his hand. "Good luck."

"I'd like a little, for a change," Hal Fry said, and then added at once when he saw the doctor's expression, "I'm sorry. I mustn't make it hard for everybody else, just to try to make it easier for me . . . I'll manage. Don't worry."

"All right," the doctor said. "I'll be in again later."

For a time after he left, the senior Senator from West Virginia lay staring up at the empty white ceiling, not moving, scarcely thinking, scarcely conscious of his body and the terrible invader to which it was playing host. He lay thus for perhaps fifteen minutes, drained of thought, emotion, energy, feeling; and then, just as there was beginning to approach the edge of his consciousness the first terrifying intimation of exactly where he was and what he was suffering from, there mercifully came a knock on the door, a hand reached around and tossed in a hat, and a second later he saw the amicable countenance, tired but reasonably cheerful, of his colleague from Iowa.

"Hi, buddy," Lafe said, recovering the hat, shucking it and his overcoat off onto the foot of the bed, and dropping into a chair. "How goes it?"

"Pretty good," Hal said, stuffing a couple of pillows behind his head so he could half-sit up, managing a smile. "Why the hat thrown in ahead of you? Have you done anything you shouldn't?"

"No. Except to phone Orrin and ask him to call and talk to us here."

"You didn't tell him—" Senator Fry began in angry alarm, but Lafe shook his head.

"He knows. You know Orrin. He doesn't know exactly what it is, but he knows it's damned serious. I expect he's going to try to persuade you to resign and take a rest."

"Rest for what?" Hal Fry asked dryly. "I haven't got anything to rest for. Except—more rest."

"Well, I thought that would be your position. You want to stay on the job, don't you?"

"Wouldn't you?"

Lafe smiled.

"I'm on your side. I was already, but I just wanted to know how you felt about it, now that—now."

"I haven't changed . . . You look tired. Have you had any sleep at all?"

Lafe yawned.

"Not much. I rode up on the plane with Terry, which was mildly interesting but not conducive to too much sleep. He's very worried about that little riot back home."

"I should think he should be. Is he going back?"

"I doubt if he will. He's stubborn, like you. I got the idea he's going to stick too, at least until the debate's over."

Senator Fry's eyes darkened and an expression of grave sadness crossed his face, but he was not, as his colleague thought he might be, concerned about himself.

"I am so sorry about Seab," he said softly. Lafe sighed and nodded.

"He wouldn't give up, either. The world," he added with a rather wan attempt at humor, "is full of a lot of stubborn people. But it was a great tragedy, for the Senate and for the country. Though some of the country may not realize it yet."

"And Cullee. I sometimes think race is going to tear this nation apart."

"Not unless we let it. Not unless we all give up and stop trying to be fair and kind to one another."

"That's part of the reason why I feel I have to keep going," Senator Fry said. "It's a contribution, I hope . . . Although I expect," he said with a half-smile as the phone rang, "that I'll be told differently."

"You'll be surprised, I think. He isn't worried about that. He's worried about you, personally. Orrin's very generous, underneath the prickly exterior."

Hal nodded and picked up the phone.

"I know . . . Hello? Yes, Orrin, how are you?"

"How are you?" the Secretary asked. "That's what I want to know. Is Lafe with you?"

"Yes, he is. And I'm fine."

"That's a lie," Orrin Knox said flatly, "and I wish you'd stop telling it to me. What have they found?"

"Nothing that will prevent me from completing the job here."

"Damn it, don't play games with me. We can't afford it, in days like these."

"You can't afford not to let me keep going, in days like these."

"It's cancer, isn't it?" the Secretary demanded. "Is it terminal?"

"Orrin," Senator Fry said, "I'm not going to tell you, and I don't think the doctors will, and I don't think Lafe will. Now, you've just got to trust me. I won't push my strength past what it can bear. You have my word on that. Isn't my word good enough for you?"

"Of course I can remove you from the delegation," the Secretary remarked thoughtfully. "Or Harley can, rather."

"Sure," Senator Fry said with a sudden harsh bitterness, "and kill me right now. That would be great . . . Look," he said, waving off Lafe as he started to reach for the receiver, "the President Pro Tem of the Senate is dead and a very fine young Congressman has been beaten up as a result of all this. And you want me to run away. What the hell do you think I am?"

"I think you're a very brave man and a very fine public servant, but I don't want you to do anything foolish with your health."

"I said I won't. Orrin, I *must* see this job through up here. It means—well, perhaps you know, perhaps you don't. It may be"—his voice broke a little, but he hurried on—"the last thing I do for the country, and you've got to let me do it. Now, please, Orrin. Lafe will tell you." And this time he did relinquish the phone to his colleague, who came on the line in a no-nonsense fashion.

"See here, Orrin, suppose you just let this situation rest up here, O.K.? We're both keeping an eye on it, it's all right, and we won't do anything to endanger either the country or Hal. Now, lay off! O.K.?"

"The President and I have got to know what the situation is," Orrin said stubbornly. "That makes sense, doesn't it? It isn't so unreasonable, is it? Go ahead, tell me it is."

"Of course it isn't. But you've got to understand the—the feeling up here, too. All sorts of things are involved, past, present—future. I give you my considered judgment it would be fatal to insist, Orrin. But you go ahead if you want to. We can't stop you."

"Well," the Secretary said, and paused. "How long?" he asked after a moment.

"Not very," Lafe said. "That's why—"

"All right. Put him back on."

Lafe nodded to Hal and handed back the receiver.

"Hal," the Secretary said, "I think you're an idealistic, wide-eyed, romantic damned fool, but—I guess that's how a lot of things get done in this world, by people like that. So—you go ahead. But I'm trusting you to watch your own health."

"I will. And, Orrin—"

"Yes?"

"I thank you very much."

"Who said I had any choice?" the Secretary asked with a return of humor.

"I seemed to be facing an outright rebellion in the delegation. Hell of a thing to have happen at a time like this. How does it look up there right now?"

"Not bad," Hal Fry said, responding gratefully in kind to his businesslike tone. "We're in pretty good shape now that Congress has acted."

"Well, keep me advised, step by step, will you? When will you be back over there?"

"Tomorrow morning."

"But—" Orrin began, then stopped. "O.K. Have Lafe call me tonight if there's anything I ought to know. If you need me up there, I'll try to make it, but I'd prefer not to because of this visit from the President of Brazil. We've all got a lot to talk about down here. Don't hesitate to call if you want me, though."

"Right. We'll try not to bother you."

"Bother me all you like. It's what I'm here for. And, Hal—for God's sake, take care of yourself, will you?"

"I will. Good-by, Orrin, and thanks."

"O.K."

After the conversation ended there was a silence in the room for several minutes, broken finally by the Senator from West Virginia.

"Thank you, too. It was most kind."

"No more than I'd expect from you in a similar situation," Lafe said. He frowned. "Actually, things don't look quite as good as we'd like, over there."

"Oh?" Senator Fry asked in some alarm. "How so?"

"Well, Terry and Felix seemed very cheerful this morning, in the Lounge. And I had a strange little talk with the S. G. Beware a wild majority, he said. What would you suppose that means?"

Hal Fry's eyes widened.

"You don't suppose they'd try—"

"If they thought they could get away with it, they'd try anything."

"I'm coming back down with you right now," Hal said abruptly, reaching for the bell cord by his bed and ringing it vigorously for the nurse. "Get my clothes out of the closet there, will you?"

"Now, wait a minute—" Lafe began, but his colleague brushed aside his protest impatiently.

"Come on, come on! We've got work to do."

"Yes, sir," Lafe said with a smile. "So we have."

"Mr. Stanley of New Zealand, please," the young lady at the telephone desk said sternly into the microphone. "Madame Vinagradof of Romania, please call the Delegates' Lounge . . . Mr. Haiutara of Japan, please . . ."

Seated already at one of the telephones along the wall of the Lounge, exchanging pleasantries with the Foreign Secretary in London, the British Ambassador wondered with some impatience who wanted him now via this cow-voiced female whose voice mooed so commandingly over the hubbub of the crowded Lounge. Whoever it was, he or she would have to wait a bit, for the voice from London was gradually abandoning pleasantries and getting down to the business in hand, namely how things were shaping up for the vote tomorrow on the Labaiya Amendment and, more importantly for Britain, on the basic resolution to demand immediate independence for Gorotoland.

As precisely as he could, Lord Maudulayne told him, though he considered it a damned difficult spot from which to telephone. Most delegates tried to confine their calls from the Lounge to relatively innocuous matters, since you never knew who might be tapping the wire or listening in at the main switchboard. Probably no one was, but it was something of an article of faith that somebody might be. Therefore calls like this were customarily made from one's own headquarters in Manhattan. However, the Foreign Secretary had tracked him down here and so, to his best knowledge, he was giving him the information he sought.

Not that his best knowledge was very good, Claude Maudulayne was forced to admit, at least to himself, because he, like Felix Labaiya, found the world a haze of dusky incertitudes at the moment. The two-thirds requirement for the resolution might just—just—save passage of the demand for Gorotoland's independence. As far as the Americans were concerned, he thought they were safe; or were they? He had the intimation, from his many conversations today with the Commonwealth and others of something moving under the surface of the waters, of vague, slippery, not-clear possibilities, and half-formed, half-hinted, half-organized projects.

"I don't like the feel of it," he said absently. "Something's in the wind."

"Eh?" said London blankly, and he realized that he had not been paying the slightest attention to his superior as the latter worried along.

"I *beg* your pardon," he said hastily. "I didn't mean for us; our situation is relatively clear. I meant for the Americans."

"Are they going to take a pasting?" the Foreign Secretary asked with a suddenly much more cheerful interest that broke through his general gloom about Gorotoland.

"I don't know," Lord Maudulayne said thoughtfully. "On the surface it appears impossible, and yet—"

"Congress' action has been very well received here. I thought possibly it might have been there."

"Yes and no. There's a very peculiar mood here, right now."

"Isn't there always? I thought it was chronic."

"There are moments when it is more chronic than others," Lord Maudulayne said. "Are we prepared to rescue the M'Bulu when the sky falls in upon him?"

"I suppose," the Foreign Secretary said wearily. "I suppose. Although of course that, too, will cause a great uproar there. How does he seem this morning?"

"Disturbed and wary, but he tells me he's going to stay until the debate ends. He seems confident of the outcome. Both outcomes."

"Isn't it nice that we're here to depend upon?" the Foreign Secretary said. "How do you tolerate him?"

"Oh, in his own strange way," Lord Maudulayne said, "he's a rather likable fellow. There's a curious innocence about it all, you know. I think fundamentally it's a complete lack of any moral sense whatsoever—like a giant child running about the world in pretty clothes tossing hand grenades into other people's open parlor windows."

"One hundred and thirty-seventh in direct descent," the Foreign Secretary said dryly. "That's more than you and I can say. And of course he isn't the only child that's loose in the world these days."

"How true."

"Well: I shall not keep you further. I think it would be well if we refrained from the Kashmir debate this afternoon. It would only inflame matters tomorrow, I'm afraid."

"My feeling exactly. I shall keep you advised."

"Good man."

"I see the two Senators coming in the Lounge, so—if you will forgive me—"

"Carry on."

"Right-ho."

There passed through Lord Maudulayne's mind as he watched the slow progression of the two Americans along the Lounge, nodding here, smiling there, being intercepted by many outstretched hands and effusive greetings, the thought that the Senator from West Virginia, despite the rumors about his health, looked determined and relatively rested, while the junior Senator from Iowa appeared tired and strained and without some of his usual comfortable amicability. The British Ambassador was also rather amused by the hearty welcome they were receiving; it had its little ironies. The thought was put into words a second later as his colleague from France came to his side from the other end of the Lounge, carrying a cup of coffee.

"One would think," said Raoul Barre, "that such a triumphal progress could only indicate a triumph. Would one not?"

"One would," Lord Maudulayne agreed. "Shall we get a table and talk to them about it?"

"It might be well," the French Ambassador said. He gestured with his cup toward the window. "I shall find a place for us, if you will—"

"Back directly," the British Ambassador said, starting off toward the Americans just as two Malinese, an Egyptian, and the Indian Ambassador stepped forward to offer their cordial greetings. Out of this jolly grouping he rescued Hal, Lafe, and K.K. and led them through the gossiping delegates, who opened a path for them rather like the waves parting for Moses and his friends, Lord Maudulayne thought. Lafe volunteered to get coffee for the four who did not have it, and in a few moments they were all comfortably seated, sipping thoughtfully and waiting for one another to make the first move. Finally Krishna Khaleel did so with a rather nervous little chuckle.

"Well, my dear Hal, we are so pleased to see you back and looking so well, in view of all the—er—unpleasant—rumors going about, you know."

"Oh, I expect I'll be around for a while," Senator Fry said calmly, though inside his head the dizziness had begun again and was stealthily growing.

"I expect I'll be around, much as I imagine you'd all like to have me elsewhere in the next couple of days."

"Oh, now!" the Indian Ambassador said in a shocked voice. "How can you say such a thing!"

"Indeed, Hal, how can you?" the French Ambassador inquired. "And what makes you think that K.K. and his colleagues don't want you here? Are you implying that they would wish you elsewhere when the Assembly votes on the proposition they favor so highly? How can you!"

"It is not that at all," K.K. said stiffly. "His presence is always welcome. In any event, I do not think the presence or absence of individual men will affect the course of history in the United Nations."

"I say, how ego-destroying!" Lord Maudulayne exclaimed. "You mean we might as well all go home?"

"Now, as usual, you are joshing me," the Indian Ambassador said sadly. "However"—he brightened—"I do not think joshing will be so fitting to-morrow, perhaps!"

"Looks good to you, does it, K.K.?" Lafe inquired. "Got us on the run, have you?"

"It is not a matter of 'having you on the run,'" the Indian Ambassador said somewhat testily. "You seem to impute a degree of hostility toward your country which does not exist here. It is all quite impersonal, believe me. Certain things are inevitable, that is all. It is purely in the spirit of history that your friends are acting here. We feel nothing but the most friendly things for you. I assure you of it."

"Mr. Tuatutu of Western Samoa, please call the Delegates' Lounge," said the young lady over the loudspeaker. "Mr. Hartley-Smith of Jamaica, please . . . Miss Mary-Alice Czinzki of the United States, please . . ."

"The executioner was friendly," Senator Fry remarked. "That's good to know."

"Assuming you get 'executed,' to use your distasteful term," Krishna Khaleel said. "Really, Hal, it is all done in the utmost spirit of helpfulness."

"Well," Lafe said comfortably, "I expect it's all academic anyway, because it does take two-thirds, and I don't think Felix has it." His tone remained comfortable, but his attention concentrated on the Indian Ambassador. "Does he, K.K.?"

"You know," K.K. said with an airy shrug, "I really am as puzzled about that as you are. One hears so many things, here in the Lounge and around the corridors, does one not? Two-thirds—four-fifths—three-fourths—six-tenths—seven-eighths—" He laughed merrily. "Who knows? We shall just have to wait and see. And now," he said, putting down his cup and rising briskly, "I must be off. I have an important speech to deliver on Kashmir, you know. It is important that we make our position clear."

"It is indeed," Hal Fry assured him. "We shall all listen with interest to your exposition of history's imperatives."

"They control us all, do they not?" the Indian Ambassador asked cordially. "It is so foolish to oppose them . . ."

"That was enlightening," Lafe remarked as their friend hurried away. "I still feel things are under way that we don't know about. What do you two hear?"

"I get the distinct impression that something is, yes," Lord Maudulayne said. "But it's devilish difficult to pin it down."

"There are certain things that could happen," Raoul Barre observed. "Not if the Assembly abides by its own rules, of course, but, then—" He shrugged. "When did that consideration ever stop it?"

"How strange it is," Hal Fry said, and for the moment the strangeness of it did indeed blot out the dizziness and the pains, "that at this moment the United States, having voluntarily passed a resolution meeting all the objections of the Assembly, having done exactly what a majority of its members seemed to want, should not know what the Assembly is going to do tomorrow. We have acted in complete good faith, we have every right to be completely confident of a friendly and favorable vote—and yet we aren't. What a commentary!"

"And not on us," Lafe remarked.

"Nor, of course," the British Ambassador observed with a certain wryness, "is that all. We, too, have acted in good faith on Gorotoland; and we, too, face the possible interference of the Assembly. Assisted in this instance, I might point out, by the likely support of our good friends in the United States."

"So where does it all end," Raoul Barre asked, "this attempt to satisfy what K.K. refers to as the spirit of history, as it is claimed to exist in this peculiar era? And can it be satisfied, by any of us who attempt to adhere to traditional principles of fair dealing and civilized behavior? I think that this, perhaps, is one of the fundamental questions we must ask ourselves . . . I think that we must do much conferring, between now and tomorrow. The spirit of history may not have a place for us," he added with a dry little twinkle, "but I am not prepared to admit it, just yet. I think diligent effort can still persuade the Assembly to honor its own rules. What happens under them, of course, is a matter for each of us to decide."

"Yes," the British Ambassador said with a smile. "Shall we go to the Assembly Hall? It must be time for K.K. to begin his statement on Kashmir."

"I think we'll stay behind and map strategy for a minute or two," Senator Fry said. "We'll see you there shortly."

After they had left, he and Lafe remained staring out upon the cold gray water as the Lounge gradually emptied and grew quiet around them. In the Assembly Hall the Ambassador of India would be starting upon his explanation of how the spirit of history warranted affirmative nonaggression against Kashmir, the Ambassador of Pakistan would be replying bitterly, the Ambassador of Panama would be engaging in still more of the endless conversations with other delegates in which they themselves must soon engage, the Soviet Ambassador and many another Ambassador would be busily preparing the morrow for the Americans; but for the moment they were silent, as if gathering themselves together, enjoying a brief respite before the strenuous hours and days to come.

"How do you feel?" Lafe asked quietly. "Going to make it?"

"Oh, sure. I feel quite dizzy, I have cramps in my chest and stomach and somebody is working on the small of my back with a pickax, but otherwise I'm fine." He managed a smile. "I'm all right, really. Don't worry. We haven't got time to worry. There's too much to do."

"I'll try not to, but I'm only human."

"I haven't got time to be," Hal said; and then with a bleak irony repeated, "I literally *haven't* got time to be. Let's go along to the Hall. Just being there will be helpful, right now . . . Speaking of being here, have you heard anything from Cullee?"

"No. I guess the poor guy's so badly banged up that he may still be in the hospital, for all I know."

"He ought to be here, if he possibly can. Can you call him pretty soon? The radio said he was in Bethesda Naval Hospital this morning, but he may be home by now."

"I'll call as soon as the morning session ends. He may not want to, but—"

"He has no choice," Hal Fry said harshly. "Any more than I have."

But as he lay half dozing, half-thinking on the bed where he had engaged in so many triumphant encounters with his wife, the Congressman from California was far, at that moment, from agreeing. His right eye was closed, he could barely see out of his left, his face was painfully swollen, a patch of court plaster masked a gash across his forehead, a sling supported his sprained left wrist and elbow, and over all his body it seemed to him that wherever anything touched him new agonies developed, whenever he moved new searing pains made themselves known. He was a messed-up sad sack for sure, he told himself with a hopeless little sigh as he lay there, a messed-up good-for-nothing wreck who had found a bitter harvest down his long, dark street.

For the one who had brought it to him, his mind was too tired at the moment to feel anything but a weary contempt. He had passed beyond anguish and anger with LeGage, had arrived finally at an emotional disengagement that now permitted him only a tired pity for the one who, in his judgment, was gone hopelessly far down his own dark road, and with no profitable or sensible end to it, either.

"All this was between you and me," he whispered through lips so swollen they could hardly form the words. "Just you and me, 'Gage. And you couldn't even do it yourself. You had to hire somebody. Poor 'Gage. Poor little old 'Gage."

There drifted across his infinitely weary, unhappy mind vague wonderings about other people: Sue-Dan was probably laughing about it right now, Orrin Knox was probably—what was he doing? Feeling sad or worried? Or was he amused, too, thinking how cleverly he had persuaded little Cullee Hamilton from Lena, S.C., to do his work for him? Or maybe not.

Maybe he was after 'Gage. Maybe he was sad and sick about it, too; maybe he and the government and the nice old President were trying to find Cullee's beaters. Yes, he thought, maybe that might be more like Orrin; but of course he didn't know . . . He didn't know much, really, except that he ached and pained and hurt all over.

Now as he lay there, where they had brought him half an hour ago by ambulance from Bethesda, he wanted nothing so much as to be allowed to sleep and forget it all. Maudie had fluttered around, clucking and exclaiming and giving him little sympathetic squeezes on the arm that only shot further agonies through his body, though he didn't have the heart to tell her, and right now she was downstairs fixing him some soup, though he had told her as best he could that he didn't want anything to eat right yet. Any minute now she'd be back, bustling and fussing and mothering him, trying to make him eat when all he wanted to do was rest for a while, just rest . . .

Idly his mind wandered in and out through recent days, his triumph in the House, the filibuster last night before he had started on his fateful journey home, his talks with Orrin and LeGage, his bitter arguments with Sue-Dan, his triumphant appearance at the United Nations— The UN. His mind tried to concentrate on it for a moment, paused, and tried to concentrate on it again. Was there something he was supposed to be doing about the UN? Wasn't there something—?

"Oh, yes," he whispered aloud again, forcing the words out between puffed lips. "Supposed to be debate." But today? Tomorrow? When? His exhausted mind did not know.

Nor, right then, did his exhausted mind care. Dimly he felt that he wanted to have no part of the UN ever again, didn't want to see it, didn't want to hear of it, didn't want to be part of any of its crazy schemes. It was too much for him—everything was too much for him. He had done his best to be a decent citizen, and they had all ganged up on him, Sue-Dan and LeGage and Orrin and the President and the UN and everybody.

"Guess I better just hide my head in a hole and keep quiet, now," he whispered. "Guess I better just not climb out of that hole ever again."

"Well, you alive, anyway," Maudie said, coming into the room with a tray. "I didn't know, a while back. What you mumbling about over there? What's that about a hole?"

"I want to sleep, Maudie. Please go away."

"You want to sleep," she said firmly, "but they told me to keep you awake and give you some soup; that's best for you. Didn't need to tell me, I knew that already, but they told me anyway, so now it's official. Anyway, you're not crawling into any hole. Not while I'm around."

"Wasn't talking to you," he whispered wearily. "None of your business."

"Got nobody else to be my business," she said tartly. "You it. So get your mouth ready; I'm going to give you this soup."

"Not too hot," he protested, almost whimpering at the thought. "Please, not too hot."

"It's medium," she said, drawing up a chair beside the bed and taking a careful spoonful. "Open . . . Swallow it!" she demanded sharply. "Don't dribble it like a little baby. Swallow it, I said!"

"I'm swallowing," he whispered, with the first stirrings of annoyance. "Get it in right, maybe I can swallow it right."

"I'll get it in right. You just concentrate."

"Concentrate yourself—" he began, but a spoonful of soup stopped him and he half choked, half gagged on it. But it went down.

"That's better," she said, readying another. "Now what's this about a hole? What kind of talk is that?"

"Guess I'll crawl into a hole and not get out. Don't guess I have any business trying to do anything else."

"More soup," she said firmly, giving him another spoonful. "What do you mean? Don't understand you, must say. You mean just because of a little old beating, you going to run away? Is that Cullee Hamilton talking?"

"You didn't get the beating," he whispered, his annoyance growing at her busy intervention; and, with the annoyance, of course, he was already beginning to feel a little better.

"I got good and scared," she said. "Guess I lost a few years' growth out of it, even if I didn't have a hand laid on me. I know you got hurt," she said, more gently. "I feel it for you. But it's no way to talk, crawling into holes. You got more to do in this world than that."

"Everything's gone wrong," he said, despair returning. "Tried to do what's right, and everything's gone wrong."

"More soup," she said, giving him another spoonful, which went down more easily this time. "Now, you shush and listen. I know you been hurt right badly, and I hope they get who did it and give 'em what they got coming. If I'd had a gun last night, I'd have done some, myself. But you can't just stop and quit. The world don't run that way. People got to keep going, 'specially in your position. You got to help keep things steady, Cullee. That's your job."

"Fine shape to keep things steady. Look at me."

"I'm looking at you. Been a long time since I see such a mess. But you still there underneath it, I do believe, and they can't change that, can they? Wouldn't like to think they could." She gave a little chuckle. "'Spect I'd have to find me somebody else to be a slave to, if I thought that could happen. Don't believe it can, and I don't believe *you* believe it can, either, once you get to feeling more like yourself again. It won't be long."

"I'm so tired . . . so tired. It isn't worth it."

"You just want me to tell you it is so you can talk yourself around to it again. You know it is. Now finish this soup and stop your nonsense."

"But—" he began feebly. The phone rang on its stand by the bed.

"Probably the President telling you to snap out of it," she said, lifting the receiver. "Yes? Who's this? . . . Yes, he is, Senator. Just a minute."

"Who—?"

"Senator Smith at the United Nations."

"But I don't want—"

"Take it," she ordered, laying the receiver on the pillow and holding the mouthpiece close to his mouth. "He's a nice man and he wants to talk to you. Take it!"

"Hello?" he said, managing to raise his voice a little so that Lafe could hear him, distant but distinguishable.

"Cullee, I'll tell you when I see you how sorry we all are about this. Right now, we need you up here. How soon can you come?"

"I can't come."

"Why not?" Lafe demanded sharply. "We need you. It's imperative you come up and help us in the debate tomorrow."

"I'm not well," he whispered, his voice almost fading completely, "and, anyway, I don't see why I should do anything—"

"You're a member of the delegation, if nothing else; that's why," Lafe said in the same sharp tone. "And the United States needs you."

"But I—am—not—well."

"Is that the only reason?"

"I don't see why I should do anything any more," he muttered stubbornly. "Anyway, I'm sick."

"Are you listening, Cullee?"

"I'm listening."

"Let me tell you about the acting chief United States delegate to the United Nations," Lafe said with a savage bitterness that instantly silenced the Congressman and broke through the sick haze so that he was abruptly alert and listening intently, "and then see how you feel about it."

The bright, perceptive face of the master of ceremonies appeared once more dead-center on the little screen. Behind him his guests could be seen chatting away, still furnishing background as the program came to an end. They were people of indubitable distinction, a peace-loving nuclear physicist from a great university, an aging young playwright, an earnest lady literary critic whose flaring nostrils and hectic manner indicated more than one little problem behind all that erudition, and LeGage Shelby. It had been a lively evening, distinguished more by the zeal with which the participants had vied in condemning their own country than by the constructive suggestions they seemed able to offer to correct its shortcomings. Now, like all good things, it was coming to an end.

"Talk—Just Good Talk—is the purpose of TALK," the master of ceremonies said smoothly. "Thank you so much for letting *us* talk to *You*."

"That was fascinating," the President said, snapping off the machine. "Don't you agree?"

"Why were you looking at it?" Orrin Knox inquired. "Nothing better to do in this peaceful world tonight?"

The President smiled.

"I like to find out from time to time what a certain segment of the better brains are thinking. It breaks the monotony, somehow. It also restores my faith. In myself. . . . I thought I'd give a little study to the reaction to the developments at the UN. How was your visit with Cullee?"

"All right. He's pretty badly banged up, but he thinks he can make it tomorrow. He's going to take the train up tonight, as a matter of fact."

"He doesn't want to quit the whole business now?"

"No, on the contrary. He seems very determined to get up there, which pleases me. He'll be a real help, I think."

"It would be disastrous if he weren't there," the President said. "No indication as to who was responsible?"

"He's sure it was LeGage. There's an element in DEFY that can be called on for that sort of thing, and he seems to think that was it."

"I must say LeGage looked and sounded very tense on the program just now. Though he was, if anything, milder than his white countrymen in attacking their mutual country."

"What's the general pattern been so far tonight. Mostly critical?"

"Yes," the President said. He frowned and his voice became more serious. "But that's to be expected; it doesn't worry me. The thing that does is that we seem to be getting quite a violent reaction from the country on Cullee's resolution and on our decision to try to accommodate the UN instead of opposing it. Seab's death seems to have produced a flood of wires from all over the country, not just the South." He sighed. "I do wish he hadn't felt he had to do what he did. Or I wish we could have stopped him. Or something."

"I know," Orrin said soberly. "I know . . . My God," he said in a tone of sudden anguished protest, "I didn't want to kill Seab! I valued him as I have few friends in all my life. But he just wouldn't listen. He just wouldn't get out of the way. He could have compromised with Cullee so easily, and it all could have been worked out."

"It wasn't his way. And you didn't kill him, so don't brood about that. Maybe I did, or Bob, or fate or history or the times we live in. Or maybe he killed himself, with his stubborn old heart that wouldn't yield an inch on what it believed in. I don't think any one thing was responsible. It rarely is, in this world . . . Although, of course," he added with an expression of sober distaste, "that little monster Van Ackerman helped it along."

"I wish we could get him," Orrin said simply. The President nodded.

"He runs next year, I believe. I'm going to give some attention to it, out there in Wyoming."

"Good," the Secretary said. "I'll help . . . Mr. President"—and a troubled urgency came into his voice—"Harley—have I become a trimmer, in this job? Have I stopped being Orrin Knox? Should I have advocated saying to hell with the UN and given you my advice in that direction instead of the opposite? I don't know," he said, staring bleakly out across the dark Ellipse to the Washington Monument rising pure and untroubled against the night. "Maybe I have changed. Maybe I've let the world's problems make me too weak. Maybe I ought to quit."

"Maybe you ought to stop dramatizing yourself," the President suggested comfortably. "That might be the best thing you could do for yourself. I am very well satisfied, and I think the country is too, on the whole. You didn't exactly start with no enemies at all, you know, but I don't think they've increased too much. Except, as I say, there is this reaction right now. But, even there, I expect I would have done the same thing, even without your advice."

"Would you?" the Secretary asked in an unconvinced tone. "I wonder."

"Oh, yes," the President said. He gave a mischievous little smile. "You don't really doubt that I'm President, do you?"

"No," Orrin said with a somewhat rueful answering smile. "Not at all. But I still—wonder about myself. On the other hand, there are so *damned* many problems that won't admit of an easy solution." He sighed. "But I still don't know."

"What's the matter? Something's under all this Hamlet-like melancholy tonight. Has something gone wrong up there at the UN?"

The Secretary frowned.

"Nobody knows. Hal called a little while ago and said there are all sorts of rumors going around indicating we might conceivably not win that vote. Yet it takes two-thirds and I'm sure we've got enough to beat it. Even if we lost by a majority, it still wouldn't be any two-thirds. So we've got it licked. And still—"

"That may be just pre-vote nerves," the President said, "but I tell you one thing. If we lose that vote after all we've done here, after humbling ourselves as we have and placing trust in the good faith of the Assembly, after losing Seab and Cullee getting beaten up, and all the bitterness and strain we've undergone about it, the reaction we're seeing now isn't going to be anything to the reaction we'll see then. I wouldn't be at all surprised but what there'd be a nationwide revulsion and a real demand to get out of the UN. Also to fire the man who advocated co-operating with it on this issue. So you see, many things ride on that vote." He looked thoughtfully at the papers on his desk. "Not that I *would* fire him, of course; you have my word on that. Or that I would take us out of the UN. But it would be a rocky passage for a while."

"Do we ever have any other kind?" Orrin Knox asked.

"How is Hal?"

"On the job."

"Is he all right?"

"He's quite ill, I think. But he insists on staying, and I think we must allow him that. He gave me his word to withdraw if he found he couldn't take it, but he seems to regard this debate as the summation of his career, somehow—"

"If not his life," the President suggested softly. The Secretary nodded.

"If not his life. So I think we should let him do it."

"I agree. I just wanted to know. Are you going to the memorial service for Seab tomorrow in the Senate?"

"Oh, yes. I think we both should, as a matter of fact. Don't you?"

"I do. I think it was a little irregular of Bob to set it after adjournment, but I know the Senate wouldn't have wanted it otherwise."

"No, it had to be done right away. No one ever deserved it more."

"Yes," the President said. He stood and stretched. "Thank you for coming by. I think I'll turn in. Brazil gets here at 11 A.M., you know. You'd better come here and ride out to Andrews Air Force Base with me to meet him."

"Surely."

"And now go home and stop worrying. We've all done what we thought we had to, and I think we've all done it honorably, and now all we can do is await the event. Isn't that right?"

"I guess so," the Secretary said, still not sounding entirely convinced. He turned back at the door to look searchingly at the comfortably portly man who watched him with a kindly thoughtfulness from behind the Presidential desk. "If you ever want my resignation . . . you know you only have to ask."

"What did Cullee say?" the President inquired. "Did he blame you?"

"No. As a matter of fact, he was very kind to me and didn't blame me at all. I was quite touched."

"All right, then. There's another judgment to add to mine. Now will you stop worrying?"

"Well—" The President waved him away.

"Go on home, will you? Just go on home and tell Beth your troubles. Don't bother me!"

"I may do just that," the Secretary said gratefully. "I just may."

After the door had closed behind him, the President sat down again at his cluttered desk in the upstairs study where so many fateful things had happened over the years in the long, haunted history of the White House and looked quizzically at the books and papers piled upon it. Downstairs, over in the West Wing where he had his principal public office, he had a desk that was neatly kept and looked reasonably efficient in the periodic pictures of it that press and television gave the public. That, however, was something of a Presidential conceit. In the upstairs study, a man could relax and let the image go hang when he wanted to. His own real working desk was overflowing with odds and ends whose mysterious inner order was known to him and him alone.

Not, of course, that Lucille hadn't tried to invade it and impose her own concept of order upon it the minute they moved into the White House, and this despite the fact that he thought he had long ago fought out at home the battle of the neat desk. "It's just like it's always been," he had protested vehemently when she had started straightening and putting away. "I know," she said, "but this is the White House. You weren't President, then." "I was *me*," he said, and after a while, when he had gone back to the original confusion several times, she had given up. By then she had taken her cue from him and adjusted to their new quarters as comfortably as he had. In fact, she had finally confessed that she had been silly to be so impressed at first. "You have to run the Presidency," she said sagely. "You can't afford to let it run you." "That's great philosophy," he agreed, "as long as you're not the President. Try it sometime."

But at least in his desk, and in the house, and in his private and to a considerable degree his public life, he had succeeded fairly well, with her assistance. She was a wonderful wife to him, in all her roly-poly pink fluffiness that roused the easy satire of the ladies of the press. Underneath the exterior that fooled so many people there resided one of the shrewdest political minds he knew. At the same time, it wasn't an anxious political mind, like so many in this ambition-ridden town. She would have been quite content to be at his side if he had remained a furniture manufacturer in Grand Rapids instead of entering upon the strange set of curious chances that had raised him, in a period of his party's desperation, to be, first, Governor of Michigan, and then Vice President to his brilliant and dominating predecessor. She had given him a loving heart, a peaceful and comfortable home, two daughters, both now happily married in the Midwest, and the constant strength of her devoted loyalty and encouraging presence. There wasn't much more a man could want, as he faced the problems into which fate and destiny had hurtled him.

Both he and Orrin, he reflected, were very lucky men to be so blessed in their wives. Beth Knox was the same type, loving, loyal, devoted, with a shrewd mind of her own that complemented and rounded out her husband's even as she rounded out his life. There must be something about a lot of wives in these newer generations, he thought; not too many of them, at least in this town, seemed to possess the secret of wifehood that had been given to such as Lucille, Beth, Dolly Munson, and some few others he could think of. Not too many nowadays were helpmates in the old sense. Cullee Hamilton's marriage was unhappy now, he knew; Lafe Smith's had never really gotten launched before it ended; the Labaiyas' could hardly be called ideal; and so it went. Many an uneasy relationship existed in the beautiful city that demanded of its more glamorous residents a clear eye, a steady hand, and a sure foot if they were to keep an even balance in the midst of all its temptations of power, and fend off the busy little claws of position and jealousy and ambition that could in time tear down all but the most solid citadels.

When it came to wives, he thought with a gentle little smile at his own fancy, the older models seemed to be the best models. With the newer ones, something too often seemed to go wrong with the automatic transmission. With the older ones you could feel comfortable doing what he was now about to do, as he lifted the receiver of his private telephone and dialed a number in Spring Valley. He could see the book-lined study where the phone was ringing, the desk, cluttered like his own, where both the man and the lady of the house worked together on speeches and legislation and all the other matters that now concerned them. It was a homey room, and he had a warm feeling about it, increased when he heard the gravely pleasant voice of its proprietress say hello.

"Beth," he said, "I've just sent home a worried man to you. I think you should repair his morale with your kindly ministrations."

She chuckled.

"I always do, Mr. President. What makes this so special?"

"A lot of things, I think. Seab's death. What happened to Cullee. Uncertainties about our course in this present matter. Things that are happening in the world—the lot. It's not so easy being Secretary of State in times like these."

"Or President, either. I think you both manage very well."

"Thank you. I try, as he does. It isn't always very clear what the course is, but—we go ahead. Largely, I suspect," he added humorously, "because there isn't anywhere else to go. But, seriously—he does seem quite disturbed tonight. Unusually so, for Orrin. I've told him not to worry, and I want you to know that he has no cause for it from me. I'm thoroughly satisfied with the job he's doing."

"I'm sure you are, and we both appreciate it. I know he has been very worried about this whole situation. A good deal of what he's felt he must do has gone against his basic feelings about it—he would have been much more impatient and much more critical if he were still in the Senate, of course. But he is really trying hard to adapt himself to this new position, understand its demands and necessities, and view the world from the different perspective that it requires. It isn't always easy." She gave a rueful little laugh. "Foggy Bottom isn't the Hill."

"No more is the White House. It's amazing the difference a mile of Pennsylvania Avenue can make. Well: I just wanted you to know that he really does have my complete confidence and support. I also wanted to give you my love and thank you for helping him. That helps me, too. And it helps the country, of course. We're all in your debt."

"You're very kind, Harley. You're one of this world's really good people, I think. I feel very fortunate that we have you there, right now."

"Thank you, my dear, I value that. One other thing, that I forgot to ask him when he was here. Have you heard him say where Hal Fry is?"

"I believe he's in Harkness Pavilion tonight. I'm dreadfully worried about that."

"So am I. We don't know quite what it is, but evidently it's something pretty final. Such a tragedy, on top of the others he's had. I just wanted to call him and tell him we're with him."

"Again, you're very kind."

"It's a small gift, to stay the world."

"It may be all we have," she said.

"Yes," the President agreed thoughtfully. "Yes."

"Give Hal my love too, will you?"

"I will. And, as I say—boost your old boy's morale for me."

"I will, Mr. President. Thank you so much for calling. My love to Lucille."

"Thank you."

That was one good wife, and waiting down the hall, probably reading quietly, was another, ready to hear whatever he wished to tell her about the problems of the day.

There really wasn't a great deal, except that they never decreased, only increased, and that each time one diminished another surged into urgency to take its place. It was a never-ending flood, and there really wasn't much to say. Here he was—and there they came—and that about summed it up. There was no getting out of the way, no finding someone else upon whom to shove off final decisions, because there wasn't anyone else. He was It, and in the crucible of Geneva so soon upon his taking office he had realized that by some fortunate fluke of fate and character he was going to be able to carry the burden without either maudlin self-pity or self-blinding egotism. He just kept going along, doing the best he knew how, meeting each new challenge as it arose, refusing to be stampeded into fear or persuaded into overconfidence, and somehow one day followed another and the world was still here, and maybe, in a few little areas, somewhat more hopeful than it had been the day before. That was about all one could expect in this age, he had decided, and he was content that he possessed the character and the ability to lead the country forward in this slow, inch-by-inch progress toward some hoped-for era of stability and peace that remained very far off but might yet be attained if the decent element in mankind could but be given sufficient time, patience, and devoted determination.

It was in that spirit that he had accepted Orrin's ideas, which substantially paralleled his own once he understood the full nature of Terrible Terry's visit and its ramifications, concerning how best to meet the situation in the United Nations. It had been asking much of the country and the Congress to accept what many Americans regarded as a deliberate self-humiliation in the face of an unprincipled international demand. But they had been willing to follow him and the Secretary because they had confidence in their honor and good intentions.

Now the Secretary was much disturbed, and so apparently were their representatives at the UN, because of some last-minute rumors that the voluntary act of the Administration, carried out in good faith and with good intentions, might not be regarded as sufficient. He could not believe that the judgments of the Assembly could be so shallow; nor could he believe, if it came right down to a matter of basic influence, that the United States could be overridden on an issue that would require a two-thirds majority to do what the enemies of the United States wished to do. He was satisfied that his Administration had done and was doing everything necessary both to meet the honest demand and to thwart the punitive harassment. So he did not feel, on this night before the final debate, that any of them should feel upset or uncertain about it.

Particularly must Hal not feel so, burdened as he was by personal harassments far more dreadful than any of the rest of them had to bear. The President could only imagine the dark passage through which the senior Senator from West Virginia must be moving now, its terrors made even more terrible by the fact that he had gone through similar passages before.

Except, of course, that none could be quite so terrible as the certainty of one's own death, conferred by a fate that must seem capricious and evil and unfair beyond all rationalization.

It was for this reason, far more than any worry that he might have that Hal would fail him in the debate, that he wanted to talk to him now. Yet it must be in exactly the right tone, neither overly pitying nor overly business-like, or it would defeat its own purpose. He thought for a while, staring thoughtfully out upon the shining obelisk of the Washington Monument, before he picked up the phone again and put through his call.

The last brisk nurse had popped in with orange juice, the last bright intern had painstakingly made him recite his medical history all over again, silence had fallen at last upon the great hospital—and there had descended upon him at once the most completely devastating feeling of depression he had ever known. Now the busy pursuits of his day at the United Nations were far away. Now he must face his situation without devised and deter-mined distraction, without thought-muffling activity, without anyone or any-thing to help him. Nothing he had experienced up to this moment could compare with the wave of desolation that swept over him now.

Out of his despair he cried out to a God who had apparently forsaken him, in stumbling words and half-formed phrases that made little sense save agony as he whispered them into the darkened room. In some pain-wracked harking-back that he could not explain and whose impulse and origin he could not remember, he kept saying over and over again, like a little boy, "Why are You mad at me? Why are You mad at me?" Somewhere he had heard the question before, somewhere far away, but where or when he could not say; nor could he understand why God did not give answer to so anguished and sincere an inquiry.

So passed time, how much he did not know, as the long night deepened and with it his awful loneliness. There came the moment eventually when the last defense, a great bitter rage, welled up and he told God that he no longer believed in Him, that He did not exist, that He was a mockery, that no Deity Who could visit upon a man so many pointless agonies could possibly make claim to further faith or respect. And after that, in due course, out of the shattering silence of the universe that followed this anguished repudiation, there came the slow, steady, inevitable restoration of faith; the benison of a great humility; the knowledge, implanted in him in childhood and never far from his thoughts in all his troubles, that God was with him always and that no rejection, however bitter, however violent, however ter-rible, could remove His loving presence or drive It from the world.

And with this, finally, there came the beginnings of peace; the tentative, struggling, but ever-stronger return of serenity; the gradual regrowth of certitude and hope; the acceptance that passeth understanding, out of the love that passeth understanding. Gradually he stopped raging, stopped crying, stopped worrying, stopped forever being torn apart by alternatives and might-have-beens. For reasons he could not understand, for purposes not of his making, he had been given a path to follow in his closing days on earth: So be it. Thus had the Lord directed him, and thus would he do. Never again in the time remaining would he be a victim to doubt and despair. God was not mad at him, and though he did not understand God's reasons, he would believe in them and go forward in the calm certainty that, in some way he perhaps would never understand, they made sense and would give him strength to do for his country whatever tasks still lay ahead.

It was thus with a growing serenity and peace that he heard the phone ring and, lifting the receiver, heard a quiet voice saying, "Hal, this is Harley. How are you feeling?"

"I'm feeling fine," he said, and there was in his words a vigor and a joy that thrilled and startled them both; and the President responded to it with a joy of his own.

"I am so happy to hear it, and I can tell in your voice that you mean it."

"I do, Harley," he said eagerly, "I do. I've been lying here thinking—and praying—and somehow, suddenly, it's all begun to make sense. I didn't think I'd make it, a little while ago, but—but now I do. I don't know why, exactly, unless it's God helping me, but—I just do. So you needn't worry about me, any more."

"Well, I think that's wonderful," the President said. "Wonderful for you, and wonderful for all of us."

"Harley," he asked, still eagerly, and still almost like a little child, a happy child now, wanting to share with someone what had happened to him, "do you ever have experiences like that, in what you're doing? I mean, when it seems as though there's no way out, and you feel an awful despair and start thinking there isn't any God, and then—all of a sudden, when you've finally told Him to go to hell and you're all through with Him—you suddenly realize He's still there, that He's been there all the time, watching over you just the same as always?"

"Yes, I do," the President said after a moment, when he found he could speak again. "You don't know how often it happens in this office."

"It's a wonderful thing, isn't it?"

"It's a wonderful thing. And it's wonderful to hear you so happy in it. I wanted you to know, also, that you have all our love, down here. We're all of us thinking of you and wishing you well. We know you will do well tomorrow; we have no doubts."

"Thank you so much, Harley. You don't know how much that means to me."

"You have our love," the President repeated. "Sleep well."

"I will," he said. "Oh, now I will. Good night, Harley, and God bless you."

"You, too."

"He has," Hal Fry told him with an unshakable conviction. "In my friends—in my country—in His love. I'm all right, Harley. Don't worry about me any more."

"I couldn't," the President said. "Not any more. Good night, old friend. May you have a good journey and come safe to harbor."

"I will," he said with an eager confidence. "I will."

He lay completely still for perhaps five minutes after their conversation ended. An utter calm, an utter peace flooded into his heart and took gentle dominion of his mind. His exhausted body relaxed. He slept, as deeply and sweetly as a child.

3

On the elevated dais above the green marble podium, the Secretary-General sat all alone in the third of the three seats there, staring out upon the gleaming Assembly Hall as it slowly filled for the resumption of debate on the Labaiya proposals. The President of the Assembly, involved since yesterday in a futile argument with Guiana about its invasion of Surinam, had not yet appeared, and indeed the S.-G. wondered whether he would be able to, so heated and unproductive have the conversations been, so long drawn out and tiring. Last night's emergency session of the Security Council had merely put the final seal on it. The Netherlands' attempt to have Guiana condemned for aggression had been vetoed by the Soviet Union, though the United States in the person of Senator Smith had argued for it, repeating the same arguments his country had used on several such occasions in recent years. This had not won the United States any friends, of course; it was just one of those gestures toward principle that the Americans, aided by the British and French persisted in making from time to time. He supposed it would perhaps add one or two more votes that had previously been doubtful when the Assembly voted later today. The votes would not, he thought sadly, be added on the American side of the ledger.

For himself, the S.-G. had reached the point where he refused to be emotionally concerned any longer about the visit of Terence Ajkaje, the Labaiya Amendment, the outlook for the United States, or anything else involved in the issue. He had spent many long and fruitless hours trying to persuade some of his more hotheaded compatriots from Africa to take a more moderate stand, only to receive blank stares, insolent answers, and, finally, bitter accusations. Similarly, his attempts to warn the United States, such as the hint he had offered yesterday in the Lounge to Senator Smith, had apparently been ignored, if they had even been understood. Evidently America in this matter was as self-confidently blind as her opponents were determinedly antagonistic. He had been in the middle of it long enough, and he was having no more.

Even so, he could not escape a feeling of regret at the way things were apparently going to develop. Many of his deepest instincts, many of his most deeply held beliefs and emotional attitudes, the mental equipment he had brought from Nigeria to his famous office had, like those of Orrin Knox in another context, been modified and changed and drastically revised by the realities of world events. Two years ago he, too, might have joined in the dangerous yet delightful game of Smack America; he, too, might have joined in pouring scorn and sarcasm upon any nation so naïve as to argue that the Charter's machinery to halt aggression should be applied equally to all. Now he knew that Smack America was a child's game when placed alongside the earnest efforts of that strangely confused yet worthy nation to set its racial house in order. And he knew that the Charter had already been flouted so many times by aggression tacitly approved by the Assembly and the Security Council that now it was only the flimsiest protection to anyone.

It was no wonder, therefore, he thought as he watched the Africans in their colorful robes, the Indians and Arabs in their flowing gowns, and all the rest come in chatting and bowing and waving in the steadily growing noise and tension, that he should feel a sad disgust with so many of his fellows of the colored races.

They were great ones, he thought, for twisting the Charter out of shape to suit their own race-sick purposes. The day would come when they would pay for it, and dearly.

But this was obviously not to be that day, if all the things he heard in his aerie on the thirty-eighth floor were correct. No good could come from what was contemplated here, for the colored races, for the UN, or for the world. The gravest consequences might flow from it for them all if it went forward as planned.

Despite his determination to have none of it, and despite his woeful and startling explosion to Cullee Hamilton, he could not, as he contemplated these consequences, refrain from turning over in his mind the possible ways in which he could intervene to point them out. He perhaps could state them more directly than anyone else would wish to do, unless the Americans might feel themselves really hard pressed and so finally abandon niceties. His intervention would help to keep them from feeling that way and would also help to ward off the disastrous results he could see if they became sufficiently disillusioned.

He doubted, however, whether he should volunteer a statement. Perhaps if Tashikov should attack him, which was quite possible—the Soviet Ambassador often did it on the slightest of pretexts, apparently just to keep his hand in—then possibly he could take the floor in reply. Or perhaps he could arrange with someone else to give him an opening. To do so would bring him sharp criticism from many delegations, but he did not care. This was one of the times when they were playing with the future of the UN itself. He might not have much influence, but he intended to use what he had in the service of the organization, whether the organization liked it or not.

Anyway, he told himself with an ironic humor, one couldn't have the sort of thing that was being readied here by Felix Labaiya and his friends just at this time, right on the eve of the annual reception and dance that he and the President of the Assembly gave together each year. The annual United Nations Ball was scheduled for next Monday night, and to the planning for it he had been devoting most of his time in the past few days.

He knew that this had been in part a deliberate attempt to find in all the details of catering and arrangement an antidote for thought about the issue now nearing decision in the Assembly; but also there was another motive.

There was something quite touching about this annual occasion when the nations danced together, and it deserved the best of attention and the best of moods to do it honor. It was always a glittering and pleasant affair—and something more. It was one of those poignant moments that occur once in a while on the East River when men tell one another, "*This* is the way it *ought* to be," and manage to persuade themselves for a few brief swings of the Netherlands' pendulum that it is not entirely beyond the realm of possibility that it may yet, someday, still be.

This fleeting, precious moment means rather more, in the United Nations, that it might if set in the humdrum context of the everyday. In Turtle Bay, where the frequent meanness of the performance must be matched daily against the greatness of the hope, it is somewhat more significant, in its wistfully sentimental way, than it would be elsewhere. It was suddenly very important to the Secretary-General that the annual Ball be held once again in the spirit of kindness and courtesy and optimism which each year transformed the unhappy divisions of the United Nations and for a few hours seemed to place genuine harmony within the grasp of those who danced the night away across the gleaming expanses of the Main Concourse.

But now it was time to put aside such thoughts for the time being, for the rotund little President from the Netherlands, tired but determined, had appeared to take his seat at the Secretary-General's side, the galleries were full to overflowing, and in the great recurring semicircles of fluorescent-lighted desks that mounted from the well of the hall to the back of the room, all seats were filled with the gossiping, chattering, excited sons of man. Tension was beginning to grip the Assembly, and into it the President rapped his gavel several times with a nervous, commanding air.

"The plenary session of the General Assembly is now in session," he announced at 3:17 P.M. "The subject matter of today's session is the amendment offered by the delegate of Panama to his resolution calling for immediate independence for Gorotoland. Delegates will remember that debate on this amendment was put forward a week on Friday last at the request of the delegation of the United States.

"In order to refresh delegates' memories on the subject matter of this amendment, I shall ask the Secretary-General to please read it to the Assembly."

The S.-G., straight-backed and erect, his silver hair and classic black features weathered by his years of age and dignity, began to read in his softly slurred British accent the words of Felix Labaiya:

"Whereas, the distinguished representative of Gorotoland, acting in the greatest traditions of human freedom and decency, has been savagely attacked in a city of the United States of America; and,

"Whereas, this attack grew directly from policies of racial discrimination in the United States of America, which decent men everywhere deplore and condemn; and,

"Whereas, the continued existence of these policies in the United States tends to place the United States in direct violation of the principles of the Charter of the United Nations, and therefore casts grave doubts upon the qualifications of the United States to continue as a member of this body;

"Now, therefore, this resolution is hereby amended to direct the Security Council, acting on behalf of the United Nations, to make an immediate investigation of racial practices in the United States, looking toward the end of such racial practices, and offering the full assistance of the United Nations in this task so that the United States may truly conform to the principles of the Charter and be fully worthy of membership in this great body."

"The Chair," the President said, "finds that the precedents as to how we proceed at this point are somewhat hazy, since we have already had a debate and several votes concerning this proposal. However, since the votes did not occur on the substance of the amendment, the Chair will rule that debate will be resumed as though *ab initio*, providing that is agreeable to the Assembly." He paused, there were no interruptions, and he went on. "The first speaker on today's list is the mover of the amendment and resolution, the distinguished delegate of Panama."

"I say," the London *Daily Express* whispered, "isn't that Hal Fry coming in over there?"

"So it is," the New York *Times* agreed.

"Reports of his death were apparently somewhat exaggerated," the *Christian Science Monitor* remarked.

"He looks all right to me," said the London *Observer*. "Maybe it was all just psychological warfare by the State Department to throw everybody off."

"No," the Chicago *Tribune* said. "I know he was in the hospital. But I must say he looks reasonably chipper now."

And so he did, as he came in with Lafe Smith and two U.S. delegation secretaries, just as the President called upon Felix, and took his seat with a matter-of-fact air alongside the British Ambassador. His vision was blurring a little; there were occasional sharp cramps through his back, chest, and stomach; he was, if truth were known, more than a little dizzy; but otherwise, at the moment, he was feeling pretty well. Above all, he was feeling well in his heart and mind, and that was the important thing. He had three different kinds of capsules in his pocket, but he was determined not to use them—he was confident he would not have to. He greeted Lord Maudulayne with a smile so natural that once more the British Ambassador dismissed the rumors he had heard so often the past several days in the Lounge.

"Good morning," he said, shaking hands. "You look as though everything were all right."

"Everything is all right," Senator Fry said. "Except," he smiled and nodded toward the podium, "Felix, up there. He's definitely all wrong."

"Lafe," Lord Maudulayne said, leaning forward and speaking across Hal, "I thought that was a stout defense of principle you made in Security Council last night. Very fine."

"Fat lot of good it did," Lafe said in a disgusted tone. "Thank you, though. I get so damned fed up with the hypocrisy here sometimes that it's all I can do to avoid throwing up."

"You would have been proud of him," Lord Maudulayne said, sitting back, and Hal nodded.

"I know. It may not accomplish much, but it seems to me that we, and you, and the rest of us who feel the same way, have got to do it each time, just for the record. Somebody may be around to read it, if the whole thing collapses. Maybe it will furnish some pointers someday, for the next time."

"I can just see them," the British Ambassador said dryly, "scratching themselves and puzzling over one of our transcripts by the light of a tallow flare in some cave somewhere in the desolate ruins of what used to be Manhattan . . . But you're right; it has to be done. Do you plan to get into this debate?"

"I think we'll have to," Hal Fry said. "It depends on what our friend has to say. It doesn't sound very friendly so far."

Nor did it, as the Ambassador of Panama, small and dark and trim and neat, completely self-contained as always, spoke earnestly to the now-quiet Assembly.

"Mr. President," he was pointing out as their attention returned to the podium, "much will no doubt be made here by distinguished representatives of the United States of the fact that in the past week the Congress has indeed passed the resolution of the Congressman from California.

"It is true that the resolution offers Gorotoland $10,000,000, which is a figure the United Nations cannot match.

"It is true that it offers a vague apology to the M'Bulu for indignities suffered by him in the state of South Carolina.

"It is true that it offers a vague pledge to give further study to improving the conditions of the Negro race within the United States.

"The truest thing about it, Mr. President," he said with a small, tight smile, "is that it is vague."

There was a ripple of laughter and a scattering of applause here and there across the crowded chamber.

"Now, Mr. President, what was the margin by which the Congress passed this noble resolution, which will presently be offered here as an excuse to us not to pass my amendment? Was it an overwhelming vote, Mr. President? Why, certainly not. It was a margin of five votes in the United States House of Representatives. It was a margin of six votes in the United States Senate. There would seem to have been, Mr. President, some slight reluctance on the part of the Congress."

Again there came the ripple of laughter, more scornful now.

"And what was said about the resolution, and what was said about us here in the United Nations? My distinguished colleagues, let me read to you. I have here three interesting quotes. One is from the chairman of the House Foreign Affairs Committee"—there were a few boos—"another is from a most sadly lamented statesman, the late Senator Cooley of South Carolina"—more boos, some laughter, some applause—"and the last is from the Majority Leader of the United States Senate"—ironic laughter, more boos. "The chairman of the House Foreign Affairs Committee had this to say about us—"

And he was off into Jawbone Swarthman's more impolite and derogatory comments.

Poised alertly beside the Indian Ambassador, who had kindly invited him to occupy a seat on the floor with his delegation, Terrible Terry could hardly keep to himself the excited elation that filled his being. Now it was coming at last, the independence for Gorotoland for which he had worked so long and hard—he had no doubt of it. And coming at last, if the plans he and Felix and the rest had been formulating so carefully over the past week came successfully to fruition, was the proper judgment of history upon the arrogant and unthinking Americans who had permitted an inexcusable racial situation to exist long past the terminal point of history's patience.

Child in pretty clothes wandering about the world tossing hand grenades into open windows he might be, in Lord Maudulayne's casual and cutting description, but Terence Ajkaje was something more; a complex human being, as so many are complex, fitting one description this moment and another description the next, depending upon time and circumstance and the matters that engaged his attention. Capable of the most ruthless cruelty, the most carefree vindictiveness, the most irresponsible misuse of history's forces, he was also capable of the most genuine and burning indignation at certain abuses in the world. He could suppress his own fellow blacks in Gorotoland with a harshness rarely matched in the United States of America, but when it came to the situation in that great land, he felt a passionate anger whose inconsistency never occurred to him at all.

Perhaps in some strangely twisted fashion this was a tribute to America, which was not supposed to allow the sort of thing he himself officially condoned every day of his life in his own country. Perhaps like so many in the UN who practice the most vicious racial discrimination at home while denouncing it with an hysterical exasperation where it occurs in the United States, he felt in some odd subconscious way that somebody had to furnish an example and that America, by falling short of perfection, fell short of her duty as humanity's conscience in these matters. He could not have analyzed it as he sat there, towering and glowering and concentrating with all the force of his great intelligence upon the speech of the Ambassador of Panama. Now nothing filled his mind but this, not even the situation in Molobangwe. Having reached his decision to remain, he had dismissed it. Now all his being was given passionately to the issue at hand, with the fierce single-ness of purpose that had brought him steadily upward along his dangerous course since the long-ago days when *Time* magazine had noted the presence of "A Little Fresh Heir" in his dilapidated and dusty land.

Sensing his concentration—for the M'Bulu was one of those people whose thinking is sometimes louder than others' conversation—K.K. was moved to jog his elbow and say airily, "My goodness gracious me, what a thunder-cloud you are this afternoon, Terry! Is this any way to act upon the eve of your country's independence, I ask you!"

"I was just thinking," Terry said with his sudden gleaming smile, "how dismayed our friends of the United States will be when they learn that deci-sions here will not be confined to that alone. What do you think they will do?"

The Indian Ambassador shrugged with a pitying smile.

"Oh, who knows? Protest. Exclaim. Attempt to secure postponements and adjournments and other diversionary things. But it will simply prove what I have told Hal and Lafe right along: you cannot deny the current of history. It will not matter, essentially, what they do. They will be helpless."

"Will they?" Terry asked, his eyes narrowing as he studied the American delegation, far across the room. "I wonder."

"Have faith!" K.K. chided him merrily. "Have faith, dear friend! Listen! Felix is preparing the way well. Everyone will be taken by surprise."

"Hardly everyone," the M'Bulu said.

Whatever the truth of this, the Ambassador of Panama *was* preparing the way well as he talked along, purposely keeping his indignation down, his sarcasm muted, his recital of the reasons for approving his amendment cogent and reasonable according to his point of view and that of many in the Assembly.

Again he stressed, more in sorrow than in anger, the theme that he was acting in the best interests of the United States, that he was a friend to America, that all her friends here in the United Nations simply wanted to help her achieve that condition of full maturity and civilization that would only come when her Negro citizens were accorded their full equality. In one sense, he said—this sense which was so important to the peoples of the earth, so many of whom had only recently come to nationhood under the aegis of the world organization—the United States itself could be called an "underdeveloped country" (the phrase, so beloved of the American State Department, brought a burst of laughter from many delegations)—under-developed in her treatment of the Negro, underdeveloped in her concepts of human dignity, underdeveloped in her inability, so far, despite more than a century of freedom for the slaves, to grant to all of their descendants the real freedom that could only come with absolute equality in all phases of her society and national life. This was what he and other genuine friends of America wanted, he said earnestly; this was all.

"But, Mr. President," he said, and now he told himself with a mounting inner tension that he must be most gentle and dulcet, "it must be confessed that the United States to some extent seems reluctant to bring this about, and that is why my delegation and I and some others here in the Assembly have felt it necessary to propose the action outlined in my amendment. Just as many other states have been encouraged by decisions of the Assembly to do what is right and honorable in the eyes of history, so it is our hope that the United States may be similarly persuaded—not by our condemnation, Mr. President, which is really not intended in my amendment—"

"Bro-*ther!*" said the New York *Daily News.* "He means it," the London *Daily Express* said indignantly. "Can't you see that?"

"—but with our help, offered sincerely and in a friendly spirit by this body that represents the combined conscience of the world."

He paused and took a sip of water. Before him the nations sat silent and attentive, and in the galleries the audience, as multicolored and variegated as the delegations themselves, leaned forward intently.

"Mr. President," he said abruptly, and something in his tone made the Press Gallery, the United States delegation, and many another sit up, suddenly alert, "because it has become apparent that to continue to designate this issue as an 'important matter' within the meaning of Rule 85 of the General Assembly would hamper it by the requirement of a two-thirds vote for passage, I now exercise my right as its author to withdraw the amendment from the resolution on Gorotoland—I reintroduce it herewith as a separate resolution—and I move that it be declared by the Assembly to be *not* an important matter and therefore requiring only a simple majority for passage."

At once the great chamber exploded, its patterns of color and costume breaking and falling apart into a moving, shifting mass of agitated people, many delegates leaving their seats to confer with one another in little groups in the aisle, many reporters hurrying from the Press Gallery to file stories, visitors in the public galleries exclaiming and turning to one another, voices raised in conjecture, counterconjecture, elation, approval, disapproval, wonderment, or dismay all across the big concave bowl. Into the hubbub the little red-cheeked President of the Assembly banged his gavel furiously for order, growing redder and more indignant as he pounded. Over and above the noise of the rest there could be heard the sound of someone in the United States delegation shouting "Point of order!" and presently it became clear that the cry came from Senator Fry. In five minutes or so, having finally secured some semblance of gradually returning decorum, the President gave him recognition and he proceeded with reasonable speed down the aisle and up to the podium.

"Mr. President," he said, feeling excited and tense, feeling the dizziness and pain, but telling himself impatiently, The hell with it, there isn't time to worry about that now, "I make the point of order that there is nothing in the rules to permit the distinguished delegate of Panama to take this action. Therefore it is out of order and his amendment must stand as an integral part of his original resolution on Gorotoland, which obviously *is* an important matter and *does* require two-thirds.

"I make the point of order that he is out of order in trying to do something he cannot do, under the rules."

There was again an explosion of sound, and the Soviet Ambassador, pounding furiously on his desk with the flat of his hand, was also on his feet, shouting, "Point of order, Mr. President; point of order! Under Rule 82—"

"The distinguished delegate of the Soviet Union—" the President began, but Senator Fry, at a cost no one knew but himself, shouted, "Mr. *President!*" in so commanding a voice that the President's voice died abruptly.

"Mr. President," Hal Fry said sternly into the silence that fell with equal abruptness, "one point of order at a time, if you please. I demand a ruling on mine, which I have every right to make. I too, I thank my good friend from the Soviet Union, have in mind Rule 82, which specifically states, and I quote: 'A motion—a *motion*, Mr. President—may be withdrawn by its proposer at any time before voting on it has commenced, provided that the motion—the *motion*, Mr. President—has not been amended.' I request the ruling of the Chair on my point of order."

For several minutes the President, the Secretary-General, and the Deputy Secretary-General conferred, heads together, over the book of rules. A tense hush fell on the great room, yet it was not really silent; it was impossible for it to be, so many people were moving, rustling, whispering, conferring.

"The Chair," the President said finally, "finds himself in agreement with the distinguished delegate"—he paused, not for the dramatic effect it was, but because he was literally out of breath from excitement—"of the United States—" there was a great shout of "NO!" from many delegations—"that there is no provision in the rules for the action of the distinguished delegate of Panama, and therefore the Chair must rule that he is out of order."

"Mr. President," Felix said with a cold anger, "the Chair and the delegate of the United States say there is nothing in the rules to authorize my taking the action I have taken. By the same token, there is nothing in the rules to deny me the right to do so. Therefore, it is up to the Assembly to decide, Mr. President. I appeal the ruling of the Chair."

"Mr. President—" Hal Fry began, but the President rapped his gavel firmly.

"No debate is permitted on either an appeal or a point of order, I will remind the distinguished delegate of the United States." He passed the box of names to the Secretary-General, who drew one and handed it to him. "The voting will begin with Morocco. A vote of Yes will uphold the appeal and reverse the ruling. Morocco!"

"*Oui.*"

"Nepal."

"Yes."

"Netherlands."

"No."

"New Zealand."

"No."

"Nicaragua."

"*Abstención.*"

"Niger."

"*Oui.*"

"Nigeria."

"Yes."

"Norway."

"No."

"Pakistan."

"Yes."

"Panama."

"Yes," said Felix coldly.

"Paraguay."

"*Sí.*"

"Peru."

"*Sí.*"

"By jove," the Manchester *Guardian* said with an excited relish, "I think you're taking a licking. I think they're going to do it!"

"I think they are, too," agreed the New York *Times* glumly. "What price the rules?"

"Labaiya's entirely right," the London *Evening Standard* said triumphantly. "Thank God the Assembly has sense enough to back him up."

"Which God is that?" the New York *Journal-American* inquired dryly. "Obviously not ours."

"On this vote," the President said into the hush that fell fifteen minutes later, "the Yeas are 59, the Nays 56, 5 abstentions, others absent, and the appeal is upheld. The ruling of the Chair is voided."

"Mr. President!" Felix shouted from the floor, hurrying again to the rostrum, "I *move*, Mr. President, that I be permitted to withdraw my amendment and reintroduce it as a resolution."

"You have the motion," the President said. "All those in favor will say—"

"Roll call, Mr. President!" shouted Vasily Tashikov. "Roll call!"

"Roll call is requested," the President said, reaching for the box and drawing a number. "The voting will begin with Iraq."

"Yes."

"Ireland."

"No."

"Israel."

"No."

"Italy."

"No."

"Ivory Coast."

"*Oui.*"

"Jamaica."

"Yes."

"Japan."

"Yes."

"Jordan."

"Yes."

"Kenya."

"Yes."

"Laos."

"Yes."

"Lebanon."

"Oui."

"The vote on the motion," the President said twenty minutes later, "is 60 Yes, 45 No, 6 abstentions, others absent. The motion is approved."

"Mr. President," Felix said into the silence that followed, "I now introduce my resolution, incorporating in its entirety the language of my previous amendment to my resolution on immediate independence for Gorotoland."

He paused while applause and shouts of approval swept across the floor.

"Mr. President, I move that my resolution, just introduced, be—"

"Mr. President!" Hal Fry called, walking again to the rostrum, not sure whether he could make it but forcing himself to concentrate on putting one foot before the other and finding to his surprise that they were behaving very well. "Point of order, Mr. President."

"The distinguished delegate of the United States need not state it," the President said, his rosy face looking quite pouty with annoyance. "The Chair is aware of the situation. The new resolution of the delegate of Panama obviously cannot take precedence over his original resolution on Gorotoland presently pending before the Assembly. The question therefore recurs on the recommendation of immediate independence for Gorotoland."

"Requiring a two-thirds vote," Senator Fry said with a passable attempt at humor, and a ripple of laughter, not unfriendly, ran across the floor.

"Requiring a two-thirds vote," the President agreed. "I do not believe any-one disputes that."

"I didn't know about my friend from Panama," Hal said, "I thought he might."

Again there was laughter, increasingly friendly. The Assembly was relax-ing, now that the prospect of a long debate was before it and now that a majority, however narrow, had achieved its objective of approving Felix's surprise maneuver.

"Also, Mr. President," Senator Fry said, "since the new resolution of the delegate of Panama will come before us *de novo*, there will be no parlia-mentary blockage of debate such as exists on points of order and appeals from rulings. The new resolution will be open to full debate."

"That is correct."

"It will have it," Hal Fry promised, and left the rostrum amid a wave of laughter, and some encouraging applause.

"The question now occurs," the President said, "on the first resolution of the distinguished delegate of Panama, to give United Nations support to immediate independence for Gorotoland. The Chair will confess that this sudden turn of events has left the Chair in somewhat of disarray as to speakers, since it was not expected that the Assembly would reach this resolution until tomorrow. The list of speakers has therefore not been made up. Is it the desire of the delegation of the United Kingdom—?"

He paused and looked down doubtfully upon the restless throng, as over on the side a hand was raised and someone called, "Mr. President!"

"The distinguished delegate of France," he said with some relief as Raoul Barre came forward.

"Mr. President," the French Ambassador said, "obviously this development has caught many of us by surprise. The President is not alone," he added in a tone that brought laughter, "in being disorganized by it. I wonder, since the hour is approaching 6 P.M. and many of us in the natural course of events will soon be feeling the pangs of hunger, whether it would not be feasible to recess the Assembly until 8 P.M. This would provide time for dinner, time to complete the speakers' list, and time for many of us to reappraise the situation as it now exists. I so move, Mr. President."

"All those in favor," the President said. There was a great roar of approval. "All those opposed—" There was silence.

"Obviously it is approved," he said, and amid a burst of jovial talk the Assembly disintegrated into its many human components and streamed and straggled out of the hall to its many destinations for dinner.

At 6:02 the delegate of the Malagasy Republic placed the first overseas telephone call from the Lounge, to his capital of Tananarive in the far-off Indian Ocean. By the time the call was completed twenty-three minutes later, thirty-nine similar calls from other delegations were clogging the lines out of Turtle Bay.

At 6:20 the Ambassador of the United Kingdom, the Ambassador of France, and the Ambassador of Niger conferred hastily on a sofa overlooking the Japanese temple bells on the First Avenue side of the Secretariat Building and then split up to hurry busily away to other conferences.

At 6:23, the Ambassador of Panama, similarly engaged, decided to find himself a seat in the lobby off the delegates' entrance to the Lounge and let would-be conferrers come to him—there were so many of them—rather than bother to seek them out.

At 6:45, CBS-TV, NBC-TV, and ABC-TV had a joint interview with the M'Bulu, looking happy and excited and supremely confident as he stood, tall and gracious in his gorgeous robes, at the Assembly Hall entrance and told the world that nothing, now, could stop immediate independence for Gorotoland.

At 6:46 Senators Fry and Smith, at U.S. headquarters, began a four-way telephone conversation with the President and Secretary of State in Washington. At its conclusion at 7:05 the President and Secretary of State rejoined their ladies and the President and First Lady of Brazil in the Blue Room of the White House for a quiet family chat before the state dinner at 8 P.M. Senators Fry and Smith went back across First Avenue to the brightly lighted Secretariat Building, gleaming against Brooklyn in the chilly winds of night. The air was wet and raw and an occasional little flurry of snow gave promise of worse to come. Out in front, the flags of the nations, normally taken down at sunset but always flown during a night session, snapped like pistol shots in the rising wind.

At 7:10 the members of the Afro-Asian bloc emerged from a closed emergency meeting in Conference Room 9, refusing to answer the questions of the large group of reporters that surged forward to meet them but giving—by a combination of knowing looks, confident smiles, and scornful grins—an impression that all was under control as far as they were concerned. So their meeting was promptly interpreted, at any rate, in a dozen hasty news stories and TV-radio reports sent out to the waiting world.

At 7:30 in the Delegates' Dining Room, Senator Fry, looking a little drawn but otherwise in good shape, had a hasty bowl of soup with the Ambassador of Niger, who had, to his surprise, searched him out and asked him to do so. Senator Smith, at another table across the room, did the same with his little friend from Gabon. Several of the more astute newsmen, noting these things, were not so sure that the Afro-Asian bloc was as united as it seemed.

At 7:45 the Soviet Ambassador swept into the Dining Room with Ghana, Guinea, and Guiana and took his usual table by the window overlooking the esplanade. They settled down, laughing and talking with an ostentatious animation, ordered a drink, and prepared to eat a leisurely meal, while all around the crowded room eyes and whispers took due note of their presence.

At 8:13, proving that the Soviet Ambassador and his friends had been entirely right not to hurry, the first handful of delegates began to straggle back into the Assembly Hall for the session called for 8 P.M.

At 8:43, everyone finally in place and the hall once more abuzz and aglitter with the colorful and contentious spokesmen of the nations, the President rapped his gavel and the session began. The delegate of the United Kingdom was recognized and walked with a businesslike dignity to the rostrum.

"Mr. President," Lord Maudulayne said slowly, arranging his papers on the lectern before him, "it is not the purpose of the United Kingdom to delay these proceedings very long. We have made our arguments on this matter repeatedly, both in this chamber and in other chambers of the United Nations. You know where we stand.

"It is the belief of Her Majesty's Government that the Territory of Gorotoland is not yet completely ready for the independence proposed in this resolution. This belief has been strengthened by events of recent days in the capital of Molobangwe—events which," he added dryly, "were undoubtedly prevented from getting out of hand only by the presence of Her Majesty's Government in the territory and the knowledge, on the part of those responsible for the disturbances, that the Government were prepared to move if necessary to assure the continuation of the leadership of His Royal Highness the M'Bulu.

"My government," he added with some irony, "are not altogether surprised that His Royal Highness has refrained from expressing either his acknowledgment or his gratitude for this fact, but they do think that it should at least be stated for this record."

There was some laughter, some comment. In the Indian delegation the Ambassador looked indignant, but his enormous guest remained impassive, a politely attentive expression on his face which disclosed nothing, conceded nothing. Lord Maudulayne stared down upon him with an equal impassivity for a moment, then went on.

"Her Majesty's Government have established an orderly, phased, progressive development of complete freedom in Gorotoland, with independence to become fully effective one year from the tenth of this month. One year is not too long to wait to insure such an orderly transition. This organization is still concerned with problems of the Congo and elsewhere which arose because its pressures produced a *dis*orderly transition to independence.

"I do not think," he said, ignoring a wavelet of boos that flickered across the Assembly, "that we want to create for ourselves another such headache to add to those we already have.

"There is no doubt in the minds of Her Majesty's Government that immediate independence for Gorotoland would produce chaos, armed conflict, civil war, and, very likely, the defeat, if not the death, of the M'Bulu himself.

"Therefore, we respectfully ask of this Assembly that it defeat the first resolution of the distinguished delegate of Panama and permit us to continue the orderly transfer of power in Gorotoland which has already been put into effect by Her Majesty's Government."

"Phew!" said the London *Daily Express*. "How pious can you get?"

"You mean you don't agree?" the *Christian Science Monitor* inquired with some irony. The *Express* snorted.

"It's all uranium, of course."

"I didn't know Gorotoland had any uranium," the *Monitor* said skeptically. "In fact, I don't think it does."

"You'll see," the *Express* said darkly.

"Oh, come off it," the *Manchester Guardian* said impatiently. "Gorotoland hasn't got two sticks to rub together to make fire, let alone uranium. All the same, I'll agree His Lordship is insufferably noble tonight. I wonder how that will go over with the duskier breeds without the law. Who are now within the law. Who now *make* the law, God rest Rudyard Kipling and Cecil Rhodes."

"Would it matter what he said?" the New York *Herald Tribune* inquired. The *Guardian* smiled.

"Not really, I suppose . . . I say," he remarked with some interest as the British Ambassador returned to his seat, "what's going on over there in your delegation? Is the U.S. going to speak now?"

"We weren't scheduled to until later," the *Herald Tribune* said with an equal interest. "Niger was next. But maybe they're going to yield to us."

And this was what occurred, as the tall delegate of Niger raised his hand and walked quickly down the aisle to the rostrum, there to announce in liquid French that his delegation would, if it pleased the Chair, yield its position on the speakers' list to the United States. There was some muttering, but the President recognized the United States in a firm tone of voice, and it subsided. Lafe Smith rose and came down to the rostrum.

"This ought to be fascinating," the London *Daily Mirror* said cheerfully. "I expect now you chaps will really let us have it."

"Why?" asked the New York *Times*.

"Oh, because. Now that Labaiya's amendment is back as a resolution, needing only a majority, you've got to get your votes where you can find them, haven't you?"

"Maybe we'll favor independence for Gorotoland just because we think it's the best thing to do," the *Times* suggested.

"Oh, my," the *Mirror* told him. "I see Maudulayne isn't the only pious one here tonight."

But it was not in a pious tone of voice that the junior Senator from Iowa began his brief remarks, for he did not feel in a pious mood. He was, for one thing, in a state of tension about his colleague, though Hal seemed to be making it all right and only a sick tiredness around his eyes and a certain pallor in his face revealed to those who looked closely that he was not feeling well. Lafe had been able to understand and accept the mental attitude that seemed to have come upon his friend, but of course the physical inroads of his disease did not stop just because he had been able to rise beyond them mentally. They kept right on gnawing away, and Lafe lived now in constant fear that Hal might suddenly collapse at some moment of tension in the Assembly, his gallant heart brought low by the grim and graceless betrayals of the body.

He was also worried, and deeply, as all the delegation was and as all the friendly states that supported them were, by this new turn of events here on the floor. Felix's move had admittedly caught them by surprise, even though they had received some inkling of it in the past twenty-four hours. They had not realized that it would be done in the fashion it was, which, by use of points of order, appeals, and things not specifically stated in the rules, had permitted him to get away with it virtually without challenge. Debate had not been possible under these circumstances, and now it must wait until tomorrow, with another twenty-four hours intervening, during which the Panamanian Ambassador and his friends could do more politicking on the basis of the accomplished fact of his new resolution. The United States was precluded from immediate answer, save in a further round of the endless talks among delegations that composed so much of the business of the United Nations; and that of course lacked the force and drama of an immediate answer here.

Well: that was tomorrow's problem, and what he was about to do now, even though it was in line with what he had always believed best from the very beginning, would not make it any easier. Therefore, he told himself firmly, up and at 'em, boy. Take a leaf from Felix and hit 'em between the eyes before they know what's coming.

"Mr. President," he said calmly into the rustling hush that fell upon the enormous chamber, "the United States will vote No on this resolution."

"No?" exclaimed the Daily Express in aggrieved astonishment. "What the hell's got into the U.S., anyway?"

"What fools!" the Manchester Guardian said excitedly. "What fools. Now you're bound to lose on the other tomorrow. You can't possibly win!"

"Oh, I don't know," said the New York Herald Tribune, feeling strangely elated for some reason he could not quite analyze. "We'll just have to see about that!"

Into the rush of exclamatory, disbelieving sound that came from all over the hall in the wake of Lafe's statement, the President banged his gavel sternly, and after a minute or two the chamber quieted down again. Lafe had waited patiently, and now went on in the same firm voice.

"The United States will vote No, Mr. President, because we agree entirely with the distinguished delegate of the United Kingdom that even more important at this stage of the United Nations' development than giving freedom is the orderly giving of freedom."

"No!" shouted someone from one of the African delegations.

"Yes. We know that is not the fashion here, right now. It was not the fashion in the Congo, as the delegate of the United Kingdom pointed out, and the UN still suffers from what happened, is still happening, and apparently always will happen, in the Congo. We know orderly transition was not the fashion in some other places, and they, too, are still on the UN's doorstep. Is it the intention of this Assembly to turn Gorotoland into another Congo? If so, go right ahead. You will do it without the vote of the United States. Or," he added coldly, "its financial support if you should find it necessary to try another intervention."

"Brave talk," said the London *Daily Telegraph* to the *Christian Science Monitor,* "but wait until somebody hollers 'Communist!' and watch Uncle Sam scramble to get aboard." The *Monitor* gave him an uncomfortable smile.

"Mr. President, it is apparent by now that the crying need of this organization is a body of established law and precedent *and respect for it,* no matter who it hits. It will not hurt Gorotoland to wait a year for freedom, if that freedom is transferred with safeguards that will really help it to last. It will hurt Gorotoland, and it will hurt this organization, to rush one more unprepared nation headlong into a liberty it doesn't know how to handle."

Again there were murmurs and mutters from the floor, ugly in tone, now, and not amused.

"Mr. President, it would be very easy for the United States to seek to win favor in this Assembly by advocating a course we cannot in good conscience advocate. It would be easy to buy votes for tomorrow in this way. We do not think we are that hard up in the world, yet. But possibly we are losing votes for tomorrow by taking this course. If so, that is as it must be.

"We would like to vote with so many of you who will support the resolution of the Ambassador of Panama, but we do not believe Gorotoland is ready for it. Therefore, as I said, we will vote No. We urge all who believe in the orderly transition of power—and, more importantly, all who believe in developing for the United Nations a tradition and a precedent of respecting the orderly and peaceable way of doing things, to also vote No."

A great chorus of boos, met and matched by appreciative applause from many sections of the floor and galleries, swelled up in his face as he left the rostrum and walked back down onto the floor. In the other aisle Krishna Khaleel hurried down, waving an arm above his head and crying, "Mr. President!" as he came.

"The distinguished delegate of India," the President said, and the hall again fell silent as the dapper little figure of the Indian Ambassador mounted the steps, bowed to the President, and turned to the lectern.

"Mr. President," he said in his clipped British accent, "the delegation of India will, as is well known, vote Yes on this resolution. But we do not wish to waste the time of this great Assembly by a recital of old arguments, sensible and sound as we believe those arguments to be. Instead, we would rather permit the one man most concerned here today to speak to you. He is the guest of my delegation on this floor at this moment. With your kind permission, Mr. President and distinguished delegates, I would like to present to you His Royal Highness the M'Bulu of Mbuele, for such time as he may need."

"Is there objection to the request of the delegate of India?" the President inquired, and a roar of "NO!" went up from the floor.

"Oh, Lord," Hal Fry murmured to Claude Maudulayne. "Here we go again."

"I just hope he's wearing his clean clothes," the British Ambassador remarked.

He was, and he looked magnificent in them as he completed his bow to the President and turned to face them. His inner elation was carefully controlled, his face impassive, his demeanor calm. Inside he was telling himself with a marvelous delight how splendidly and with what powerful magnetism he was commanding the attention of the nations. He was entirely correct, and he knew he would continue to be so, for he knew this was no occasion for dramatics but just for the simple, overwhelming impact of his presence and his arguments.

"Mr. President," he said in his guttural British accent, "distinguished delegates: I thank you once again for the high honor you do me in permitting me the privilege of this rostrum when I am not yet a member of your organization."

"You will be soon!" someone cried from the floor, and a gust of laughter and applause gave approval. Terry smiled and bowed.

"Much has happened since I spoke here last, Mr. President. The Congress of the United States has passed a resolution. Many arguments and statements have been made in many places concerning the merits of independence for my country. Many arguments and statements"—and he permitted himself a sudden grin that brought an answering wave of amusement—"have been made about me. But—nonetheless—here we all are once again, in the great hall of the Assembly, faced with the decision of the only body that matters in this affair, the United Nations itself."

There was applause for this from many delegations.

"Mr. President, the distinguished delegates of the U.K. and the U.S.—both, I am proud to say, have become personal friends of mine in these recent weeks that I have been here for my cause—say that my country is not yet ready for independence. They say independence has been promised in a year. They say the orderly transition of independence is more important than independence itself.

"Mr. President"—and he sounded genuinely puzzled—"how can they say these things?

"My country has had a functioning government—it is true, under the guidance of the Crown in recent decades, but nonetheless with great internal control—for centuries.

"If freedom is coming to us in any case, what is the magic of waiting a year?

"And, finally, Mr. President, to say that orderly transition of freedom is more important than independence itself is, it seems to me, to put one's finger exactly on the essential difference that divides so many new states from the old.

"Mr. President," he said, and now he permitted himself a stronger passion, "it is my belief that nothing is more important than freedom! Nothing is more sacred than freedom! Nothing is greater than freedom! Nothing—nothing, nothing, nothing, nothing"—and he pounded on the lectern so furiously it almost broke—"can be permitted to stand in the way of freedom!

"Freedom, Mr. President," he shouted as the answering roar of approval began to gather and rise from the floor in response to his exhortation, "is all that makes men great! It is all men have to live for! Without freedom, what good is life! Give us our freedom, my dear friends of the Assembly! Do not listen to the words of the fearful and the self-interested! Do not listen to the colonialist oppressors!

"Give us our freedom!"

And into the bellow of sound that came up, many delegates standing and applauding and shouting hysterically, he turned to the President, bowed gravely once more, turned back and bowed once again to the Assembly, and with a slow and stately tread came back up the aisle, shaking many eagerly thrust out hands that greeted him along the way.

"I would say that does it," the Chicago *Tribune* remarked. The Manchester *Guardian* nodded.

"All over but the shouting. And there's more than a whisper left of that."

So there was, as the night dragged on and a total of twenty-five delegations made the speeches they felt they must make before The Problem of Gorotoland could come to a final vote. The casual customs of UN debate, which even more than that of the U. S. Senate encourages the unchecked expression of ego and the uncontrollable flow of verbal diarrhea, was allowed full rein. It was not until 1:14 A.M. that the last speech, delivered by the gracious, half-apologetic delegate of Italy, speaking in what he obviously believed to be a lost cause, came finally to its conclusion.

The President said at last, into the tired hush that fell at last upon the Assembly:

"The question occurs on the resolution of the delegate of Panama, to state the desire of the United Nations that the Territory of Gorotoland, now administered by Her Majesty's Government in the United Kingdom, be granted immediate and full independence. On this resolution, which under Rule 85 of the Assembly is an 'important matter,' two-thirds of those voting must approve in order to secure passage."

The Secretary-General handed him the box of names; he reached in and slowly drew one.

"Wish us luck," Lord Maudulayne whispered, and Senator Fry, by now appearing very tired and with a curiously drained look that disturbed his English friend, said with a reasonable approximation of an ironic smile, "We'll need it."

"The voting will begin," the President said, "with Turkey."

"No," said Turkey.

"Uganda."

"Yes."

"Ukrainian S.S.R."

"Da."

"U.S.S.R."

"Da."

"United Arab Republic."

"Yes."

"United Kingdom."

"No."

"United States."

"No."

"Upper Volta."

"*Non*," and there was a startled hiss of breath.

"Uruguay."

"*Sí*," and there was another.

"Venezuela."

"*Abstención.*"

"West Indies."

"Yes."

"Western Samoa."

"Yes."

"Yemen."

"Yes."

"Yugoslavia."

"Yes."

"Afghanistan."

"Yes."

"Albania."

"Yes."

"Algeria."

"*Oui.*"

"Argentina."

"*No.*"

"Australia."

"No."

"Belgium."

"*Non!*" And there was mocking laughter.

"Bolivia."

"*Abstención.*"

"Brazil."

"*Sí.*"

Excitement grew in the hall as the vote moved gradually to its conclusion, and when the President finally spoke it burst and overflowed into wild exclamations of protest or approval.

"The vote stands at 74 Yes, 37 No, 5 abstentions, remainder absent, and, accordingly, two-thirds of those present having voted in favor of the resolution, it is hereby—"

"Mr. President! Mr. President! Mr. *President!*" someone shouted insistently. Immediately there was a rush of boos and protest, for some instinct, even before they knew what he would say, indicated to many that this might be an attempt to upset the vote.

"The distinguished delegate of Gabon—" the President began, and a roar of "No!" greeted his words. He flushed at once and pounded angrily with the gavel.

"Any delegate has the right to address the Chair and speak to the Assembly providing he is in order!" he shouted. "The delegate from Gabon *is* in order. The Assembly is *out* of order! *The Assembly will be quiet!*"

"By George," the *Daily Express* said with a grin to the New York *Herald Tribune*, "I think he means it."

Apparently the Assembly, though with reluctant murmurs and mumbles, thought so too, for after a moment it fell gradually into silence as Gabon came swiftly down the aisle, bowed to the President, and turned to the room.

"Mr. President, the delegation of Gabon abstained on this vote. The delegation has changed its decision and wishes to vote. On this resolution"—and his voice rose in challenge—"Gabon votes—No!"

"Hot dog!" Lafe Smith said exultantly. "I knew that little guy wouldn't let me down! Now it's 74 to 38, and that isn't two-thirds!"

"Thanks to Raoul," Hal Fry pointed out, leaning forward tensely, his pain temporarily forgotten in the excitement of the moment.

"France voted with us, too," Lord Maudulayne said in a surprised voice. "Apparently my fears were groundless."

"But wait a minute—" Lafe said in a suddenly worried voice, and they fell abruptly silent as once more there came a call of "Mr. President!" from the floor.

"The distinguished delegate of Bolivia," the President said into the tensely rustling hush.

"Bolivia also abstained," her delegate said laconically. "Bolivia also wishes to vote. Bolivia votes *Sí!*"

"I knew it," Lafe said, pounding a fist into a palm. "I *knew* it. Here comes Venezuela. I must say for Felix—"

"He planned it well," Lord Maudulayne said glumly.

"Venezuela, too, abstained," her delegate said into a chained excitement almost more than the delegates could bear. "Venezuela, too, will vote. *Sí!*"

And in the midst of the thundering noise that ensued he walked quickly back to his seat as the President pounded for order. When he had it, he spoke into the quivering silence.

"The vote on the resolution now stands at 76 Yes, 38 No, 2 abstention, remainder absent, and the resolution for the immediate independence of Gorotoland is approved by this Assembly . . . This plenary session of the General Assembly on The Problem of Gorotoland is now concluded," he said, his words almost lost in the rush of excited sound as delegates and galleries rose and began milling about in excited groups. "The plenary session of the Assembly on the second resolution of the distinguished delegate of Panama on The Matter of the United States, will convene at 3 P.M. on Mond—"

"Mr. President!" Hal Fry and Vasily Tashikov shouted together. The President recognized Hal.

"Mr. President," he called as the Assembly, now in almost complete informality as its members, moving toward the exits, turned back for a moment of attention to hear him, "there is no point in delaying this. The United States suggests that the next plenary convene at 3 P.M. today, instead of Monday."

"The next plenary session," the President said as Vasily Tashikov nodded his head in satisfied agreement, "will convene at 3 P.M. today."

There was a scattering of applause as the gavel fell. The Problem of Gorotoland was settled. Ahead still lay The Matter of the United States.

Across the big concave bowl, now draining rapidly of its colorful, cantankerous occupants, the giant figure standing with the Indian delegation and the small, neat figure in the Panamanian delegation caught each other's eyes and bowed. Felix Labaiya's smile, as always, was slight and self-contained, the smile of a man who had planned well, expected to do well, and done well. The M'Bulu's happy grin was broad and carefree, that of a prizefighter who had finally bested his opponent. As if to strengthen the comparison, he raised his hands above his head and clasped them together in the traditional victory gesture. There was a sound of laughter and friendly applause from all around, and in the glow of it he told himself that the gods were still with Terence Ajkaje, just as always. He had the vote he had fought so hard to get, and while he had thought earlier that it might be his death warrant, now that the triumph was actually his he did not really think so—he could not really think so, so happy and supremely confident did he feel. He would stay one more day, now, to help Felix as Felix had helped him, and then he would fly home and, with the kind assistance of the British, put things to rights in Molobangwe. There, he now felt sure, triumph awaited him, after so great a triumph here in this world assemblage that once and for all had recognized the 137th M'Bulu of Mbuele for the great one he was in the councils of mankind.

Seeing his happy aspect, and grasping intuitively something of the emotion that must be behind it, the Ambassador of Panama felt triumph too, though the last thing he would ever have done was to have shown it by so revealing a gesture as that of Terrible Terry. Outward displays were not Felix's way; nor did he have time for them. His major task still remained, though it now appeared much simpler in the wake of the Assembly's support for his parliamentary maneuvers and the size of the favorable vote on Gorotoland.

He looked with a glance that was half calculating, half pitying, toward the American delegation, where Senator Fry, gray-faced and tired, was moving slowly out with Senator Smith. We shall meet this afternoon, Felix Labaiya promised them. We shall meet this afternoon and see who wins the final toss.

Lafe waved to him and automatically he waved back. But there was no cordiality on either side, only the cold, carefully appraising look of opponents who know a battle to the death still lies before them.

After they had crossed First Avenue in the mixture of sleet, snow, and freezing rain that now had the city under siege, the two Americans went briefly up to Hal's office in U.S. headquarters before catching a cab, Lafe to go to the Waldorf for much-needed sleep, Hal to return to Harkness for another treatment and sleep until time to come back for the next plenary. In the office they put through a call, as directed, to the White House and the Knox home in Spring Valley. Once again a conference call was set up and their two superiors, sleepy but increasingly awake as they talked along, analyzed with them the import of the day's events.

"Is Cullee there?" the President asked, and Hal said yes, he was, but had preferred, and they had agreed, to defer his appearance until debate actually came on Felix's new resolution.

"I think it's as well we didn't have him with us today," Lafe said. "He's still feeling pretty rocky and of course looks like the very devil—"

"Which is all right," Orrin said from the Spring Valley house.

"It doesn't harm us," Hal agreed. "He'll feel better tomorrow, and be more impressive then. I think it's well for them to see how he looks; they're always saying nobody in America cares about the racial problem. Somebody cared, right enough."

"Which has made Cullee care, too, in a way he didn't imagine he could before, I think," Orrin said.

"How ironic it is," the President said, "that in the affairs of the world these days, nations must stage-manage their effects as carefully as though they were on Broadway. Terry with his splattered robes, Cullee with his beaten body—" He made a sad sound, of tiredness and disgust. "What an age."

"Yet it must be done," the Secretary of State said. "That is how many of the nations reach their decisions nowadays, on the basis of emotions stirred up by things like that."

"I know," the President said. "It does not always give me great faith in the future of the globe. Good night, all. I think we know where we stand for this afternoon. Thank you for everything, and best of luck in the debate."

"What will we do if—" Hal Fry began, and left the question hanging.

"We will do whatever the situation requires," the President said. "When it requires it. Sleep well."

The farewells said, the call ended, hats and coats on, lights turned off in the office, the two Senators stood for a moment looking across at the Secretariat, surging upward into the night, its many brightly lighted windows, where charwomen worked as the hour reached 2 A.M., obscured and shrouded by the weather. The building seemed almost to drift against the night, without anchor or reference point for the eye to tie it to, all else blocked out by the scudding storm. Out of the north door of the Main Concourse they could see a few last stragglers hurrying home across the lighted esplanade. In front of the Delegates' Entrance, directly below, two tiny figures were methodically hauling down the sopping flags.

"It's curious," Lafe said. "So much happens there during the daytime, but somehow I always think of it as being at night. It always seems to be a night place—for night people—"

"—doing night things to the world. I wonder if it will ever fulfill what mankind hoped for it when it first began."

"Who knows?" Lafe asked soberly. "Who knows? . . . But, here!" He clapped his colleague on the back. "You're desperately tired and it's past 2 A.M. Let me run you up to the hospital."

"I'll drop you and go on alone. I can make it all right."

"Can you?" Lafe said, studying him closely. Hal smiled.

"Whatever the situation requires," he quoted the President. "When it requires it. Come on."

Downstairs, while they waited for a cab to come along the now quite deserted avenue in the hostile storm, their eyes were inevitably drawn once more to the great building rising into the mists above them.

A night place—for night people—doing night things.

And the hope?

It was still there somewhere.

It had to be.

There Wasn't Anything Else.

4

Looking down once again upon the crowded and colorful scene as he once more patiently awaited the arrival of the President of the Assembly, the Secretary-General could see that, of all those who would contest the issue, the acting chief delegate of the United States appeared to be the most eager to commence. Certainly he was the first of the major participants to appear in the chamber, arriving with one of his delegation secretaries at 2:45 P.M., well in advance of the time the plenary would actually begin.

He looked, the S.-G. thought, somewhat tense and under pressure, but that was understandable. Apparently his medical examination, despite the rumors running through the corridors, had given him a clean bill of health, for here he was again today, evidently in good shape and ready for battle. It was true that there was a certain luminous grayness about his face, but then, the S.-G. thought with a shiver, who wouldn't be gray in the kind of weather that howled upon Manhattan outside? That is, he corrected himself with a small inward amusement, anyone who could *turn* gray would be gray. Those who were black could only look pinched and shrink with the rest in the storm that had lasted all night and was only now easing, after piling the streets with heavy snow. It seemed to him that he could feel the cold right here in the chamber, overheated as it was, so foreign was this type of weather to that he was native to in West Africa.

Along with that, it seemed to him, there was another coldness in the room, the coldness of men contending in bitterness and determination for different and conflicting ends and ambitions. He had spent much time in the white man's world, but gods and ghosts still walked his mind at times, and this was one. There were presences here today, moving among the living and influencing their actions; presences going back to the earliest colonialism and the first slave-trading days in Africa—not only white presences that had profited, but black presences that had profited, as well.

The burden of all the world lay heavy upon this issue. What the Indian Ambassador had lately taken to referring to, with a pixyish relish, as the "shade of difference" united many in guilt even as it divided them in purpose.

What could he do about it, where could he logically and with honor participate in the struggle imposed by history upon mankind? Perhaps, old man, he told himself bleakly, there is no place for you. Perhaps you will fail here, as in all the rest.

For his part, as he stood at the head of the aisle leading down to the section marked for the United States delegation, managing to smile and shake hands with other delegates as they arrived, Senator Fry, too, was feeling the winds of the years and the certainty of a harsh contention. As much as could be expected, he was ready for it, after a long sleep under sedation that had lasted until almost noon. But he wondered if any of them, really, whatever their condition, was ready for it, and whether this might not be one of those occasions when men attempted to deal with forces of history so great that they could not, in reality, be controlled or managed—when the only feasible human purpose must be to channel them as much as possible into ways that would not damage too much the structure of a reasonably sane society.

Whether some of his fellow delegates realized this he did not know as he stood there watching them form into little groups, chat for a moment, break up, form other groups, move restlessly here and there among the aisles, waving and greeting one another as the chamber filled. There were many purposes here, within the shadow of the resolution of the Panamanian Ambassador on The Matter of the United States; and he was well aware that a majority of them were hostile to his country and that it was questionable if his country could defeat them.

In the delegation and among its friends, he thought things were as favorable as possible under the circumstances. Certain strategies had been worked out, certain plans made, for the debate. With equal attention to detail, he knew, plans and strategies had been organized by the other side. The votes that had permitted Felix to bring the issue here in this form, and the vote with which Gorotoland's independence had been approved, might on the face of them be taken to predict a simple and inevitable defeat for the United States on the companion issue. Yet it was not that simple or inevitable, as many hints and indications coming into the delegation during the morning had made clear.

Again, as in the first debate when Terry had made his dramatic appeal after the episode in Charleston, there appeared to be two conflicting impulses: one to rush forward in a storm of emotion and condemn the United

States, the other to recognize the United States' many contributions to the UN and draw back before condemnation went too far. What he would do in the event the first impulse prevailed, he did not know. He had no instructions other than the President's cryptic "what the situation requires, when it requires it," and so he was in no position to use the possibility of future action as a weapon in debate. He did not know what the possibility was.

Neither was there any further means of diplomacy or pressure open to the delegation. Everything had been exhausted by now. The type of horse-trading with funds and promises and warnings that all the nations resorted to on major issues had run its course. Nothing was left but persuasion and argument in open debate; and there, basically, all that remained was emotion, since reason and logic had automatically been forced to a secondary place by the impassioned prejudices and preconceptions that surrounded this highly emotional matter.

Nonetheless, he thought as he tightened his grasp on a little bottle of pills in his pocket, it should not be the move of the United States to be the first to raise the emotional cloud around this. His country had a case, in logic and justice, and it should be presented that way first. That would be consistent with the basic American concept of the United Nations—more idealistic, perhaps, than that of most. To that concept, as well as to his country's own interests, he felt her delegation must try to be true.

He would begin, then, after Felix made his opening statement, on that theme which in these recent months, and especially in these past hours, he conceived to be a theme worthy of a man's endeavors. There had come to him, in these two nights of certainty about his condition, a swift draining-away of more mundane matters, a rapidly diminishing concern for the affairs that occupied men less starkly confronted by their own mortality than he. Now his life was narrowing down to some final justification, some essential reality worthy of the sacrifice the Lord had placed upon him for some reason he could not understand. But perhaps the reason was simple. Perhaps it was to clear his mind and life so that he could make one last appeal to mankind to honor the promise it had made to itself here on the East River. Perhaps it had been done so that he could be free to urge his fellow men to honor, along with it, those qualities of tolerance and decency and love that they can sometimes achieve when all else is gone and they are left to realize at last their desperate need of one another in the night that surrounds the universe. Perhaps only one in his particular position at this particular time could do it.

It could be, he thought as a sudden wave of dizziness shot through his head and his eyes began to blur again with the reddish tinge, that this was it.

"Good afternoon," he said automatically to the delegate of Guinea as they arrived together at the Delegates' Entrance; but the delegate of Guinea, after a startled and scornful look, did not reply. Very well, you bastard, he told the delegate of Guinea in his mind. Don't speak, and see if I care.

But he did care, the Congressman from California admitted honestly to himself as he gave a deep, unhappy sigh and followed the flouncily spiteful delegate of Guinea in. He did care that there was so much hostility in the world, that things were on so personal a level here on this embittered issue, and that his own difficult position was so little appreciated and understood by those whom pigmentation should have made his brothers but politics and prejudice had made his enemies. He did care, for this was one extra little burden added to the rest that made life, at the moment, a heavy thing to bear.

Not that he would not or could not bear it, of course, for even without the example of Hal Fry before him, sketched in bluntest terms by Lafe Smith in the telephone call that had brought him back to his duty here at the UN— even without good old Maudie, who had also been getting him here in her own loving, cantankerous way—he had his own character to rely upon. It was not a character to give in easily, no matter what the pressures. He was quite sure now that he would in any event have been right where he was, entering the Secretariat Building and turning toward the corridor to the Assembly Hall where there waited the fate of the new Labaiya Resolution and the judgment of the nations upon his own.

He did not know, as he turned left and joined the throng of delegates, spectators, and press who were taking the escalator to the second floor and proceeding toward the Assembly Hall down the long green-carpeted corridor, whether his wife or his friend would be here at this particular moment. Somehow he thought they might be, on this occasion, however carefully they had stayed away from the Senate. He had noticed the banners of DEFY among those that waved in a self-conscious straggle in the little parklike area across First Avenue where the police were accustomed to herd UN demonstrators, and it was not unlikely that the chairman was somewhere about. Perhaps even now he was conferring with Felix and his other friends in the Lounge or sitting with an air of ostentatious importance in the public gallery of the Assembly Hall. Sue-Dan, too, no doubt wearing stylish clothes and an expression as defiant as she dared, very likely might be there. He would just have to try not to see them, he told himself with a dogged determination. He really didn't want to see them, so unsure was he of what he might do to LeGage after what LeGage had caused to be done to him, and so sure was he that from his wife he would receive just more hurtful words and hurtful actions.

Well, one thing was sure, anyway: he hadn't been turned from his purpose in Washington, and he wasn't going to be turned from it here. The United States was his concern, as imperfectly expressed, maybe, as most people expressed it, yet a passionate and overriding solicitude that dominated his thoughts and his actions, particularly right now. LeGage and all the dutiful echoers of his absolutist line in the white press and the colored press had done their best to throw him off balance; they hadn't succeeded, so they had beaten him up—in a sense all of them had beaten him up, not just LeGage's bullies. Sue-Dan had chimed in with her two-bits worth and tried to knock him off balance, too.

And yet he, Cullee, was still here, right where he had been, plowing along, confused about a lot of things, maybe, not very perfect, not very smart or brilliant, maybe, but knowing a couple of things that he'd take over them, any day: He knew he was honest, and he knew he was doing the right thing for his country, and, so as far as he was concerned, that was enough for him. As far as he was concerned, they could take a running jump and go to hell. They had shoved him off and they thought he'd come back, maybe, begging and crying and doing what they wanted. Well, they didn't know old Cullee, even after all these years. If anybody did any coming back, it would be them, and maybe even that wouldn't be enough. He had more important things to worry about now.

He shook his head impatiently as if to clear it of them, and it did seem to, a little.

He was aware as he walked along that the crowd was thinning around him, that those nearest him were falling away, that he was being left to move forward in a little isolated space that marked him out from the rest. Thus separated, his tall figure moved ahead, presenting to the hurrying crowd a picture he was not ashamed for it to see: his face still misshapen and puffy; a patch still across his forehead where the gash, fortunately only skin-deep, was beginning to heal; his left arm in a sling; his gait half limping and awkward because of the pain that still crippled his body. Let them look at what hate could achieve, he thought grimly. Let them think about it a little. It will do them good.

"I say," the delegate of Kenya remarked to the delegate of Uganda as they came along a few paces behind, "that is a little crude, that physical display. Do they expect that actually to impress us?"

"Some people," said the delegate of Uganda, "have no taste."

Half an hour later, the plenary session finally convened, the hall filled once more with tense and rustling life as the excitement of issues fiercely met and battles about to be joined gripped all its occupants, the Ambassador of Panama stood for a moment with his hands rigid upon the lectern and looked out upon the acrimonious descendants of Adam in all their shapes and shadings. He had slept hardly at all in forty-eight hours, and if he had stopped to think about it, the strain would certainly be telling upon him now. But he had not had time to think, and a keen excitement had buoyed him up all through the many conferences and telephone calls and private talks that had followed the Assembly's dramatic and surprising support of his position in last night's session.

He had not known, when he withdrew his amendment and reoffered it as a resolution in its own right, what the response would be. He had gambled that a majority would go with him, and a majority had. He had not known, when the vote came on Gorotoland, whether two-thirds would be with him, though he had made some careful plans for it. The plans had paid off.

Now he did not know what the decision would be on his resolution calling the United States to the bar of history to answer for its racial practices; but here, too, he was hopeful. He was aware of the hesitations that intimidated many all over the world, but he was also aware of the instinctive hostility to America's social attitudes that was at war with the hesitations. It was his task now to play upon the hostility as he could—not violently and antagonistically, as some others could be counted upon to do before the debate concluded, but with the delicacy and finesse that he knew was one of his greatest talents and most became him.

"Mr. President," he began quietly as the rustling diminished and the enormous hall settled down, "I do not think, at this late hour in the Assembly's consideration of this serious matter now before it, that there is any need for extended discussion on my part.

"You all know the terms of the resolution. You all know the racial conditions in the United States which have prompted me to introduce it.

"Some of you know this from first hand experience." There was an angry little murmur of agreement. "Others of you soon may. All of you whose skins are not white know that any time, as you move about this country, on the business of the United Nations or simply as tourists, you too may suddenly be subjected to rejection, insult, or even physical danger because of your color." He paused for a moment, then asked slowly: "Does this seem right to you?"

A roar of "NO!" replied, and the tension in the hall shot up several levels.

"No more does it to me, and that is why I, who have the closest family ties with the United States, have introduced this resolution. It is an attempt to help the United States—to try to persuade the United States to be the true home of democracy that we who are her friends desire her to be."

"And give her a black eye in the process," Senator Fry murmured to Lord Maudulayne, down on the floor. The British Ambassador smiled and gave a quizzical shrug.

"I know it is fashionable in some circles in the United States," Felix went on, "for some enemies of this organization to say that my resolution is designed simply to embarrass the United States in the eyes of the world."

"He heard you," Lord Maudulayne said, and Hal Fry, responded with an amused nod that felt as though it almost took off the top of his head.

"This is a childish interpretation. Nothing is further from my mind, or from the minds of those here in the United Nations who sincerely believe in racial democracy. Only enemies of the United Nations itself would attribute such motives to anyone here.

"Only reactionaries would say a thing like that of the United Nations.

"Our motives are honorable and our purposes are clean.

"We are not vindictive. We are not hostile. We are not unfriendly. The United Nations does not operate, ever, on such unworthy motivations.

"We reject all such reactionary attacks upon the United Nations, and we do so proudly!"

"Oh, bro-*ther*," the New York *World-Telegram* murmured to the Manchester *Guardian* as an explosion of approving applause responded. "How noble can you get?"

"You ain't seen nothin' yet," the *Guardian* murmured back.

"Earnestly, then, and honorably," the Ambassador of Panama said with a quiet emphasis as the favoring outburst died down, "I present to you this resolution that will give the strong encouragement and assistance of the United Nations to the United States as it strives to correct its deplorable racial practices.

"I commend it to the good faith of all who truly believe in democracy—not just the mouthing of democracy, but the practice of democracy.

"I commend it, particularly, to the United States itself, whose distinguished senior delegate I have asked repeatedly to support it. He has refused on behalf of his country. So, Mr. President, regretfully but acting in the right, this Assembly must do for the United States what the United States will not do for itself.

"Justice and honor dictate this course, Mr. President. Injustice and dishonor, only, support the other.

"I appeal to you to see the right and act in the right."

And with a graceful little bow to the Assembly and its President, he left the rostrum and walked at a dignified pace up the aisle to his seat, surrounded by prolonged applause, many delegations standing, as he did so.

"Well, that wasn't so bad," Lafe remarked, and Hal smiled.

"Not what I expected."

"I imagine others will provide it. How do you feel? Are you going to be up to this? I'm perfectly willing to take the first phase of it if you—" Hal shook his head.

"I'm all right. It isn't very bad today. With a little luck"—he paused, and for just a second, before he thrust it resolutely away, a sadness briefly clouded his eyes—"I'll manage all right."

"The next speaker," the President announced, "is the distinguished delegate of the United States."

There came a ripple of anticipatory comment, a heightening of excitement; all those delegates who did not understand English put on their earphones and switched to the English channel. Senator Fry came slowly down the aisle, nodded briefly to Terry and K.K. as he passed the Indian delegation, ascended the rostrum, and bowed to the President. Then he turned and stared out into the closely watching eyes of the nations, the hovering and merciless gaze of the television cameras looking down from the glass-enclosed studios high along the walls above.

It could be seen, on many screens in many places over the world, that he was holding himself very erect as he prepared to speak. His face looked a little thin, but his expression was steady and outwardly untroubled. To the millions who studied his appearance, there seemed to be a certain tension about the way he held himself, but, otherwise, nothing. They did not know, and he was not about to tell them, that it had been all he could do to get down the aisle without falling. In the terrible irony of his disease, almost none of its symptoms appeared on the surface. He looked like a kindly, earnest, pleasant-faced man, a little tired and under an understandable tension in view of the attack on his country. With an effort whose cost no one but he could know, he began to speak in a reasonable, unhurried voice.

"Mr. President, the distinguished delegate of Panama has spoken of racial conditions in my country and of his noble motives in asking this Assembly to intervene in them. I shall not comment on his remarks, except to say that it is possible to oppose his point of view, and oppose such action by the Assembly, without being an opponent of the United Nations.

"That charge, which is flung against anyone who dares to say that the UN is not perfect in every respect, is both childish and self-defeating."

There was a murmur of protest, and into it he spoke more sharply for a moment.

"You and I are the United Nations, and *we know* we aren't perfect. All of us here realize that there are shortcomings and weaknesses in the organization, and I think we all agree that only if they are eliminated can the UN be the instrument of hope that it was originally intended to be."

"Just so you don't spell out too carefully what they are," the New York *Times* observed to the Denver *Post*. "*Then* we can all agree."

"It is this," Hal Fry said, "that I should like to discuss for a moment. It is, essentially, the same issue that was presented in the early hours of this morning in our debate on the resolution concerning Gorotoland. It is the UN itself that is on trial here, not the United States."

At this there was a laugh, deliberately raucous and rude, from somewhere on the floor. He turned upon it, though the sudden movement increased the dizziness and also brought a sharp surge of nausea that took a second or two to abate. When it did, he spoke without niceties.

"Some delegate laughs. Some cowardly, nameless delegate laughs."

There was a gasp of surprise, but he went on strongly while below Claude looked at Lafe with a quizzically questioning air.

"Who is he laughing at, Mr. President? The United States? I think he is laughing at the UN. I think he is laughing at the hopes of the world. I think he is laughing at himself, for his laugh is symbolic of just that mood of intolerance and impatience and injustice that has come to hang over our deliberations here in recent years like an ominous cloud.

"The death of the UN lies in that cloud if it continues, Mr. President. And delegates who sneer and laugh and voice intolerance and hatred and disrespect for one another's good faith and one another's problems only make it worse."

There was an uneasy stirring of sound at both his tone and his words, and in the midst of it the eyes of the delegate of Belgium caught the eyes of the delegate of Portugal. With a sardonic gravity, they winked.

"Mr. President, too often, of late, we have permitted the dead hand of history to rest upon the deliberations here. Nations, some of them new here and some of them understandably hurt by the past, have attempted to turn the UN into a vengeful instrument against those they blame for that past. But that world is dead."

Someone shouted "No!" but he ignored it.

"What do you do, Mr. President," he asked with an earnestness springing from a genuine anguish of spirit compounded by the steadily increasing pain of his body, "after you have punished the past? Do you keep on punishing it, forever after, long after it is only a distant memory?

"What happens to the UN when everyone is free and all the decisions of history have been turned upside down and made over again?

"What then? *What then, if in the process you have set aside law and justice and orderly progress and decent dealing between men?*

"What happens to you, having turned the UN into an instrument of vengeance, when you attempt to turn it back into an instrument of peace?

"It cannot be done, Mr. President. It will have been twisted and torn too far. *Nothing can ever again establish the rule of law in the affairs of men if law is permanently flouted here.*

"It is this we should be concerned about, Mr. President, not the punishments of the past. Particularly not when, over most of the earth's surface, including my own country, those responsible for the past are working sincerely and diligently to correct its errors."

Again there was laughter, knowing, sardonic, superior, unyielding. An expression of anger crossed his face, but he concluded gravely and without rancor.

"Mr. President, the Congress of the United States has passed the resolution for which this debate was temporarily suspended. My government has acted in good faith to keep its word to the nations. We ask now that the nations keep their word to us.

"I respectfully ask that you defeat the resolution of the Ambassador of Panama."

To a mixture of applause and boos, about equally divided, he bowed to the President and came slowly back up the aisle, his face looking very tired and sad for a moment, so much so that many delegates nearby commented to one another. But in a minute or two he straightened his shoulders again, took a deep breath, and came on up the aisle to his seat.

"Good work," Lafe said encouragingly as he sat down, but he shook his head.

"It wasn't all I wanted to say," he confessed in a disappointed voice, "but no matter."

"There'll be another chance later. This won't end for a while, yet."

"It won't," Hal said wryly, "but I may." Then at Lafe's alarmed look he smiled and put his hand on his arm. "No, I'm all right."

"Really?"

"It's not bad," Hal said, telling the lie he must. "And if it is, I have the pills. I haven't taken any, though," he added with pride, "and I'm not going to, if I can help it."

"Good," Lafe said, turning to look toward the rostrum as a wave of applause indicated a new speaker, obviously eagerly awaited. "Here comes Guinea, and now I expect we're in for it."

This they were, as the stark young delegate of Guinea stood before the Assembly like an ebony carving from his native land and waited for the susurrus to die down. When he began to speak, it was in no conciliatory or reasonable voice. Here was an avenger of the past, with a vengeance.

"Mr. President!" he snapped in French as many earphones went on and many dials were spun for translation. "The distinguished delegate of the United States talks piously about the United Nations and concludes by saying that his country has kept its word with us, therefore we should keep our word with it.

"When did we give any word to his country, Mr. President? I do not remember that it was any bargain. I remember the colored American who authored the resolution in Congress, who is no brother of ours"—there was a shout of approval and in the U.S. delegation Cullee Hamilton scowled and stirred angrily—"begged us to stop debating and promised us that the Congress would pass the resolution. But we made no promises in return, Mr. President. We made no promises, because we assumed," he said with a scathing sarcasm, "that if the United States were as honorable as the United States always says it is, we would not have to make promises in order to persuade the United States to do the right thing.

"That is why we made no promises, Mr. President!"

A roar of laughter and applause greeted this. The delegate of Guinea hardly paused to let it die down, so absorbed was he in his attack and so swiftly did his hurrying words come tumbling out.

"Mr. President, the delegate of the United States talks about the dead hand of the past. It is all very fine talk for one whose country last felt the hand of colonialism in 1776. Some of us felt it only yesterday. Our memories may be more vivid than his, Mr. President, about colonialism!"

Again there was a burst of applause as he rushed on.

"Furthermore, it is all very well for him to attempt to cloud the issue and conceal it by talking noble things about the United Nations. He does not have to lecture us on the United Nations, Mr. President. We are grown up enough to know about the United Nations. What we are talking about here are the shameful racial conditions in the United States. Why does he not give us a little lecture on that, Mr. President? Why does he not talk to us about the shame of his own country, Mr. President? That is what we want to hear about from him!"

Applause, wilder now, greeted this.

"Mr. President, no truer words were ever said than those uttered by the distinguished delegate of Panama, author of this resolution.

"You know—I know—anyone of color knows—what the true situation is in this pious nation that lectures the world on international morality. Whole areas of this country are closed to those of us who are not white. We cannot eat in certain places. We cannot travel in certain conveyances. We cannot live in certain sections of cities. We cannot do this, we cannot do that. No more can Americans of color—though our distinguished friend from Congress, who by some mistake of nature looks black even as he talks white

—no doubt will try to pretend to us that these things do not apply to his own race. He knows they do, Mr. President! We all know they do! What a flaunting and a shame to mankind, Mr. President! What a flaunting and a shame!"

Applause and shouts, deeper and uglier now, welled up from the floor.

"Look at this, Mr. President!" he cried, suddenly producing from somewhere in the folds of his brilliant robes a copy of the early-afternoon edition of the New York *World-Telegram*.

"What do we read here? I will tell you. There died in Washington on Thursday, after a speech trying to defeat the resolution of our white-black, black-white friend from the Congress, one of the most powerful racists in the United States, Senator Cooley! No friend to you, my friends. No friend to me.

"And so what happened this morning? The Senate of the United States held a special memorial service in its chambers to honor this great racist. And who attended? The President of the United States! The Secretary of State of the United States! Most of the leading members of the government of the United States! To do honor to this old racist, Mr. President! That is how sincere the United States is about the racial question, Mr. President! That is the good faith of the United States!"

He raised the paper and shook it angrily above his head, several pages slipping out and fluttering about him to the floor. "That is what the United States really thinks, Mr. President. Honor to a racist!"

"Oh, Lord," Lafe said in a tone of angry disgust, making no attempt to keep his voice down in the excited babble that followed. "Will they *ever* understand?" In the British delegation Lord Maudulayne leaned forward and answered him down the row. "No. They never will."

"Mr. President," Guinea said, "there is no argument capable of justifying these things. There is nothing anyone can say that will thwart the aroused conscience of mankind on this issue. It is not the United Nations which is on trial here. It is the United States. No pious lectures from anybody, white or black, or black-white or white-black, can change that fact, Mr. President.

"Let us vote for this resolution! Let us show the racists of the United States what the judgment of mankind is upon them! Let us register humanity's disapproval as it should have been registered long ago!

"My country is not afraid to do it.

"Is yours?"

And as a great roar of "NO!" welled up, he turned, bowed to the President, bowed to the Assembly, and came down.

"Well!" the London *Daily Telegraph* remarked in the press gallery. "That rather puts it up to you chaps, doesn't it?"

"I guess it does," the *Associated Press* agreed crisply. "And here comes Cullee Hamilton to do it."

"But not looking like the Wreck of the Hesperus," the *Telegraph* protested with a groan. "Oh, my God, now! How corny can you be?"

"About as corny as Terry a week ago. I don't remember any great protest then."

"But these buggers won't see the connection. It's psychologically all wrong, I tell you. Wait and see."

It was not until Cullee reached the rostrum and turned, however, that the full impact of his appearance struck the Assembly, and then it was several moments, as he bowed to the President and came to the lectern, before the angry and scornful murmurings began. Once started, they mounted rapidly as he stood there looking with an angry scorn of his own upon the restless crowd. There broke out in the Soviet delegation a pounding of desks and a harsh booing that was instantly taken up across the floor. Cullee turned without expression and gazed impassively at the President, who nodded and pounded angrily with his gavel. At first it seemed to do no good. Then the hostile noises gradually subsided enough so that he could be heard against them.

"If the Assembly does not accord its speakers common courtesy in this debate," he said, his round cheeks aflame with indignation, his whole plump little body seeming to quiver with anger, "then the Chair will suspend this meeting!"

"The Chair has no right to suspend a meeting!" someone shouted from the floor, and the President crashed down his gavel upon the words as though he would drive it through his desk.

"The Chair, the Secretary-General, and the Deputy Secretary-General will leave this podium. What will you do to run the meeting then, you who have so little regard for the dignity of the United Nations!"

"Mr. President!" Vasily Tashikov cried, jumping up and rushing down the aisle. "Point of order, Mr. President! Point of order! The Chair has no right to abandon the meeting! The rules do not permit it, Mr. President! The rules do not permit the Chair—"

"Then the delegate of the Soviet Union *will take his seat!*" the President cried, spitting out the words. "And this Assembly will *proceed in order!*"

And presently, grumbling and pouting and resentful, like an unruly group of children, those delegations that were responsible for the demonstration gradually quieted, while those other delegations that had not participated waited with a silent but ill-concealed impatience for the debate to proceed.

"Mr. President," Cullee said into the queasy calm that ensued, "I wish to thank the distinguished delegate of Guinea for his polite, pleasant, dignified, honorable, kind, decent, tolerant, fair, helpful, and constructive address. He has called my country vicious names. He has called me vicious names. If he thinks he can scare either, he has another think coming.

"I want you to look," he cried with a sudden, rising anger as a sullen muttering of protest again broke out on the floor, "I want you to look at what can happen when a man tries to be all those decent things that the delegate of Guinea is not. Yes, I want you to look! Yes," he shouted as the protests mounted to a renewed chorus of booing, "I want you to look at me and see what you think of it. You looked at my friend, that big old pretty Terry, when he came here the other day in his dirty diapers and showed them to you!" ("My *God*," said the London *Daily Express*. "Here's fun!") "Now you look at *me*, all you loud talkers who know so much about my country. Maybe you don't think anybody cares about the racial situation in the United States. You'd better think again. Somebody cared enough to beat me up. *I* cared enough to do what I did in the Congress, and what I'm doing here right now. I tell you, smart boys, *we* care, and we know a lot more about it than you do, I can tell you that!"

There was a great roar of boos, but, encouraging to him and sending the excitement in the hall to even greater pitch, there met it this time a thunder of approval and applause.

"Now, Mr. President," he said when both abated, "the delegate of Guinea, who knows so much, weeps and moans about what is going on in the United States about race. Does he know what the situation was thirty years ago? Does he know how much it's improved today? Sure! It's easy to pick out bad places and beat your breast about them, and *I'm not saying* that my country is perfect. But I am saying that my country has made great strides and that she'll continue to make great strides. And without a lot of black busybodies running around here pretending to talk like statesmen and acting like fools."

"Woweee!" Lafe said softly in the delegation as the boos began. "I don't know, Cullee, boy. Maybe you'd better take it easy, chum."

"He's all right," Hal said, through the screen of pain that was gradually becoming more intense, creeping and creeping over his body, clouding the world. "He's O.K. It's meet fire with fire, now, I guess."

"I guess," Lafe said, though doubtfully.

"Mr. President, the fine delegate of Guinea who knows so much about my country makes a lot of stuff because the President of the United States and the Secretary of State did honor to Senator Cooley. I honor him myself. He was a friend of mine! Yes, he was!" he said, as the sound of protest rose again from the floor. "I didn't agree with him and he didn't agree with me. I think he was wrong in what he always believed on race and in what he set out to do to my resolution in Congress. But at least he was a man. He fought in the open. He wasn't"—and a scathing sarcasm entered his voice—"some sneaking little jackal running around snapping at the heels of the United States. He believed what he believed, and I believed what I believed, and we set out to beat each other if we could.

"Well, I won, thanks to my colleagues in the Congress, and he lost. But we respected each other as human beings, and it didn't make any difference how we disagreed; at least we were decent to each other. And I say to you like my good friend from the Senate, Senator Fry, that's what we're talking about right here.

"It's what you want to make of the United Nations, not what you want to do to us. We'll survive that, if that's the way you decide to vote. But the day will come when the UN won't survive it, if you keep on like this, attacking everybody's good faith and being intolerant of what decent people are trying to do. And then when somebody jumps on *you*, little smart boys, you can go whistle.

"The UN won't be able to help you, and the world won't care."

Again there was an angry exclamation of protest from many places across the floor, some desk-pounding from the Communists, the customary UN show that more often than not greets the expression of uncomfortable truth. He shook his head impatiently and plunged on to his conclusion.

"One other thing," he said, and a cold anger came into his voice. "About this black-white, white-black business the clever boy from Guinea made so much big talk about. I don't make any apologies, to you or anybody, for trying to help my country work out her problems. She is *my country*—maybe you can get that through your heads—and I'm going to keep right on doing what I can to help her. We have lots of problems in the United States, and maybe race is the biggest right now, but I've made my choice on whether we can settle it by trying to work together or by trying to beat each other's heads in.

"I think we've got to work together, and I'm sticking to that even if it means getting *my* head beaten in. It was! Two nights ago! But here I am, and I'm not changing because some cowards jumped me from behind. I'm not changing because some sneerers jump me from in front here, either. We've got more important things to do in my country than worry about that kind of stuff.

"Now," he said, more calmly, into the silence that had settled upon his audience as its more vocal members had finally realized that he would not be intimidated by their outbursts, "you think it over. You aren't just voting on us. You're voting on yourselves, and on the UN.

"We can take care of ourselves, if we have to, in this world. *But you can't.* You'd better think awhile, before you weaken this thing further."

He paused and then spoke his final sentence softly into the silence.

"You'll be pretty lonely, if it isn't here any more to protect you."

For several moments after he left the rostrum and strode back up the aisle, an uneasy silence continued in the great hall. Then, abruptly, the boos began again and, opposing them, the shouts of approval and applause. In the general uproar the London *Daily Express* turned to *United Press International* with a quizzical grin.

"Such magnificent candor!" he said dryly. "Do you think it will sway the nations?"

"It ought to be at least as good as the shoe-pounding," UPI remarked. "And maybe more to the point."

"We shall find out," the *Express* noted with a pleasant anticipation. "The Shoe-Pounder-in-Residence approacheth."

As Vasily Tashikov came rapidly forward down the aisle, it could be seen by all the watching eyes 'round about that in the United States delegation Representative Hamilton was greeted with handshakes and congratulations by his colleagues and that the British Ambassador, too, leaned over to shake his hand. It could be seen that Senator Smith clapped him with especial fervor on the back, and that Senator Fry spoke with him briefly with a tired but cordial smile. It could be seen that after this first flurry died down, the Congressman engaged in a private whispered talk with the Senator from West Virginia, and to some nearby it seemed that the import must be even more serious than the issue at hand, so concerned did the Congressman seem. The Senator from Iowa, too, leaned over presently and entered in; but if they were trying to persuade Senator Fry to leave the floor, as some suspected, it was obvious that they failed, for he shook his head slowly and firmly and remained where he was, slumped slightly in his seat, his hands resting on the desk before him. It could be seen that his colleagues looked at one another over his head with expressions of deep concern and worry; but there, for the moment at least, the matter seemed to rest.

The Soviet Ambassador was, as always, blunt, explosive, and to the point as he saw it.

"Mr. President," he said with a heavy sarcasm as earphones went on and dials were switched to the Russian translation, "we have been treated to lectures here this afternoon. It is all we have been given—lectures. Lectures, lectures, lectures! How noble is this United States, Mr. President! Just ask its representatives and they will tell you. They will tell you and tell you and tell you and tell you!

"Well, Mr. President"—and the sarcasm became more biting—"perhaps it is being forgotten how noble the United States really is. Perhaps it is being neglected here. Perhaps all these words of the distinguished representatives of the United States are hiding it. Perhaps it is time to hear once more from the man who really knows these colonialist racist oppressors in their own land as they really are.

"Mr. President, I ask permission of this Assembly that the great fighter for freedom in Africa of the colored races, who will soon be seated among us now that his nation has been voted approval by this Assembly, the distinguished M'Bulu of Mbuele, be accorded the courtesy of the microphone to speak to us before we vote."

"You have heard the request of the distinguished delegate of the Soviet Union—" the President began, but he was interrupted by a cry of "Point of order!" from the floor. Senator Fry was coming down the aisle again, walking with a careful slowness that caused a busy whisper in his wake. But he went forward doggedly, climbed rather than ascended the rostrum, and turned to face them at the lectern.

"Mr. President," he said, his voice sounding heavy with fatigue—("What *is* the matter with that man?" the Manchester *Guardian* demanded of his neighbors in the press gallery, but none could give him answer)—"my delegation did not object, some days ago, when His Royal Highness was allowed, without regard for the rules of the Assembly, to speak at length in a harsh and bitter attack upon the United States. We did not object when he spoke last night, because that was a concern of the United Kingdom, not ours. We will not object to his speaking here again once his nation has become independent and has been accorded membership among us.

"But we do object now, Mr. President, at this stage in this debate, to a rehash of old arguments and old attacks. The Congress of the United States has given His Highness full apology and recompense for any hurt he may have suffered while visiting this country. We see nothing to be gained by going over it again.

"Accordingly we make the point of order that the M'Bulu's nation is not a member of this Assembly, and so he is not entitled to the right to speak in this forum at this time."

"The Chair believes the point of order of the distinguished representative of the United States is well taken—" the President began. The Soviet Ambassador's cry broke across his words.

"Appeal the ruling!" he shouted. "Roll call! Roll call!"

"Roll call!" echoed many voices, and the President, with an expression of annoyance, reached into the box of names and drew one as Hal Fry returned slowly to his seat. "The voting is on the ruling of the Chair denying the M'Bulu the right to speak. A vote Yes will uphold the appeal and reverse the ruling. A vote No will uphold the ruling. The voting will begin with Iceland."

"Yes," said Iceland.

"India."

"Yes."

"Indonesia."

"Yes."

"Iran."

"Yes."

"Iraq."

"Yes."

"I rather think you shouldn't have tried it, you know?" the London *Observer* remarked ten minutes later. "It just puts your strategic weakness on the record again."

"On the appeal of the Chair's ruling," the President announced sourly five minutes after that, "the vote is 61 Yes, 54 No, the appeal is upheld, and the ruling is reversed. His Royal Highness the M'Bulu."

"What it really does," said the *Wall Street Journal*, "is put the weakness of the rules on the record."

"Not at all," said the *Observer*. "It just depends on who they're being used for, that's all."

"Or against," said the *Wall Street Journal*.

"Mr. President," said Terrible Terry in his guttural way as the wave of frenzied applause that greeted him finally died out, "I am not, as you see, wearing my dirty diapers today."

There was a shout of laughter. With a cheerful smile he nodded and went on.

"I am not wearing them because I do not think this Assembly needs to be reminded of what they symbolize. I think this Assembly is fully aware of what they symbolize. I think this Assembly knows who it is who really has dirty diapers, Mr. President." He frowned and spat out the words with an angry emphasis. "*It is not the decent peoples of this earth, Mr. President!*"

A burst of applause welled up. He nodded with a sternly satisfied air and went on.

"No, it is not the decent of the earth. It is not those who know how to treat their fellow men fairly and honorably, whatever their color. It is the racists and colonialists and the blind fools who crush people for their color who wear the dirty diapers of the twentieth century, Mr. President! I say that to my friend from Congress, and I say to him: Look at the diapers of the United States, Mr. President! Look at your own country's diapers! That is where the dirt is. *Not anywhere else!*"

Again there was a roar of approval, and it was noted that in the U.S. delegation the Congressman from California was being persuaded by his colleagues not to go to the rostrum and demand the right of reply. After several moments of heated argument, he was apparently convinced and settled back down in his seat, a fearful scowl upon his face.

"I committed a great crime in this United States that preaches to all the world," the M'Bulu said with a harsh sarcasm. "I took a little girl to school. That is a great crime in the United States, for little children to go to school—*if they are black*. It is also a crime for some of us, as my good friend from Guinea says, to go to certain places, live in certain places, eat in certain places, live in certain houses—*if we are black*."

There was an angry murmur and he raised his hand to stay it.

"But, Mr. President," he said in a tone of elaborate tiredness and disgust, "why recite again the sorry list of sorry things in this unhappy land that tells the world how noble it is? We all know what they are. We all know that they will not be corrected without the outside pressures of world opinion—at least they will not be corrected as speedily as they should be.

At least they will not be corrected fast enough to keep pace with us, who are free"—his voice rose in a series of steadily mounting challenges—"who are decent—who know how to treat other people—who believe in real freedom and democracy! I say to you, Mr. President," he concluded as a wave of approving sound began to gather across the floor and surge toward him in growing excitement, "let us pass this resolution! Let us declare the conscience of mankind! Let us tell this United States that humanity expects it to practice what it preaches—if it would have us respect it in the world!"

A crashing explosion of sound swept the chamber as he turned, bowed gravely to the President, bowed to the Assembly, and stepped down. Again from the American delegation, after a hasty conference with his colleagues, terminated by their approving nods, the Congressman from California came forward.

"Mr. President," he said, "I shall not waste any time replying to Terry. He has done enough damage to my country, and I hope he is happy with it. He can go home in triumph now, and maybe they won't cut his head off because he's been such a big boy over here. Anyway," he said as an audible gasp from the Assembly greeted his remark, "that's his problem, not ours."

"Young Cullee's really on the warpath, isn't he?" the *Christian Science Monitor* said. The London *Daily Mirror* nodded.

"I hear there's been a little hanky-panky between his wife and the distinguished M'Bulu. These things rankle, you know."

"Oh, is that his only motivation?" the *Monitor* inquired.

"What else?" asked the *Daily Mirror*.

"Mr. President," Cullee said, "it is not the purpose of my delegation to delay a vote on this resolution." A skeptical ripple of amusement met this, but he went on calmly. "No, it really isn't. But we do believe that there might be some profit to the Assembly in hearing the comments of the one man among us who represents some continuity in the United Nations. I have not consulted him on this. I do not know that he is ready to speak or wishes to speak. But I do know that he is black, and I do know that he is devoted to this organization, and I do think that perhaps his thoughts will be of some interest.

"Mr. President, I should like to inquire if the distinguished Secretary-General would wish to address us at this time?"

So here it was, the S.-G. thought in the minute or two that he sat considering, while below him the Congressman from California looked up with a questioning air, in which respect and curiosity and a certain irony walked side by side. In the challenge of those eyes, much more than in the hundreds of others that watched him in a fascinated blur from floor and galleries, he could see himself mirrored. What now, old man? he asked himself with a bitter skepticism. You wanted a chance to speak, though you are afraid of it in your heart. What will you do, now that it has come?

A minute later, his body having answered before his mind did, he found himself standing at the lectern, dignified and patriarchal and appearing to be wise; yet even as he began to speak he did not know exactly what, from all his tumbling thoughts, would emerge.

"Mr. President," he started slowly, while the Assembly accorded him what it had accorded no one else so far in the debate—an almost complete silence— "I have always thought that the Secretary-General embodied, to some degree, the conscience of mankind—at least I have thought he should try to do so. Sometimes I know this has not been easy for my predecessors. Sometimes it has not been easy for me.

"It is not easy for me now.

"Yet I must attempt it, for I regard it to be my duty.

"The Assembly is seized here today of an issue upon which, obviously, great emotions rest. Members of the Assembly have made that amply clear, on both sides. Yet is there not some higher responsibility than that of emotion? Is there not a duty to the United Nations itself?"

The first uneasy stirrings began below him, but he went steadily ahead.

"Were I to yield to my emotions, Mr. President, I should perhaps find it pleasant to join with my good friend from Guinea and with His Royal Highness in an appeal such as they have made. *Yes!*" he cried, as an angry murmur began to rise. "Yes, that is right! Try to tell *me* I am not black! Try to tell *me* I have not fought for free Africa all my life! Try to tell *me* I do not believe in justice and democracy! Try to tell *me* those things, and I will say you lie!"

He paused and stared out upon them sternly, until the murmur died and there was again a silence, restless but attentive, in the big blue-and-tan bowl.

"Well, then. So I do not believe that such an appeal serves the interests of the United Nations, or of humanity. No more do I believe that the racial practices of the United States, which this resolution condemns, serve the purposes of the United Nations, or of humanity. So what is the solution, as between those two positions?

"Mr. President," he said solemnly, and now there was an almost painful concentration upon his words over all the great hall, "I do not believe this resolution should pass."

A sudden loud cry of "NO!"—a babble of sound—a roar of boos: he waited for them to subside, his expression indicating nothing, his classic head held rigid and unyielding.

"This may be an irregular expression of opinion from the Secretary-General. Yet I deem I must express it in view of the dangerous emotions stated here.

"Now, look you!" he said, as though lecturing children, which, in some cases, he was. "Do you not think the United States is aware, now, if it had any doubt before, of what the world thinks about certain of its unfortunate social habits? Do you think it has to be made clear by the formal condemnation of this Assembly?"

Someone shouted "YES!" He ignored it.

"I warn you of what the delegation of the United States has refrained from warning you: Such action could very well induce among the people of the United States a revulsion that would have the gravest effect upon future United States support of this organization."

Again there were boos, but this time not quite so confident—a little hesitant, a little unsure.

"Yes. That is something you should think about.

"Furthermore, the distinguished senior delegate of the United States is correct. There is too much backbiting here. There is too much vindictiveness. There is too much attempt to rewrite the wrongs of the past on this floor, and in so doing to turn them into the wrongs of the present and the future.

"The United Nations is at issue here, just as much as any racial practices of any one of its members. *Many* of you do not have perfect racial practices in your own countries. But all of you have the greatest stake in preserving the United Nations as an instrument for peace and a protection for all powers under a rule of law. You are trying to ignore law here, as you have on other matters in recent years. You will do it too much, one day. And that will be the end.

"Mr. President," he said simply into the hush that followed, "I have spoken. Not to please anyone, but because I, an old man who will soon be leaving this world, would like to see it continued with some hope of decency and understanding among nations. Condemn me for it if you like. I have spoken."

And with a grave inclination of his stately head he returned to his seat beside the portly little President and looked out impassively upon the Assembly. You have done it, old man, he thought. You need not be ashamed of yourself any longer.

There followed for several minutes thereafter a puzzled and uneasy stirring over the floor, particularly in the United States delegation, where there seemed to be some dispute as to what should be done next, and who should do it.

"Is it the wish of the delegation of the United States—?" the President began uncertainly. Senator Fry raised his hand and came slowly forward, holding his body in a curiously bent way that indicated how painful its movements were becoming to him. There was a stir of interest and much comment through the chamber.

"Lafe," Cullee said, sliding over into Hal's vacated seat beside him, "I'm worried as hell about that man."

"So am I," Lafe said with a frown. "He's apparently feeling much worse, but he won't admit it."

"It's seemed to me in the last few minutes that he was much more tense. I wish we could make him go lie down."

Lafe sighed.

"He won't. He's literally a dying man, but he won't stop until he drops."

"But can't we make him?" Cullee asked. Lafe shook his head.

"This is the way he wants it, and the President and Orrin O.K.'d it, and so we've just got to support him as long as he wants to keep going."

"I feel the way I did the other night with Seab," Cullee said unhappily. "I don't like to see men eaten up by their duty."

"You've been, a little," Lafe said, managing a smile. "Who are you to talk?"

"Well, I can't claim like that. That's different."

"Only in degree," Lafe said, his eyes going back with worry to Hal, now slowly climbing the stairs to the distant rostrum. "Listen. And we'd better be ready to go to him if he needs us."

But for the first few moments of his new appearance before the Assembly the senior Senator from West Virginia did not appear to need help, though all his symptoms were now rampaging through his body. Only his bow to the President showed it—generally in the right direction but sufficiently off center so that the comment from the floor grew louder. He turned back to the lectern, which he gripped with a painful desperation, and managed to begin his statement, slowly and carefully, with a tight and rigid control. It did not last.

"Mr. President, the delegation of the United States wishes to commend and thank the Secretary-General for a . . . courageous expression of . . . opinion. It is . . . not the purpose of the delegation . . . of the United States . . . to delay . . . any longer . . ."

"What's the matter" Cullee said sharply, and he and Lafe both stood up.

"Come on," Lafe said. "Let's go!"

". . . a vote . . . on this matter," Senator Fry said with an increasing slowness and almost, it seemed, a drowsiness. "And therefore, Mr. . . . President . . . we ask for an . . . immediate . . ."

There was a flicker of movement, the faintest suggestion of sound, and suddenly he wasn't standing there any more. The rostrum was apparently empty, and from their seats above, the President and the Secretary-General were hurrying down even as others came hurrying up from the floor. A wave of excitement and shock filled the room, comment and question and the half-happy anticipation with which human beings greet the visiting of disaster upon one of their number. Many delegates stood and craned forward to see. Down the aisle Lafe and Cullee came running, reaching their fallen colleague simultaneously with the Secretary-General, who knelt at once beside him and cradled his head in his lap.

"The doctor will come," the S.-G. assured them hastily, and even as he did so, Hal's eyes opened in a gray face and somehow, from somewhere, he managed a small, self-deprecating smile with which to greet his two frantic friends.

"What a spectacle," he whispered. "I'm sorry."

"You're getting on back to that hospital right now, buster," Lafe said with a fright that made his words sound angry. "We've had enough of this nonsense!"

"Not nonsense at all," Hal contradicted, his voice growing a little stronger and steadier. "This is all an elaborate plot . . . by the American delegation . . . to gain sympathy. You wait and see."

"Plot or no," Lafe said firmly, "you're getting on back."

"No, I'm not," Hal said, some color beginning to return to his face. "It was just a temporary dizziness. I've got some pills in my pocket—" He held out a hand to the S.-G., who helped him sit up, as above them the President, returning hastily to his seat, rapped the gavel and announced into the stillness that followed:

"Delegates are advised that the distinguished delegate of the United States seems to have suffered a slight fainting spell, but he is already feeling better, and I think we can continue in a few moments, if delegates will be patient."

"Give me a glass of water," Hal said. "It's those two-tone jobs in my right pocket. Let me have one." He managed a smile. "Or two." He rubbed his forehead. "That was a damn-fool thing to do, but I just—just—blacked out, I guess."

"You *must* get back to the hospital," Lafe said, but his colleague waved him off as the Secretary-General handed him a glass of water and Cullee, squatting down beside him, got the bottle from his pocket, shook out a couple of pills, and put them in his hand.

"That's better," Hal said, swallowing them down. "Now give me a lift, Lafe. Don't just stand there like a dope. Here, damn it!"

And he held out a hand, which his colleague finally took, reluctantly, and together he and Cullee brought Hal to his feet, where he stood for a moment, rocking slightly, as a burst of applause, for the moment genuinely friendly, came from floor and galleries.

"Now get back," he said, again with a little smile. "I still have the floor."

"But—" Lafe protested. Hal waved him off and moved with a reasonably steady tread to the lectern as Lafe and Cullee and the S.-G. stood in a little protective group nearby. The President rapped his gavel and silence fell.

"As I was saying when I was so rudely interrupted," Hal Fry said in a ragged but somehow cheerful voice, and there was a wave of laughter, still friendly and encouraging, "the United States does not wish to delay a vote on this resolution. Therefore, Mr. President, we ask an immediate roll call."

A burst of approving applause, swelled with a note of real warmth, came as he left the rostrum, closely accompanied by his two colleagues but moving under his own steam, and came slowly back up the aisle.

"The vote occurs on the resolution of the delegate of Panama on The Matter of the United States," the President said, reaching into the box of names. "The voting will begin with Ethiopia."

An abrupt singing silence fell on the hall, and into it Ethiopia gave her expected answer, clear and firm.

"Yes."

"Federation of Malaya."

"Yes."

"Finland."

"No."

"France"—and there was a quick intake of breath as Raoul Barre called out his one crisp word:

"*Oui!*"

"Gabon."

"*Oui.*"

"Ghana."

"Yes!"

"Greece."

"No."

"Guatemala."

"*No.*"

"Guiana."

"Yes."

"Guinea."

"*Oui!*"

"Haiti."

"*Oui!*"

"Honduras."

"*No.*"

"Hungary."

"Yes."

"Iceland."

"Yes."

"I still think—" Lafe was saying in the delegation, but Hal Fry shook his head.

"I'll go back pretty soon," he said. "This will be over in a little while, and then I'll go . . . Look, Lafe," he said softly, "I'm not under any illusions. The next will be worse. And the next. And the next. And the next . . . When I go back to the hospital tonight"—and a bleakness that wrung the hearts of his two colleagues as they leaned close to listen came suddenly into his eyes—"I won't be coming out again. I know that. So just—let me stay. O.K.?"

Lafe bowed his head.

"As you say."

"Anyway," Hal said, more lightly. "I'm not through yet. I may have something else to say."

"Now, damn it—" Lafe began again, but again Hal stopped him.

"I may not. But again I may. We'll have to see the note on which this ends. After all," he said with a last show of humor, "who else is better equipped to give a valedictory, if that is what it should have to be?"

"You break my heart," Cullee told him simply.

"Listen to the vote," Hal commanded lightly, though the dizziness and pain were back again and the pills were not really helping very much. "That's more important than hearts, right now."

And as the long roll call moved on, it did become important, quite literally the most important thing in the world at that moment, so that as it neared its end the great room was gripped with an almost unbearable tension and excitement in which only an occasional sharp intake of breath, a muffled exclamation, the sound of someone accidentally hitting the metal shade of his desk lamp with a pencil, broke the silence. Many delegates were keeping their own tallies, and from them there spread like lightning across the floor the startling word: the vote was coming down to its finish in a tie. Four names remained, and the President called them out with an almost defiant loudness that betrayed his own excitement:

"Denmark!"

"No."

"Dominican Republic!"

"*Sí.*"

"Ecuador."

"No."

"El Salvador!"

"*Sí!*"

"On this vote," the President said, his voice trembling slightly, there are 60 Yes, 60 No, 2 abstentions, others absent."

He paused for a moment, while all over the chamber there was an explosion of bottled-up emotion.

"Under Rule 97," he went on, reading from it as it lay before him on his desk, " 'If a vote is equally divided on matters other than elections, a second vote shall be taken at a subsequent meeting which shall be held within forty-eight hours of the first vote, and it shall be expressly mentioned in the agenda that a second vote will be taken on the matter in question. If this vote also results in equality, the proposal shall be regarded as rejected.'

"Therefore, if it is the pleasure of the Assembly, it is the intention of the Chair to call a subsequent meeting of this plenary session for 3 P.M. on Monday next—"

"Mr. President!" someone called from the floor, and down the aisle to the rostrum there could be seen advancing the dapper figure of the French Ambassador, walking in a purposeful but unhurried fashion as a wave of noisy speculation followed in his wake.

"Mr. President," Raoul Barre said calmly, "all delegations have discussed this matter at great length both publicly and privately in recent days. Therefore it is quite likely that no votes will be changed should a subsequent meeting be held.

"Furthermore, I do not know how others feel, but my delegation is sick of it, we believe the time of the Assembly has been employed enough in this matter, and we are not disposed to consider it any further.

"Therefore: since another vote would result in the same tie, which in turn would result in the defeat of this resolution, my delegation, which voted Yes, will now change its vote and vote No, thus guaranteeing the defeat of this resolution, which in our opinion is inevitable anyway, and clearing the agenda for other matters before this Assembly."

"Mr. President!" the Soviet Ambassador shouted into the uproar that followed. "Mr. President, it is out of order for a delegate to change his vote after the result is announced!"

"There is nothing in the rules that says so, Mr. President," Raoul Barre said in a bored and contemptuous tone. "Furthermore, I do not remember the distinguished Soviet delegate being so tender of procedure early this morning when several votes were changed after announcement of the first result on Gorotoland. In any event, we have changed our vote now. There it stands. Does anyone wish to join the distinguished Soviet delegate in shouting about it?"

"Mr. President!" Vasily Tashikov cried in an anguished voice. "Mr. President!"

"I hear the delegate," the President shouted, furiously banging his gavel. "I hear the distinguished delegate, who will be in order! So will this Assembly be in order! . . . Now!" he said explosively when a reasonable facsimile of calm had been restored. "Does any other delegation wish to change its vote, one way or the other?"

For a touch-and-go minute there was a busily waiting silence.

"Very well, then. On this vote the total is 59 Yes, 61 No, 2 abstentions, others absent, and the resolution is defeated."

"Thank *you*, Raoul Barre," Lafe said in the delegation, knowing very well what Raoul knew—that another vote might very well go against the United States, and that he had in effect smooth-talked the Assembly into letting him prevent it. "God knows why, Raoul Barre, but thank *you*."

"If there is no further business—" the President began, but once again someone cried "Mr. President!" and in a tired voice he said, "The distinguished delegate of Portugal."

Immediately tension returned. A wave of boos greeted the slight, mustachioed figure of the Portuguese delegate as he mounted the rostrum. He spat, rather than spoke, into the microphone.

"So now we see, Mr. President, the fine results of trying to appease those in this body who are unappeasable! Now we see that the United States, like everyone who tries to bow to pressures no self-respecting nation should bow to, reaps, like everyone, the same reward.

"Now we see, in this vote which came so close to majority condemnation of the United States that in the eyes of the world it *is* condemnation and cannot be explained away as anything else, how pointless it is to try to make friends in this body by crawling to those who are too ignorant and too hostile to be anything but enemies.

"Now we see," he said, his voice rising against the surge of boos that began to rise against him, "what this United Nations is worth. How empty are its pretenses, Mr. President, how shabby its performances! How futile it is to abandon honor and integrity in the hopes of being rewarded by its members! How pointless to run like a scared mouse before this cat which wants nothing but to gobble you up!

"This is what you get, I will say to my friends of the United States. This is what you receive when you try to appease certain nations here. This is what you receive when you abandon principle and try to make humble bargains against your old friends and your own best interests.

"What has it profited you, to treat as you have my country, and Belgium, and South Africa, and others? You tried to please your new-found friends, but you have found they are not friends, even so.

"May you learn from this what the United Nations really is, before it is too late for you!"

And, to the applause of some few delegations but the hisses of many more, he left the rostrum, a fierce scorn upon his face, and returned to his seat, looking neither to right nor to left along the jeering aisle.

"Now," Hal Fry said, struggling slowly to rise, "I must. Get the President's attention for me."

"But, Hal, *damn* it—" Lafe protested.

"Get it, I said!"

"Mr. President!" Cullee shouted, jumping to his feet. "Mr. President!"

"The distinguished delegate of the United States," the President said uncertainly. "Which delegate is it who wishes—?"

"Senator Fry," Cullee said.

Abruptly the hall quieted once again to a close and watching attention as slowly down the aisle, walking with a carefulness that betrayed his weariness and pain in every movement, came the senior Senator from West Virginia. But he did not falter, and when he turned to face them at the lectern his head came up with an earnest and commanding air that stirred and gripped them all.

Of the many things going through his mind, he knew in general which he would select to say; the many things going through his body he was aware of as a sort of great, dark wall of pain hanging between him and a world that, though it now seemed far away, must yet be spoken to. He did not know at that moment, so agonizing was the pain that had defied the sedatives, whether he could even utter words aloud.

Yet he felt he must, and he thought that if he could keep off the dizziness a little bit he could manage. If he held himself very tightly with the aid of the lectern, if he made no sudden gestures to induce further dizziness and nausea, if he kept his mind and attention firmly on the words that it seemed to him must now be said, then he might make it.

He took a deep and trembling breath and began to speak, slowly and carefully, but without pause or other outward sign of the terrible storm within.

"Mr. President, the United States could not leave alone upon this record, as the final words to be said about the United Nations in this debate, the comments just made by the distinguished delegate of Portugal.

"The United States can realize what prompts this bitterness. Just as it can realize, I hope, the bitterness on the other side that has filled much of this debate and resulted in a vote which is, as the delegate of Portugal truly says, for all practical purposes a condemnation of my country.

"Yet, Mr. President: That debate is over, now. That decision has been rendered. Those hostile words and feelings, the United States now hopes, can be put aside and left to history. It is now a question of where we go from here.

"Mr. President," he said, and a note of deeper urgency came into his voice, "I would like to tell you something that I would not tell you if I did not think it would help you to listen more seriously to what I have to say."

He paused, and in the press gallery and everywhere through the Hall, men leaned forward with a rapt and completely absorbed attention.

"A few minutes ago, as you saw, I was overcome by what the President kindly referred to as a temporary fainting spell. I wish"—and he smiled faintly with a wistful ruefulness that almost killed his two colleagues, who had followed him down and were now sitting nearby with the delegation of Tanganyika in the front row of seats—"that the President had been right. I wish it had been temporary."

He paused again for a moment and then, after some obvious inner struggle, managed to keep his voice steady and went on.

"The word 'temporary' no longer belongs to me. Everything I now face is permanent.

"My visit to the hospital, of which many of you have heard, was not encouraging. The disease I have is leukemia." There was a sudden great intake of breath all around the chamber, but he still managed a slight, wry smile. "No votes can be changed on that."

"Oh, God, I wish he didn't have to," Lafe whispered with an agonized expression to Cullee on the floor.

"So, my friends, I have no more axes to grind in this world. Everything is—over—for me. And therefore, perhaps, you will believe me when I say that I am truly concerned about the lack of tolerance and mutual understanding and, if you will forgive the word—because, for me, at least, it no longer has any embarrassment—love, for one another, that seems to be characteristic of our associations here.

"I would like to think, Mr. President," he said, and it seemed to them as they examined him more closely that there was now a certain luminous quality about his skin, a first outward intimation of his ravaging disease, "that the time has come for an end to hate in the world. I would like to think that we have reached a point in human history where we might all realize that hate is no longer effective, that hate, indeed, is fatal.

"Mr. President, I suppose that in a sense I have been guilty of it, for I have had deep suspicions of the Soviet Union. It has seemed to me that hate has been more of a conscious and consistent policy there than it has in any other nation or area. Yet perhaps it is time to put aside that part of the record, too, and appeal to all of us, without regard to nationhood or political policy but simply as human beings to deal with one another kindly and charitably in all things.

"Mr. President"—and there was no doubt that he had them completely now, so silent and attentive was the whole of his colorful audience—"what is the situation of the world at this moment? We all know what it is.

"Armies stand poised. Nuclear arsenals are full to overflowing. Rockets rest at the ready on launching pads around the earth. The arms race mounts and mounts and no one yet has managed to cancel out the logic of history which has always said, before, that arms races have but one ending.

"Hand in hand with all this go suspicion and mistrust and jealousy, bad faith and bitterness, envy and hate. The peoples of the earth huddle in terror before the weight of disaster they have mustered to their command. Nothing but awful destruction seems to lie ahead for humanity, and no fine words and no brave slogans seem any more able to prevent the blowing-out of the tiny flame of hope.

"Oh, Mr. President!" he cried, and his anguish both mental and physical lent his words a vivid power. "How does mankind stand, in this awful hour? Where does it find, in all its pomp and pride and power, the answer to its own fateful divisions? Where on this globe, where in this universe, is there any help for us? Who will come to our aid, who have failed so badly in our trusteeship of the bounteous and lovely earth? Who will save us, if we do not save ourselves?

"I say to you, my friends, no one will. No one will. We are wedded to one another, it may be to our death, it may be to our living. We cannot escape one another, however hard we try. Though we fly to the moon and far beyond, we shall take with us what is in our hearts, and if it be not pure, we shall slaughter one another where'er we meet, as surely on some outward star as here on earth.

"*This* is the human condition—that we cannot flee from one another. For good, for ill, we await ourselves behind every door, down every street, at the end of every passageway. We try to remain apart: we fail. We try to hide: we are exposed. Behind every issue here, behind the myriad quarrels that make up the angry world, we await, always and forever, our own discovery. And nothing makes us better than we are.

"Mr. President," he said, and his voice, beginning to fill with a dragging tiredness, came up in one last powerful surge of effort. "I beg of you, here in this body of which men have hoped so much and for which they have already done so much, let us love one another!

"*Let us love one another!*

"It is all we have left."

With an infinite weary dignity he bowed to the President and the Assembly and came slowly down the steps, no applause, no stirring, no sound breaking the stillness, to his waiting colleagues.

"Well," he whispered with a wistful little smile as they took his arms to brace him on his now quite unsteady walk up the aisle, "at least this time I didn't fall down."

"No," Lafe said in a choked voice. "You didn't fall down."

"If there is no further business to come before the Assembly," the President said "this plenary session is now adjourned."

Five

A SHADE OF DIFFERENCE

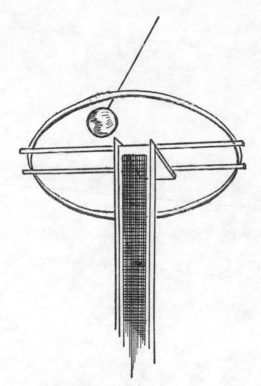

But, of course, so reluctant are men to seek the love that binds them, in contrast to the eager diligence with which they pursue the hate that divides, that by next morning the effect of the speech of the senior United States delegate to the United Nations had been pretty well dissipated around the world.

There were still many millions of ordinary folk in many places over the earth who were profoundly moved and touched and would not soon forget his gray, strained face and desperately earnest words, and who thought that possibly, in the seats of power and communication, so urgent an appeal might perhaps have some moderating effect. But they were only the ordinary folk. In far too many seats of power and communication it was tacitly understood at once that nothing like that could be allowed to interfere with the course of events.

As the speaker had truly implied, love *was* an embarrassing concept, too simple and too direct and too naked and too desperate for those who produced the clever editorials, the smooth radio-television commentaries, the bland, self-serving statements of the leaders of men. Suavely, with respect for Senator Fry's brave effort but with a gentle irony concerning the impossibility of what he proposed, the disturbing subject was put back in its proper place and allowed to do no harm to the plans of the mighty as they whipped on the hurtling juggernaut of the hapless Twentieth Century.

Nor, in fact, was it only the mighty who so reacted; for even among the ordinary folk the human suspicions, the human envies, the human fears and worries and mistrusts came back almost at once after the initial emotion of the speech had died away.

"It's all very well to tell *us* to love *them*," people said, from Shanghai to Seattle, from Tierra del Fuego to Hudson's Bay, in Zanzibar and Yap, in Moscow and Washington, in London and Paris and New Delhi and Athens and all the points between. "The real problem is to get *them* to love *us*."

And so, as always when some human voice gives expression to the deepest yearnings of the human heart, mankind paused for a brief, shivering moment to weep hastily for its own fate and then plunged hurriedly back into the blind pursuit of it.

It was generally agreed that Senator Fry's speech was very noble, and it was apparent already that it would be widely quoted and requoted in many places for as many years as the world had yet to run—but it was seen that it was, after all, only a speech.

Humanity had more pressing things to attend to.

And so, as always, few dared to love.

And the globe spun on.

In the two days following, while the Secretary-General saw to the final arrangements for the annual United Nations Reception and Ball, and while the nations studied the new posture of world affairs in the wake of the Assembly's almost-condemnation of the United States, the various participants in the visit of the M'Bulu and all its ramifications assessed their positions as the episode passed into history.

For Terrible Terry himself, towering at Idlewild in his gorgeous robes before the B.O.A.C. plane that would carry him home, smiling and waving triumphantly to the reporters and cameramen who had gathered to see him off, it seemed that history had given him half the garland while still retaining its grip upon the remainder. He did not show it to those who saw and photographed his cheerful face, nor did he acknowledge it in the happy and confident words in which he permitted himself to be quoted, but it was in a strange mixture of moods that he was leaving the United States.

He did not know, at this moment, what he would find in Gorotoland, or how, or whether, he would survive it. He was not physically afraid, for he had a fierce courage that convinced him that he would win out, whatever the obstacles; but along with it, unfortunately for his complete peace of mind, went an intelligence sophisticated enough to know that sometimes courage was not enough. He might *not* win out, when all was said and done. That would depend on many factors—his people, his cousin, the Communists, the British, his mother, himself. In these complicated days a chieftain needed more than paint, dried bones, a shield, a spear, and the conviction of his people that he was invincible. Invincibility required many things, nowadays: the gods that watched over him would have to be not only well disposed but well equipped. He waved and chatted, but there gnawed at his heart many doubts and misgivings now that he actually faced his return. It did not help him any to see approaching four familiar figures from Washington, or to be told, as they greeted him with a slightly ironic cordiality at planeside, that he would have two of them for company at least as far as London.

"But how delightful!" he exclaimed, as the watching reporters hovered close around. "How delightful, Senator Munson; how delightful, Mrs. Munson! And you, Mr. Secretary? Could we not persuade you and Mrs. Knox to travel with us, too, to brighten up the journey?"

"I'm afraid not, Terry," Orrin Knox said. "We just came up to have dinner with these two and see them off. Then I think we'll stay in town tomorrow and attend the UN Ball tomorrow night. Sorry you couldn't be there."

"Oh, you know how it is," Terry said. "Affairs call one home. There is always something."

"Yes, I know," the Secretary agreed, a trifle dryly. "Well, perhaps next year. After all, you'll be a member then."

"Yes," the M'Bulu agreed, and for a moment nothing but the most complete satisfaction showed in his face and filled his heart. "Yes. So I will."

"Are you going straight on from London?" Dolly Munson asked. "We'll be at the Dorchester, and perhaps if you'd like to have dinner—?"

"Oh, no, thank you, thank you," Terry said quickly. "I must hurry on."

"Can't wait to get back, eh?" the Majority Leader couldn't resist asking, and the listening reporters crowded closer for the M'Bulu's answer.

"You know how it is," he said cheerfully. "Affairs of state, affairs of state!"

"They *are* time-consuming, aren't they?" Beth Knox agreed gently, in a tone that caused Terry to give her a sudden sharp glance. But he covered it with a laugh.

"You and your husband should know, Mrs. Knox. Indeed you should."

"Well, have a good trip," the Secretary said, as the jets began to whistle and the stewardess appeared and looked down upon them questioningly from above. "Robert," he said, shaking hands, "rest well. You deserve it. Dolly, my dear, take care of him." He leaned down. "A kiss to travel on."

"Yes," she said, returning it. "You be careful, too. Beth"—they kissed and looked at one another soberly for a second—"you take care of this one, too."

"I will," Beth said. "Do have a wonderful time, both . . . And you, Your Highness," she said as the Munsons went up the steps and disappeared inside. "A safe journey home."

"And safety when you get there," Orrin Knox said quietly as the reporters retired and the cameramen drew back for a last shot of them shaking hands.

"Thank you," Terry said, suddenly sober. "It is kind of you to wish me that after—after—" He stopped.

"We are a strange people," the Secretary said. "Don't try to understand us. Travel well."

"I shall," the M'Bulu said. "And now," he added with a sudden change of mood and a wink to them both, "I must pose once more for my public." And, ascending to the door of the plane, he turned and did so, laughing in the glare of the flashbulbs and the night lights of the great airport, roaring with activity all around, while from a window nearby the Munsons waved down to the Knoxes and the Knoxes waved back.

"Well," Orrin said as they watched the plane lift off and dwindle rapidly into the night, "there goes an interesting young man."

"Which," Beth said, "probably ranks as the understatement of the year."

"Yes," he said, tucking her hand under his arm. "Brrh, it's cold out here! Let's get on back . . . And a curiously appealing one, too, in his own strange way. I wonder, though—I still wonder whether I handled that correctly. I just don't know."

"I suppose I'm partly to blame, too," she said as they walked rapidly along. "Even though the Secretary of State told me Cullee's resolution was *his* idea, I still think I had something to do with suggesting it." She smiled. "So if you aren't happy with the results, blame me."

"I know," he said glumly. "I know. But—Seab, for instance. And Cullee getting beaten up. And then this gray fizzle at the UN, after everything we'd done . . . You wonder. At least I do."

"Cullee doesn't hold it against you. And I'm sure Seab didn't either. He was a fighter; he respected fighters. And as for the UN—well, I don't see that we could have done much else, regardless of the outcome. Anyway, Harley's satisfied; I'm satisfied. Most people are, I think. So why look back?"

"I didn't used to, much. But the world intrudes, now . . . What are you going to do tomorrow—shop out the town?"

"Want to join me?"

"I suppose I should be over at the UN, but what the hell. Even Secretaries of State have to relax sometimes. Yes, I will."

"Good."

"And now," he said soberly, "one more task and then we can go back to the Waldorf and go to bed."

"Yes," she said, equally subdued. "I hope he will know us."

"I don't know," Orrin said. "Lafe's going to meet us there first, and maybe he'll have the late word."

And, as they met him in the hushed corridors of Harkness, he did; but it was not what they had hoped to hear, though it was what they feared. Hal, he told them, had collapsed completely when he and Cullee brought him back to the hospital. He was now in partial coma and under heavy sedation, unable to see anyone.

"The doctors," Lafe said in a saddened voice, "don't know when, if ever, he will be able to—see anyone again. I'll keep in touch with him, and if there is a better period before—before—I'll let you know, Orrin, and maybe you can fly up. But they don't hold out much hope now."

"Well," the Secretary said after a moment, "if he comes to at all before he goes—you tell him how proud his country is of him, will you? I think Harley is going to give him the Distinguished Service Medal later this week, but of course that probably won't mean anything to him. If by any chance he does have a good period again, I think Harley wants to come up and give it to him here in person. But I suppose that's very problematical, at the moment."

"Very. They doubt that he'll come back at all, now. The strains of the session yesterday pretty well rushed it along, I gather. He was under terrific tension. Cullee and I tried to make him take it easy, but he wouldn't, so— there we are."

"If he had called it off, of course," Beth said, "then he wouldn't have left the world his speech. So, maybe—maybe the Lord knew what He was doing, and you didn't."

"Speech . . ." Lafe mused. "It was a great one, but I wonder what difference it will make, in the long run."

"Sometimes speeches live in ways we can't calculate or understand," Orrin said. "It wasn't such a bad legacy to leave the world. I wouldn't mind going out with something like that behind me."

Lafe nodded.

"No, you're right. Neither would I. I'd be proud . . . Though I think," he added in a voice suddenly moved with emotion, "that he blacked out before he really had time to be."

"What about his son?" Beth asked softly, and Lafe managed a little smile.

"I went up to see him this morning."

"Oh? How is he?"

"The same. But you know something, Beth? I'm going to work with that boy. I really am. Hal sort of—entrusted him—to me, a few days ago. He asked me to look after him, and I will. I just can't accept the idea that anyone as fine-looking as that, and as bright as Hal has told me he was as a child, is just—gone—forever. I don't think Hal really ever accepted it, and I refuse to, too." He gave a thoughtful smile, something faraway and touching in his expression. "He's a challenge to me," he said softly. "I'm going to bring that boy back, someday, Beth. You wait and see."

"Oh, I hope so," she said earnestly, putting a hand on his arm. "My dear Lafe, I hope so."

"I will. I will . . . Well: you're staying for the ball tomorrow night? It should be fun."

"Yes," Orrin said, "and tomorrow we're going to shop out the town, so I'm told. Why don't you have breakfast with us and come along?"

"I'll have breakfast with you, but I won't go shopping. I want to do some reading at the Library, I think, and then come back here and talk to some of the doctors about cases like Jimmy's." He smiled. "I've got a lot of homework to do in that area, if I'm to go about it correctly."

"Yes," Beth said. "I think that's the right thing to do. Now"—she added gently—"now that you have a son."

"Yes," Lafe said; and, quite surprisingly for one whom much of the world considered to be generally light of heart and frivolous of purpose, sudden tears came into his eyes. "Yes."

To the President of the United States, sitting at his desk in the upstairs study, thoughtfully reading the editorials in the newspapers and the great sheaf of telegrams piled before him on this gray Sunday in snow-wrapped Washington, the aftermath of the glittering passage of the heir to Gorotoland was also bringing its second thoughts and sober reappraisals.

It was obvious already that a new and grave turning in foreign policy had come in the minds of his countrymen as a result of the Assembly's vote on Felix Labaiya's second resolution. Try as they might, previously friendly journals were hard put to it to find in their editorial hearts quite the measure of earnest endorsement of the United Nations that they had found before. There was the reluctant and cautious admission that just possibly the organization might be moving in directions that would bring it into sharp and perhaps fatal disrepute with the great commonalty of the United States. There was the wistful and aching hope that somehow this would not be so. There was the anguished reiteration of the theme that It Must Survive—There Isn't Anything Else. And there were the customary stern and self-righteous admonitions to him, the President, to Keep Calm, Judge Fairly, and Not Act Hastily In The Heat Of The Moment.

Well, they needn't worry—he wasn't going to do that. But there was no mistaking the correctness of their fearful analyses of the public reaction. Of the telegrams flooding into the White House at the rate of some five hundred an hour, possibly twenty were in wholehearted approval of the actions of the United Nations with regard to the Labaiya resolution; all the rest were as violently critical as the regulations of the Federal Communications Commission would permit. He had also received a number of worried telephone calls from various members of the Senate and House, at home in their states and getting a terrific backlash against the UN from their constituents. He gathered from the worried voices of old friends as they came to him from around the continent that there was a shocked and indignant feeling of "They can't do that to *us*" that promised rough going in the months ahead for the policies he deemed best.

Without attempting to judge, for the moment, the merits of the dispute or the decision, he could understand, in a way that many of his countrymen had not until now been able to match, exactly why they could, indeed, "do that to us." Perhaps for the first time, Americans were beginning to perceive how certain of their racial policies inflamed and antagonized the newly independent world. He could understand how those policies had arisen, in human error and human blindness; he could know what was the genuine truth of it—that his Administration, like all recent Administrations, had devoted itself to correcting those policies as speedily and honorably as could possibly be done. But he could also know that the past histories of many who now had the power to make their harshly antagonistic judgments felt in the UN had made it impossible for them to concede or realize these things.

This was but another example of one of the constantly recurring tragedies of history: the fatal timetable between cause and effect, the fatal inability of the understanding of the one to catch up with the blind prejudice aroused by the other.

In a minor degree, which had turned out to be a very major one before the M'Bulu's visit was done, he himself had been responsible for such a lag. His initial refusal to give Terry the hospitality he desired, which the President still felt had been entirely correct, plus his inadvertent press conference blurt, which he knew ruefully to have been a human mistake but quite incorrect in view of all the tender feelings involved, had given opponents of the United States exactly the lever they sought. The all-out assault of the Soviets at Geneva had failed, and he rather thought it would be some time before anything so blatant would be attempted again. Therefore, the game now was to go back to previous policies of attempting to wear down and tear down the American image wherever and whenever it could be done. In a sense, the UN debate over the Labaiya resolution had been just as serious for his country as the meeting at Geneva. He was sadly aware that his country had not emerged from it with an equal success. Not because it had not tried to, in good faith and good intention, with a Congressional resolution that did, indeed, represent a startling act of compliance from a major power; but because there was, in the UN at this time, a mood that negated such gestures almost before they began.

Just as many members of the UN were honestly blinded by their emotions to the genuine integrity of such a gesture, so a great many of his country-men were now going to be honestly blinded by their emotions against the UN.

There was, for a responsible man in such a situation, no course that could safely be based upon the sort of angry haste that the more admonitory metropolitan journals needlessly warned him against; but there was the al-most inevitable certainty that his countrymen were going to force his Ad-ministration into a most serious re-examination of the United States' re-lationship to the UN, and to the world itself, in the ensuing months. It would, he knew, inevitably color and shape the coming Presidential cam-paign. It would impose certain imperatives, even as it restricted their abilities to deal with those imperatives, upon such ambitious men as Orrin Knox and the Governor of California. And it might well force him, too, to undertake a serious re-examination of plans he had thought he could put away on a shelf of his mind and forget about until the time came to use them.

So as he waited for Lucille to come in and join him for the quiet supper they had planned together before an hour or two of reading aloud and then an early bed, the President knew very well that the M'Bulu's visit was not really over, that in a sense it was just beginning, and that much that had already been changed by it would be changed still more as the months and years went by.

As one of those who really were deeply affected by the closing speech of his senior delegate to the United Nations, the President was doing his best, as he sat there at his desk, portly and kindly and comfortable-looking, to approach the changes with love. But he did not know if in these times even love would be strong enough to withstand the winds of anger that howled through the halls of history.

For the Congressman from California, love in these afterhours of Terrible Terry's encounter with his country was a dominant thought but not yet, it seemed to him, in any way an achieved objective. He intended to stay for the UN Ball because he was mad enough at the Africans and Asians so that he wanted to annoy them with his presence just by being there, and to say to them with it: Go to hell if you think you can intimidate Cullee Hamilton or his country.

This was not, he recognized, the spirit of Hal Fry's speech, which had profoundly touched and moved him, but it was about all he could muster as he thought of the smug and superior faces that would smile knowingly at him in the gaily-decorated Main Concourse tomorrow night. If he was to achieve love, he told himself as he wandered aimlessly through Manhattan's snow-clogged Sunday streets, he would have to do better than that.

Well: let somebody love him, then; maybe that would help. He had loved a couple of people, or thought he had, and both had let him down; so let them come back and love him, wherever they were on this cold day in this cold world. Then he would think about love, and maybe after he had thought about it in relation to them he could extend himself a bit and think about it in relation to nations and peoples that would have to go some, now, to convince him that they were anything but what he had told them they were—jackals snapping at the heels of the country he belonged to and still wanted to serve with all the heart and idealism in him.

But, after all, he thought with a sudden impatience, a sudden deeply personal self-criticism as he walked slowly along, head bowed and young face stern in the drafty and near-deserted canyon of Fifth Avenue, why look for the kind of love Hal Fry was talking about, the kind of love the world needed and everyone needed, from outside? It didn't come from outside, that kind of love: it came from inside. It was something you had to work out yourself, from your own being—then maybe if you really ever achieved it inside, somebody who had also achieved it inside would come along, and you could have it together and it would really be something— then you could give it to the world too. But only after you had achieved it inside. Only then.

That's what it really has to boil down to, little Cullee Hamilton from Lena, S.C., walking down your long dark street, he told himself; that's where it has to come from, if you're to have it, right from inside. And you know it hasn't come yet, no, sir. It may be on the way, somewhere inside there, but it hasn't come yet, for all your devotion to country and your decent, stubborn heart.

Exactly because of that decency, he did not, as he walked the cold city, give himself credit for the fact that, in his deep concern for his country and his compassionate attempt to bridge the gap between the races in their difficult relationship, he had already gone some distance along the way to love.

He was too humble to realize it, but little Cullee Hamilton from Lena, S.C., had gone already a long way farther than most.

Three others also appraised their positions, in another of their three-way telephone conversations, while far above the Atlantic the towering young giant who had affected all their lives winged worriedly home.

It was not a satisfactory conversation, and it accomplished nothing save to increase a little more the tensions between them. From Sacramento, Governor Jason made clear that he would increasingly disassociate himself from his brother-in-law. From Washington, his sister made clear that she would probably have to follow his lead in the long run, if not immediately. From the St. Regis in New York, Felix Labaiya made clear that while he would regret this, he did not, perhaps, really care.

Yet, in the curious fashion of their curious relationship, none of the three was ready to terminate it, and none did. Once again, as always, it was not love but ambition that held the family together; and once again it stopped them short of a final break, though all were aware that they had inched still further toward it, now that Felix had indeed accomplished the damage to their country which neither his wife nor brother-in-law could accept.

Of all those involved in the M'Bulu's visit, he had emerged from it, in his estimation, in the best position. He had for all practical purposes done what he set out to do; and for this, he knew with a fiercely satisfied certainty, his grandfather would have been proud of him. He was proud of himself, as he contemplated the possibilities that now might open up as a gravely damaged United States sought to sort out its policies in the face of near-condemnation by the nations of the world. What had failed by a fluke on one issue might succeed handsomely on some other, now that the ice had been broken.

On the thirty-eighth floor of the Secretariat, serene in his own heart and mind for the first time in many months, the Secretary-General was patiently checking and rechecking the lists of liquor, food, and decorations presented to him by the Director of General Services for the reception and ball tomorrow night. He was calm in the certainty that, whatever the Assembly vote had been, he, like Senator Fry, had contributed some small accrual of decency to the collective conscience of mankind. His speech might not last as long as the Senator's, and yet it, too, was of a nature to give it place in humanity's memory. Possibly it, too, might yet in the long run produce some constructive results here in this argumentative congress of the world. If it could do that, no matter how little, just a very little, to help, he would be content. He thought it would, and he was content.

Now he was going over the preparations for the party, working on a Sunday because he wanted to be sure that nothing would be overlooked, no detail neglected, to make of it a happy and pleasant event for all the races of mankind. They might not be able to forget their animosities and troubles entirely, and yet it was the one occasion when they came closest to it. He appreciated the irony of this, for it was during the one night in the year when they had no business with one another that their organization came closest to that spirit of harmony which its founders had hoped it might eventually achieve in its conduct of human affairs.

But he had no intention of allowing the irony to shadow the event. He wanted this to be a happy night, and patiently, carefully, meticulously, and with a feeling of compassion and love that extended, for the time being, to all the difficult children who fought and argued so furiously in the fateful chambers below, he was doing his best to see that it would be.

2

And so it came time for the nations to dance, and from all the reaches of Megalopolis the Great City, from all the apartments, the hotel rooms, the delegation offices and headquarters, the homes and temporary resting places

of the races of man, the long line of cars and taxicabs began rolling up to the
Delegates' Entrance as the hour approached nine-thirty on a clear, cold
Monday night.

Some came in Fords, some in Ramblers and Chevrolets, some few in tiny
sports cars incongruous in the sleek parade. The choice of most, aware
of their nation's dignity and anxious to suitably chariot their own importance, appeared to have settled upon the chauffeured Cadillacs, the Jaguars
and Mercedes-Benzes provided by Manhattan's many rental agencies. Out of
these stylish conveyances there emerged powdered white faces and shiny
black, dignified tuxedos and the flamboyant raiment of the distant plains
and jungles. Bowing, smiling, laughing, nodding, they descended and moved
within, while all about, electric in the air, could be felt a sense of the high
portentousness of the nations, the touchingly hopeful pomposities of man.

Look at us, they seemed to say: We are the nations. We are the peoples.
We cannot blow ourselves off the face of the earth.
We cannot banish ourselves from history.
We are too important for that.
Look at us, how bright, how brilliant, how notable, how brave!
Do you not believe it?

Outside, overlooking First Avenue, the line of flags snapped bravely in
the wind, and indoors, as the guests deposited their coats and then turned
left from the entrance to make their way around the long curved wall that
on its other side houses Conference Room 4 on the floor below, all the proud
standards stood massed there, too, crowding the narrow passageway so that
quite often some delegate in tuxedo or flowing robe would find himself
brushing Israel, say, out of his face, while his wife did likewise with Italy
or the Ivory Coast. Potted palms and other decorative plants, reminiscent
of the homelands of many who came crowding in, stood over against the
glass wall that separated them from the night, and distantly in the Main
Concourse could be heard the sound of orchestras playing as the line moved
slowly forward in gay and happy anticipation.

Presently the long, jostling progression emerged into the Concourse, to
find waiting the pink little figures of the President of the General Assembly and his wife, the grizzled classical stateliness of the Secretary-General.
Names were given, hands shaken, greetings exchanged. Duty done on both
sides, the guests moved on into the shiny expanses where the wide-eyed
Boy and Girl Scouts, the members of the Springport, Indiana, Parent-
Teachers Association, the United Nations Study Group of the Women's
Club of Twin Falls, Idaho, and all their counterparts and copies were wont
to gather at other times to learn the exciting story of the world organization.

Now the room had been modestly transformed under the direction of the
Secretary-General—not too much, for the budget would not permit it, hampered as it always was by the refusal of some notable members to meet their
assessments—but with a potted plant here, a festoon of paper streamers there,
whirling lights behind red and blue and yellow glass that cast a flickering,

multicolored combination of light and shadow upon the Main Concourse and gave a delightful and pleasing aspect that increased the holiday mood with which the guests turned to their partners and stepped forth upon the floor.

Grouped near Sputnik, midway toward Zeus, a dance band played the latest tunes, while downstairs, on the lower level of the post office and the gift shop, another could be heard performing for the dancers there Toward the south end of the room, near the desk where Miss Burma (East), Miss Malaya (North), Miss Viet Nam (South) and Miss Thailand (West) were accustomed to comment on the unsuspecting tourists, long tables were set out with liquor and food for the buffet, and all along that part of the room, on both sides, smaller tables and chairs stood ready when the dancers should feel moved to eat or drink.

By 10:30 P.M., all the guests having arrived, both dance bands were performing at the peak of their noise and brilliance, both dance areas were filled with swooping, dashing, laughing occupants. The ball was moving at a high pitch of felicity that pleased the Secretary-General as he finally left the reception line and stood for a moment beside the information desk in the central lobby. Many distinguished persons were present, the Ambassador of Panama, Lord and Lady Maudulayne, Raoul and Celestine Barre, many another famous delegate and his lady, many members of the press, several movie stars and actors from Broadway, many members of the Secretariat, the Governor of New York, the Secretary of State, famous statesmen, famous thinkers, famous people. The affair was going well, the S.-G. could sense it. He felt well pleased. Not even Ghana and Guinea, who had submitted formal written protests to his office this morning because of his intervention in the debate, looked sour tonight. They had greeted him cheerfully and now were dancing with an air as gay and carefree as that of all the rest.

Even Vasily Tashikov, he noted with amusement, was dancing with his solid wife, and as they passed the Secretary of State and Mrs. Knox, out in the center of the swirling throng, he could see all four nod and smile with a reasonable cordiality. Even they had succumbed to the mood of the evening, he congratulated himself; even they. Was it not possible to hope, in such a moment, that someday, somehow—

"It would be nice, wouldn't it?" Senator Smith of the United States said quietly at his elbow, and he turned to see that the Senator, too, was watching the little exchange of amenities on the dance floor.

"What?" the S.-G. asked with a start at dissembling; but then he yielded to the mood of the evening and gave up the dissembling. "Yes, it would," he agreed gravely. "If only—"

Lafe sighed.

"The story of the world, summed up in two words: If only. But damn it!" he said with a sudden dark anger that the Secretary-General could understand and fully share. "This is the way it should be! This is how it ought to be! Why can't we do it! *Why can't we ever do it?*"

"I do not know," the Secretary-General said quietly. "The man who finds the answer to that, and shows us the way, will live forever in men's hearts."

"Well," Lafe said, more calmly, "it won't be you or I, that's for sure."

"But we must always try."

Lafe smiled.

"Oh, yes. I don't think either of us has any intention of stopping . . . And it *is* a wonderful party. Everything is going so well."

"Yes. I hope you will stay until the dancing ends."

"Oh, you know me," Lafe said. "Until the last note sounds." His face lighted up as a young Indonesian pair danced by. They saw him, stopped, and waved eagerly, and he waved back. "Excuse me," he said, and moved to engage them in animated conversation.

The S.-G. did not know how long he would stay. He was not as young as he used to be, he did not dance the Western or Latin dances very well, his principal wife had long been dead, and he had no particular companion for this evening. But, still, a man should enjoy the hour while he could, and so he decided to cut in, carefully selecting for the purpose one of the more matronly ladies, brilliantly saried, of the Indian delegation.

As he started forward to separate her politely from her partner, the Ambassador, he was delayed by the Congressman from California, dancing with a tall young Negress, very pretty. Cullee placed an enormous hand gently on his arm.

"Mr. Secretary-General, I would like very much to have you meet my friend, Miss Sarah Johnson of the United States. Sarah and I just met."

"How fortunate," the Secretary-General said with an amused and gentle smile for something in Cullee's tone. "For you both."

"For me, anyway," the Congressman said with a cheerful glance that his partner answered.

"It may be mutual," she said. "We'll have to tell you later, Mr. Secretary-General."

"One thing now, though," Cullee said, still holding him by the arm. "I just want to say that I am proud of you, sir, for your speech to the Assembly. I didn't know when I asked you whether you would want to or not, but I took a chance you might. I think we should all be grateful to you."

The S.-G. smiled.

"Some aren't." The Congressman made an impatient gesture.

"Oh, them! Don't worry about them, Mr. Secretary-General. All decent people are, and they're still what count, in spite of everything. Anyway, I just wanted to thank you. As an American—as a Negro—and I guess, maybe, just—well, as a citizen of the world, if one can say that."

"It's easier to, tonight. I thank you. And of course I, like all decent people, will forever be in the debt of Senator Fry."

"Yes," Cullee said gravely. "I wish he could have been here tonight, but—no chance."

"Is it all over?"

"It soon will be."

"He is a brave man, and a fine one. *There* is a citizen of the world, if the world will but listen."

"Who knows?" Cullee said gloomily. "But," he said, deliberately breaking the mood, "no place for such talk tonight. We're having a fine time at your party, sir, and we hope you are, too."

"I am about to," the S.-G. said with a smile. "I have designs on Miss India. Or, rather, I should say," he added, cocking his noble head on one side and giving her a quizzical squint as she danced by with the Indian Ambassador, "Mrs. India. Or Mother India. I think the 'Miss' disappeared long ago."

"Good luck," Cullee called as the stately old man moved off toward her. "I hope the Ambassador will let her go! . . . Now, Miss Sally J., let's dance."

"Yes, sir," she said, swinging comfortably into his arms as though she had always belonged there. "As you say."

She was puzzled by his answering expression, quizzical and sad for a moment. She could not know that he was saying to himself, Oh, no, Miss Sally J. Not yet awhile. Life isn't *that* pat.

Five minutes later, Krishna Khaleel, relieved of his pleasant but sedate companion by the Secretary-General, and the Secretary of State, similarly relieved of his by the Governor of New York, who had cut in on him and taken Beth away with a dashingly boyish smile, found themselves standing together by the information desk looking out upon the crush.

"Well, K.K., what do you make of it?"

"It is a happy scene," the Indian Ambassador said cheerfully. Then he looked cautious and somewhat puzzled. "What—what, eh? What do you mean?"

"Oh, all this mixing of the races, as we say in some parts of my country. Your 'shade of difference' does not seem so serious tonight."

"Nothing seems serious tonight," K.K. said with a smile. "No, not tonight."

"Why should it ever be?" the Secretary pressed, enjoying his little intellectual game as K.K. looked first starchy, then more relaxed.

"We do not wish it."

"No more do we. Why, then, does it come about? Are you to blame? Or are we?"

"It comes about because of history," the Indian Ambassador said. "That is why it comes about, Orrin. You know that as well as I. We are prisoners of the past. The irony of it is," he added with a rueful smile, "that it is not *our* past, yours and mine and that of all these others here. *We* did not make it. It was made by others, long before and so we must suffer. It hardly seems fair."

"No, it does not," the Secretary agreed, more seriously. "Does it not seem to you, then, that we must try to get out from under it? That we must move onto some new way of thinking about it, together?"

"Ah-ha!" K.K. cried with a sudden laugh. "Now you are leading me on down paths where Hal tried to lead us. Now you wish us to forget the past, and you know we cannot do that. *Poor* Hal," he added, suddenly sad. "Such a dear friend; such a horrible thing."

"I think he feels he may have left us something, if we will but listen."

"But not by forgetting the past. It is impossible, for us."

"I think many of *us* would like to try," the Secretary said. His companion looked at him for a long moment.

"But it is not you who suffered," he said softly.

To this, for which there was little answer—or at least none that could be understood or accepted by many who danced in happy companionship across the Main Concourse—the Secretary returned only, after several seconds of looking directly into the liquid brown eyes that looked directly into his, a shrug.

"Where does that leave us for the future, then? What will it do to the world, if we cannot escape it?"

"Alas, where does it leave you in your own land, let alone the world? How can you handle it elsewhere, if you cannot handle it here?"

"But we *are* handling it here," the Secretary protested. His companion laid a hand quickly on his arm.

"Let half the people who are in this building, which is temporarily enchanted on this enchanted night, go forth into the city of New York, and in ten minutes' time they will be able to tell you how well you are handling it here," K.K. said softly.

"And you?" Orrin Knox asked harshly. "Do you handle it so well, in India?"

"Do not mistake me, my friend," the Indian Ambassador said. "I am not one of those who thinks he is perfect, or that his country is, in this regard. Oh, no, not I! It is just that we must all realize an equal guilt."

"*I* do," the Secretary said, still in the same harsh tone. "I ask only an equal humility. Or perhaps, as Hal Fry said, an equal love."

"Ah, yes," K.K. said gently. "All living comes full circle to that, does it not? And how few perceive it!"

"More than achieve it, I think," the Secretary said. "That is what brings the tears of the ages—that in the area of love so many perceive and so few achieve."

They were silent for a time while the band played gaily and the colorful crowd danced by. The mood had changed when they spoke again, because for that, too, there was no answer.

"My lady and yours are both free," the Indian Ambassador noted. "Shall we rejoin them?"

"I think we should," the Secretary said. "Why don't we exchange partners for a dance? I know Beth would enjoy it."

"How nice!" K.K. cried with a pleased expression. "What a happy thought!"

So the nations danced on, as the night wore away beside the East River to midnight, 1 A.M., 2 A.M., 3 A.M. Quantities of liquor, quantities of food, much music, much dancing, much jovial good-fellowship filled the Main Concourse of the fantastic palace in Turtle Bay that housed the hope of men who did not always let hope enter in.

If Only and Why Can't We, those two unhappy guests at the wonderful affair, were presently pushed outside into the cold night air of Manhattan and thought of no more. The Shade of Difference, their dark and bitter companion, had been barred at the door to begin with, and would not again stalk the long glass corridors and comfortable conference rooms until he was needed. He did not mind this temporary banishment, for he knew he would be needed very soon. In the Delegates' Lounge no imperious female voices trumpeted the names of man, the chairs and sofas and coffee tables stood deserted. In the Security Council, the Assembly Hall, and the committee rooms the desks stood empty and night enfolded the scenes of yesterday's contention that would soon be the scenes of tomorrow's.

Only the Main Concourse remained brightly lighted and alive, and in it the nations danced on, above the abyss that always yawns beneath nations, which somehow become accustomed to it; and only a few of those who danced were moved, now and again, to ponder wistfully the touching human frailty of the happy sight. Above hung arrogant Sputnik, outspread stood ready Zeus, steadily on its steel wire went the Netherlands' pendulum on its endless journeyings back . . . and forth . . . and back . . . and forth . . .

Passing beneath it with his wife sometime around 2 A.M., the Secretary of State glanced up and paused. They stood together hand in hand as the gleaming ball traversed its imprisoned path in response to laws far more inexorable than any man would ever promulgate.

"It is a privilege to live this day and tomorrow," the inscription said.

How like the Dutch, Orrin Knox thought as the band swung into a new set behind them and once again the brilliant throng was galvanized to action: how like the Dutch, to expect so little of time, and ask so little of it.

And yet, perhaps, how sage a counsel to give the troubled world to see it through the strange, unhappy circumstances devised by its quarrelsome sons, as they fail to find in hatred the salvation that they might, had they but the courage, find in love.

November 1960–February 1962
New York–Washington–Sanibel–Doyles